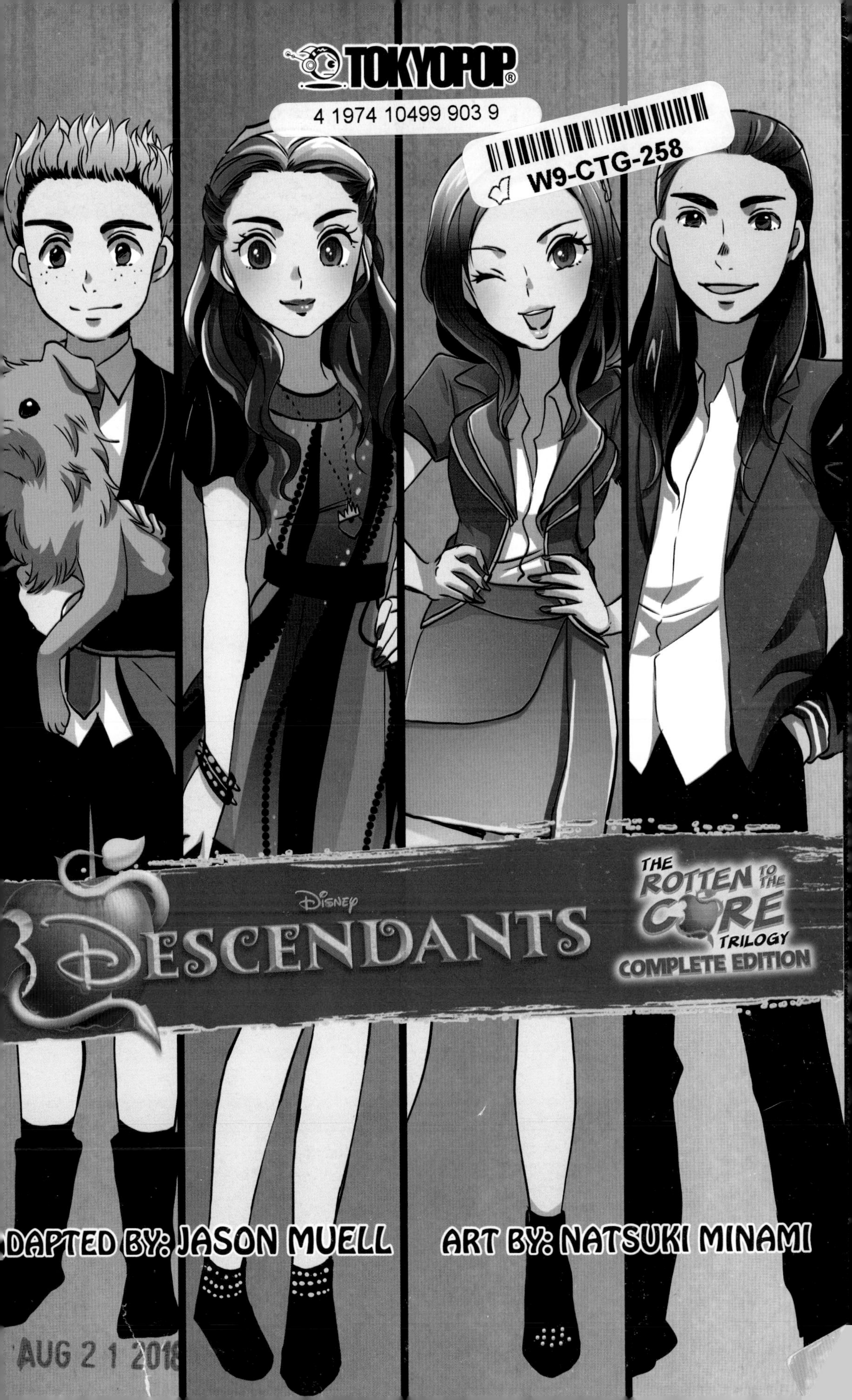
TOKYOPOP
Disney
DESCENDANTS
THE ROTTEN TO THE CORE TRILOGY
COMPLETE EDITION
DAPTED BY: JASON MUELL
ART BY: NATSUKI MINAMI

ABOUT THE
VILLIAN KIDS

MAL [DAUGHTER OF MALEFICENT]

PERSONALITY
DRIVEN, CONFIDENT, STREET SMART

STRENGTHS
LEADERSHIP AND DRAWING

ITEM OF CHOICE
SPELL BOOK

EVIE [DAUGHTER OF EVIL QUEEN]

PERSONALITY
INTELLIGENT, FLIRTY, CHARMING

STRENGTHS
CHEMISTRY AND POTIONS

ITEM OF CHOICE
MAGIC MIRROR

JAY [SON OF JAFAR]

PERSONALITY
LOYAL, PHYSICAL, ATHLETIC

STRENGTHS
SPORTS AND PARKOUR

ITEM OF CHOICE
ANYTHING NOT NAILED DOWN

CARLOS [SON OF CRUELLA DE VIL]

PERSONALITY
VERY INTELLIGENT, CARING, WITTY

STRENGTHS
TECHNOLOGY

ITEM OF CHOICE
LAPTOP COMPUTER

ABOUT THE
AURADON KIDS

BEN [SON OF BELLE AND THE BEAST]

PERSONALITY
CARING, BRAVE, IDEALISTIC

STRENGTHS
DIPLOMACY AND GOVERNANCE

ITEM OF CHOICE
CORONATION CROWN

AUDREY [DAUGHTER OF AURORA AND PRINCE PHILLIP]

PERSONALITY
CONFIDENT, CHARISMATIC, OUTSPOKEN

STRENGTHS
SOCIAL SKILLS AND ACROBATICS

ITEM OF CHOICE
CHEERLEADING UNIFORM

JANE [DAUGHTER OF FAIRY GODMOTHER]

PERSONALITY
SHY, INSECURE, EARNEST

STRENGTHS
ORGANIZED AND HARDWORKING

ITEM OF CHOICE
DIGITAL PLANNER

DOUG [SON OF DOPEY]

PERSONALITY
KIND, HELPFUL, NERDY

STRENGTHS
MARCHING BAND AND MATHEMATICS

ITEM OF CHOICE
CALCULATOR

TABLE OF CONTENTS

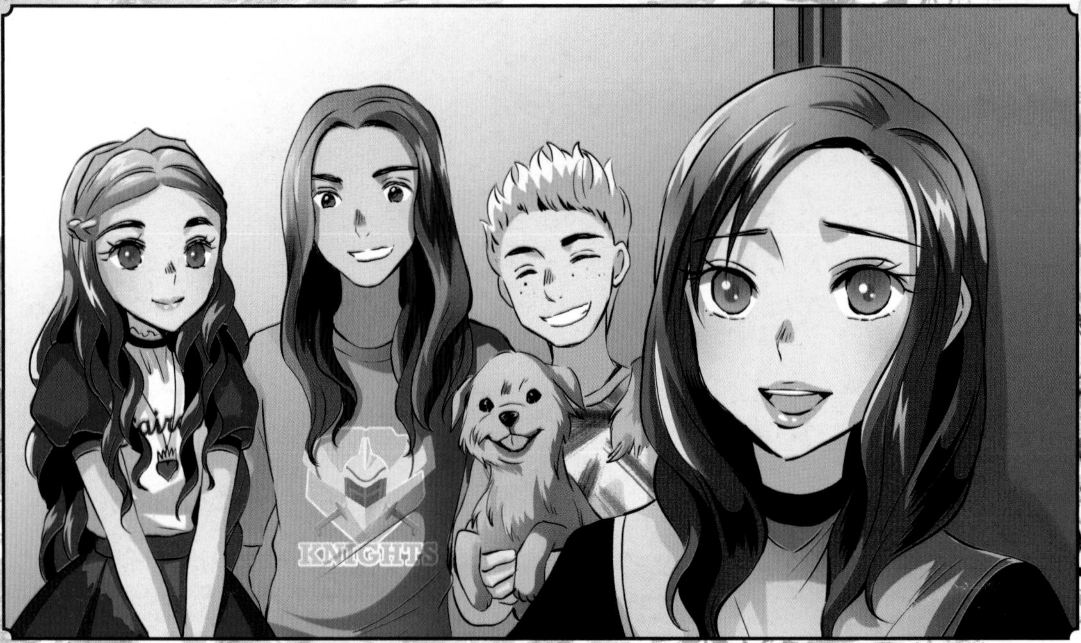
KNIGHTS

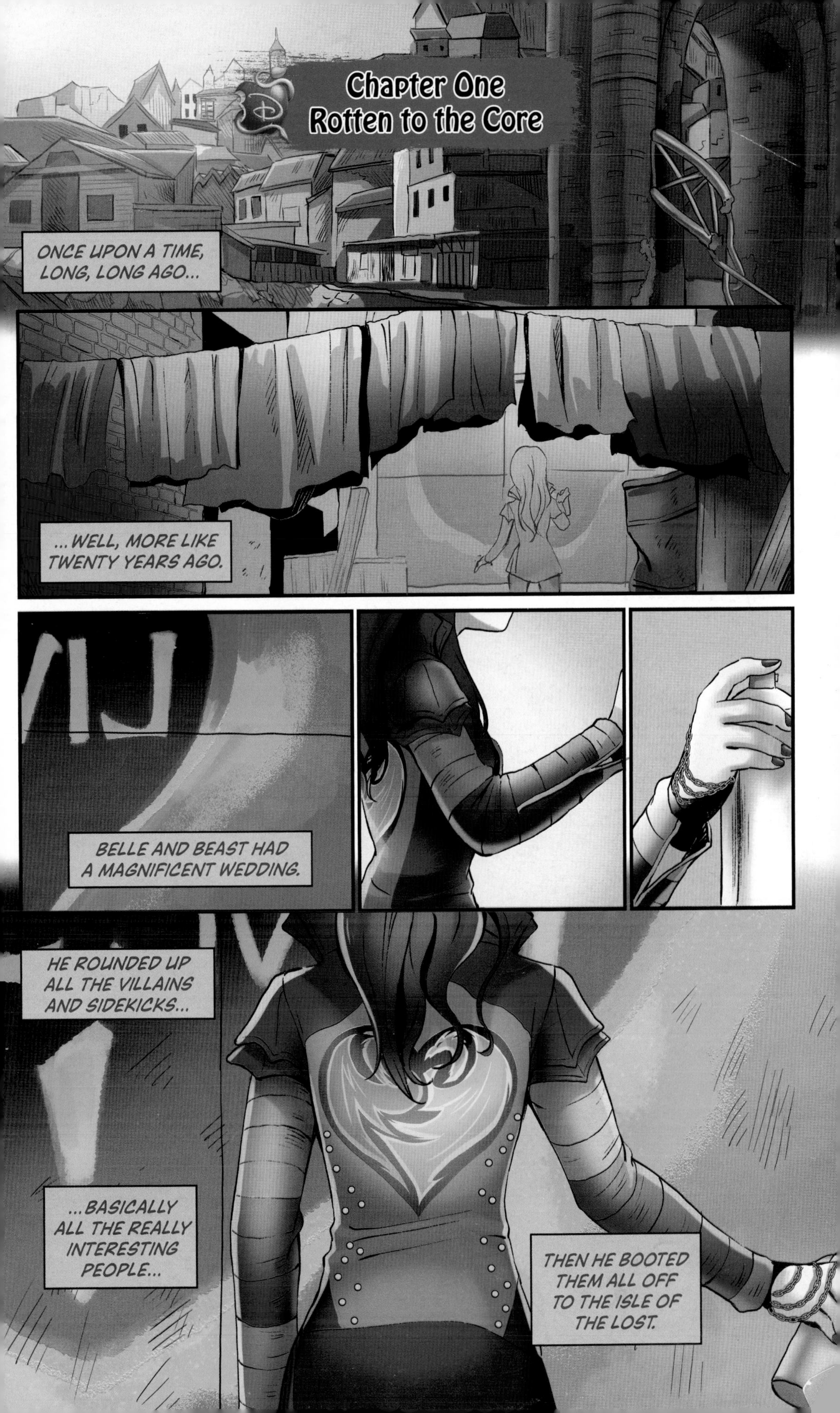

Chapter One
Rotten to the Core
ONCE UPON A TIME, LONG, LONG AGO...
...WELL, MORE LIKE TWENTY YEARS AGO.
BELLE AND BEAST HAD A MAGNIFICENT WEDDING.
HE ROUNDED UP ALL THE VILLAINS AND SIDEKICKS...
...BASICALLY ALL THE REALLY INTERESTING PEOPLE...
THEN HE BOOTED THEM ALL OFF TO THE ISLE OF THE LOST.

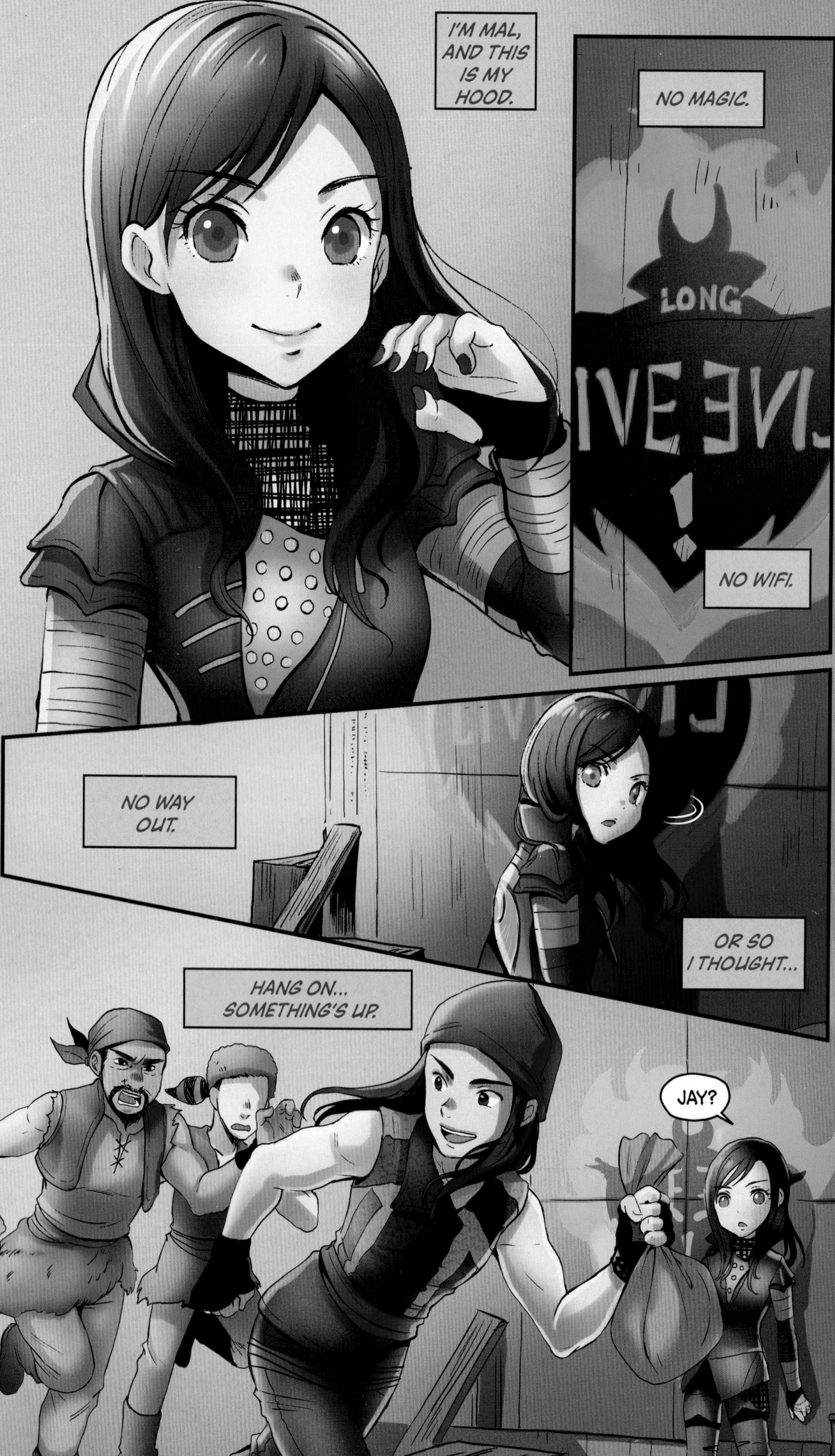

I'M MAL, AND THIS IS MY HOOD.
NO MAGIC.
LONG
NO WIFI.
NO WAY OUT.
OR SO I THOUGHT...
HANG ON... SOMETHING'S UP.
JAY?

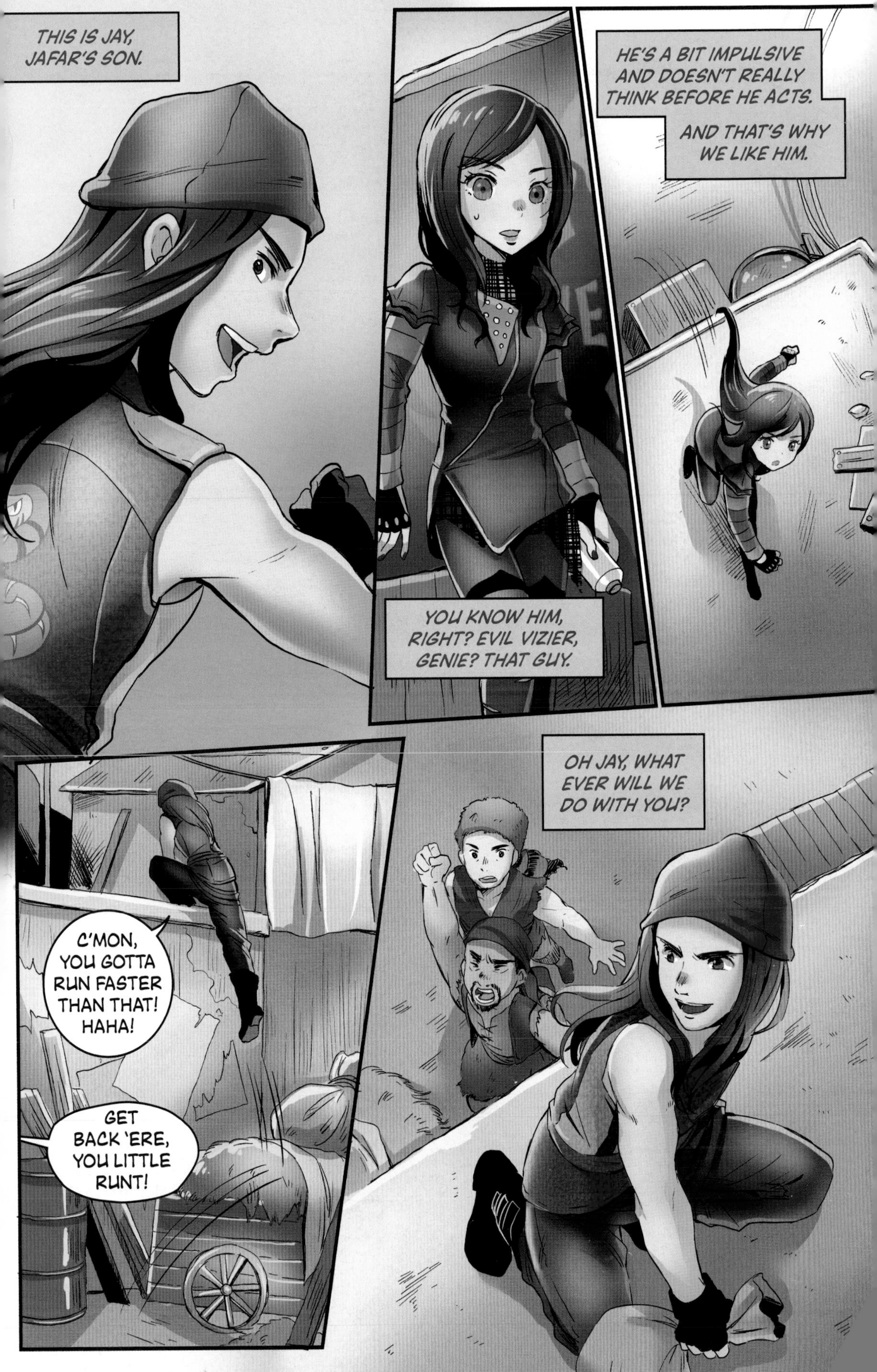
THIS IS JAY, JAFAR'S SON.
YOU KNOW HIM, RIGHT? EVIL VIZIER, GENIE? THAT GUY.
HE'S A BIT IMPULSIVE AND DOESN'T REALLY THINK BEFORE HE ACTS.
AND THAT'S WHY WE LIKE HIM.
C'MON, YOU GOTTA RUN FASTER THAN THAT! HAHA!
GET BACK 'ERE, YOU LITTLE RUNT!
OH JAY, WHAT EVER WILL WE DO WITH YOU?

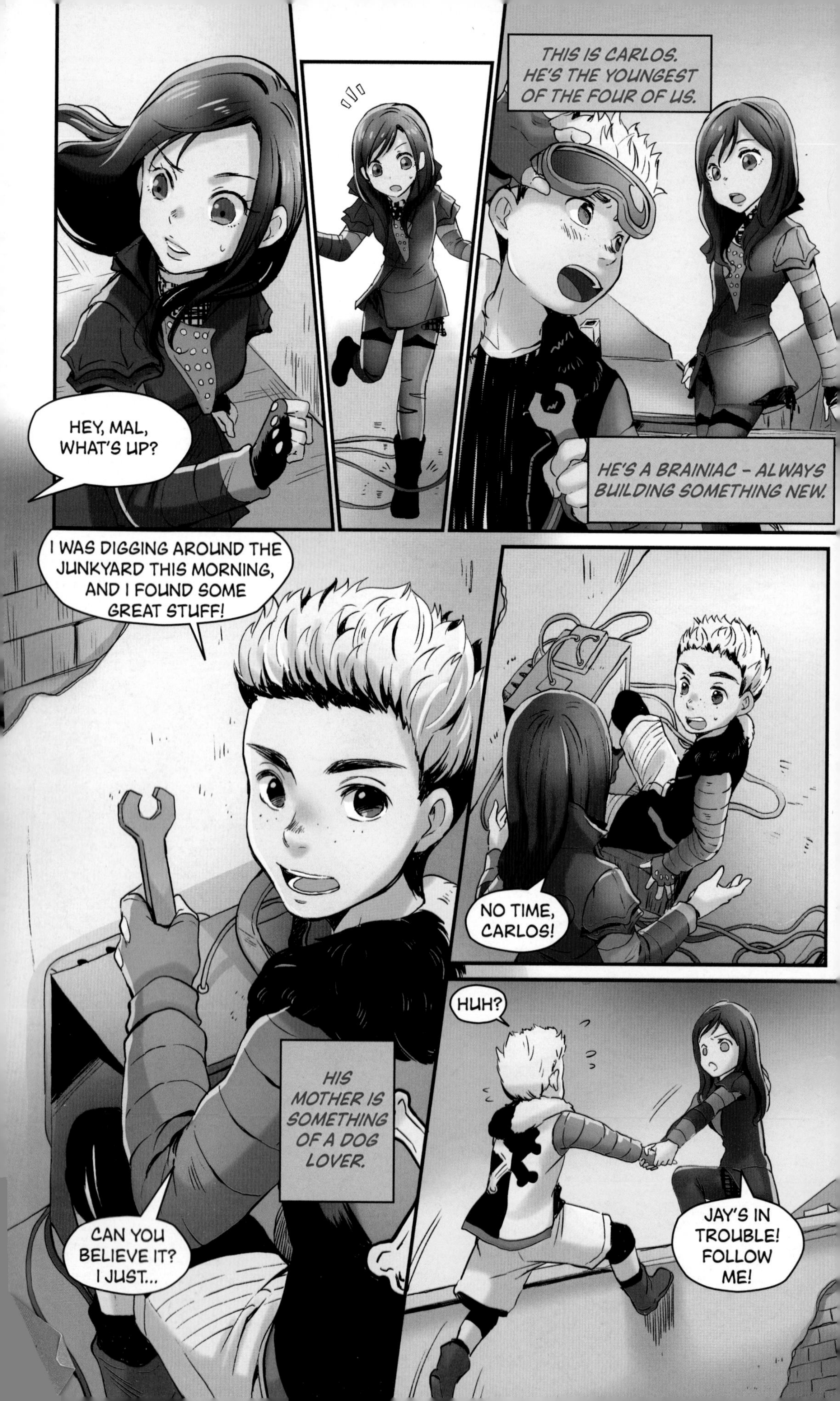
HEY, MAL, WHAT'S UP?
THIS IS CARLOS. HE'S THE YOUNGEST OF THE FOUR OF US.
HE'S A BRAINIAC – ALWAYS BUILDING SOMETHING NEW.
I WAS DIGGING AROUND THE JUNKYARD THIS MORNING, AND I FOUND SOME GREAT STUFF!
NO TIME, CARLOS!
HIS MOTHER IS SOMETHING OF A DOG LOVER.
CAN YOU BELIEVE IT? I JUST...
HUH?
JAY'S IN TROUBLE! FOLLOW ME!

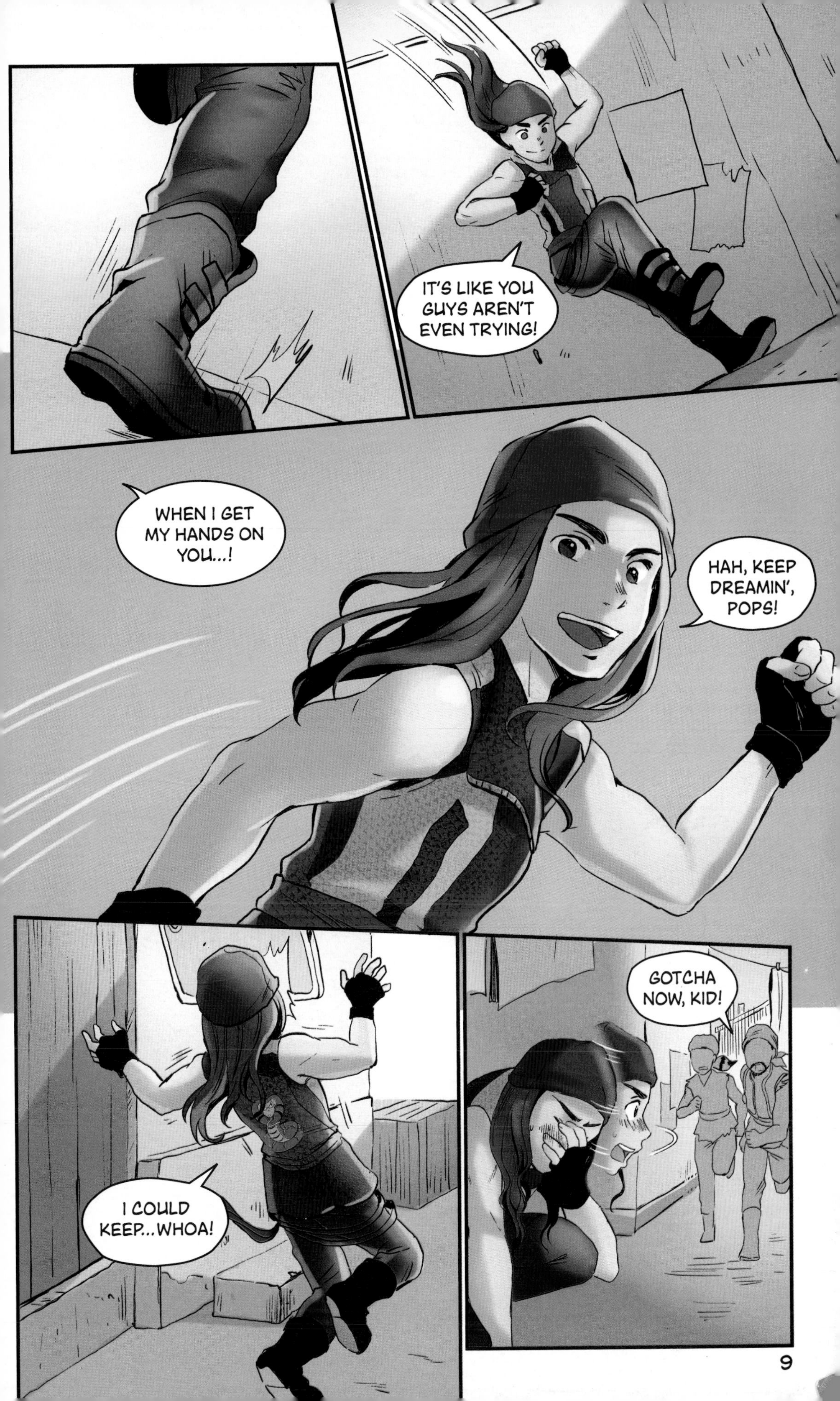
IT'S LIKE YOU GUYS AREN'T EVEN TRYING!
WHEN I GET MY HANDS ON YOU...!
HAH, KEEP DREAMIN', POPS!
I COULD KEEP...WHOA!
GOTCHA NOW, KID!

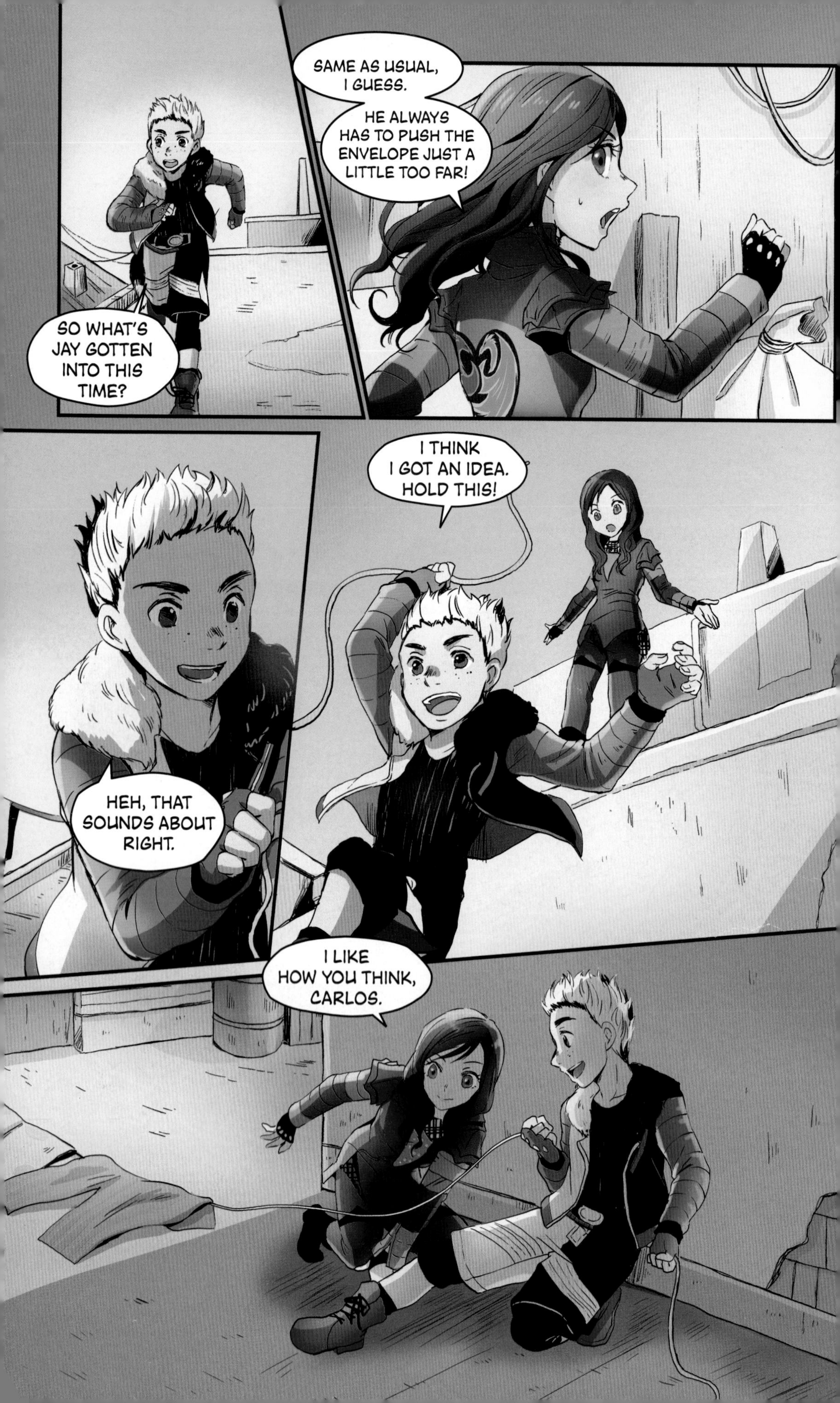
SO WHAT'S JAY GOTTEN INTO THIS TIME?
SAME AS USUAL, I GUESS.
HE ALWAYS HAS TO PUSH THE ENVELOPE JUST A LITTLE TOO FAR!
HEH, THAT SOUNDS ABOUT RIGHT.
I THINK I GOT AN IDEA. HOLD THIS!
I LIKE HOW YOU THINK, CARLOS.

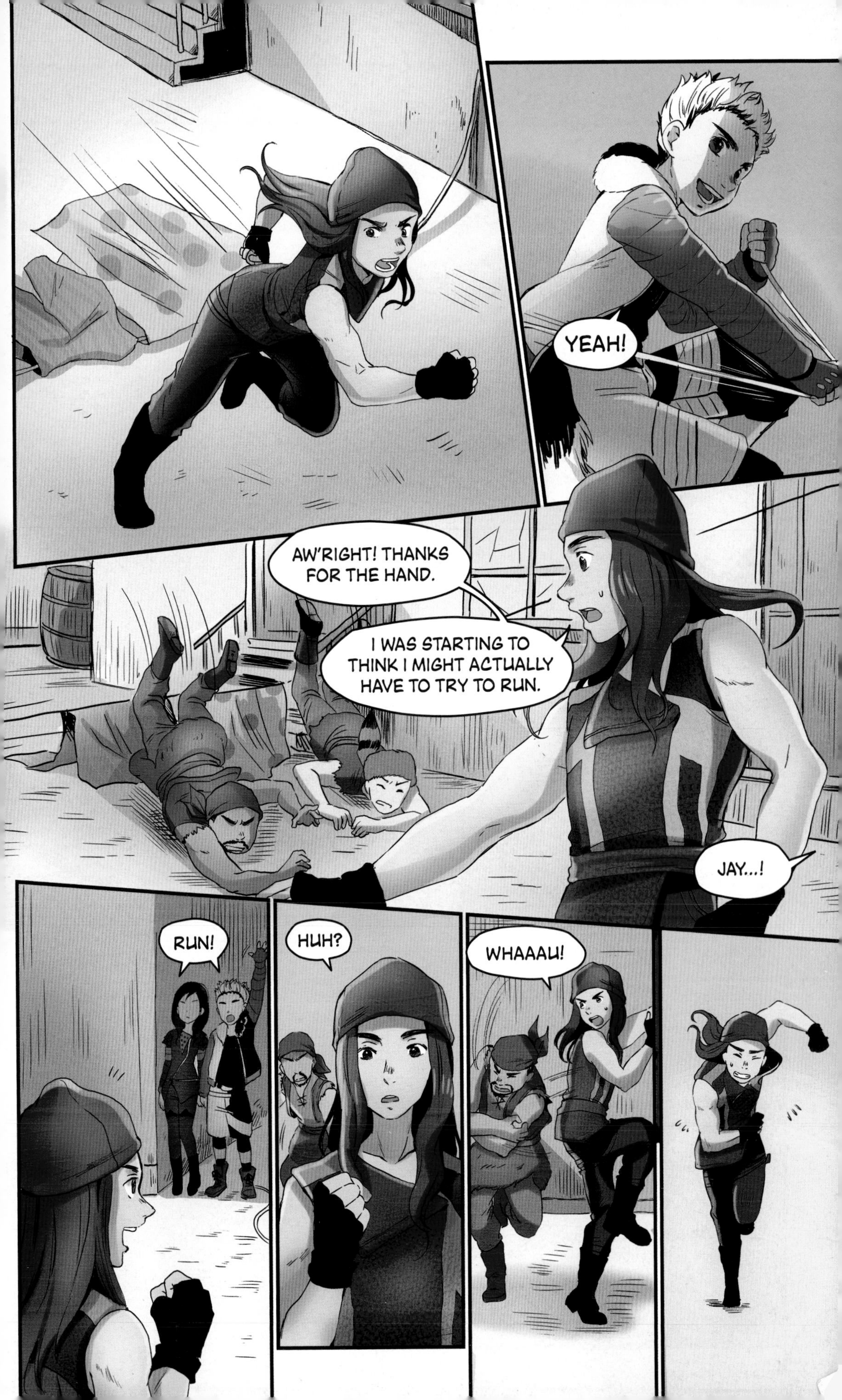
YEAH!
AW'RIGHT! THANKS FOR THE HAND.
I WAS STARTING TO THINK I MIGHT ACTUALLY HAVE TO TRY TO RUN.
JAY...!
RUN!
HUH?
WHAAAU!

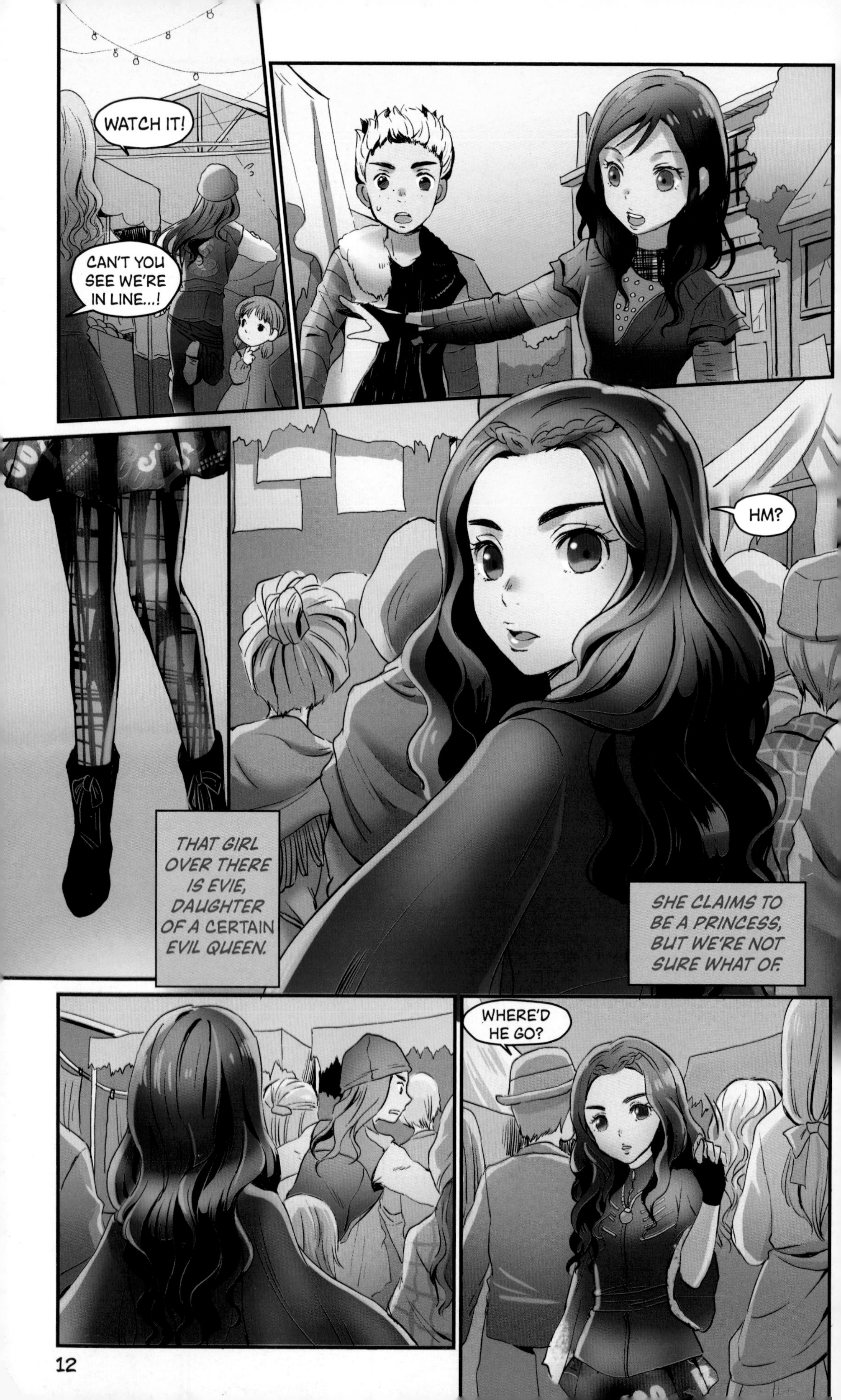
WATCH IT!
CAN'T YOU SEE WE'RE IN LINE...!
HM?
THAT GIRL OVER THERE IS EVIE, DAUGHTER OF A CERTAIN EVIL QUEEN.
SHE CLAIMS TO BE A PRINCESS, BUT WE'RE NOT SURE WHAT OF.
WHERE'D HE GO?

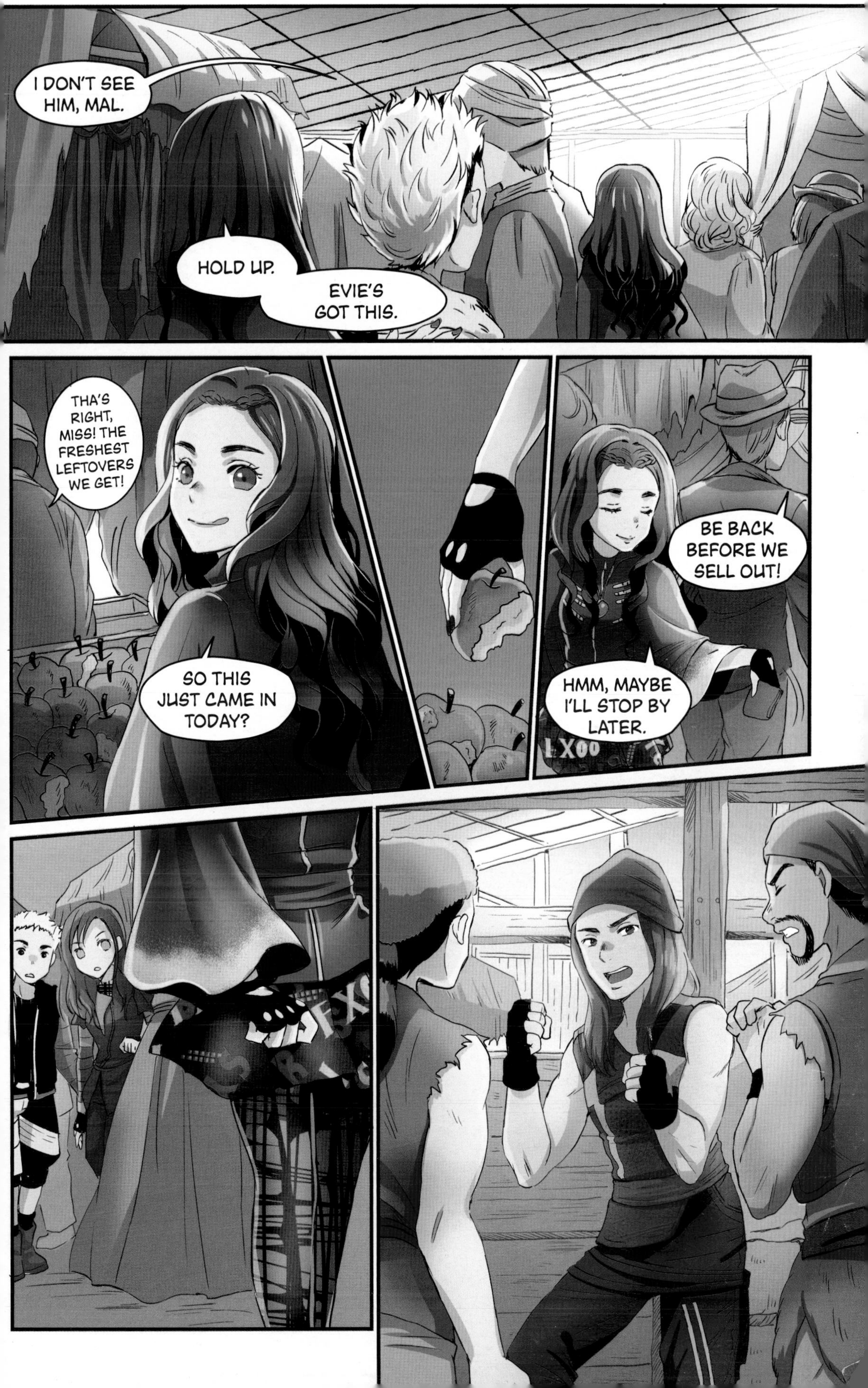
I DON'T SEE HIM, MAL.
HOLD UP.
EVIE'S GOT THIS.
THA'S RIGHT, MISS! THE FRESHEST LEFTOVERS WE GET!
SO THIS JUST CAME IN TODAY?
BE BACK BEFORE WE SELL OUT!
HMM, MAYBE I'LL STOP BY LATER.

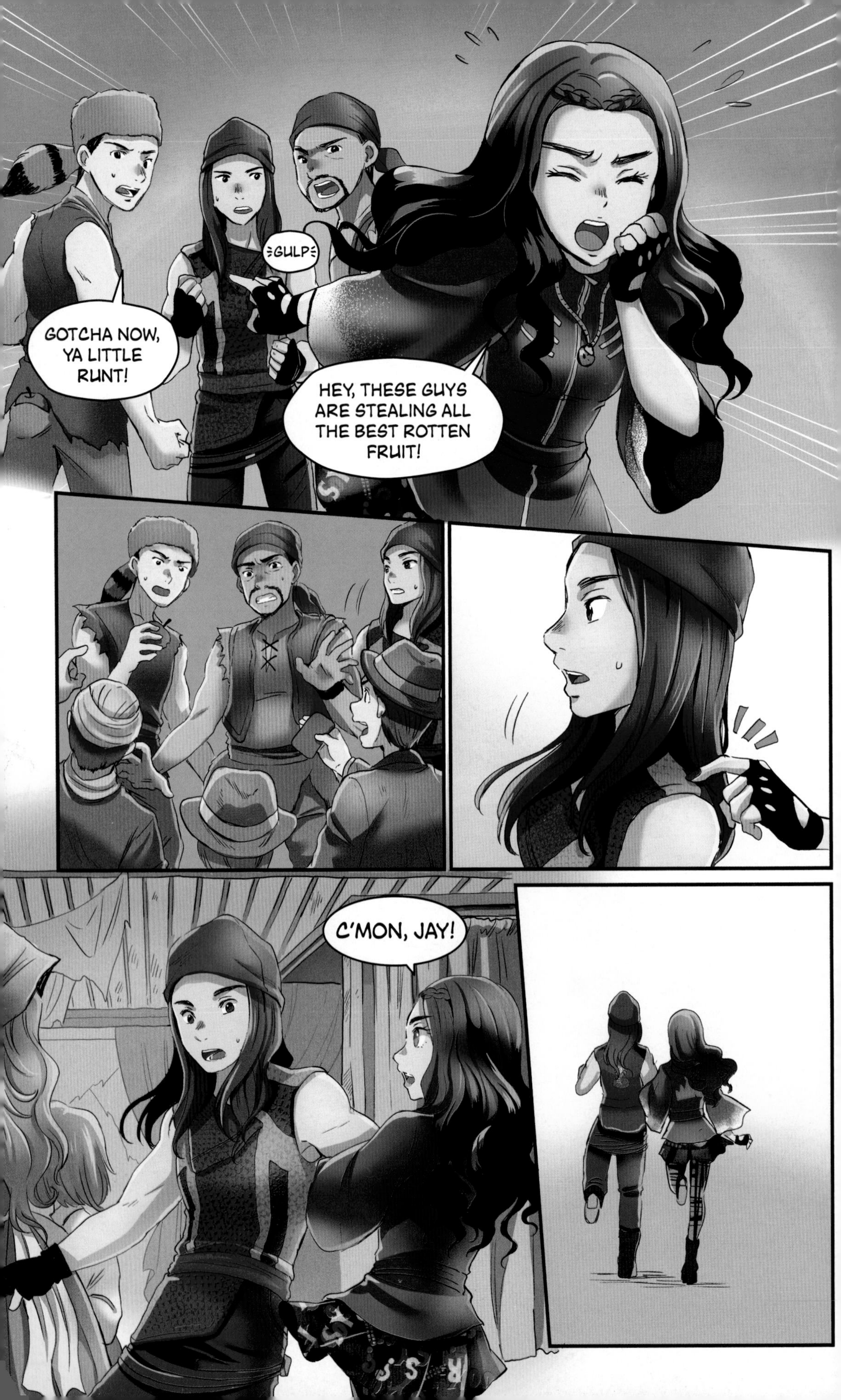
GULP
GOTCHA NOW, YA LITTLE RUNT!
HEY, THESE GUYS ARE STEALING ALL THE BEST ROTTEN FRUIT!
C'MON, JAY!

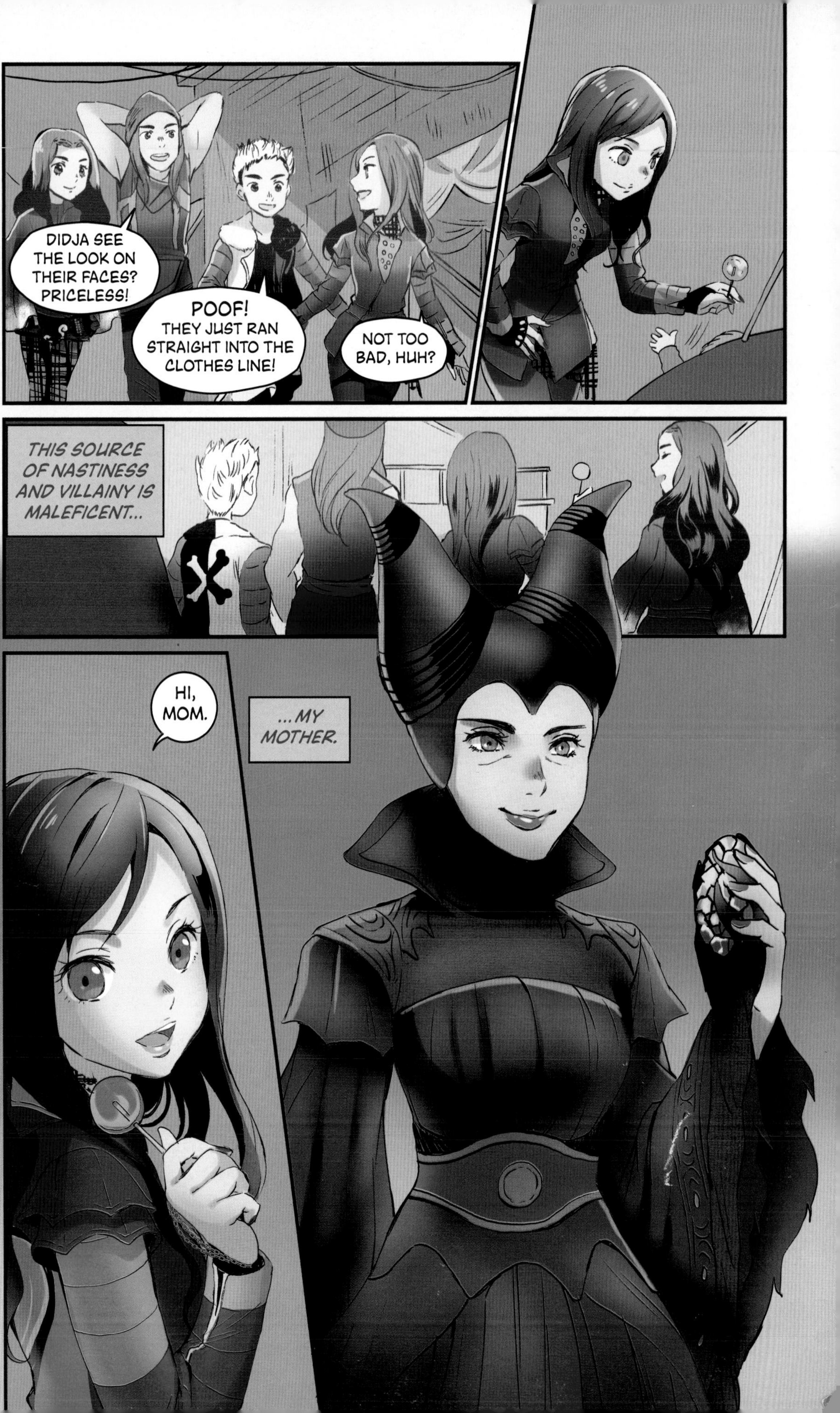

DIDJA SEE THE LOOK ON THEIR FACES? PRICELESS!
POOF! THEY JUST RAN STRAIGHT INTO THE CLOTHES LINE!
NOT TOO BAD, HUH?
THIS SOURCE OF NASTINESS AND VILLAINY IS MALEFICENT...
HI, MOM.
...MY MOTHER.

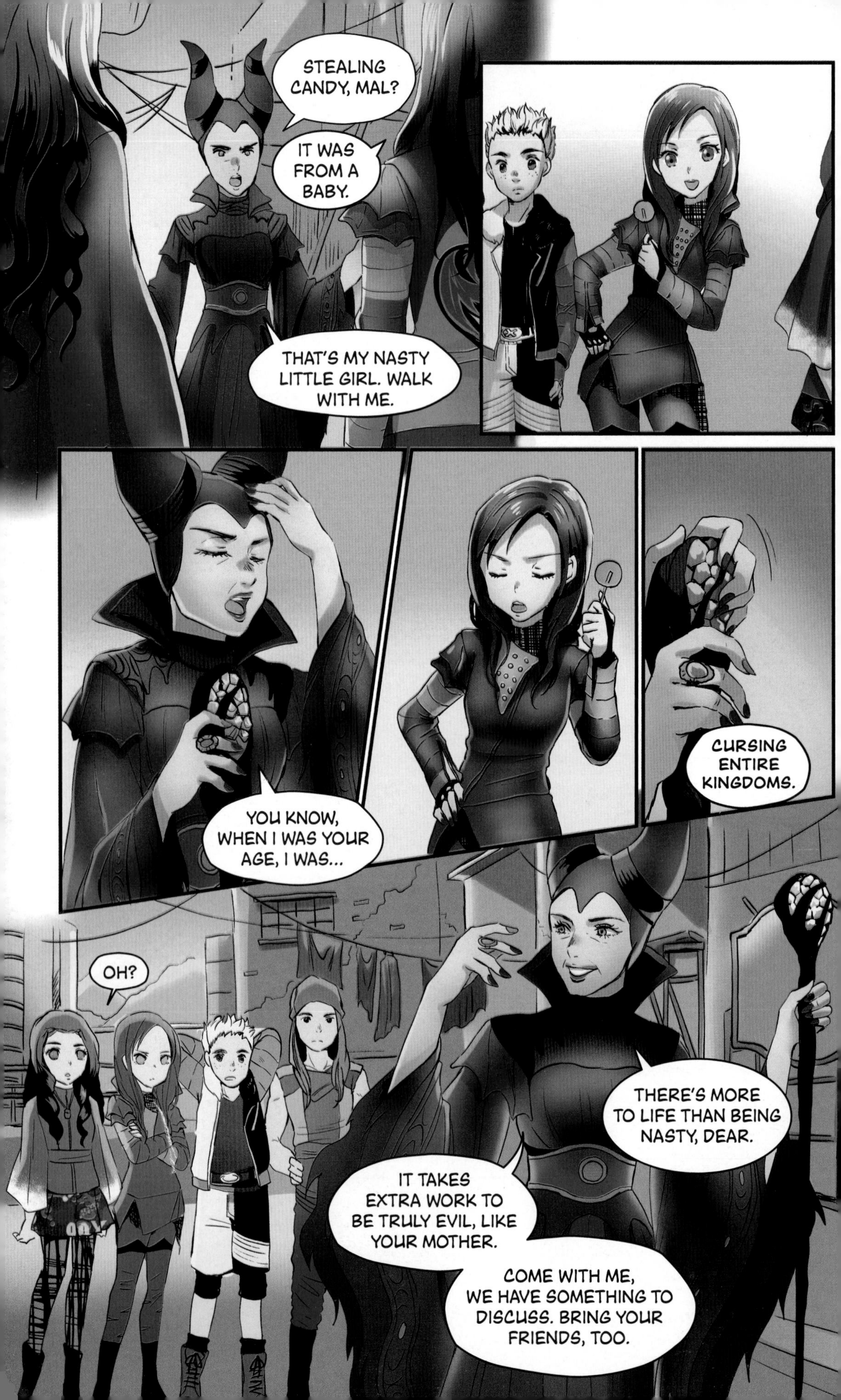
STEALING CANDY, MAL?
IT WAS FROM A BABY.
THAT'S MY NASTY LITTLE GIRL. WALK WITH ME.
YOU KNOW, WHEN I WAS YOUR AGE, I WAS...
CURSING ENTIRE KINGDOMS.
OH?
THERE'S MORE TO LIFE THAN BEING NASTY, DEAR.
IT TAKES EXTRA WORK TO BE TRULY EVIL, LIKE YOUR MOTHER.
COME WITH ME, WE HAVE SOMETHING TO DISCUSS. BRING YOUR FRIENDS, TOO.

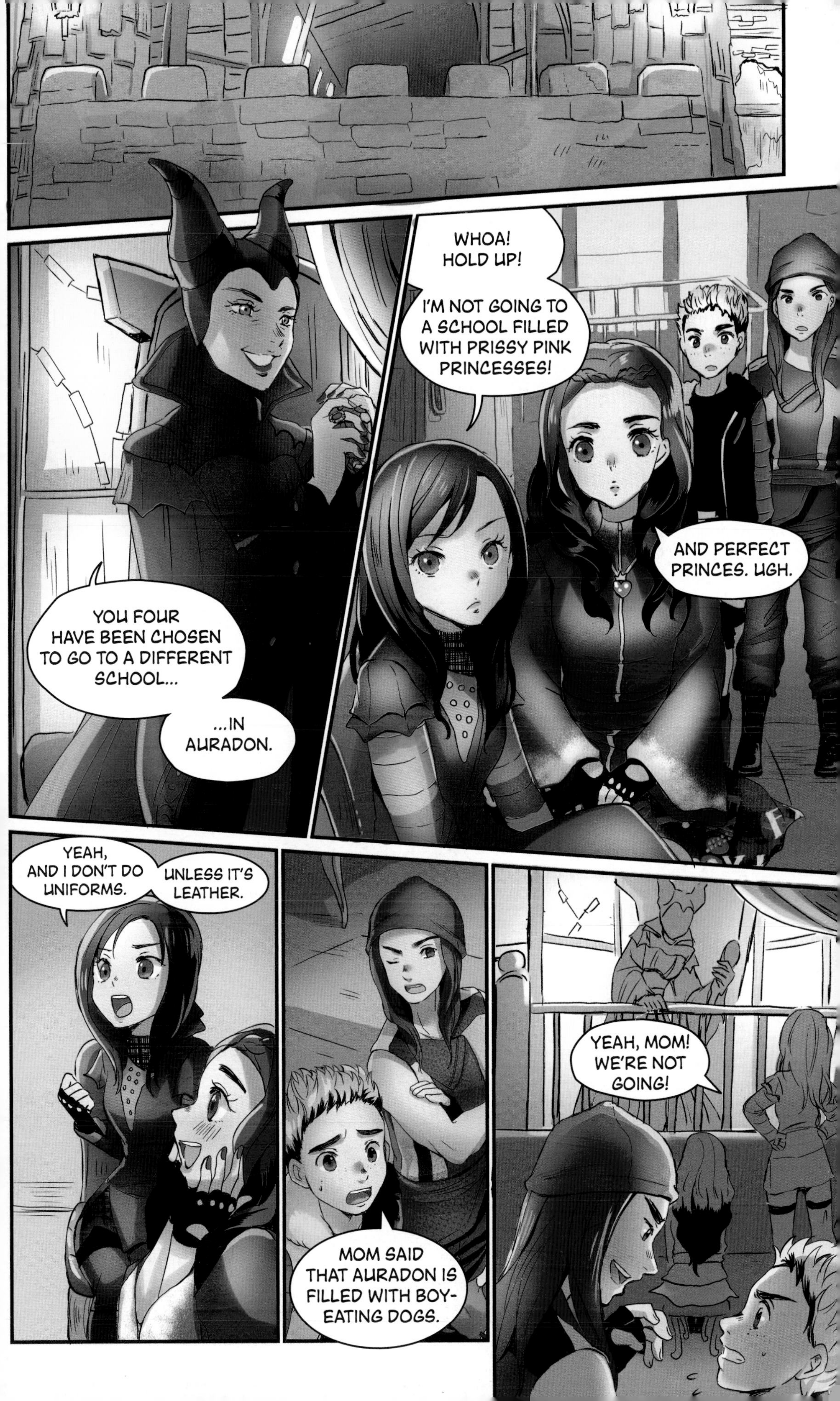
WHOA! HOLD UP!
I'M NOT GOING TO A SCHOOL FILLED WITH PRISSY PINK PRINCESSES!
AND PERFECT PRINCES. UGH.
YOU FOUR HAVE BEEN CHOSEN TO GO TO A DIFFERENT SCHOOL...
...IN AURADON.
YEAH, AND I DON'T DO UNIFORMS.
UNLESS IT'S LEATHER.
MOM SAID THAT AURADON IS FILLED WITH BOY-EATING DOGS.
YEAH, MOM! WE'RE NOT GOING!

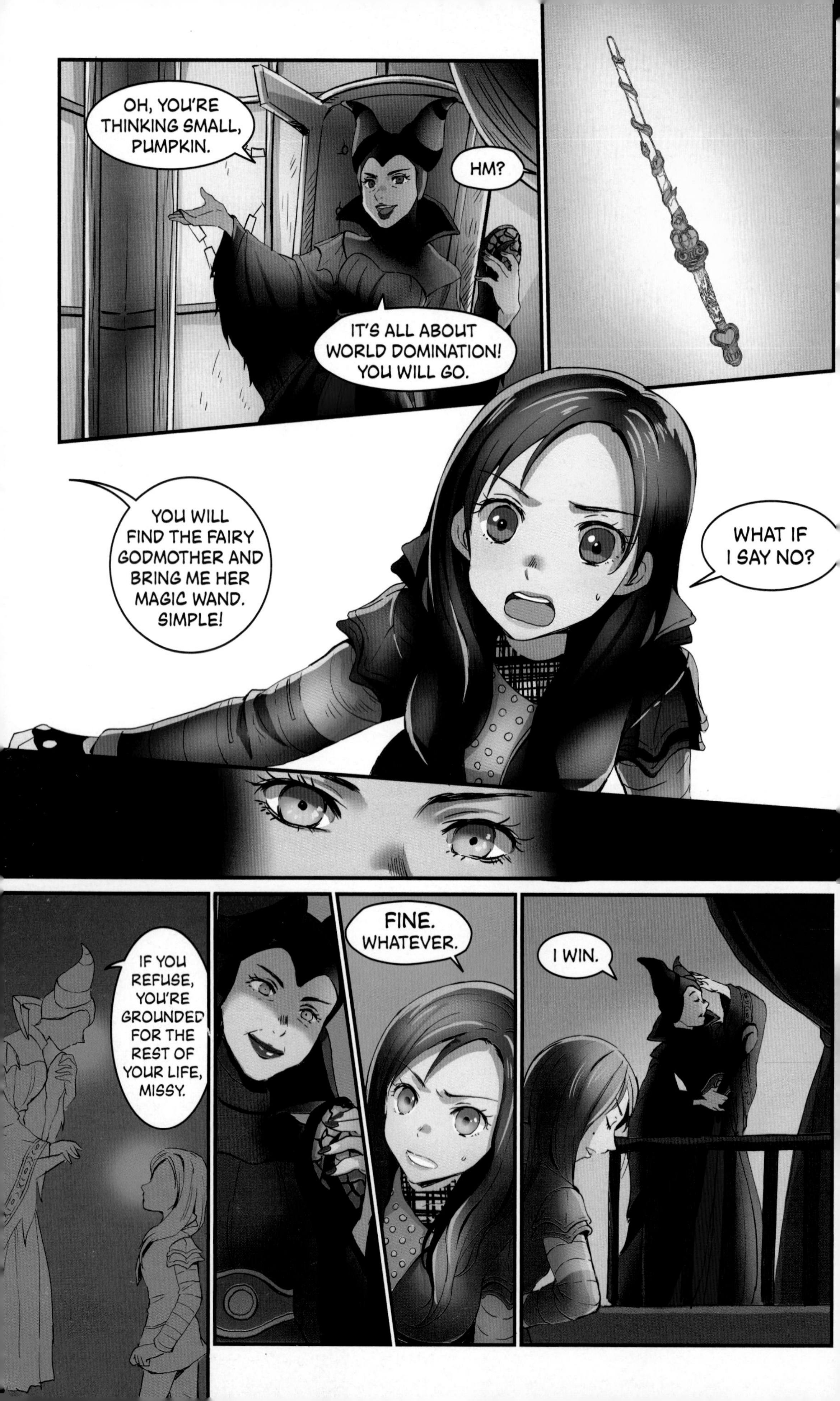
OH, YOU'RE THINKING SMALL, PUMPKIN.
HM?
IT'S ALL ABOUT WORLD DOMINATION! YOU WILL GO.
YOU WILL FIND THE FAIRY GODMOTHER AND BRING ME HER MAGIC WAND. SIMPLE!
WHAT IF I SAY NO?
IF YOU REFUSE, YOU'RE GROUNDED FOR THE REST OF YOUR LIFE, MISSY.
FINE. WHATEVER.
I WIN.

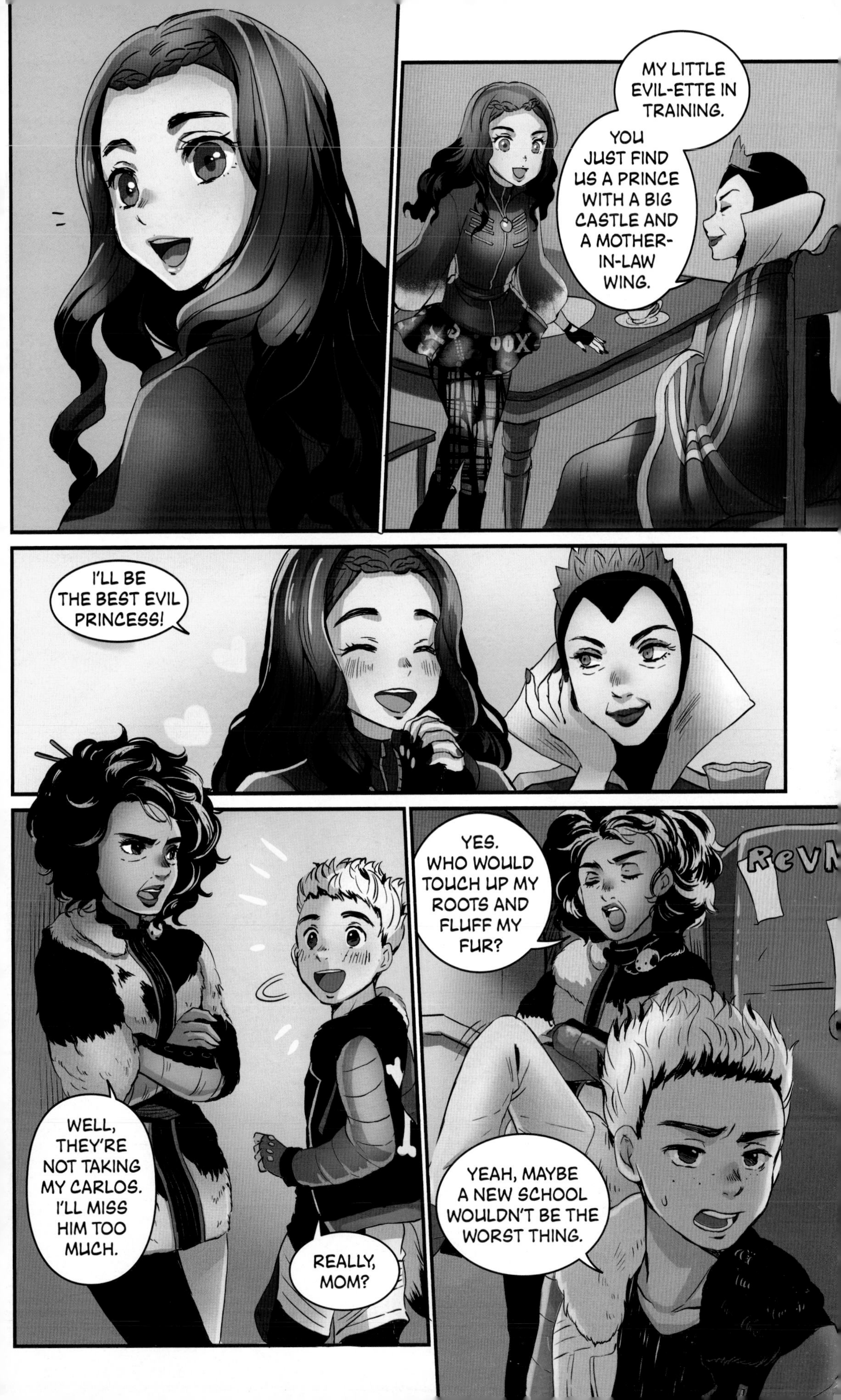
MY LITTLE EVIL-ETTE IN TRAINING.
YOU JUST FIND US A PRINCE WITH A BIG CASTLE AND A MOTHER-IN-LAW WING.
I'LL BE THE BEST EVIL PRINCESS!
WELL, THEY'RE NOT TAKING MY CARLOS. I'LL MISS HIM TOO MUCH.
REALLY, MOM?
YES. WHO WOULD TOUCH UP MY ROOTS AND FLUFF MY FUR?
YEAH, MAYBE A NEW SCHOOL WOULDN'T BE THE WORST THING.

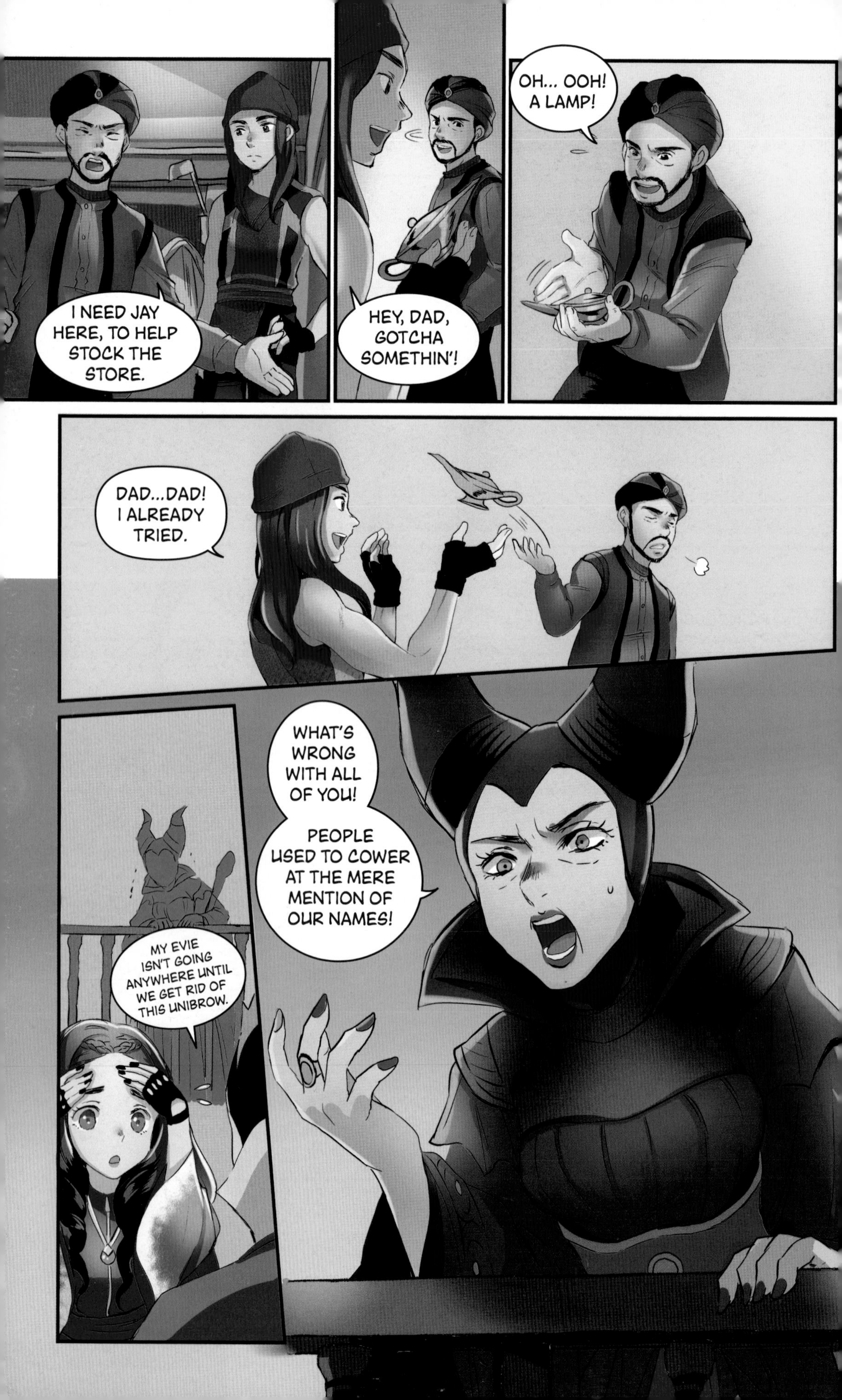
I NEED JAY HERE, TO HELP STOCK THE STORE.
HEY, DAD, GOTCHA SOMETHIN'!
OH... OOH! A LAMP!
DAD...DAD! I ALREADY TRIED.
MY EVIE ISN'T GOING ANYWHERE UNTIL WE GET RID OF THIS UNIBROW.
WHAT'S WRONG WITH ALL OF YOU!
PEOPLE USED TO COWER AT THE MERE MENTION OF OUR NAMES!

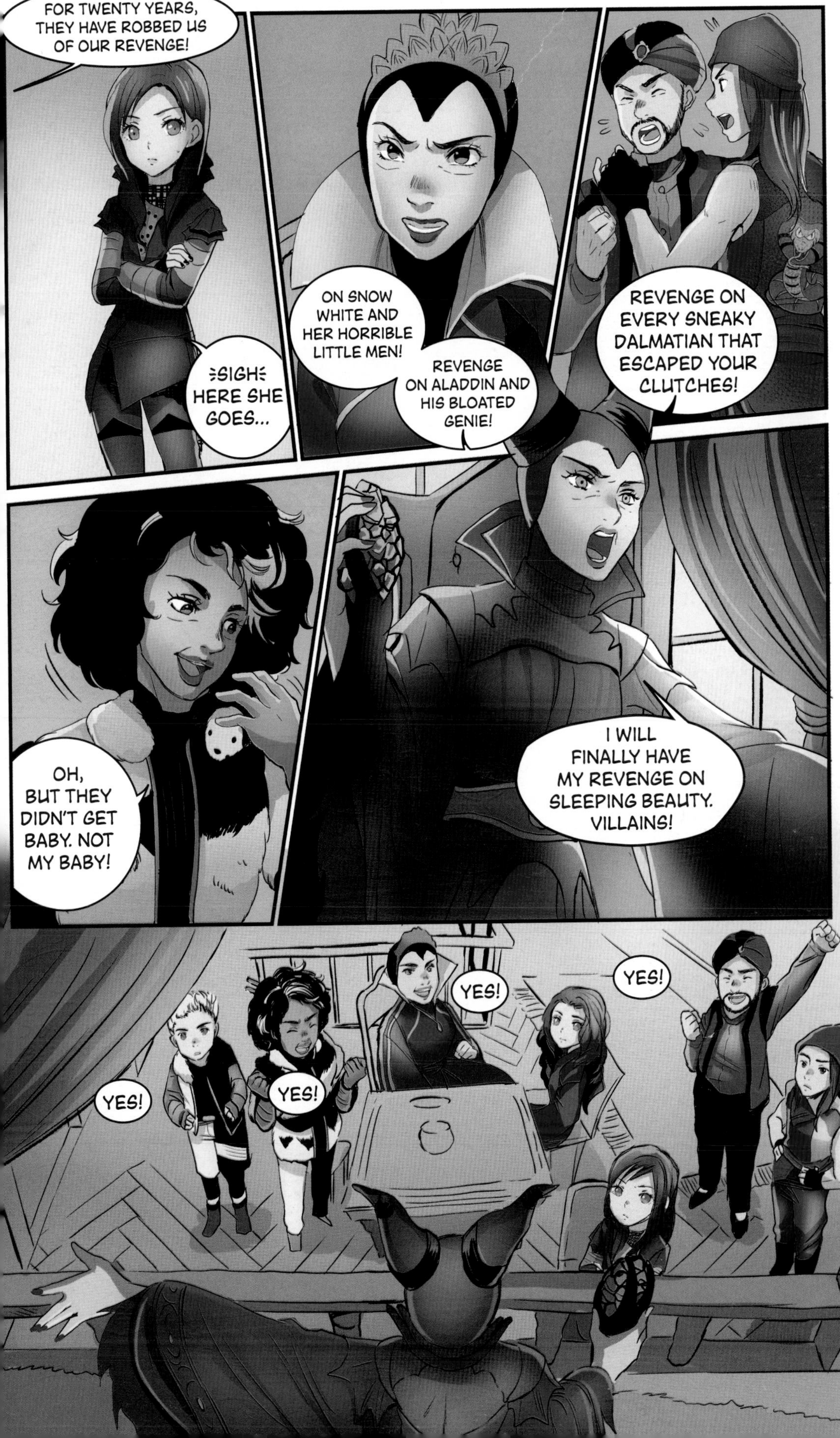
FOR TWENTY YEARS, THEY HAVE ROBBED US OF OUR REVENGE!
ON SNOW WHITE AND HER HORRIBLE LITTLE MEN!
≡SIGH≡ HERE SHE GOES...
REVENGE ON ALADDIN AND HIS BLOATED GENIE!
REVENGE ON EVERY SNEAKY DALMATIAN THAT ESCAPED YOUR CLUTCHES!
OH, BUT THEY DIDN'T GET BABY. NOT MY BABY!
I WILL FINALLY HAVE MY REVENGE ON SLEEPING BEAUTY. VILLAINS!
YES!
YES!
YES!
YES!

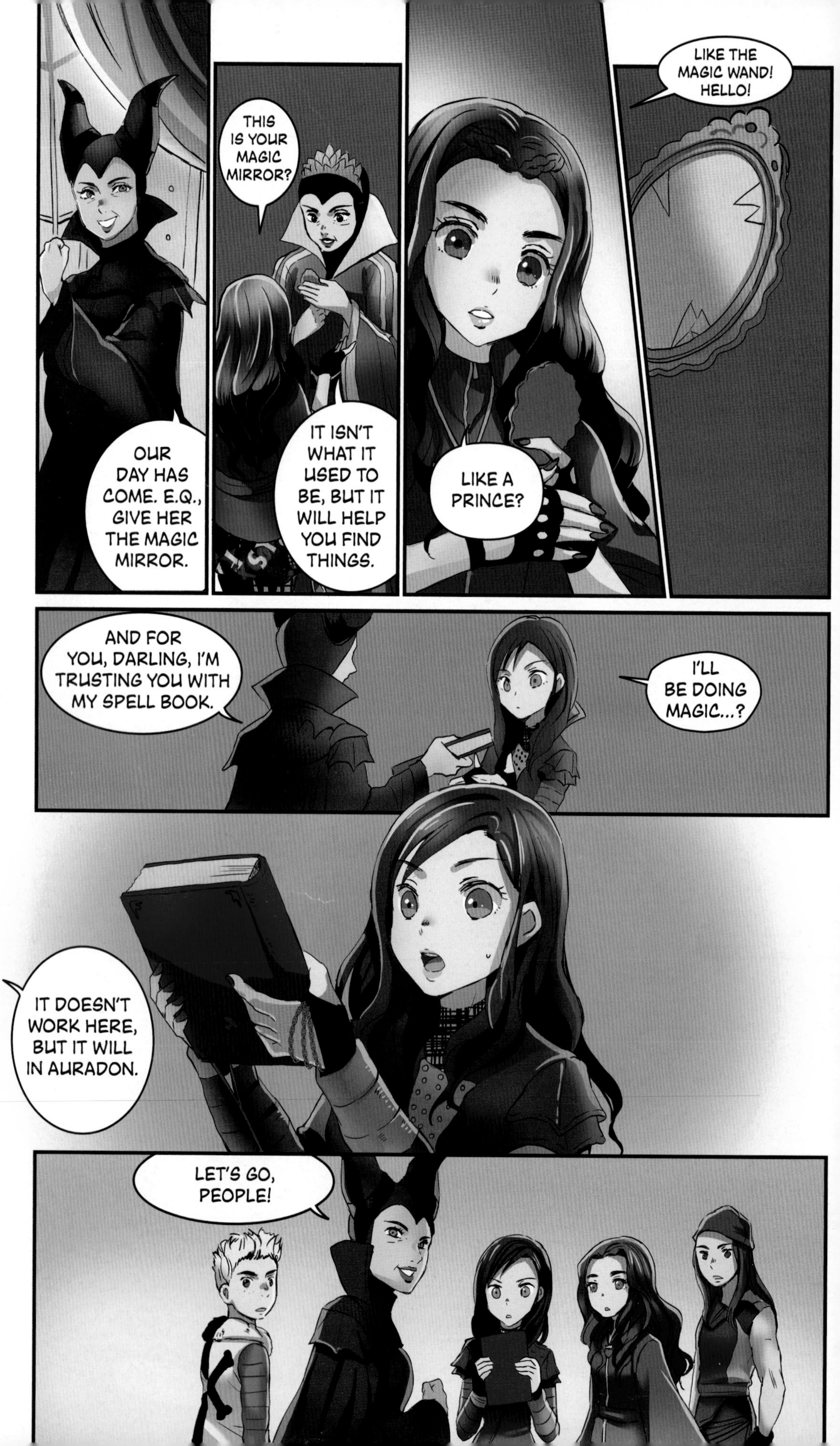
OUR DAY HAS COME. E.Q., GIVE HER THE MAGIC MIRROR.
THIS IS YOUR MAGIC MIRROR?
IT ISN'T WHAT IT USED TO BE, BUT IT WILL HELP YOU FIND THINGS.
LIKE A PRINCE?
LIKE THE MAGIC WAND! HELLO!
AND FOR YOU, DARLING, I'M TRUSTING YOU WITH MY SPELL BOOK.
I'LL BE DOING MAGIC...?
IT DOESN'T WORK HERE, BUT IT WILL IN AURADON.
LET'S GO, PEOPLE!

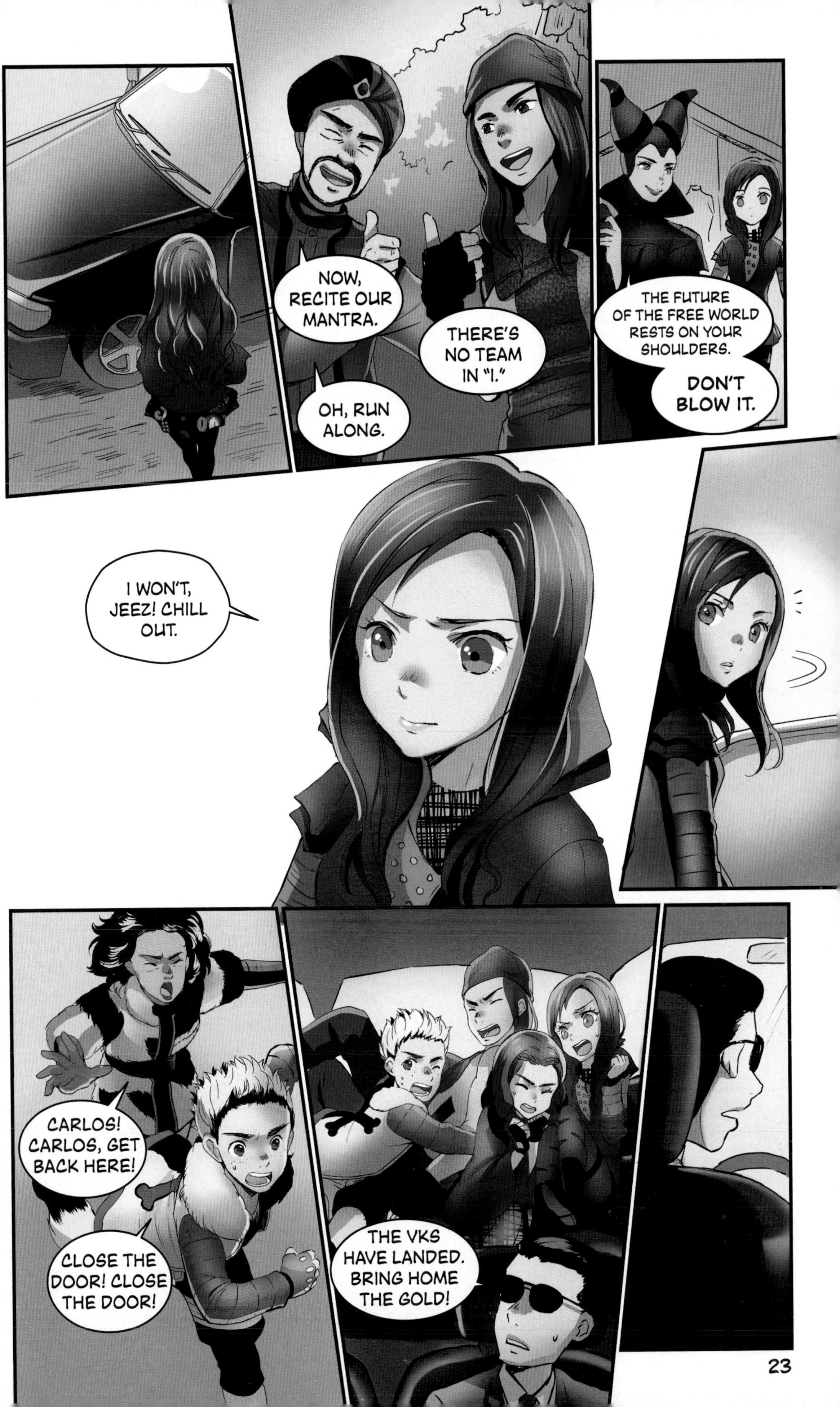

NOW, RECITE OUR MANTRA.
OH, RUN ALONG.
THERE'S NO TEAM IN "I."
THE FUTURE OF THE FREE WORLD RESTS ON YOUR SHOULDERS.
DON'T BLOW IT.
I WON'T, JEEZ! CHILL OUT.
CARLOS! CARLOS, GET BACK HERE!
CLOSE THE DOOR! CLOSE THE DOOR!
THE VKS HAVE LANDED. BRING HOME THE GOLD!

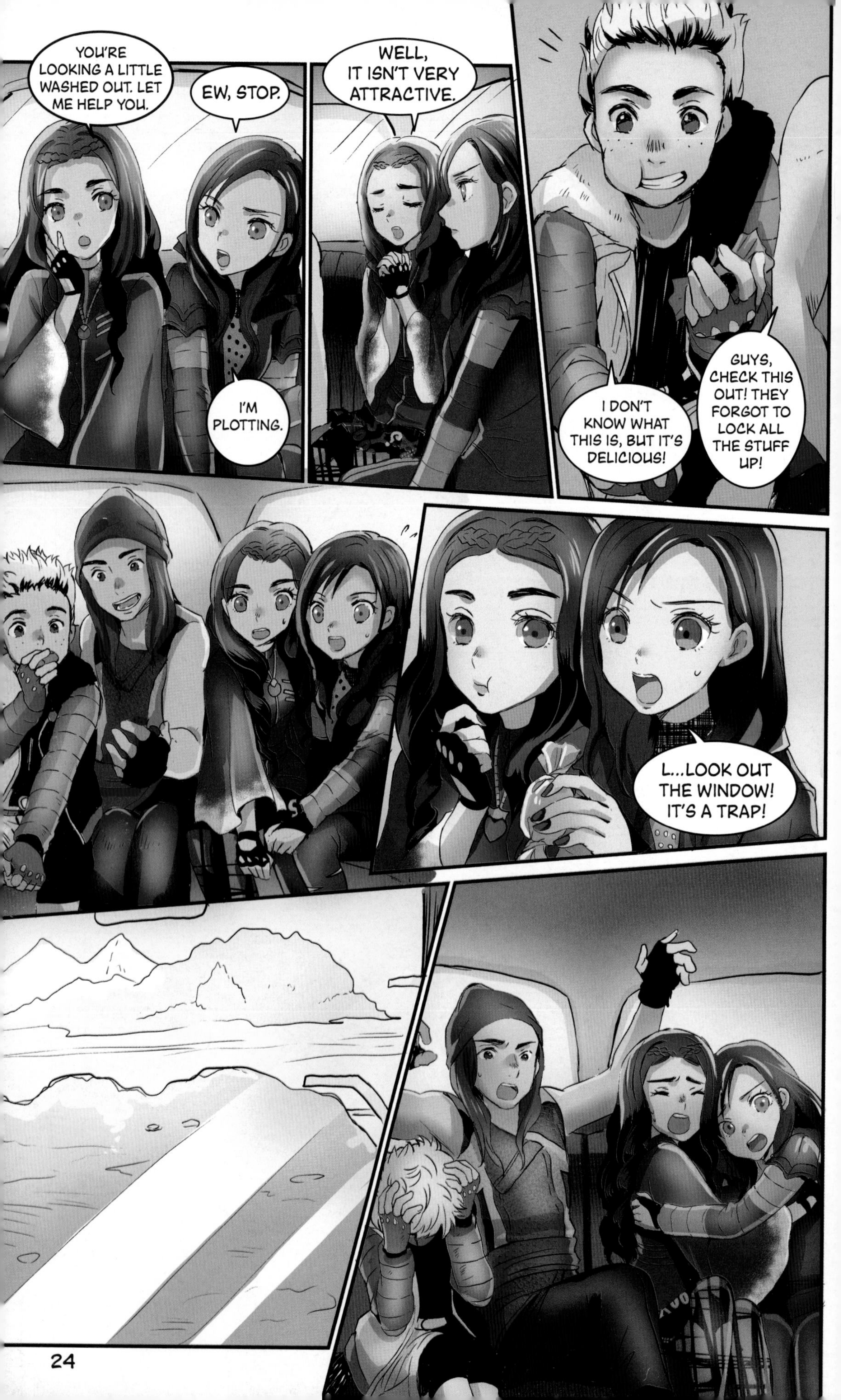

YOU'RE LOOKING A LITTLE WASHED OUT. LET ME HELP YOU.
EW, STOP.
I'M PLOTTING.
WELL, IT ISN'T VERY ATTRACTIVE.
GUYS, CHECK THIS OUT! THEY FORGOT TO LOCK ALL THE STUFF UP!
I DON'T KNOW WHAT THIS IS, BUT IT'S DELICIOUS!
L...LOOK OUT THE WINDOW! IT'S A TRAP!

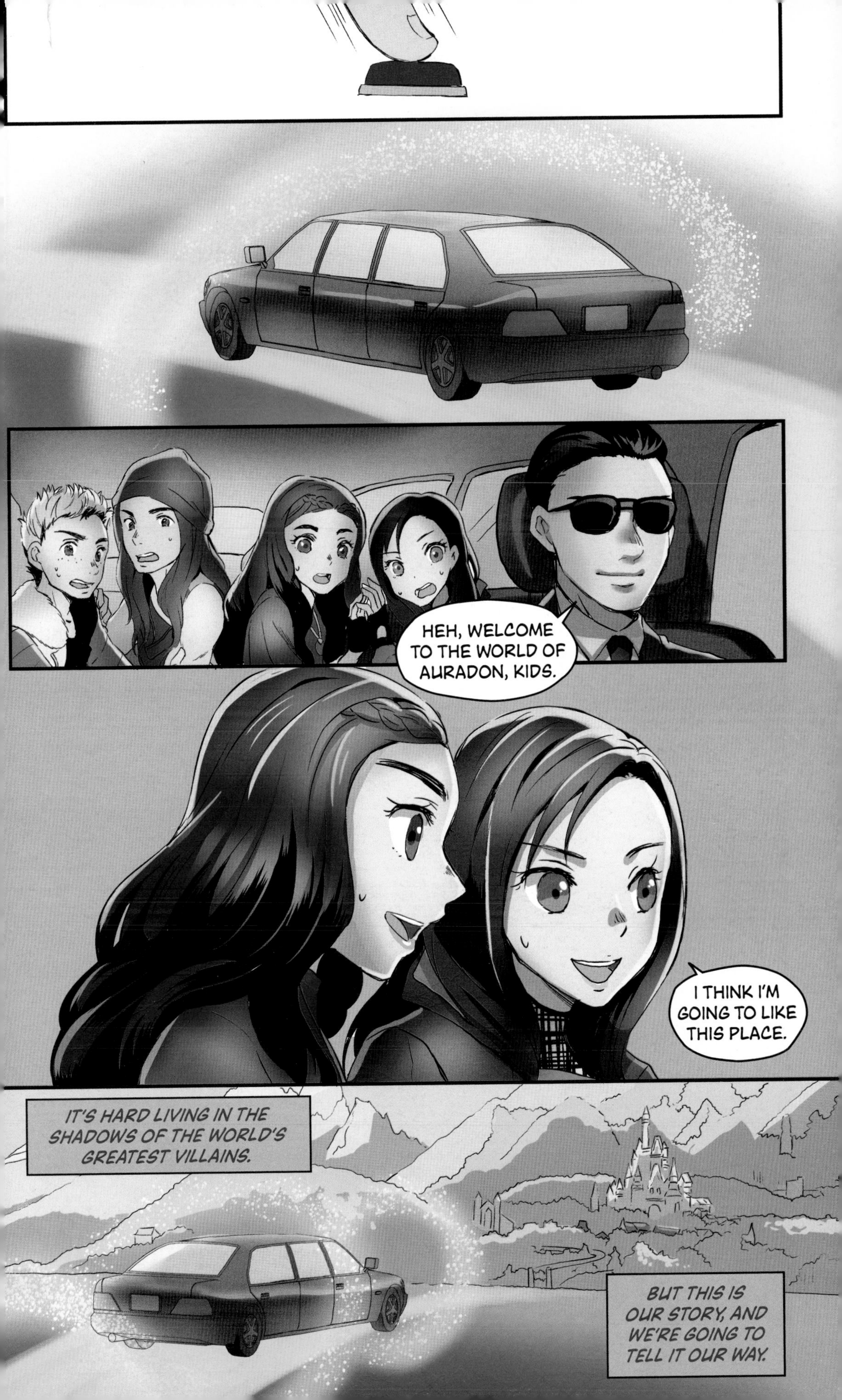
HEH, WELCOME TO THE WORLD OF AURADON, KIDS.
I THINK I'M GOING TO LIKE THIS PLACE.
IT'S HARD LIVING IN THE SHADOWS OF THE WORLD'S GREATEST VILLAINS.
BUT THIS IS OUR STORY, AND WE'RE GOING TO TELL IT OUR WAY.

Chapter Two
School Days

SO THIS IS AURADON PREP, HUH?

COMPARED TO OUR OLD SCHOOL, THIS IS SO...

SICKENINGLY CLEAN? I KNOW, RIGHT?

AH, YEAH, TOTALLY SICK. BLEH.

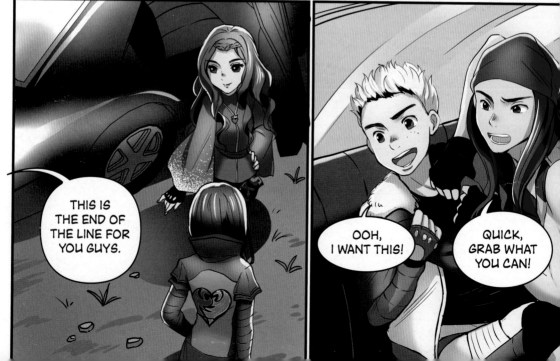

THIS IS THE END OF THE LINE FOR YOU GUYS.

OOH, I WANT THIS!

QUICK, GRAB WHAT YOU CAN!

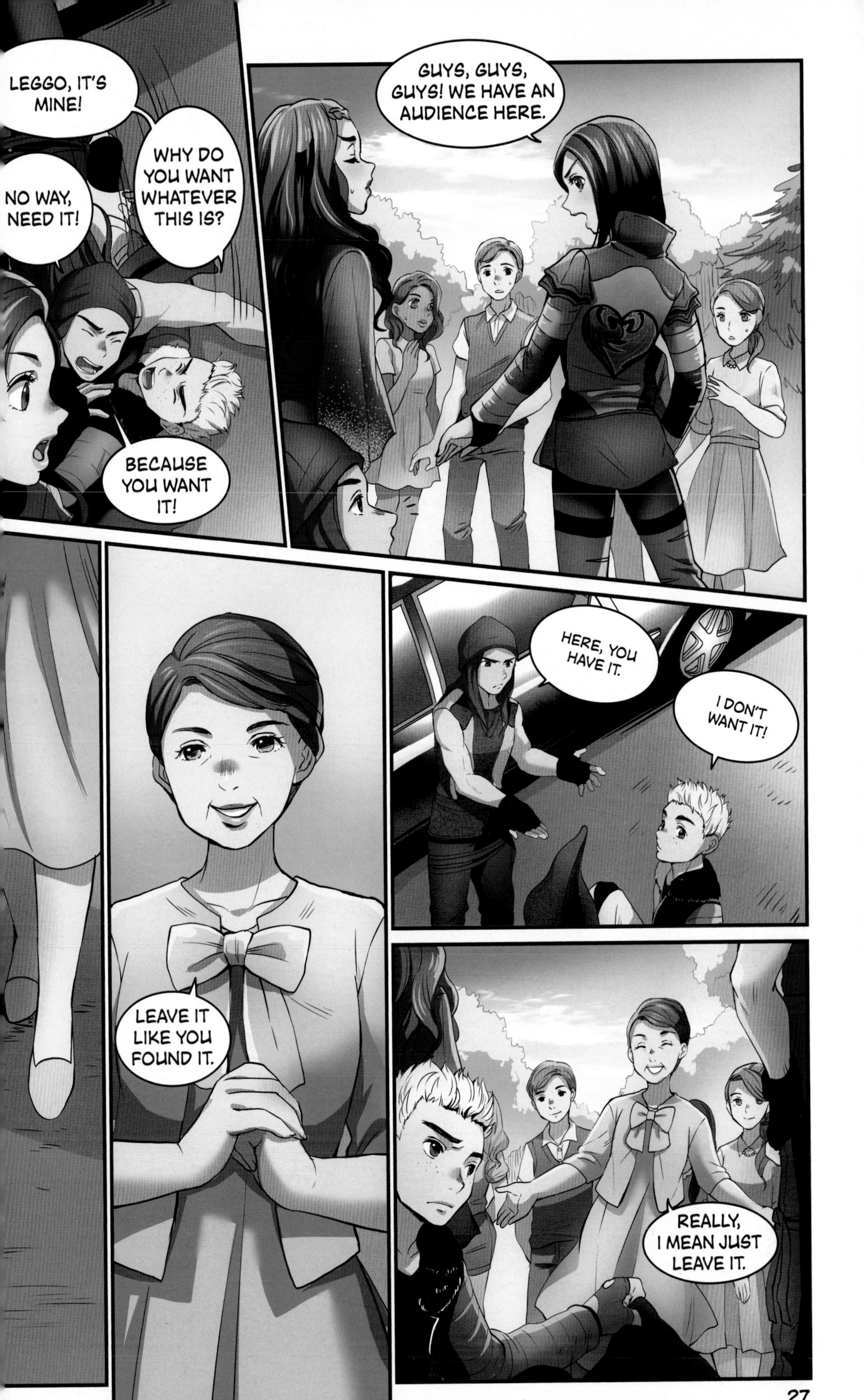
LEGGO, IT'S MINE!
NO WAY, NEED IT!
WHY DO YOU WANT WHATEVER THIS IS?
BECAUSE YOU WANT IT!
GUYS, GUYS, GUYS! WE HAVE AN AUDIENCE HERE.
LEAVE IT LIKE YOU FOUND IT.
HERE, YOU HAVE IT.
I DON'T WANT IT!
REALLY, I MEAN JUST LEAVE IT.

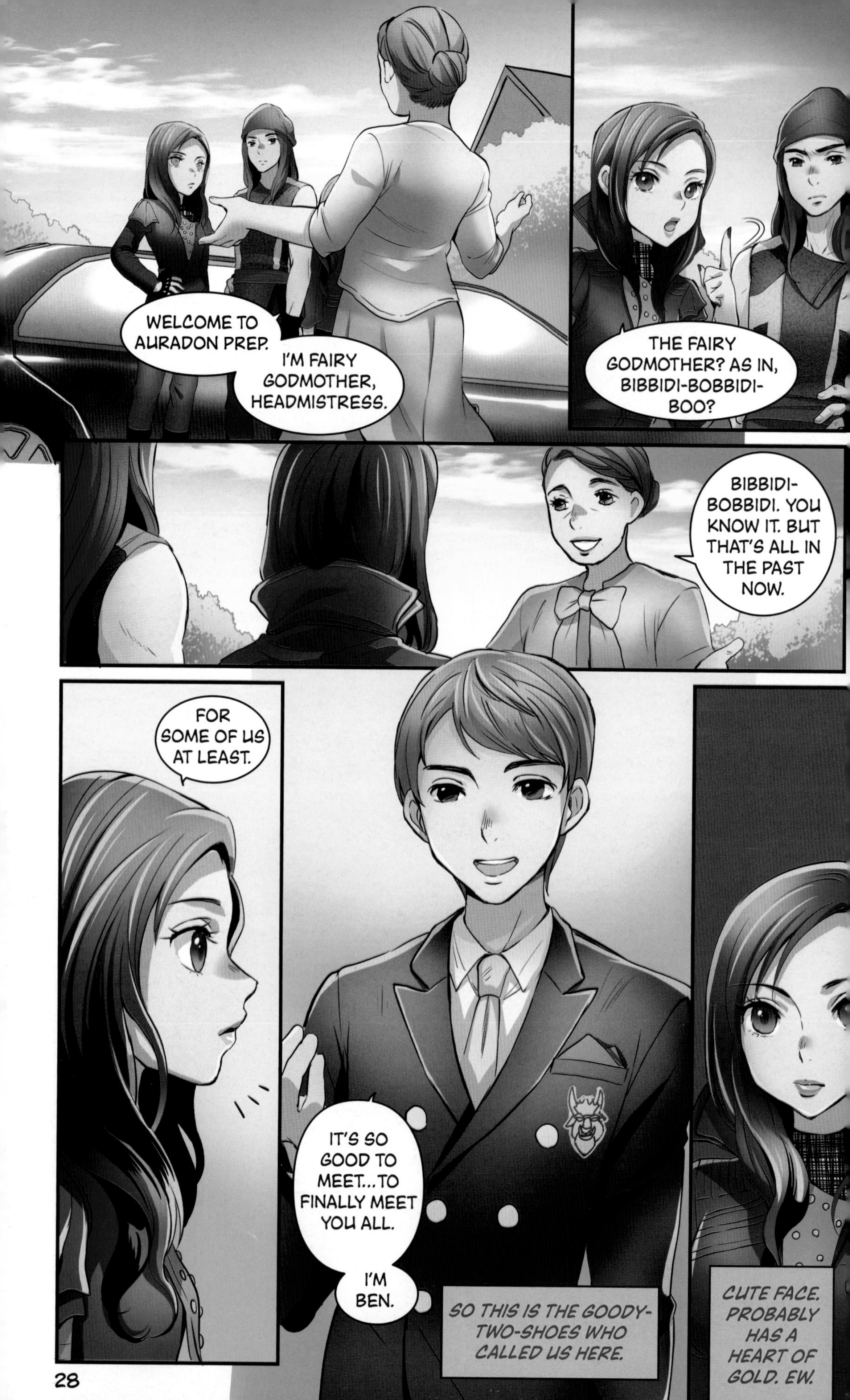
WELCOME TO AURADON PREP.
I'M FAIRY GODMOTHER, HEADMISTRESS.
THE FAIRY GODMOTHER? AS IN, BIBBIDI-BOBBIDI-BOO?
BIBBIDI-BOBBIDI. YOU KNOW IT. BUT THAT'S ALL IN THE PAST NOW.
FOR SOME OF US AT LEAST.
IT'S SO GOOD TO MEET...TO FINALLY MEET YOU ALL.
I'M BEN.
SO THIS IS THE GOODY-TWO-SHOES WHO CALLED US HERE.
CUTE FACE. PROBABLY HAS A HEART OF GOLD. EW.

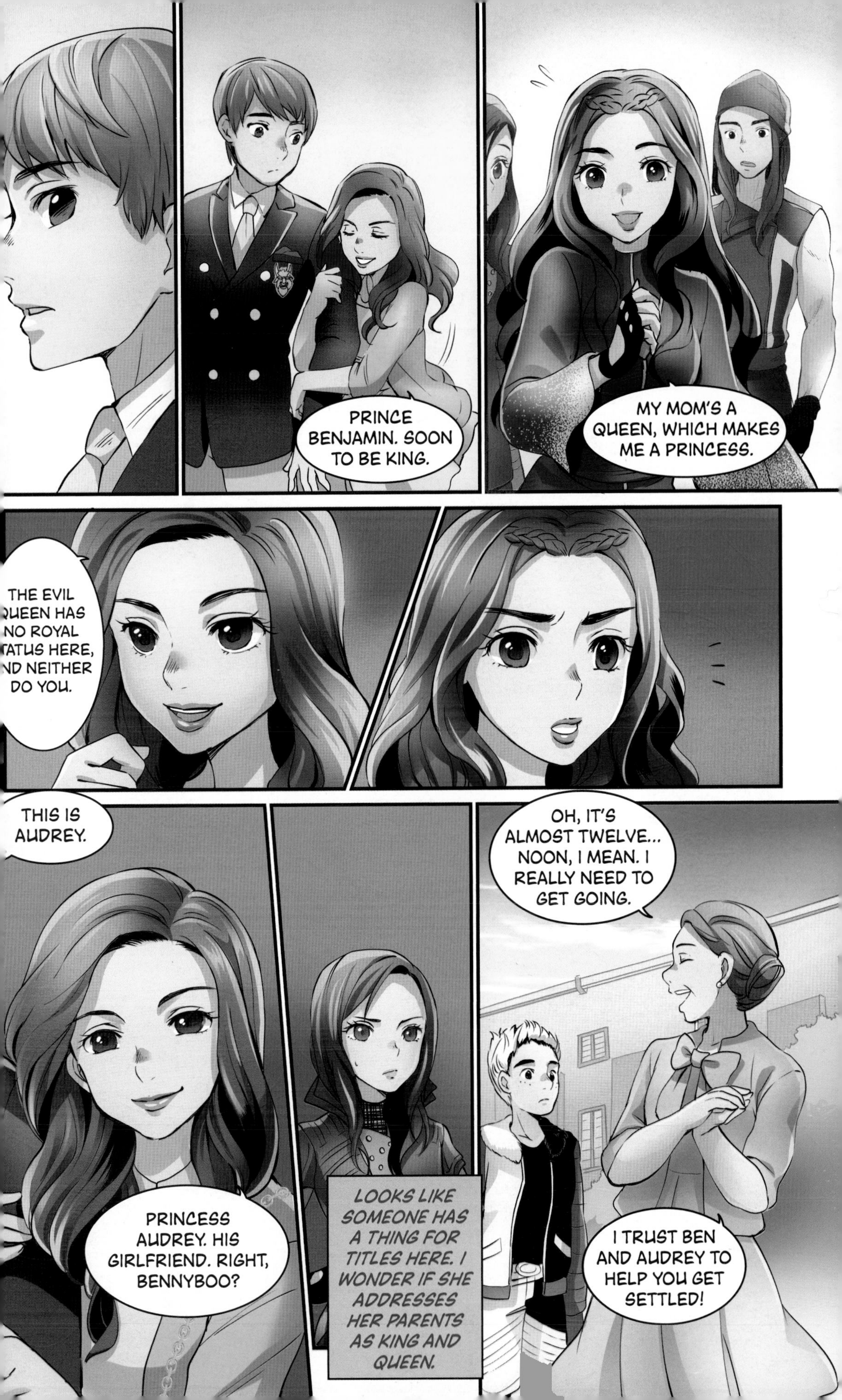
PRINCE BENJAMIN. SOON TO BE KING.
MY MOM'S A QUEEN, WHICH MAKES ME A PRINCESS.
THE EVIL QUEEN HAS NO ROYAL TATUS HERE, ND NEITHER DO YOU.
THIS IS AUDREY.
PRINCESS AUDREY. HIS GIRLFRIEND. RIGHT, BENNYBOO?
LOOKS LIKE SOMEONE HAS A THING FOR TITLES HERE. I WONDER IF SHE ADDRESSES HER PARENTS AS KING AND QUEEN.
OH, IT'S ALMOST TWELVE... NOON, I MEAN. I REALLY NEED TO GET GOING.
I TRUST BEN AND AUDREY TO HELP YOU GET SETTLED!

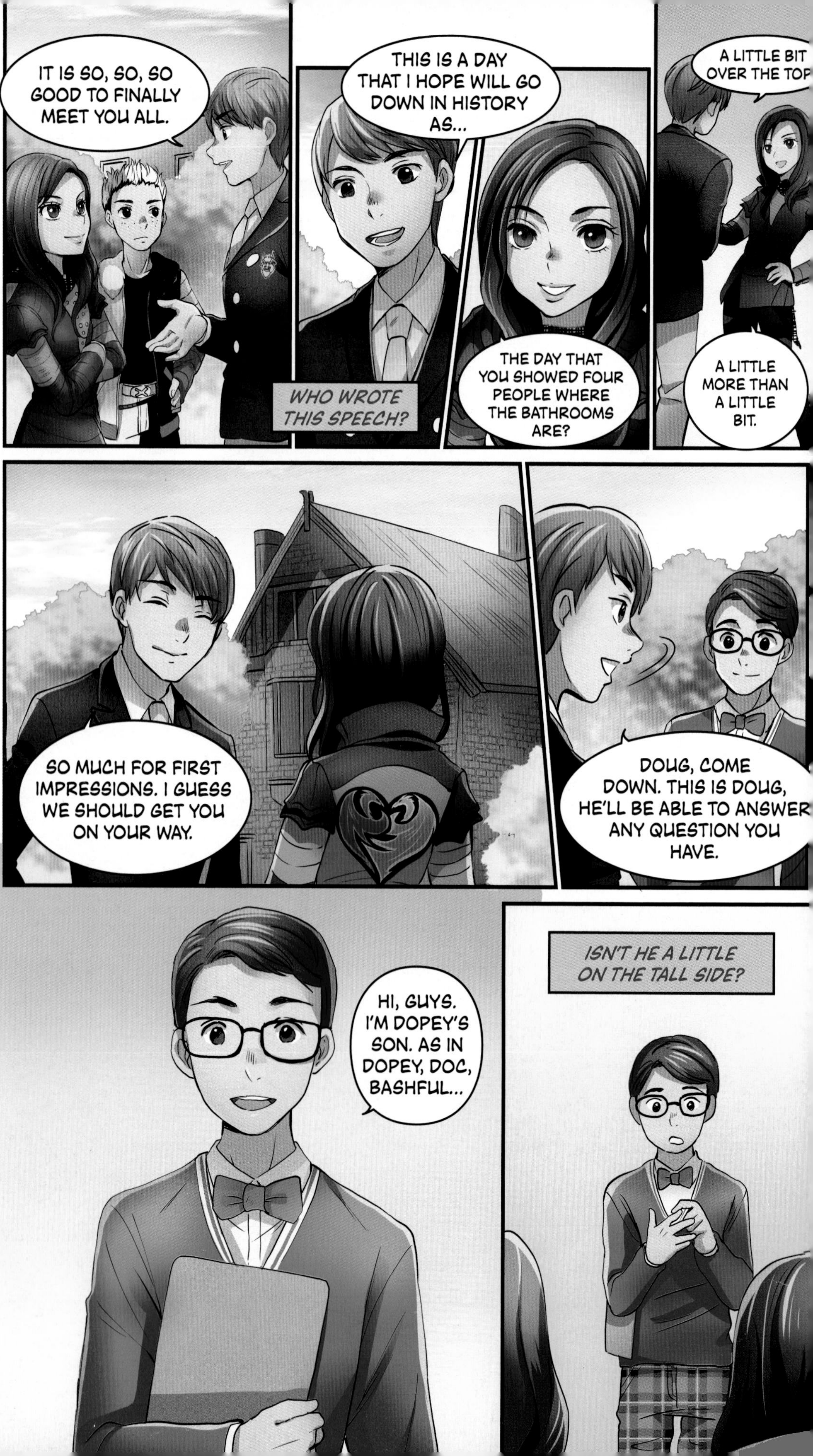
IT IS SO, SO, SO GOOD TO FINALLY MEET YOU ALL.
THIS IS A DAY THAT I HOPE WILL GO DOWN IN HISTORY AS...
WHO WROTE THIS SPEECH?
THE DAY THAT YOU SHOWED FOUR PEOPLE WHERE THE BATHROOMS ARE?
A LITTLE BIT OVER THE TOP
A LITTLE MORE THAN A LITTLE BIT.
SO MUCH FOR FIRST IMPRESSIONS. I GUESS WE SHOULD GET YOU ON YOUR WAY.
DOUG, COME DOWN. THIS IS DOUG, HE'LL BE ABLE TO ANSWER ANY QUESTION YOU HAVE.
HI, GUYS. I'M DOPEY'S SON. AS IN DOPEY, DOC, BASHFUL...
ISN'T HE A LITTLE ON THE TALL SIDE?

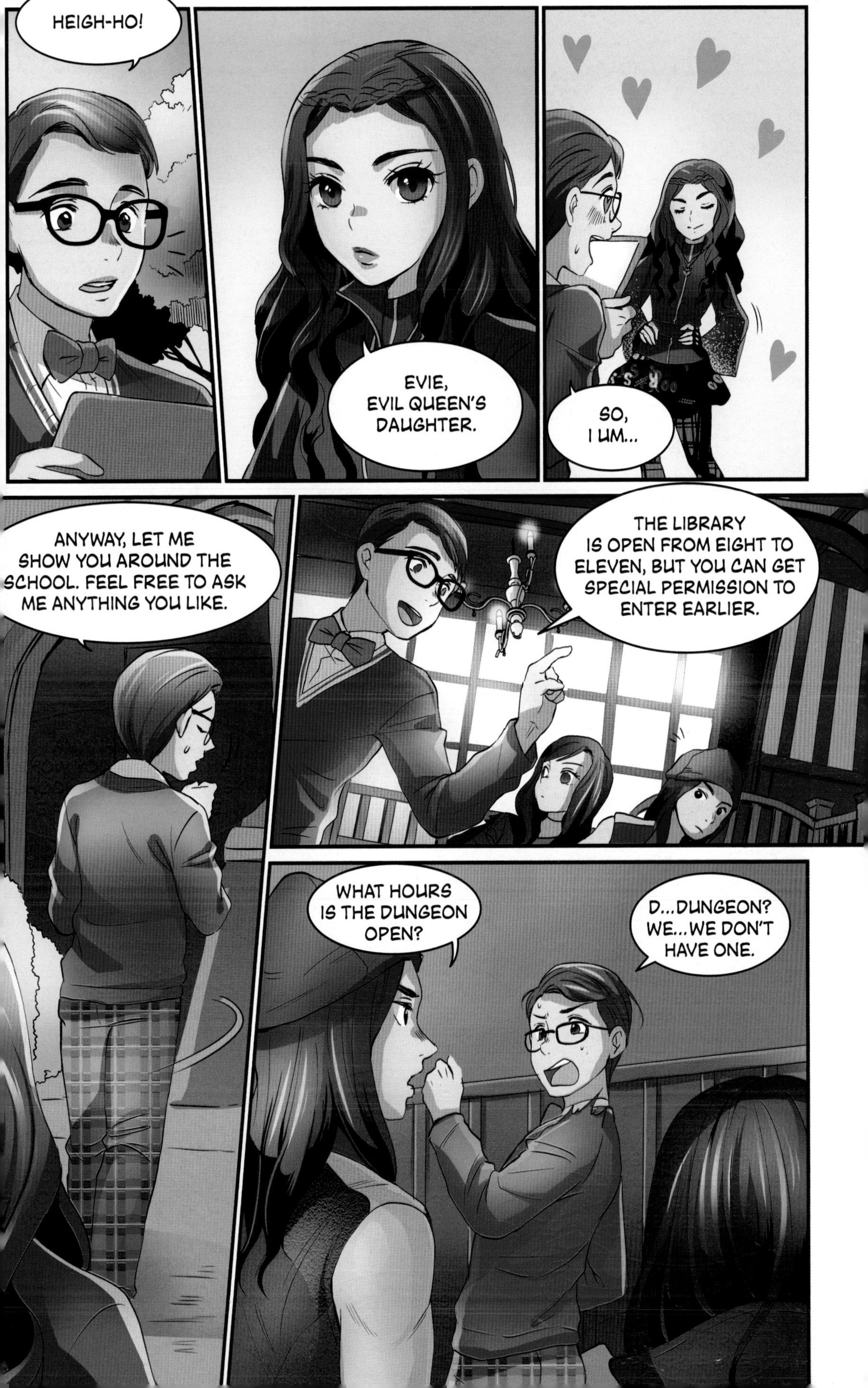
HEIGH-HO!
EVIE, EVIL QUEEN'S DAUGHTER.
SO, I UM...
ANYWAY, LET ME SHOW YOU AROUND THE SCHOOL. FEEL FREE TO ASK ME ANYTHING YOU LIKE.
THE LIBRARY IS OPEN FROM EIGHT TO ELEVEN, BUT YOU CAN GET SPECIAL PERMISSION TO ENTER EARLIER.
WHAT HOURS IS THE DUNGEON OPEN?
D...DUNGEON? WE...WE DON'T HAVE ONE.

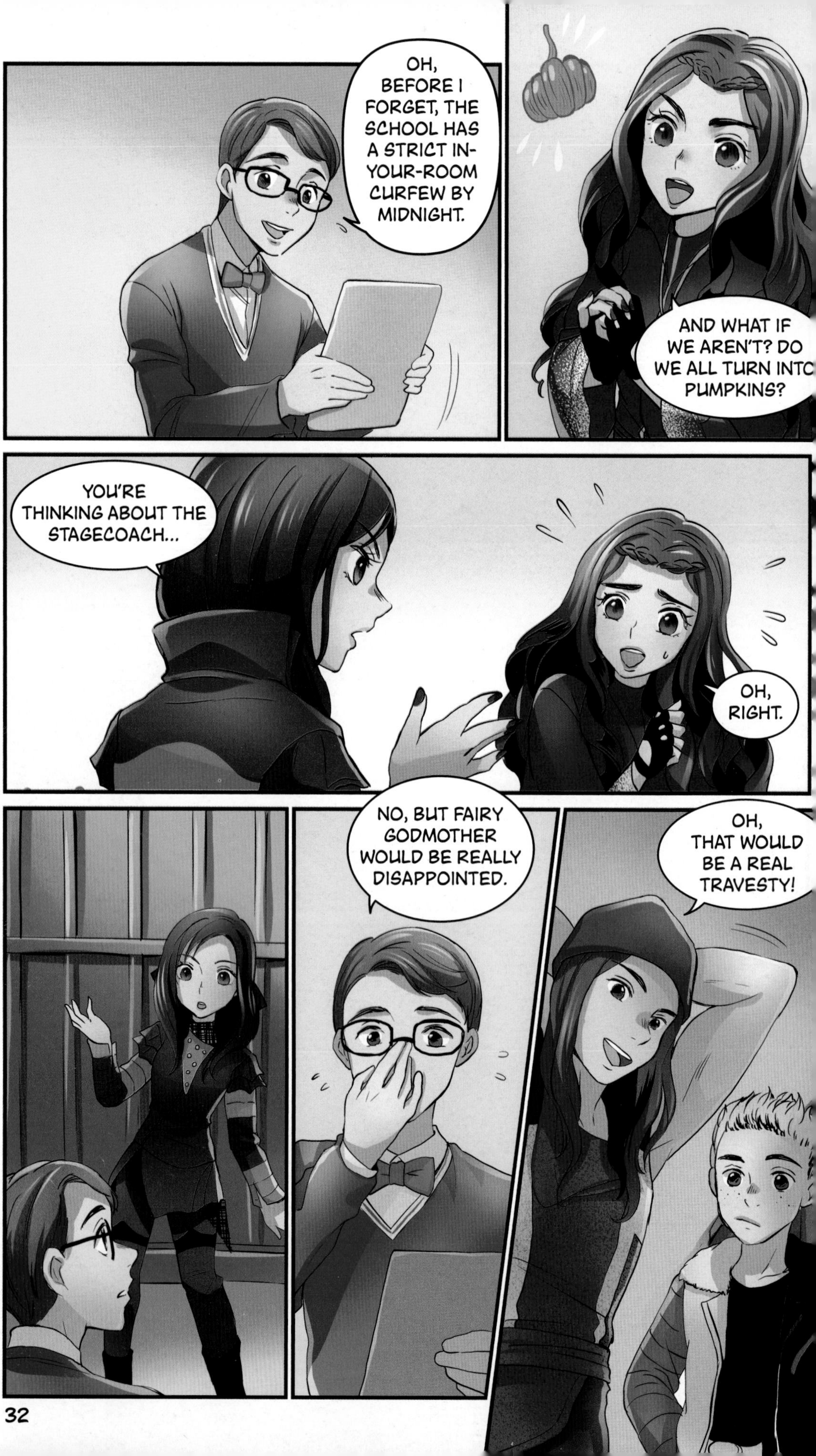
OH, BEFORE I FORGET, THE SCHOOL HAS A STRICT IN-YOUR-ROOM CURFEW BY MIDNIGHT.
AND WHAT IF WE AREN'T? DO WE ALL TURN INTO PUMPKINS?
YOU'RE THINKING ABOUT THE STAGECOACH...
OH, RIGHT.
NO, BUT FAIRY GODMOTHER WOULD BE REALLY DISAPPOINTED.
OH, THAT WOULD BE A REAL TRAVESTY!

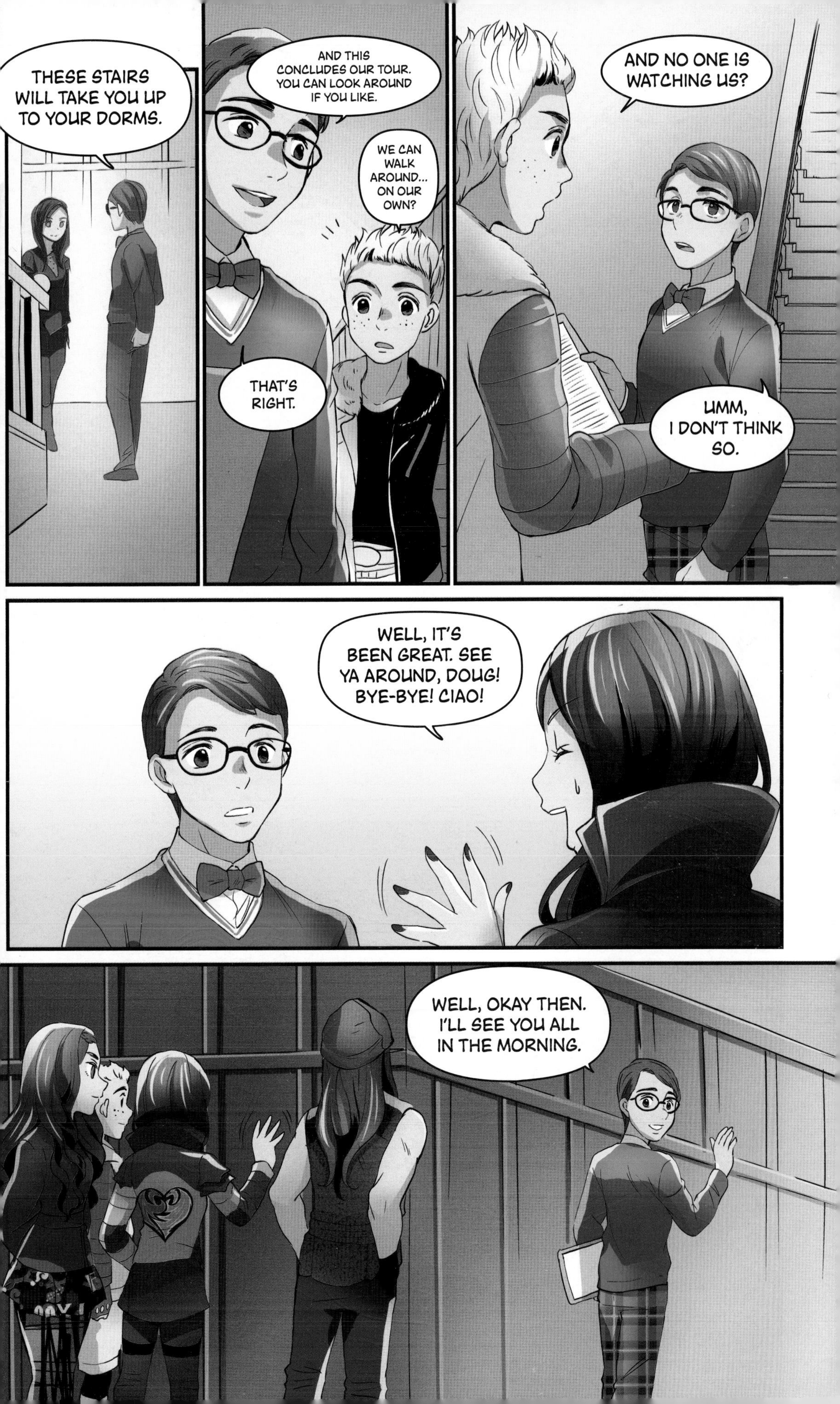
THESE STAIRS WILL TAKE YOU UP TO YOUR DORMS.
AND THIS CONCLUDES OUR TOUR. YOU CAN LOOK AROUND IF YOU LIKE.
WE CAN WALK AROUND... ON OUR OWN?
THAT'S RIGHT.
AND NO ONE IS WATCHING US?
UMM, I DON'T THINK SO.
WELL, IT'S BEEN GREAT. SEE YA AROUND, DOUG! BYE-BYE! CIAO!
WELL, OKAY THEN. I'LL SEE YOU ALL IN THE MORNING.

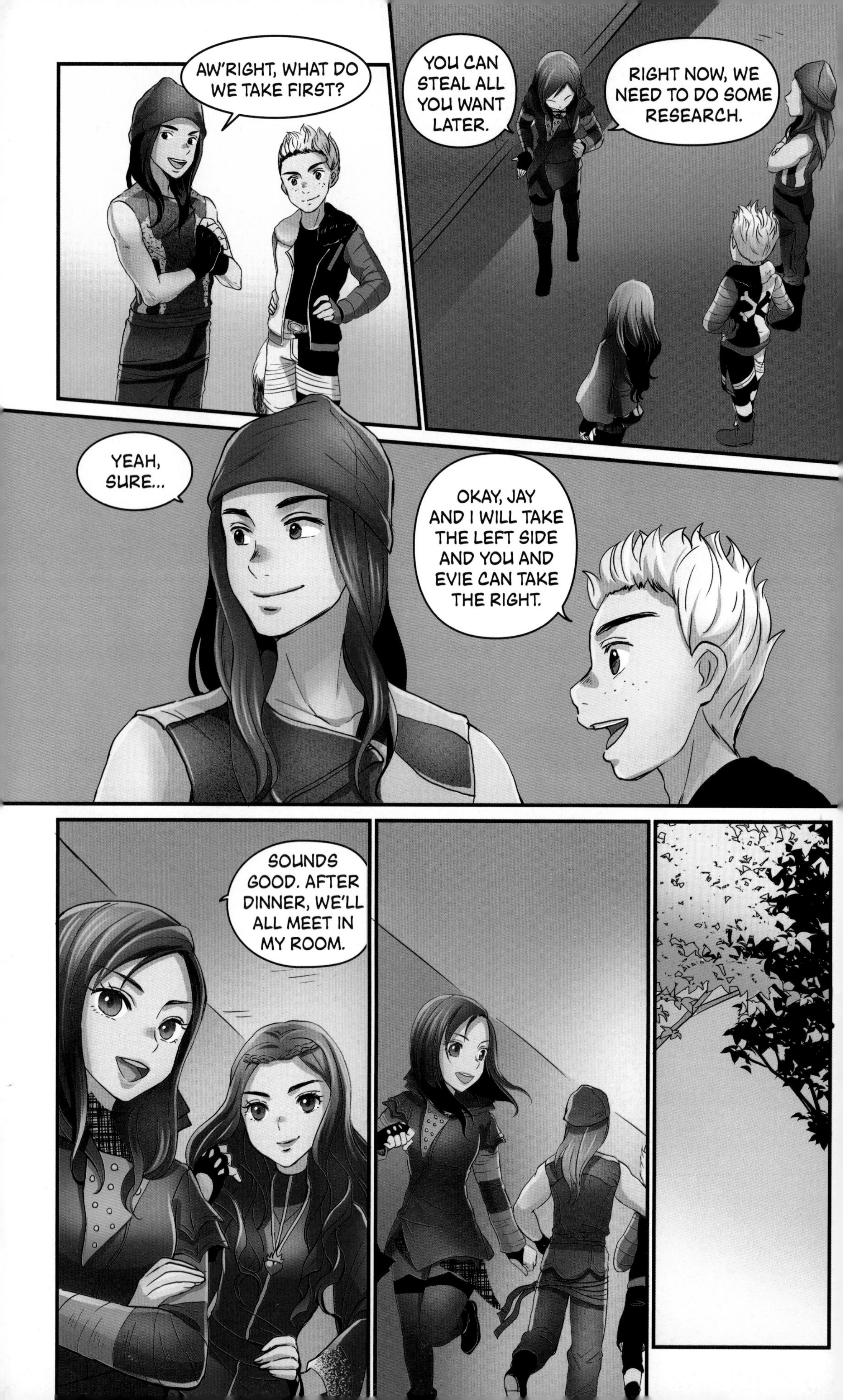
AW'RIGHT, WHAT DO WE TAKE FIRST?
YOU CAN STEAL ALL YOU WANT LATER.
RIGHT NOW, WE NEED TO DO SOME RESEARCH.
YEAH, SURE...
OKAY, JAY AND I WILL TAKE THE LEFT SIDE AND YOU AND EVIE CAN TAKE THE RIGHT.
SOUNDS GOOD. AFTER DINNER, WE'LL ALL MEET IN MY ROOM.

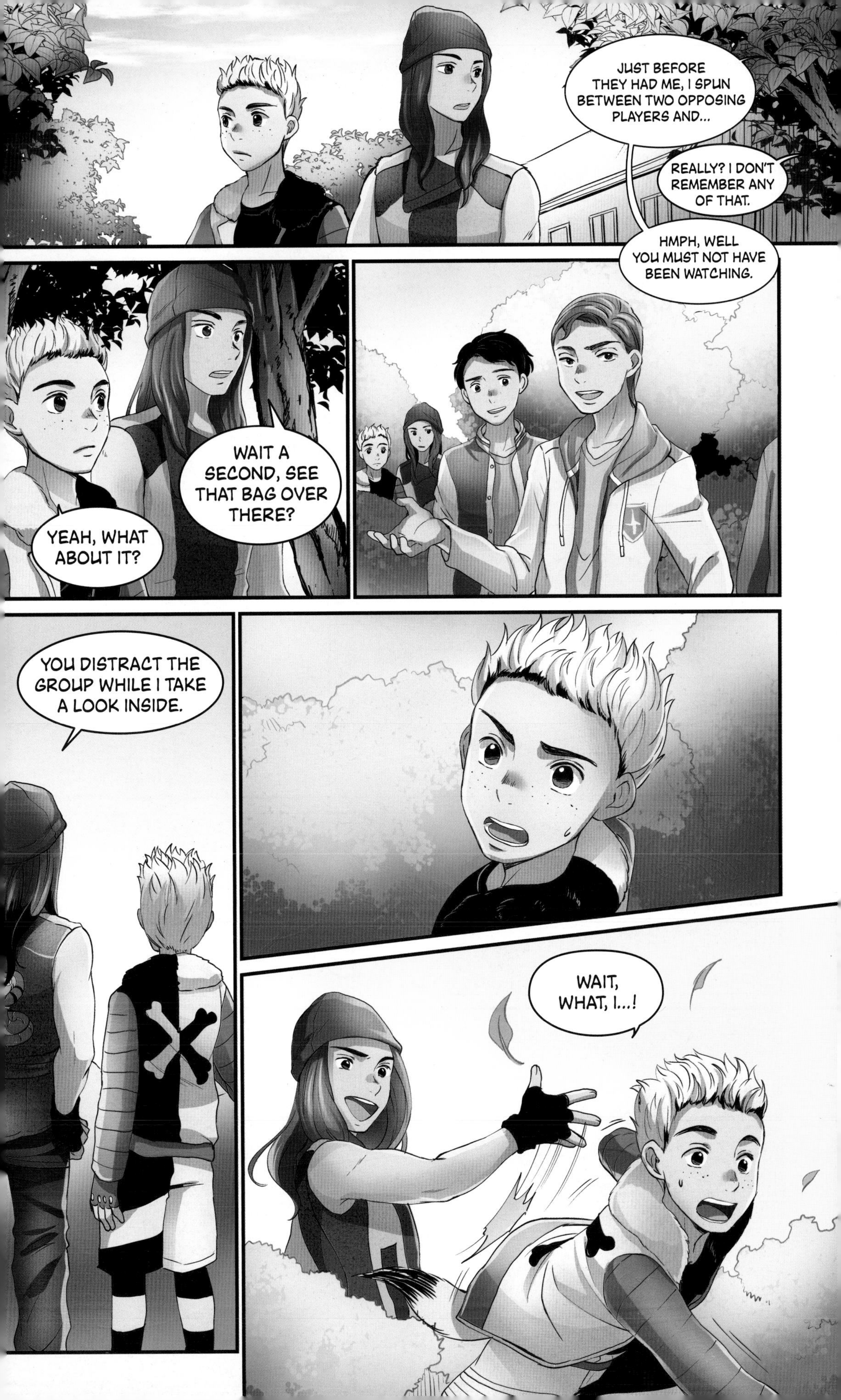
JUST BEFORE THEY HAD ME, I SPUN BETWEEN TWO OPPOSING PLAYERS AND...
REALLY? I DON'T REMEMBER ANY OF THAT.
HMPH, WELL YOU MUST NOT HAVE BEEN WATCHING.
WAIT A SECOND, SEE THAT BAG OVER THERE?
YEAH, WHAT ABOUT IT?
YOU DISTRACT THE GROUP WHILE I TAKE A LOOK INSIDE.
WAIT, WHAT, I...!

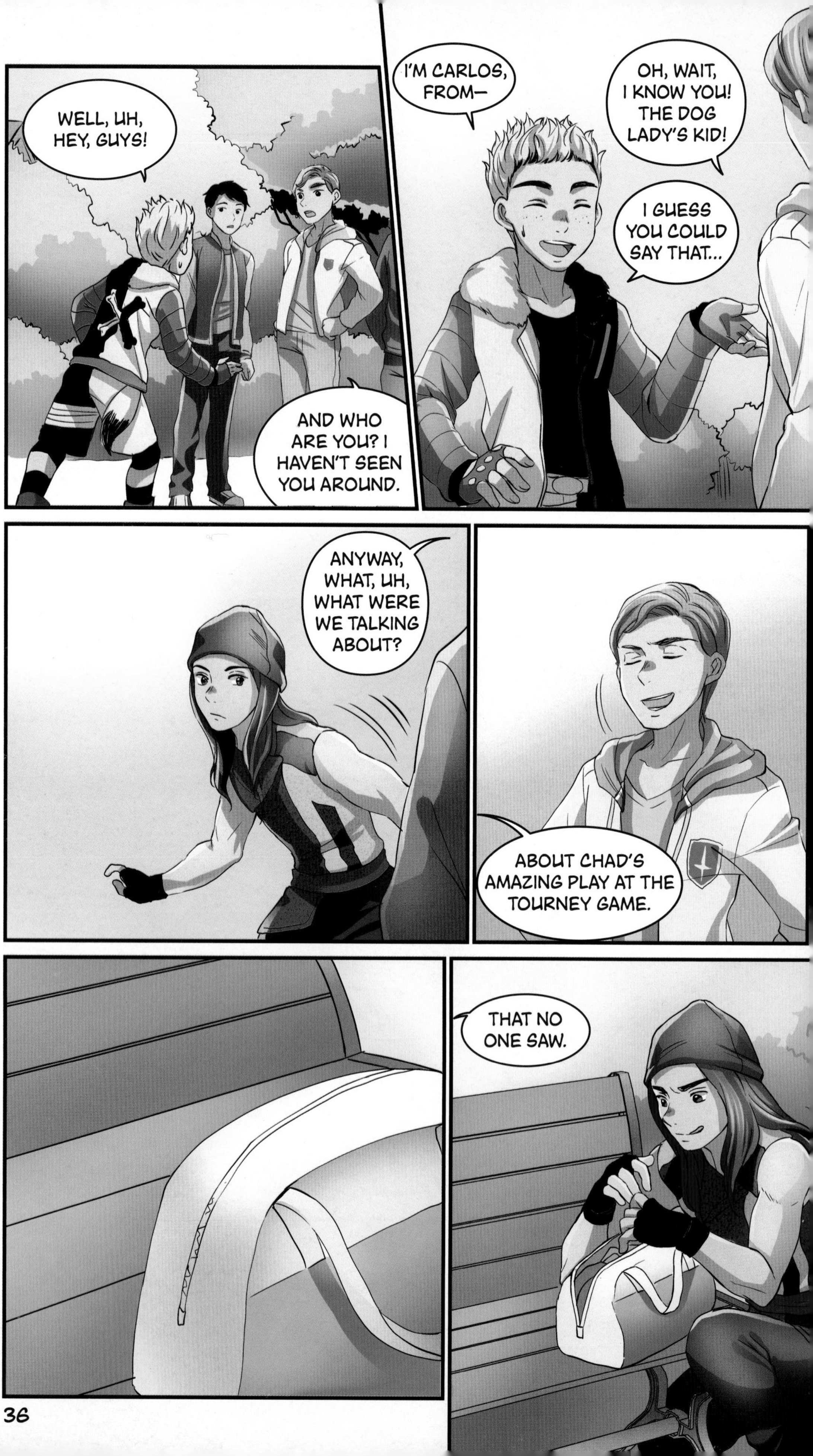
WELL, UH, HEY, GUYS!
AND WHO ARE YOU? I HAVEN'T SEEN YOU AROUND.
I'M CARLOS, FROM—
OH, WAIT, I KNOW YOU! THE DOG LADY'S KID!
I GUESS YOU COULD SAY THAT...
ANYWAY, WHAT, UH, WHAT WERE WE TALKING ABOUT?
ABOUT CHAD'S AMAZING PLAY AT THE TOURNEY GAME.
THAT NO ONE SAW.

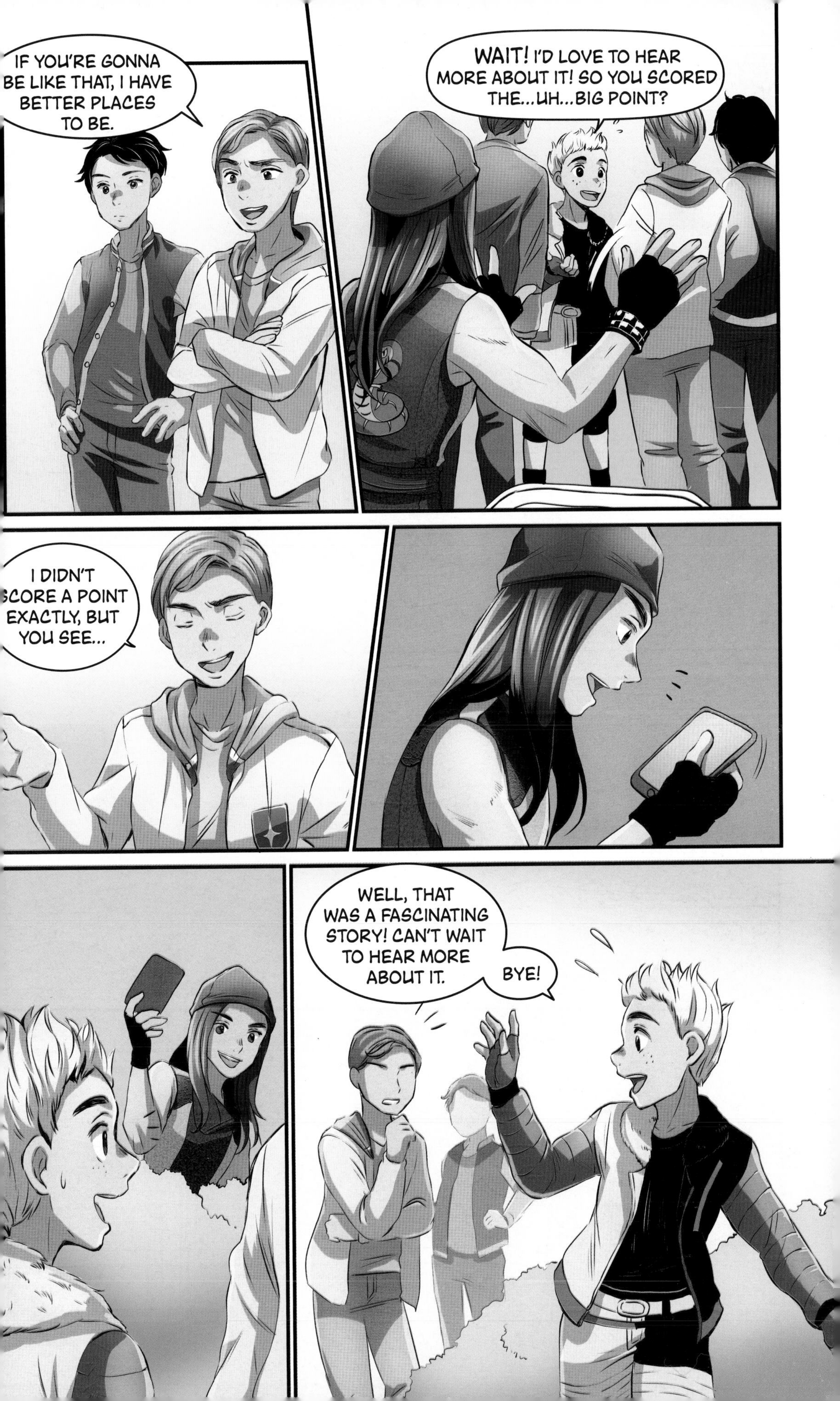
IF YOU'RE GONNA BE LIKE THAT, I HAVE BETTER PLACES TO BE.
WAIT! I'D LOVE TO HEAR MORE ABOUT IT! SO YOU SCORED THE...UH...BIG POINT?
I DIDN'T SCORE A POINT EXACTLY, BUT YOU SEE...
WELL, THAT WAS A FASCINATING STORY! CAN'T WAIT TO HEAR MORE ABOUT IT.
BYE!

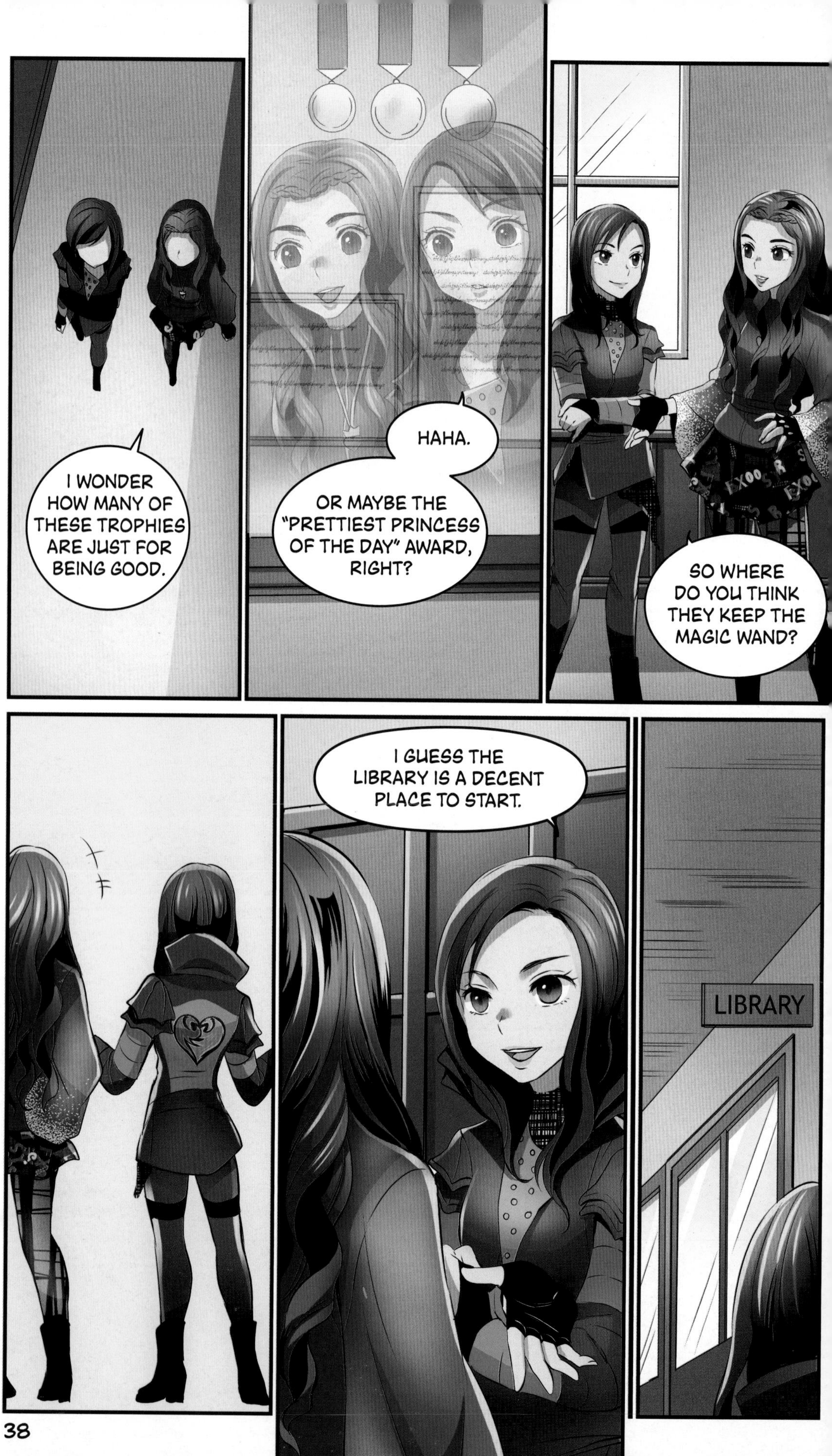
I WONDER HOW MANY OF THESE TROPHIES ARE JUST FOR BEING GOOD.
HAHA.
OR MAYBE THE "PRETTIEST PRINCESS OF THE DAY" AWARD, RIGHT?
SO WHERE DO YOU THINK THEY KEEP THE MAGIC WAND?
I GUESS THE LIBRARY IS A DECENT PLACE TO START.
LIBRARY

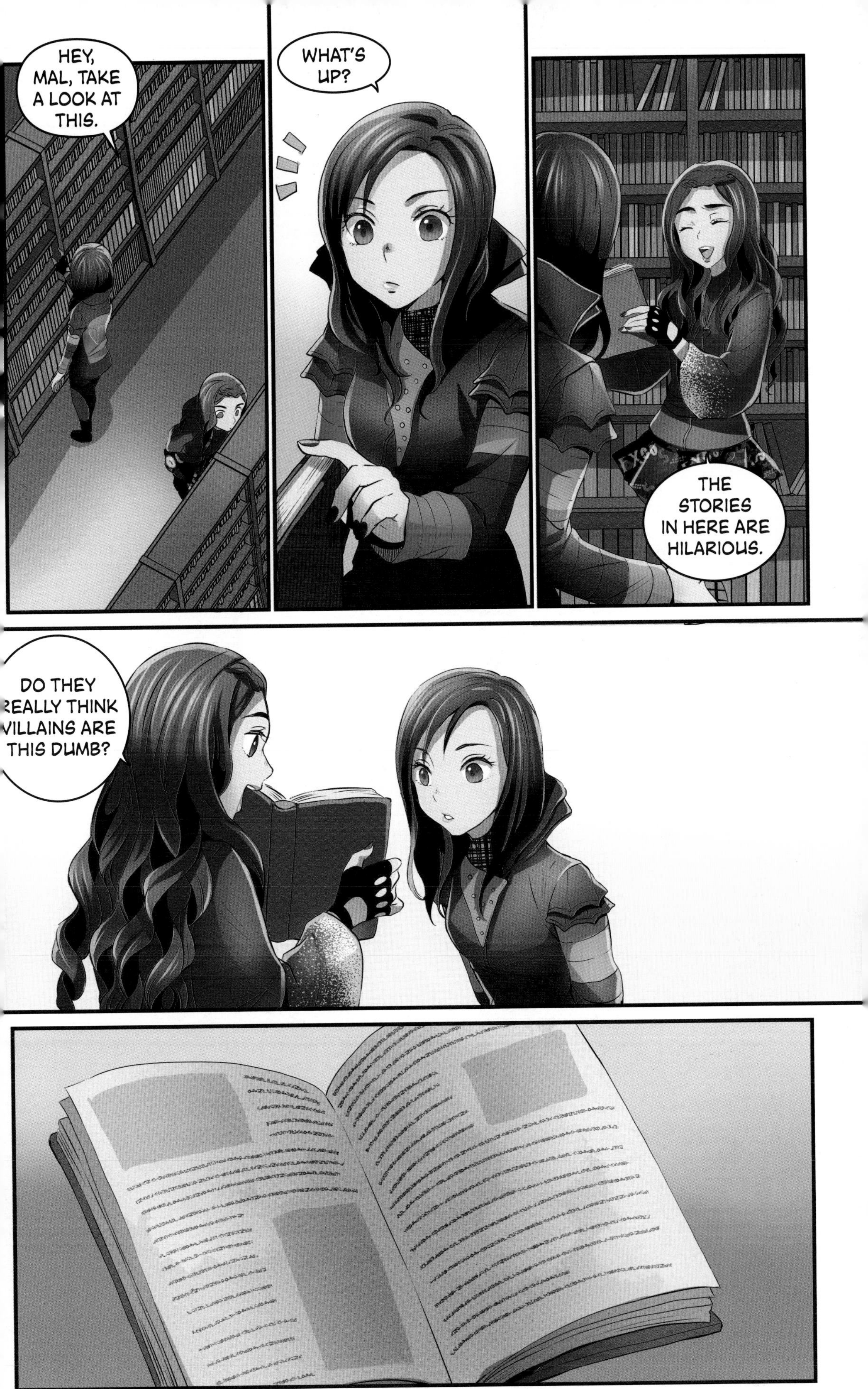
HEY, MAL, TAKE A LOOK AT THIS.
WHAT'S UP?
THE STORIES IN HERE ARE HILARIOUS.
DO THEY REALLY THINK VILLAINS ARE THIS DUMB?

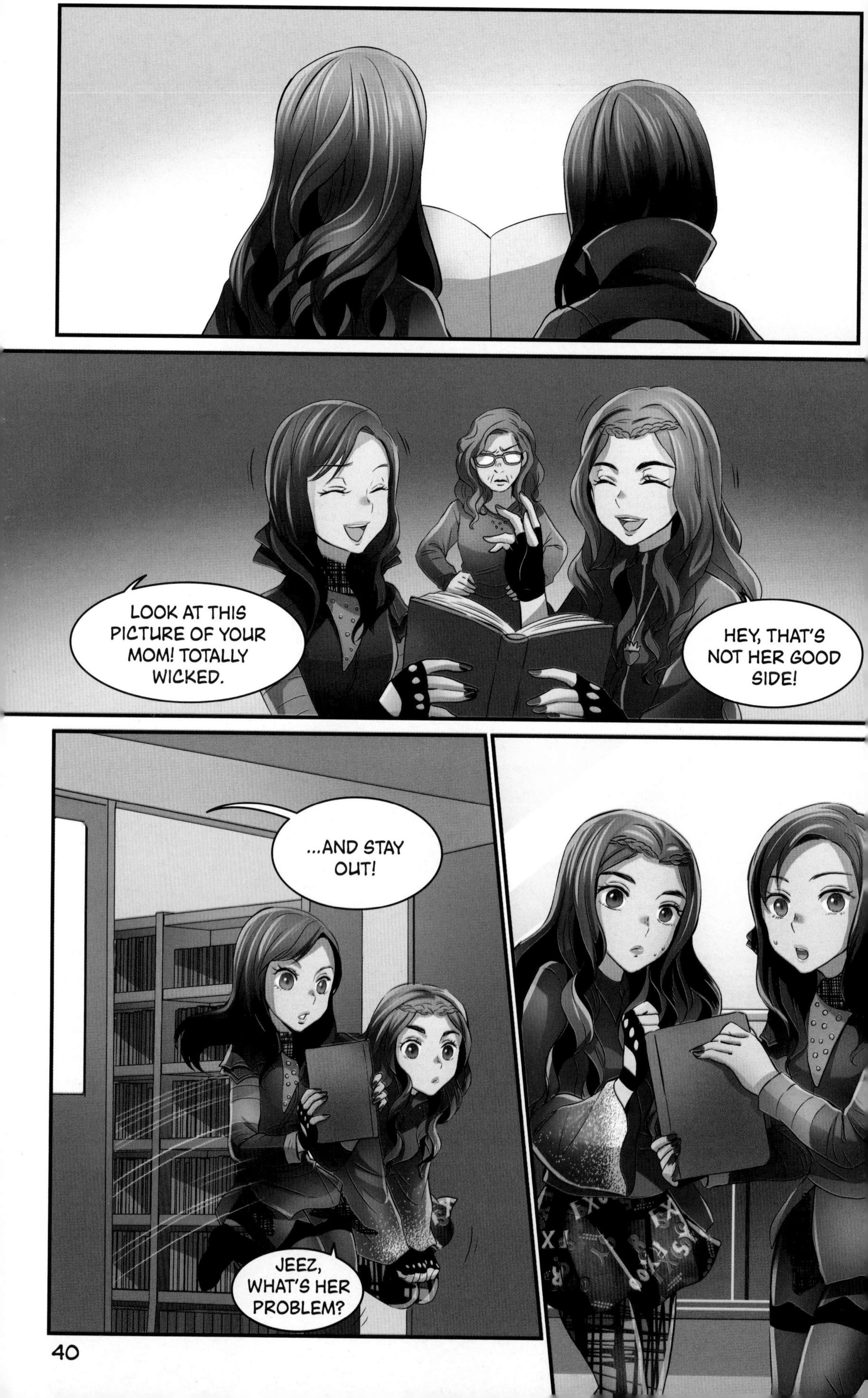
LOOK AT THIS PICTURE OF YOUR MOM! TOTALLY WICKED.
HEY, THAT'S NOT HER GOOD SIDE!
...AND STAY OUT!
JEEZ, WHAT'S HER PROBLEM?

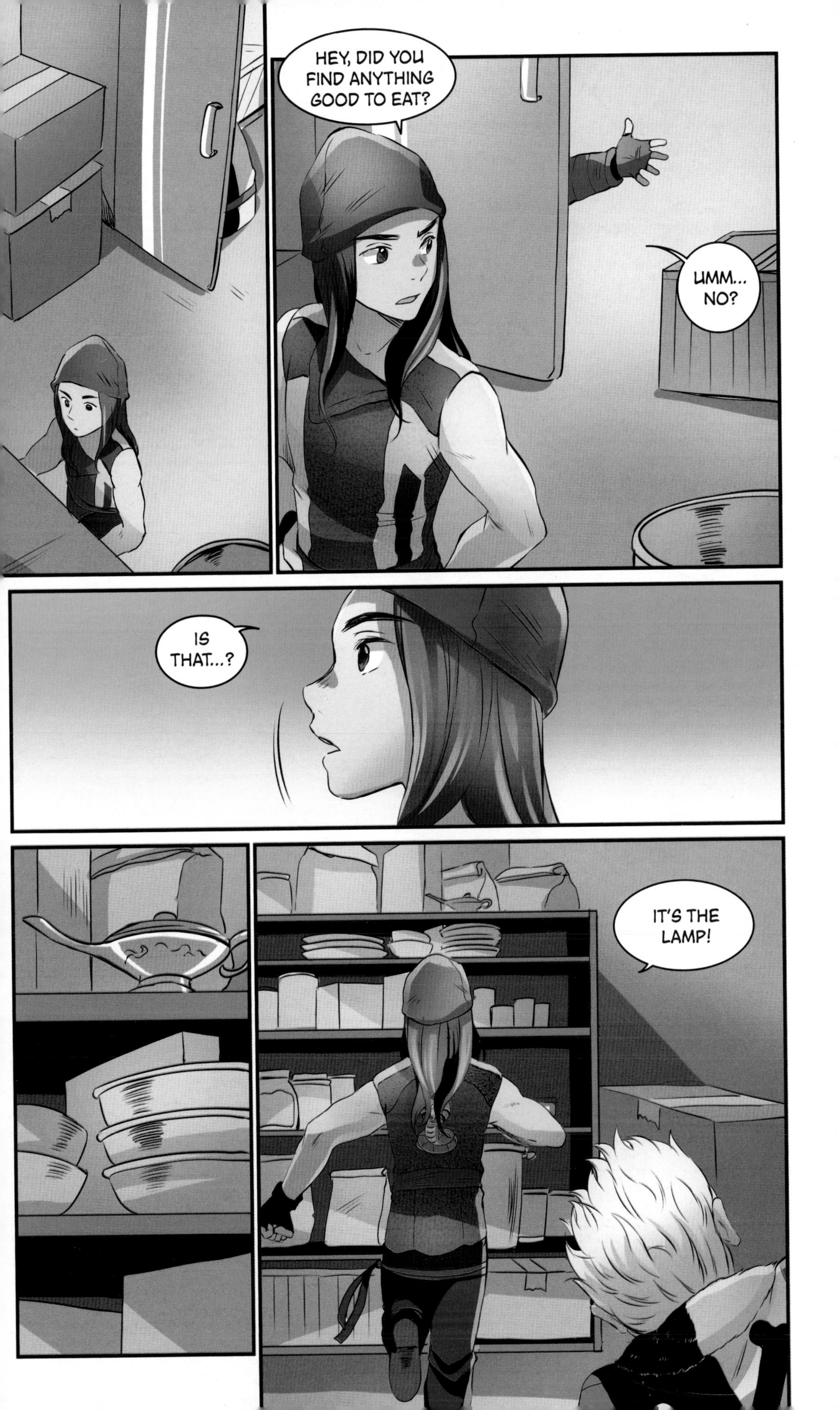
HEY, DID YOU FIND ANYTHING GOOD TO EAT?
UMM... NO?
IS THAT...?
IT'S THE LAMP!

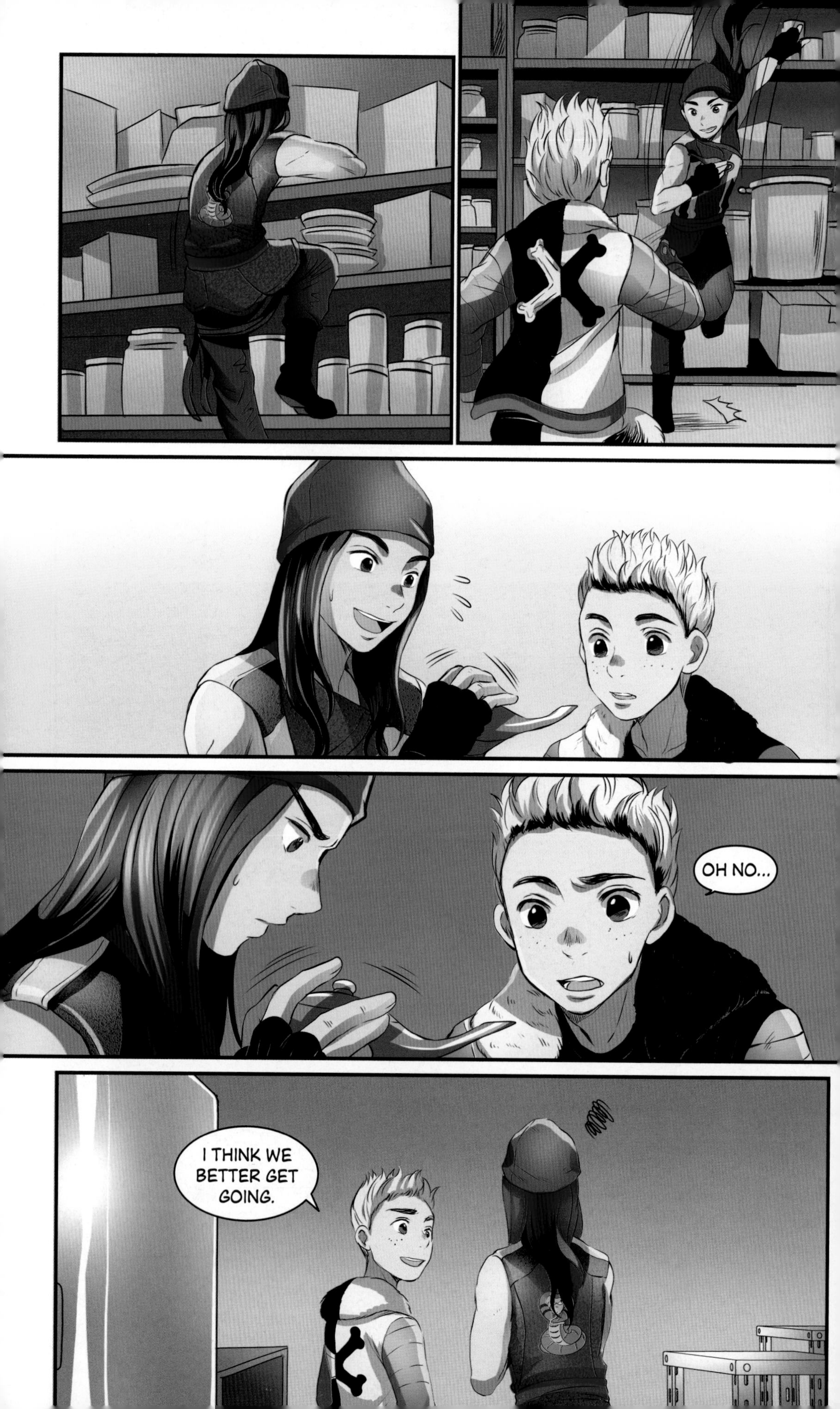
OH NO...
I THINK WE BETTER GET GOING.

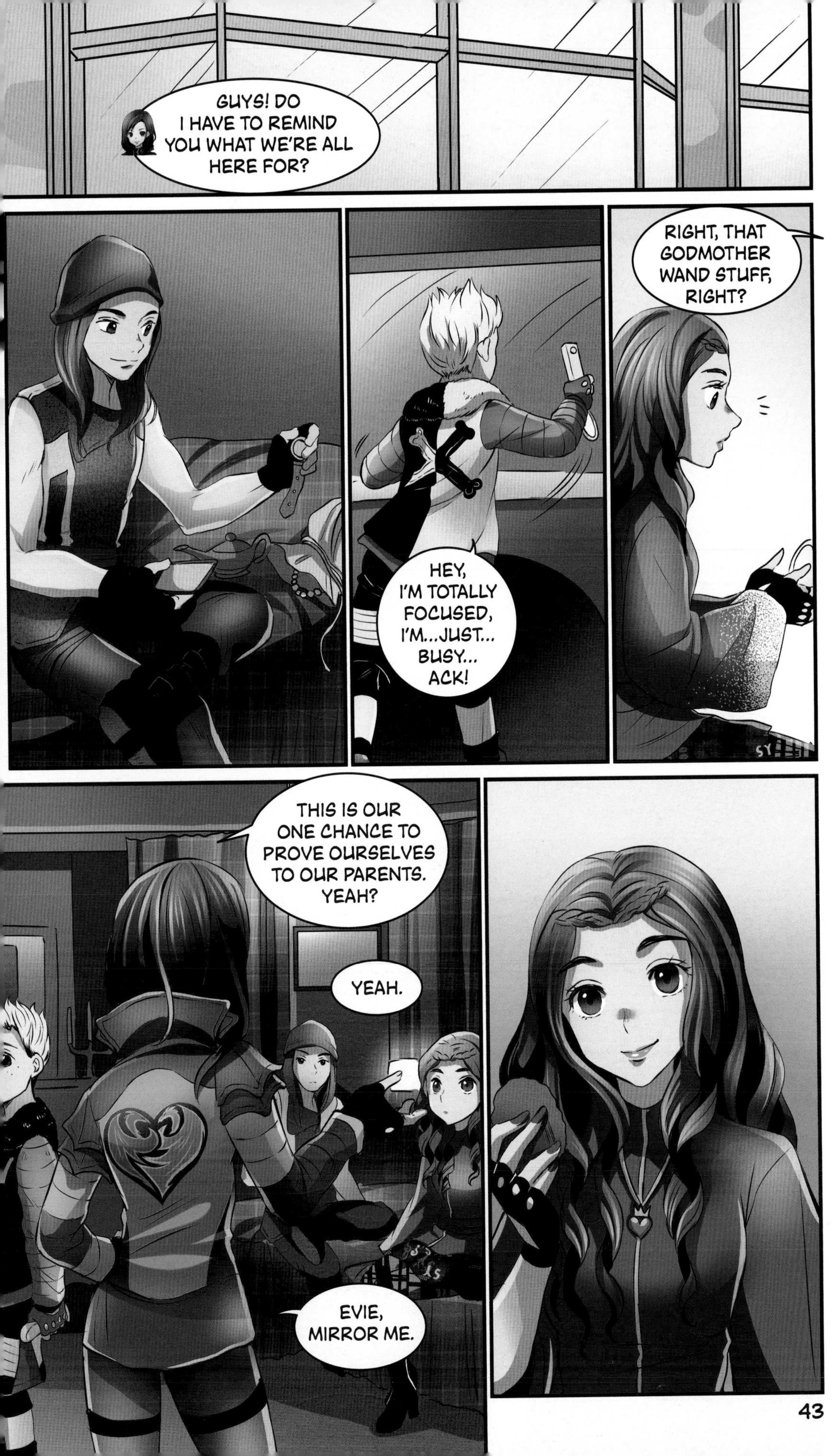
GUYS! DO I HAVE TO REMIND YOU WHAT WE'RE ALL HERE FOR?
RIGHT, THAT GODMOTHER WAND STUFF, RIGHT?
HEY, I'M TOTALLY FOCUSED, I'M...JUST... BUSY... ACK!
THIS IS OUR ONE CHANCE TO PROVE OURSELVES TO OUR PARENTS. YEAH?
YEAH.
EVIE, MIRROR ME.

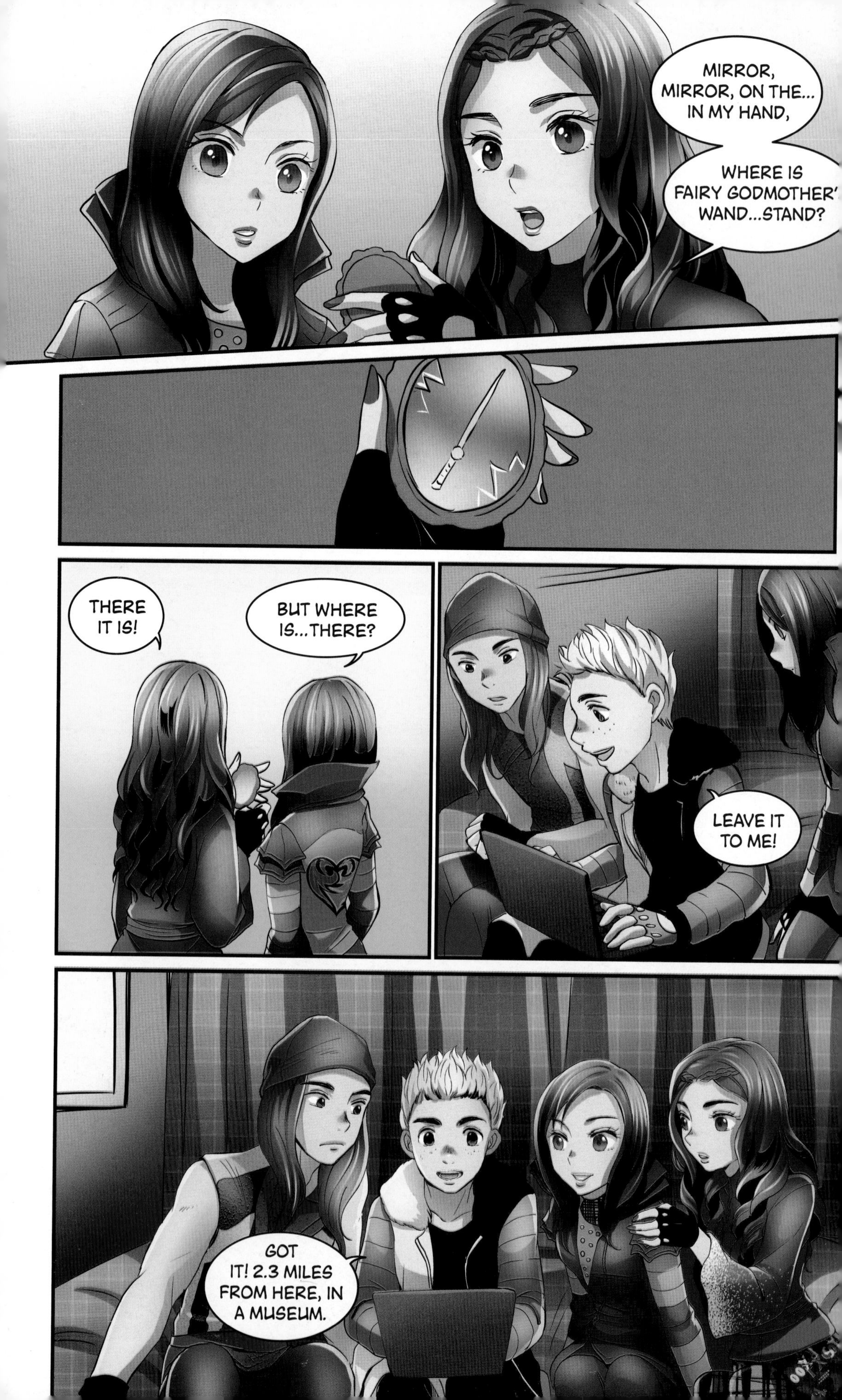
MIRROR, MIRROR, ON THE... IN MY HAND,
WHERE IS FAIRY GODMOTHER' WAND...STAND?
THERE IT IS!
BUT WHERE IS...THERE?
LEAVE IT TO ME!
GOT IT! 2.3 MILES FROM HERE, IN A MUSEUM.

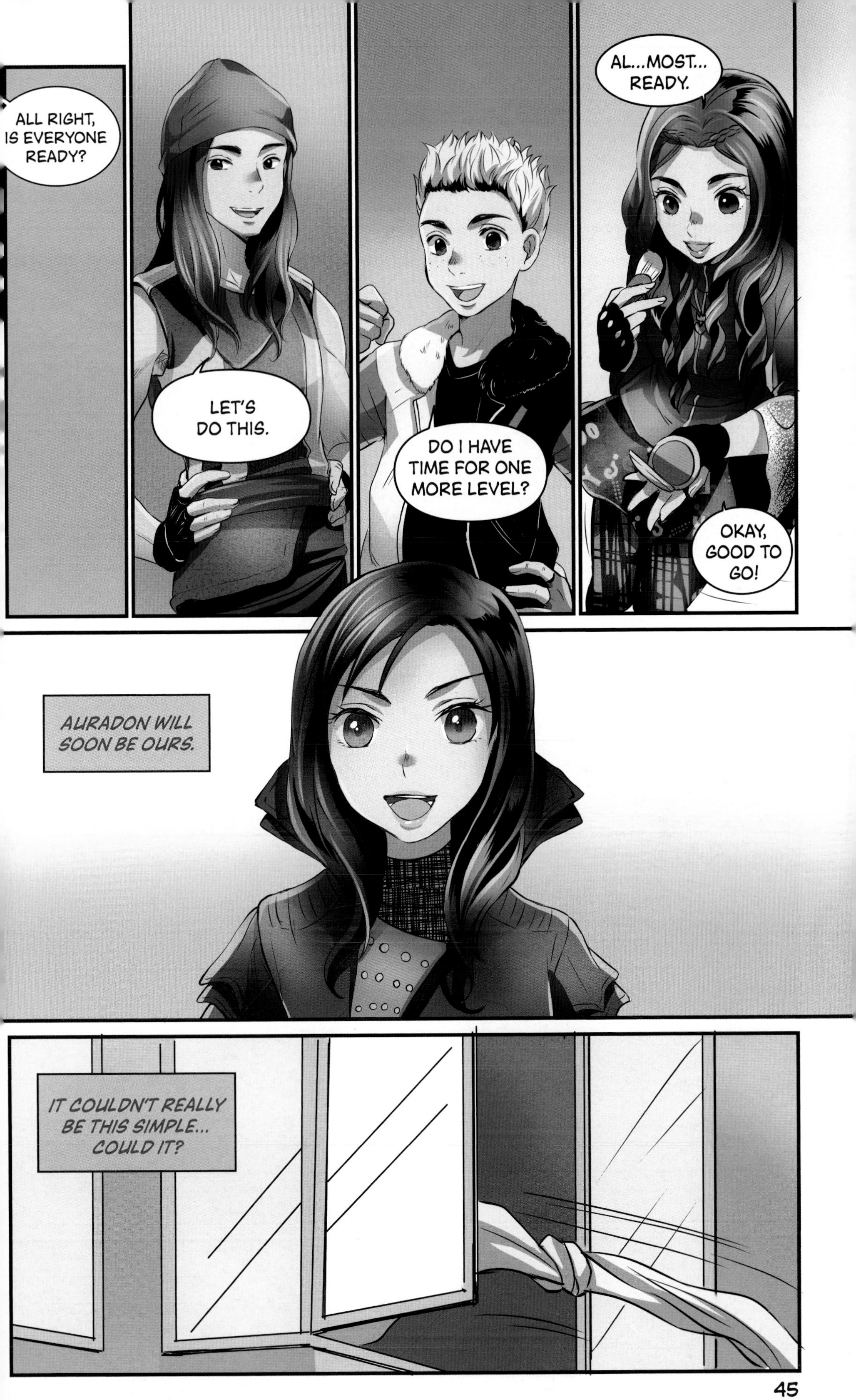
ALL RIGHT, IS EVERYONE READY?
LET'S DO THIS.
DO I HAVE TIME FOR ONE MORE LEVEL?
AL...MOST... READY.
OKAY, GOOD TO GO!
AURADON WILL SOON BE OURS.
IT COULDN'T REALLY BE THIS SIMPLE... COULD IT?

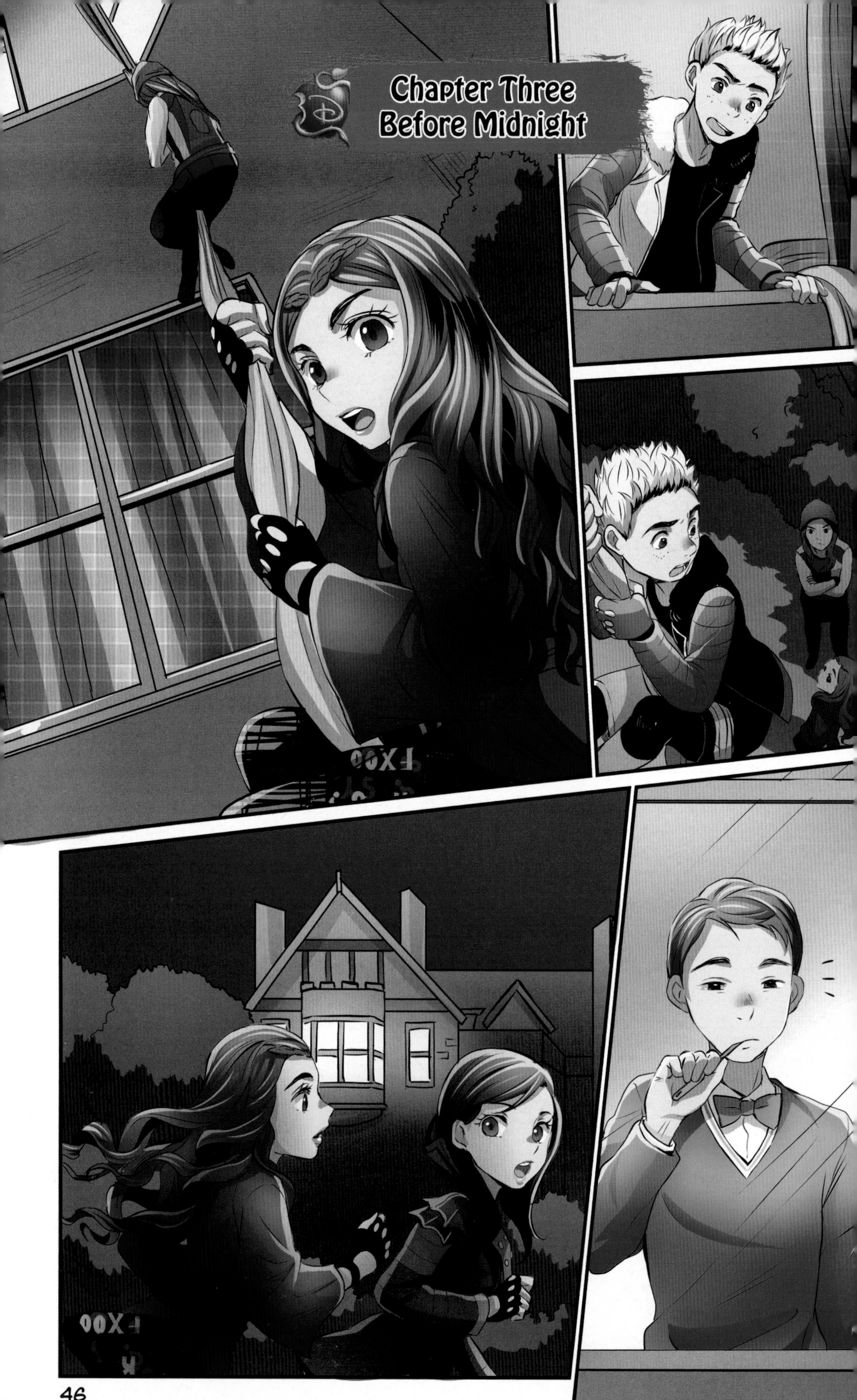
Chapter Three
Before Midnight

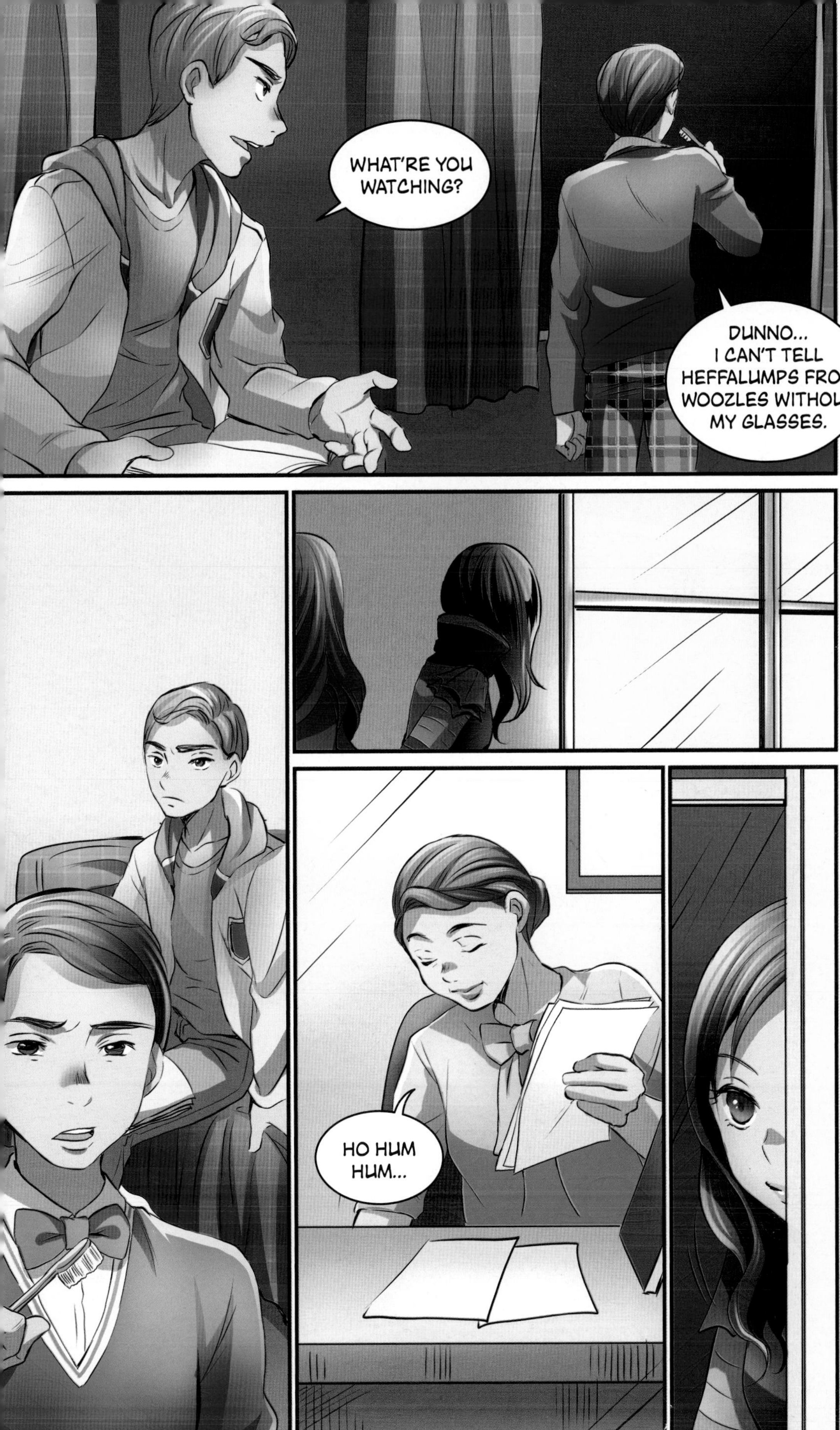
WHAT'RE YOU WATCHING?
DUNNO... I CAN'T TELL HEFFALUMPS FROM WOOZLES WITHOUT MY GLASSES.
HO HUM HUM...

ACCORDING TO THE MIRROR, WE WALK STRAIGHT FOR 0.6 MILES...

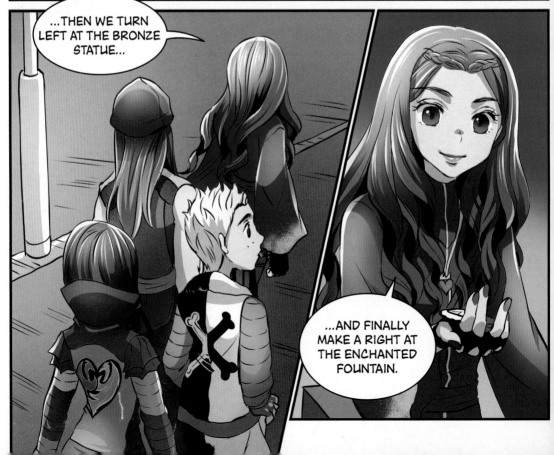

...THEN WE TURN LEFT AT THE BRONZE STATUE...

...AND FINALLY MAKE A RIGHT AT THE ENCHANTED FOUNTAIN.

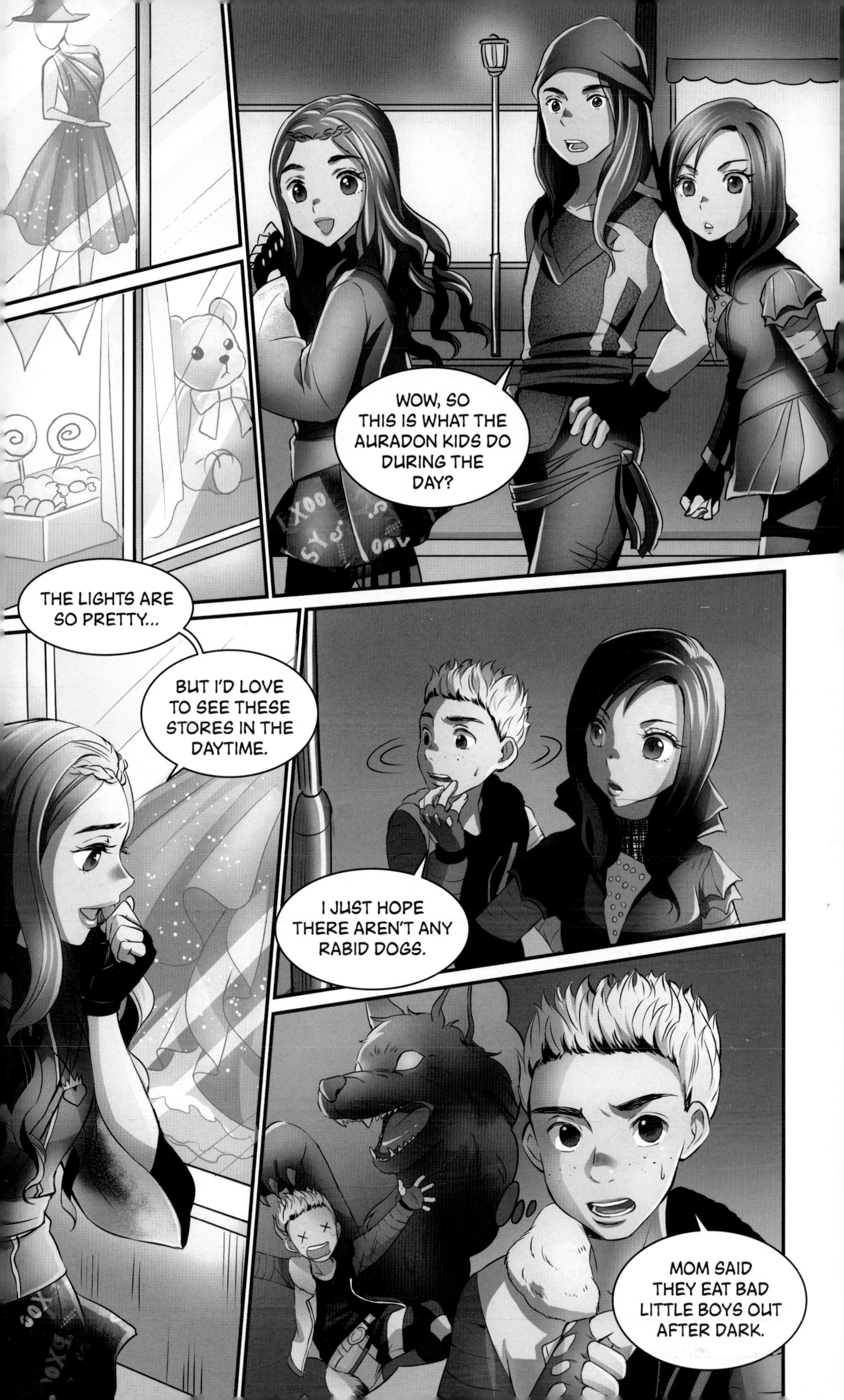
WOW, SO THIS IS WHAT THE AURADON KIDS DO DURING THE DAY?
THE LIGHTS ARE SO PRETTY...
BUT I'D LOVE TO SEE THESE STORES IN THE DAYTIME.
I JUST HOPE THERE AREN'T ANY RABID DOGS.
MOM SAID THEY EAT BAD LITTLE BOYS OUT AFTER DARK.

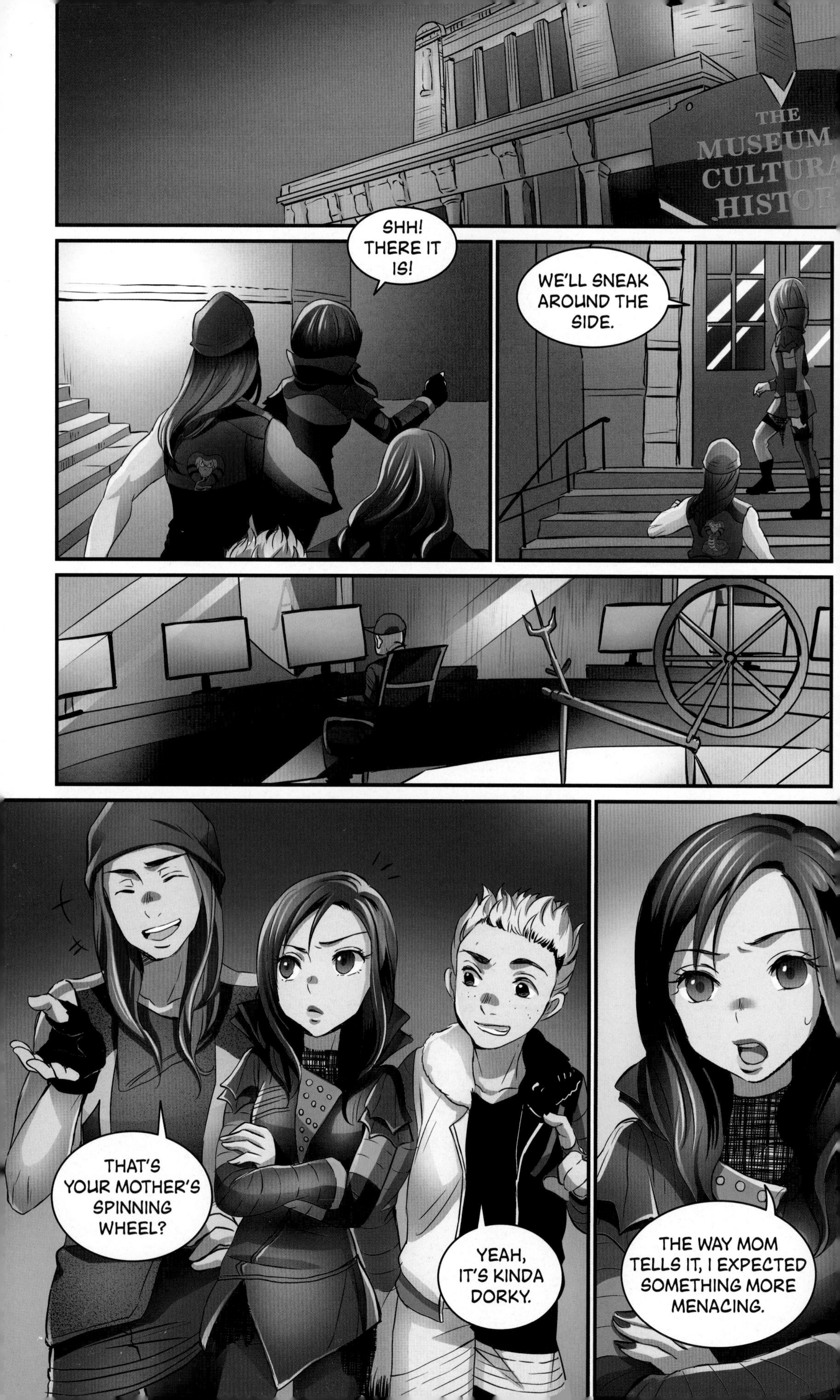
THE MUSEUM CULTURA HISTOR
SHH! THERE IT IS!
WE'LL SNEAK AROUND THE SIDE.
THAT'S YOUR MOTHER'S SPINNING WHEEL?
YEAH, IT'S KINDA DORKY.
THE WAY MOM TELLS IT, I EXPECTED SOMETHING MORE MENACING.

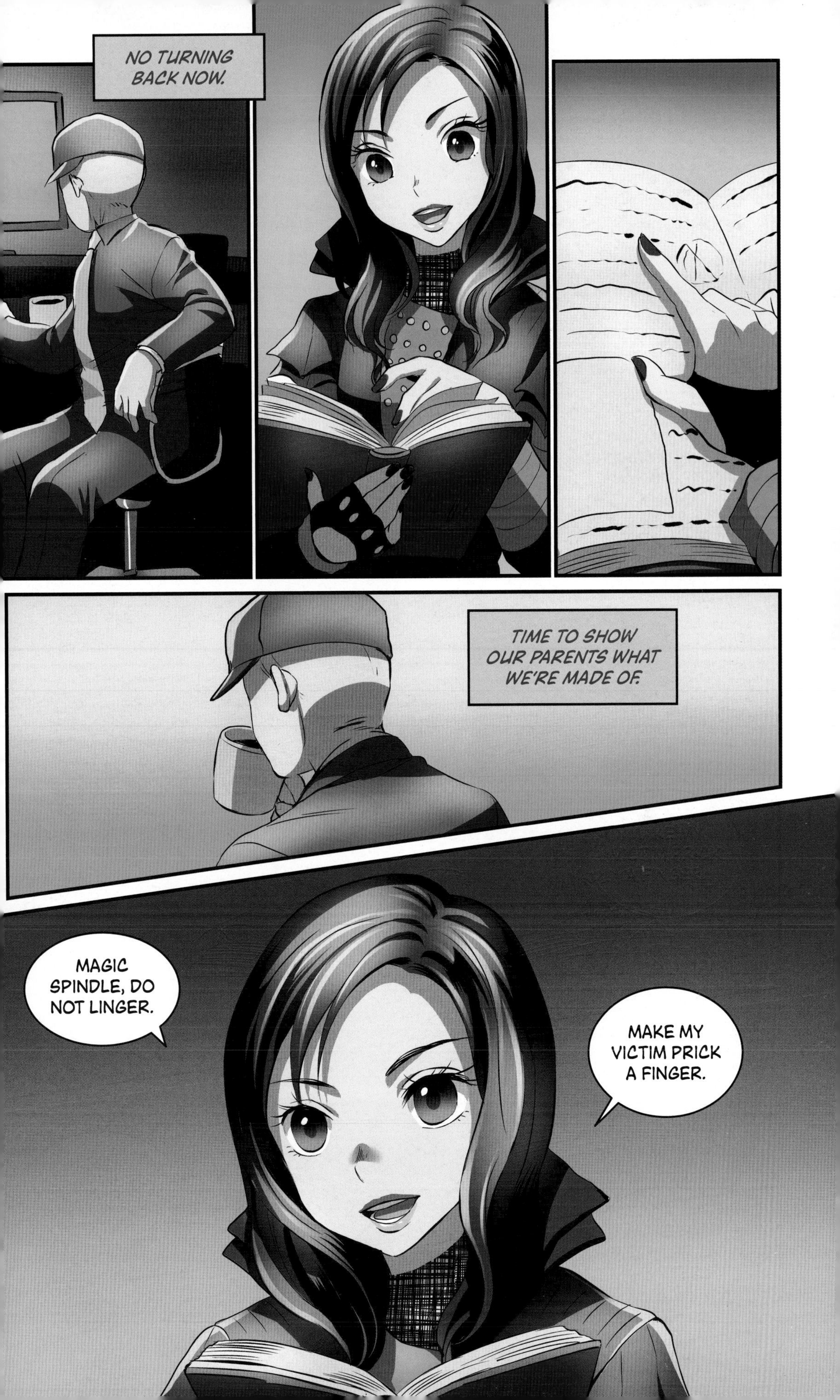
NO TURNING BACK NOW.
TIME TO SHOW OUR PARENTS WHAT WE'RE MADE OF.
MAGIC SPINDLE, DO NOT LINGER.
MAKE MY VICTIM PRICK A FINGER.

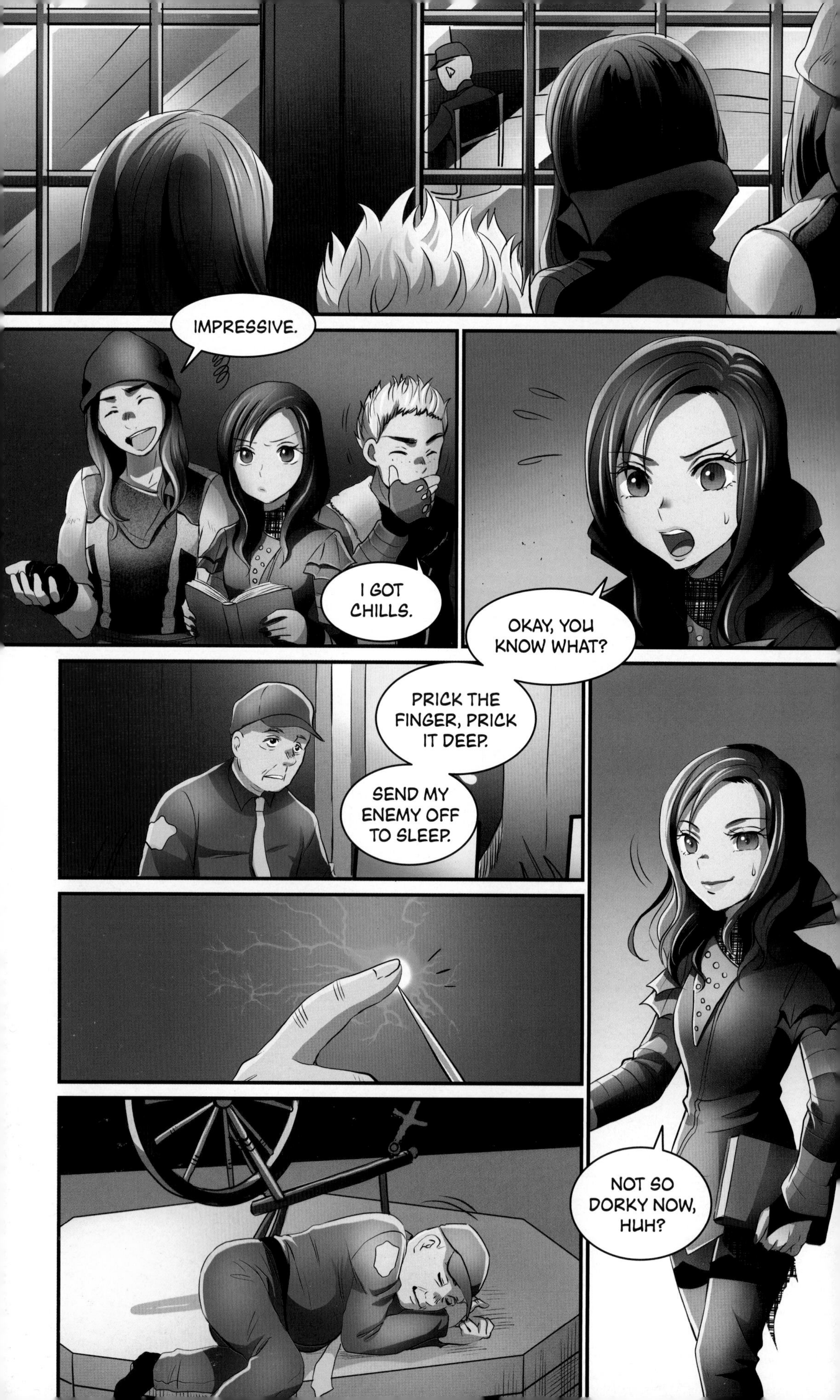
IMPRESSIVE.
I GOT CHILLS.
OKAY, YOU KNOW WHAT?
PRICK THE FINGER, PRICK IT DEEP.
SEND MY ENEMY OFF TO SLEEP.
NOT SO DORKY NOW, HUH?

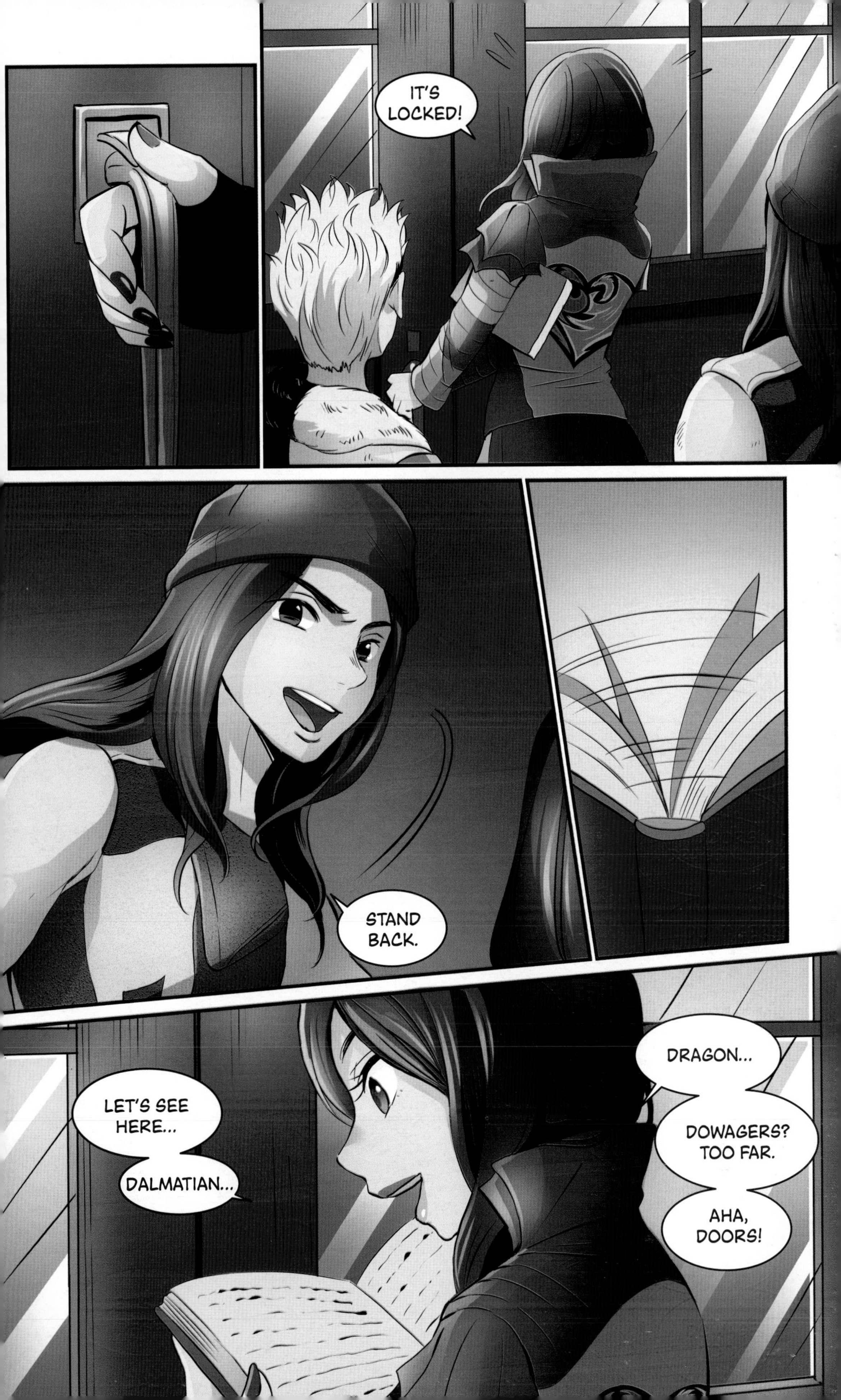
IT'S LOCKED!
STAND BACK.
LET'S SEE HERE...
DALMATIAN...
DRAGON...
DOWAGERS? TOO FAR.
AHA, DOORS!

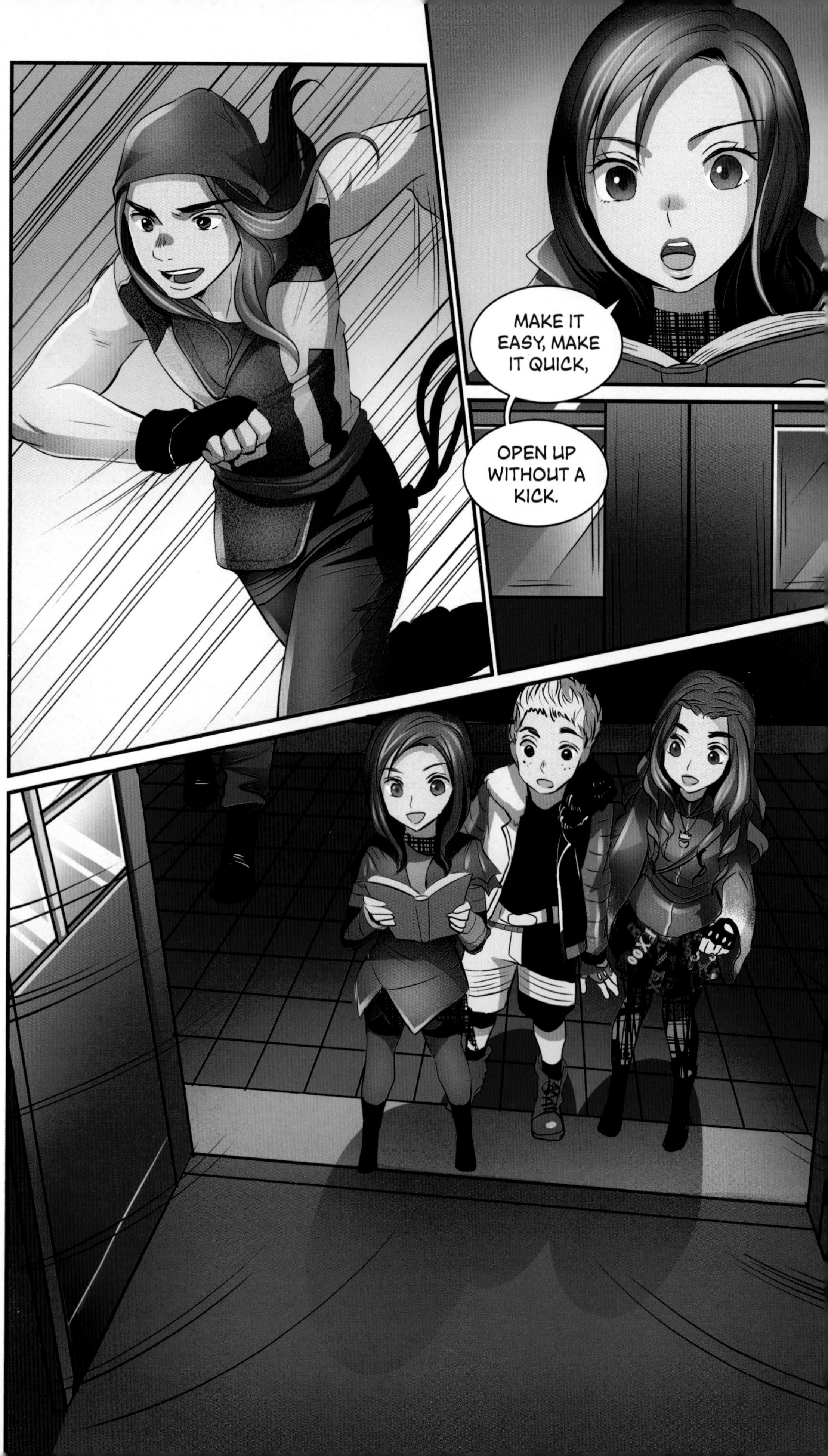
MAKE IT EASY, MAKE IT QUICK,
OPEN UP WITHOUT A KICK.

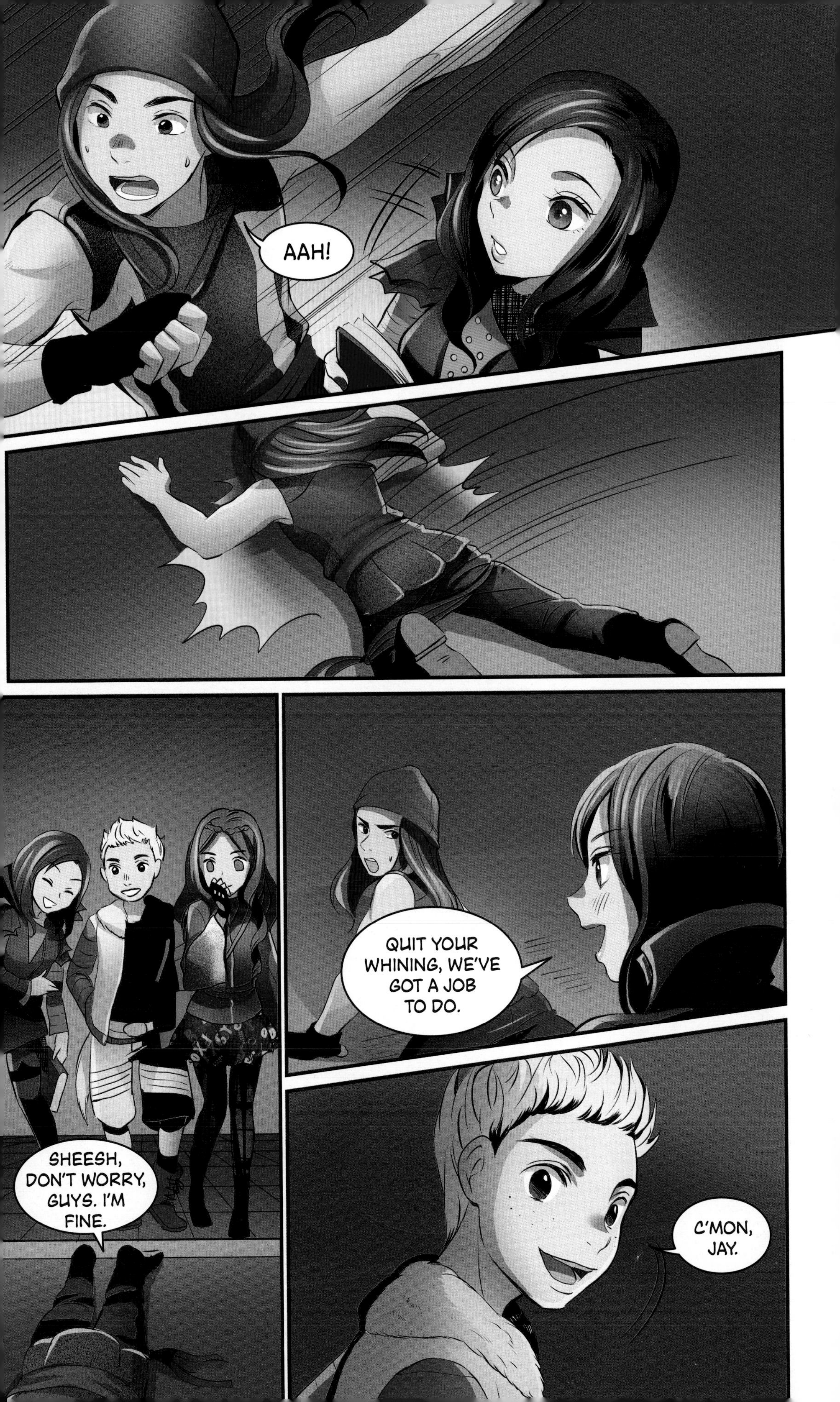
AAH!
QUIT YOUR WHINING, WE'VE GOT A JOB TO DO.
SHEESH, DON'T WORRY, GUYS. I'M FINE.
C'MON, JAY.

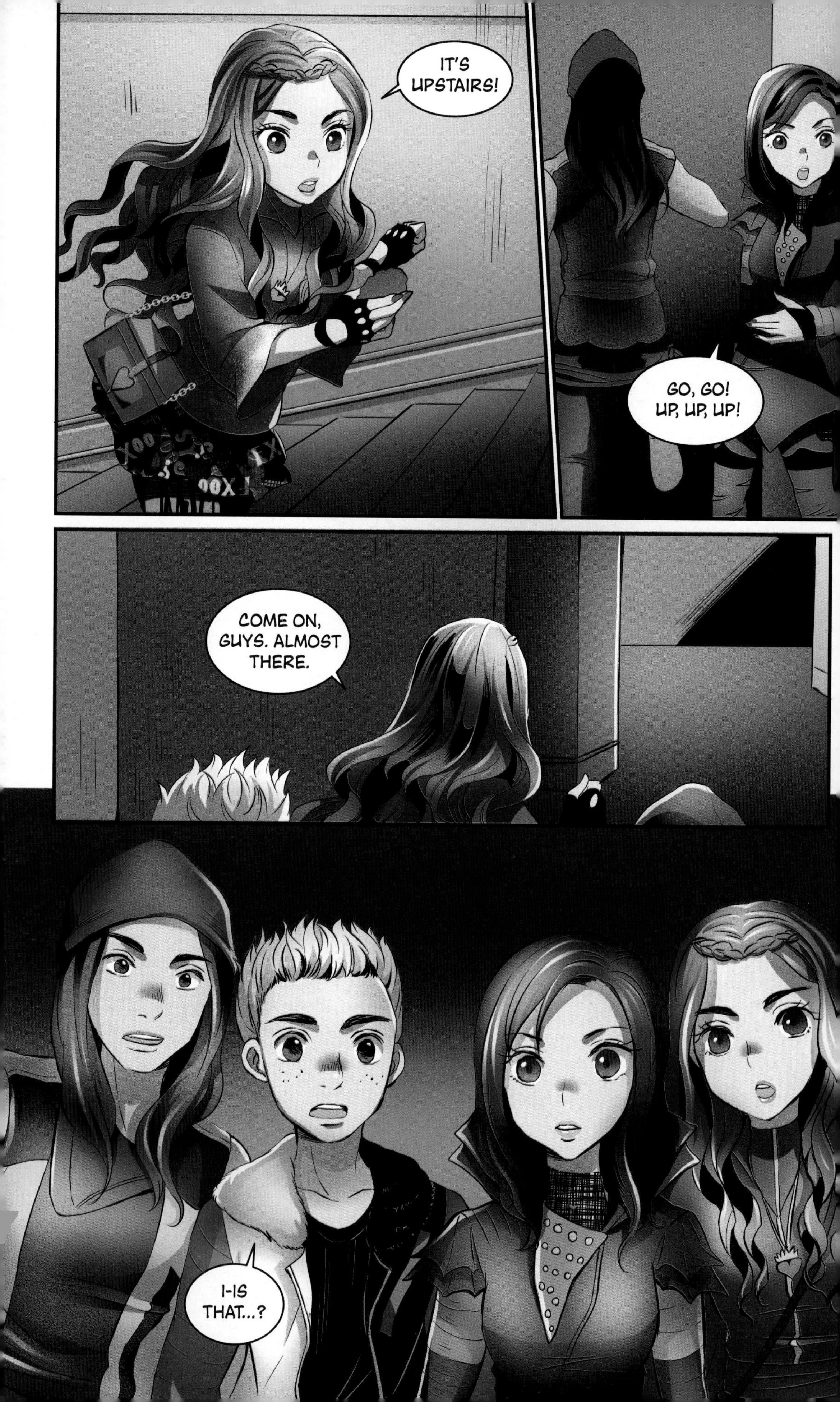
IT'S UPSTAIRS!
GO, GO! UP, UP, UP!
COME ON, GUYS. ALMOST THERE.
I-IS THAT...?

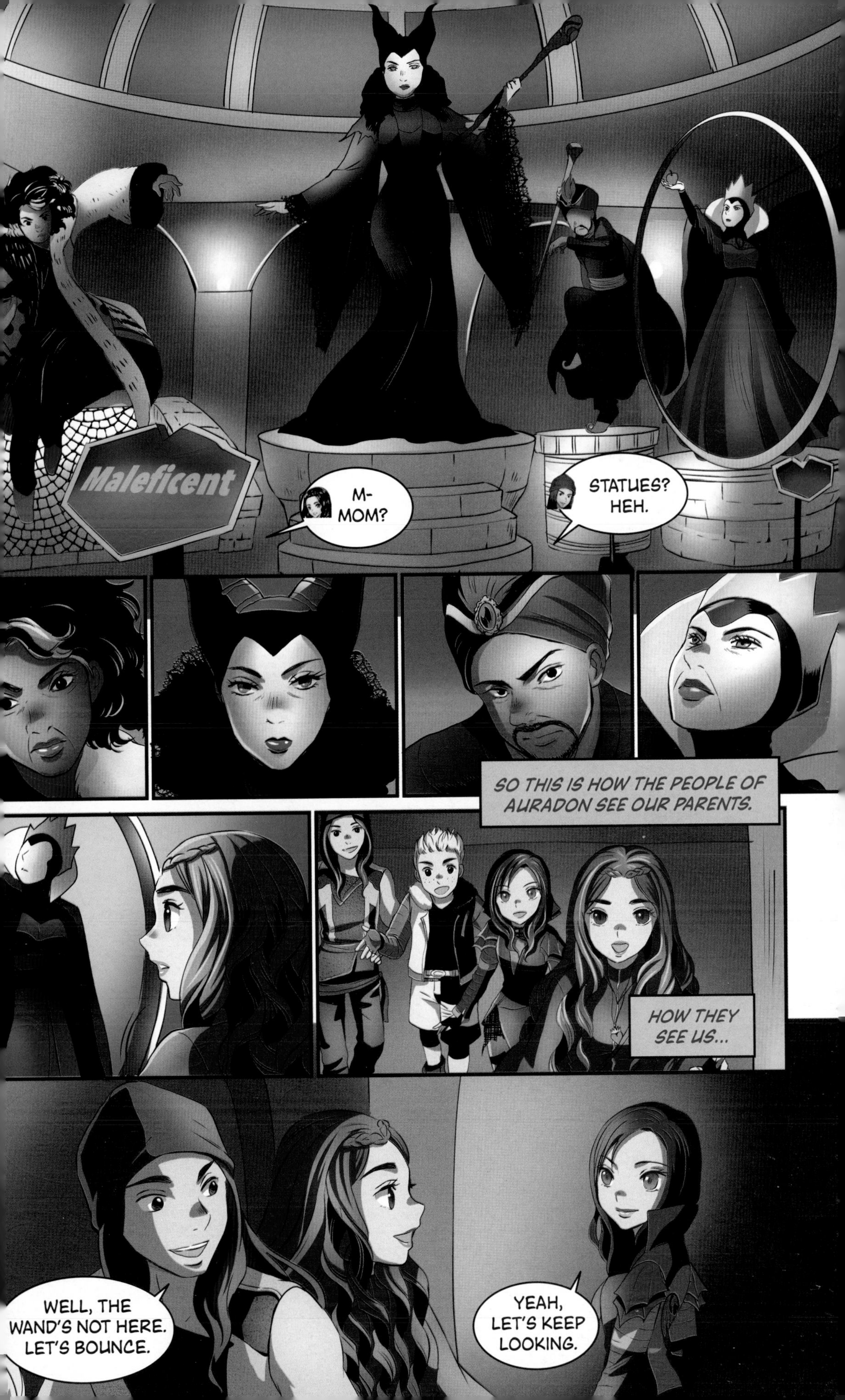
Maleficent
M-
MOM?
STATUES?
HEH.
SO THIS IS HOW THE PEOPLE OF
AURADON SEE OUR PARENTS.
HOW THEY
SEE US...
WELL, THE
WAND'S NOT HERE.
LET'S BOUNCE.
YEAH,
LET'S KEEP
LOOKING.

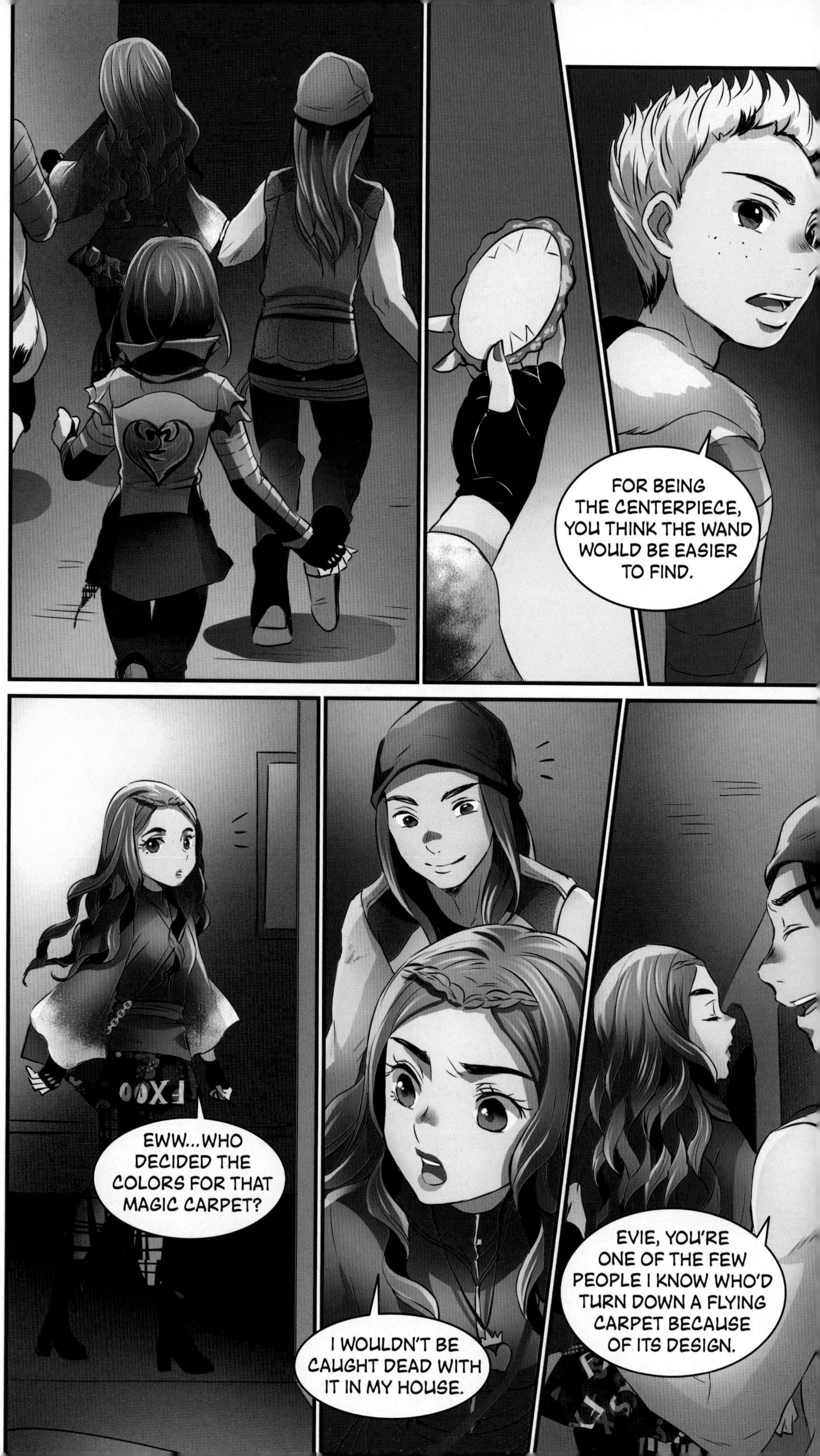

FOR BEING THE CENTERPIECE, YOU THINK THE WAND WOULD BE EASIER TO FIND.
EWW...WHO DECIDED THE COLORS FOR THAT MAGIC CARPET?
I WOULDN'T BE CAUGHT DEAD WITH IT IN MY HOUSE.
EVIE, YOU'RE ONE OF THE FEW PEOPLE I KNOW WHO'D TURN DOWN A FLYING CARPET BECAUSE OF ITS DESIGN.

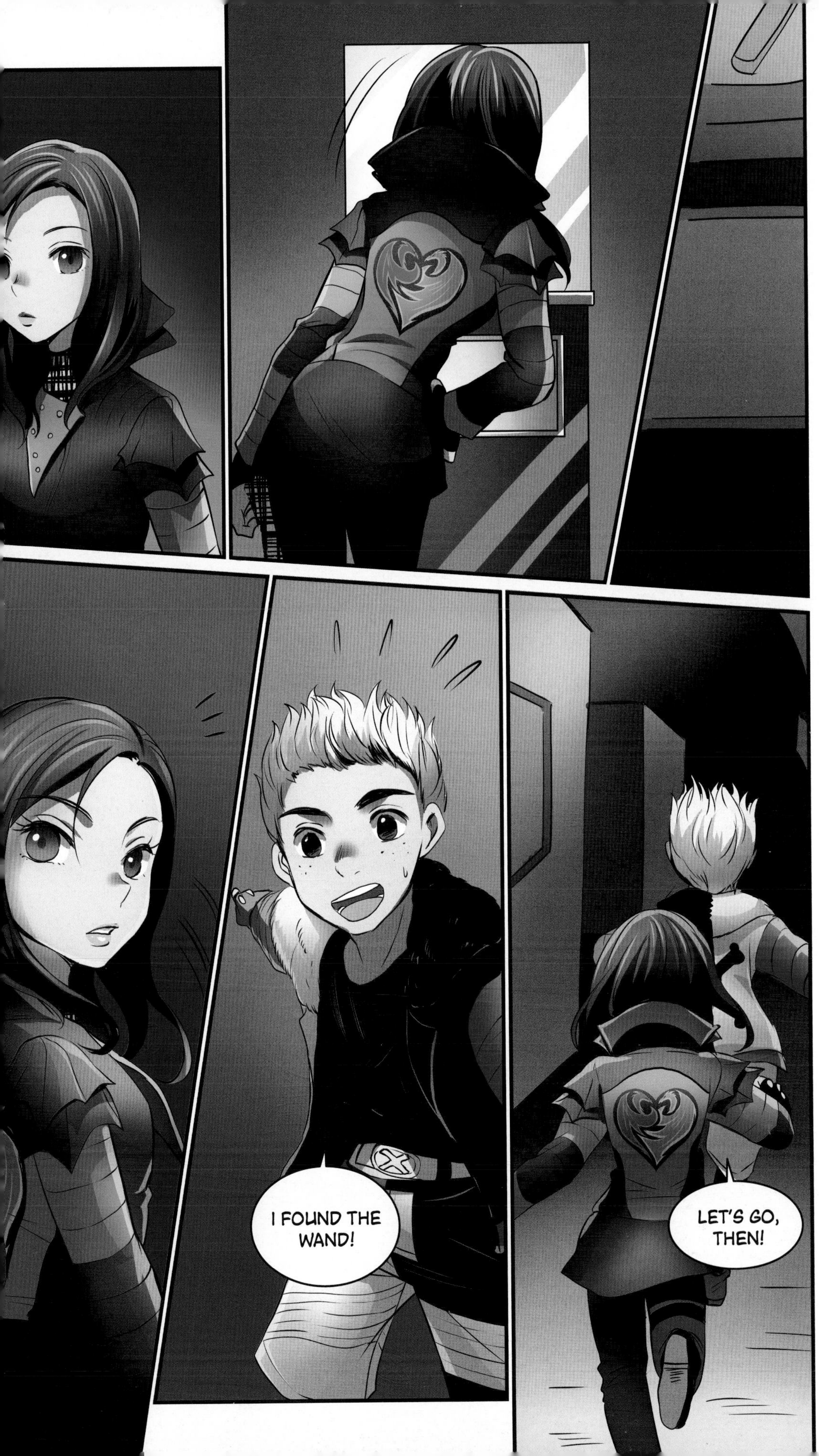
I FOUND THE WAND!
LET'S GO, THEN!

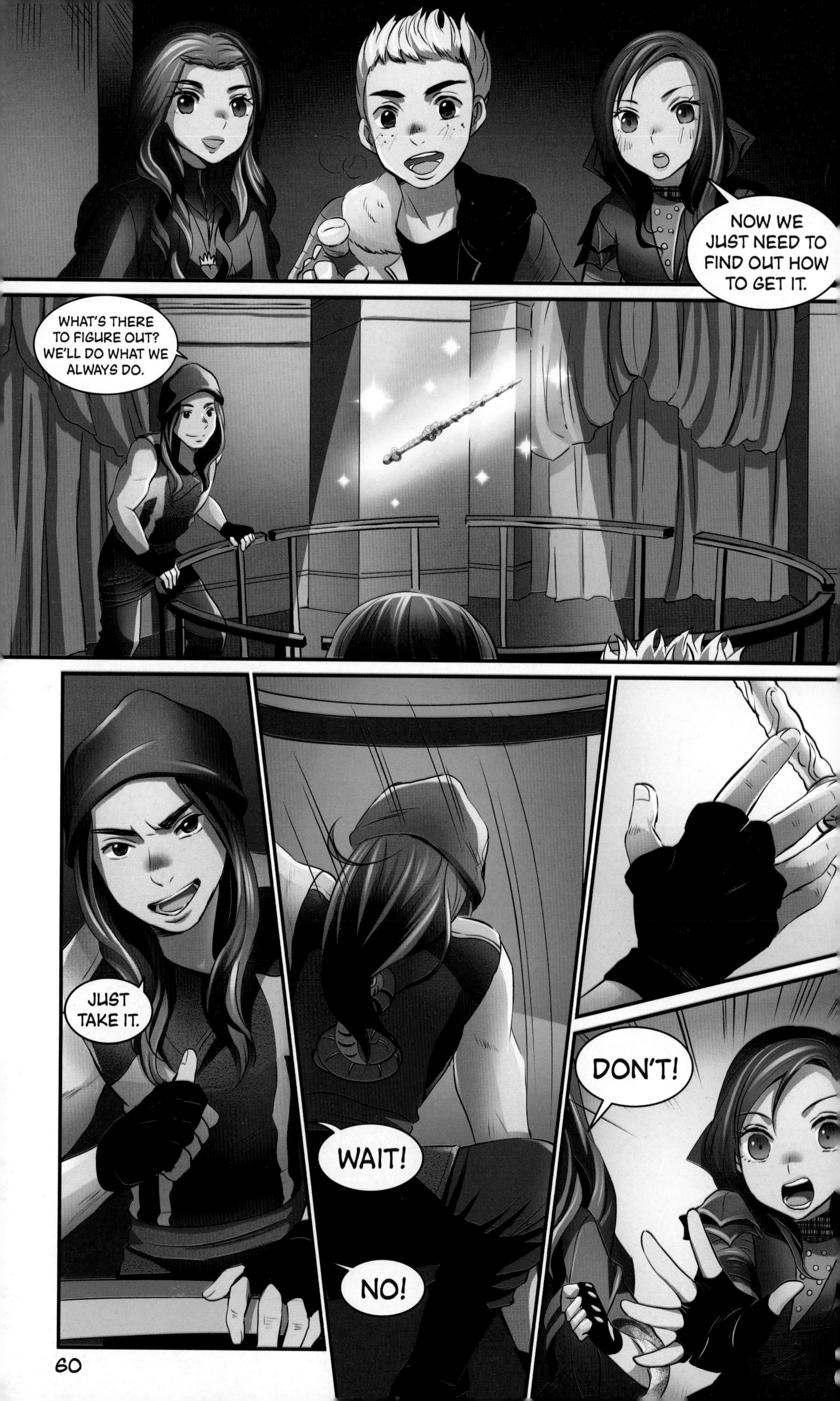
NOW WE JUST NEED TO FIND OUT HOW TO GET IT.
WHAT'S THERE TO FIGURE OUT? WE'LL DO WHAT WE ALWAYS DO.
JUST TAKE IT.
WAIT!
NO!
DON'T!

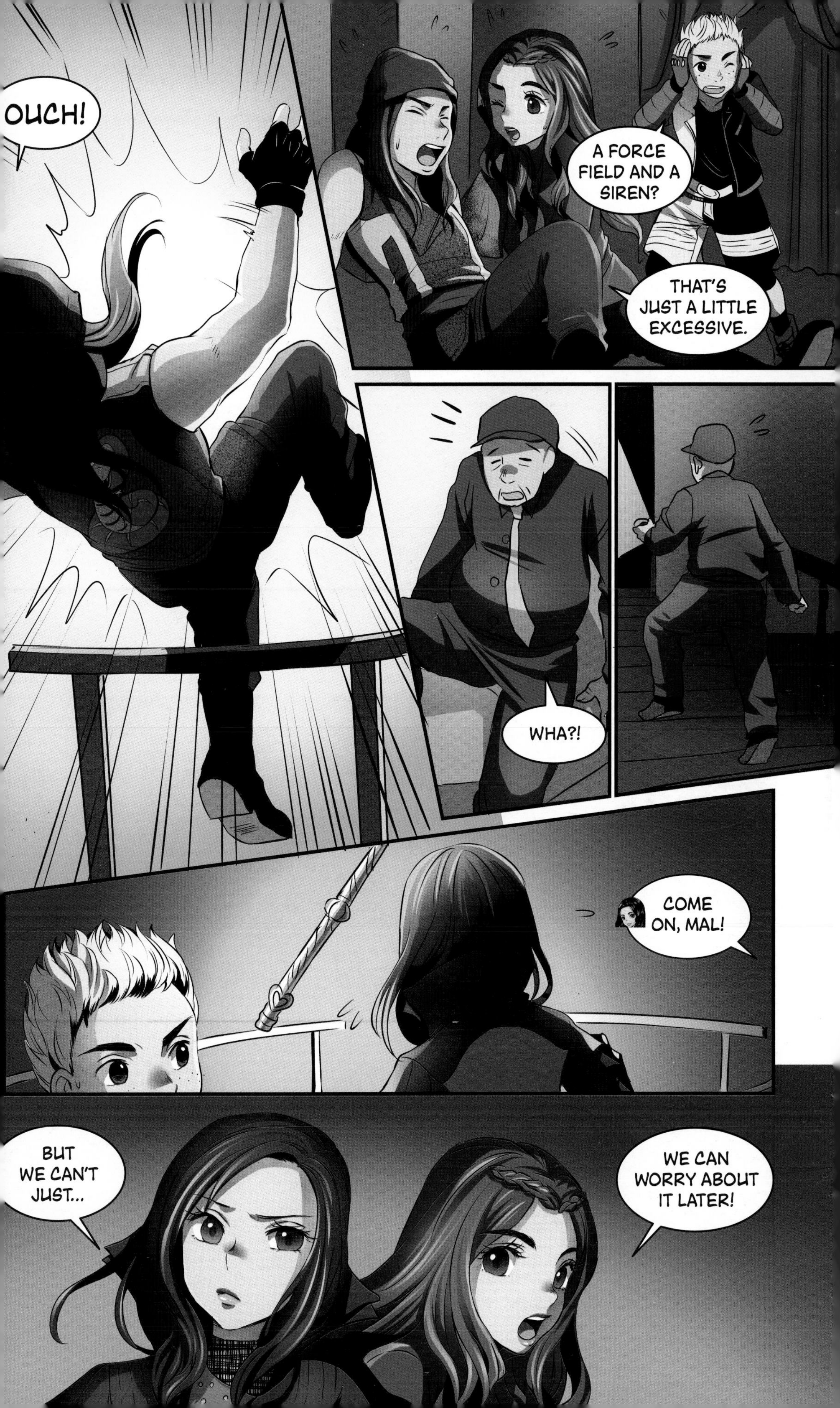
OUCH!
A FORCE FIELD AND A SIREN?
THAT'S JUST A LITTLE EXCESSIVE.
WHA?!
COME ON, MAL!
BUT WE CAN'T JUST...
WE CAN WORRY ABOUT IT LATER!

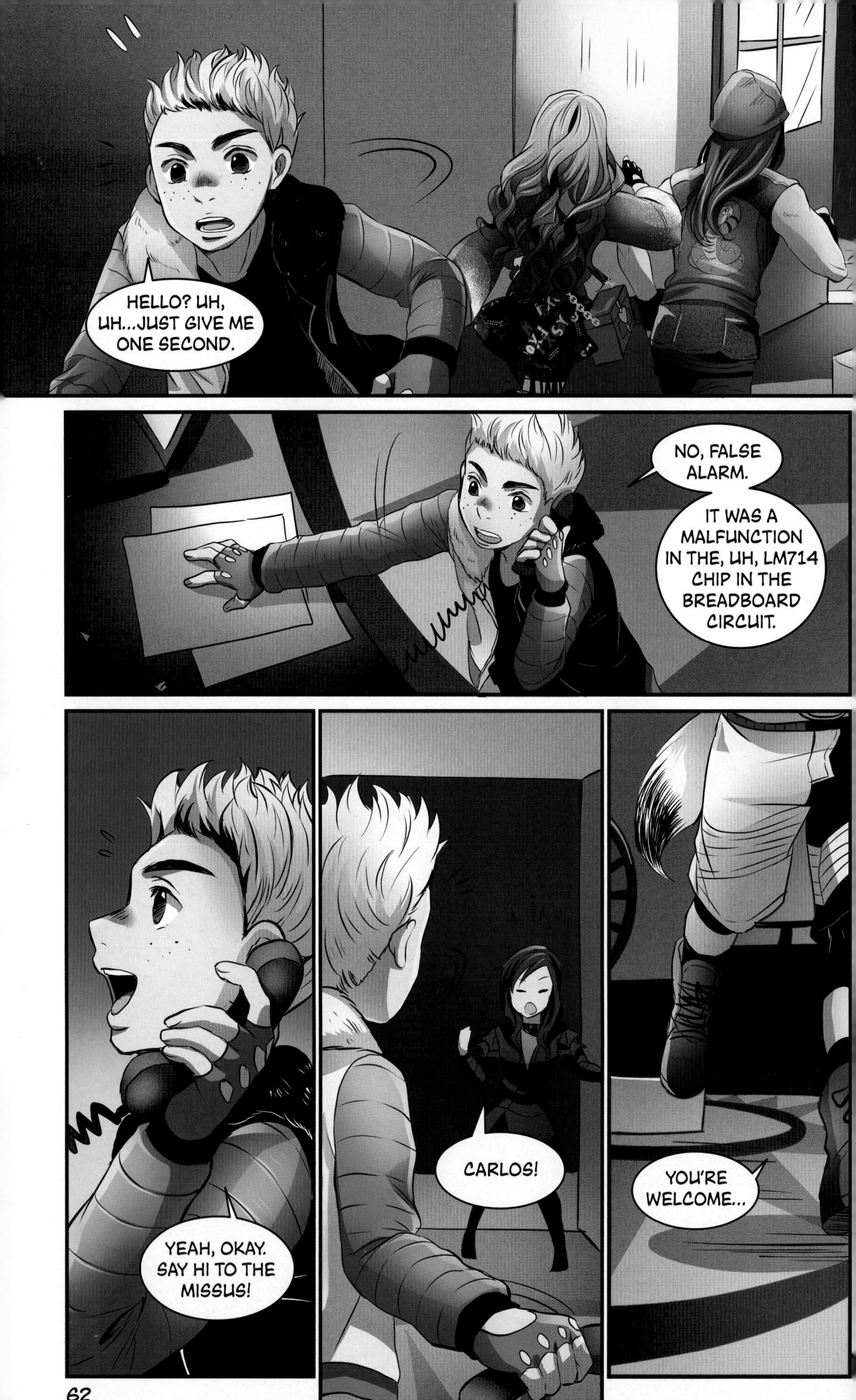
HELLO? UH, UH...JUST GIVE ME ONE SECOND.
NO, FALSE ALARM.
IT WAS A MALFUNCTION IN THE, UH, LM714 CHIP IN THE BREADBOARD CIRCUIT.
YEAH, OKAY. SAY HI TO THE MISSUS!
CARLOS!
YOU'RE WELCOME...

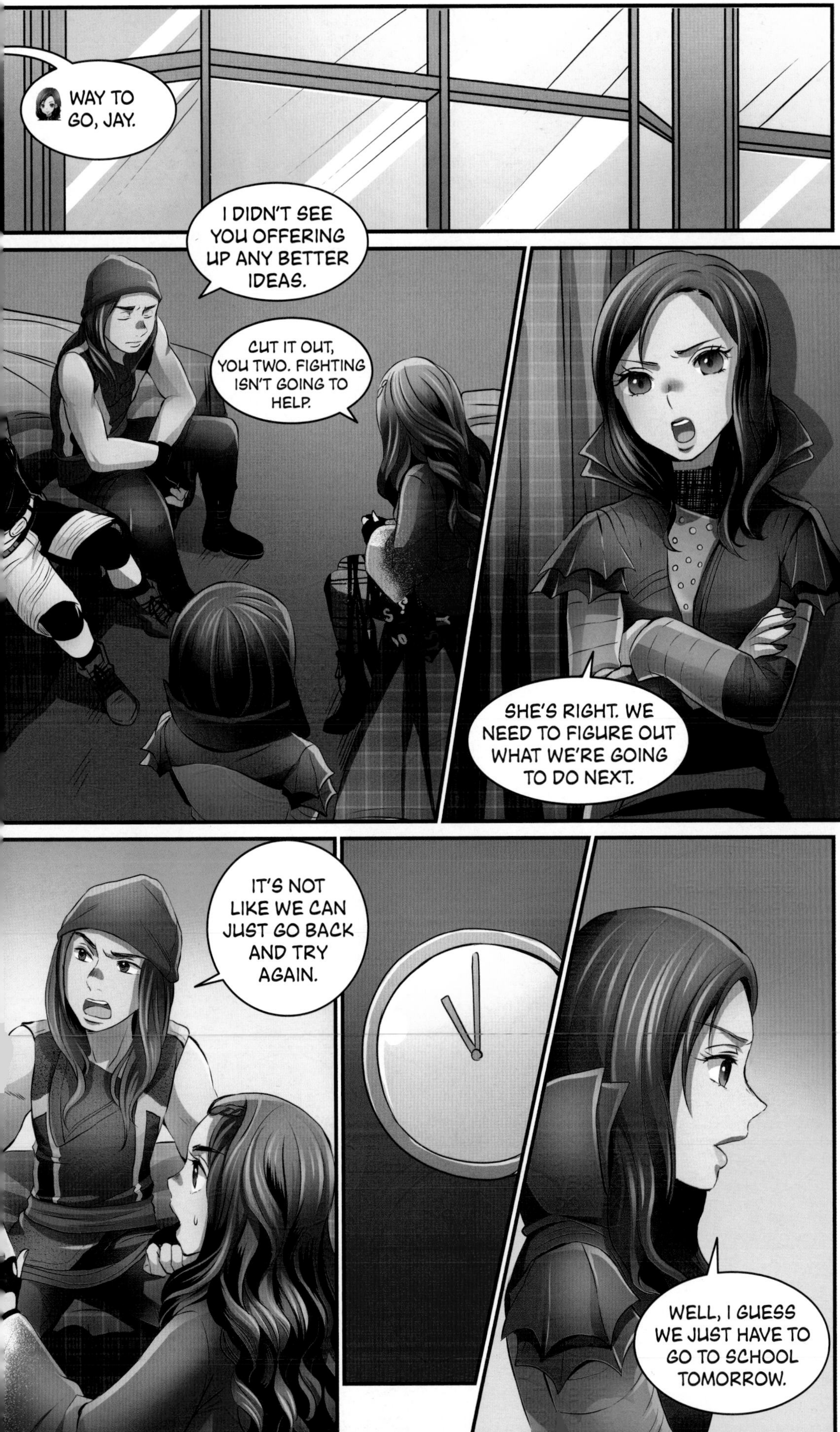
WAY TO GO, JAY.
I DIDN'T SEE YOU OFFERING UP ANY BETTER IDEAS.
CUT IT OUT, YOU TWO. FIGHTING ISN'T GOING TO HELP.
SHE'S RIGHT. WE NEED TO FIGURE OUT WHAT WE'RE GOING TO DO NEXT.
IT'S NOT LIKE WE CAN JUST GO BACK AND TRY AGAIN.
WELL, I GUESS WE JUST HAVE TO GO TO SCHOOL TOMORROW.

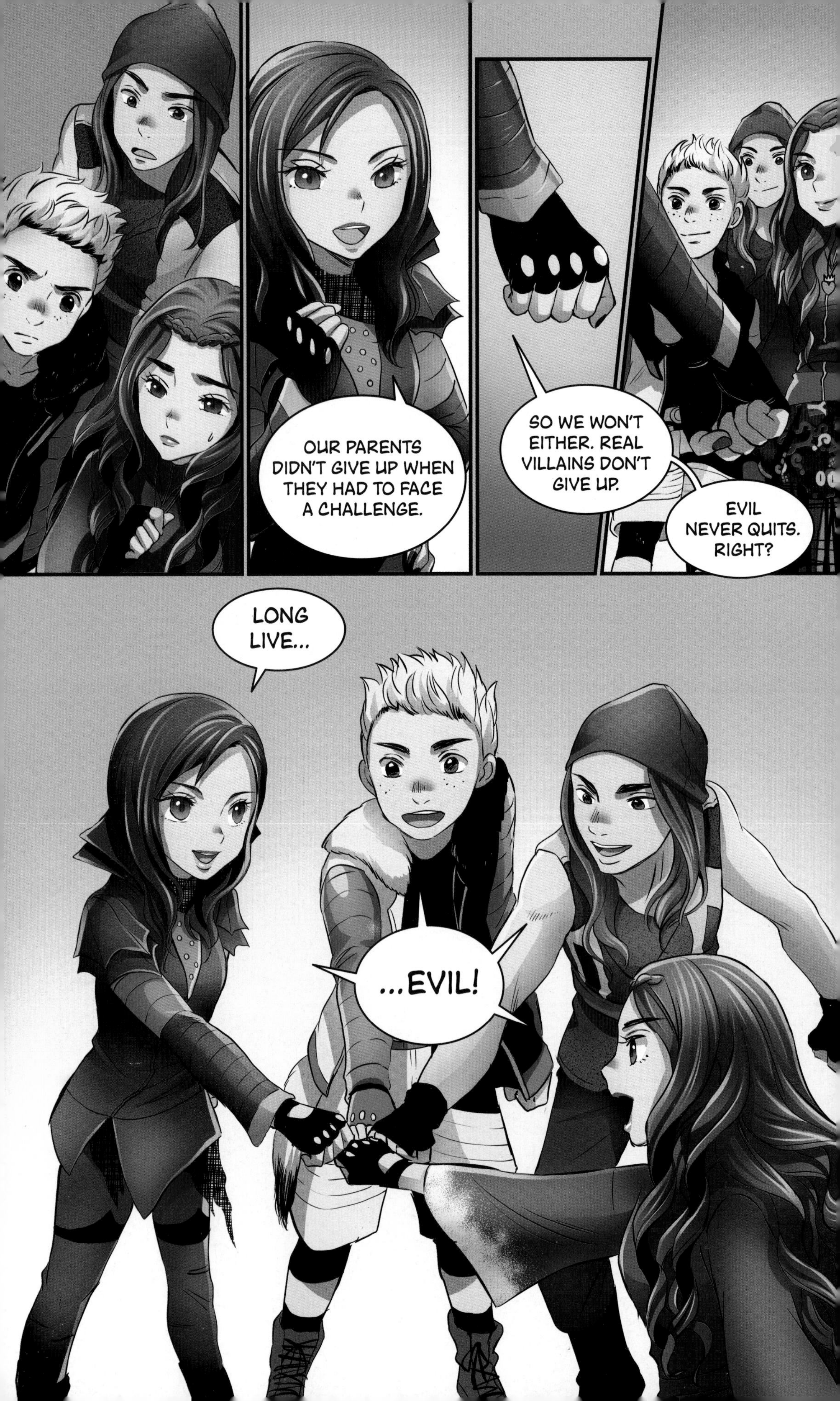
OUR PARENTS DIDN'T GIVE UP WHEN THEY HAD TO FACE A CHALLENGE.
SO WE WON'T EITHER. REAL VILLAINS DON'T GIVE UP.
EVIL NEVER QUITS. RIGHT?
LONG LIVE...
...EVIL!

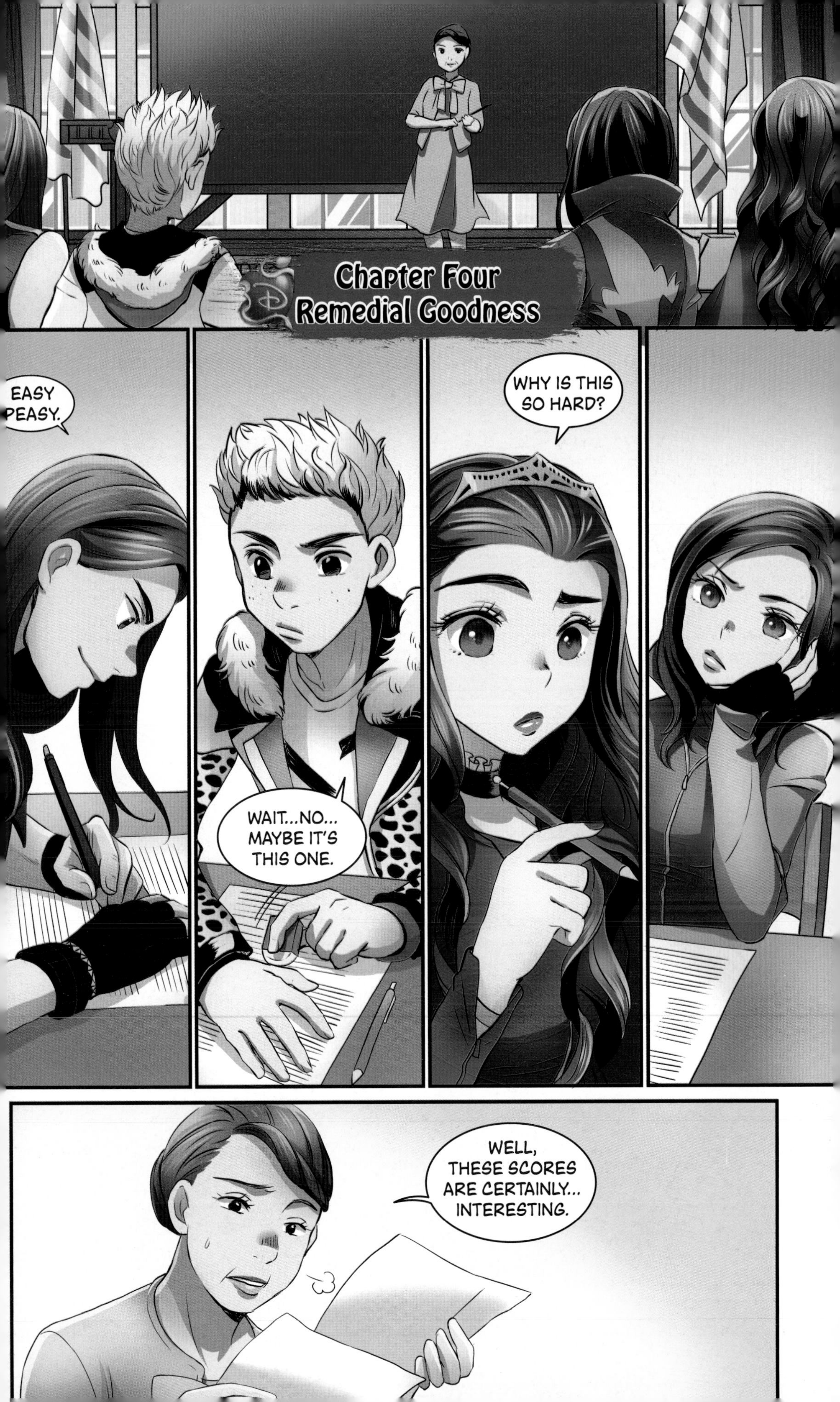
Chapter Four
Remedial Goodness
EASY PEASY.
WAIT...NO... MAYBE IT'S THIS ONE.
WHY IS THIS SO HARD?
WELL, THESE SCORES ARE CERTAINLY... INTERESTING.

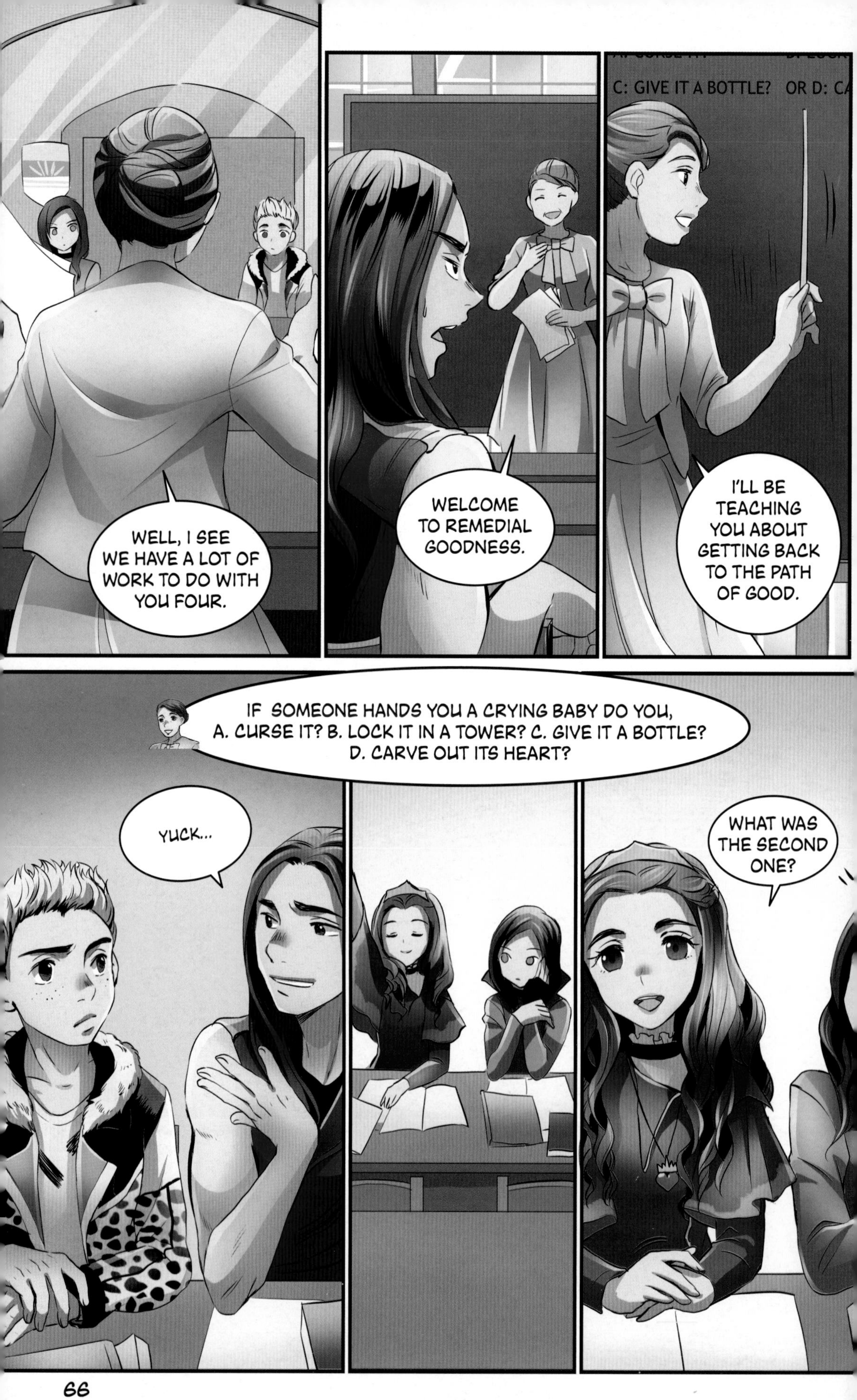
WELL, I SEE WE HAVE A LOT OF WORK TO DO WITH YOU FOUR.
WELCOME TO REMEDIAL GOODNESS.
C: GIVE IT A BOTTLE? OR D:
I'LL BE TEACHING YOU ABOUT GETTING BACK TO THE PATH OF GOOD.
IF SOMEONE HANDS YOU A CRYING BABY DO YOU, A. CURSE IT? B. LOCK IT IN A TOWER? C. GIVE IT A BOTTLE? D. CARVE OUT ITS HEART?
YUCK...
WHAT WAS THE SECOND ONE?

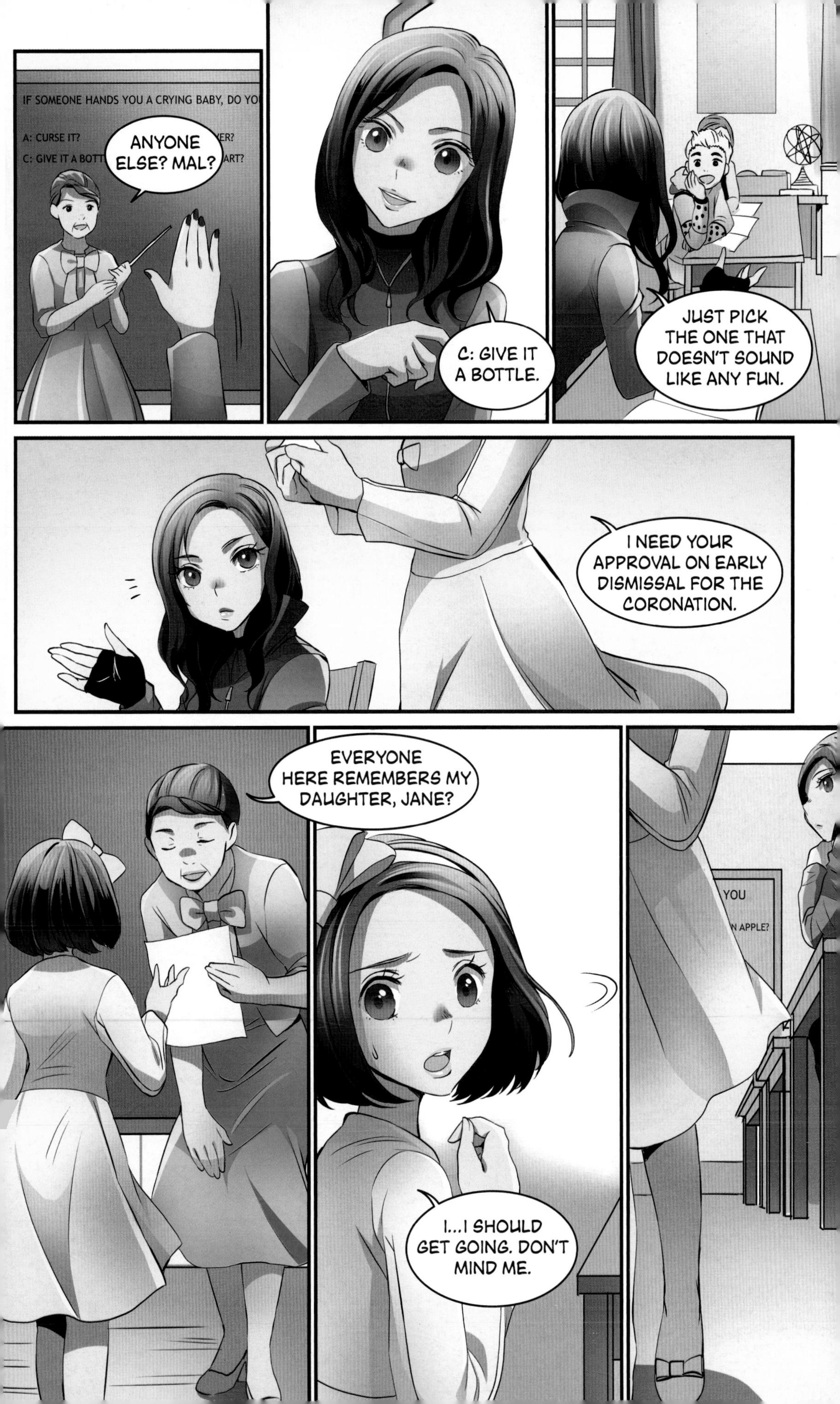
IF SOMEONE HANDS YOU A CRYING BABY, DO YO
A: CURSE IT?
ANYONE ELSE? MAL?
C: GIVE IT A BOTTLE.
JUST PICK THE ONE THAT DOESN'T SOUND LIKE ANY FUN.
I NEED YOUR APPROVAL ON EARLY DISMISSAL FOR THE CORONATION.
EVERYONE HERE REMEMBERS MY DAUGHTER, JANE?
I...I SHOULD GET GOING. DON'T MIND ME.
YOU

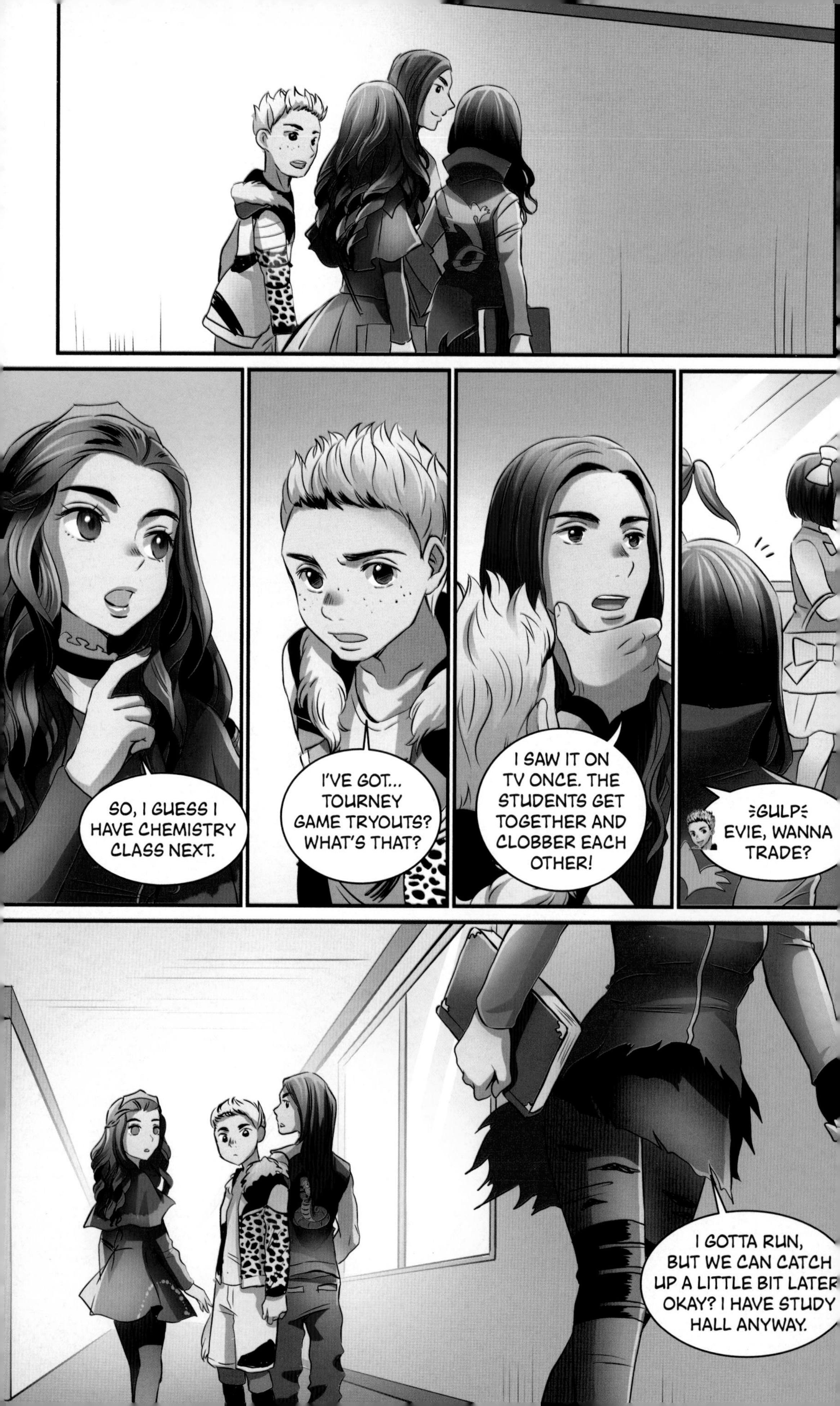
SO, I GUESS I HAVE CHEMISTRY CLASS NEXT.
I'VE GOT... TOURNEY GAME TRYOUTS? WHAT'S THAT?
I SAW IT ON TV ONCE. THE STUDENTS GET TOGETHER AND CLOBBER EACH OTHER!
GULP
EVIE, WANNA TRADE?
I GOTTA RUN, BUT WE CAN CATCH UP A LITTLE BIT LATER OKAY? I HAVE STUDY HALL ANYWAY.

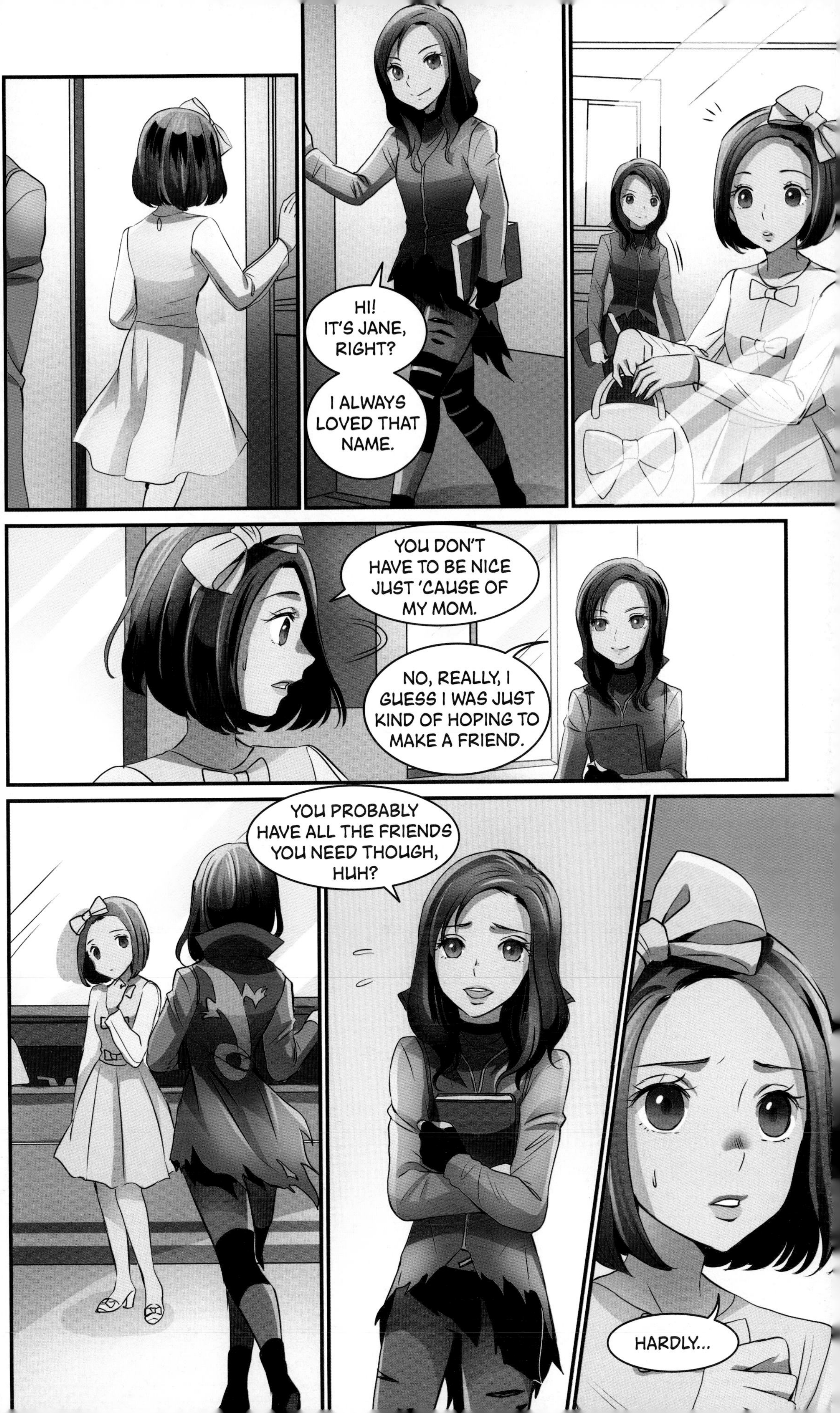
HI! IT'S JANE, RIGHT?
I ALWAYS LOVED THAT NAME.
YOU DON'T HAVE TO BE NICE JUST 'CAUSE OF MY MOM.
NO, REALLY, I GUESS I WAS JUST KIND OF HOPING TO MAKE A FRIEND.
YOU PROBABLY HAVE ALL THE FRIENDS YOU NEED THOUGH, HUH?
HARDLY...

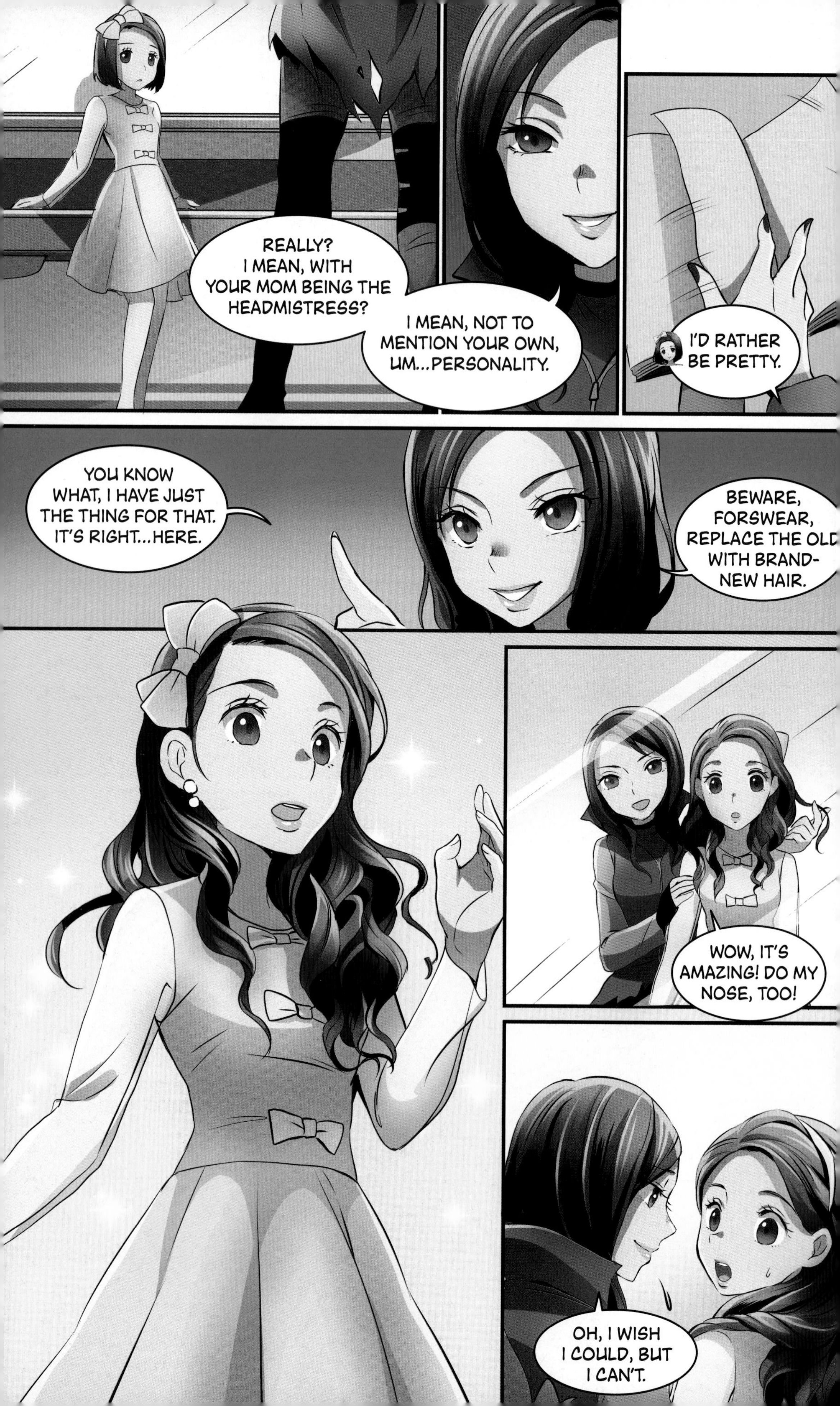
REALLY? I MEAN, WITH YOUR MOM BEING THE HEADMISTRESS?
I MEAN, NOT TO MENTION YOUR OWN, UM...PERSONALITY.
I'D RATHER BE PRETTY.
YOU KNOW WHAT, I HAVE JUST THE THING FOR THAT. IT'S RIGHT...HERE.
BEWARE, FORSWEAR, REPLACE THE OLD WITH BRAND-NEW HAIR.
WOW, IT'S AMAZING! DO MY NOSE, TOO!
OH, I WISH I COULD, BUT I CAN'T.

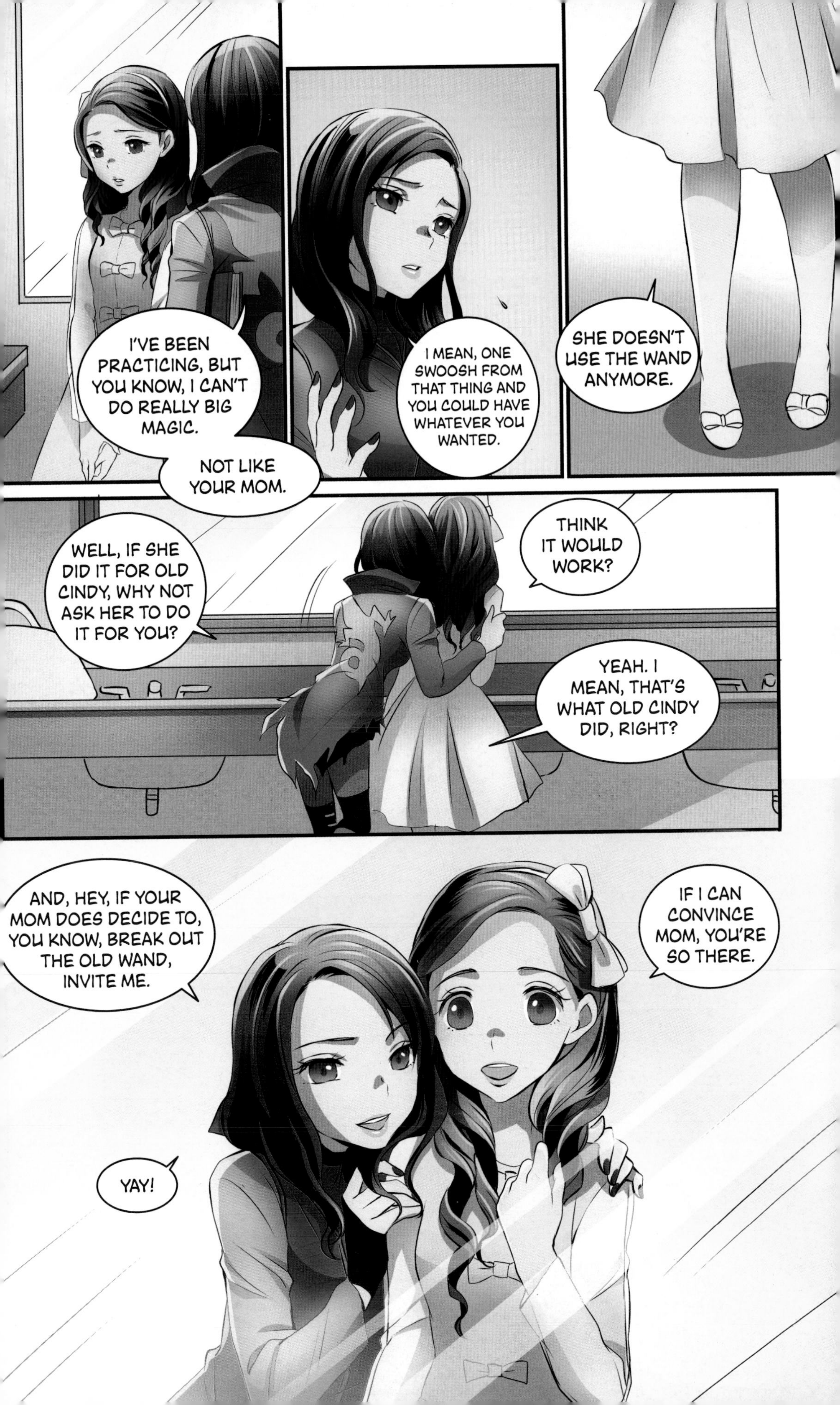
I'VE BEEN PRACTICING, BUT YOU KNOW, I CAN'T DO REALLY BIG MAGIC.
NOT LIKE YOUR MOM.
I MEAN, ONE SWOOSH FROM THAT THING AND YOU COULD HAVE WHATEVER YOU WANTED.
SHE DOESN'T USE THE WAND ANYMORE.
WELL, IF SHE DID IT FOR OLD CINDY, WHY NOT ASK HER TO DO IT FOR YOU?
THINK IT WOULD WORK?
YEAH. I MEAN, THAT'S WHAT OLD CINDY DID, RIGHT?
AND, HEY, IF YOUR MOM DOES DECIDE TO, YOU KNOW, BREAK OUT THE OLD WAND, INVITE ME.
IF I CAN CONVINCE MOM, YOU'RE SO THERE.
YAY!

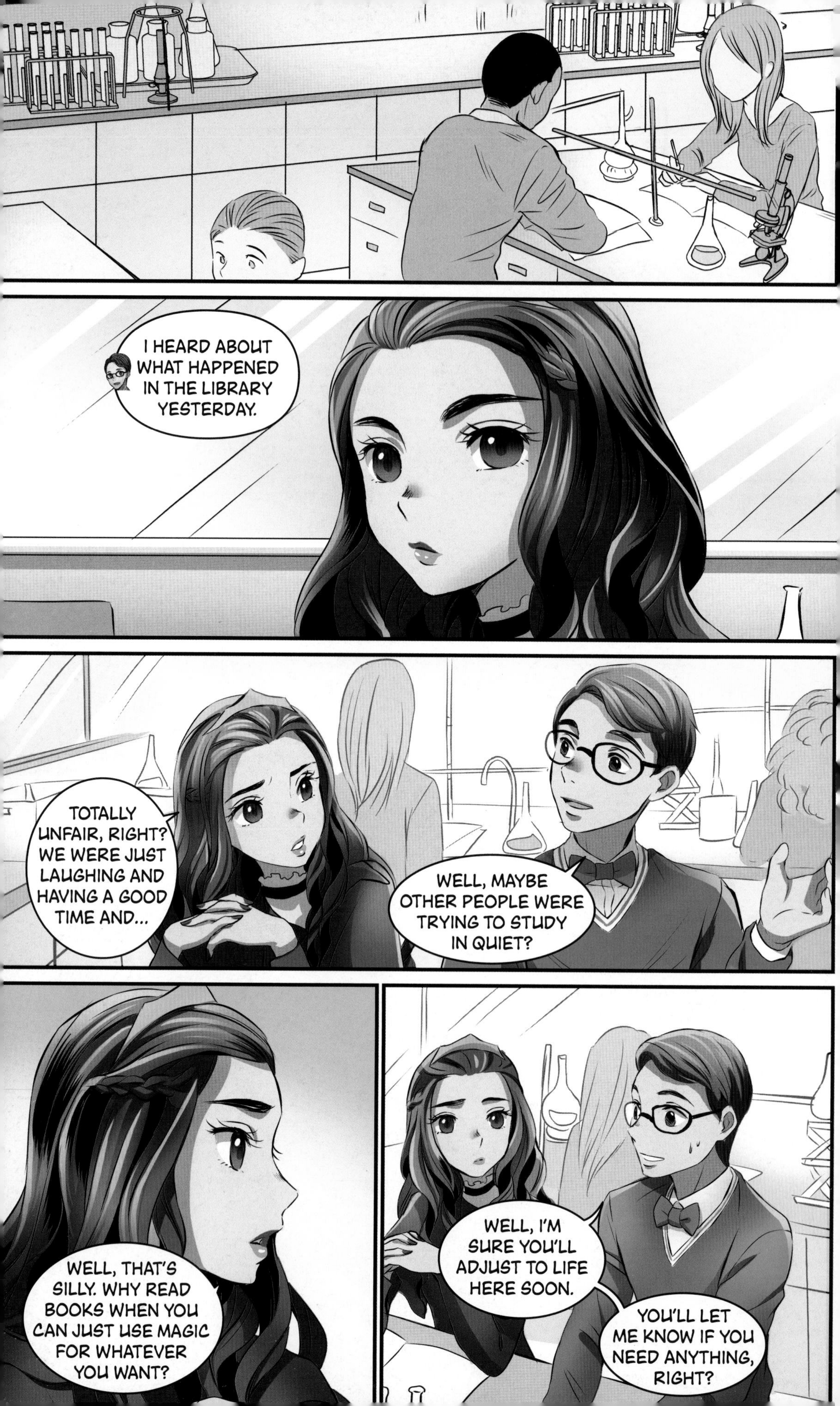
I HEARD ABOUT WHAT HAPPENED IN THE LIBRARY YESTERDAY.
TOTALLY UNFAIR, RIGHT? WE WERE JUST LAUGHING AND HAVING A GOOD TIME AND...
WELL, MAYBE OTHER PEOPLE WERE TRYING TO STUDY IN QUIET?
WELL, THAT'S SILLY. WHY READ BOOKS WHEN YOU CAN JUST USE MAGIC FOR WHATEVER YOU WANT?
WELL, I'M SURE YOU'LL ADJUST TO LIFE HERE SOON.
YOU'LL LET ME KNOW IF YOU NEED ANYTHING, RIGHT?

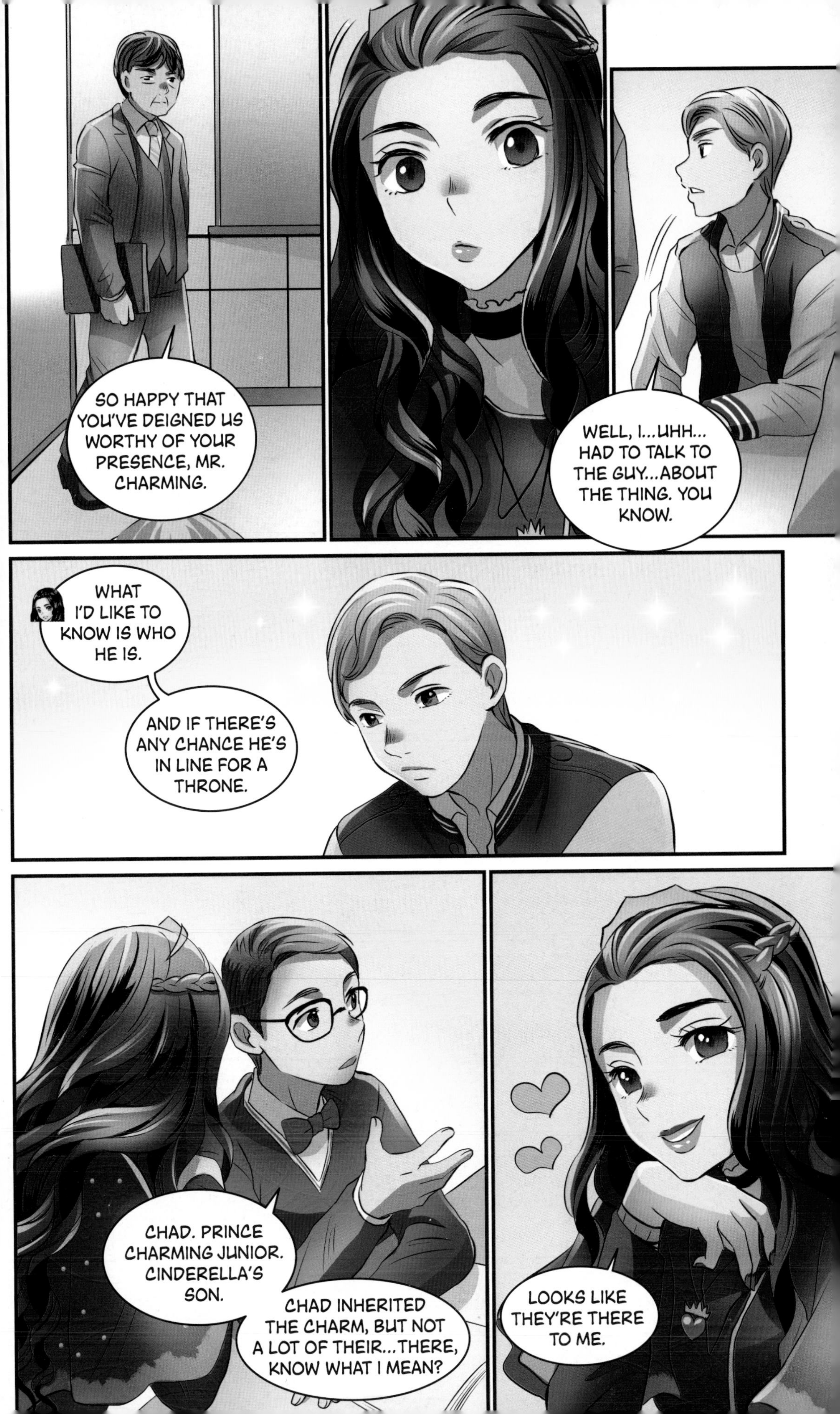
SO HAPPY THAT YOU'VE DEIGNED US WORTHY OF YOUR PRESENCE, MR. CHARMING.
WELL, I...UHH... HAD TO TALK TO THE GUY...ABOUT THE THING. YOU KNOW.
WHAT I'D LIKE TO KNOW IS WHO HE IS.
AND IF THERE'S ANY CHANCE HE'S IN LINE FOR A THRONE.
CHAD. PRINCE CHARMING JUNIOR. CINDERELLA'S SON.
CHAD INHERITED THE CHARM, BUT NOT A LOT OF THEIR...THERE, KNOW WHAT I MEAN?
LOOKS LIKE THEY'RE THERE TO ME.

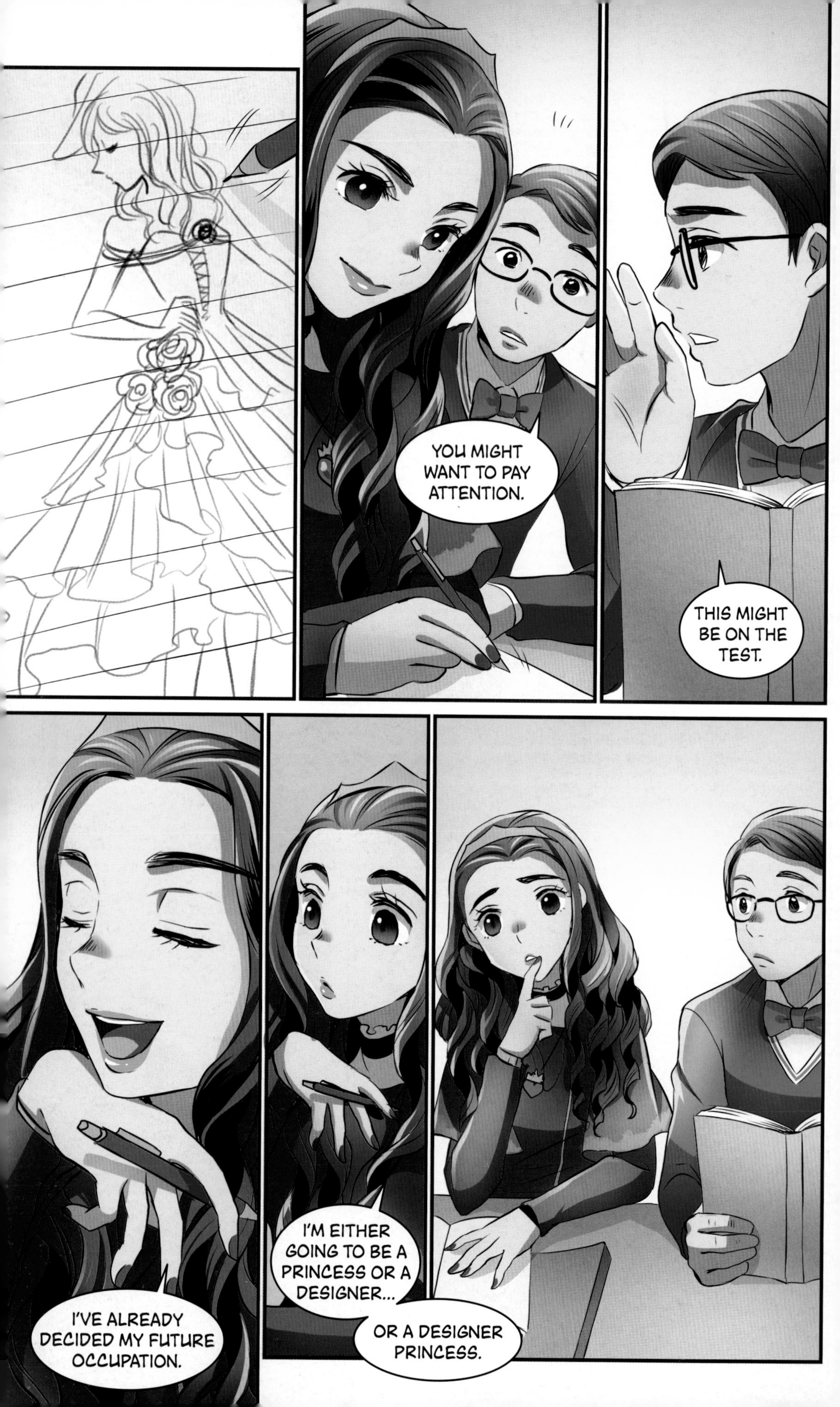
YOU MIGHT WANT TO PAY ATTENTION.
THIS MIGHT BE ON THE TEST.
I'VE ALREADY DECIDED MY FUTURE OCCUPATION.
I'M EITHER GOING TO BE A PRINCESS OR A DESIGNER...
OR A DESIGNER PRINCESS.

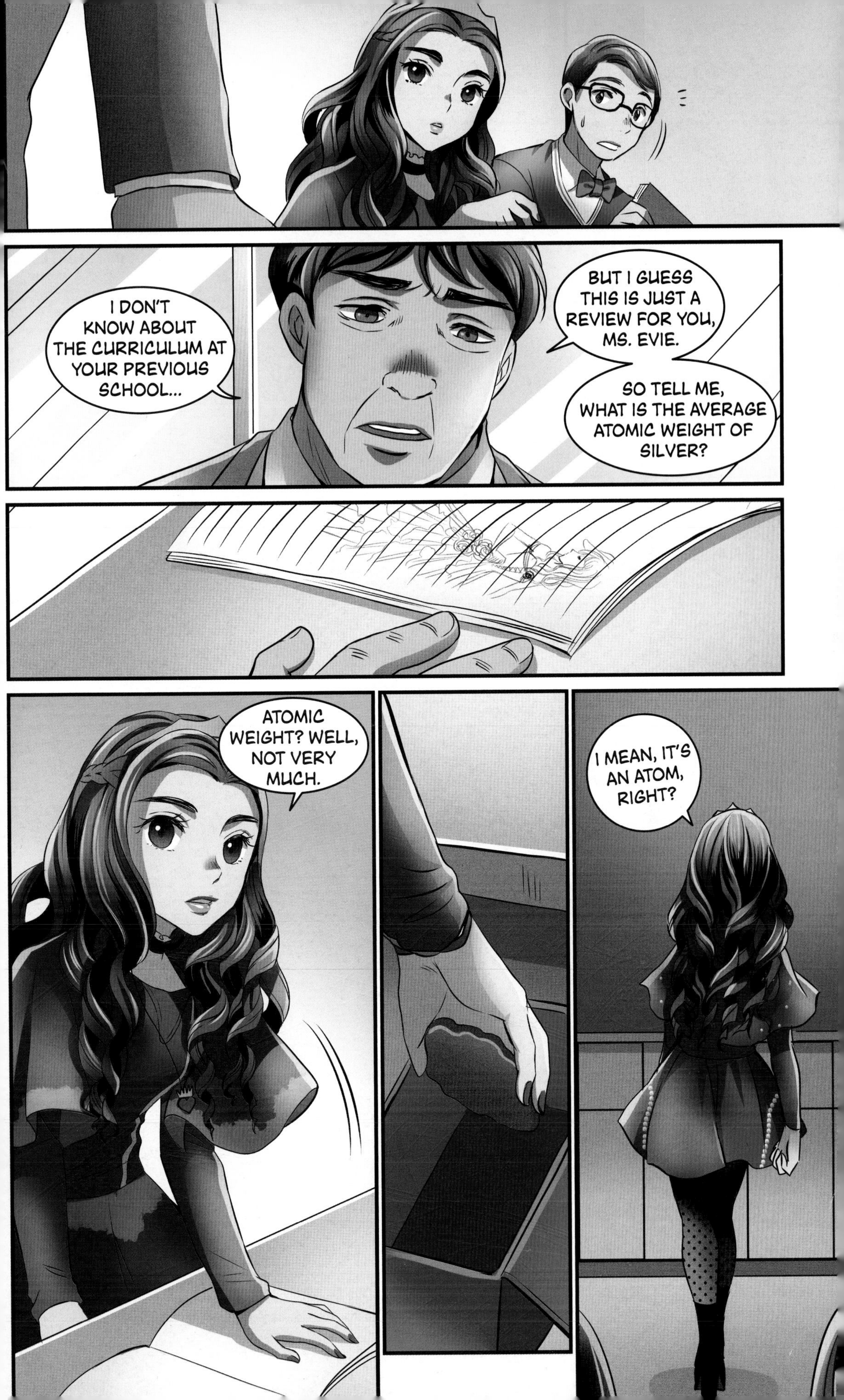
I DON'T KNOW ABOUT THE CURRICULUM AT YOUR PREVIOUS SCHOOL...
BUT I GUESS THIS IS JUST A REVIEW FOR YOU, MS. EVIE.
SO TELL ME, WHAT IS THE AVERAGE ATOMIC WEIGHT OF SILVER?
ATOMIC WEIGHT? WELL, NOT VERY MUCH.
I MEAN, IT'S AN ATOM, RIGHT?

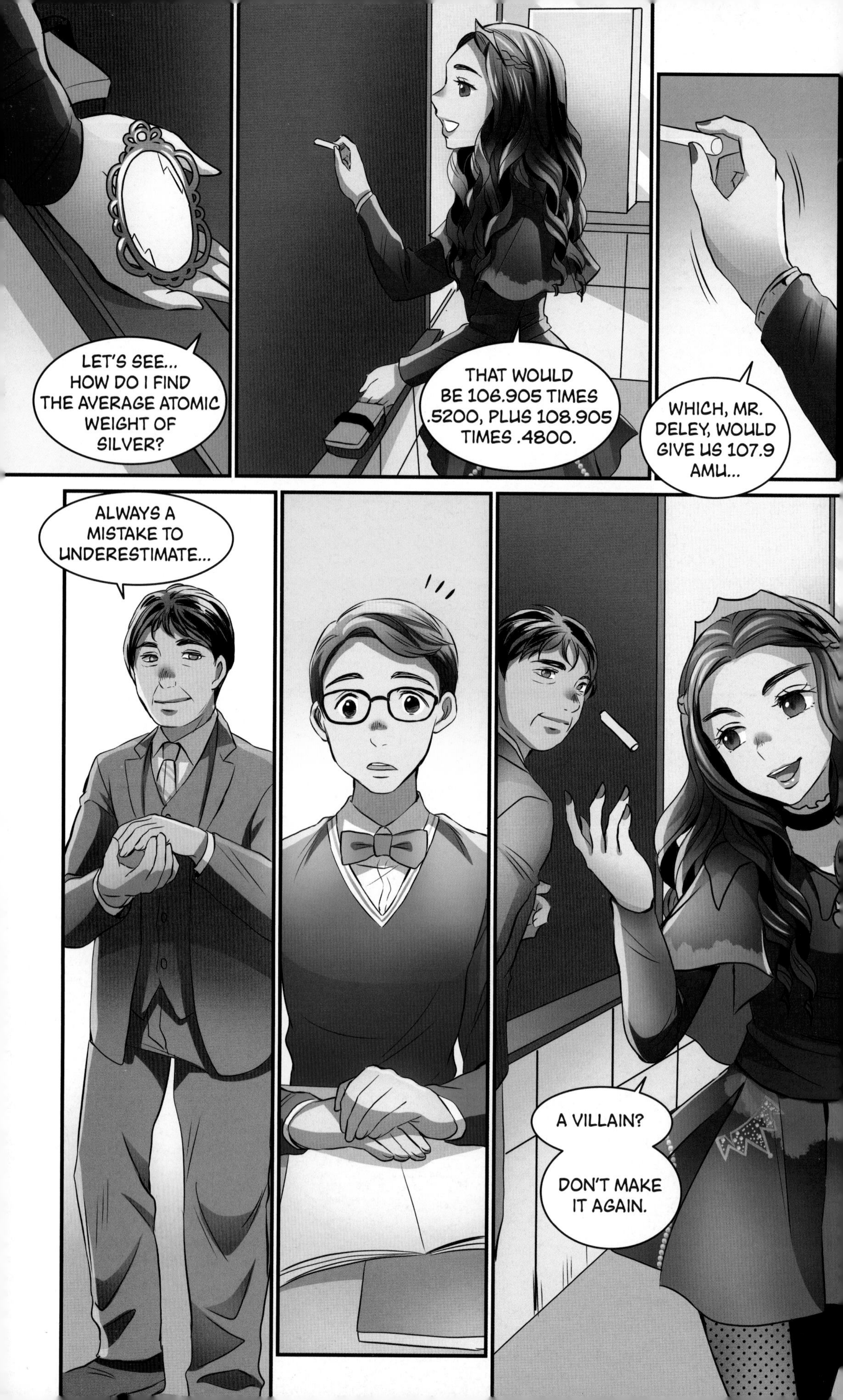
LET'S SEE... HOW DO I FIND THE AVERAGE ATOMIC WEIGHT OF SILVER?
THAT WOULD BE 106.905 TIMES .5200, PLUS 108.905 TIMES .4800.
WHICH, MR. DELEY, WOULD GIVE US 107.9 AMU...
ALWAYS A MISTAKE TO UNDERESTIMATE...
A VILLAIN?
DON'T MAKE IT AGAIN.

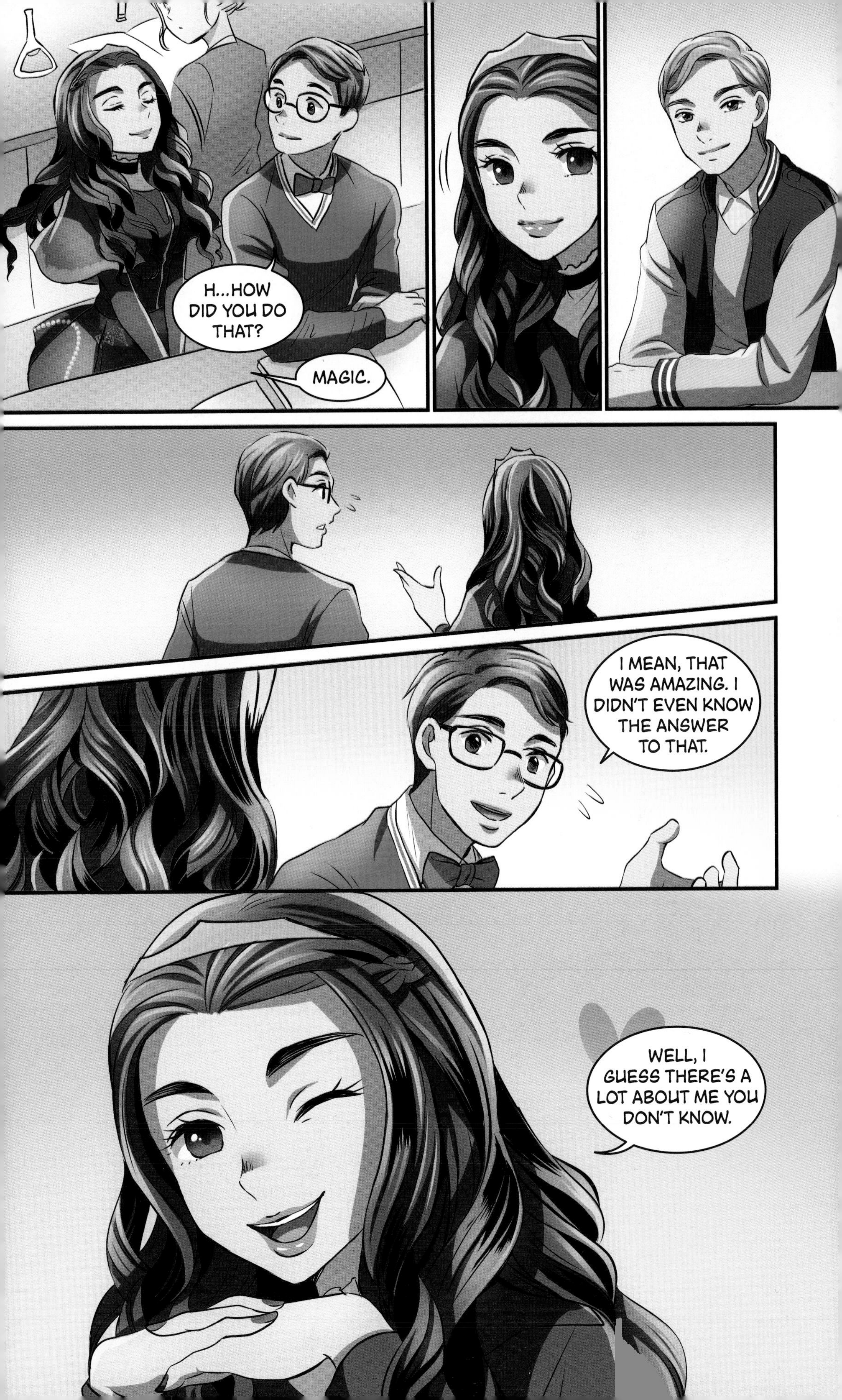
H...HOW DID YOU DO THAT?
MAGIC.
I MEAN, THAT WAS AMAZING. I DIDN'T EVEN KNOW THE ANSWER TO THAT.
WELL, I GUESS THERE'S A LOT ABOUT ME YOU DON'T KNOW.

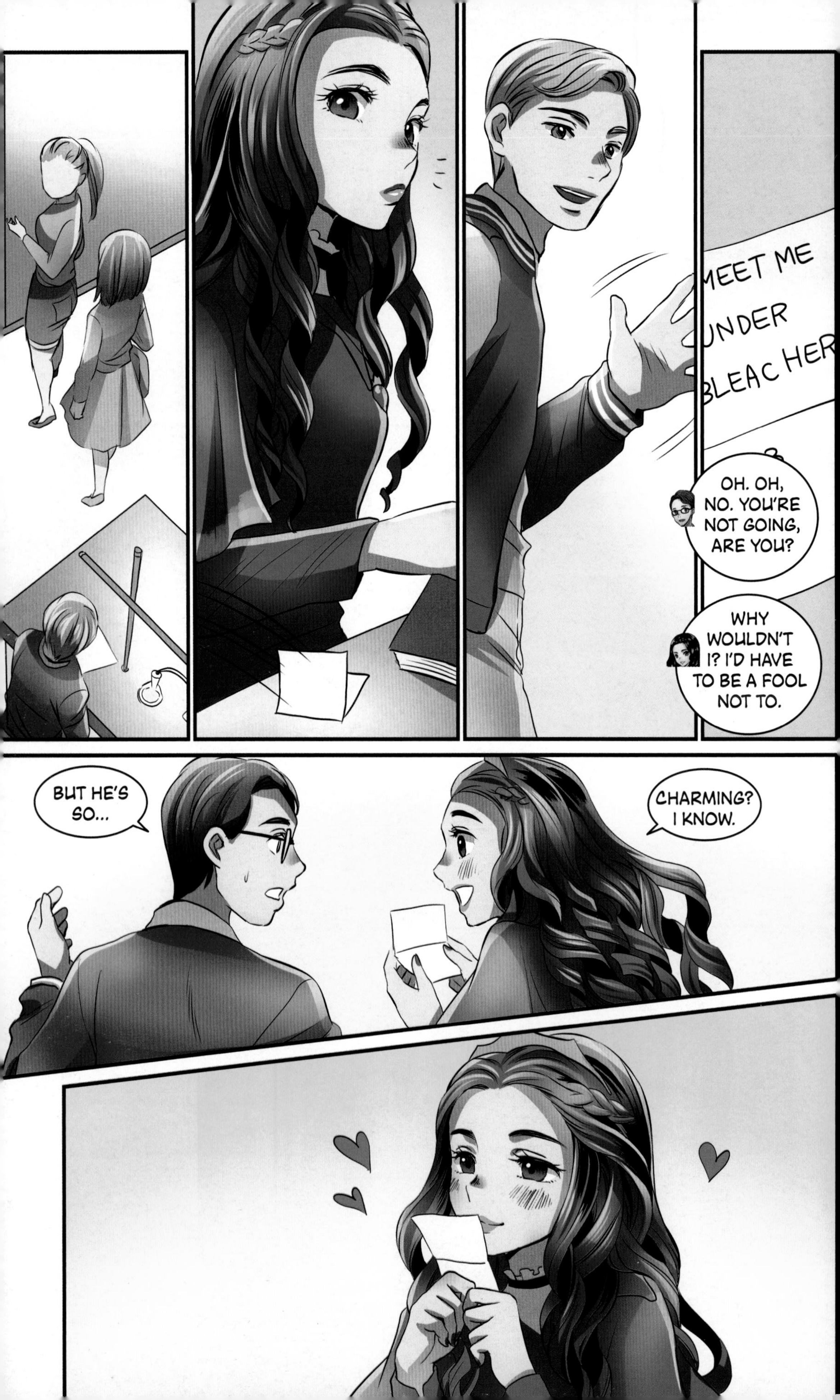

MEET ME
UNDER
BLEACHER
OH. OH, NO. YOU'RE NOT GOING, ARE YOU?
WHY WOULDN'T I? I'D HAVE TO BE A FOOL NOT TO.
BUT HE'S SO...
CHARMING? I KNOW.

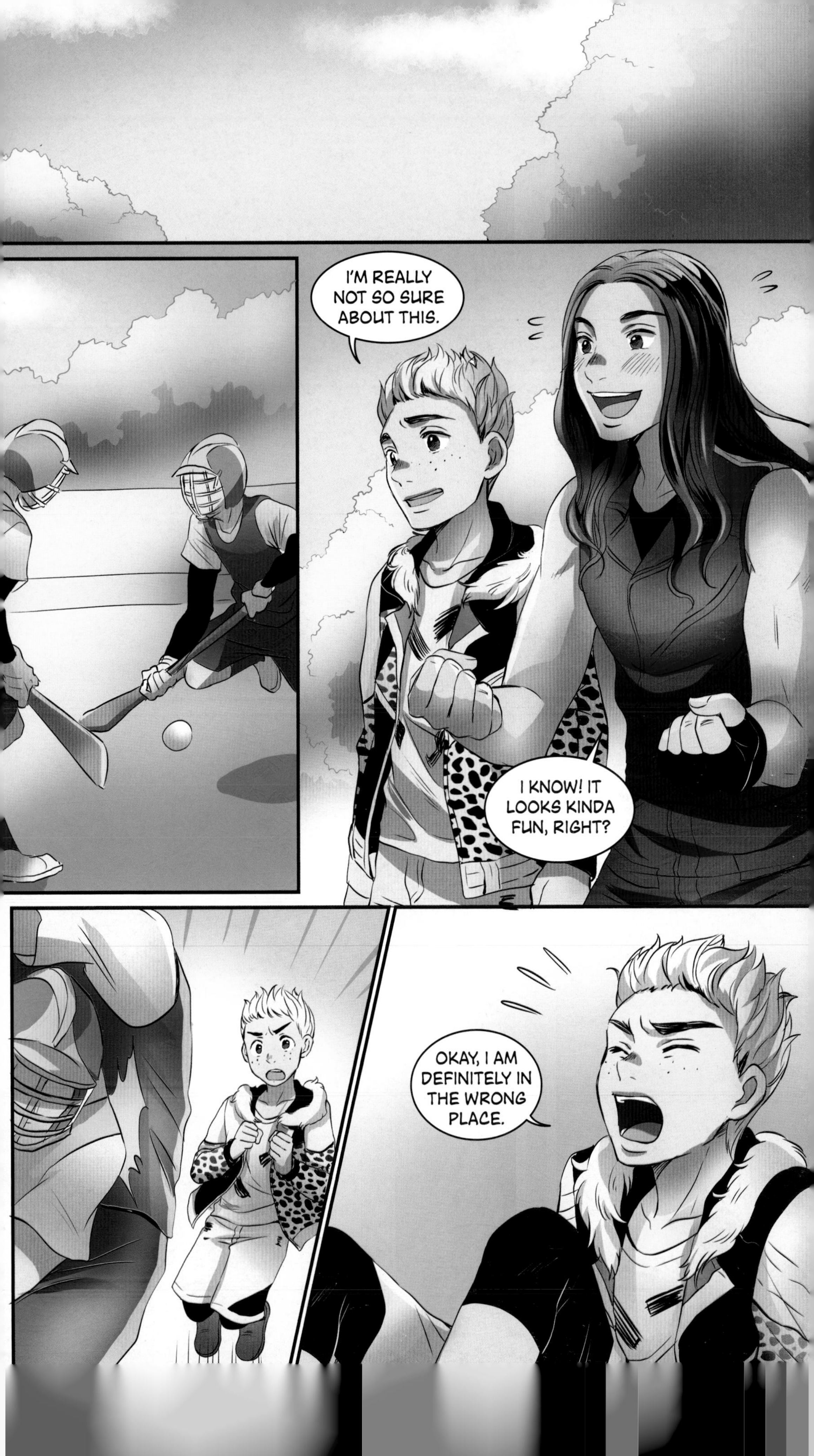
I'M REALLY NOT SO SURE ABOUT THIS.
I KNOW! IT LOOKS KINDA FUN, RIGHT?
OKAY, I AM DEFINITELY IN THE WRONG PLACE.

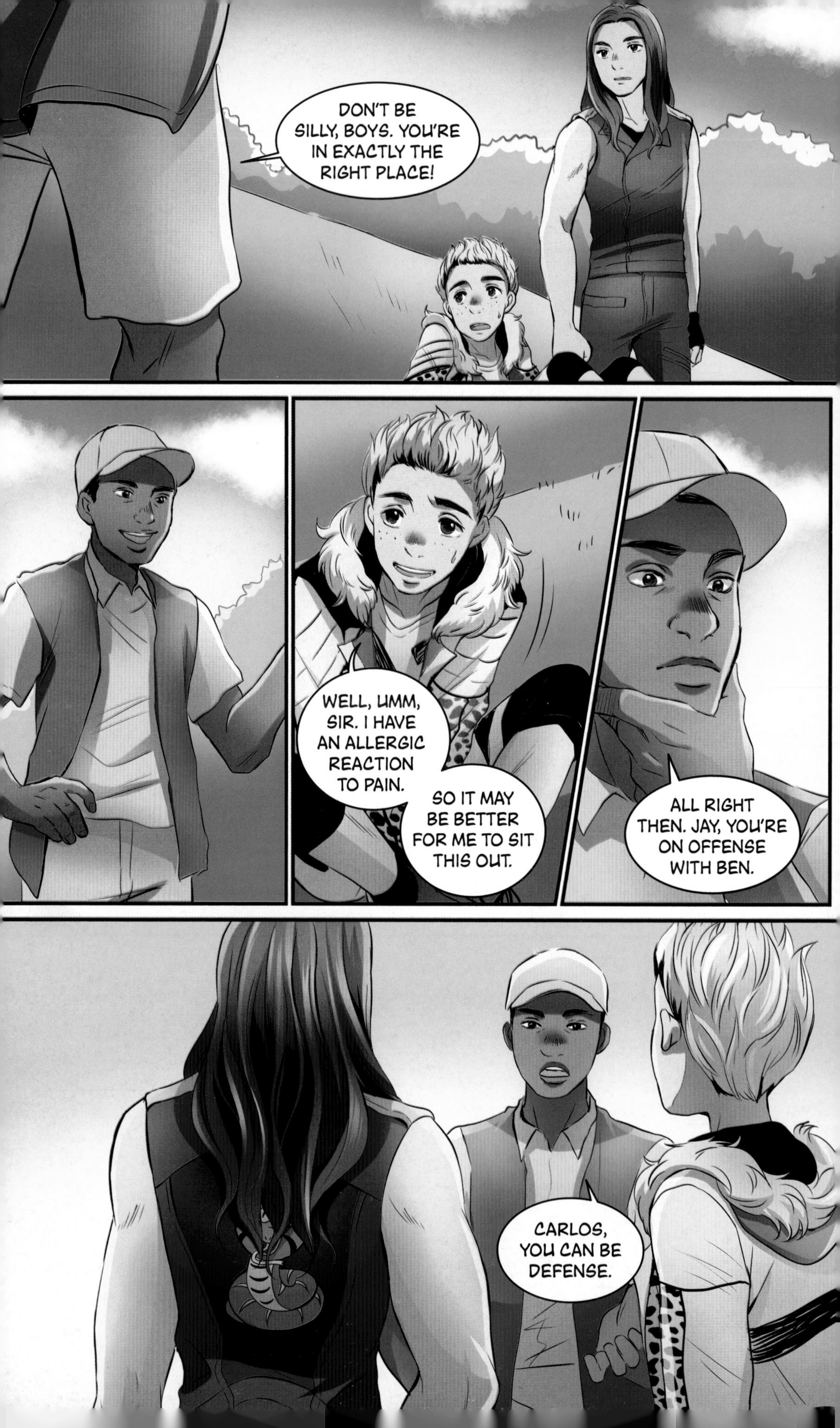
DON'T BE SILLY, BOYS. YOU'RE IN EXACTLY THE RIGHT PLACE!
WELL, UMM, SIR. I HAVE AN ALLERGIC REACTION TO PAIN.
SO IT MAY BE BETTER FOR ME TO SIT THIS OUT.
ALL RIGHT THEN. JAY, YOU'RE ON OFFENSE WITH BEN.
CARLOS, YOU CAN BE DEFENSE.

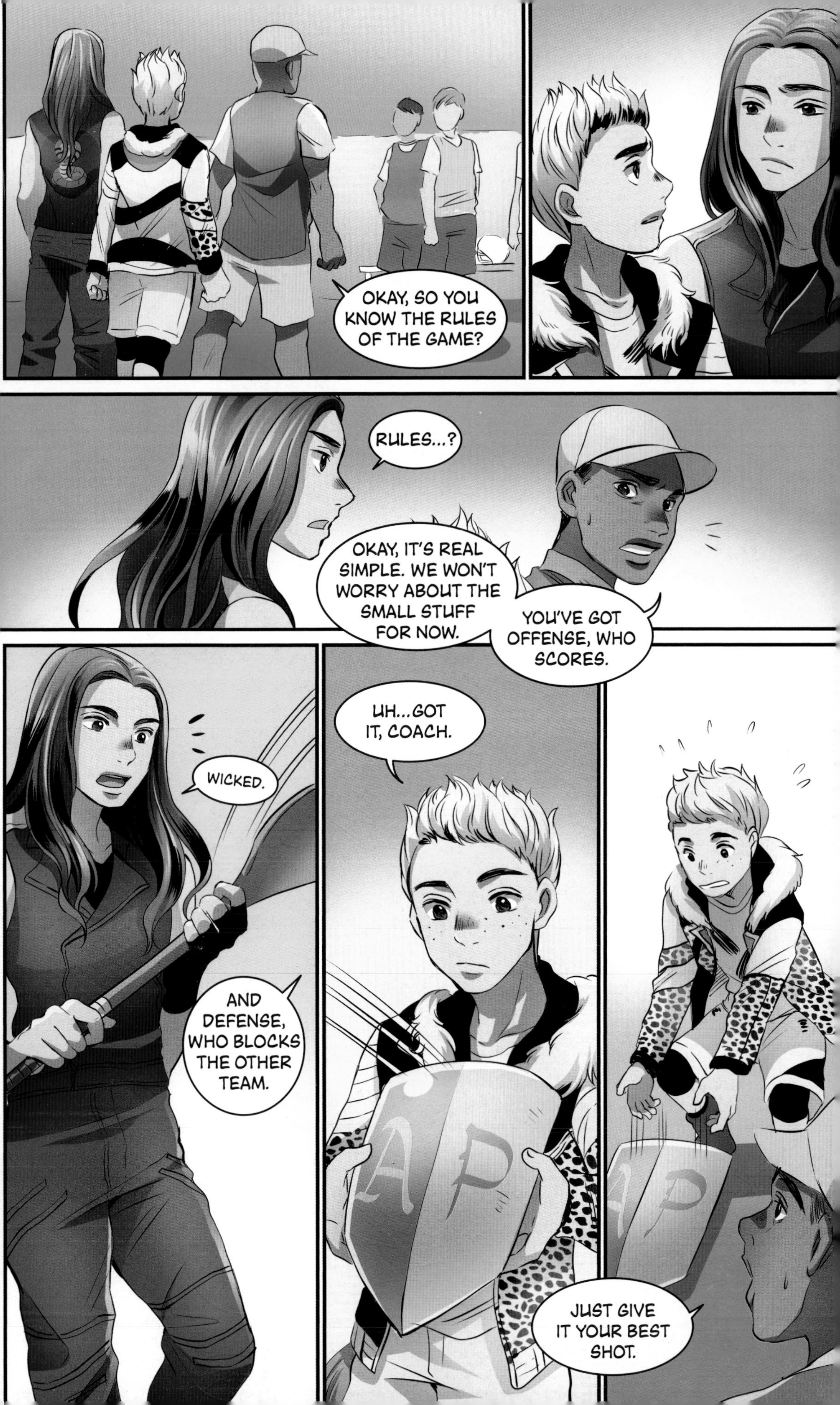
OKAY, SO YOU KNOW THE RULES OF THE GAME?
RULES...?
OKAY, IT'S REAL SIMPLE. WE WON'T WORRY ABOUT THE SMALL STUFF FOR NOW.
YOU'VE GOT OFFENSE, WHO SCORES.
WICKED.
AND DEFENSE, WHO BLOCKS THE OTHER TEAM.
UH...GOT IT, COACH.
JUST GIVE IT YOUR BEST SHOT.

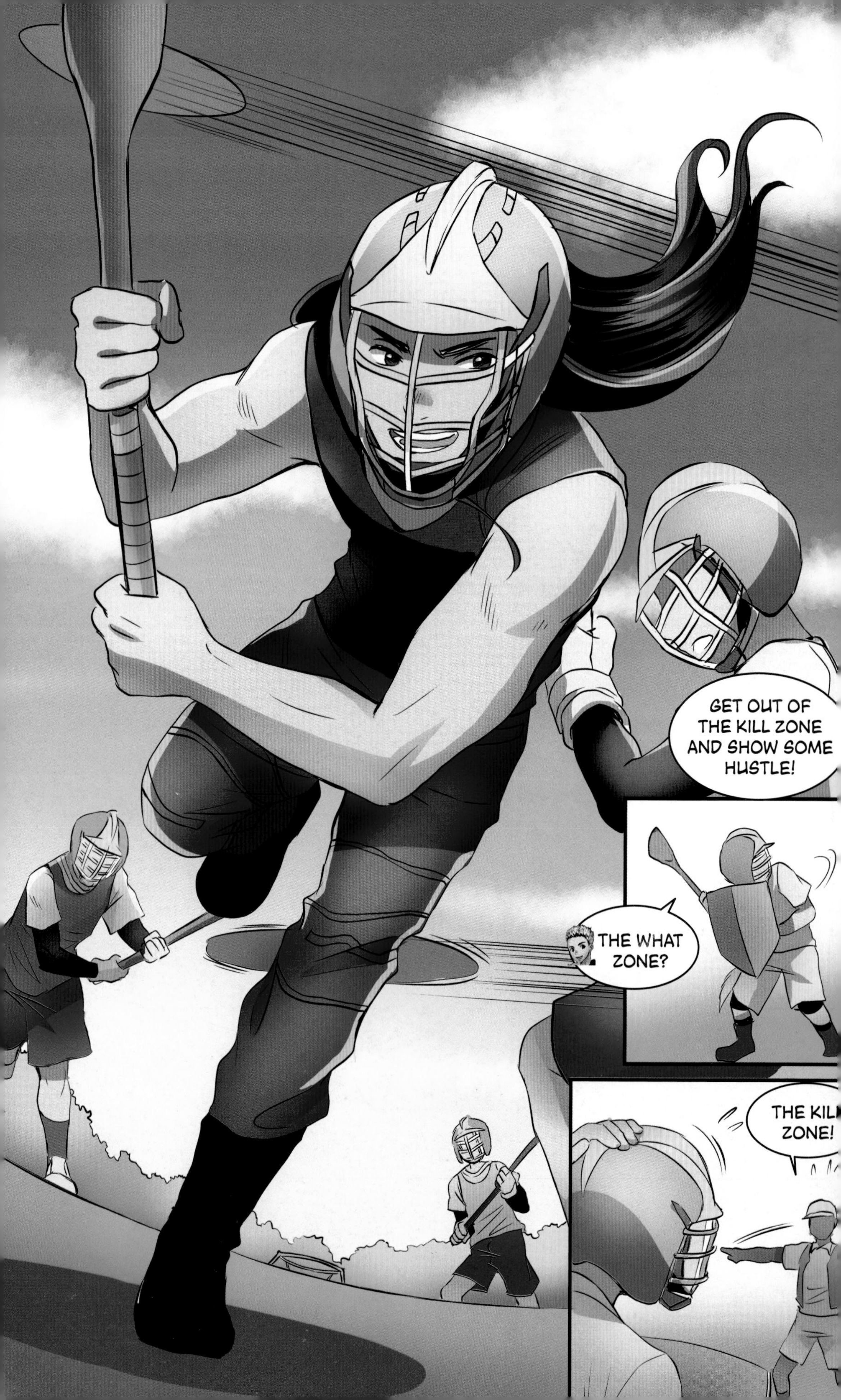

GET OUT OF THE KILL ZONE AND SHOW SOME HUSTLE!
THE WHAT ZONE?
THE KILL ZONE!

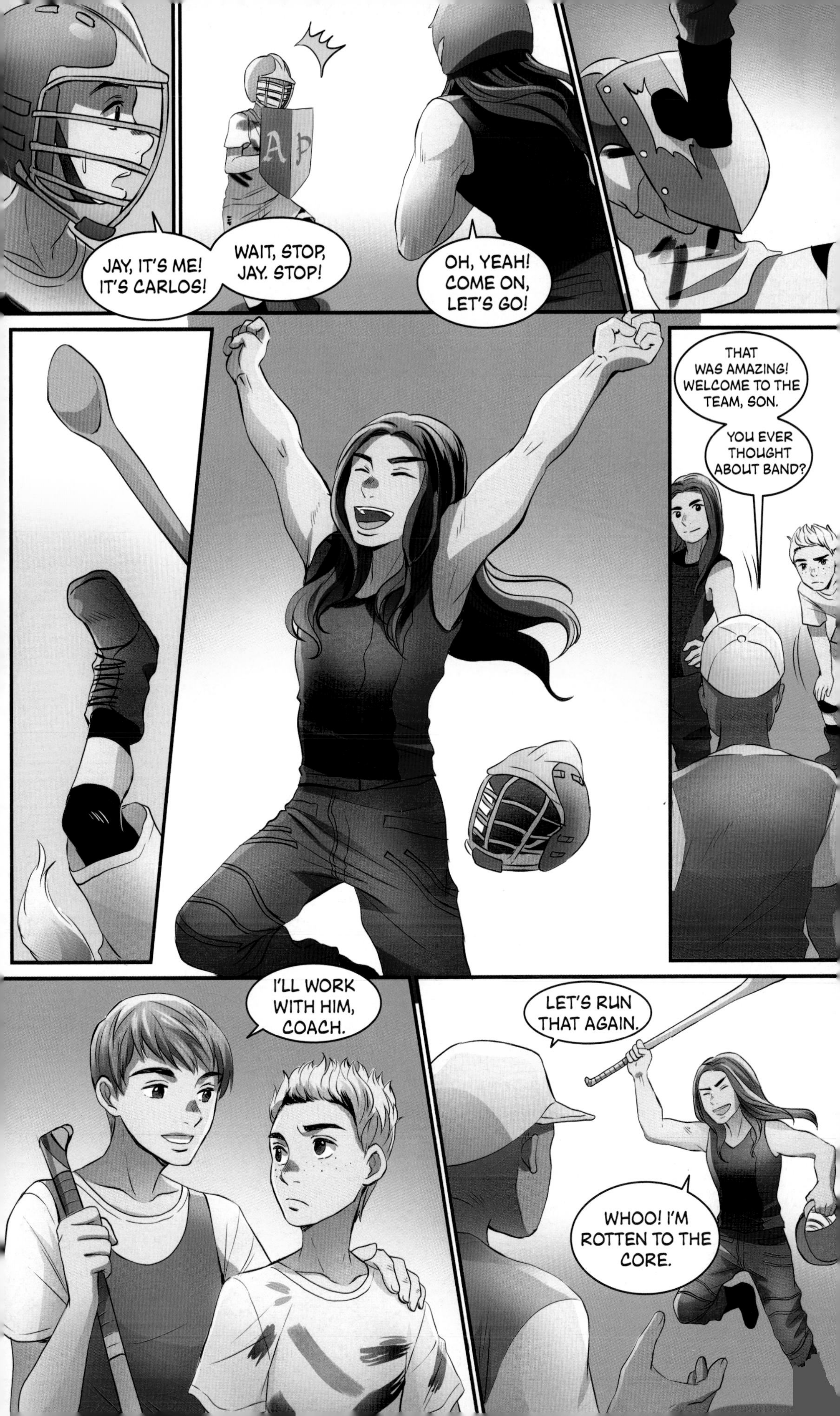
JAY, IT'S ME! IT'S CARLOS!
WAIT, STOP, JAY. STOP!
OH, YEAH! COME ON, LET'S GO!
THAT WAS AMAZING! WELCOME TO THE TEAM, SON.
YOU EVER THOUGHT ABOUT BAND?
I'LL WORK WITH HIM, COACH.
LET'S RUN THAT AGAIN.
WHOO! I'M ROTTEN TO THE CORE.

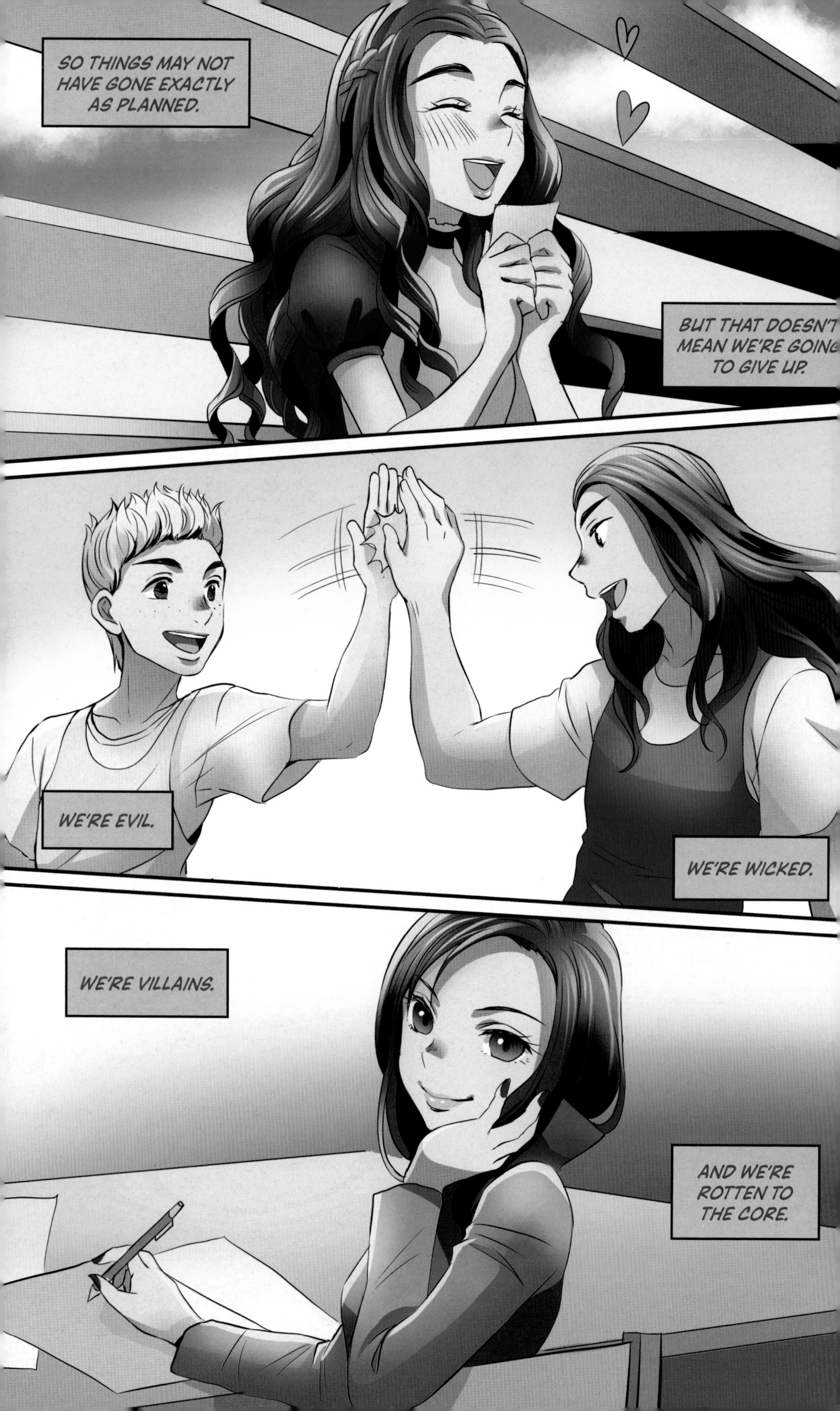
SO THINGS MAY NOT HAVE GONE EXACTLY AS PLANNED.
BUT THAT DOESN'T MEAN WE'RE GOING TO GIVE UP.
WE'RE EVIL.
WE'RE WICKED.
WE'RE VILLAINS.
AND WE'RE ROTTEN TO THE CORE.

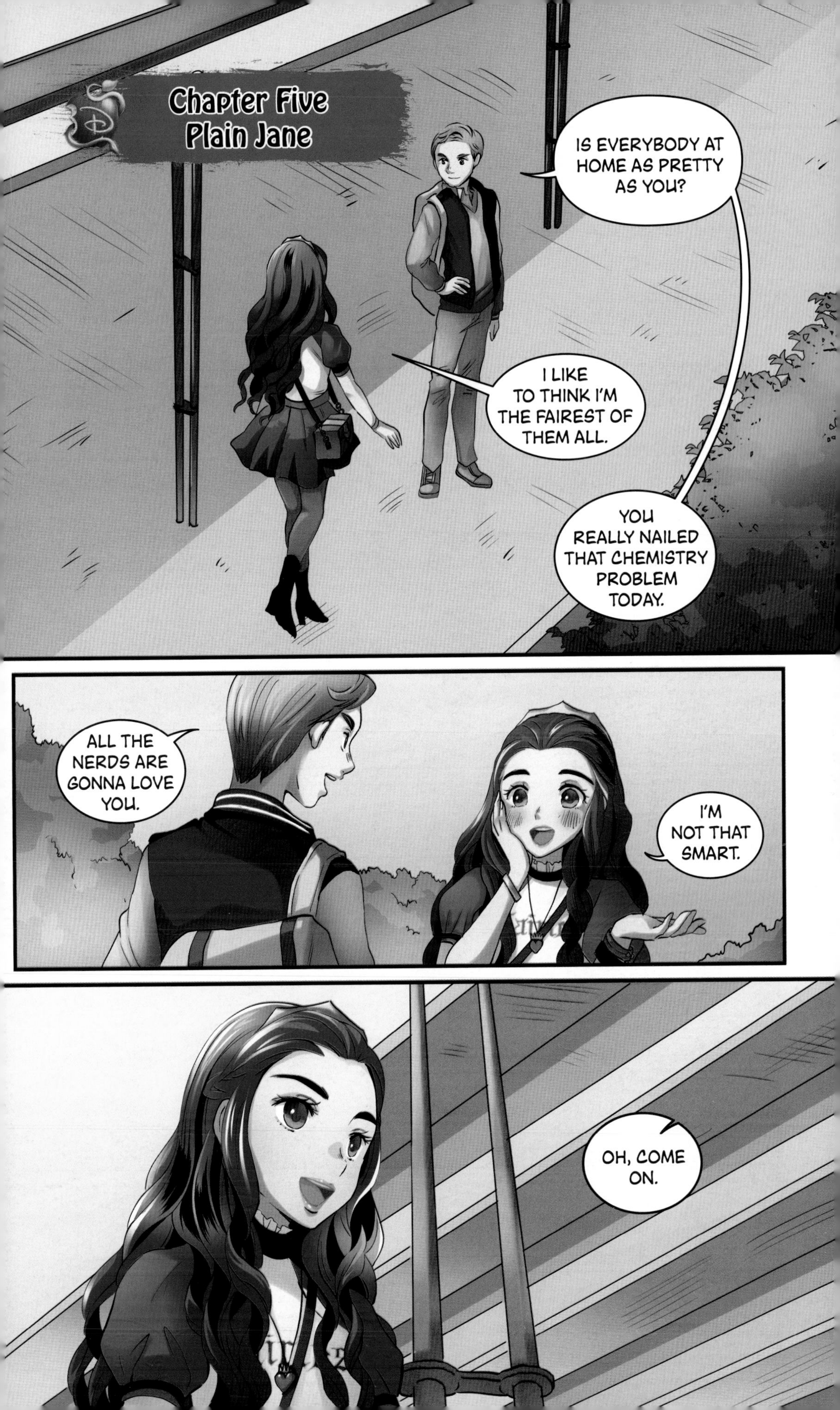
Chapter Five
Plain Jane
IS EVERYBODY AT HOME AS PRETTY AS YOU?
I LIKE TO THINK I'M THE FAIREST OF THEM ALL.
YOU REALLY NAILED THAT CHEMISTRY PROBLEM TODAY.
ALL THE NERDS ARE GONNA LOVE YOU.
I'M NOT THAT SMART.
OH, COME ON.

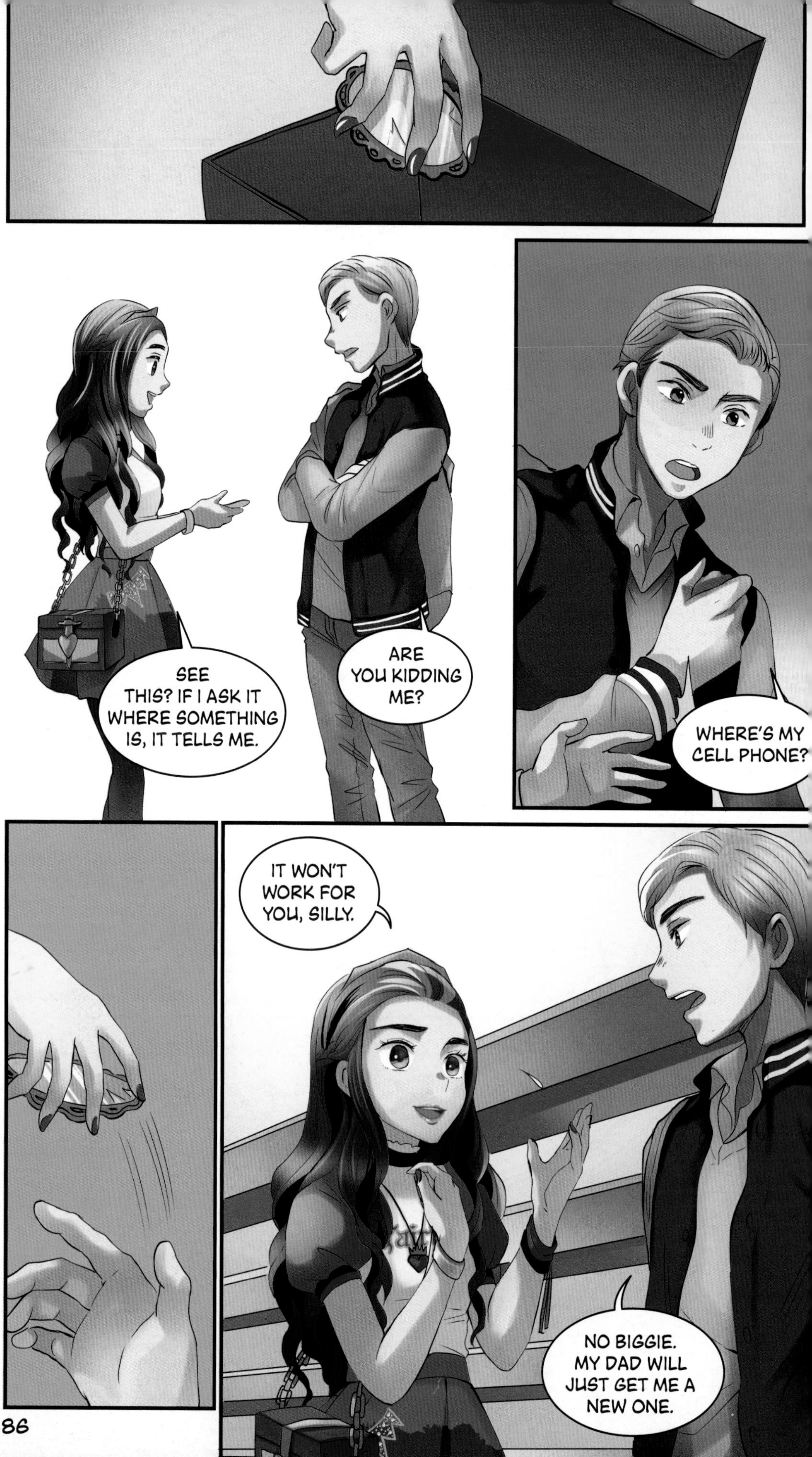
SEE THIS? IF I ASK IT WHERE SOMETHING IS, IT TELLS ME.
ARE YOU KIDDING ME?
WHERE'S MY CELL PHONE?
IT WON'T WORK FOR YOU, SILLY.
NO BIGGIE. MY DAD WILL JUST GET ME A NEW ONE.

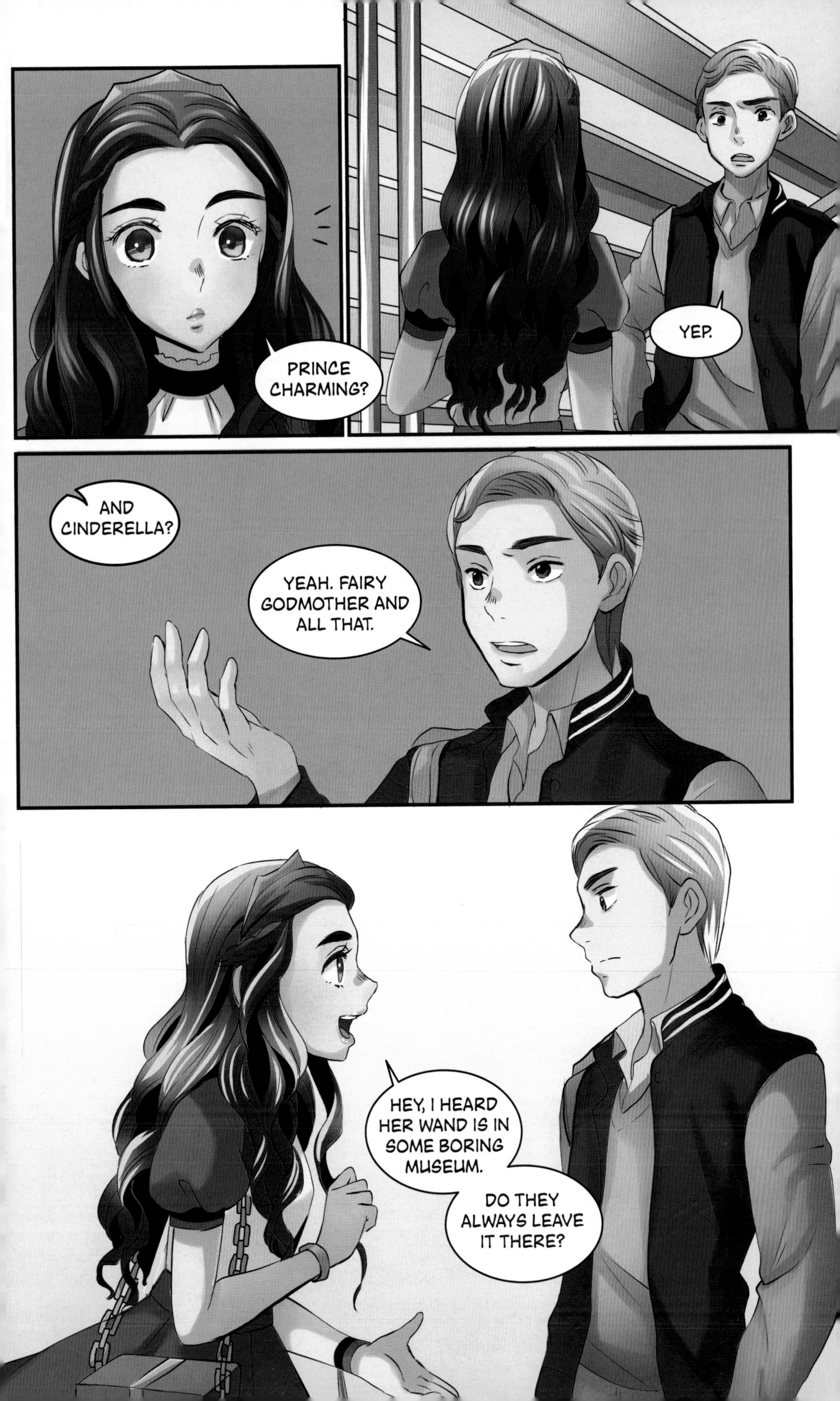
PRINCE CHARMING?
YEP.
AND CINDERELLA?
YEAH. FAIRY GODMOTHER AND ALL THAT.
HEY, I HEARD HER WAND IS IN SOME BORING MUSEUM.
DO THEY ALWAYS LEAVE IT THERE?

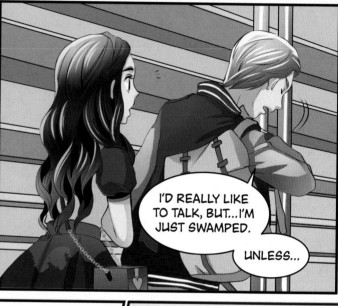

I'D REALLY LIKE TO TALK, BUT...I'M JUST SWAMPED.

UNLESS...

UNLESS?

IF YOU COULD KNOCK ALL MY HOMEWORK OUT ALONG WITH YOURS, THEN MAYBE WE COULD GET TOGETHER SOMETIME...

O...OKAY.

THANKS, BABE.

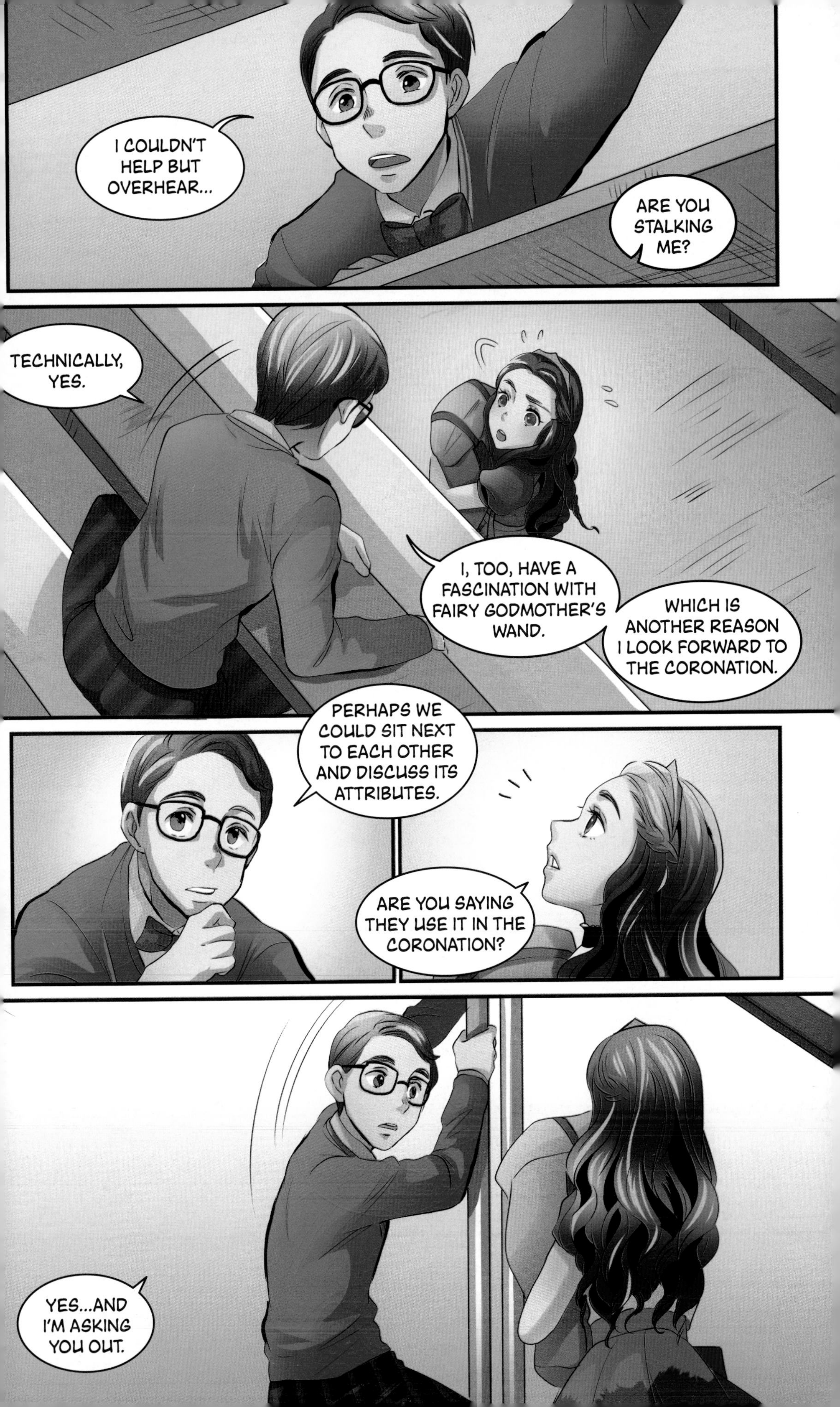
I COULDN'T HELP BUT OVERHEAR...
ARE YOU STALKING ME?
TECHNICALLY, YES.
I, TOO, HAVE A FASCINATION WITH FAIRY GODMOTHER'S WAND.
WHICH IS ANOTHER REASON I LOOK FORWARD TO THE CORONATION.
PERHAPS WE COULD SIT NEXT TO EACH OTHER AND DISCUSS ITS ATTRIBUTES.
ARE YOU SAYING THEY USE IT IN THE CORONATION?
YES...AND I'M ASKING YOU OUT.

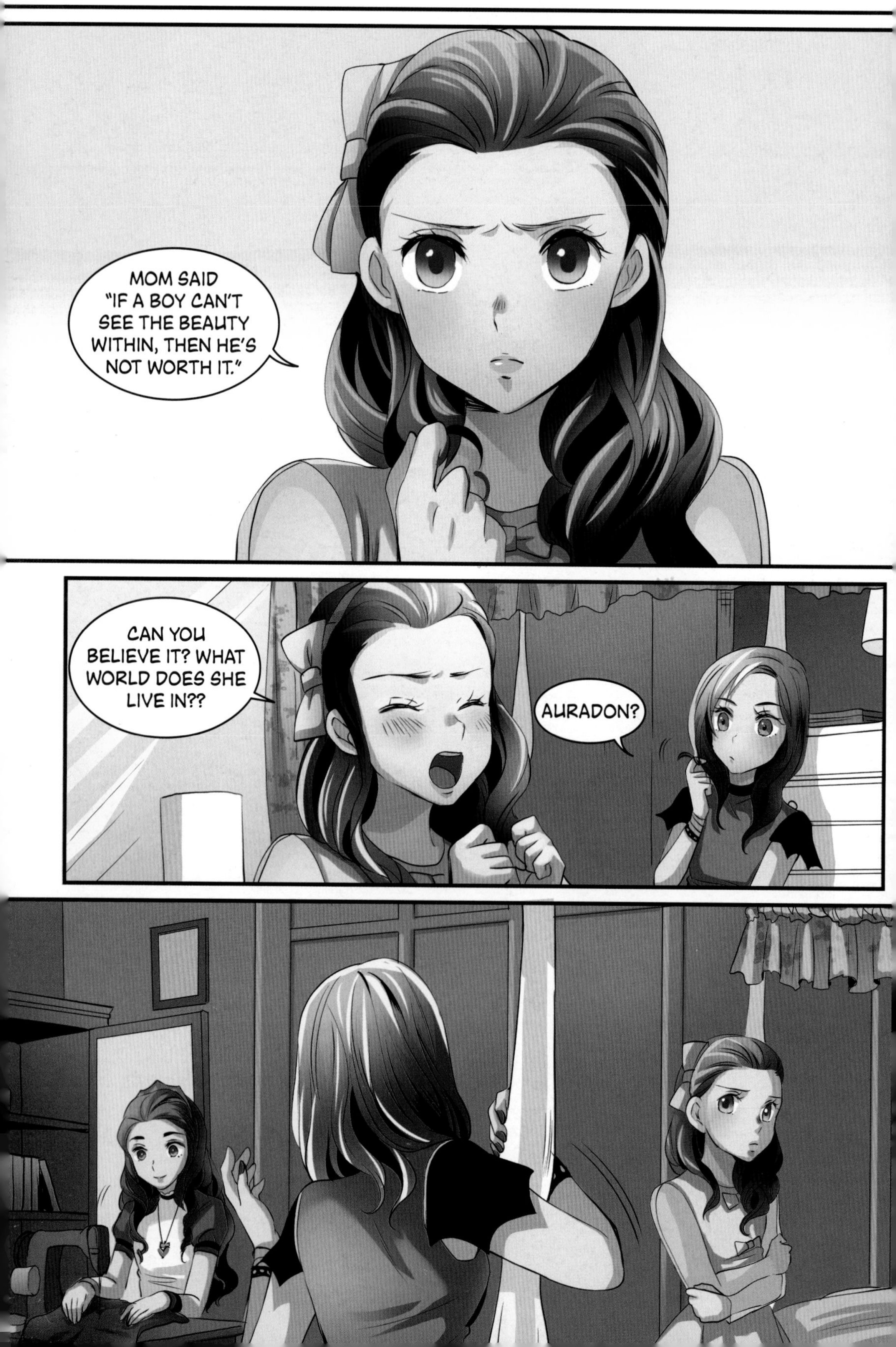
MOM SAID
"IF A BOY CAN'T SEE THE BEAUTY WITHIN, THEN HE'S NOT WORTH IT."
CAN YOU BELIEVE IT? WHAT WORLD DOES SHE LIVE IN??
AURADON?

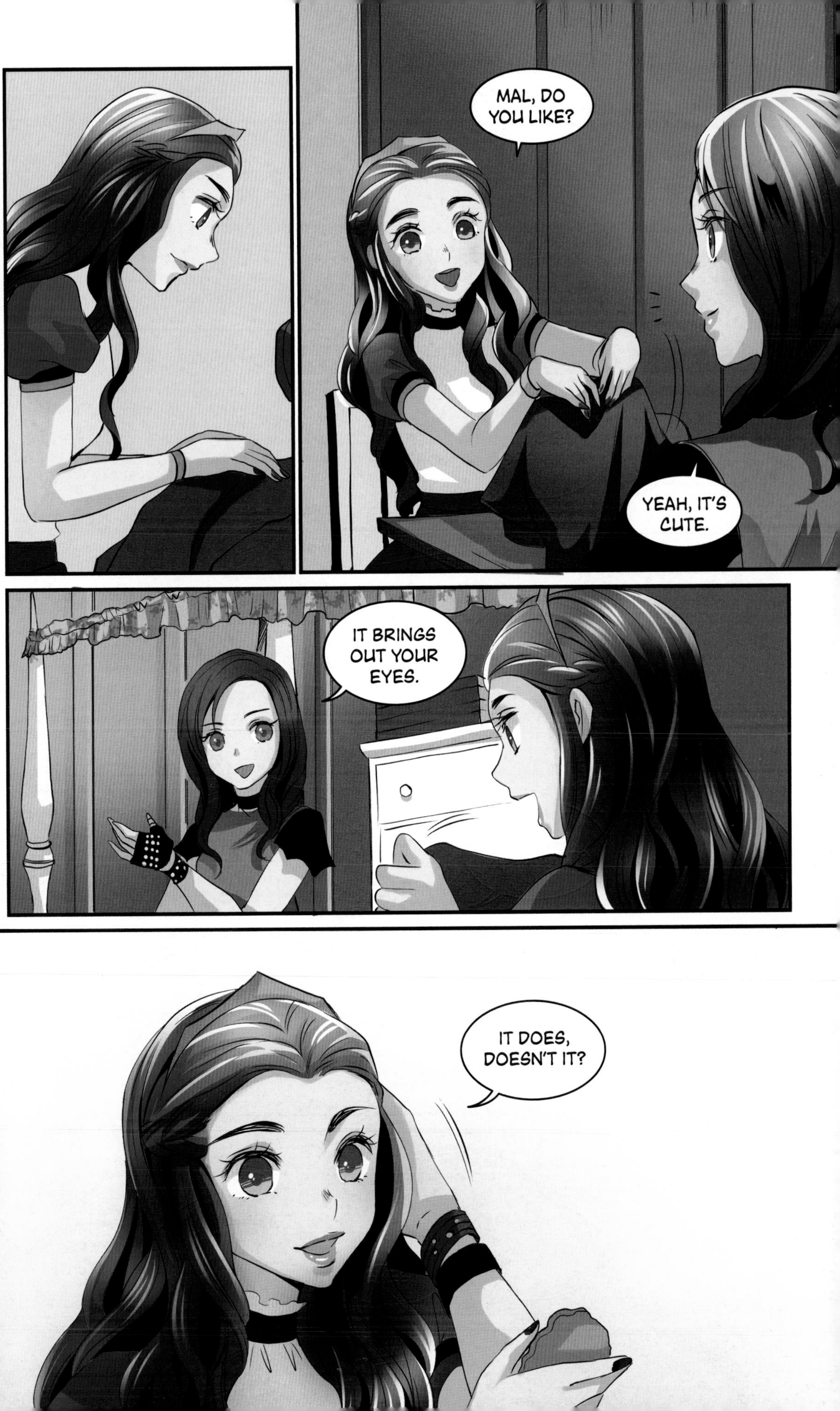
MAL, DO YOU LIKE?
YEAH, IT'S CUTE.
IT BRINGS OUT YOUR EYES.
IT DOES, DOESN'T IT?

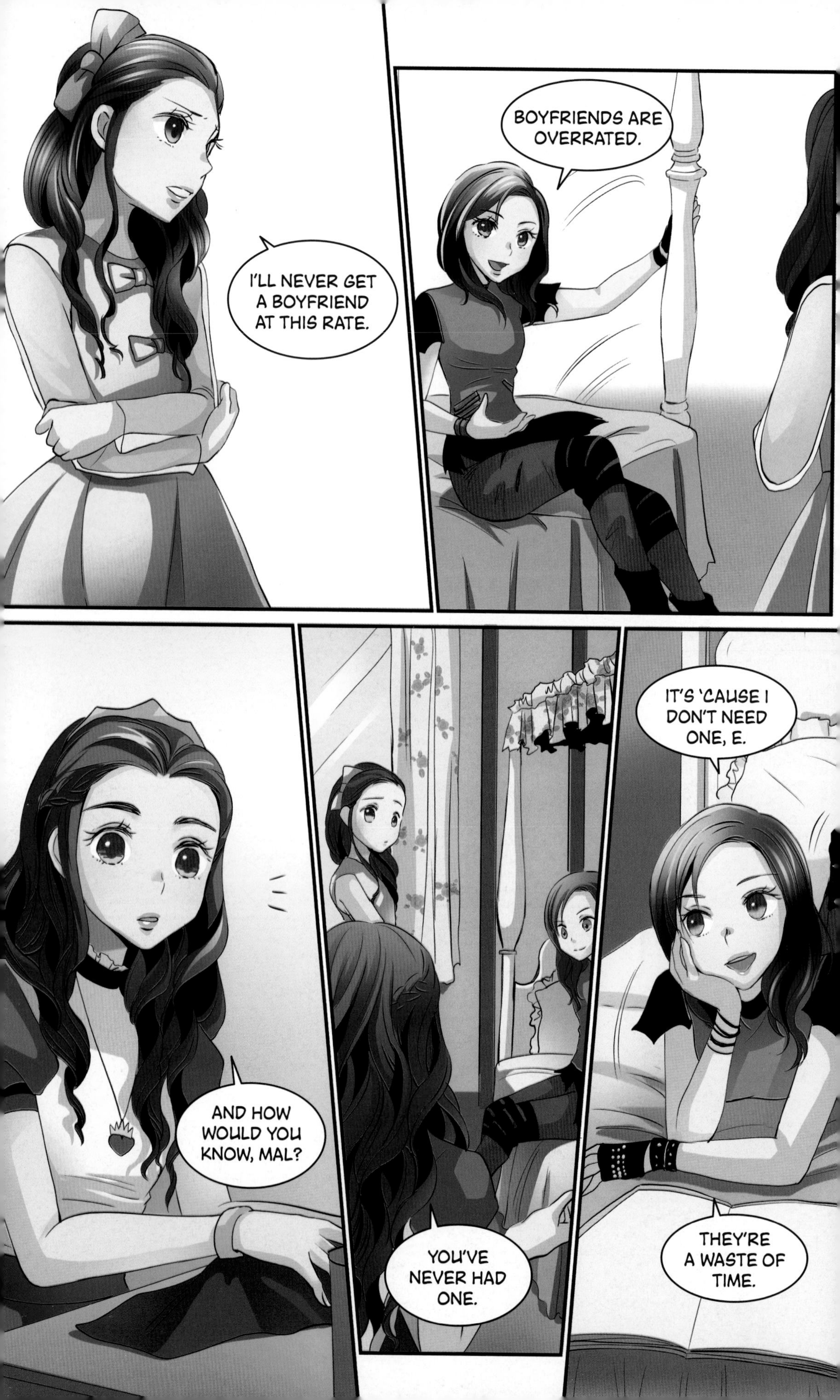
I'LL NEVER GET A BOYFRIEND AT THIS RATE.
BOYFRIENDS ARE OVERRATED.
AND HOW WOULD YOU KNOW, MAL?
YOU'VE NEVER HAD ONE.
IT'S 'CAUSE I DON'T NEED ONE, E.
THEY'RE A WASTE OF TIME.

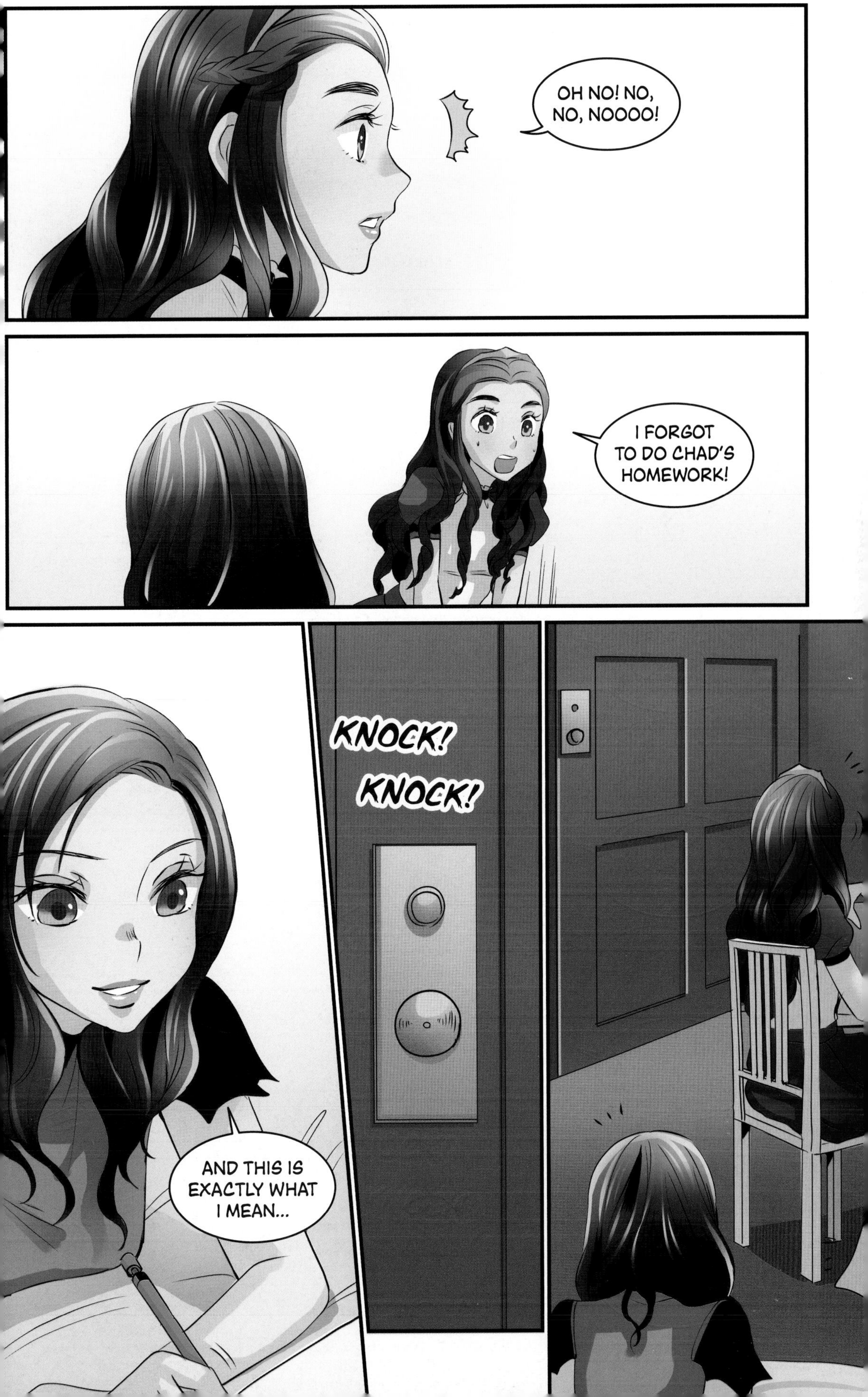
OH NO! NO, NO, NOOOO!
I FORGOT TO DO CHAD'S HOMEWORK!
AND THIS IS EXACTLY WHAT I MEAN...
KNOCK! KNOCK!

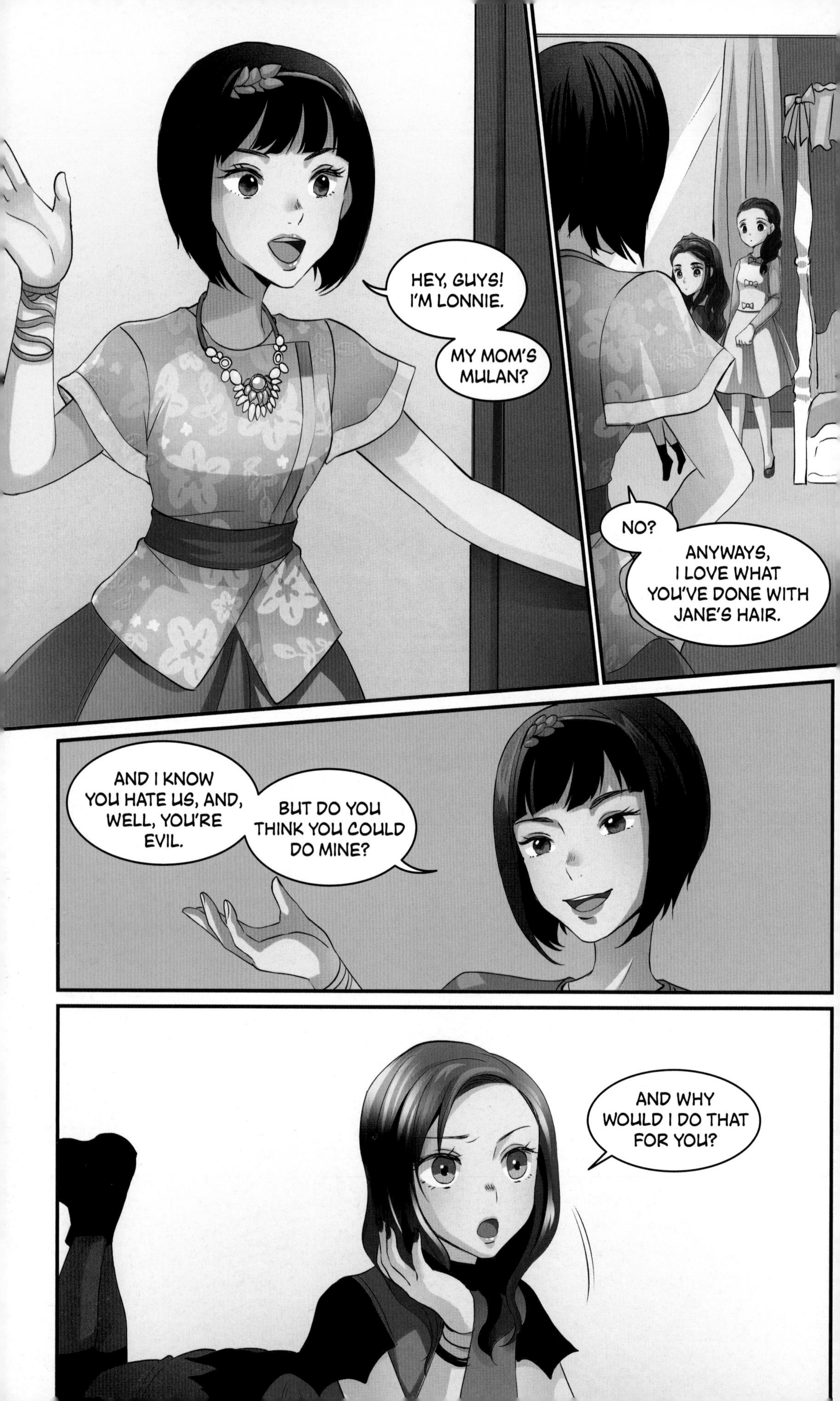
HEY, GUYS! I'M LONNIE.
MY MOM'S MULAN?
NO?
ANYWAYS, I LOVE WHAT YOU'VE DONE WITH JANE'S HAIR.
AND I KNOW YOU HATE US, AND, WELL, YOU'RE EVIL.
BUT DO YOU THINK YOU COULD DO MINE?
AND WHY WOULD I DO THAT FOR YOU?

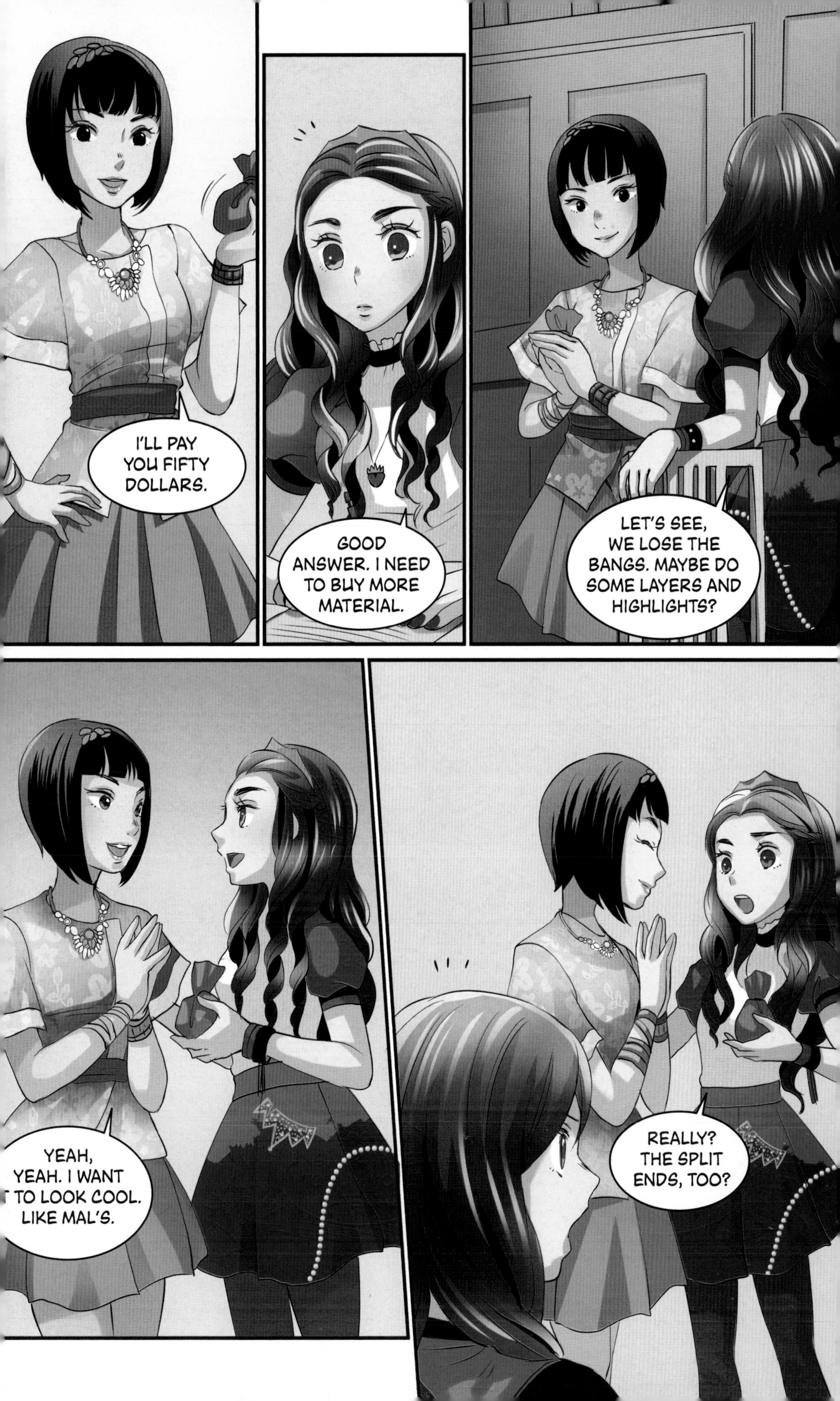
I'LL PAY YOU FIFTY DOLLARS.
GOOD ANSWER. I NEED TO BUY MORE MATERIAL.
LET'S SEE, WE LOSE THE BANGS. MAYBE DO SOME LAYERS AND HIGHLIGHTS?
YEAH, YEAH. I WANT TO LOOK COOL. LIKE MAL'S.
REALLY? THE SPLIT ENDS, TOO?

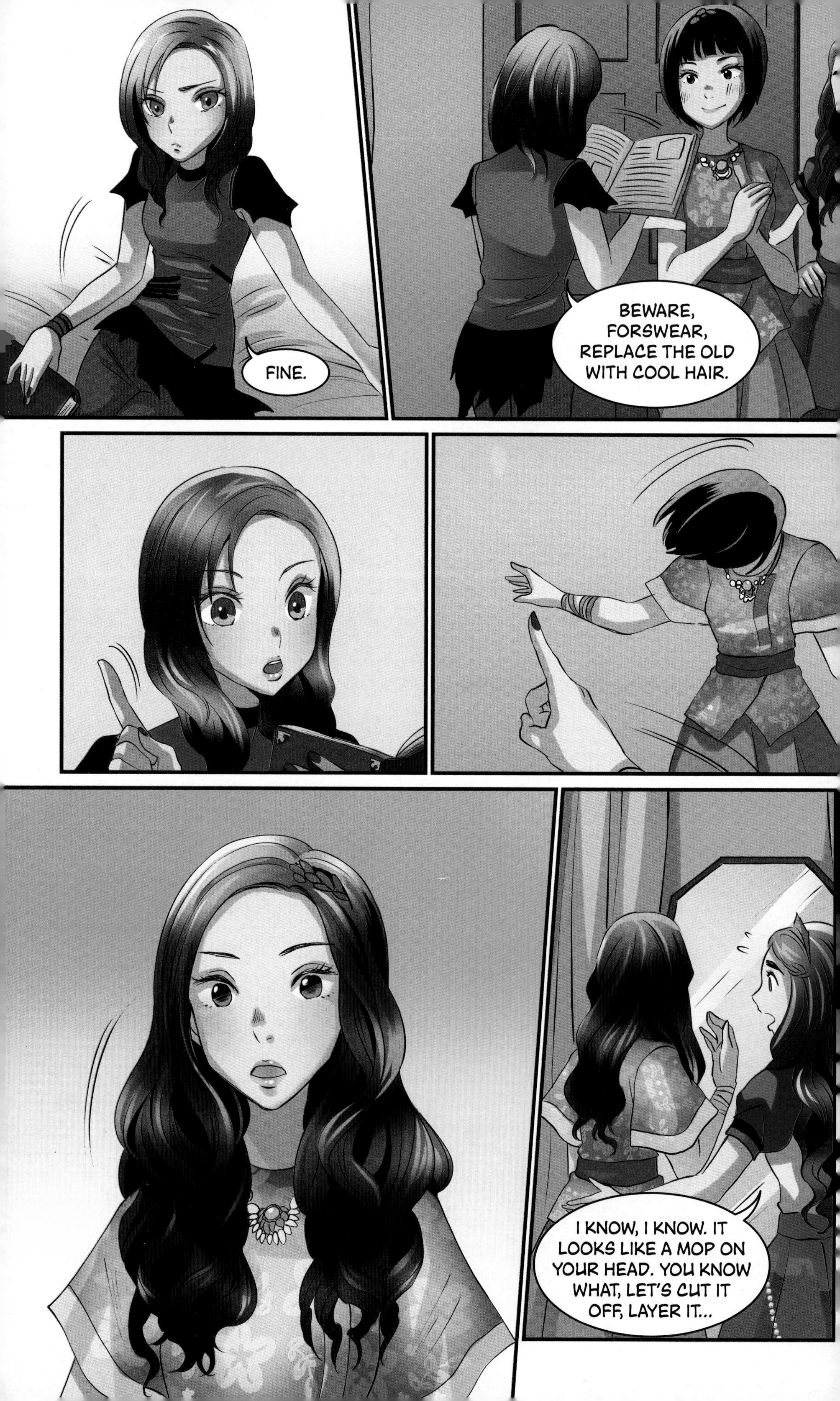
FINE.
BEWARE, FORSWEAR, REPLACE THE OLD WITH COOL HAIR.
I KNOW, I KNOW. IT LOOKS LIKE A MOP ON YOUR HEAD. YOU KNOW WHAT, LET'S CUT IT OFF, LAYER IT...

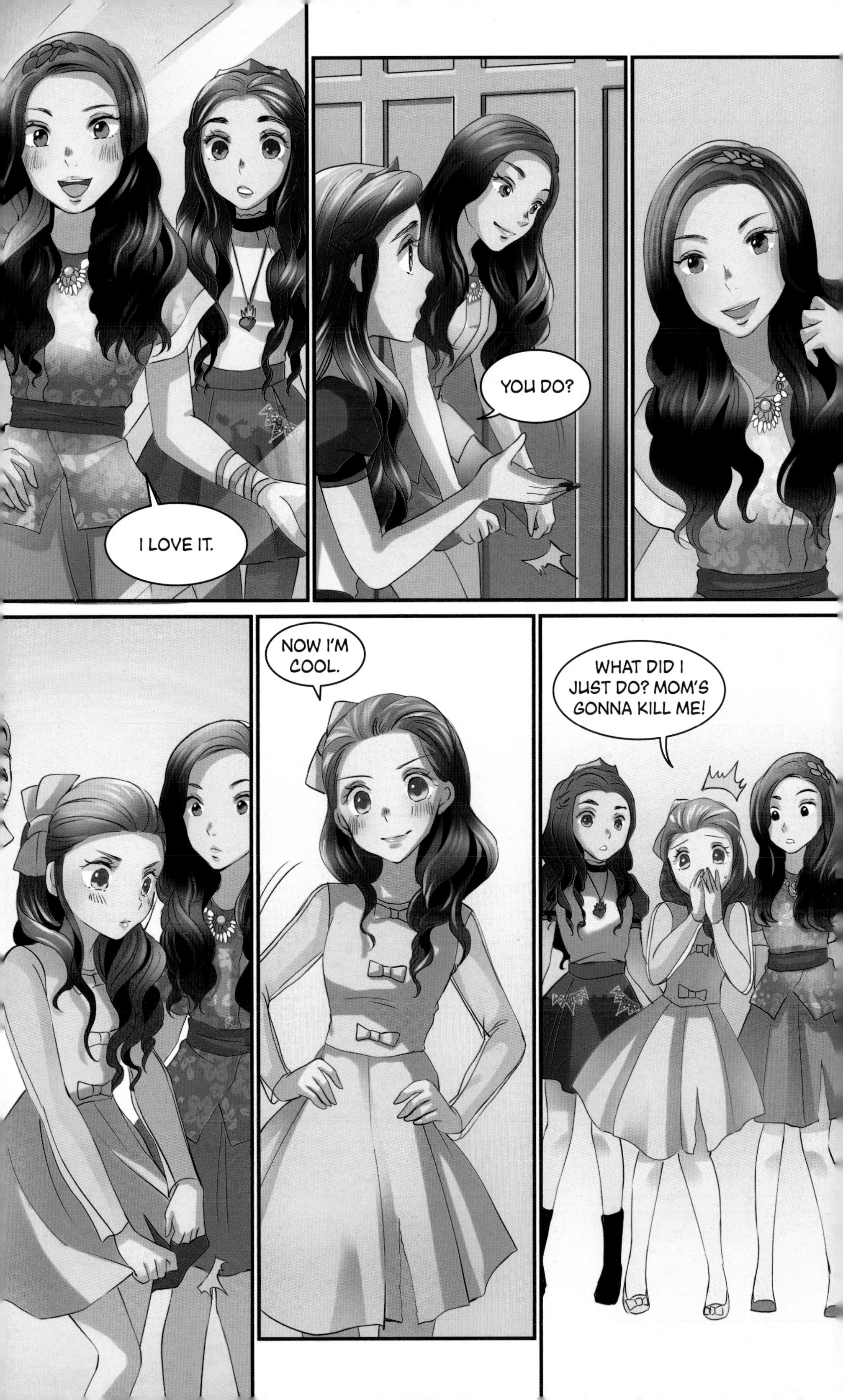
I LOVE IT.
YOU DO?
NOW I'M COOL.
WHAT DID I JUST DO? MOM'S GONNA KILL ME!

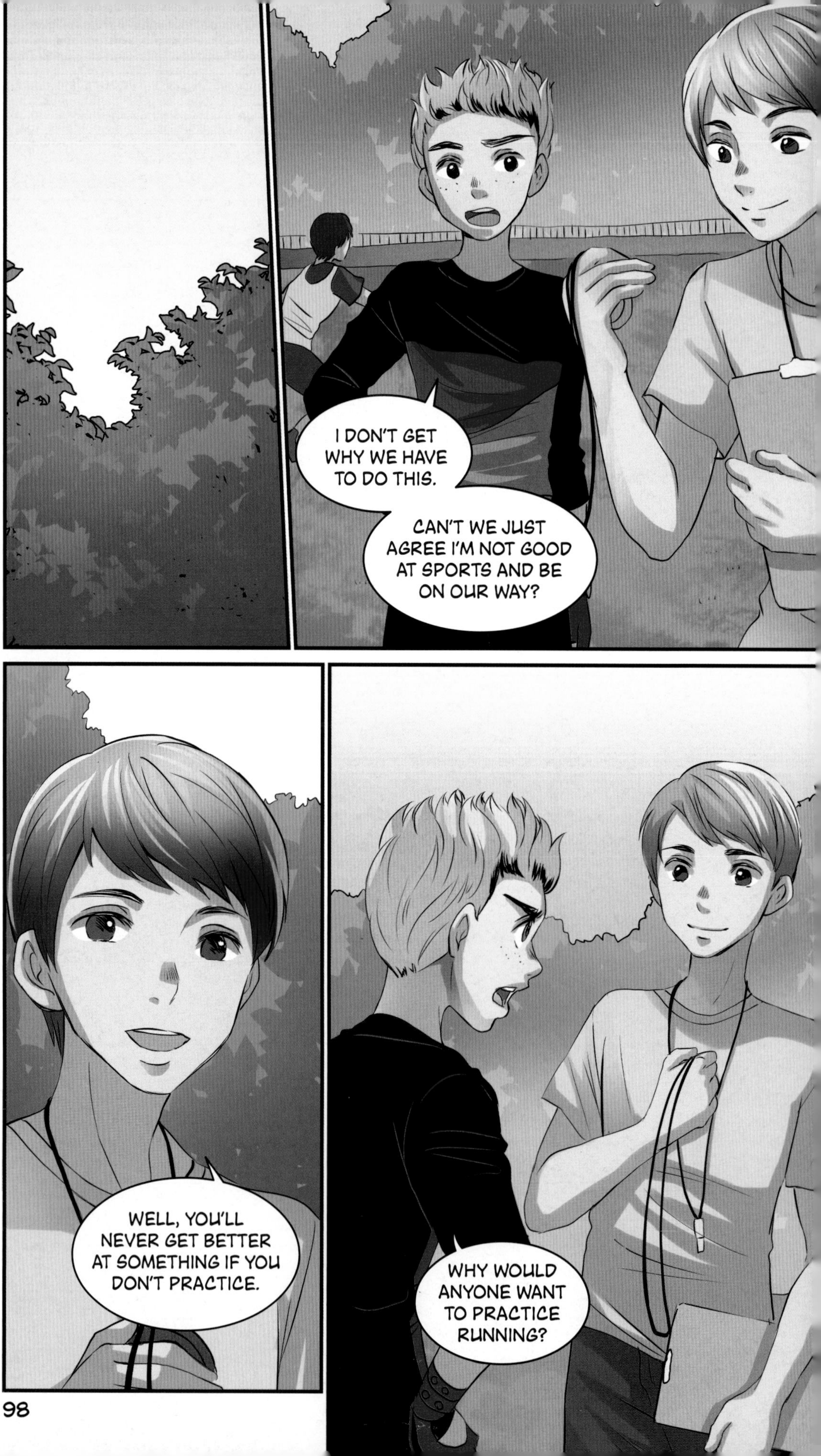
I DON'T GET WHY WE HAVE TO DO THIS.
CAN'T WE JUST AGREE I'M NOT GOOD AT SPORTS AND BE ON OUR WAY?
WELL, YOU'LL NEVER GET BETTER AT SOMETHING IF YOU DON'T PRACTICE.
WHY WOULD ANYONE WANT TO PRACTICE RUNNING?

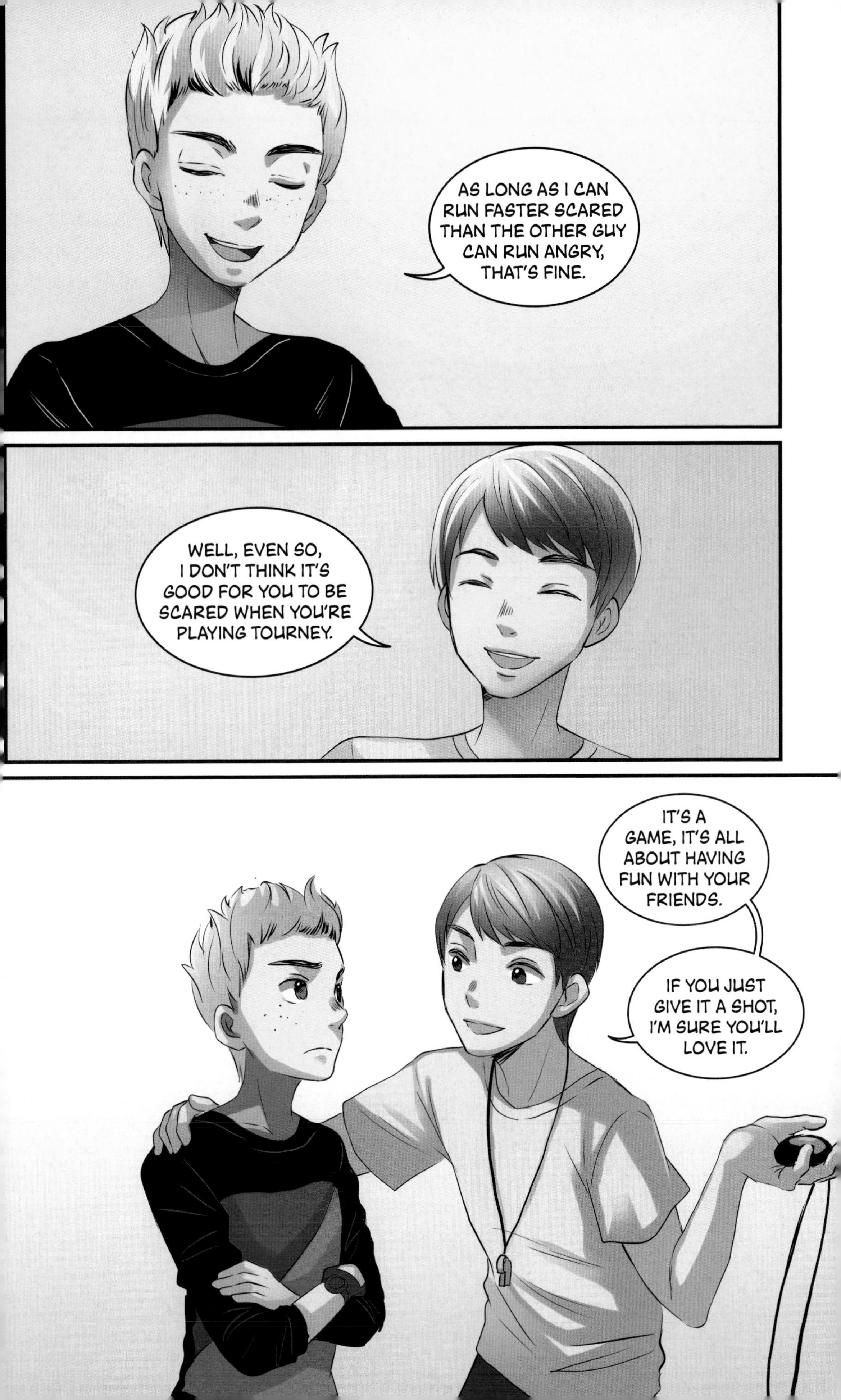
AS LONG AS I CAN RUN FASTER SCARED THAN THE OTHER GUY CAN RUN ANGRY, THAT'S FINE.
WELL, EVEN SO, I DON'T THINK IT'S GOOD FOR YOU TO BE SCARED WHEN YOU'RE PLAYING TOURNEY.
IT'S A GAME, IT'S ALL ABOUT HAVING FUN WITH YOUR FRIENDS.
IF YOU JUST GIVE IT A SHOT, I'M SURE YOU'LL LOVE IT.

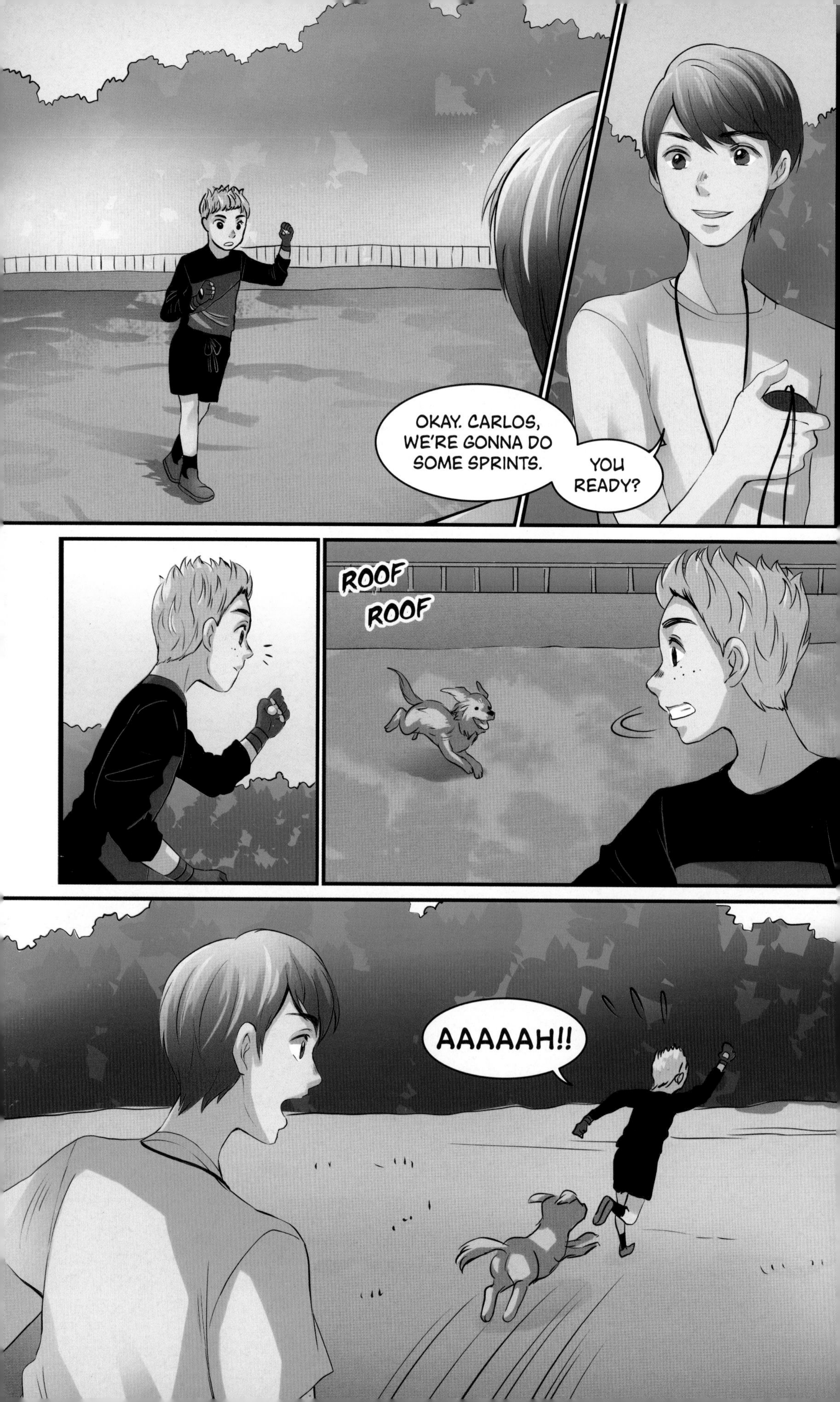
OKAY. CARLOS, WE'RE GONNA DO SOME SPRINTS.
YOU READY?
ROOF
ROOF
AAAAAH!!

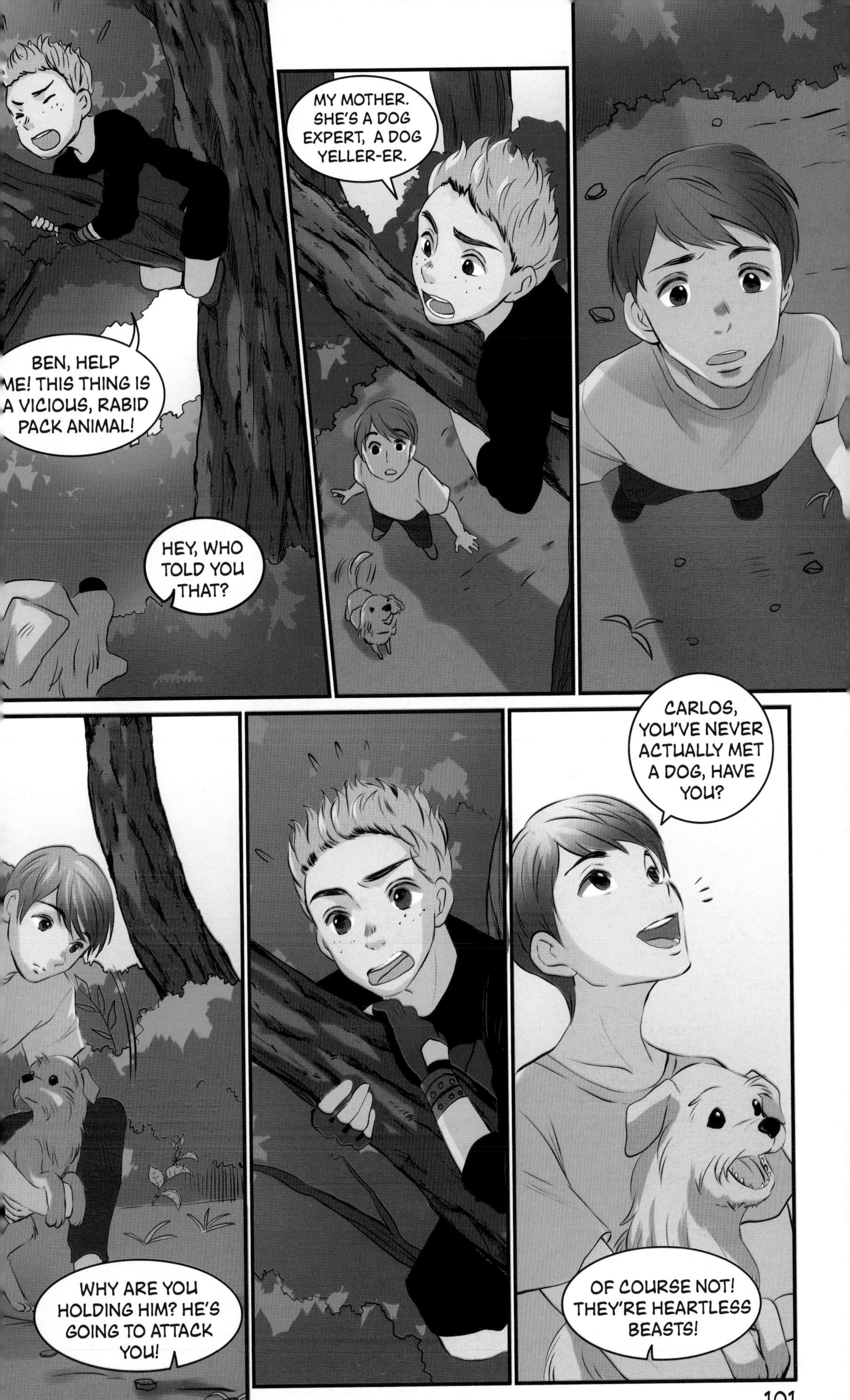
BEN, HELP ME! THIS THING IS A VICIOUS, RABID PACK ANIMAL!
HEY, WHO TOLD YOU THAT?
MY MOTHER. SHE'S A DOG EXPERT, A DOG YELLER-ER.
WHY ARE YOU HOLDING HIM? HE'S GOING TO ATTACK YOU!
CARLOS, YOU'VE NEVER ACTUALLY MET A DOG, HAVE YOU?
OF COURSE NOT! THEY'RE HEARTLESS BEASTS!

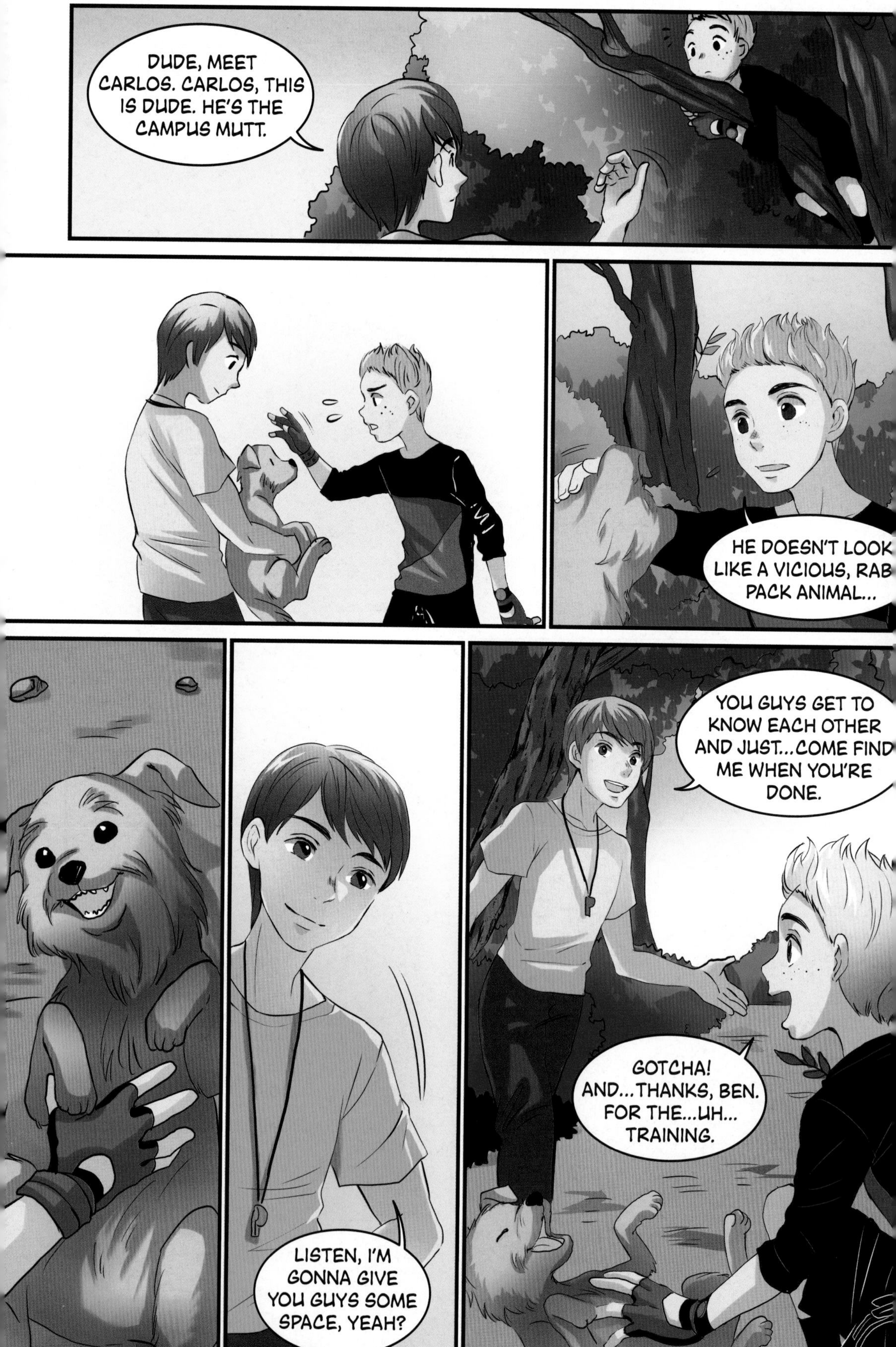
DUDE, MEET CARLOS. CARLOS, THIS IS DUDE. HE'S THE CAMPUS MUTT.
HE DOESN'T LOOK LIKE A VICIOUS, RAB PACK ANIMAL...
LISTEN, I'M GONNA GIVE YOU GUYS SOME SPACE, YEAH?
YOU GUYS GET TO KNOW EACH OTHER AND JUST...COME FIND ME WHEN YOU'RE DONE.
GOTCHA! AND...THANKS, BEN. FOR THE...UH... TRAINING.

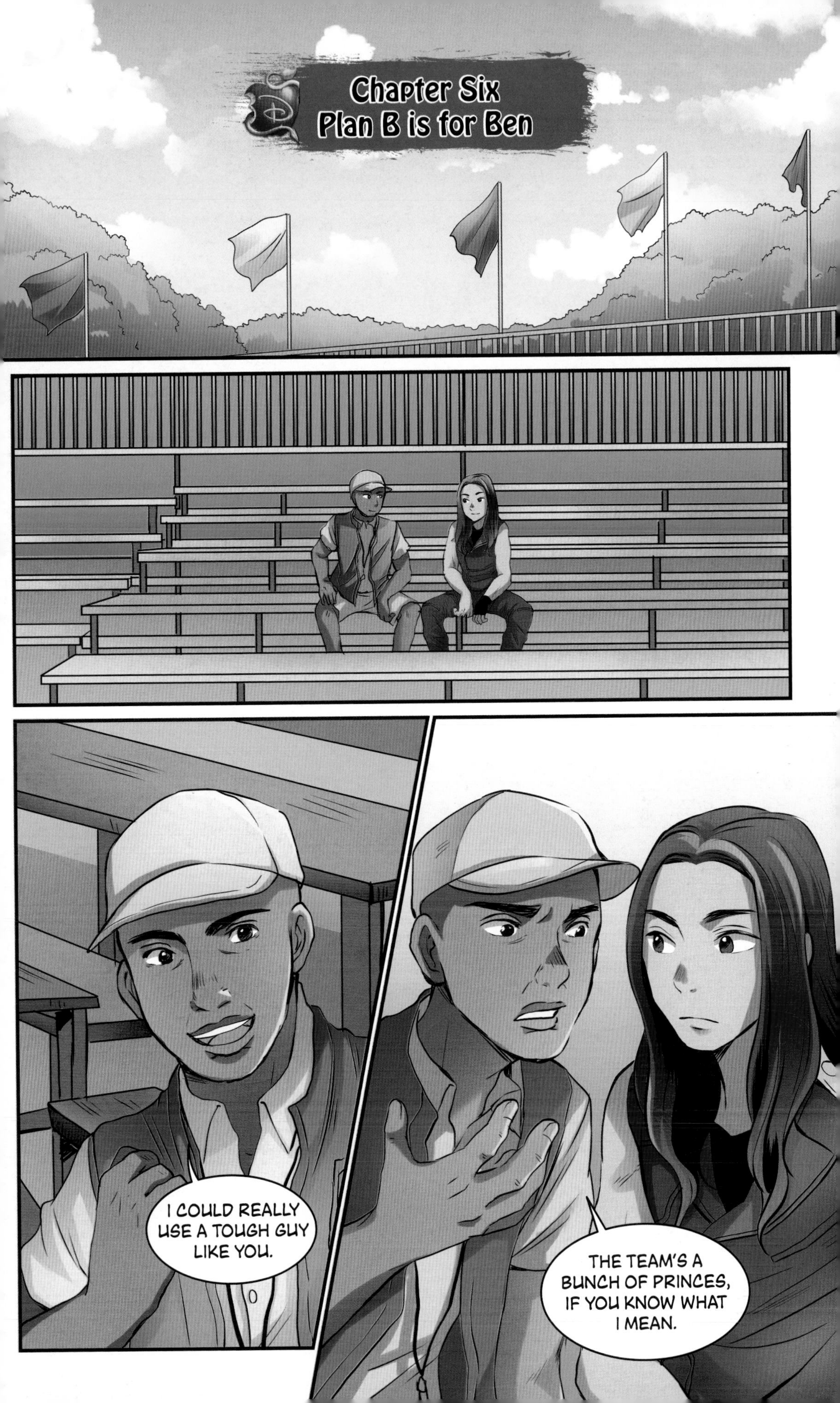
Chapter Six
Plan B is for Ben
I COULD REALLY USE A TOUGH GUY LIKE YOU.
THE TEAM'S A BUNCH OF PRINCES, IF YOU KNOW WHAT I MEAN.

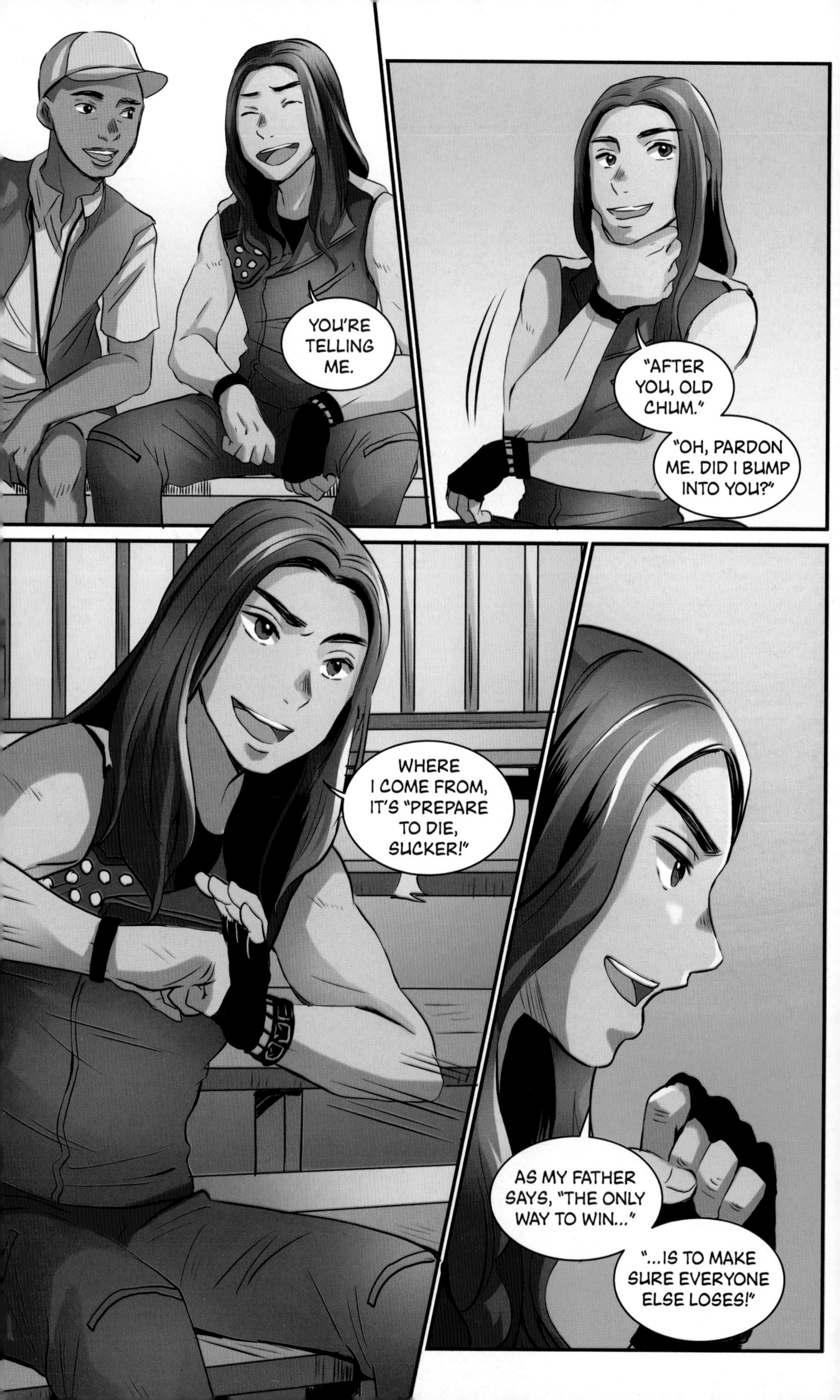
YOU'RE TELLING ME.
"AFTER YOU, OLD CHUM."
"OH, PARDON ME. DID I BUMP INTO YOU?"
WHERE I COME FROM, IT'S "PREPARE TO DIE, SUCKER!"
AS MY FATHER SAYS, "THE ONLY WAY TO WIN..."
"...IS TO MAKE SURE EVERYONE ELSE LOSES!"

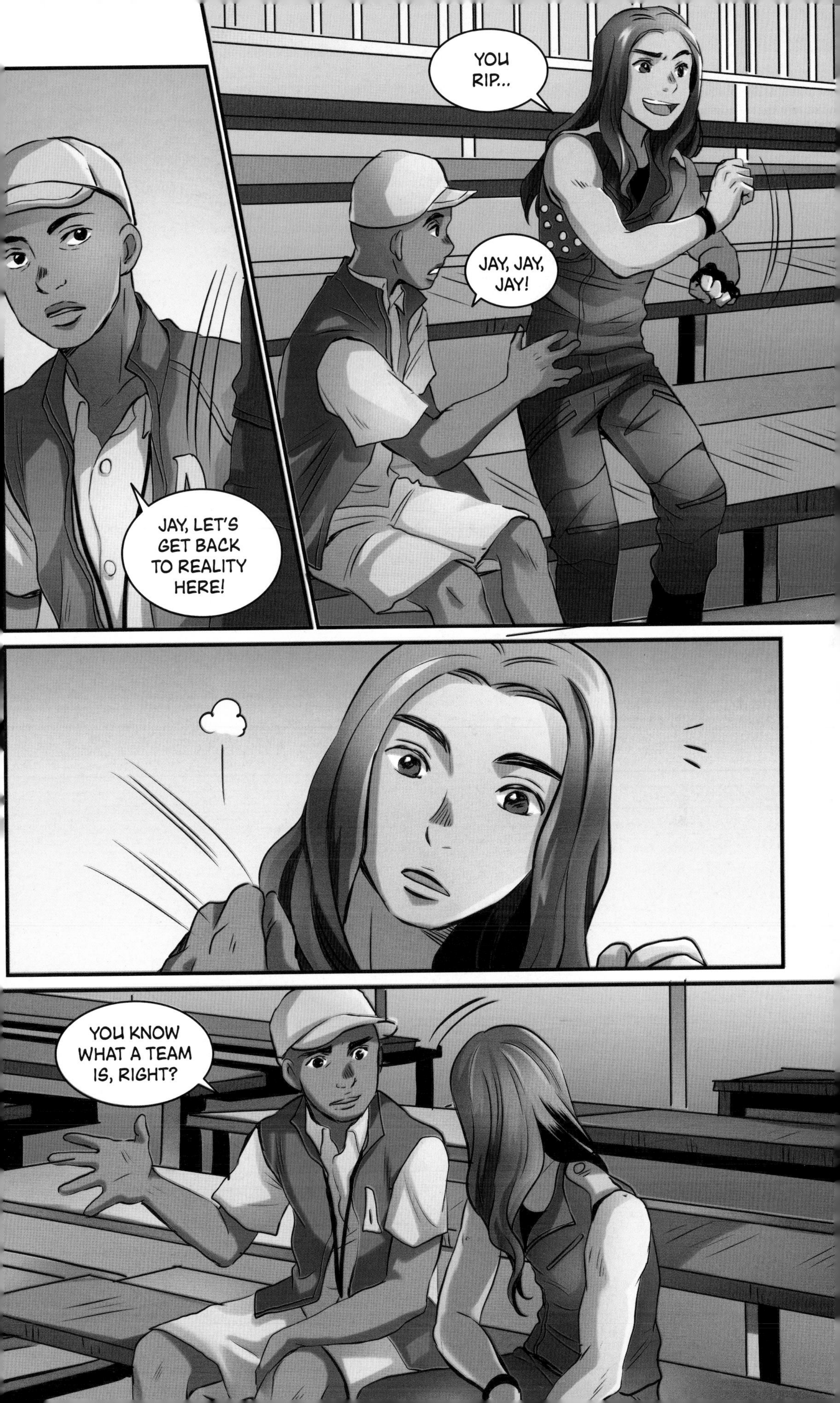
YOU RIP...
JAY, JAY, JAY!
JAY, LET'S GET BACK TO REALITY HERE!
YOU KNOW WHAT A TEAM IS, RIGHT?

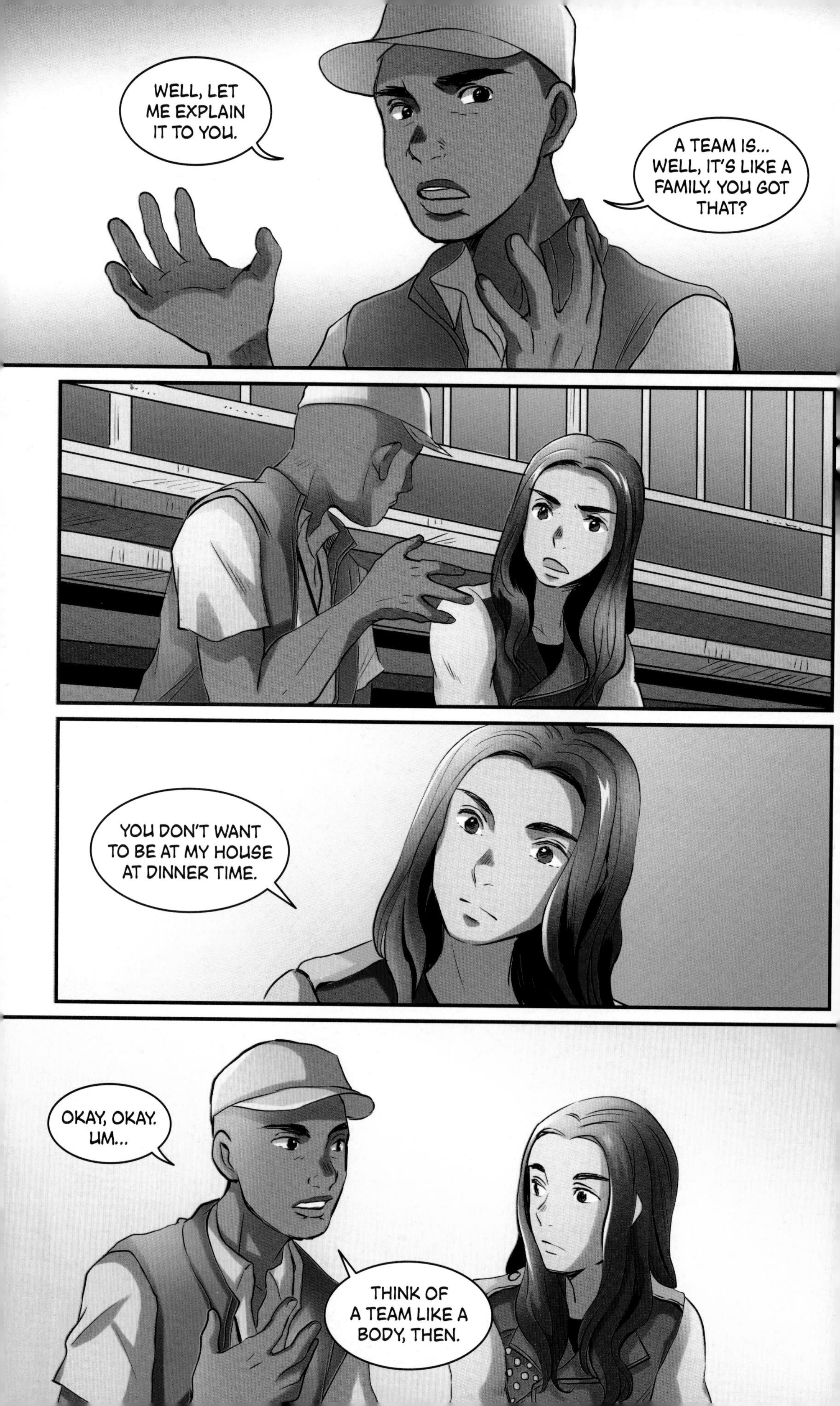
WELL, LET ME EXPLAIN IT TO YOU.
A TEAM IS... WELL, IT'S LIKE A FAMILY. YOU GOT THAT?
YOU DON'T WANT TO BE AT MY HOUSE AT DINNER TIME.
OKAY, OKAY. UM...
THINK OF A TEAM LIKE A BODY, THEN.

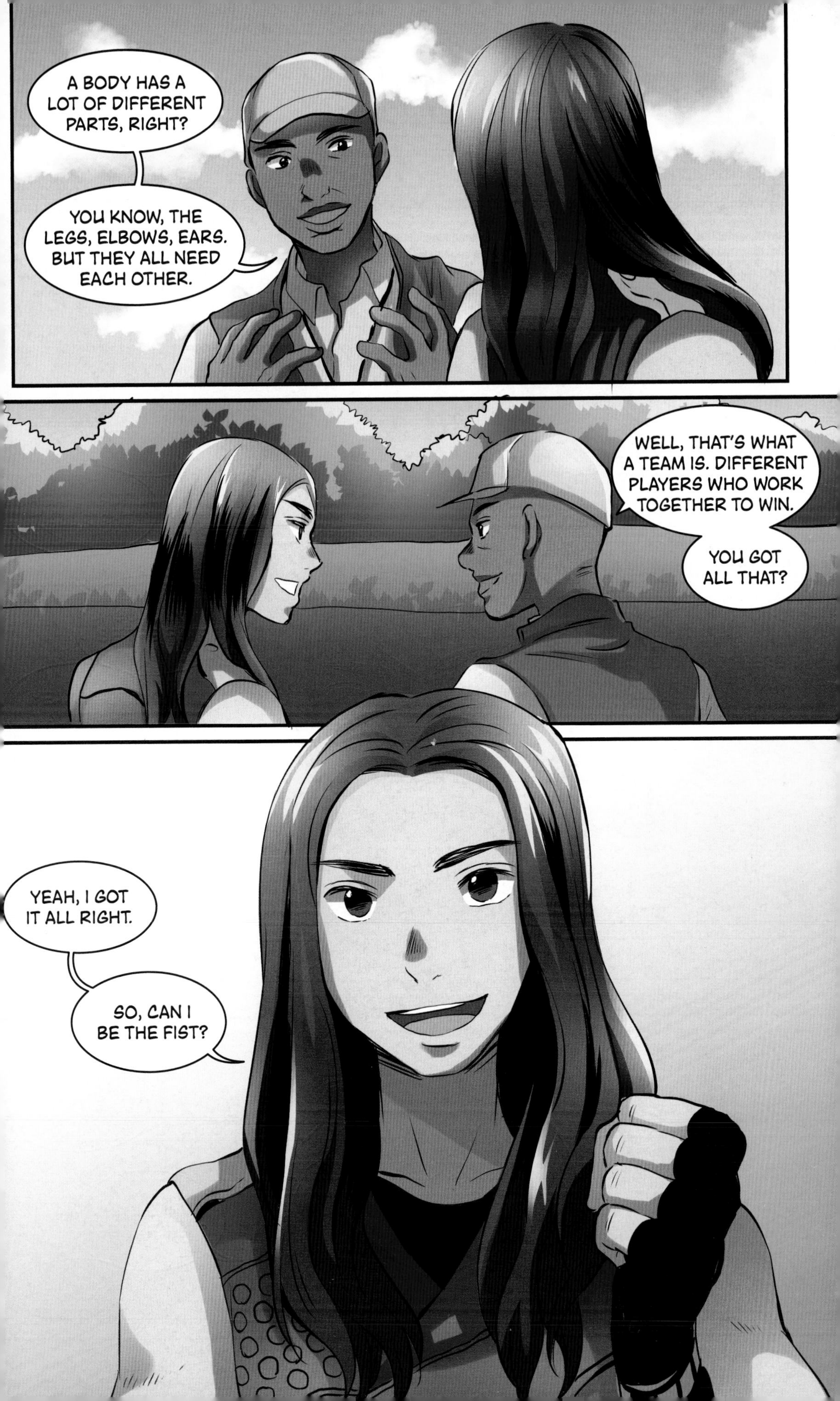
A BODY HAS A LOT OF DIFFERENT PARTS, RIGHT?
YOU KNOW, THE LEGS, ELBOWS, EARS. BUT THEY ALL NEED EACH OTHER.
WELL, THAT'S WHAT A TEAM IS. DIFFERENT PLAYERS WHO WORK TOGETHER TO WIN.
YOU GOT ALL THAT?
YEAH, I GOT IT ALL RIGHT.
SO, CAN I BE THE FIST?

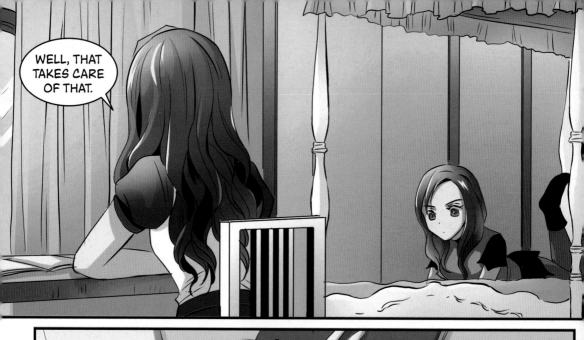

WELL, THAT TAKES CARE OF THAT.

THINK CHAD'LL HAVE MORE TIME TO TALK TOMORROW?

WHO KNOWS? SEEMS LIKE HE'S GOT HIS HANDS FULL JUST KEEPING TRACK OF HIMSELF.

I JUST WISH LONNIE WOULD KEEP HER MOUTH SHUT.

IT'S NOT LIKE I'M HERE TO BE EVERYONE'S MAGIC HAIRDRESSER!

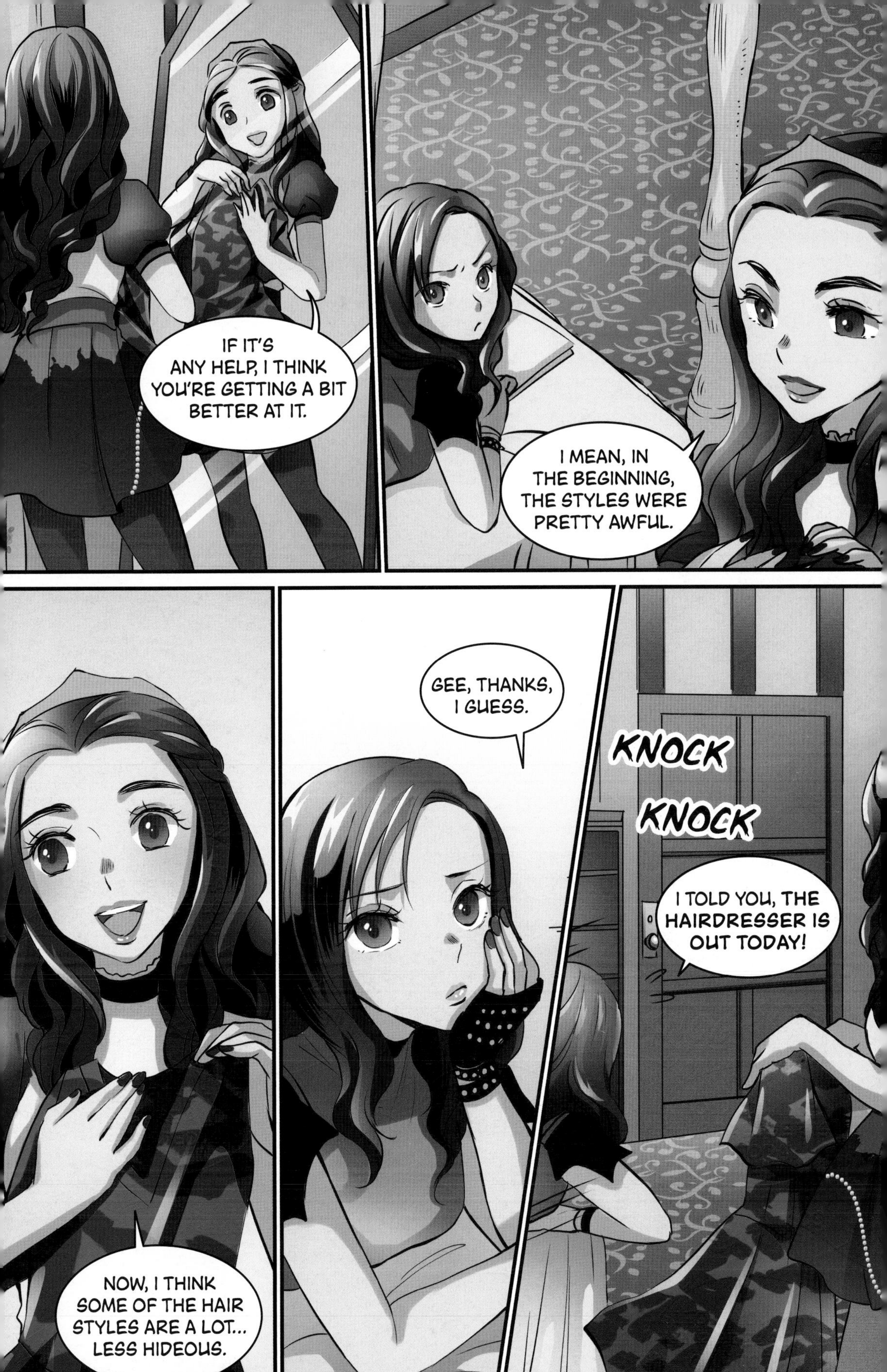
IF IT'S ANY HELP, I THINK YOU'RE GETTING A BIT BETTER AT IT.
I MEAN, IN THE BEGINNING, THE STYLES WERE PRETTY AWFUL.
NOW, I THINK SOME OF THE HAIR STYLES ARE A LOT... LESS HIDEOUS.
GEE, THANKS, I GUESS.
KNOCK
KNOCK
I TOLD YOU, THE HAIRDRESSER IS OUT TODAY!

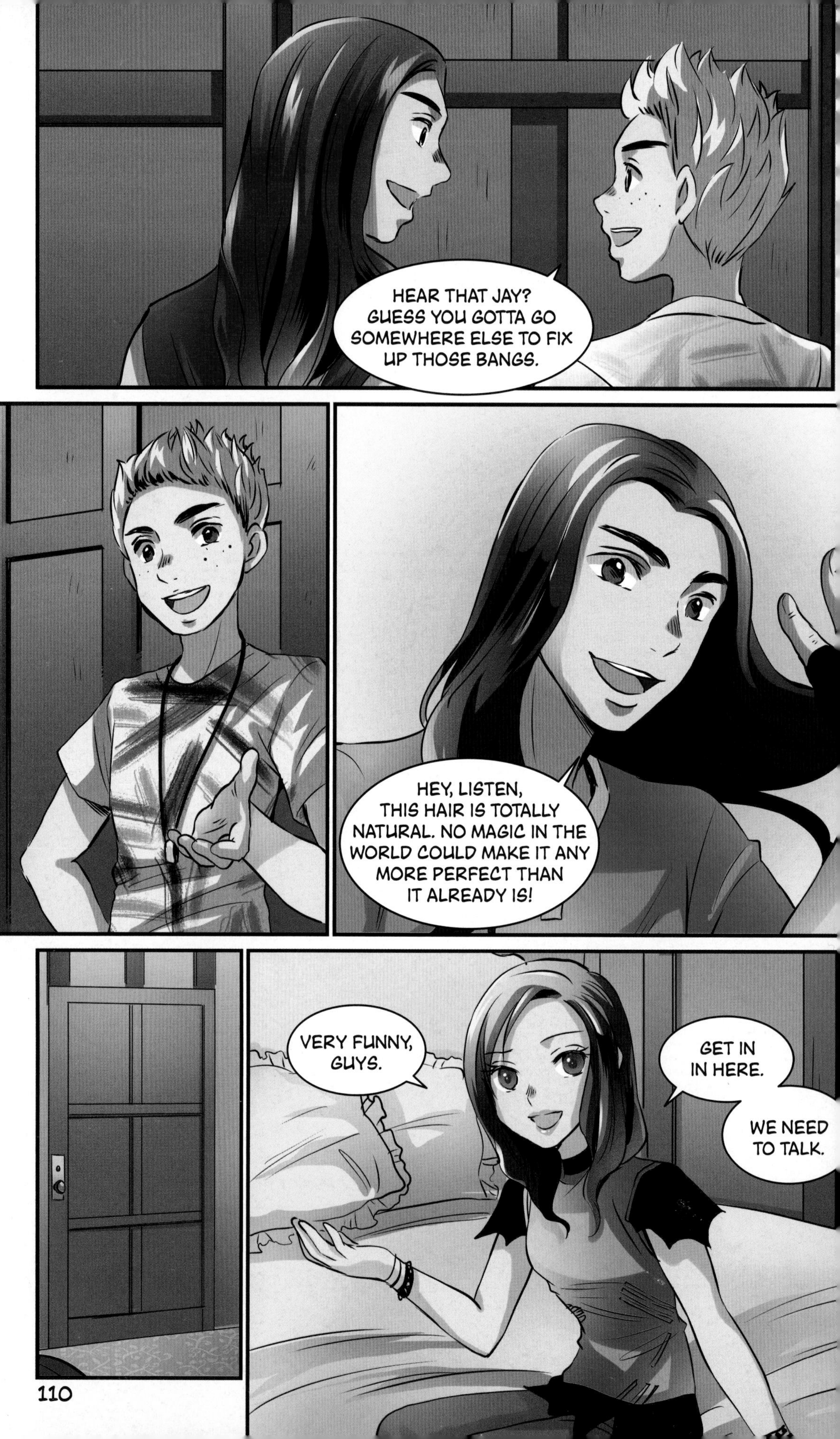
HEAR THAT JAY? GUESS YOU GOTTA GO SOMEWHERE ELSE TO FIX UP THOSE BANGS.
HEY, LISTEN, THIS HAIR IS TOTALLY NATURAL. NO MAGIC IN THE WORLD COULD MAKE IT ANY MORE PERFECT THAN IT ALREADY IS!
VERY FUNNY, GUYS.
GET IN IN HERE.
WE NEED TO TALK.

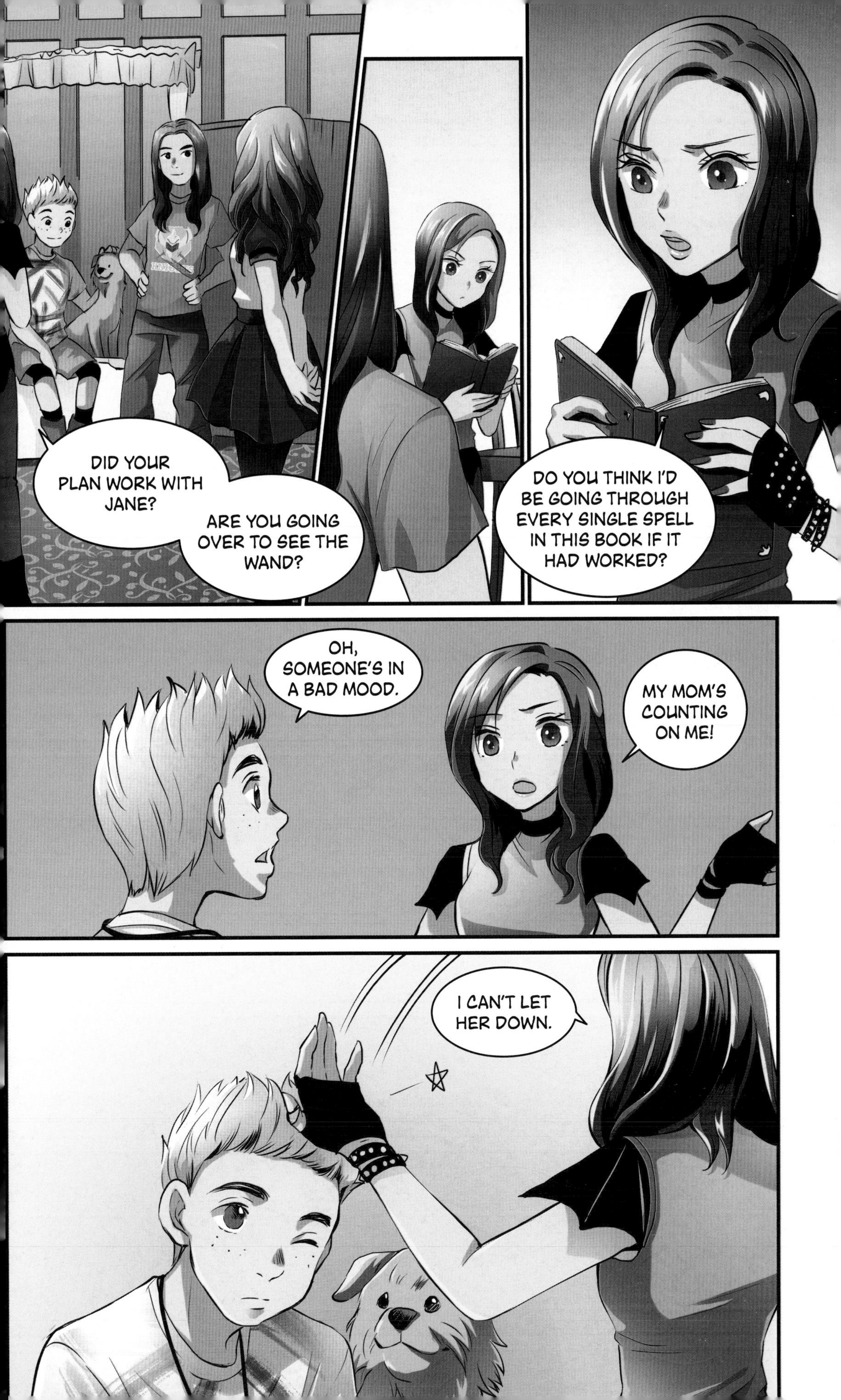
DID YOUR PLAN WORK WITH JANE?
ARE YOU GOING OVER TO SEE THE WAND?
DO YOU THINK I'D BE GOING THROUGH EVERY SINGLE SPELL IN THIS BOOK IF IT HAD WORKED?
OH, SOMEONE'S IN A BAD MOOD.
MY MOM'S COUNTING ON ME!
I CAN'T LET HER DOWN.

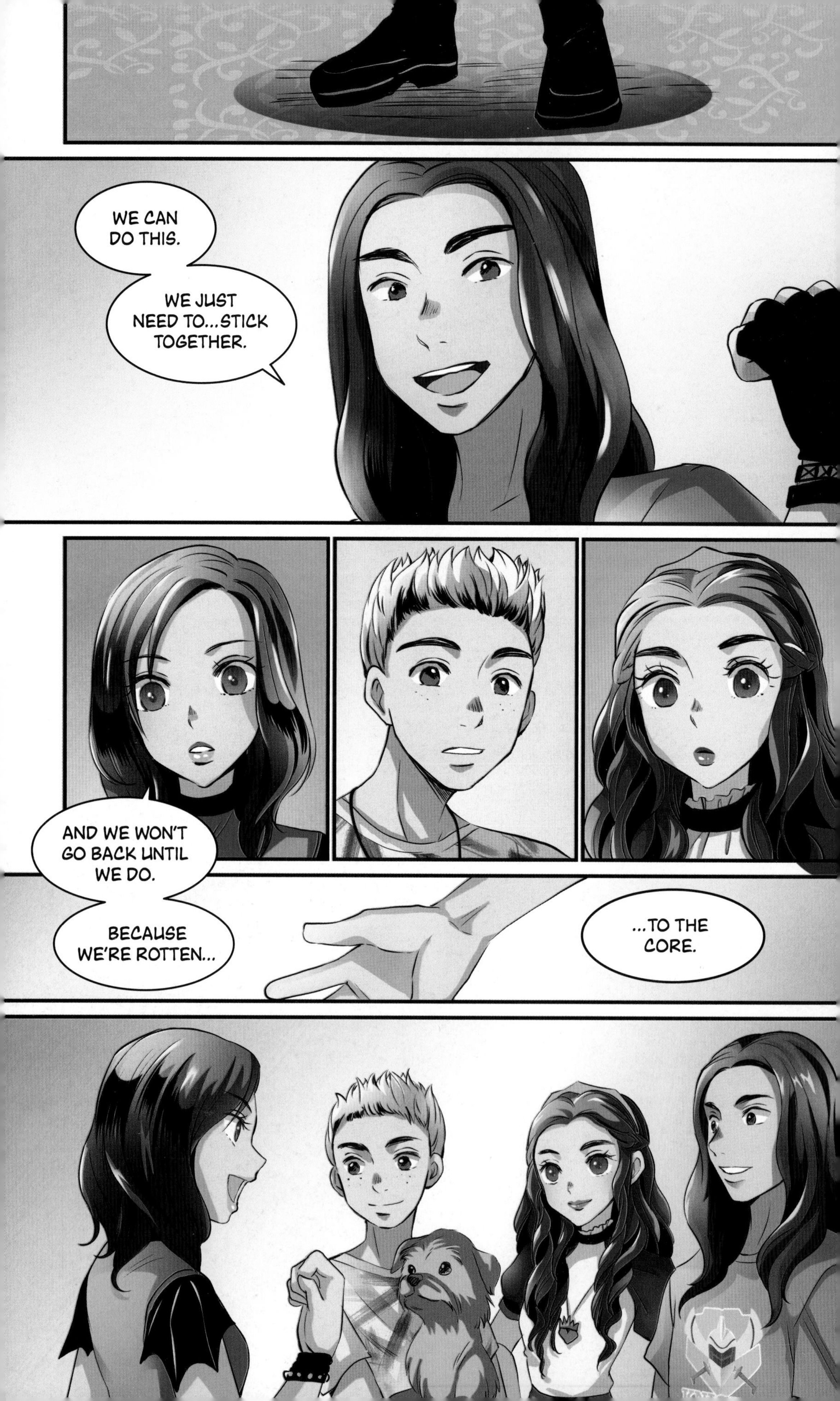
WE CAN DO THIS.
WE JUST NEED TO...STICK TOGETHER.
AND WE WON'T GO BACK UNTIL WE DO.
BECAUSE WE'RE ROTTEN...
...TO THE CORE.

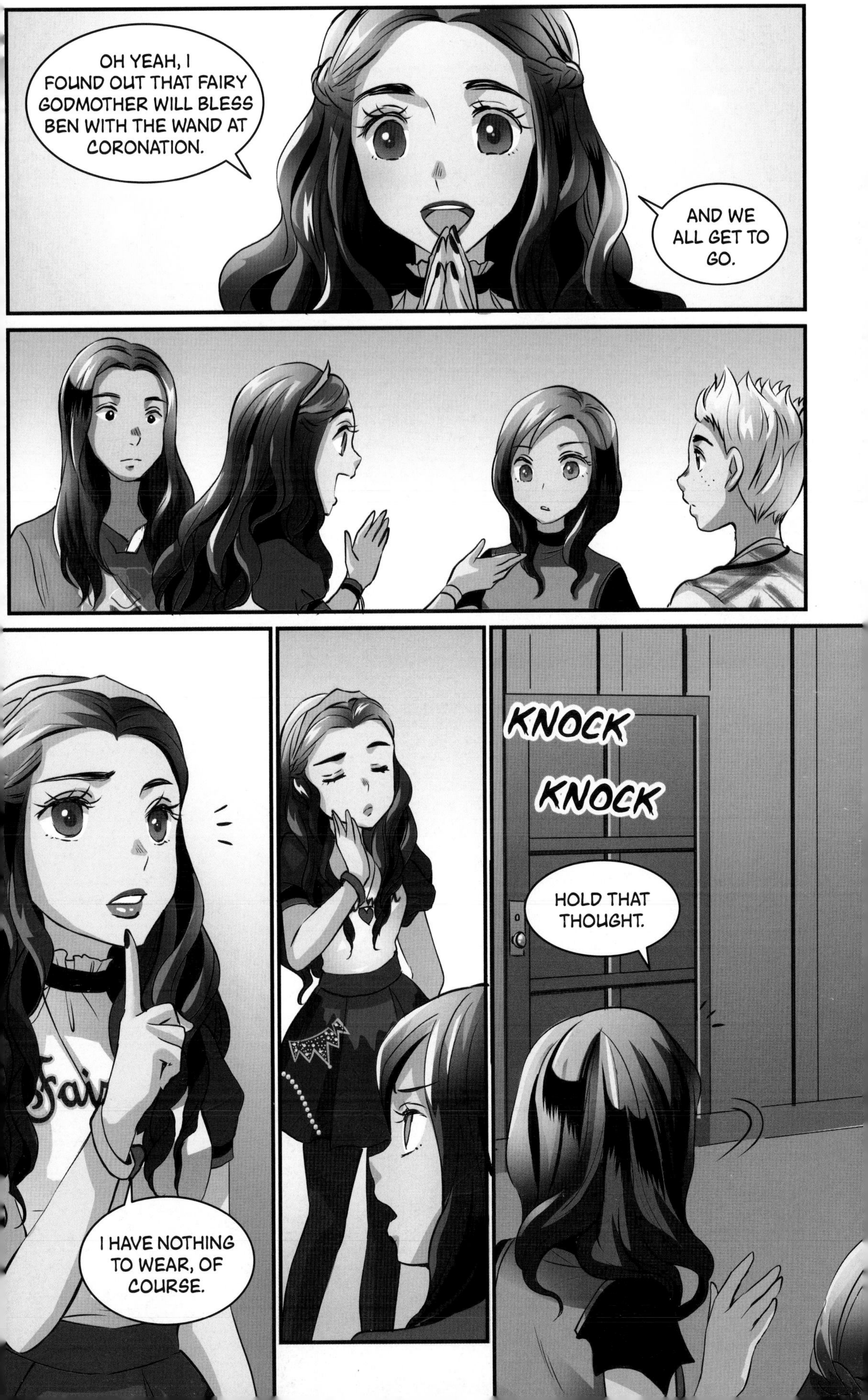
OH YEAH, I FOUND OUT THAT FAIRY GODMOTHER WILL BLESS BEN WITH THE WAND AT CORONATION.
AND WE ALL GET TO GO.
I HAVE NOTHING TO WEAR, OF COURSE.
KNOCK KNOCK
HOLD THAT THOUGHT.

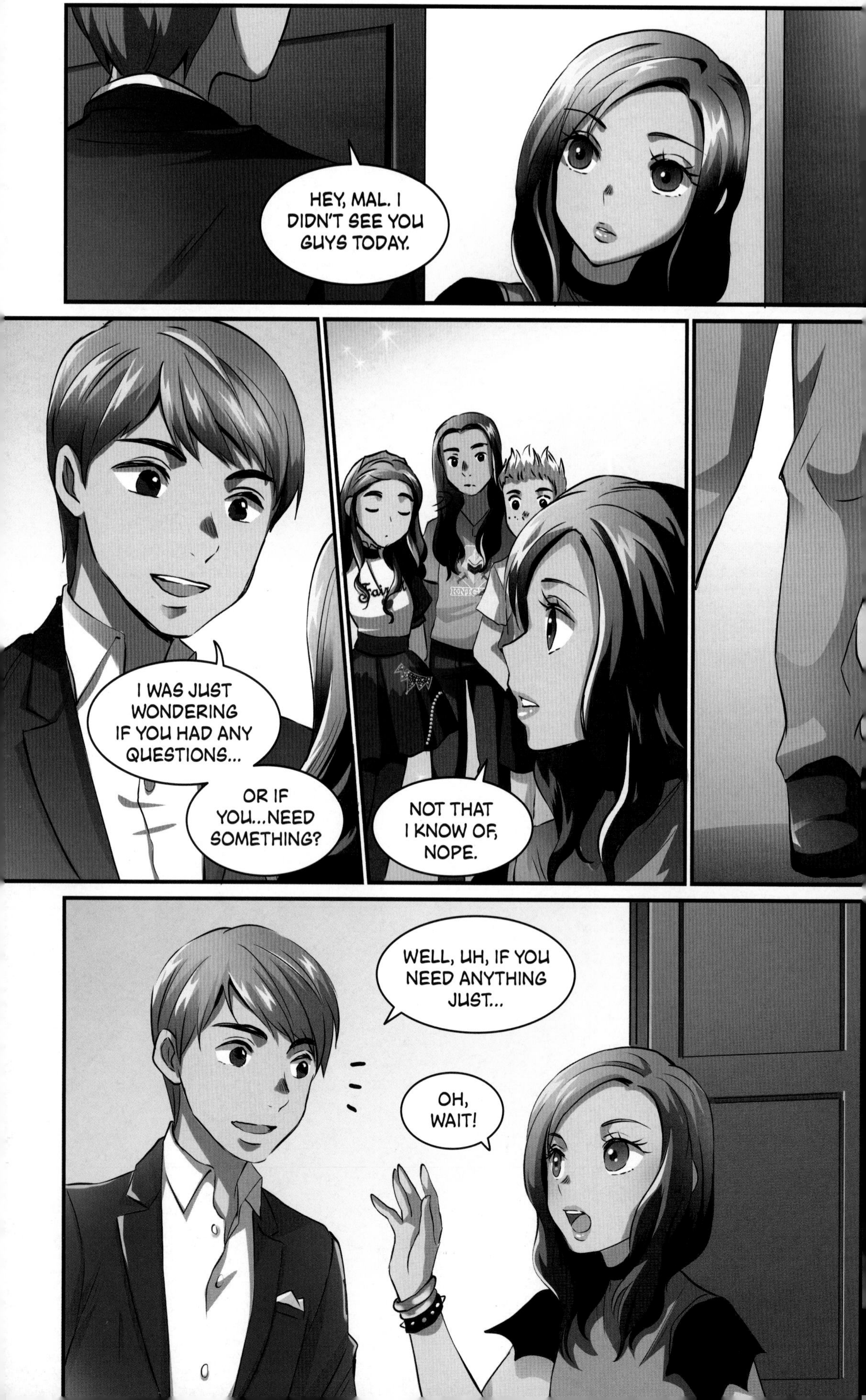
HEY, MAL. I DIDN'T SEE YOU GUYS TODAY.
I WAS JUST WONDERING IF YOU HAD ANY QUESTIONS...
OR IF YOU...NEED SOMETHING?
NOT THAT I KNOW OF, NOPE.
WELL, UH, IF YOU NEED ANYTHING JUST...
OH, WAIT!

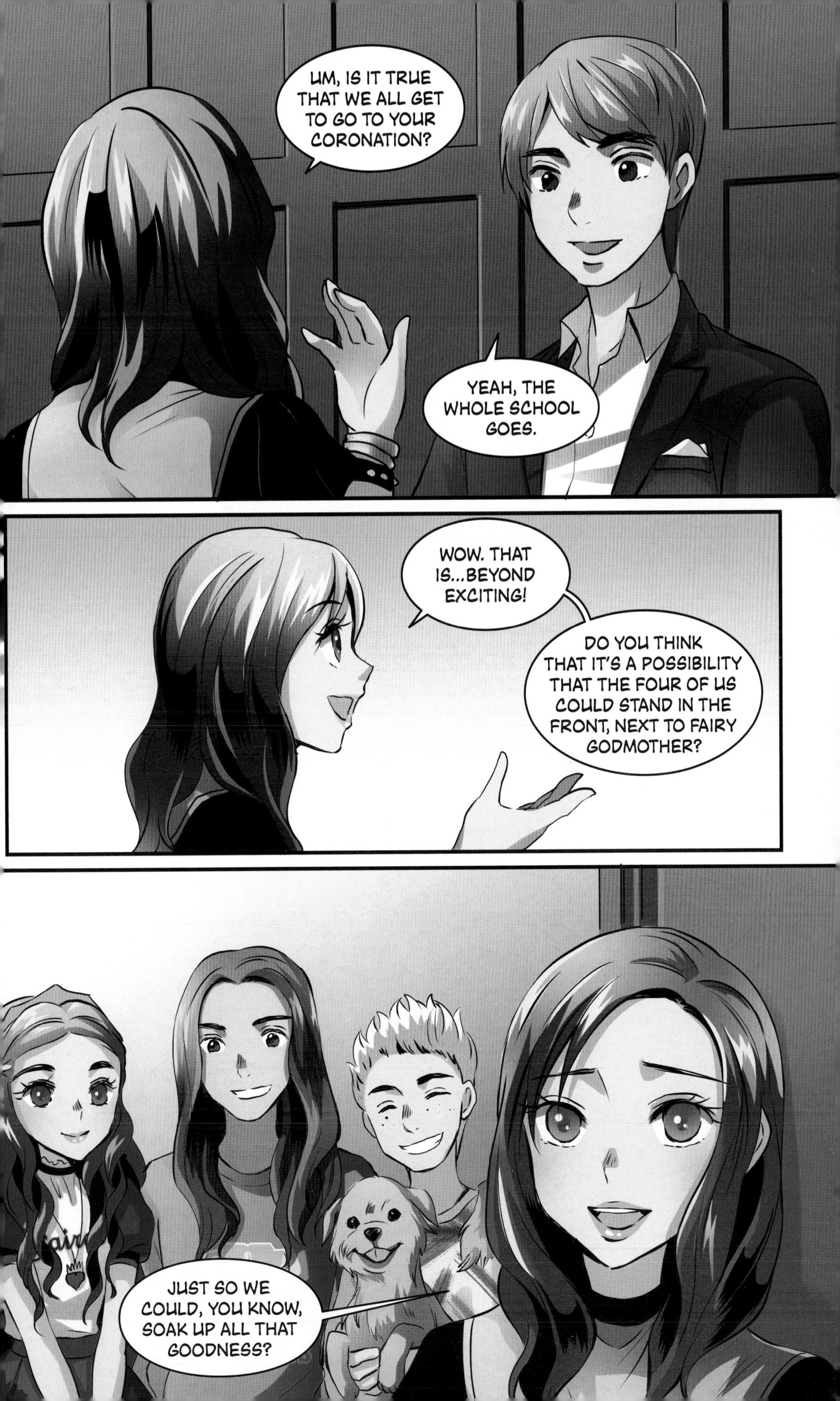
UM, IS IT TRUE THAT WE ALL GET TO GO TO YOUR CORONATION?
YEAH, THE WHOLE SCHOOL GOES.
WOW. THAT IS...BEYOND EXCITING!
DO YOU THINK THAT IT'S A POSSIBILITY THAT THE FOUR OF US COULD STAND IN THE FRONT, NEXT TO FAIRY GODMOTHER?
JUST SO WE COULD, YOU KNOW, SOAK UP ALL THAT GOODNESS?

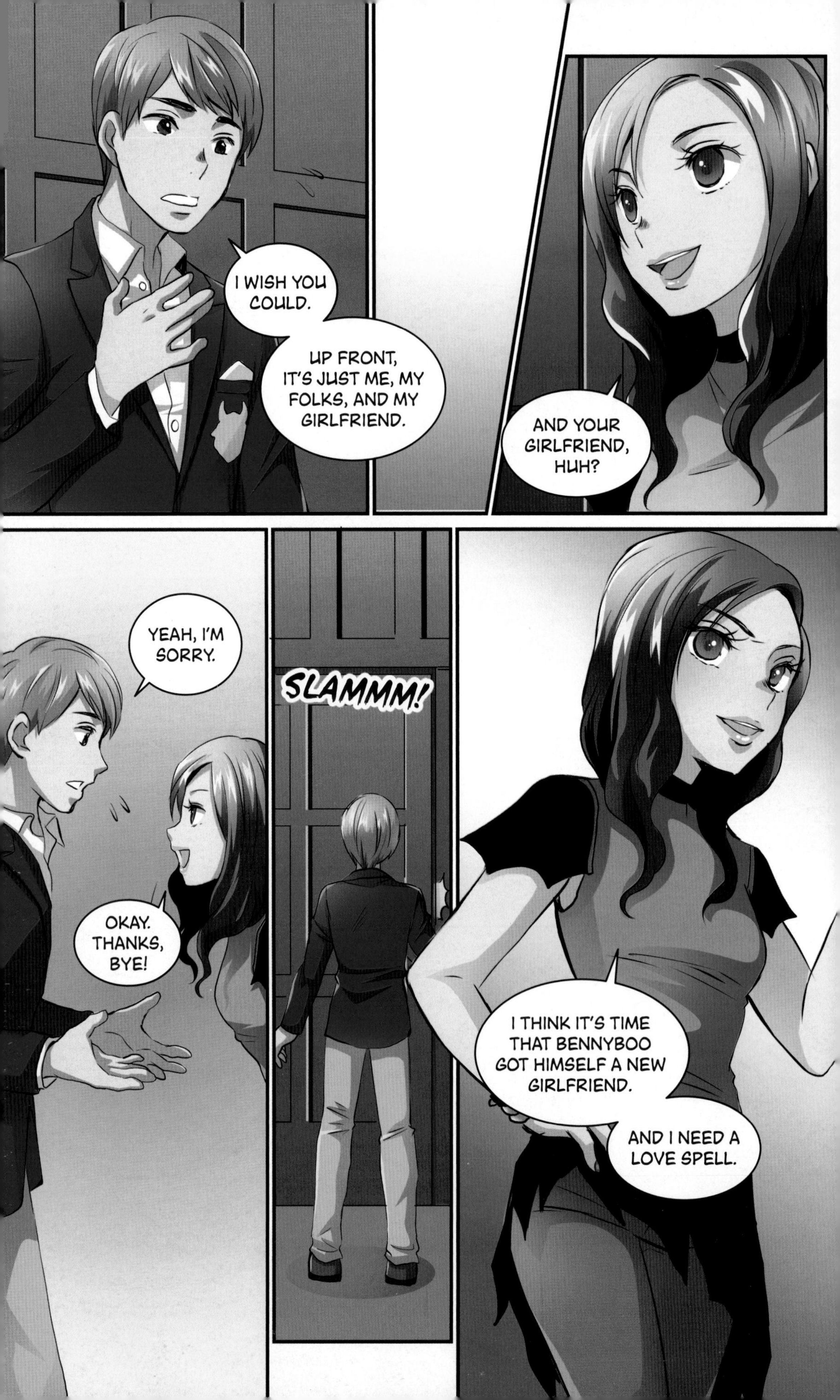
I WISH YOU COULD.
UP FRONT, IT'S JUST ME, MY FOLKS, AND MY GIRLFRIEND.
AND YOUR GIRLFRIEND, HUH?
YEAH, I'M SORRY.
OKAY. THANKS, BYE!
SLAMMM!
I THINK IT'S TIME THAT BENNYBOO GOT HIMSELF A NEW GIRLFRIEND.
AND I NEED A LOVE SPELL.

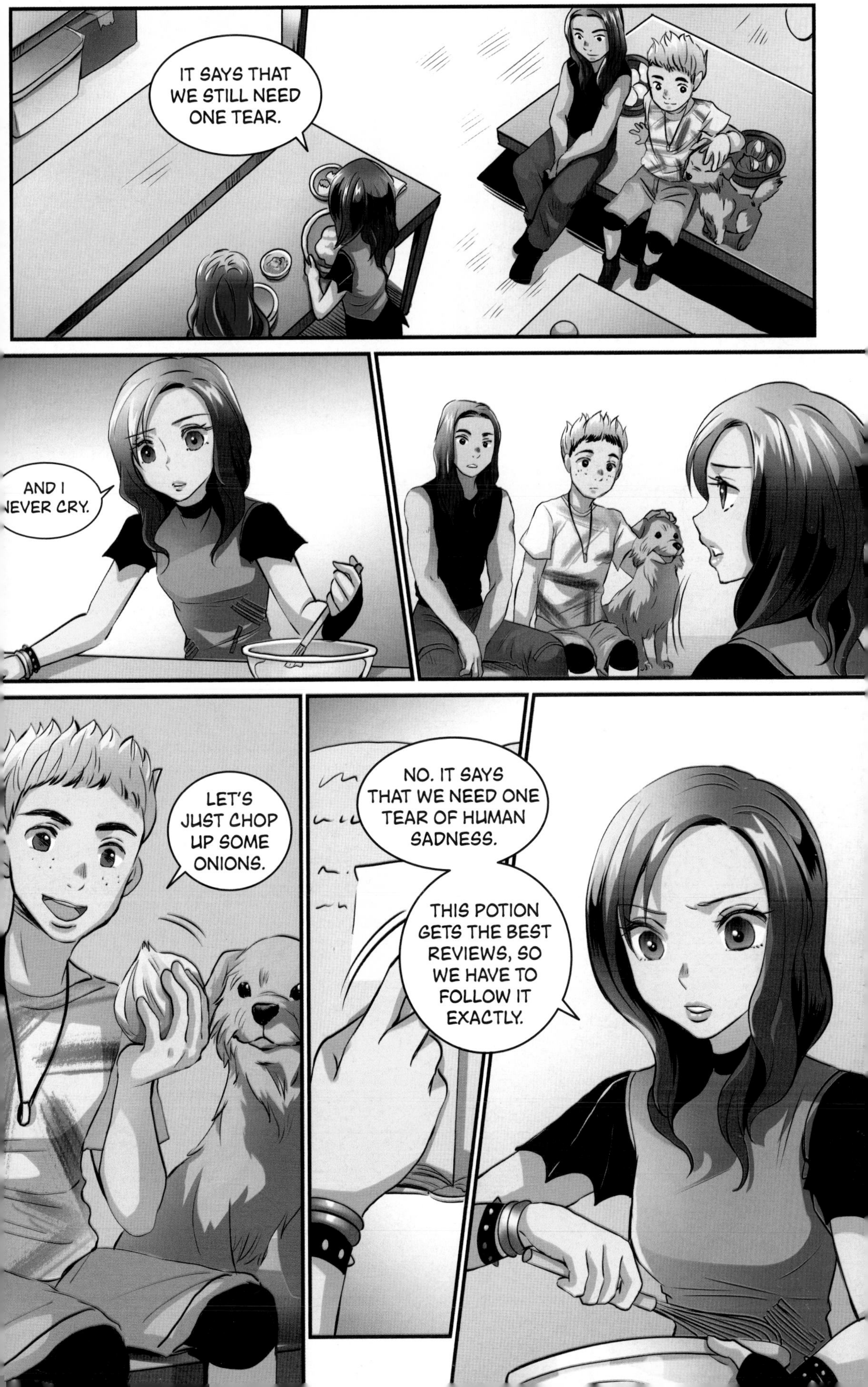
IT SAYS THAT WE STILL NEED ONE TEAR.
AND I NEVER CRY.
LET'S JUST CHOP UP SOME ONIONS.
NO. IT SAYS THAT WE NEED ONE TEAR OF HUMAN SADNESS.
THIS POTION GETS THE BEST REVIEWS, SO WE HAVE TO FOLLOW IT EXACTLY.

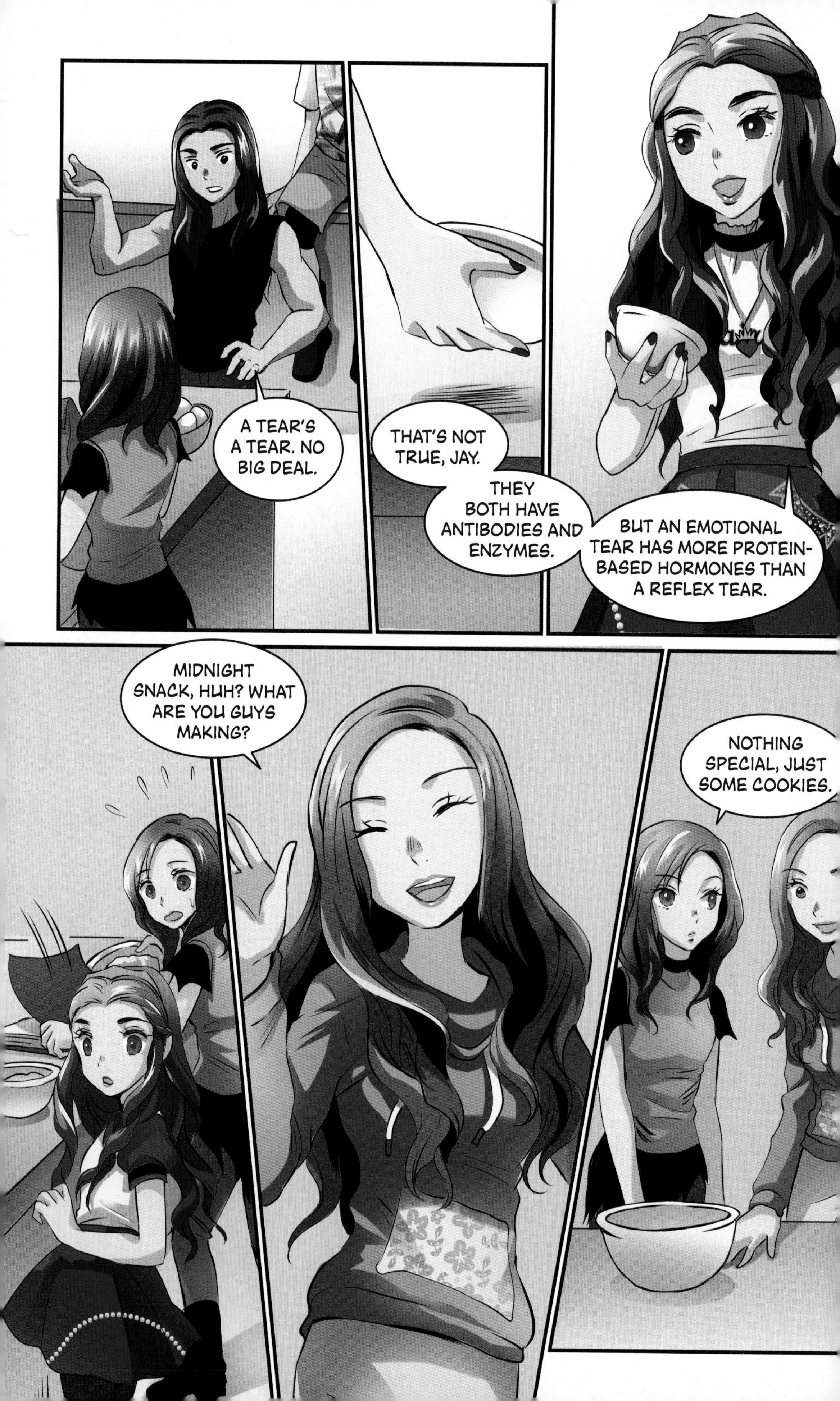
A TEAR'S A TEAR. NO BIG DEAL.
THAT'S NOT TRUE, JAY.
THEY BOTH HAVE ANTIBODIES AND ENZYMES.
BUT AN EMOTIONAL TEAR HAS MORE PROTEIN-BASED HORMONES THAN A REFLEX TEAR.
MIDNIGHT SNACK, HUH? WHAT ARE YOU GUYS MAKING?
NOTHING SPECIAL, JUST SOME COOKIES.

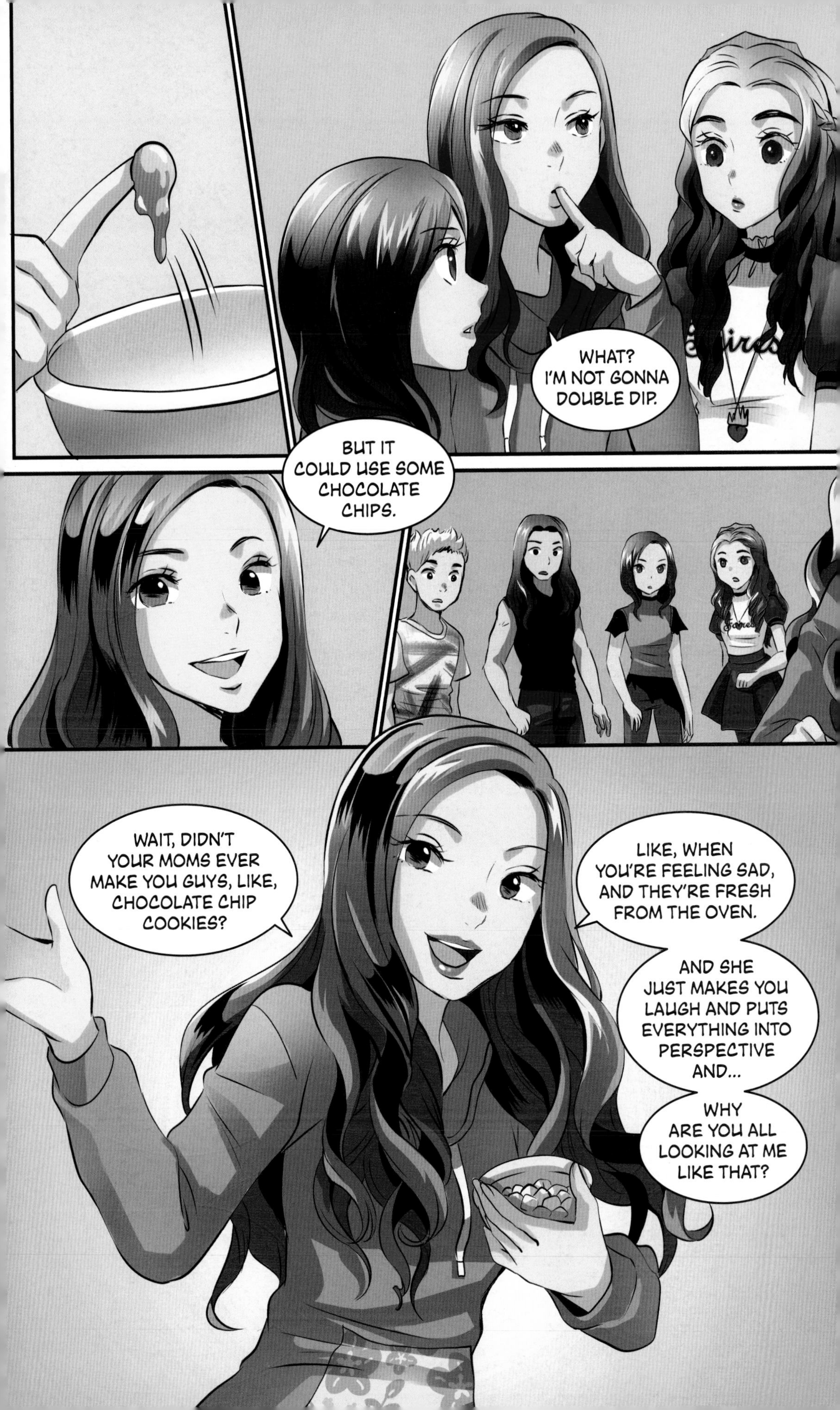
WHAT? I'M NOT GONNA DOUBLE DIP.
BUT IT COULD USE SOME CHOCOLATE CHIPS.
WAIT, DIDN'T YOUR MOMS EVER MAKE YOU GUYS, LIKE, CHOCOLATE CHIP COOKIES?
LIKE, WHEN YOU'RE FEELING SAD, AND THEY'RE FRESH FROM THE OVEN.
AND SHE JUST MAKES YOU LAUGH AND PUTS EVERYTHING INTO PERSPECTIVE AND...
WHY ARE YOU ALL LOOKING AT ME LIKE THAT?

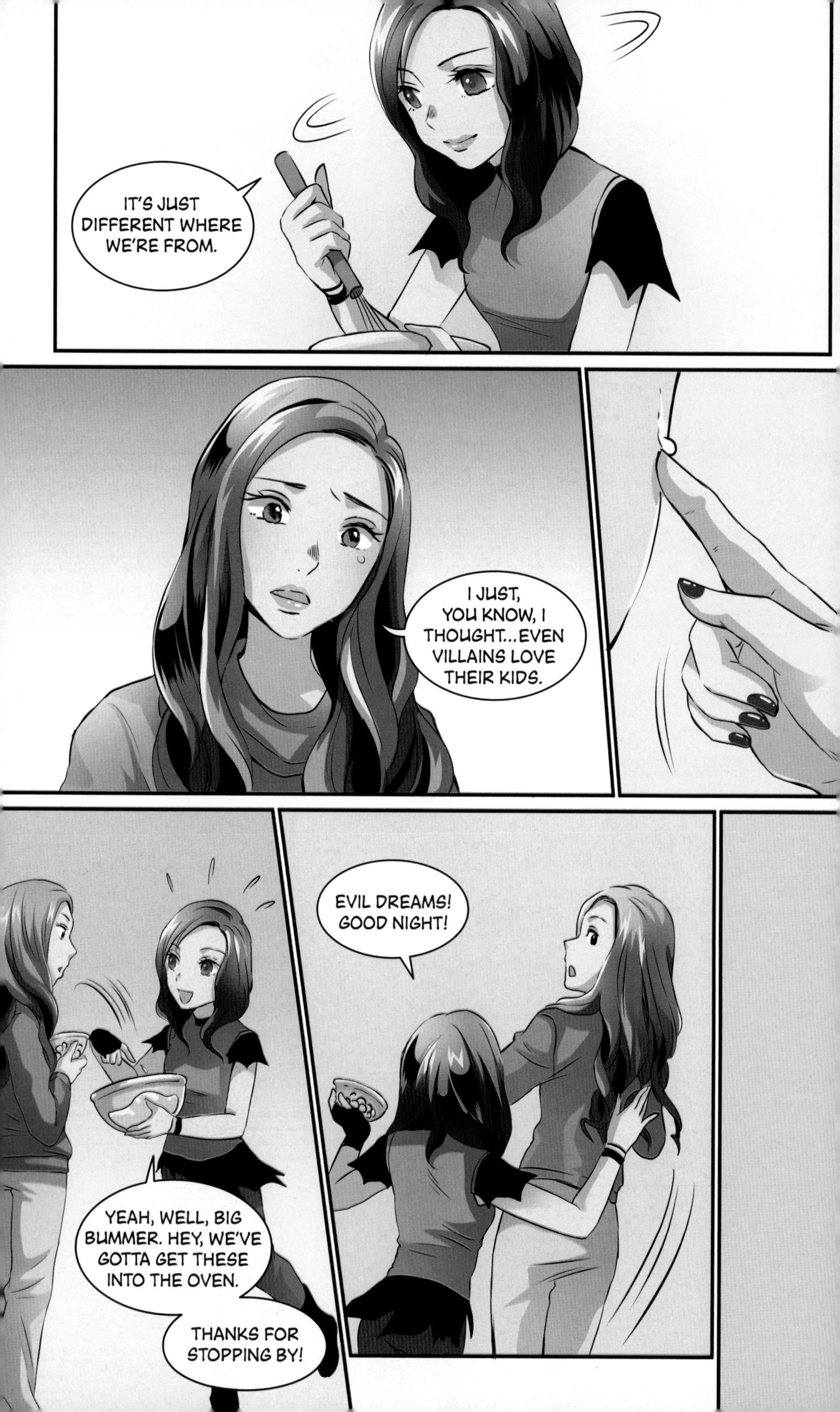
IT'S JUST DIFFERENT WHERE WE'RE FROM.
I JUST, YOU KNOW, I THOUGHT...EVEN VILLAINS LOVE THEIR KIDS.
YEAH, WELL, BIG BUMMER. HEY, WE'VE GOTTA GET THESE INTO THE OVEN.
THANKS FOR STOPPING BY!
EVIL DREAMS! GOOD NIGHT!

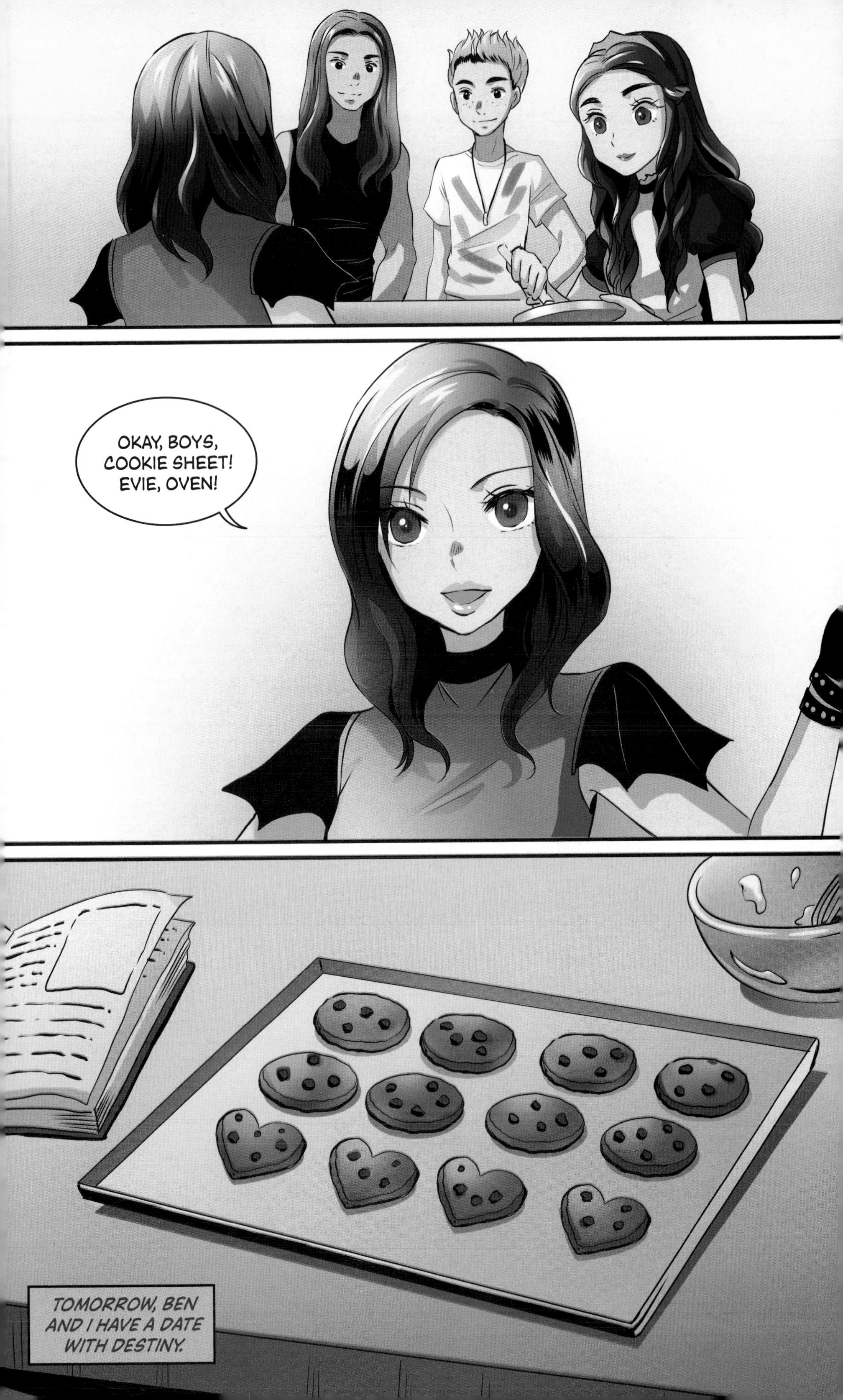
OKAY, BOYS, COOKIE SHEET! EVIE, OVEN!
TOMORROW, BEN AND I HAVE A DATE WITH DESTINY.

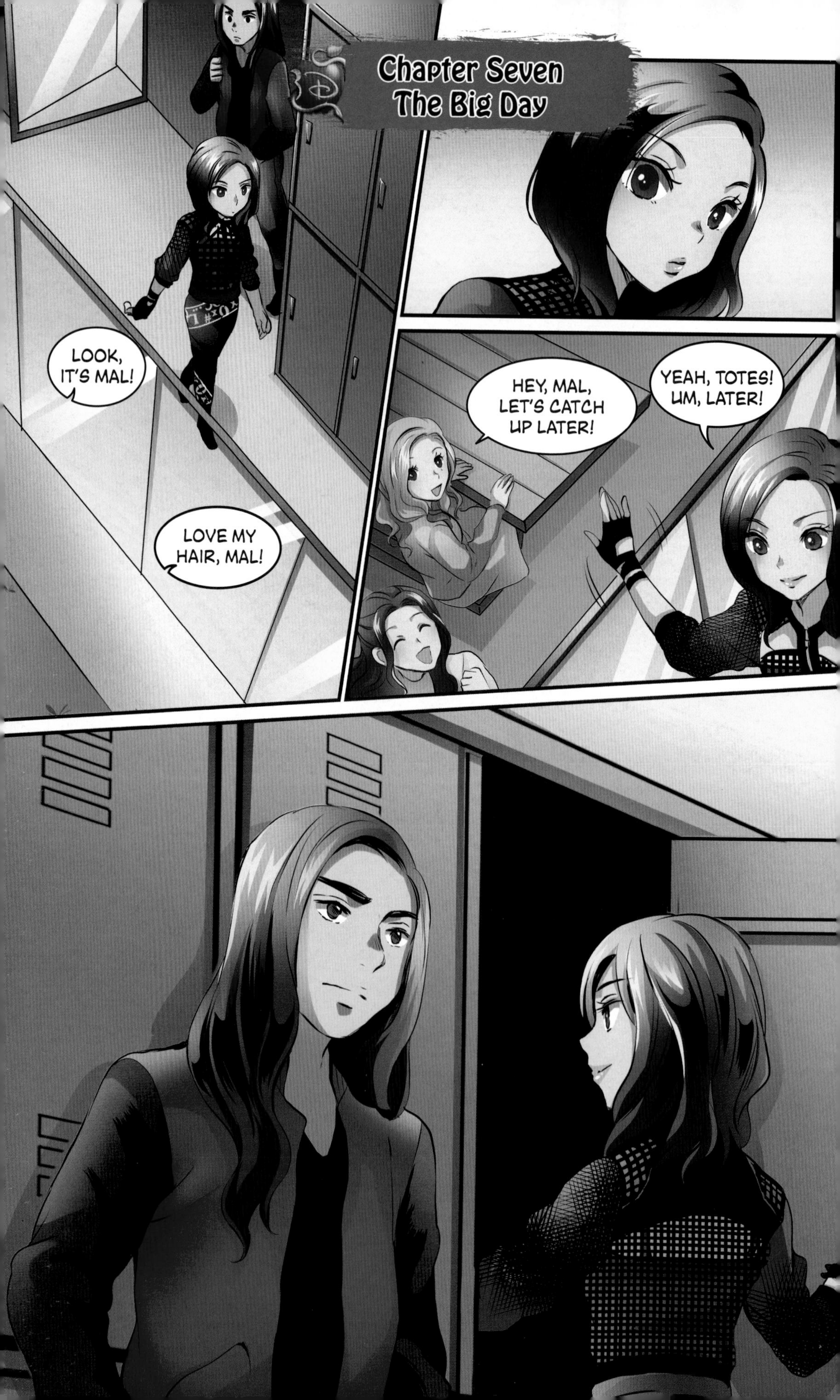
Chapter Seven
The Big Day
LOOK, IT'S MAL!
LOVE MY HAIR, MAL!
HEY, MAL, LET'S CATCH UP LATER!
YEAH, TOTES! UM, LATER!

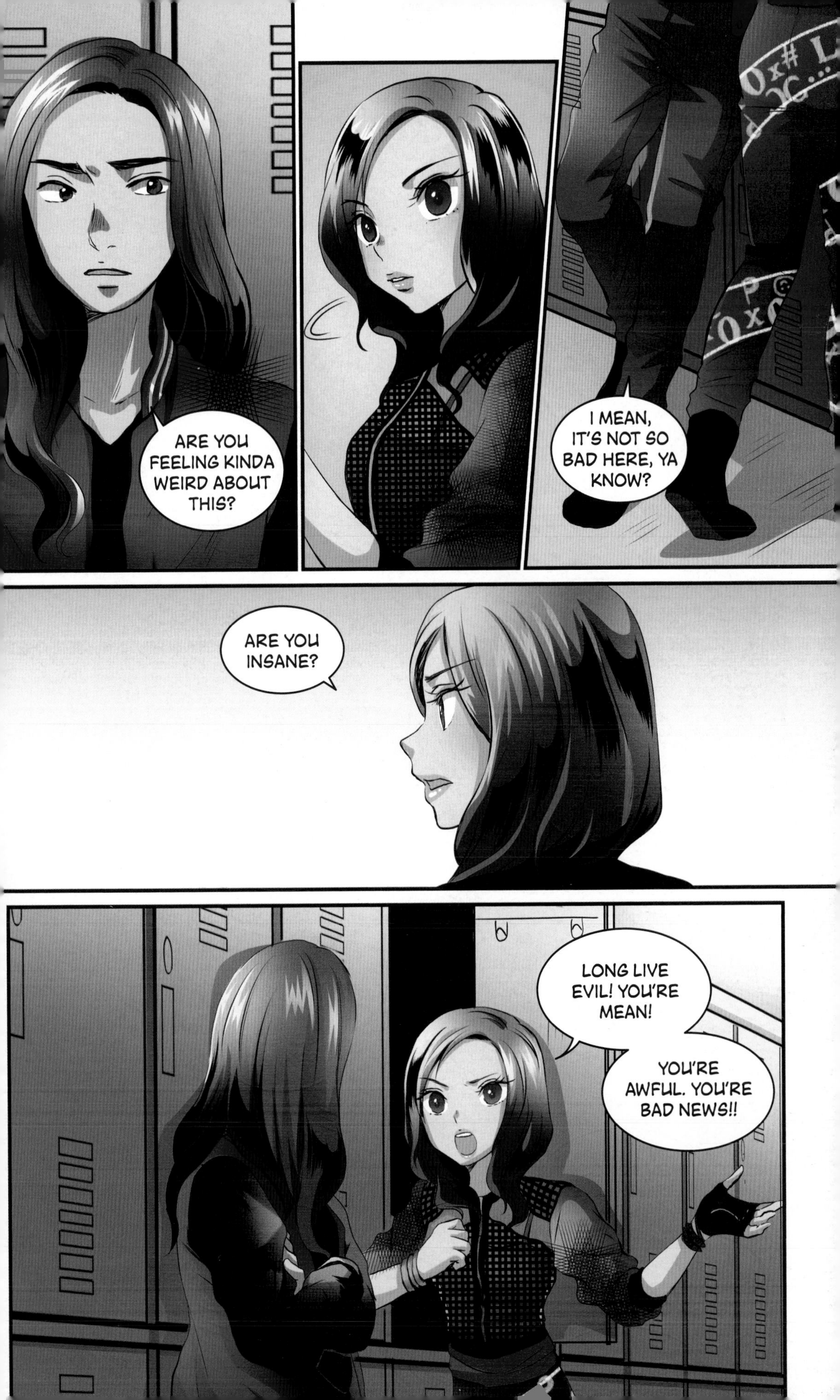
ARE YOU FEELING KINDA WEIRD ABOUT THIS?
I MEAN, IT'S NOT SO BAD HERE, YA KNOW?
ARE YOU INSANE?
LONG LIVE EVIL! YOU'RE MEAN!
YOU'RE AWFUL. YOU'RE BAD NEWS!!

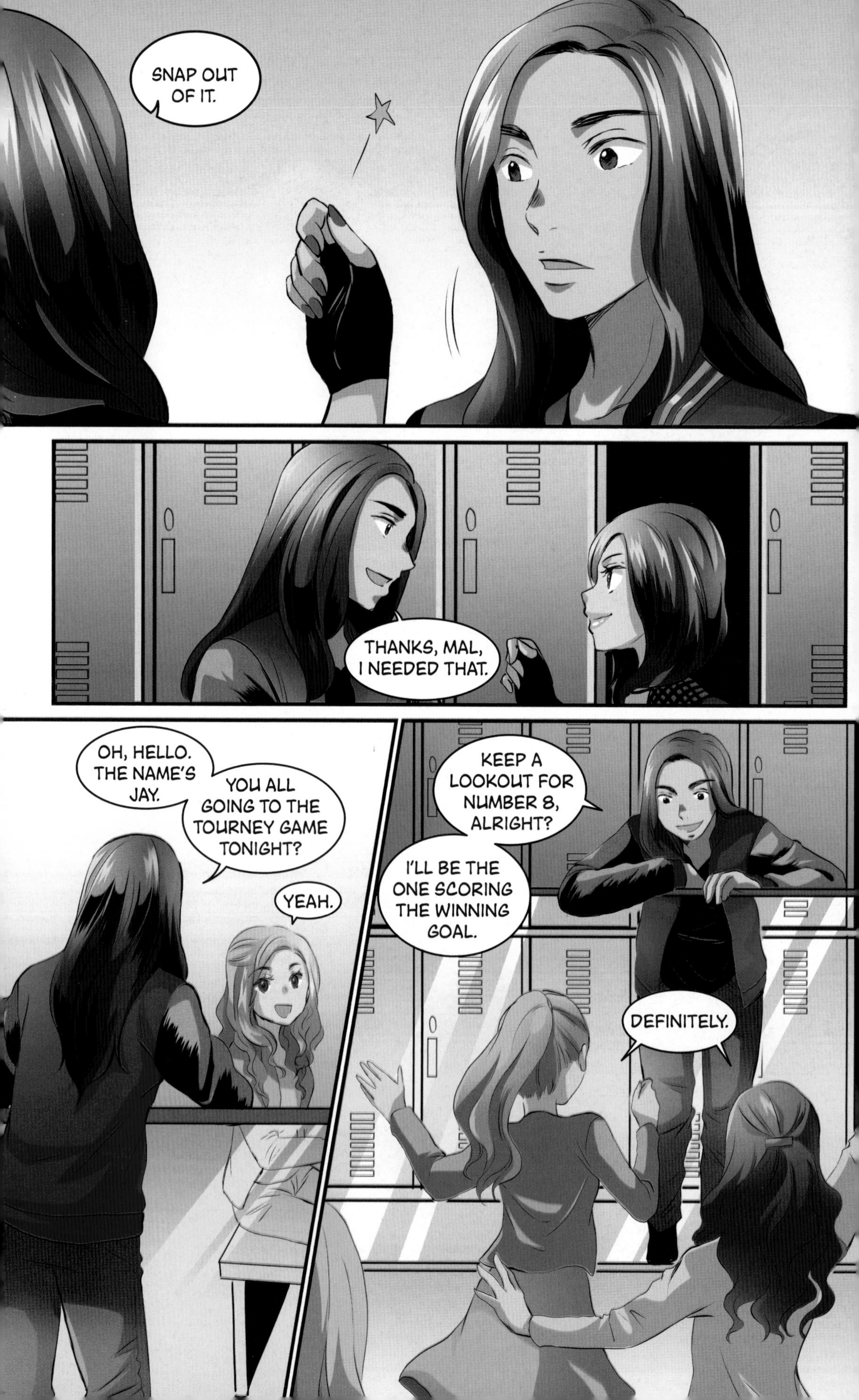
SNAP OUT OF IT.
THANKS, MAL, I NEEDED THAT.
OH, HELLO. THE NAME'S JAY.
YOU ALL GOING TO THE TOURNEY GAME TONIGHT?
YEAH.
KEEP A LOOKOUT FOR NUMBER 8, ALRIGHT?
I'LL BE THE ONE SCORING THE WINNING GOAL.
DEFINITELY.

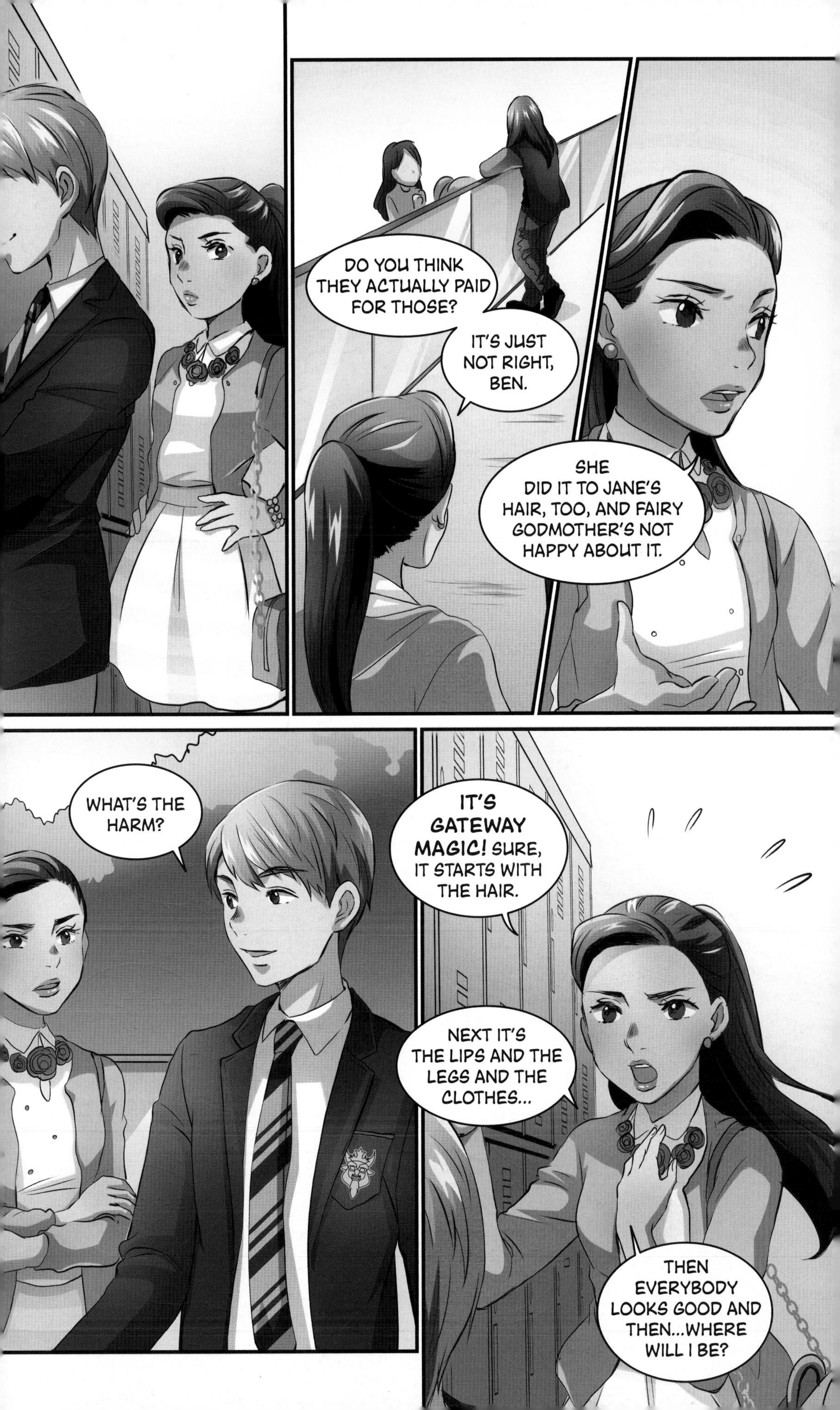
DO YOU THINK THEY ACTUALLY PAID FOR THOSE?
IT'S JUST NOT RIGHT, BEN.
SHE DID IT TO JANE'S HAIR, TOO, AND FAIRY GODMOTHER'S NOT HAPPY ABOUT IT.
WHAT'S THE HARM?
IT'S GATEWAY MAGIC! SURE, IT STARTS WITH THE HAIR.
NEXT IT'S THE LIPS AND THE LEGS AND THE CLOTHES...
THEN EVERYBODY LOOKS GOOD AND THEN...WHERE WILL I BE?

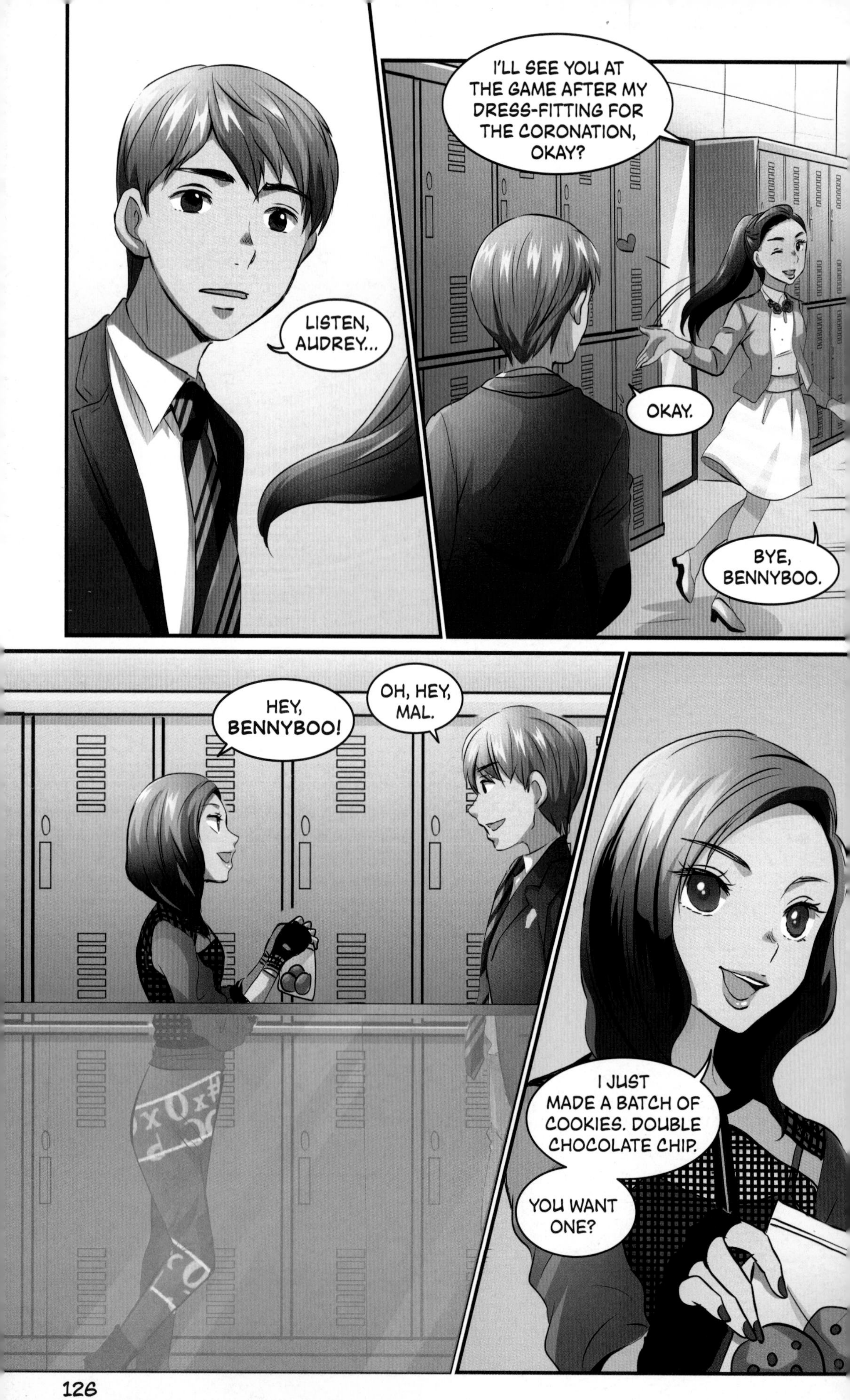
LISTEN, AUDREY...
I'LL SEE YOU AT THE GAME AFTER MY DRESS-FITTING FOR THE CORONATION, OKAY?
OKAY.
BYE, BENNYBOO.
HEY, BENNYBOO!
OH, HEY, MAL.
I JUST MADE A BATCH OF COOKIES. DOUBLE CHOCOLATE CHIP.
YOU WANT ONE?

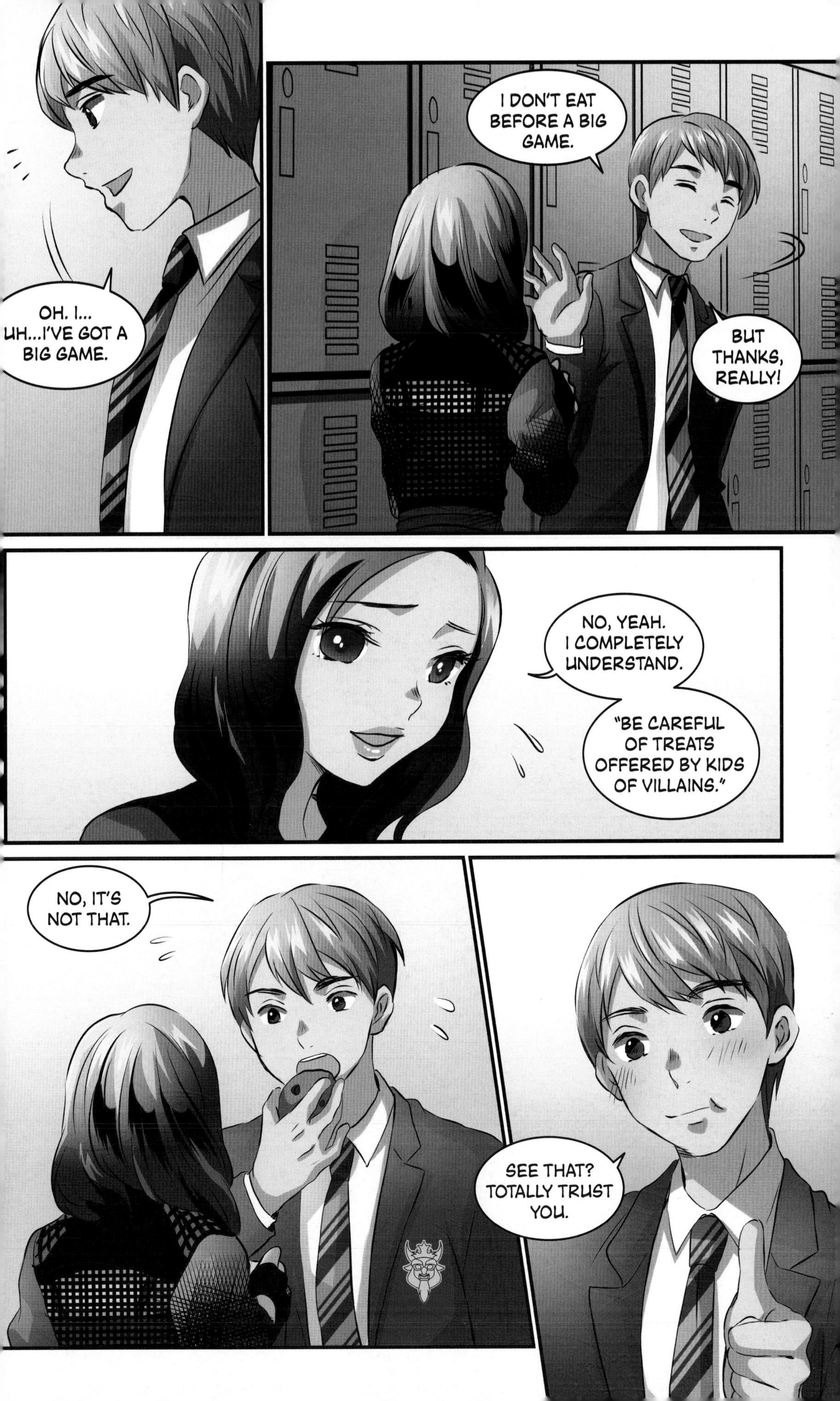
OH. I...
UH...I'VE GOT A BIG GAME.
I DON'T EAT BEFORE A BIG GAME.
BUT THANKS, REALLY!
NO, YEAH. I COMPLETELY UNDERSTAND.
"BE CAREFUL OF TREATS OFFERED BY KIDS OF VILLAINS."
NO, IT'S NOT THAT.
SEE THAT? TOTALLY TRUST YOU.

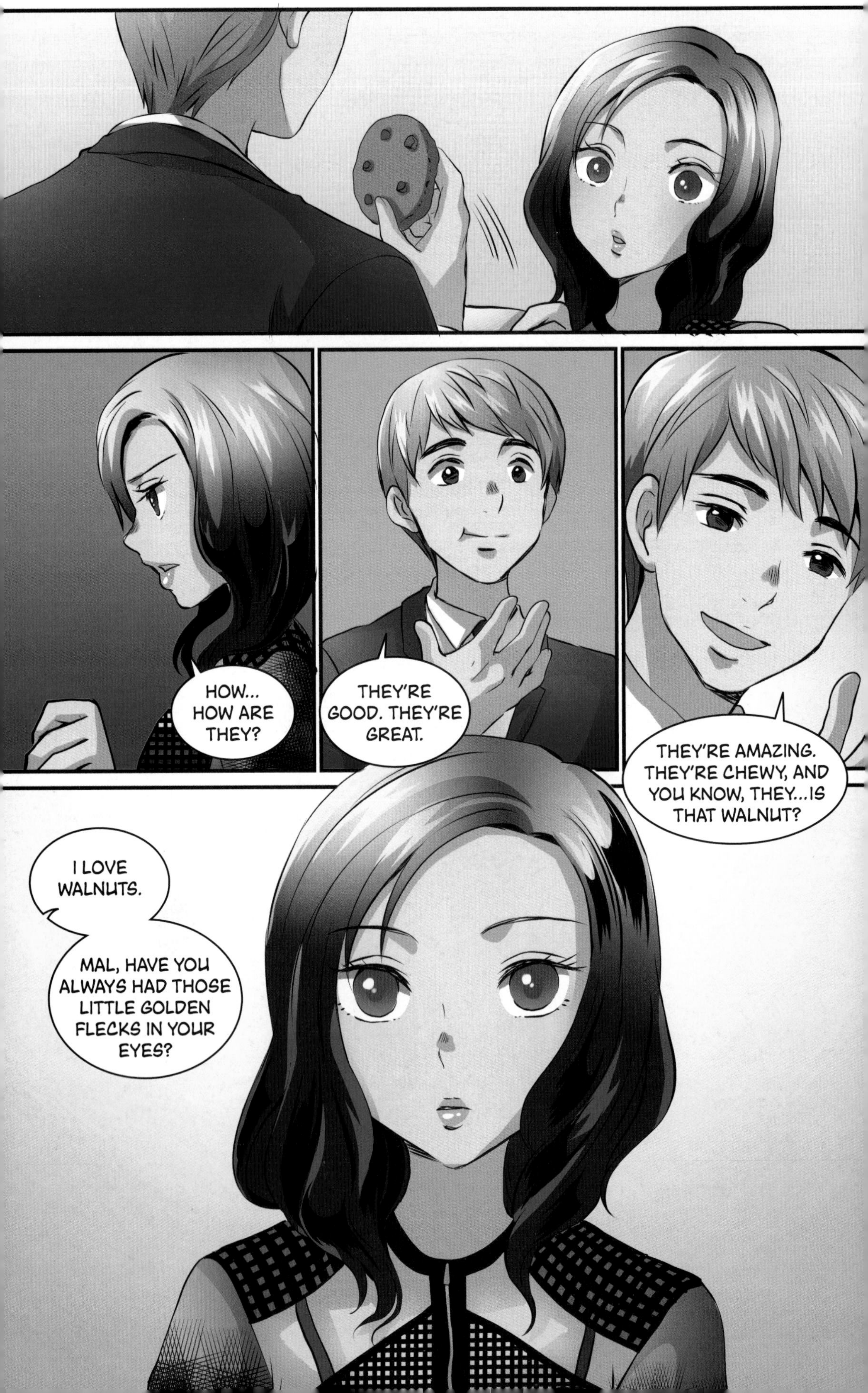
HOW... HOW ARE THEY?
THEY'RE GOOD. THEY'RE GREAT.
THEY'RE AMAZING. THEY'RE CHEWY, AND YOU KNOW, THEY...IS THAT WALNUT?
I LOVE WALNUTS.
MAL, HAVE YOU ALWAYS HAD THOSE LITTLE GOLDEN FLECKS IN YOUR EYES?

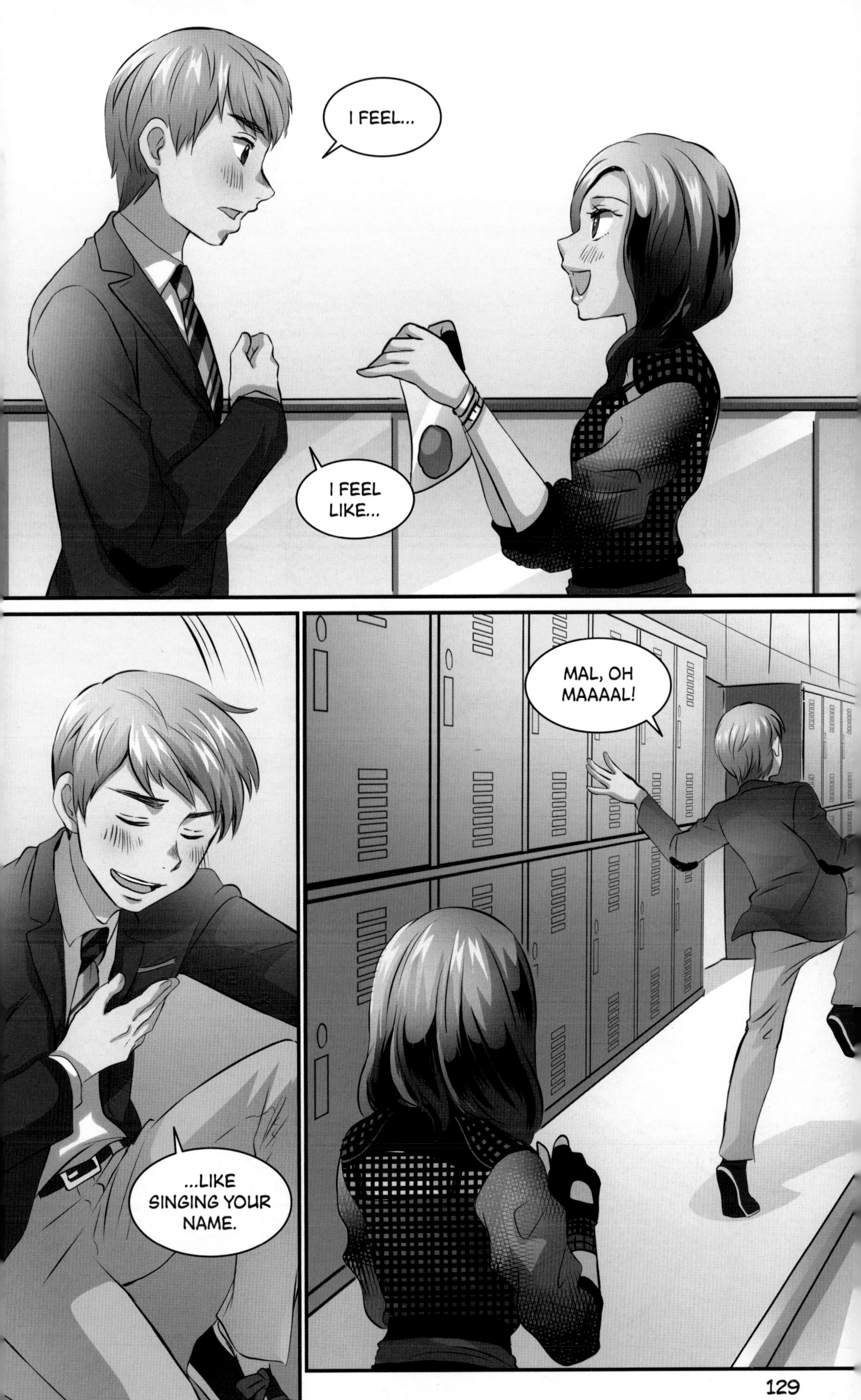
I FEEL...
I FEEL LIKE...
...LIKE SINGING YOUR NAME.
MAL, OH MAAAAL!

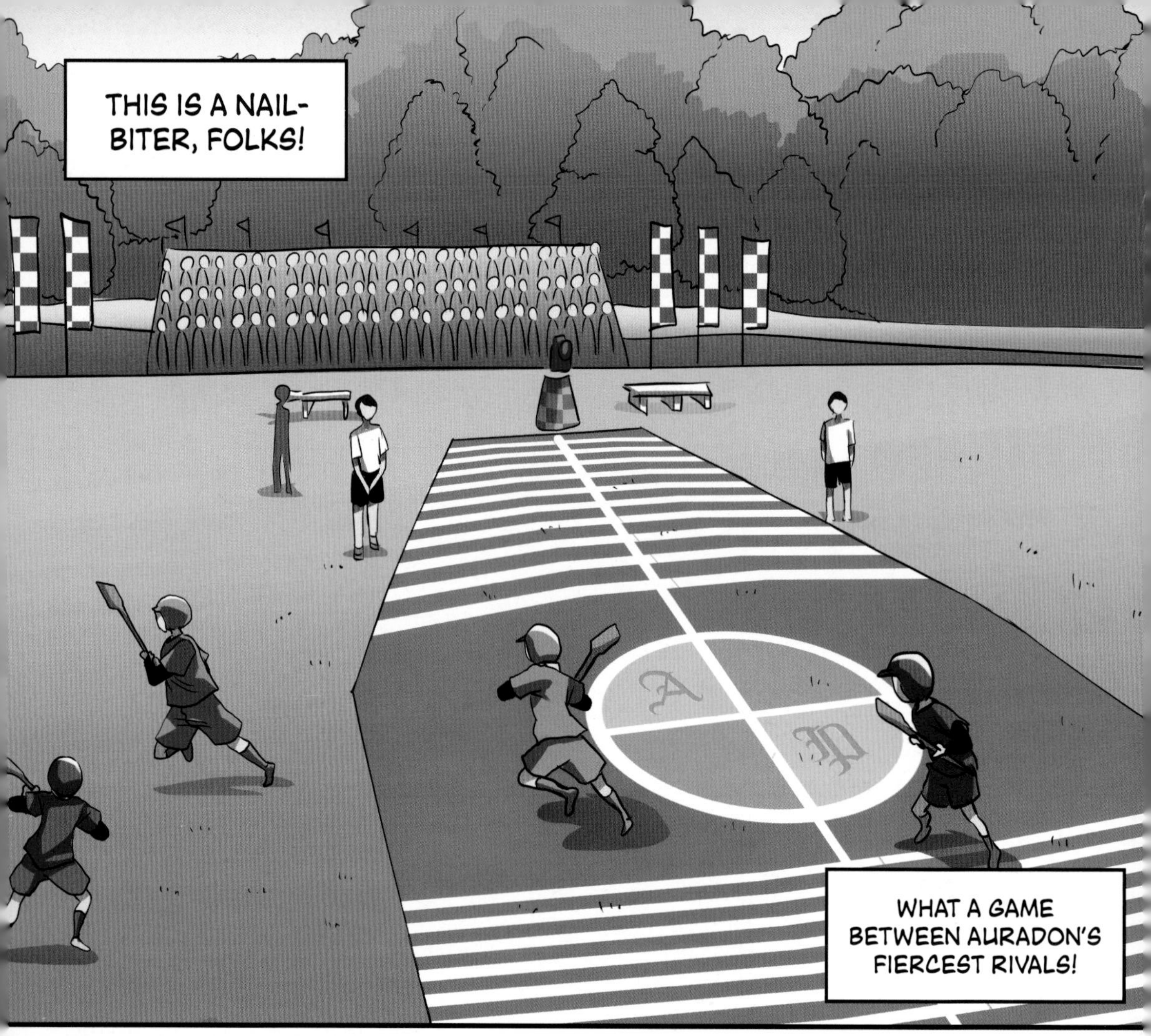
THIS IS A NAIL-BITER, FOLKS!
WHAT A GAME BETWEEN AURADON'S FIERCEST RIVALS!

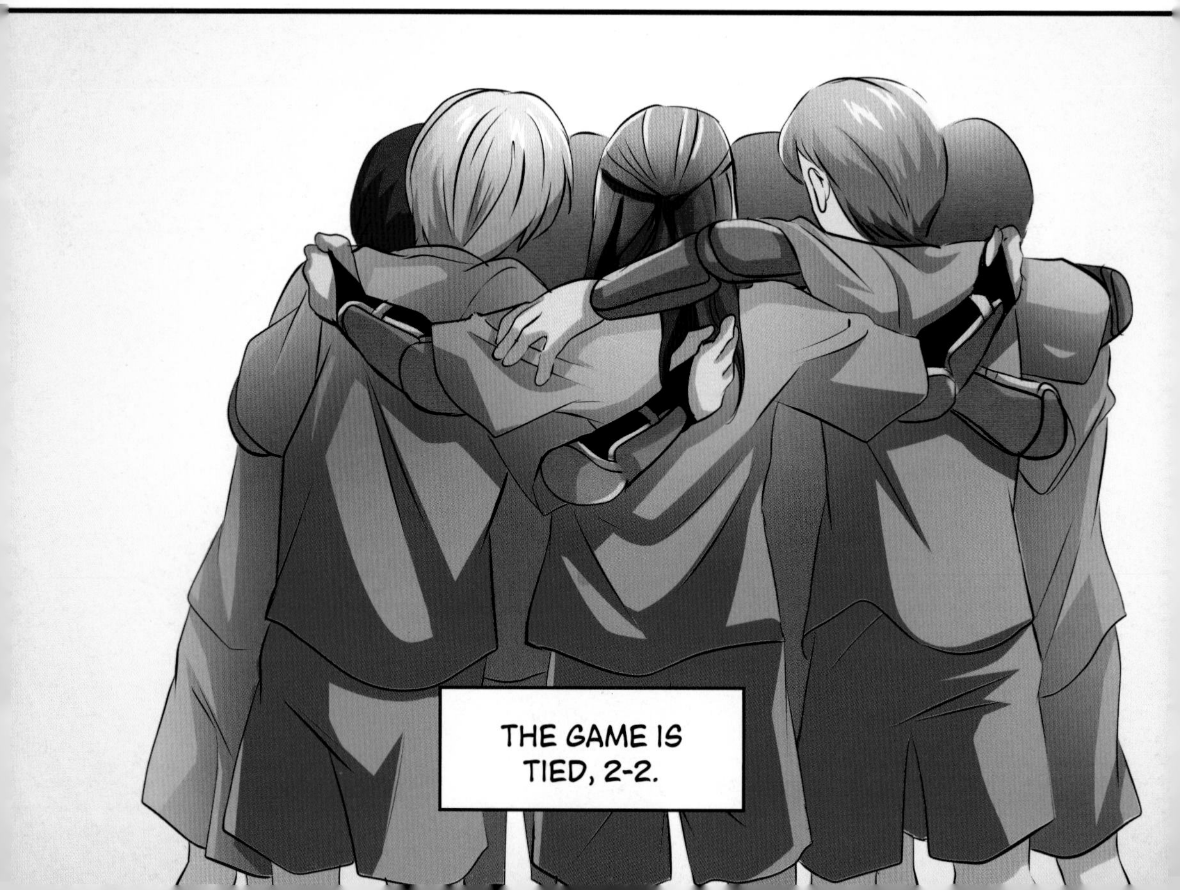
THE GAME IS TIED, 2-2.

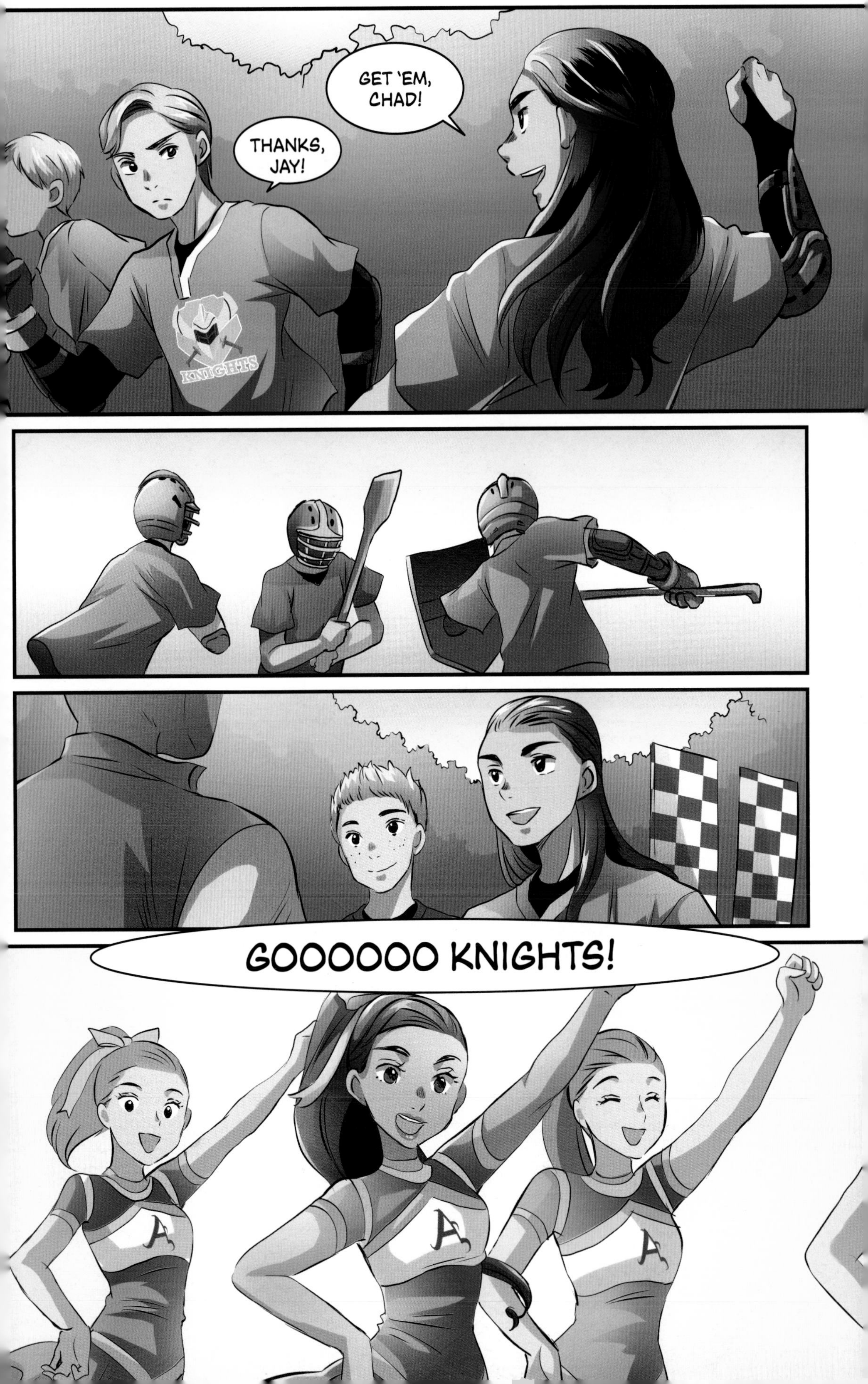
THANKS, JAY!
GET 'EM, CHAD!
KNIGHTS
GOOOOOO KNIGHTS!

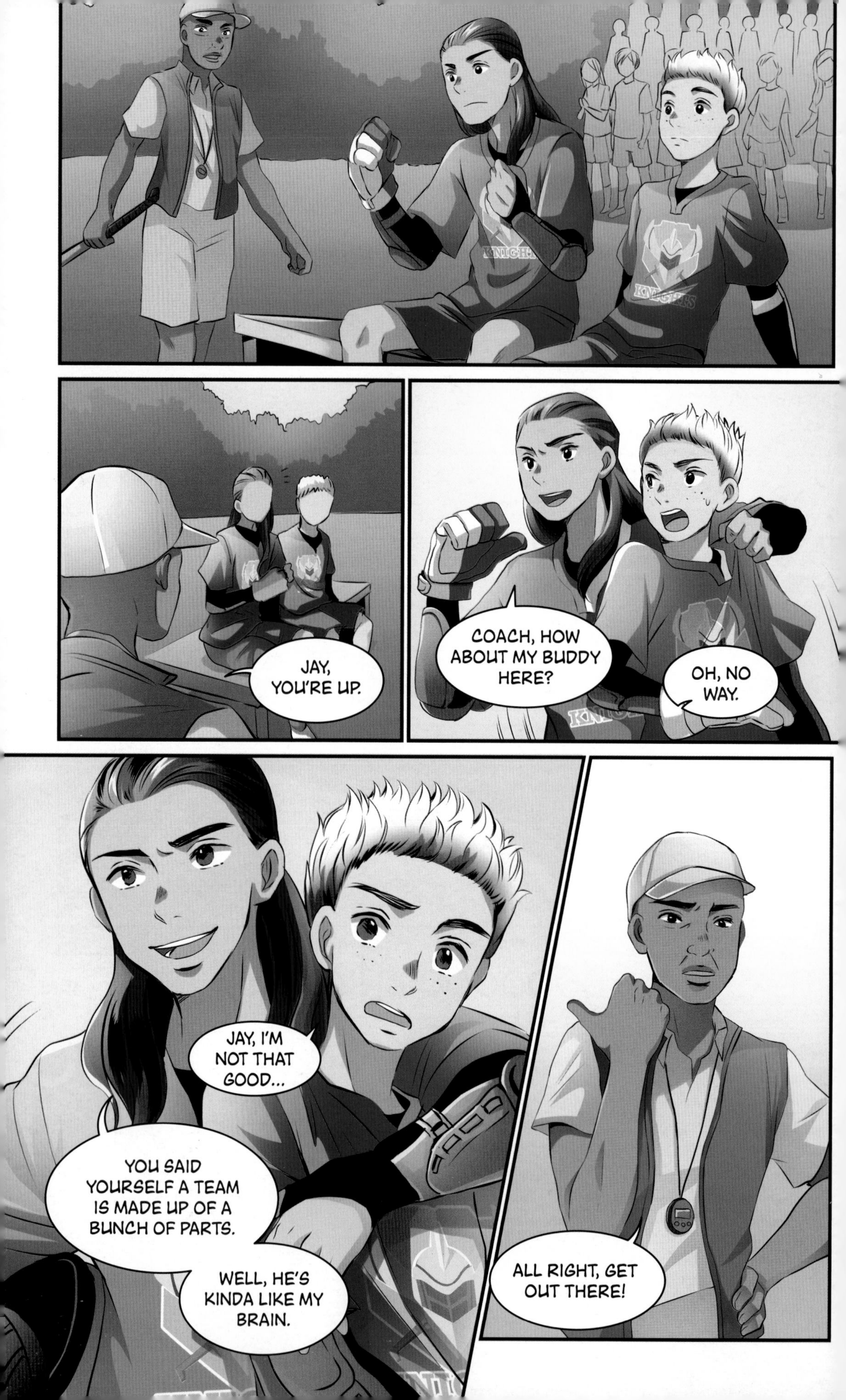
JAY, YOU'RE UP.
COACH, HOW ABOUT MY BUDDY HERE?
OH, NO WAY.
JAY, I'M NOT THAT GOOD...
YOU SAID YOURSELF A TEAM IS MADE UP OF A BUNCH OF PARTS.
WELL, HE'S KINDA LIKE MY BRAIN.
ALL RIGHT, GET OUT THERE!

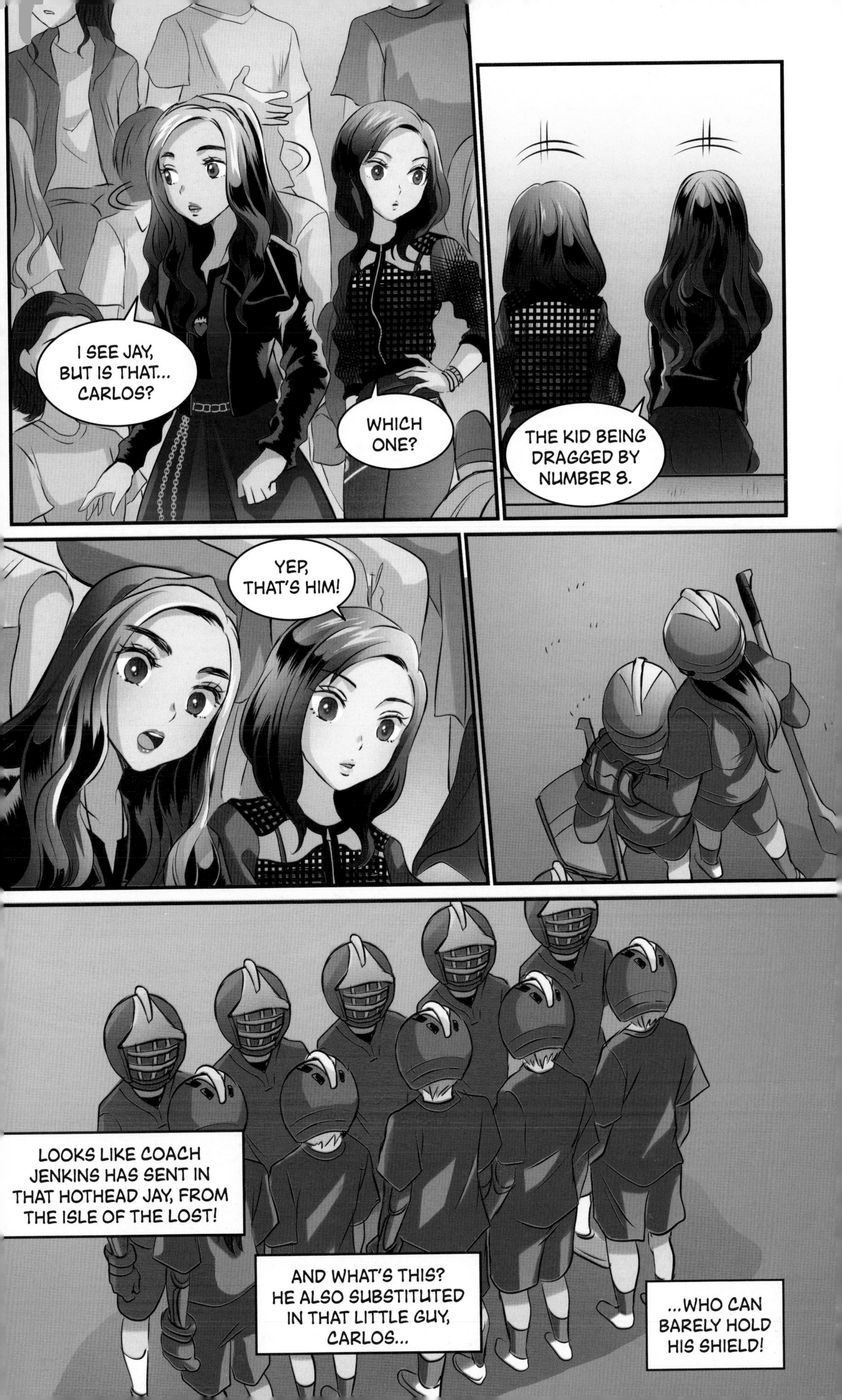
I SEE JAY, BUT IS THAT... CARLOS?
WHICH ONE?
THE KID BEING DRAGGED BY NUMBER 8.
YEP, THAT'S HIM!
LOOKS LIKE COACH JENKINS HAS SENT IN THAT HOTHEAD JAY, FROM THE ISLE OF THE LOST!
AND WHAT'S THIS? HE ALSO SUBSTITUTED IN THAT LITTLE GUY, CARLOS...
...WHO CAN BARELY HOLD HIS SHIELD!

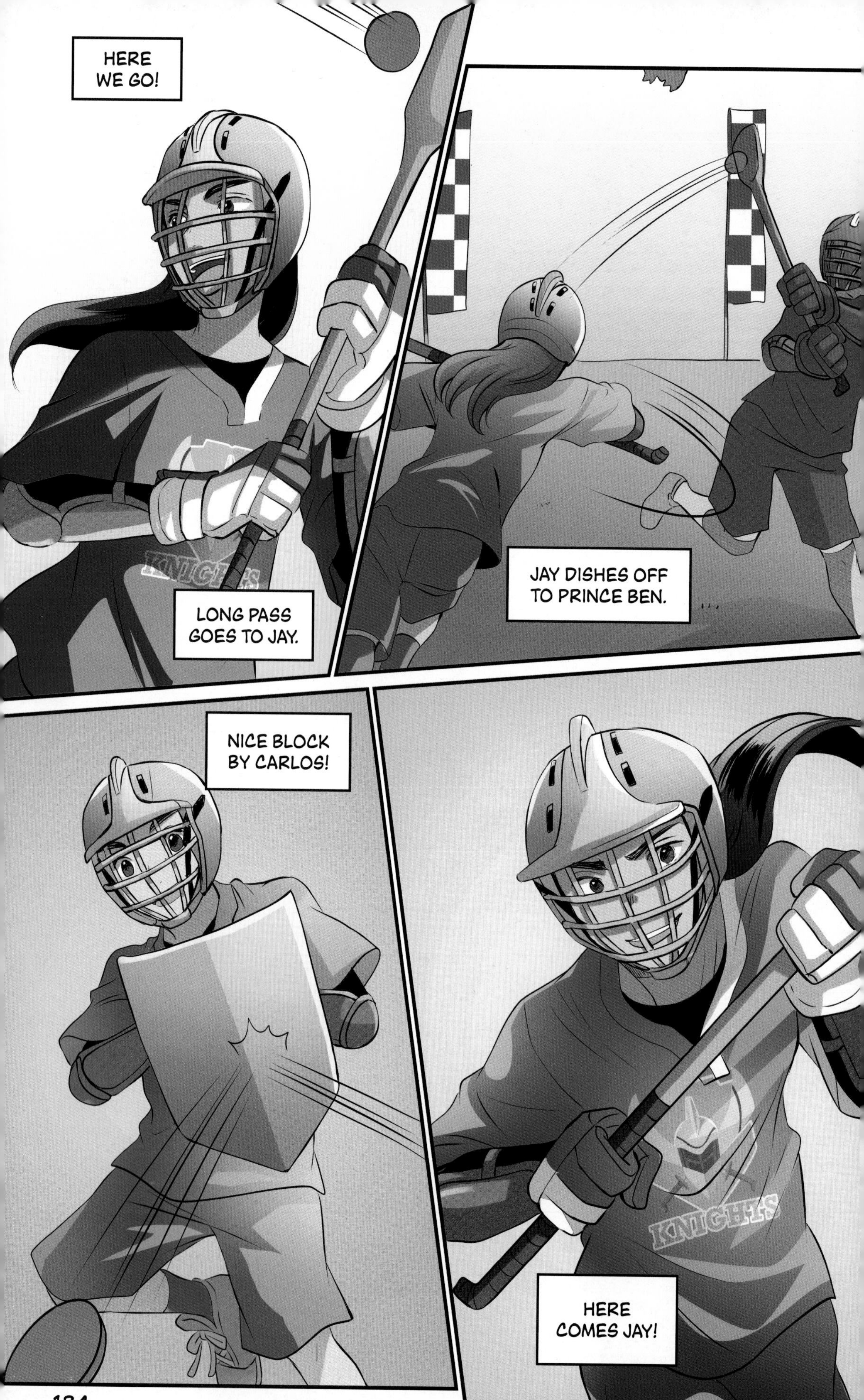
HERE WE GO!
LONG PASS GOES TO JAY.
JAY DISHES OFF TO PRINCE BEN.
NICE BLOCK BY CARLOS!
HERE COMES JAY!
KNIGHTS

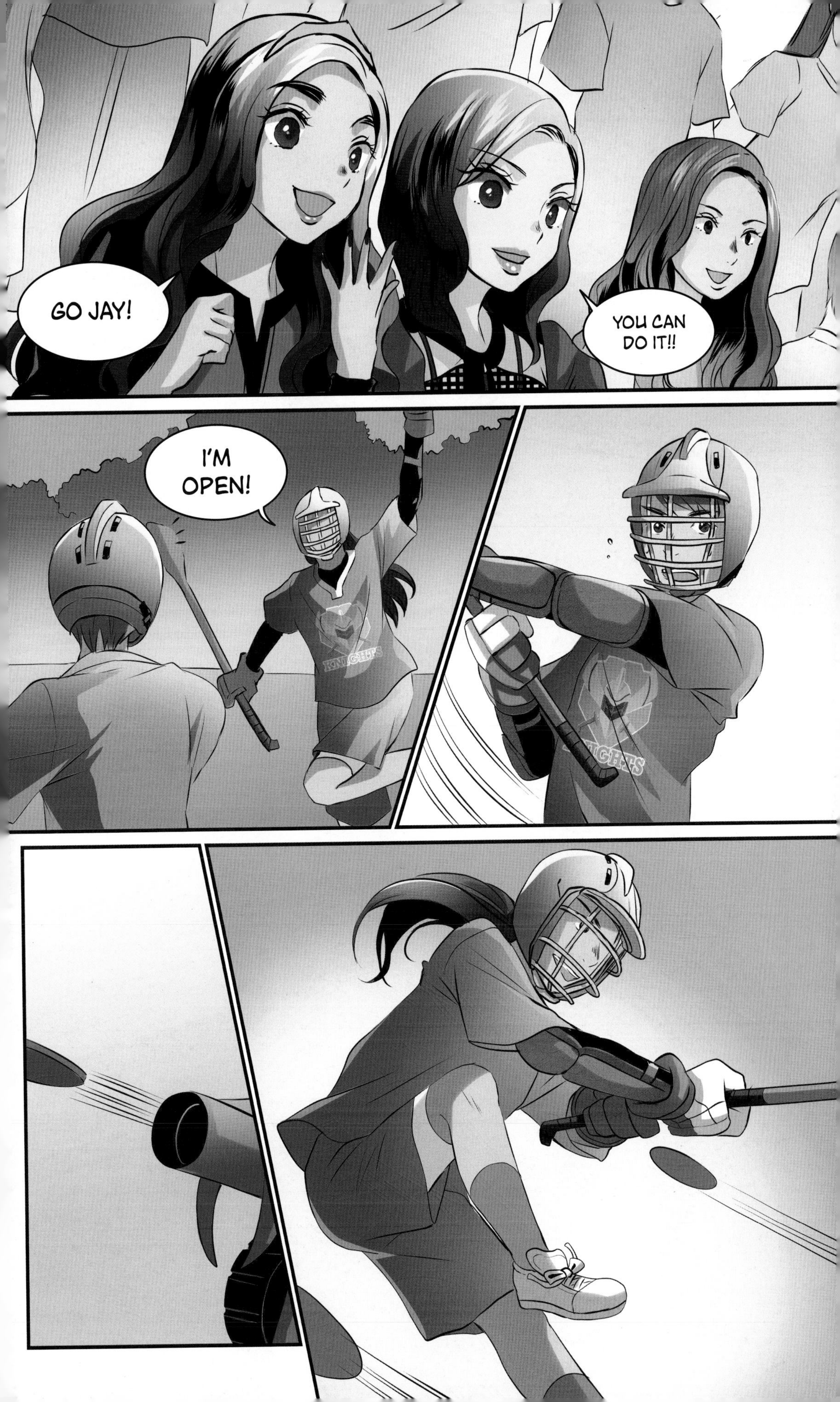
GO JAY!
YOU CAN DO IT!!
I'M OPEN!
KNIGHTS

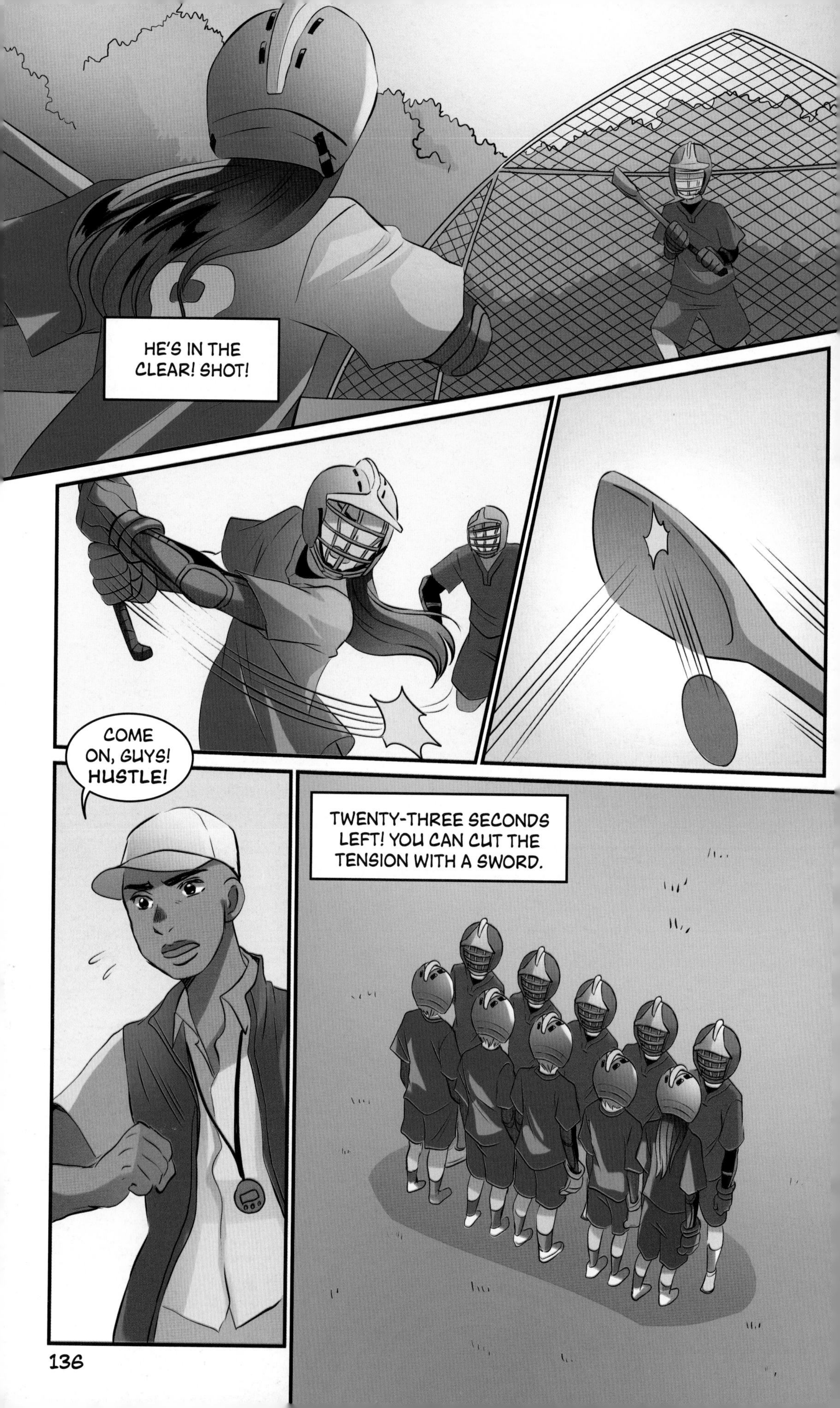
HE'S IN THE CLEAR! SHOT!
COME ON, GUYS! HUSTLE!
TWENTY-THREE SECONDS LEFT! YOU CAN CUT THE TENSION WITH A SWORD.

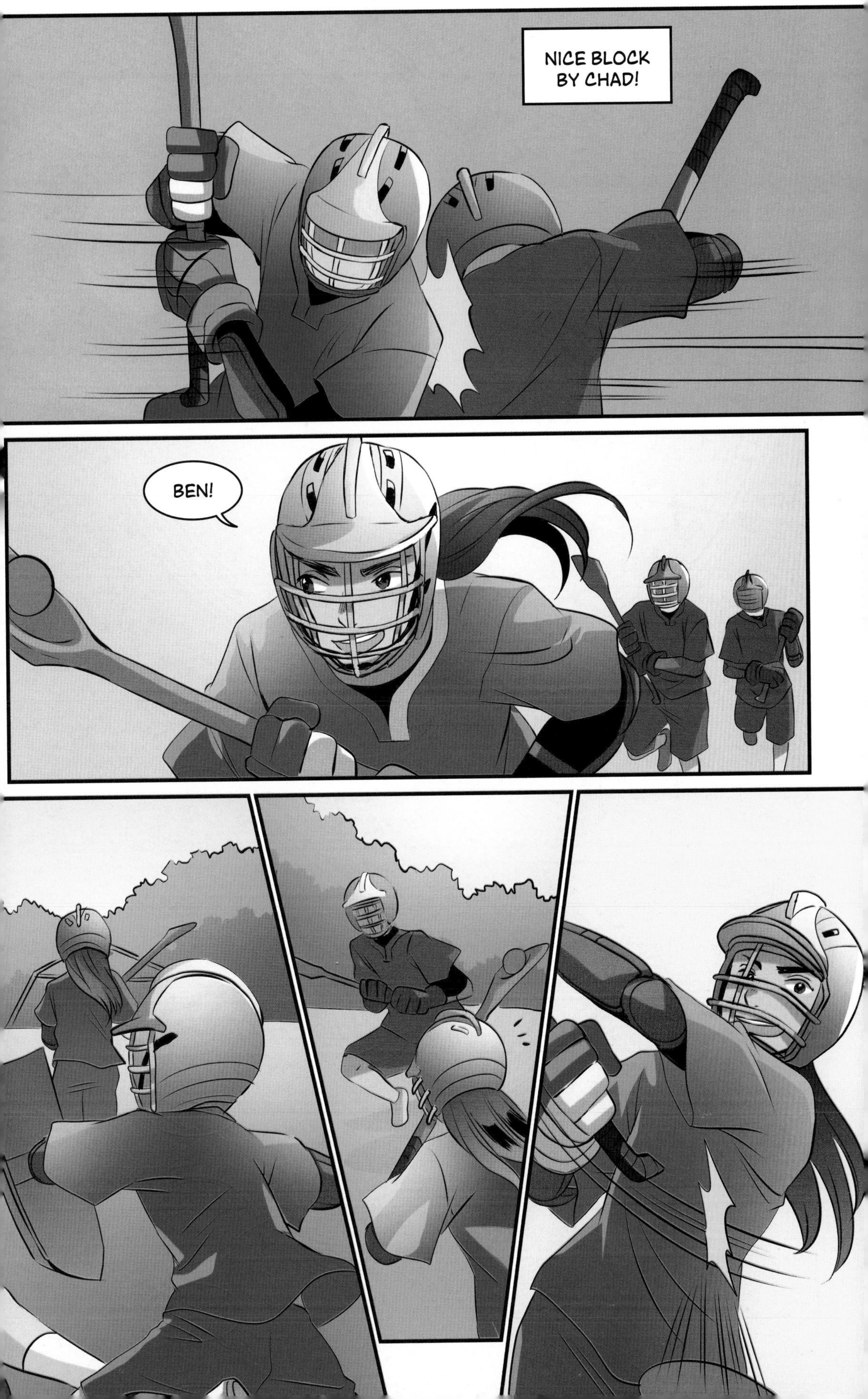
NICE BLOCK BY CHAD!
BEN!

HE SCORES! PRINCE BEN HAS WON IT!

WHAT A TEAM! INCREDIBLE!

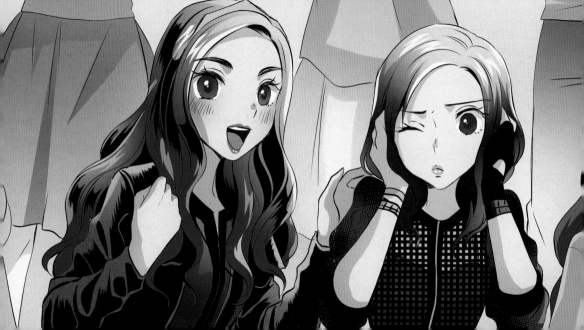

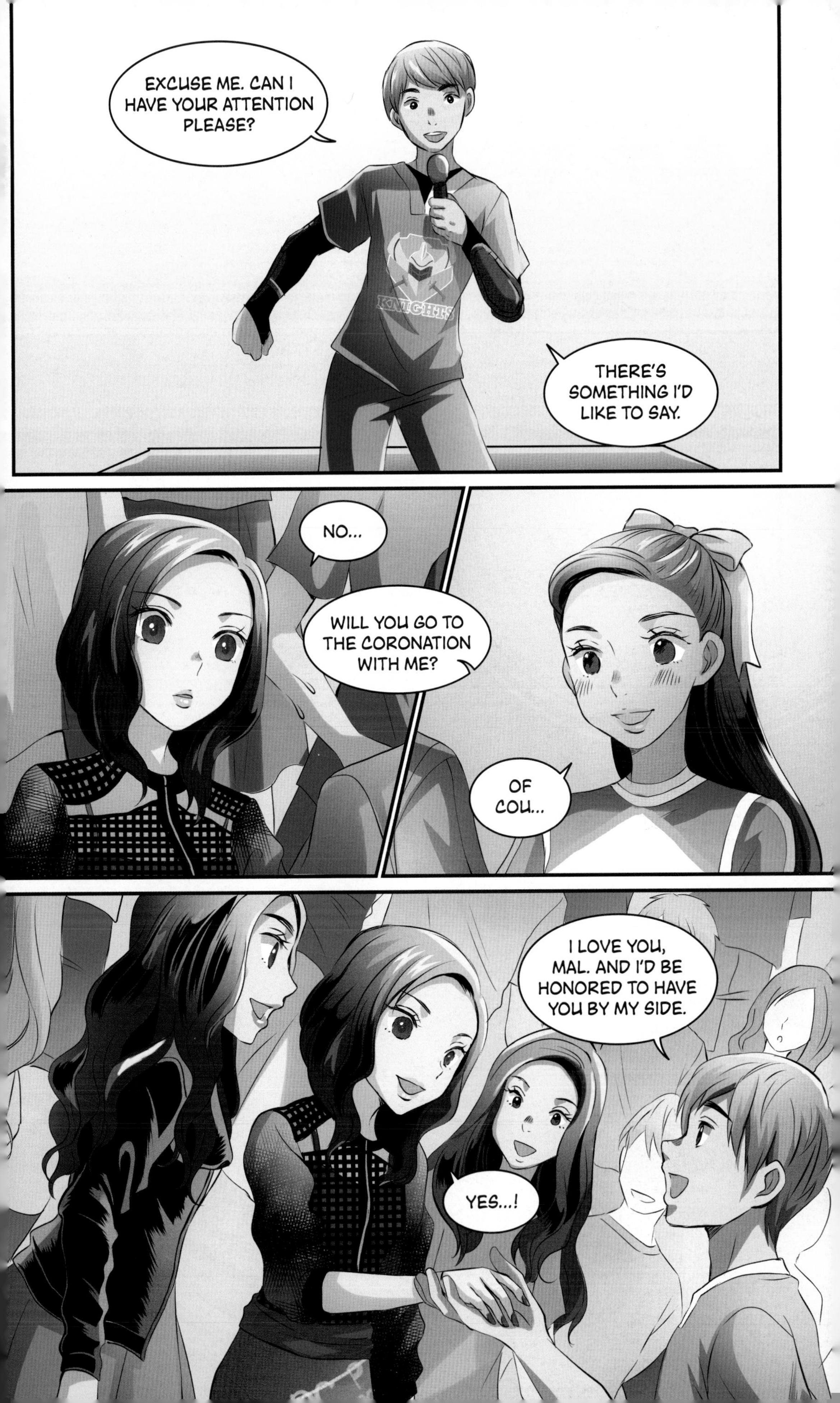
EXCUSE ME. CAN I HAVE YOUR ATTENTION PLEASE?
KNIGHTS
THERE'S SOMETHING I'D LIKE TO SAY.
NO...
WILL YOU GO TO THE CORONATION WITH ME?
OF COU...
I LOVE YOU, MAL. AND I'D BE HONORED TO HAVE YOU BY MY SIDE.
YES...!

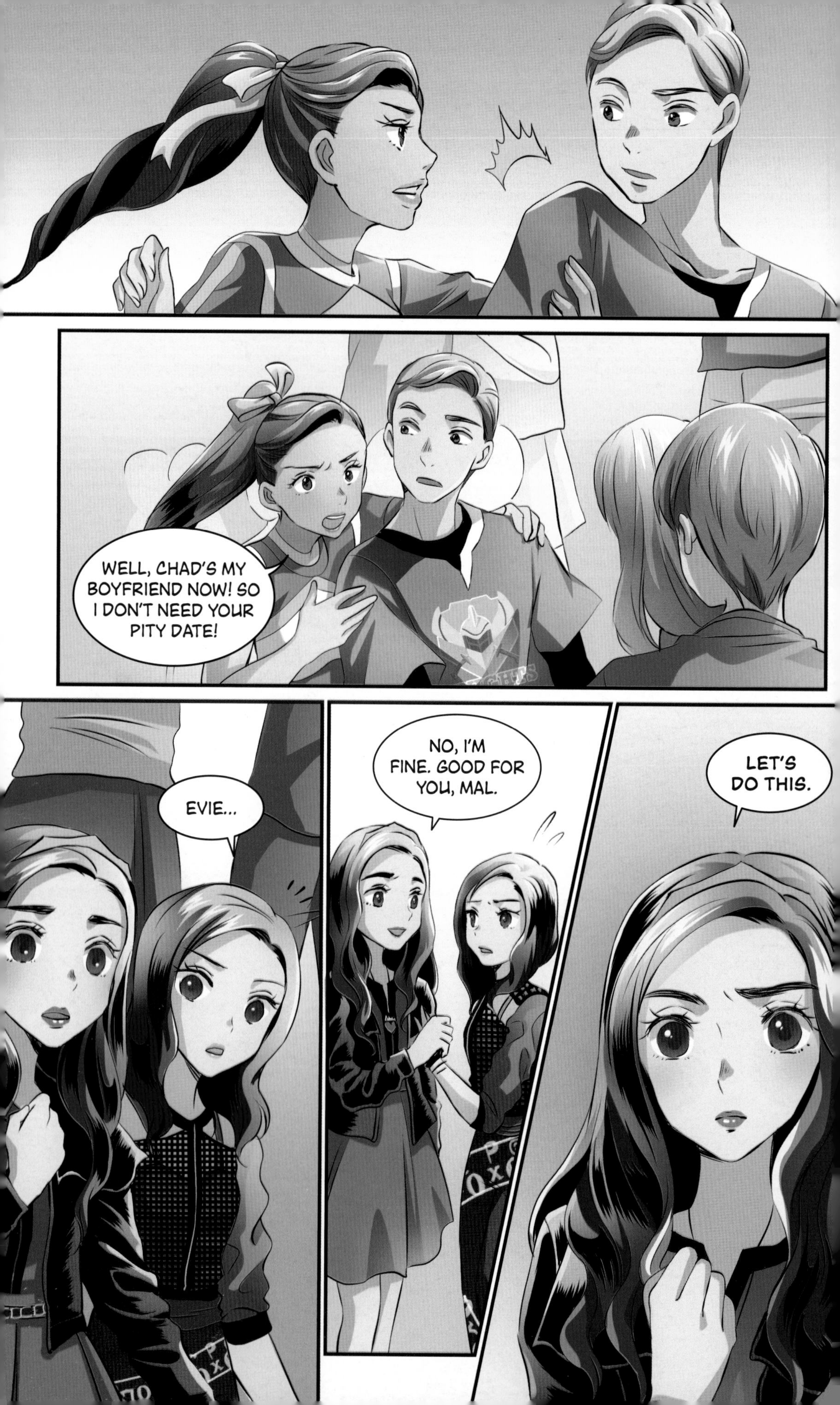
WELL, CHAD'S MY BOYFRIEND NOW! SO I DON'T NEED YOUR PITY DATE!
EVIE...
NO, I'M FINE. GOOD FOR YOU, MAL.
LET'S DO THIS.

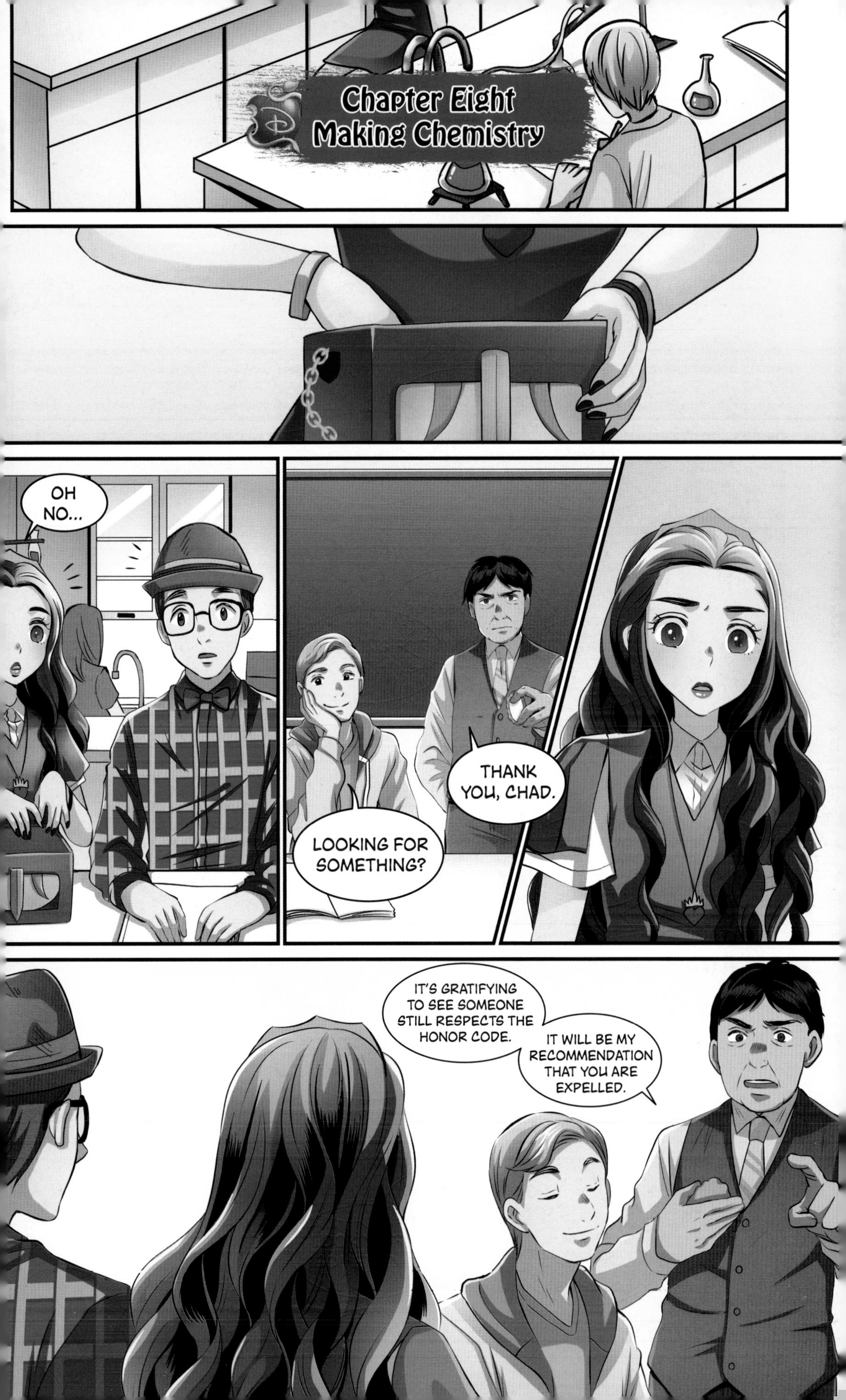
Chapter Eight
Making Chemistry
OH NO...
LOOKING FOR SOMETHING?
THANK YOU, CHAD.
IT'S GRATIFYING TO SEE SOMEONE STILL RESPECTS THE HONOR CODE.
IT WILL BE MY RECOMMENDATION THAT YOU ARE EXPELLED.

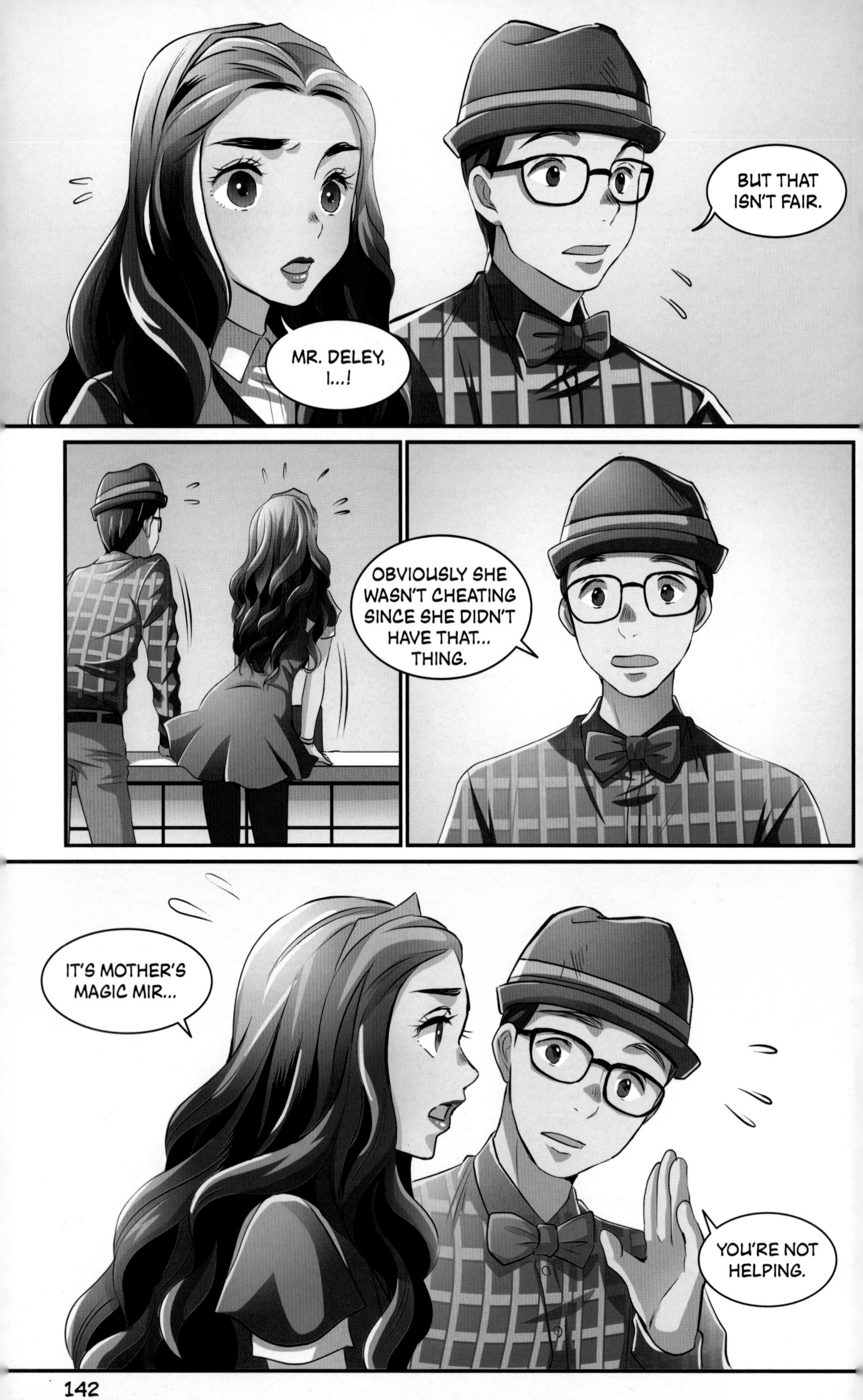
BUT THAT ISN'T FAIR.
MR. DELEY, I...!
OBVIOUSLY SHE WASN'T CHEATING SINCE SHE DIDN'T HAVE THAT... THING.
IT'S MOTHER'S MAGIC MIR...
YOU'RE NOT HELPING.

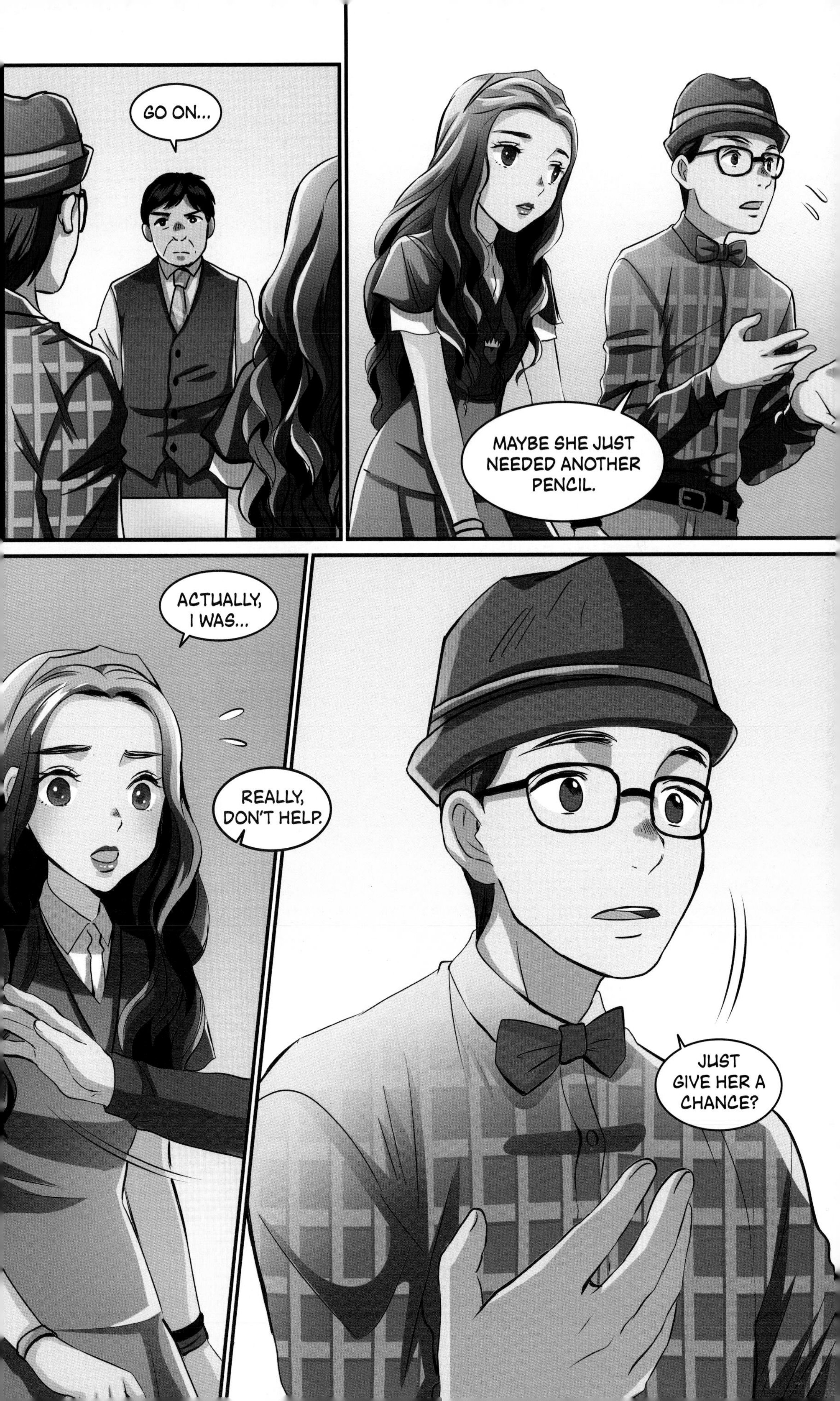
GO ON...
MAYBE SHE JUST NEEDED ANOTHER PENCIL.
ACTUALLY, I WAS...
REALLY, DON'T HELP.
JUST GIVE HER A CHANCE?

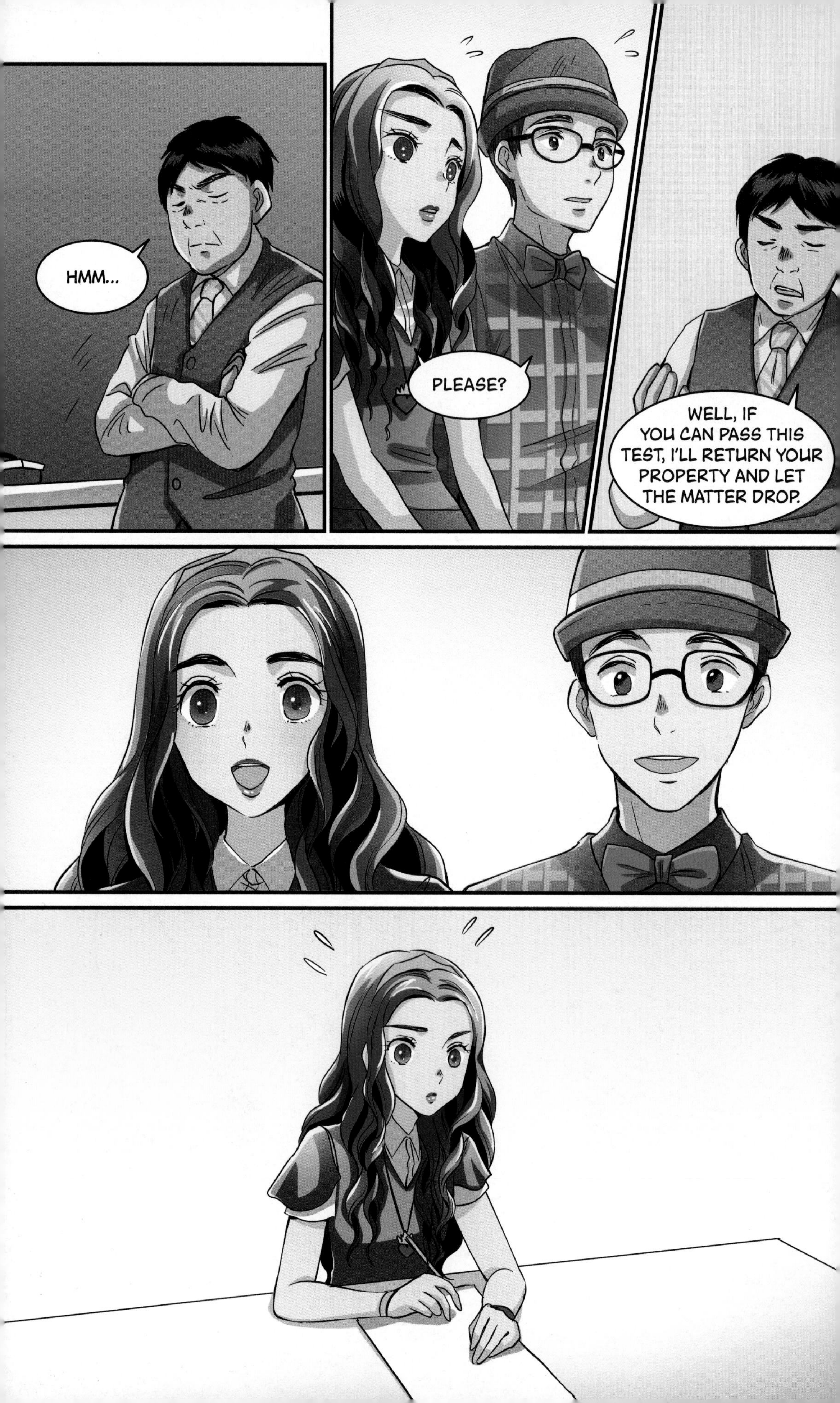
HMM...
PLEASE?
WELL, IF YOU CAN PASS THIS TEST, I'LL RETURN YOUR PROPERTY AND LET THE MATTER DROP.

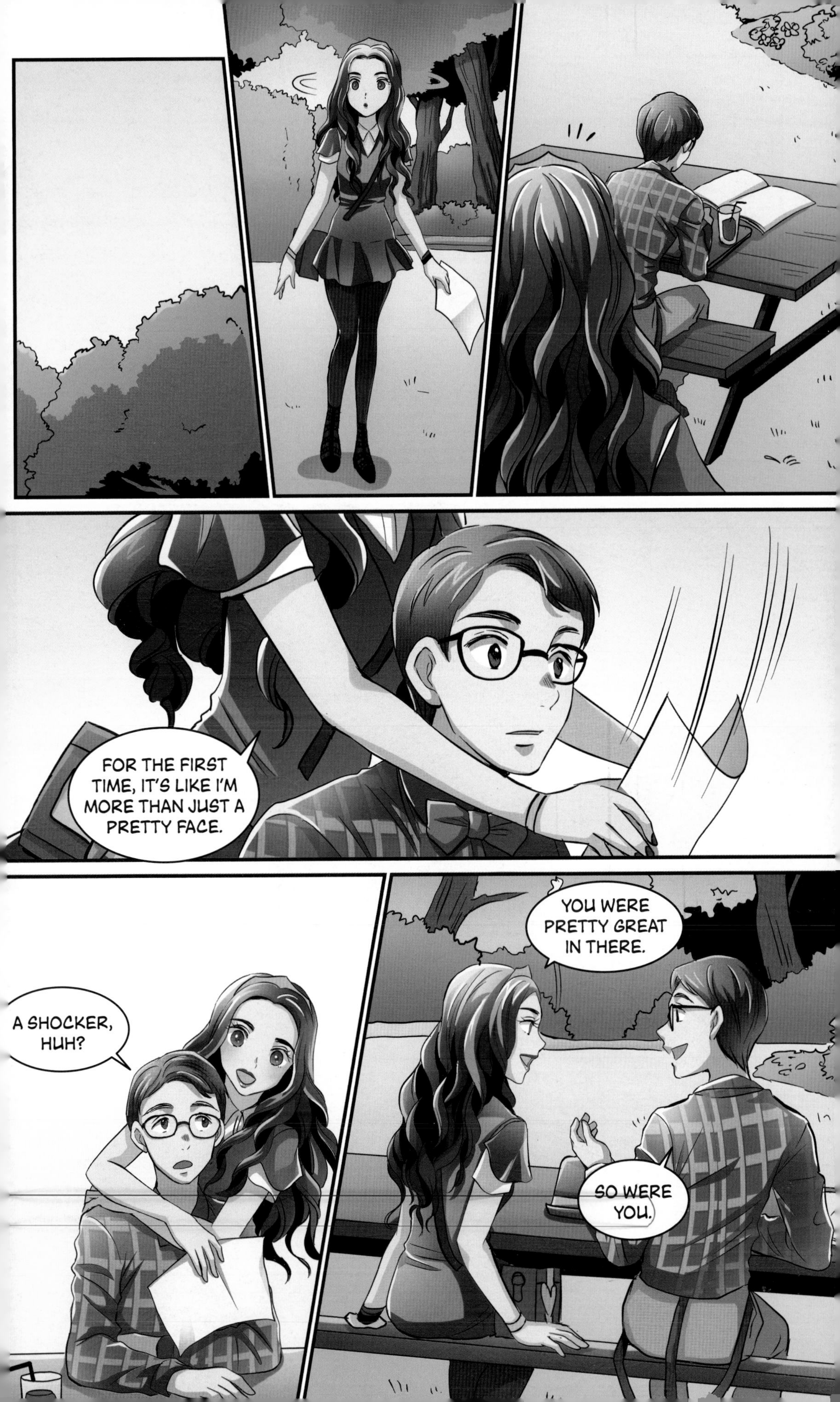

FOR THE FIRST TIME, IT'S LIKE I'M MORE THAN JUST A PRETTY FACE.
A SHOCKER, HUH?
YOU WERE PRETTY GREAT IN THERE.
SO WERE YOU.

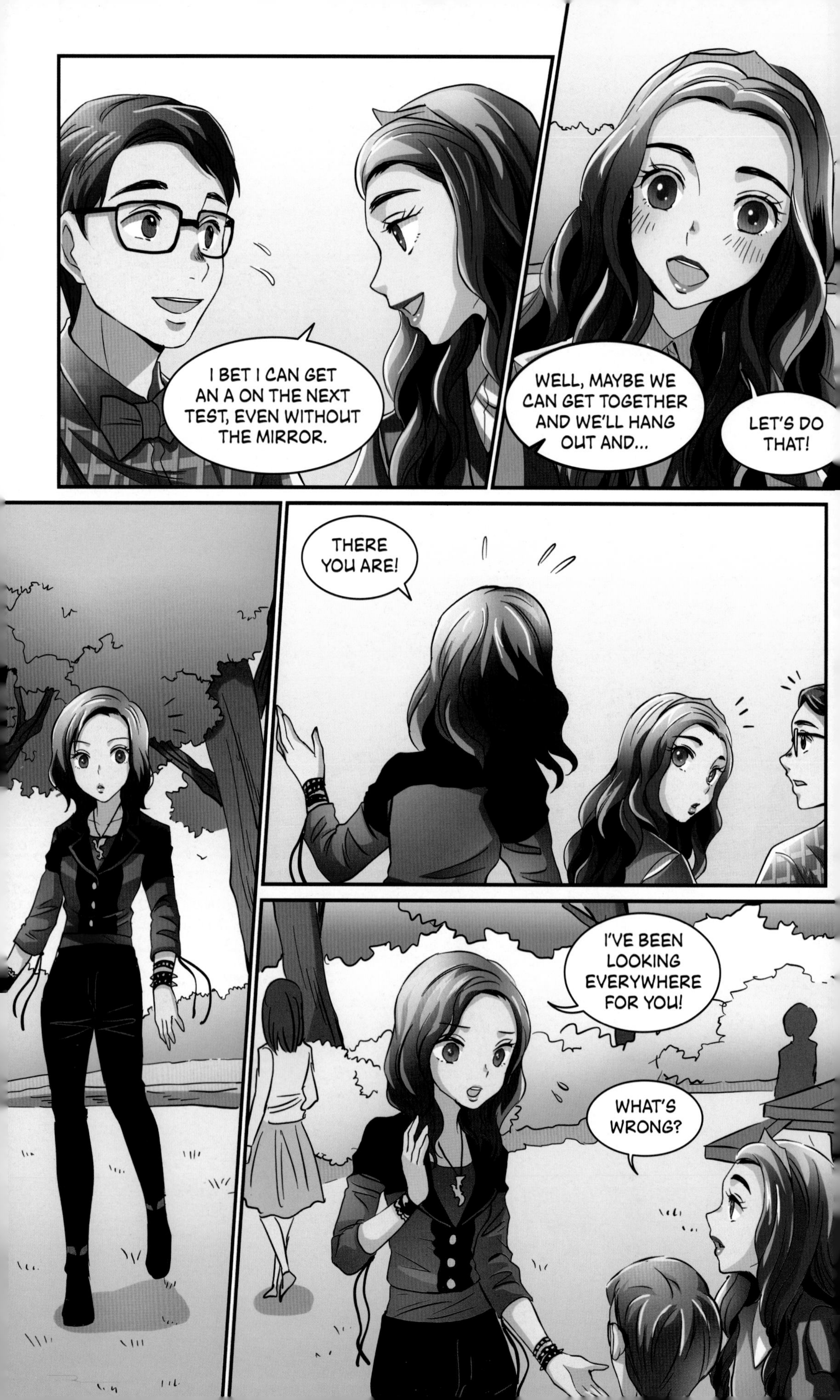
I BET I CAN GET AN A ON THE NEXT TEST, EVEN WITHOUT THE MIRROR.
WELL, MAYBE WE CAN GET TOGETHER AND WE'LL HANG OUT AND...
LET'S DO THAT!
THERE YOU ARE!
I'VE BEEN LOOKING EVERYWHERE FOR YOU!
WHAT'S WRONG?

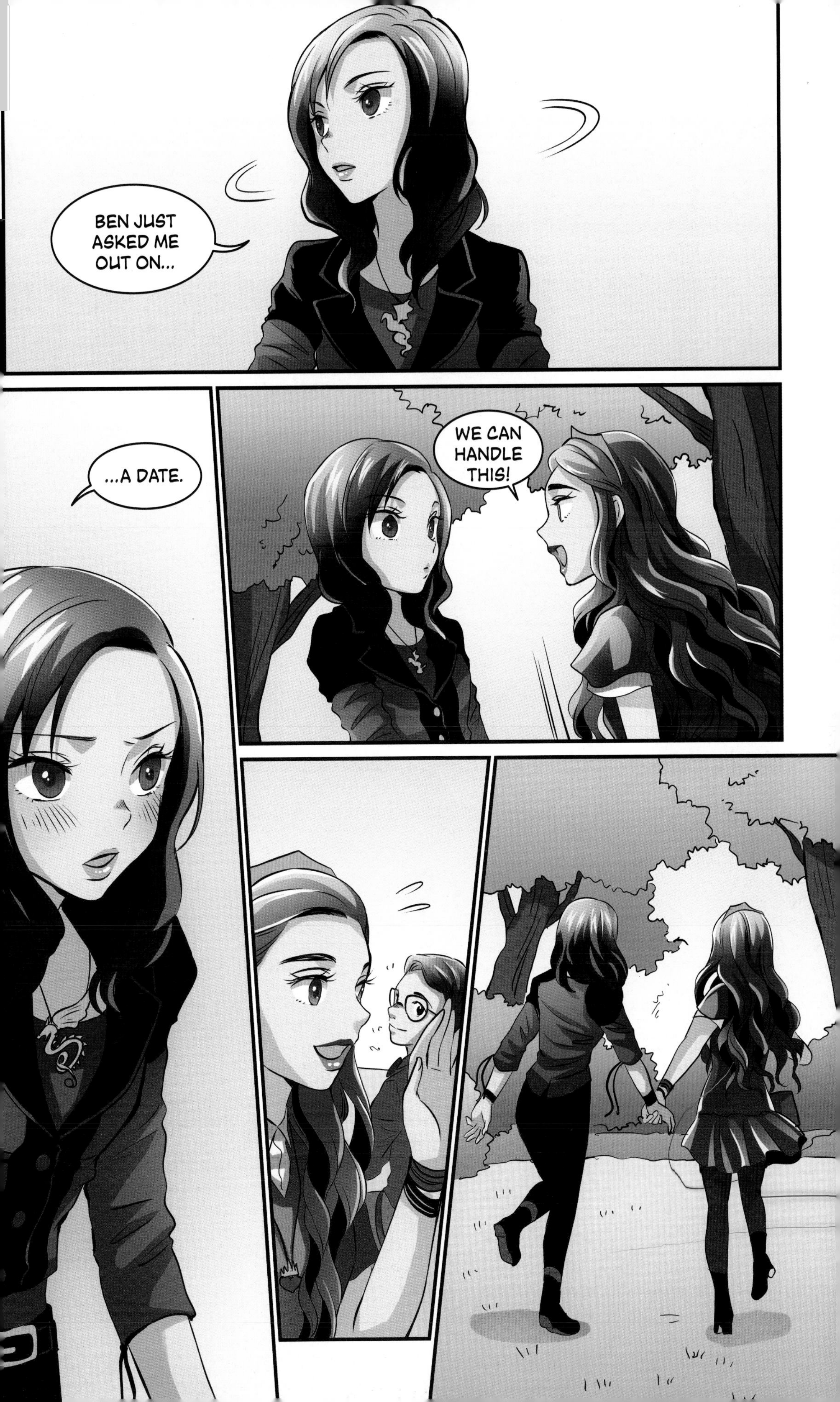
BEN JUST ASKED ME OUT ON...
...A DATE.
WE CAN HANDLE THIS!

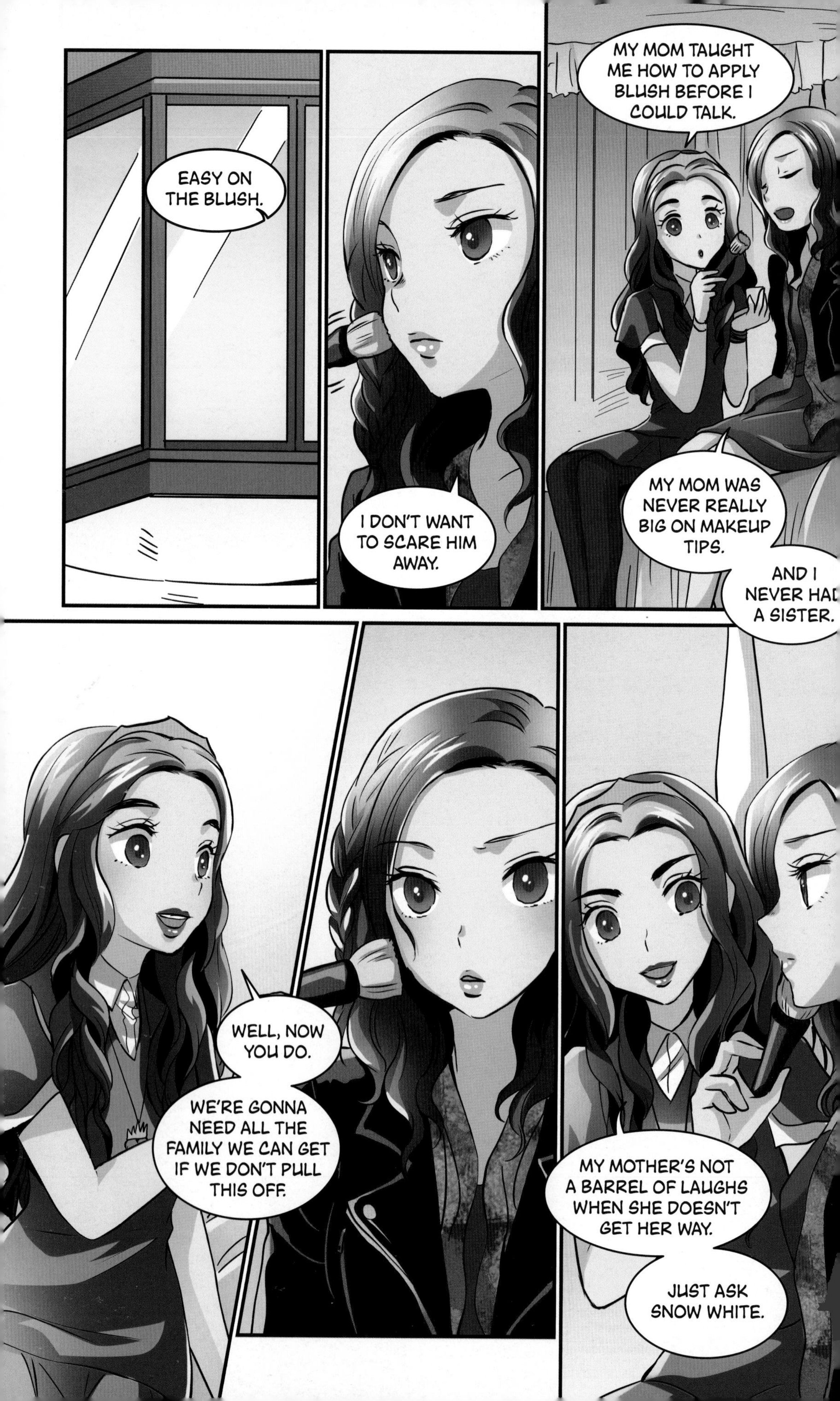
EASY ON THE BLUSH.
I DON'T WANT TO SCARE HIM AWAY.
MY MOM TAUGHT ME HOW TO APPLY BLUSH BEFORE I COULD TALK.
MY MOM WAS NEVER REALLY BIG ON MAKEUP TIPS.
AND I NEVER HAD A SISTER.
WELL, NOW YOU DO.
WE'RE GONNA NEED ALL THE FAMILY WE CAN GET IF WE DON'T PULL THIS OFF.
MY MOTHER'S NOT A BARREL OF LAUGHS WHEN SHE DOESN'T GET HER WAY.
JUST ASK SNOW WHITE.

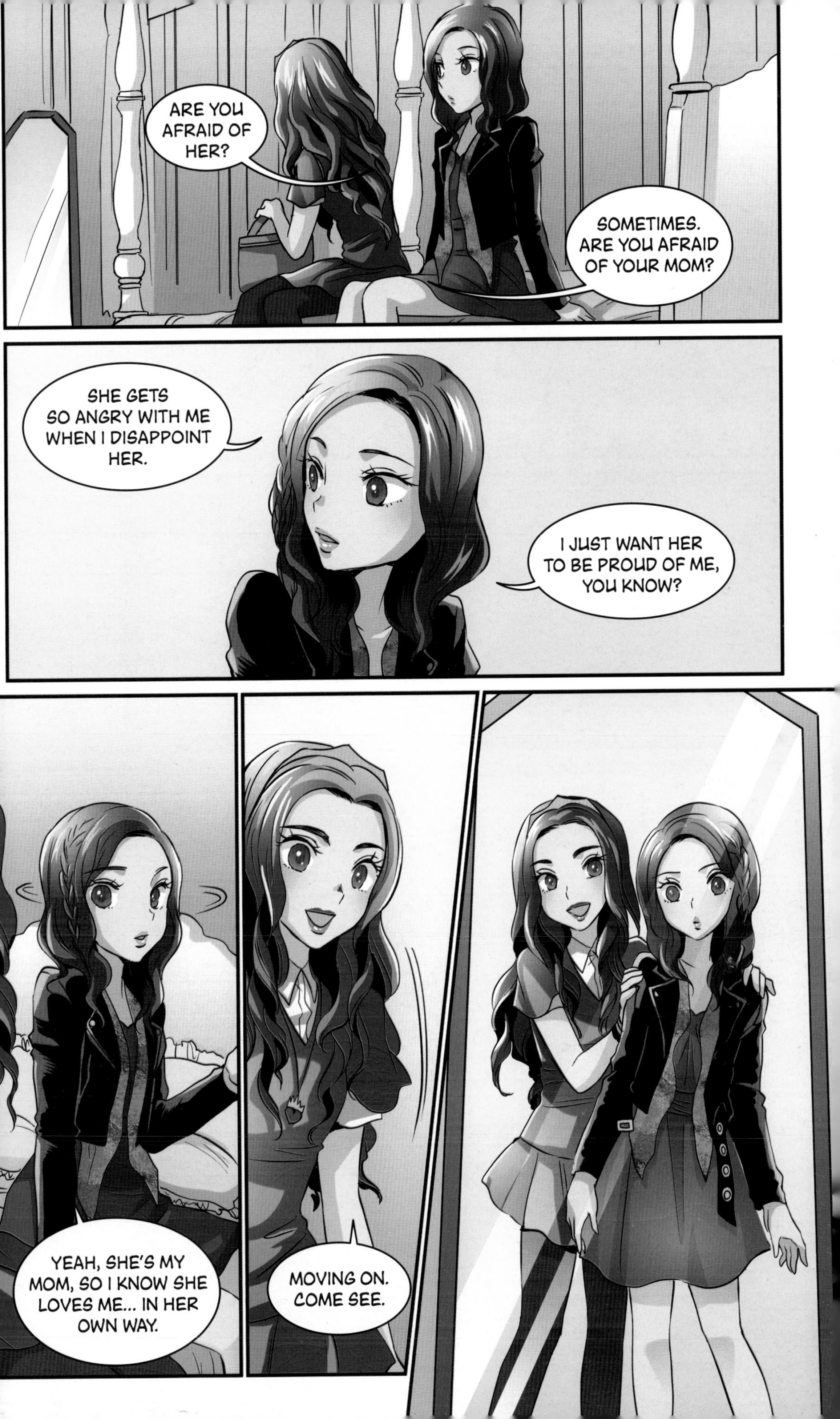
ARE YOU AFRAID OF HER?
SOMETIMES. ARE YOU AFRAID OF YOUR MOM?
SHE GETS SO ANGRY WITH ME WHEN I DISAPPOINT HER.
I JUST WANT HER TO BE PROUD OF ME, YOU KNOW?
YEAH, SHE'S MY MOM, SO I KNOW SHE LOVES ME... IN HER OWN WAY.
MOVING ON. COME SEE.

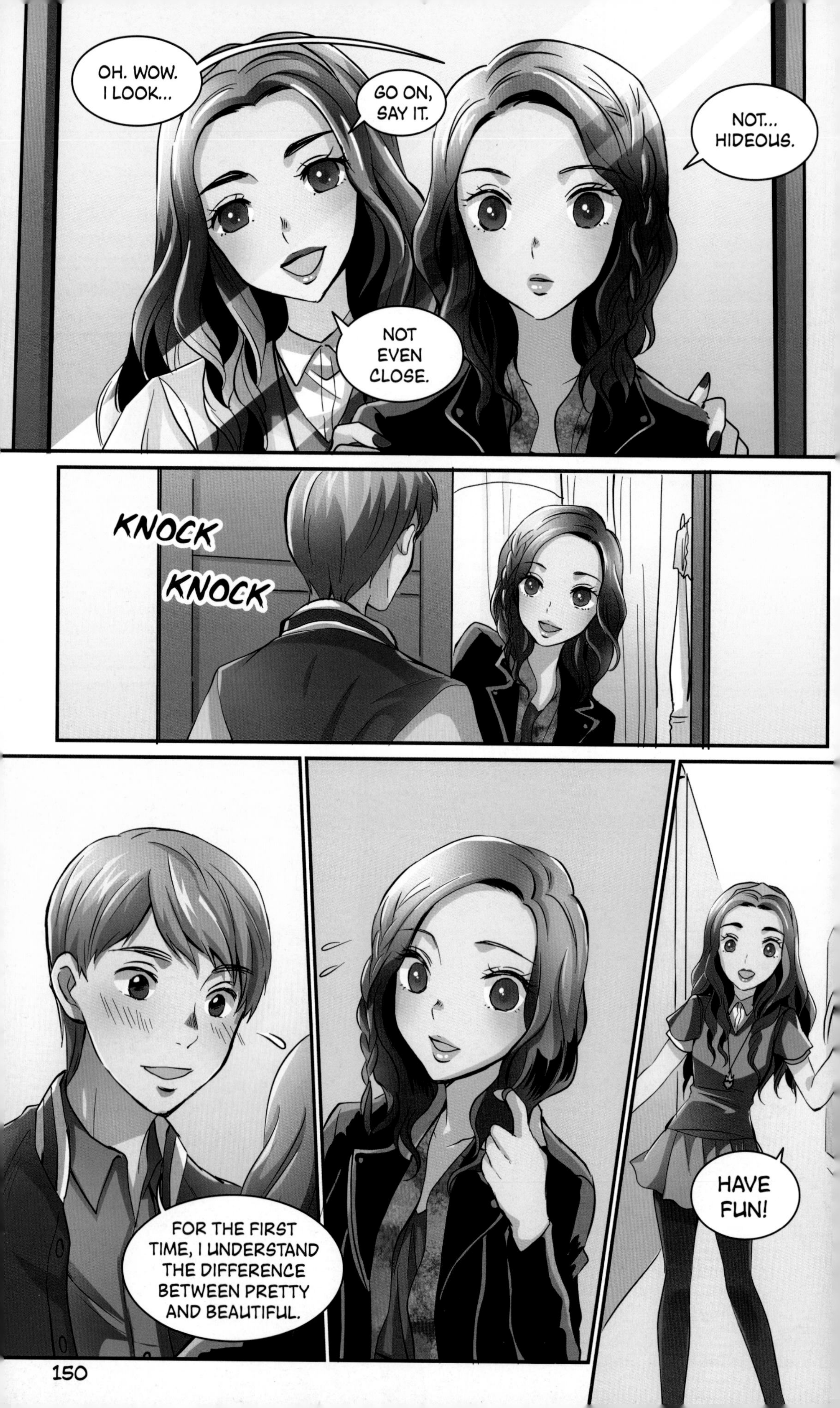
OH. WOW. I LOOK...
GO ON, SAY IT.
NOT... HIDEOUS.
NOT EVEN CLOSE.
KNOCK
KNOCK
FOR THE FIRST TIME, I UNDERSTAND THE DIFFERENCE BETWEEN PRETTY AND BEAUTIFUL.
HAVE FUN!

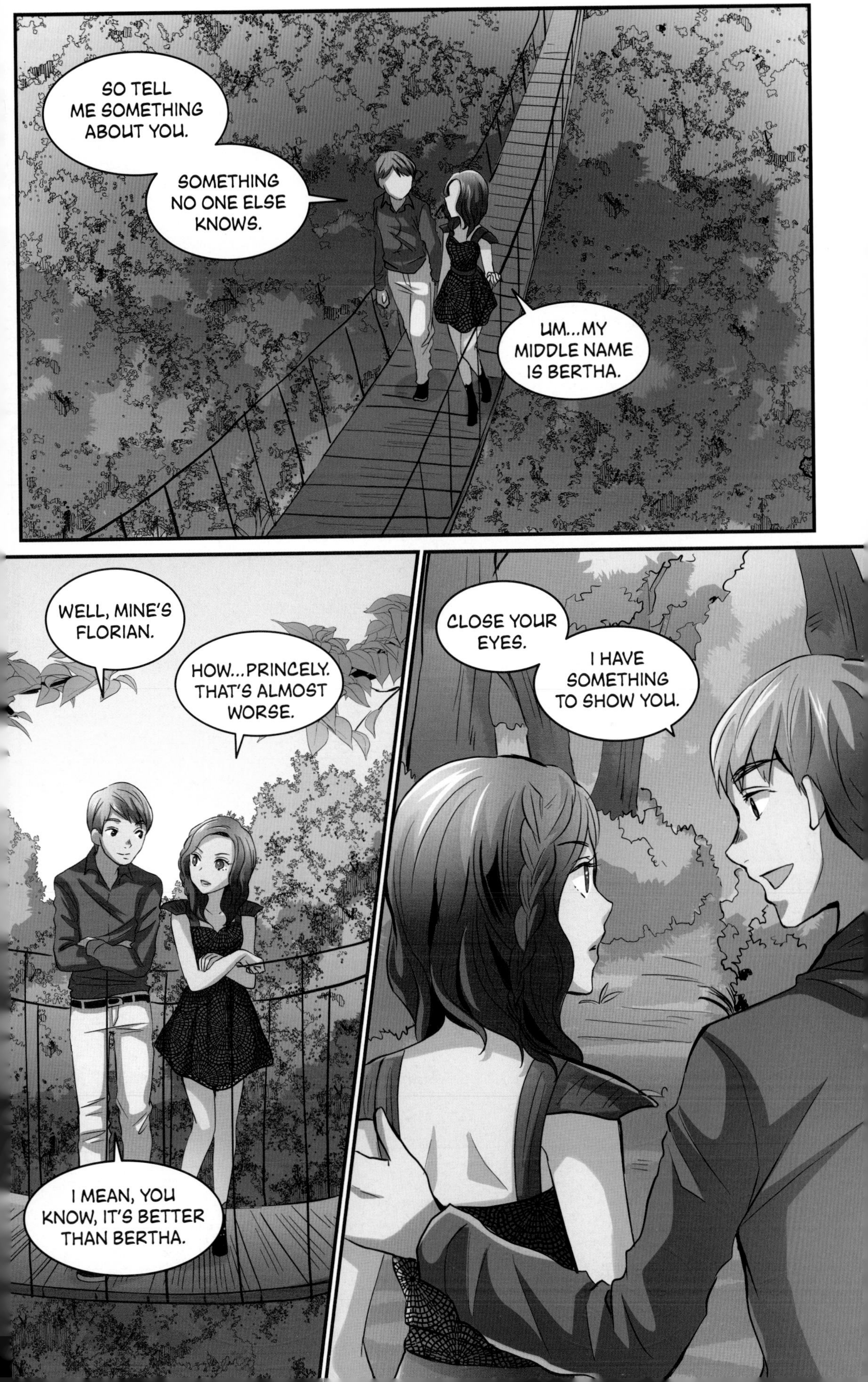
SO TELL ME SOMETHING ABOUT YOU.
SOMETHING NO ONE ELSE KNOWS.
UM...MY MIDDLE NAME IS BERTHA.
WELL, MINE'S FLORIAN.
HOW...PRINCELY. THAT'S ALMOST WORSE.
I MEAN, YOU KNOW, IT'S BETTER THAN BERTHA.
CLOSE YOUR EYES.
I HAVE SOMETHING TO SHOW YOU.

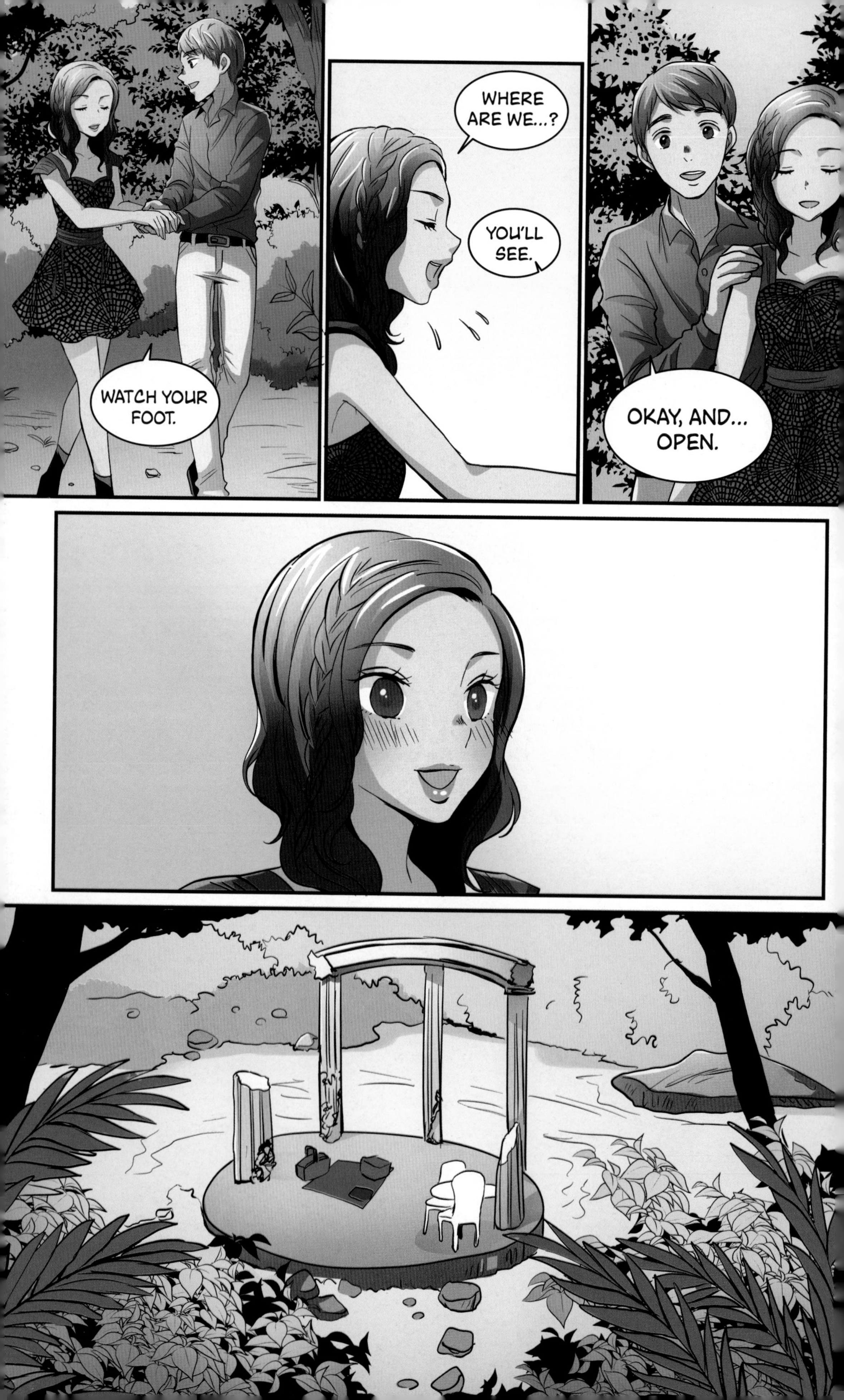
WATCH YOUR FOOT.
WHERE ARE WE...?
YOU'LL SEE.
OKAY, AND... OPEN.

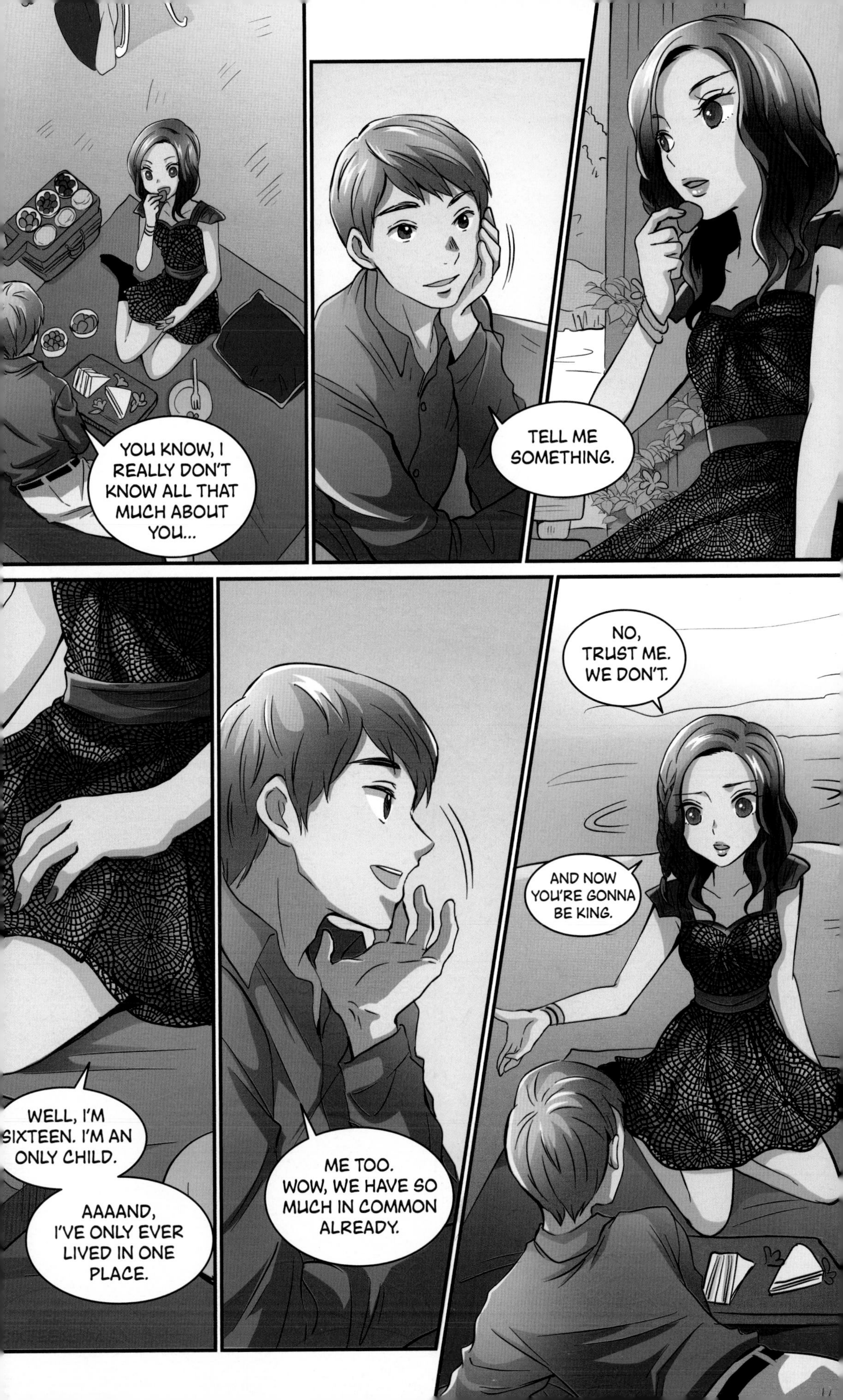
YOU KNOW, I REALLY DON'T KNOW ALL THAT MUCH ABOUT YOU...
TELL ME SOMETHING.
WELL, I'M SIXTEEN. I'M AN ONLY CHILD.
AAAAND, I'VE ONLY EVER LIVED IN ONE PLACE.
ME TOO. WOW, WE HAVE SO MUCH IN COMMON ALREADY.
NO, TRUST ME. WE DON'T.
AND NOW YOU'RE GONNA BE KING.

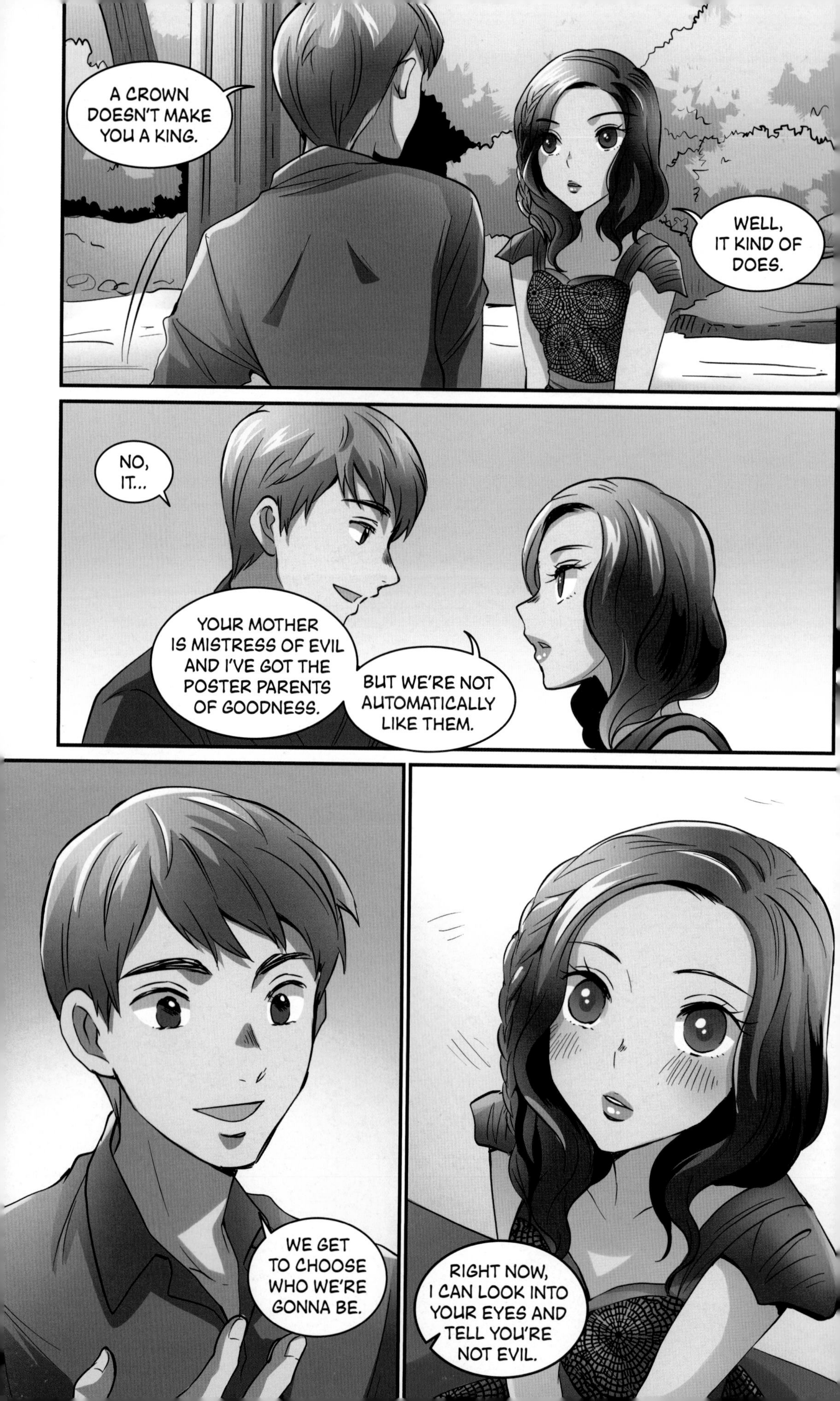
A CROWN DOESN'T MAKE YOU A KING.
WELL, IT KIND OF DOES.
NO, IT...
YOUR MOTHER IS MISTRESS OF EVIL AND I'VE GOT THE POSTER PARENTS OF GOODNESS.
BUT WE'RE NOT AUTOMATICALLY LIKE THEM.
WE GET TO CHOOSE WHO WE'RE GONNA BE.
RIGHT NOW, I CAN LOOK INTO YOUR EYES AND TELL YOU'RE NOT EVIL.

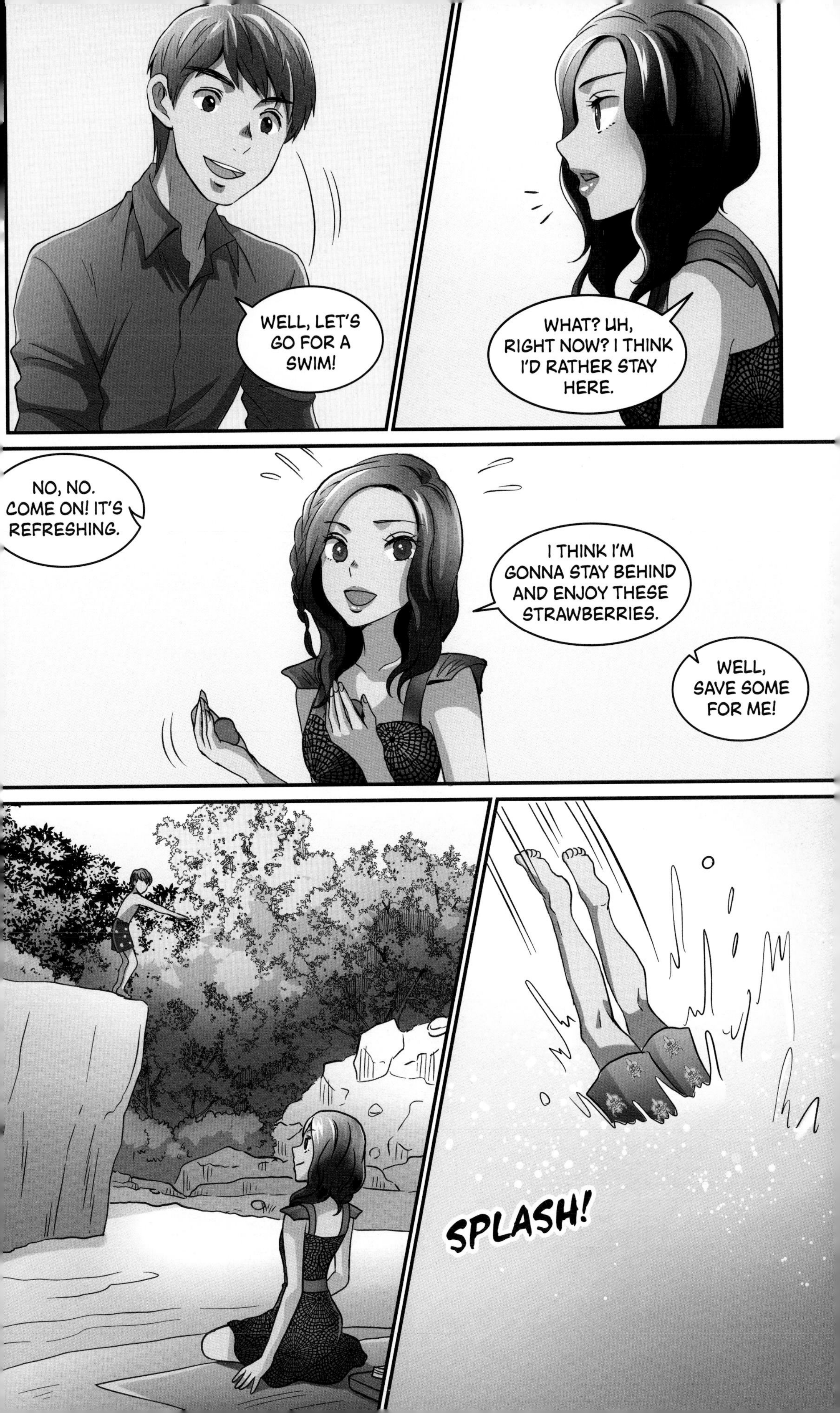
WELL, LET'S GO FOR A SWIM!
WHAT? UH, RIGHT NOW? I THINK I'D RATHER STAY HERE.
NO, NO. COME ON! IT'S REFRESHING.
I THINK I'M GONNA STAY BEHIND AND ENJOY THESE STRAWBERRIES.
WELL, SAVE SOME FOR ME!
SPLASH!

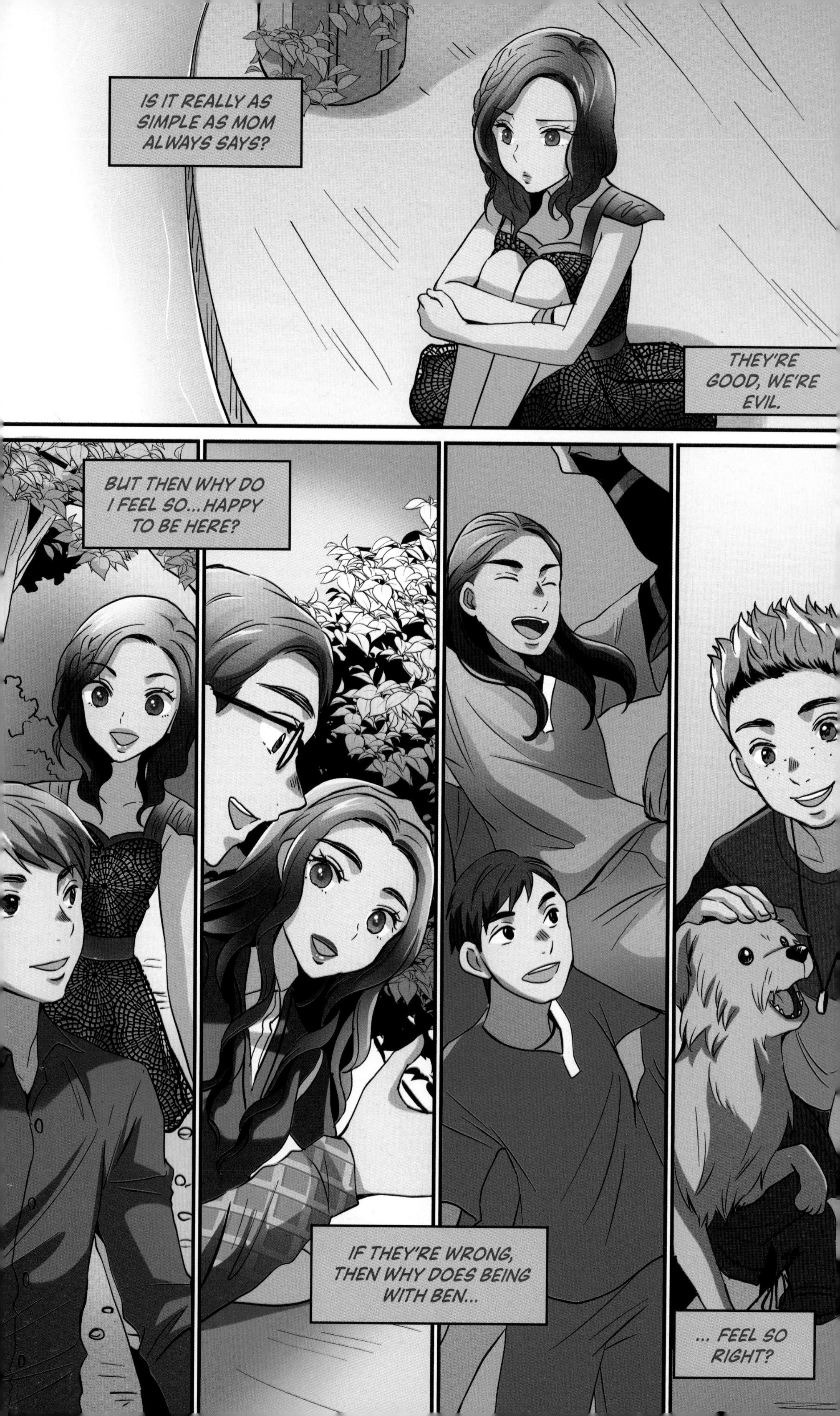
IS IT REALLY AS SIMPLE AS MOM ALWAYS SAYS?
THEY'RE GOOD, WE'RE EVIL.
BUT THEN WHY DO I FEEL SO...HAPPY TO BE HERE?
IF THEY'RE WRONG, THEN WHY DOES BEING WITH BEN...
... FEEL SO RIGHT?

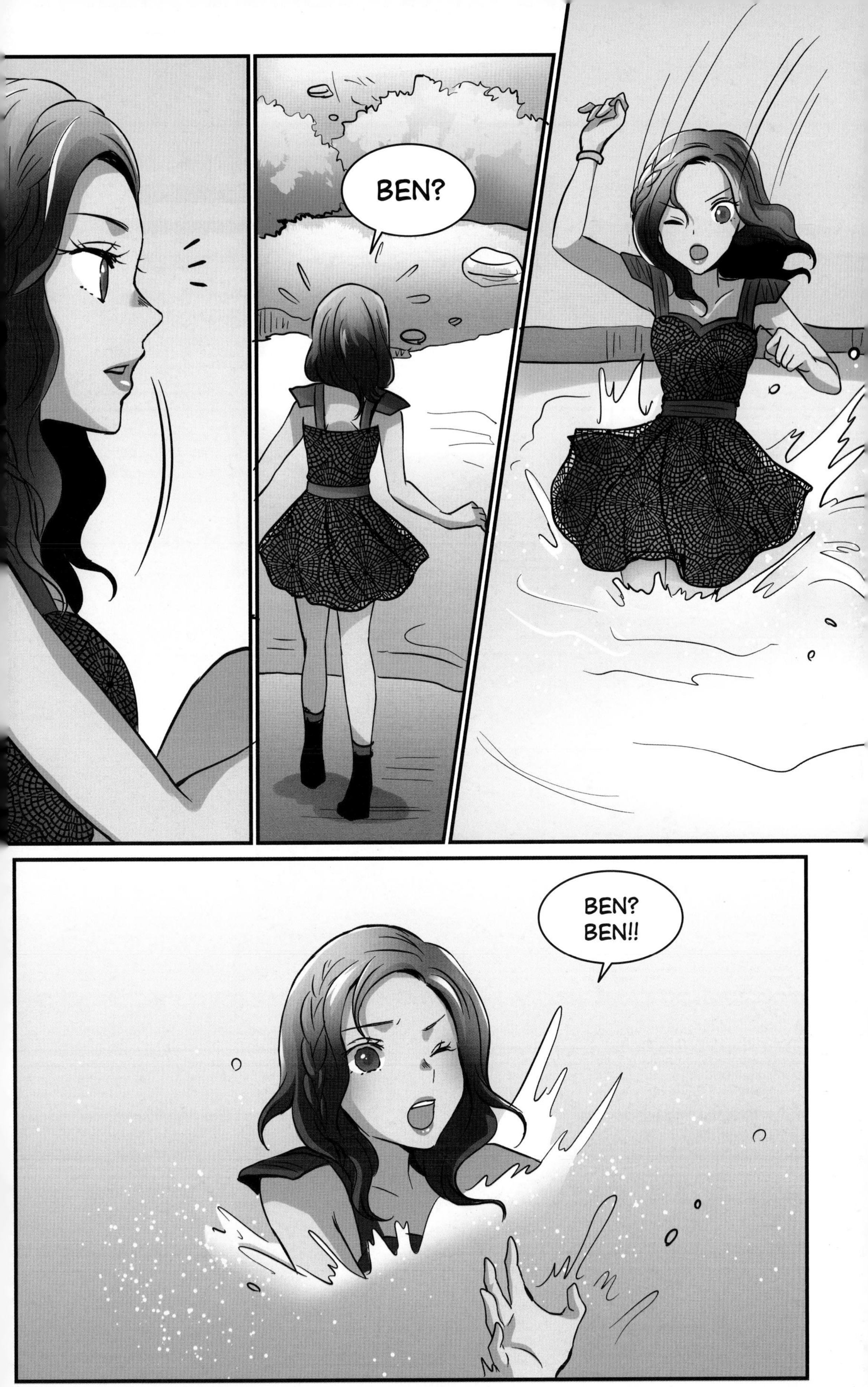
BEN?
BEN?
BEN!!

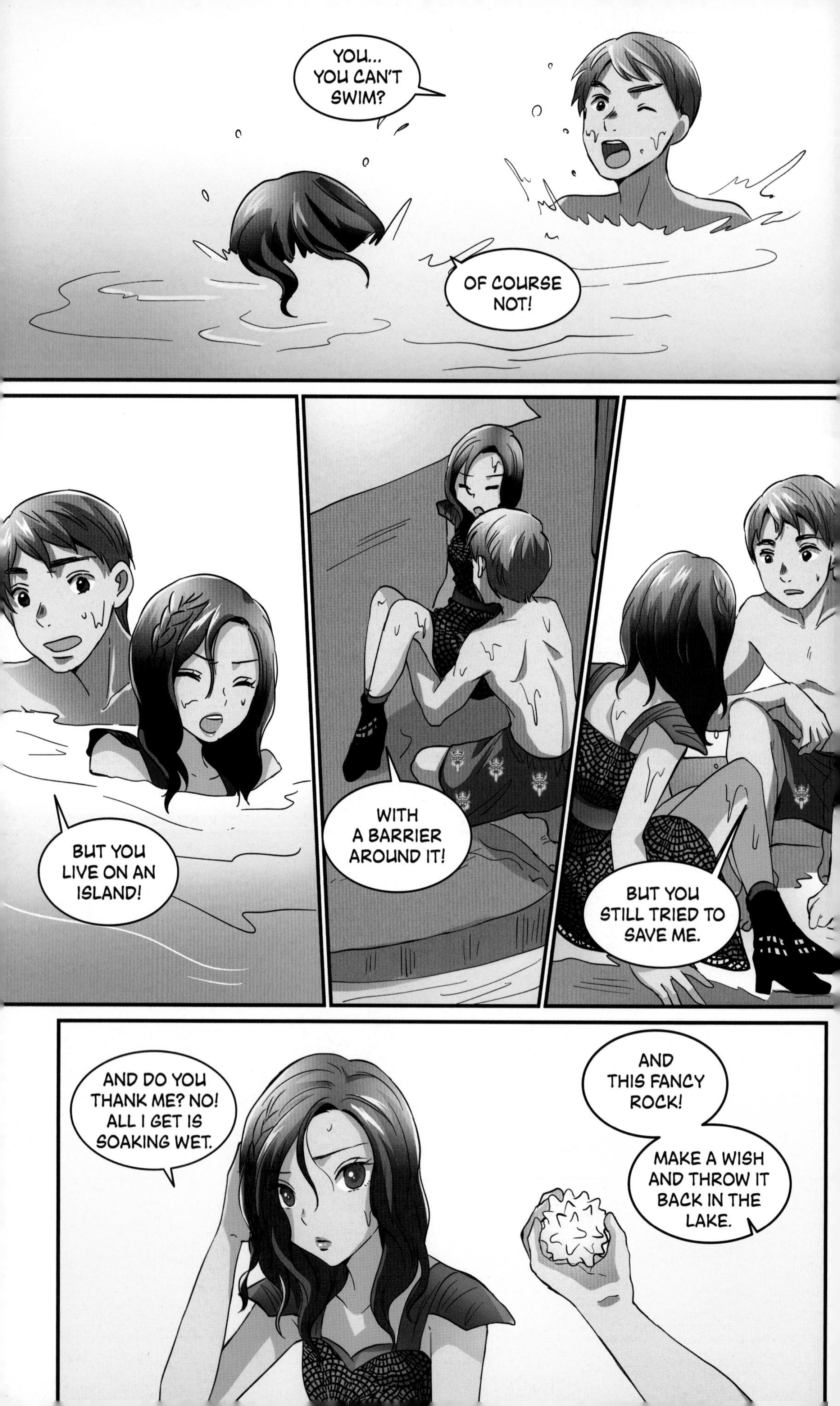
YOU... YOU CAN'T SWIM?
OF COURSE NOT!
BUT YOU LIVE ON AN ISLAND!
WITH A BARRIER AROUND IT!
BUT YOU STILL TRIED TO SAVE ME.
AND DO YOU THANK ME? NO! ALL I GET IS SOAKING WET.
AND THIS FANCY ROCK!
MAKE A WISH AND THROW IT BACK IN THE LAKE.

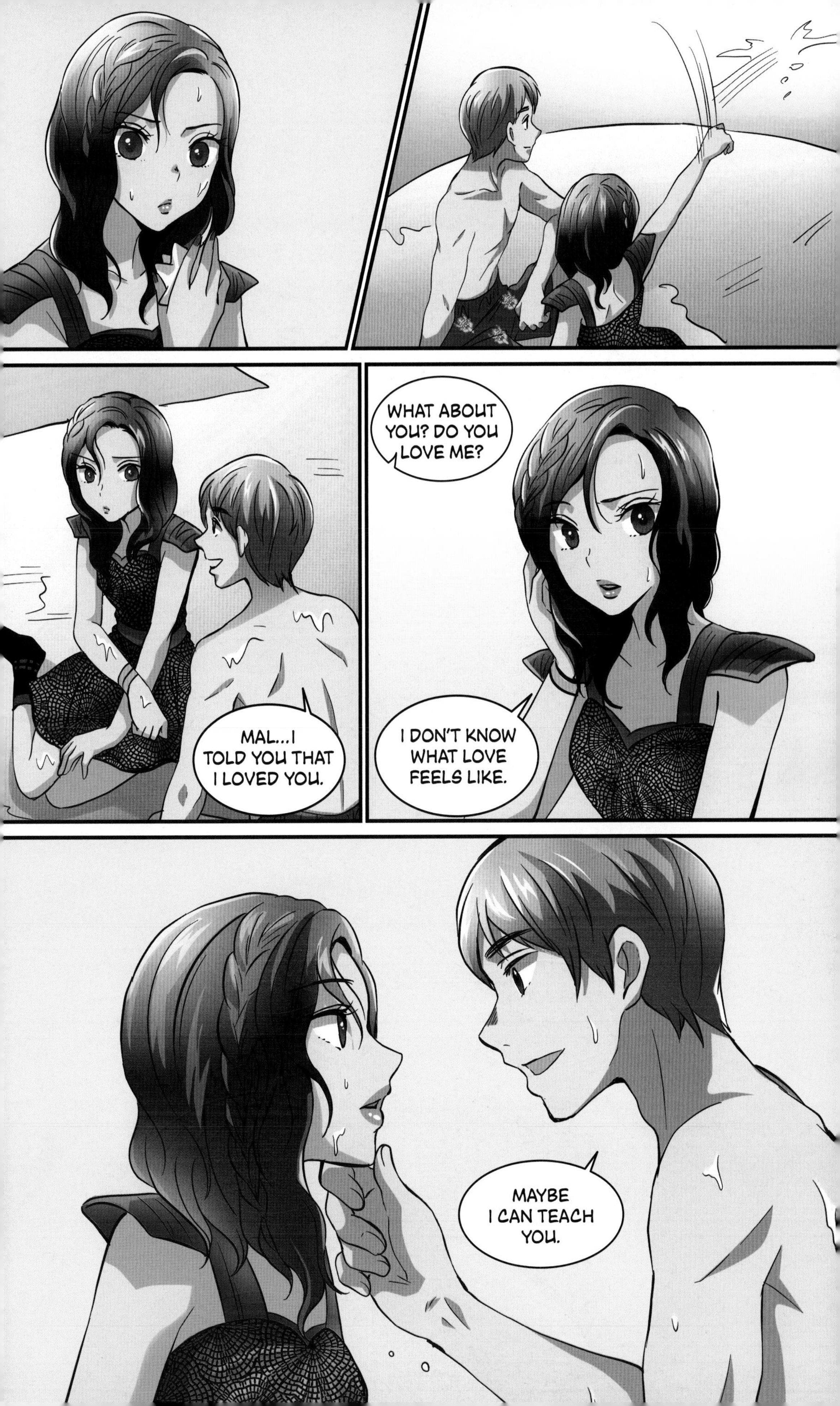
MAL...I TOLD YOU THAT I LOVED YOU.
WHAT ABOUT YOU? DO YOU LOVE ME?
I DON'T KNOW WHAT LOVE FEELS LIKE.
MAYBE I CAN TEACH YOU.

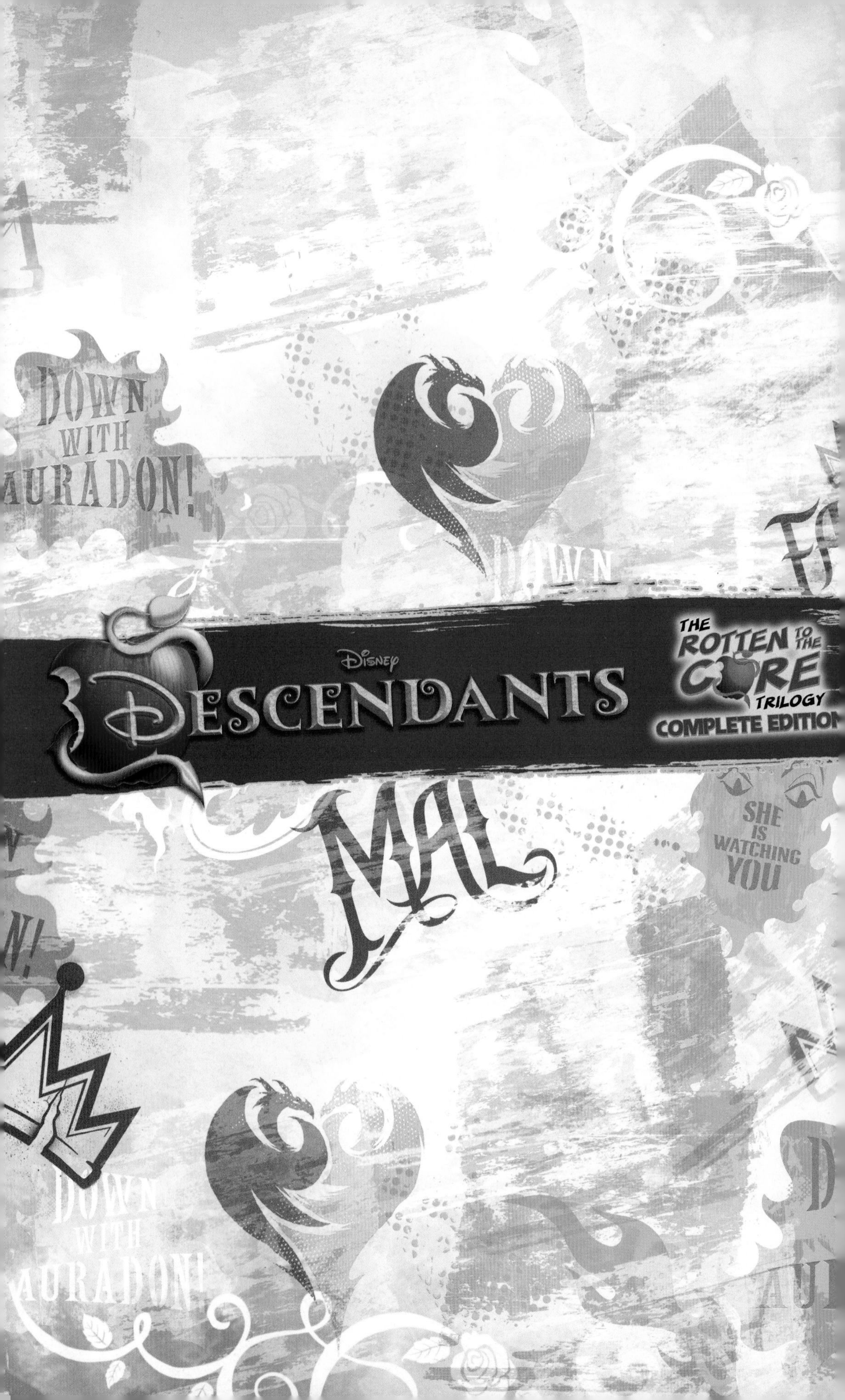
DOWN WITH AURADON!
DOWN
DISNEY DESCENDANTS
THE ROTTEN TO THE CORE TRILOGY
COMPLETE EDITION
MAL
SHE IS WATCHING YOU
DOWN WITH AURADON!

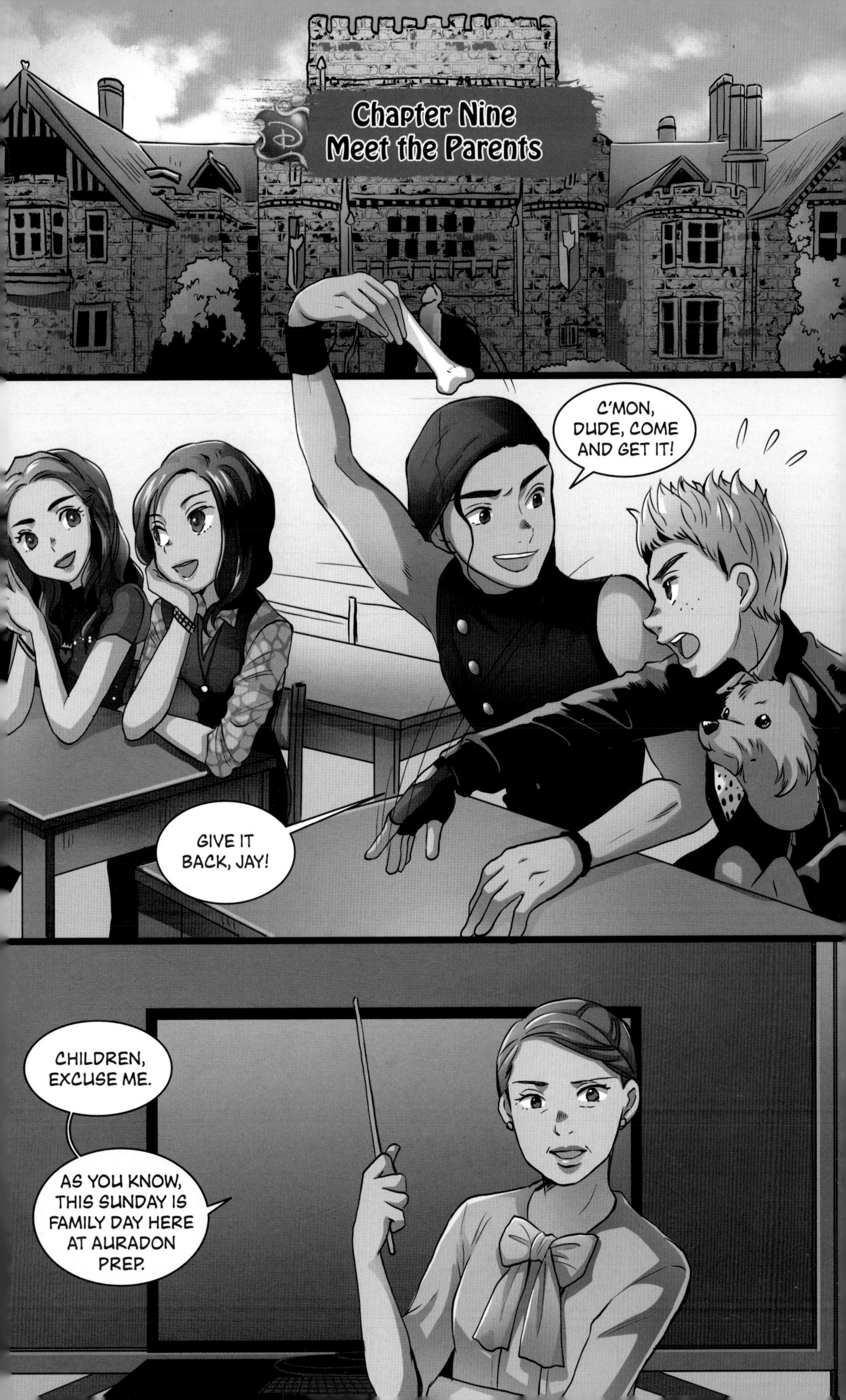
Chapter Nine
Meet the Parents
C'MON, DUDE, COME AND GET IT!
GIVE IT BACK, JAY!
CHILDREN, EXCUSE ME.
AS YOU KNOW, THIS SUNDAY IS FAMILY DAY HERE AT AURADON PREP.

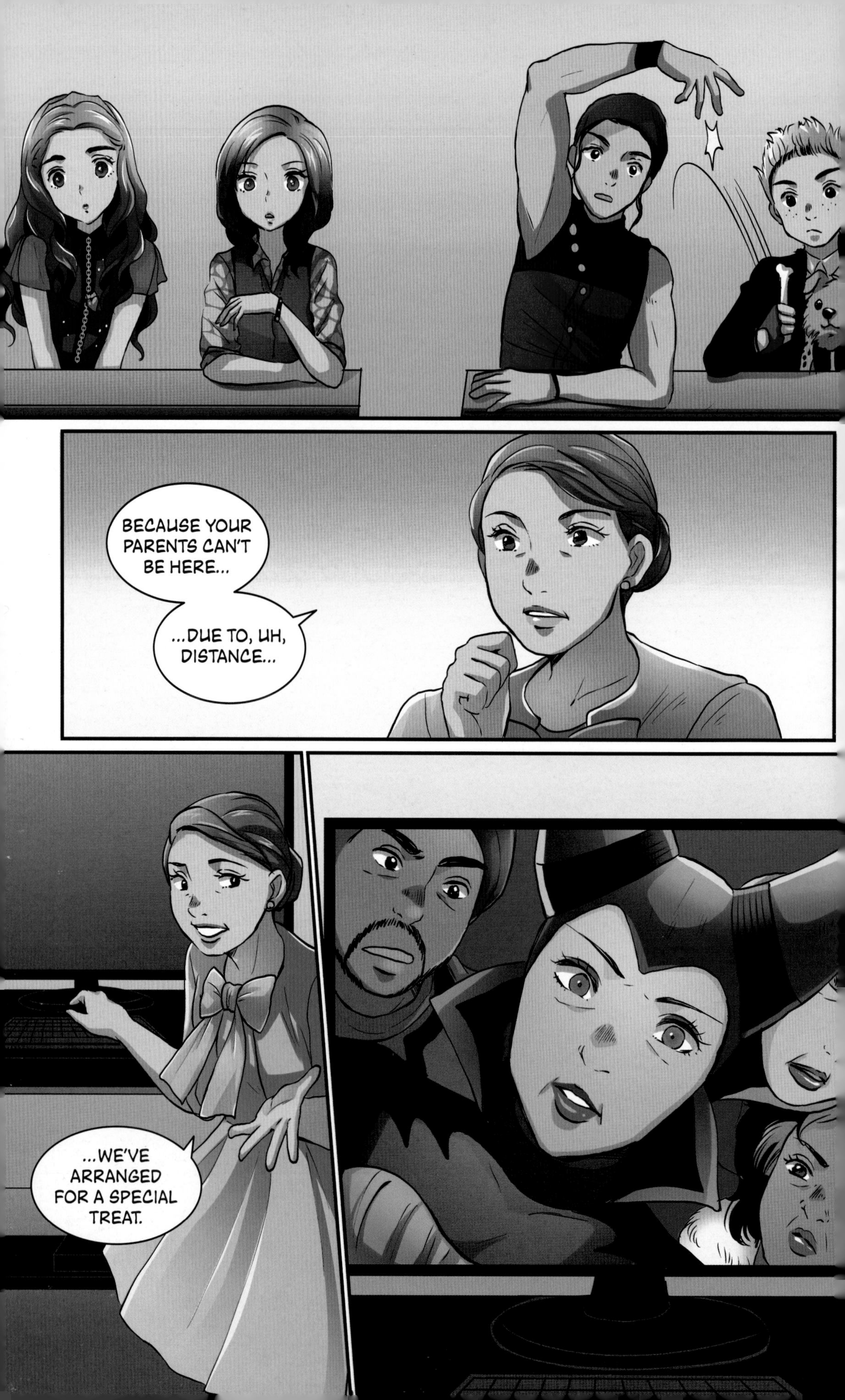
BECAUSE YOUR PARENTS CAN'T BE HERE...
...DUE TO, UH, DISTANCE...
...WE'VE ARRANGED FOR A SPECIAL TREAT.

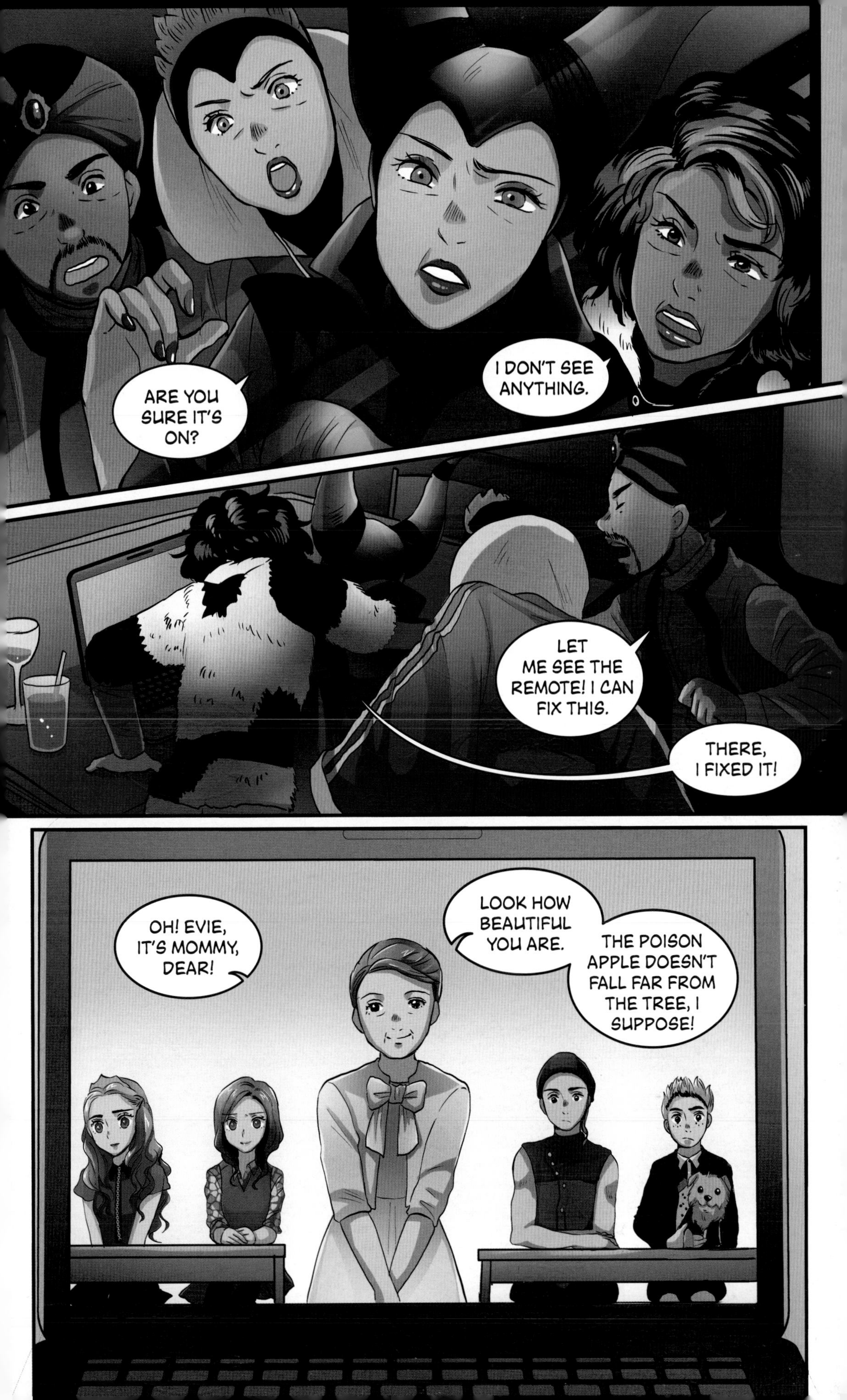
ARE YOU SURE IT'S ON?
I DON'T SEE ANYTHING.
LET ME SEE THE REMOTE! I CAN FIX THIS.
THERE, I FIXED IT!
OH! EVIE, IT'S MOMMY, DEAR!
LOOK HOW BEAUTIFUL YOU ARE.
THE POISON APPLE DOESN'T FALL FAR FROM THE TREE, I SUPPOSE!

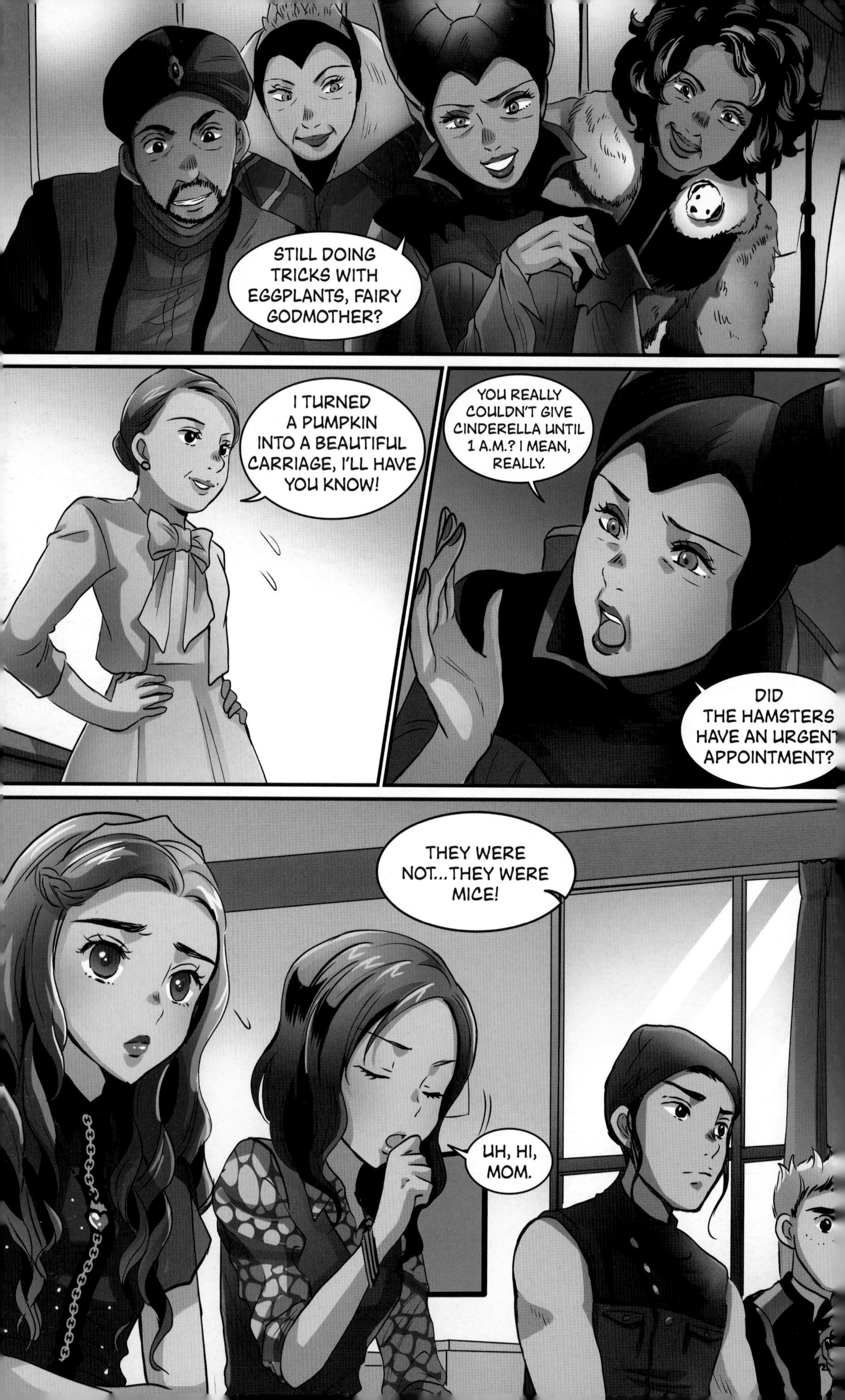
STILL DOING TRICKS WITH EGGPLANTS, FAIRY GODMOTHER?
I TURNED A PUMPKIN INTO A BEAUTIFUL CARRIAGE, I'LL HAVE YOU KNOW!
YOU REALLY COULDN'T GIVE CINDERELLA UNTIL 1 A.M.? I MEAN, REALLY.
DID THE HAMSTERS HAVE AN URGENT APPOINTMENT?
THEY WERE NOT...THEY WERE MICE!
UH, HI, MOM.

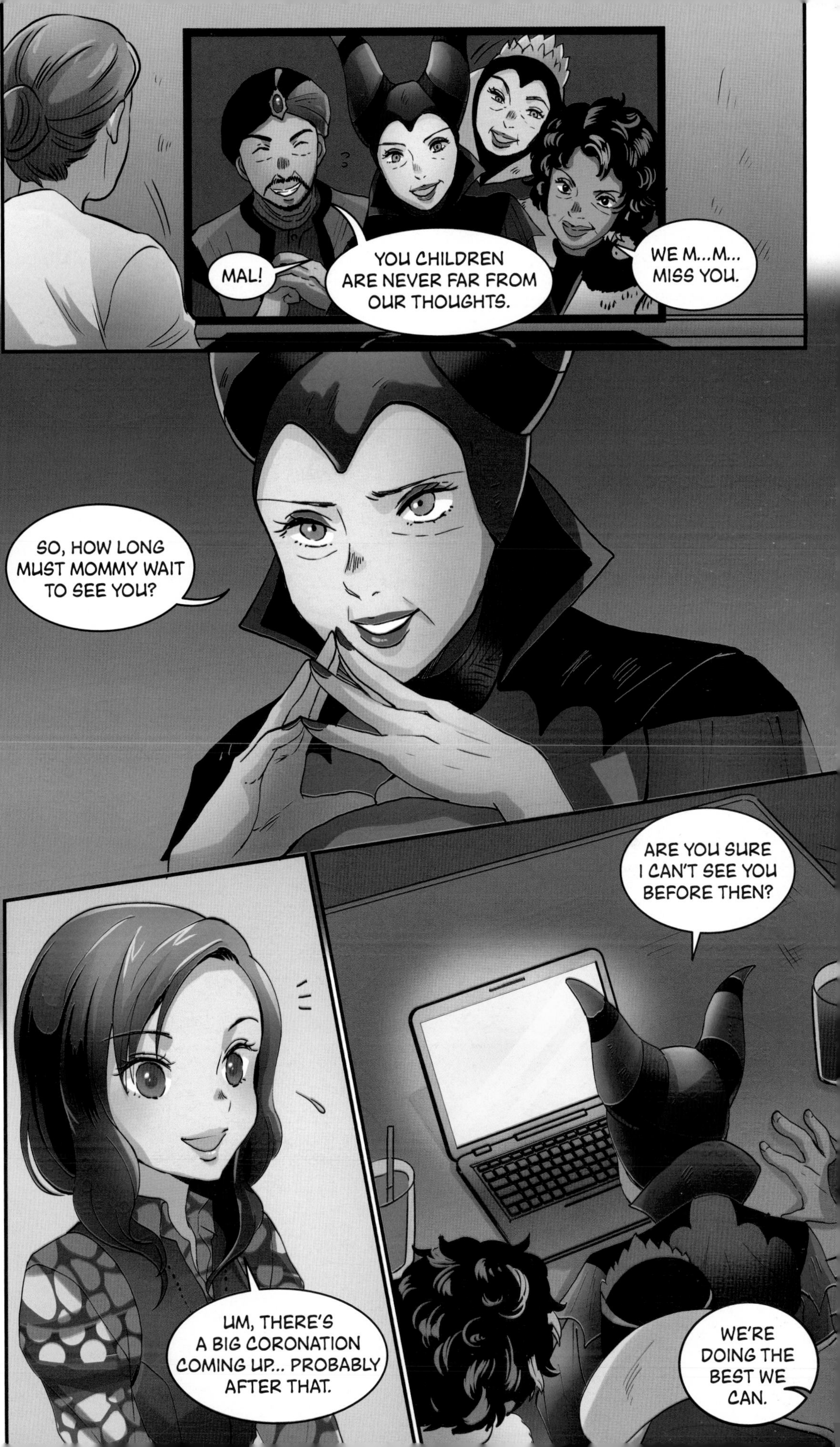
MAL!
YOU CHILDREN ARE NEVER FAR FROM OUR THOUGHTS.
WE M...M... MISS YOU.
SO, HOW LONG MUST MOMMY WAIT TO SEE YOU?
ARE YOU SURE I CAN'T SEE YOU BEFORE THEN?
UM, THERE'S A BIG CORONATION COMING UP... PROBABLY AFTER THAT.
WE'RE DOING THE BEST WE CAN.

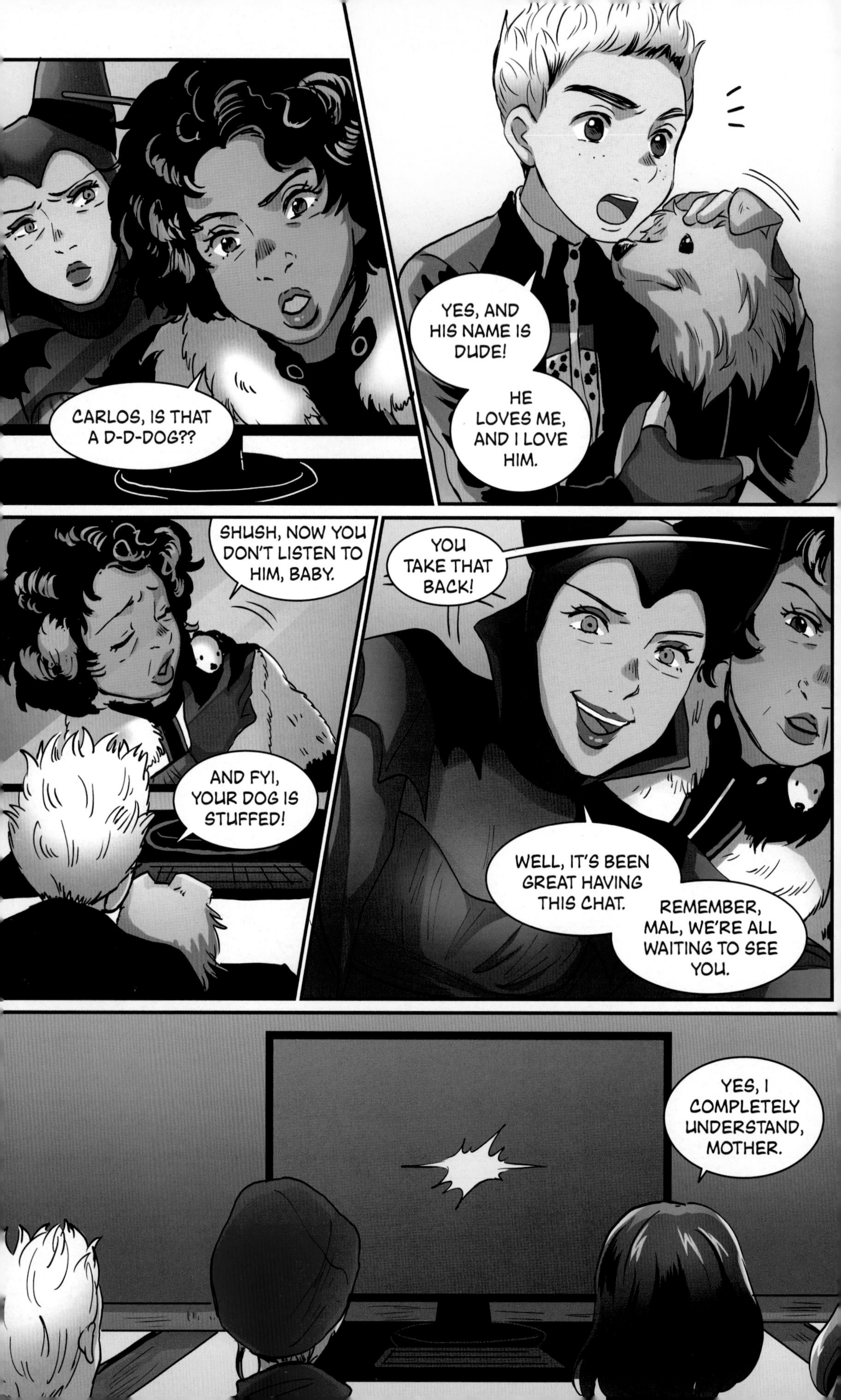
CARLOS, IS THAT A D-D-DOG??
YES, AND HIS NAME IS DUDE!
HE LOVES ME, AND I LOVE HIM.
SHUSH, NOW YOU DON'T LISTEN TO HIM, BABY.
AND FYI, YOUR DOG IS STUFFED!
YOU TAKE THAT BACK!
WELL, IT'S BEEN GREAT HAVING THIS CHAT.
REMEMBER, MAL, WE'RE ALL WAITING TO SEE YOU.
YES, I COMPLETELY UNDERSTAND, MOTHER.

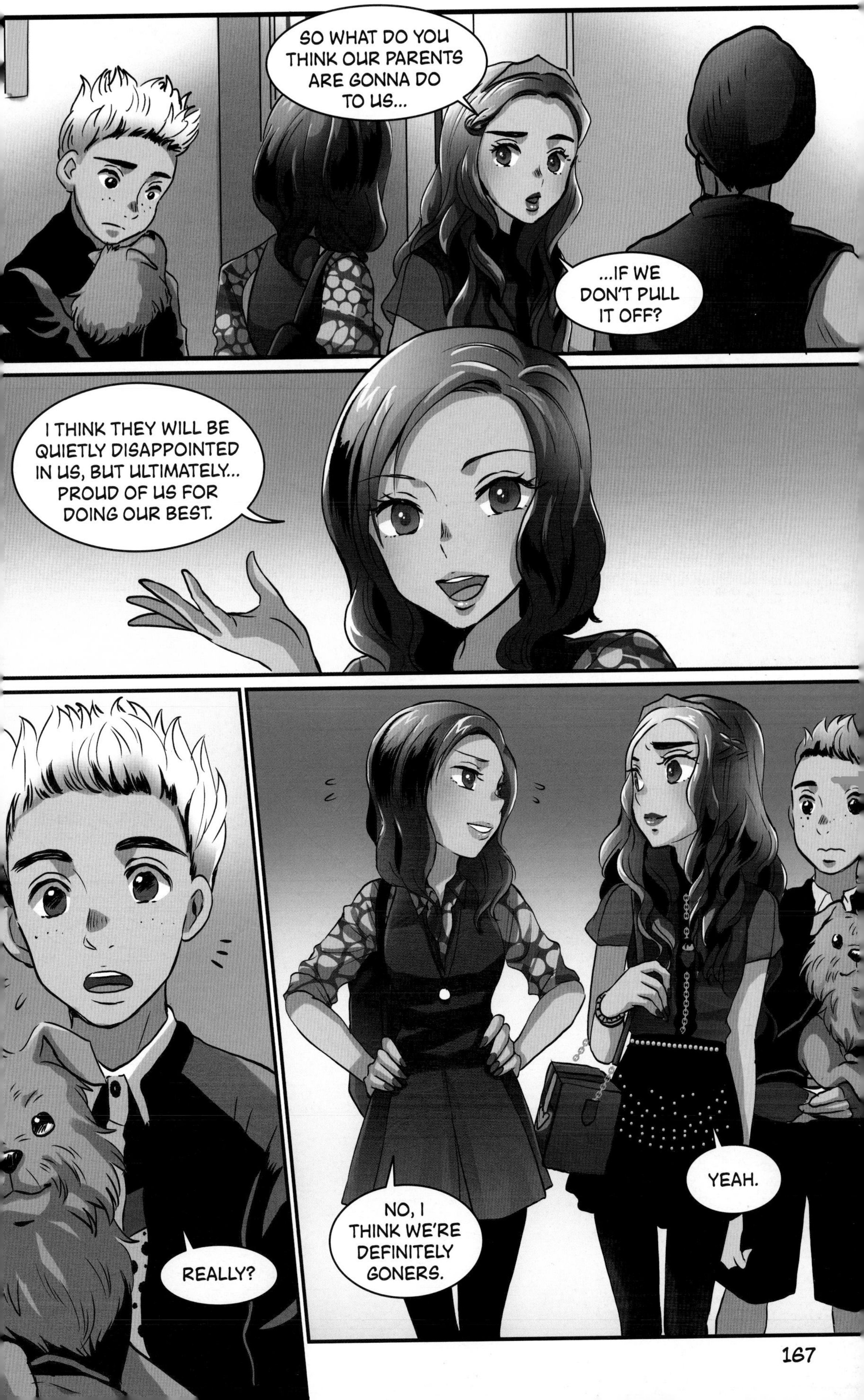

SO WHAT DO YOU THINK OUR PARENTS ARE GONNA DO TO US...
...IF WE DON'T PULL IT OFF?
I THINK THEY WILL BE QUIETLY DISAPPOINTED IN US, BUT ULTIMATELY... PROUD OF US FOR DOING OUR BEST.
REALLY?
NO, I THINK WE'RE DEFINITELY GONERS.
YEAH.

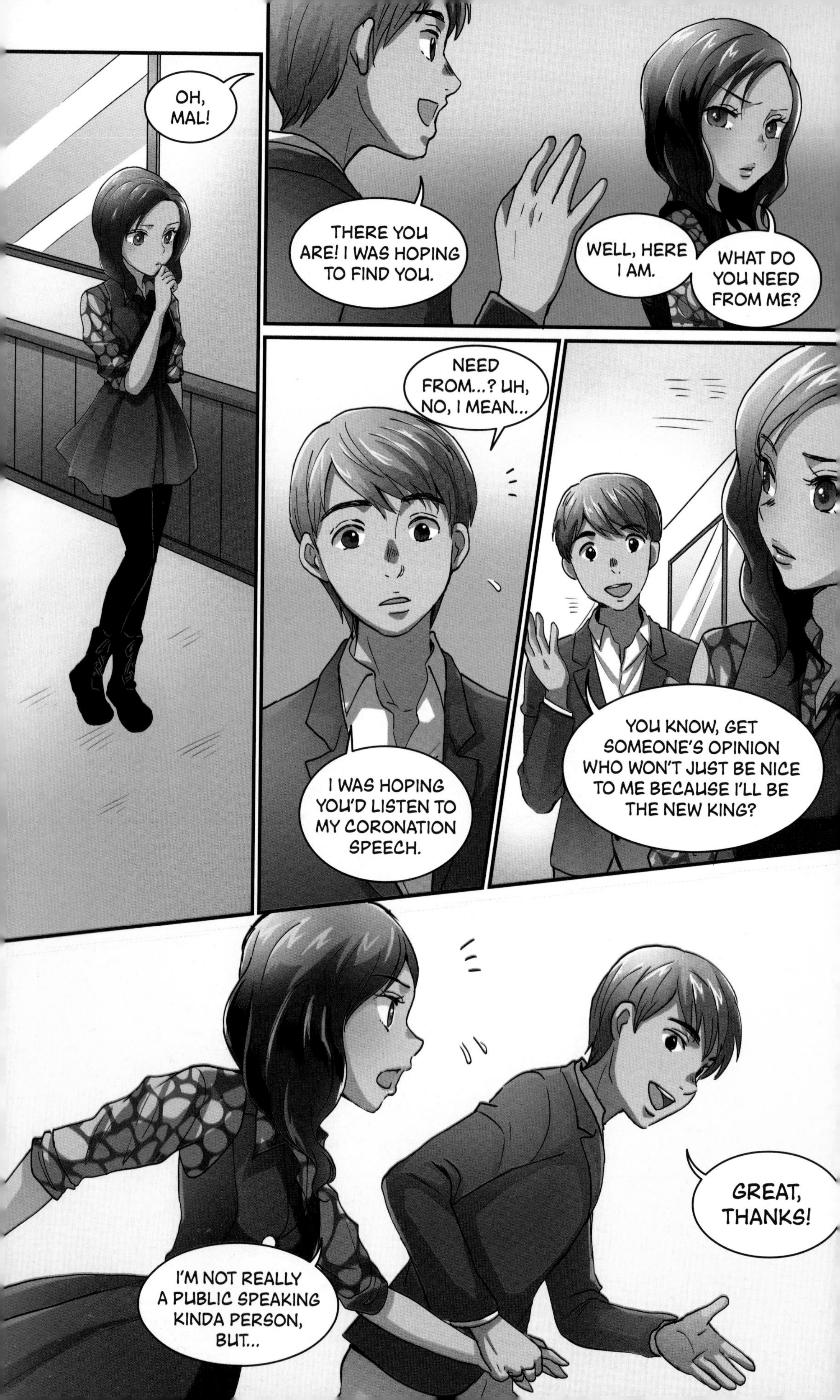
OH, MAL!
THERE YOU ARE! I WAS HOPING TO FIND YOU.
WELL, HERE I AM.
WHAT DO YOU NEED FROM ME?
NEED FROM...? UH, NO, I MEAN...
I WAS HOPING YOU'D LISTEN TO MY CORONATION SPEECH.
YOU KNOW, GET SOMEONE'S OPINION WHO WON'T JUST BE NICE TO ME BECAUSE I'LL BE THE NEW KING?
I'M NOT REALLY A PUBLIC SPEAKING KINDA PERSON, BUT...
GREAT, THANKS!

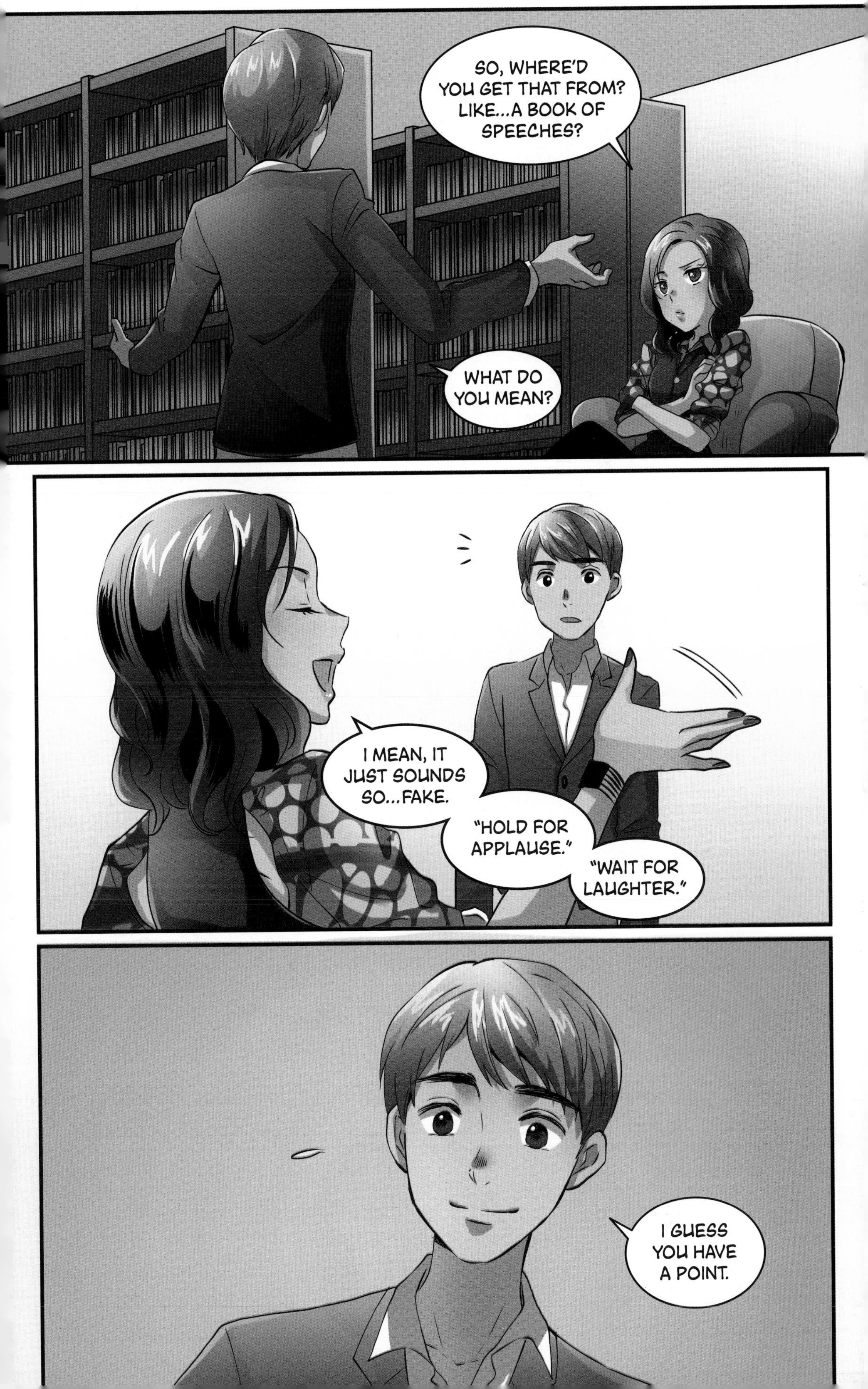
SO, WHERE'D YOU GET THAT FROM? LIKE...A BOOK OF SPEECHES?
WHAT DO YOU MEAN?
I MEAN, IT JUST SOUNDS SO...FAKE.
"HOLD FOR APPLAUSE."
"WAIT FOR LAUGHTER."
I GUESS YOU HAVE A POINT.

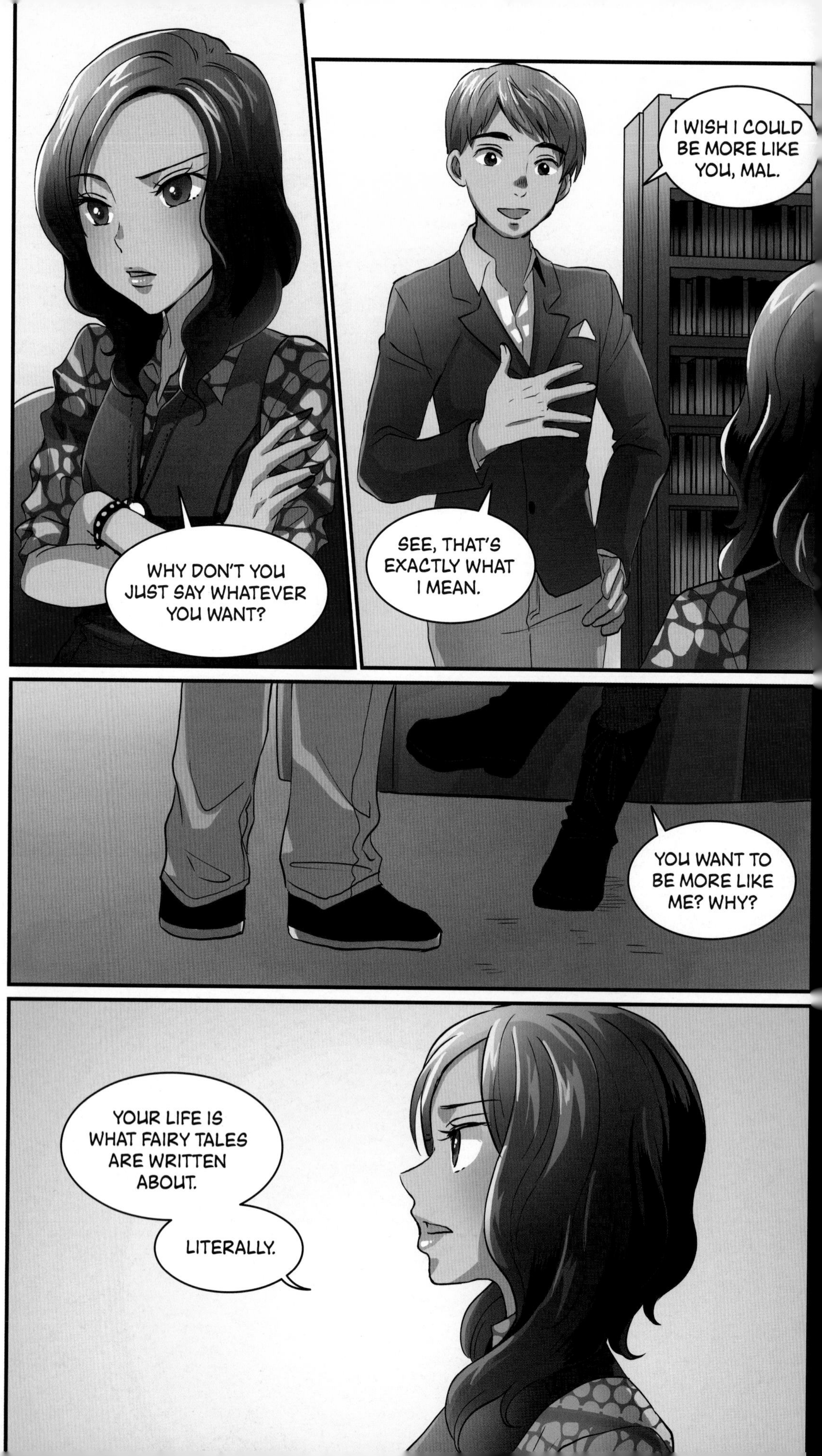
WHY DON'T YOU JUST SAY WHATEVER YOU WANT?
I WISH I COULD BE MORE LIKE YOU, MAL.
SEE, THAT'S EXACTLY WHAT I MEAN.
YOU WANT TO BE MORE LIKE ME? WHY?
YOUR LIFE IS WHAT FAIRY TALES ARE WRITTEN ABOUT.
LITERALLY.

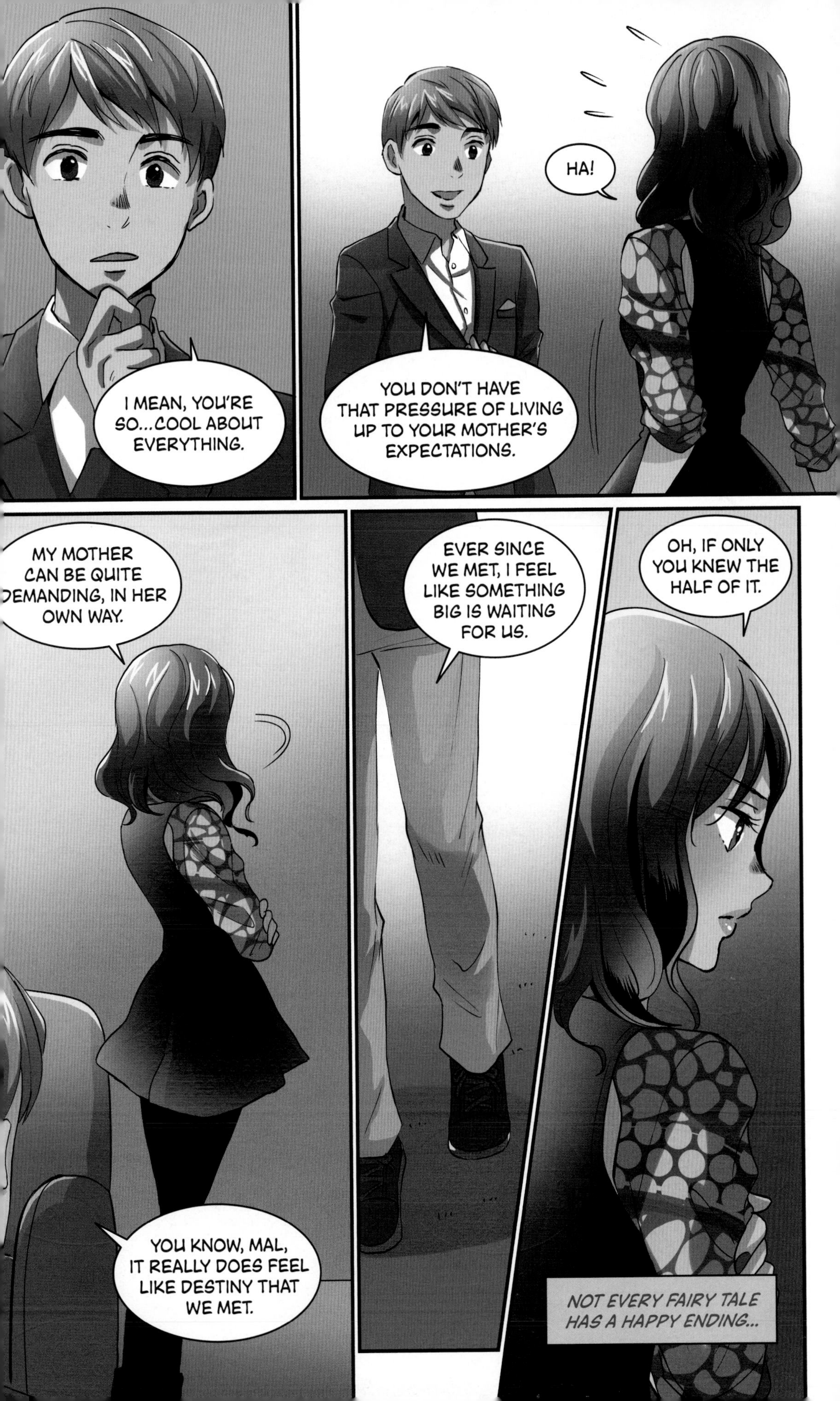
I MEAN, YOU'RE SO...COOL ABOUT EVERYTHING.
YOU DON'T HAVE THAT PRESSURE OF LIVING UP TO YOUR MOTHER'S EXPECTATIONS.
HA!
MY MOTHER CAN BE QUITE DEMANDING, IN HER OWN WAY.
YOU KNOW, MAL, IT REALLY DOES FEEL LIKE DESTINY THAT WE MET.
EVER SINCE WE MET, I FEEL LIKE SOMETHING BIG IS WAITING FOR US.
OH, IF ONLY YOU KNEW THE HALF OF IT.
NOT EVERY FAIRY TALE HAS A HAPPY ENDING...

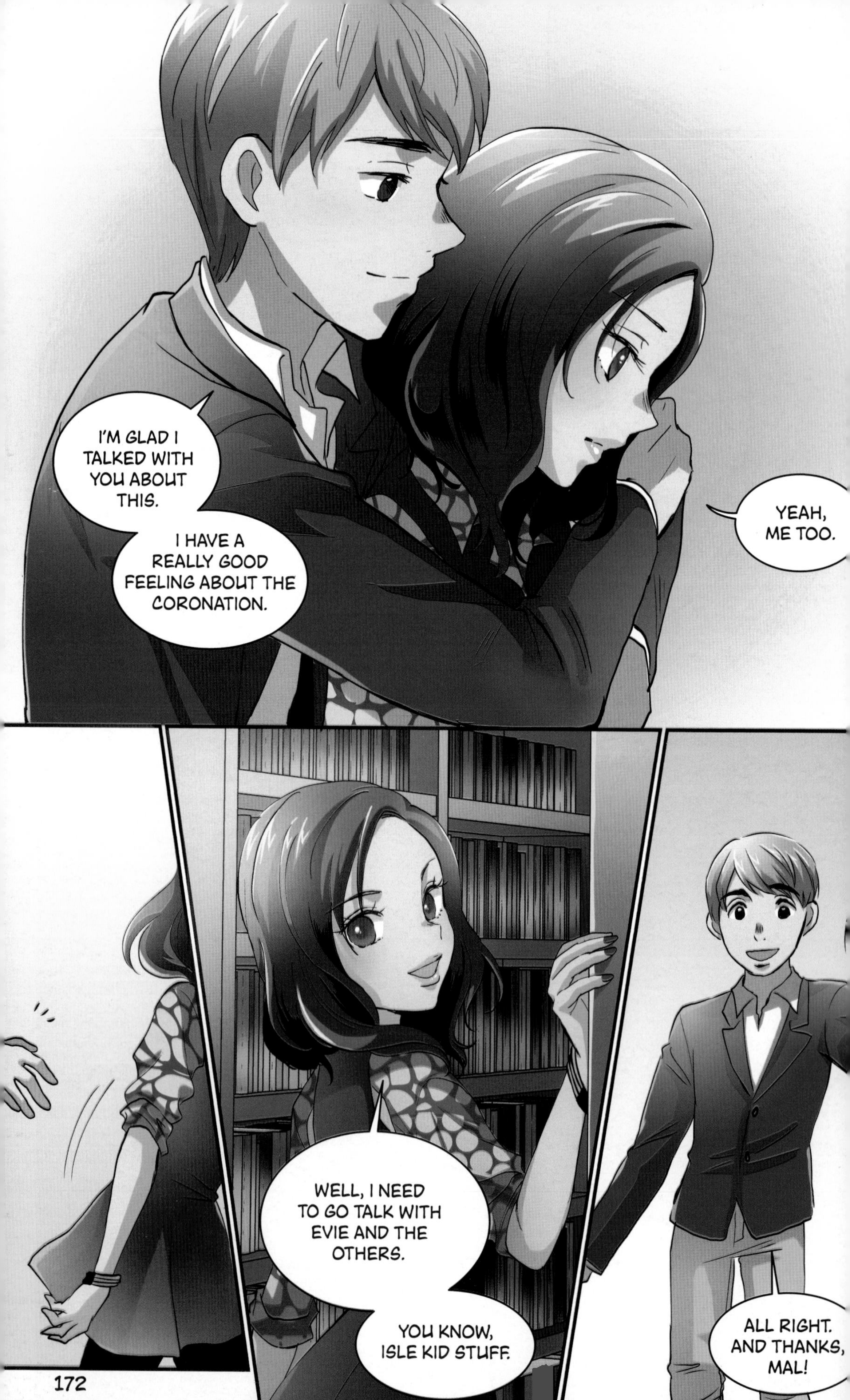
I'M GLAD I TALKED WITH YOU ABOUT THIS.
I HAVE A REALLY GOOD FEELING ABOUT THE CORONATION.
YEAH, ME TOO.
WELL, I NEED TO GO TALK WITH EVIE AND THE OTHERS.
YOU KNOW, ISLE KID STUFF.
ALL RIGHT. AND THANKS, MAL!

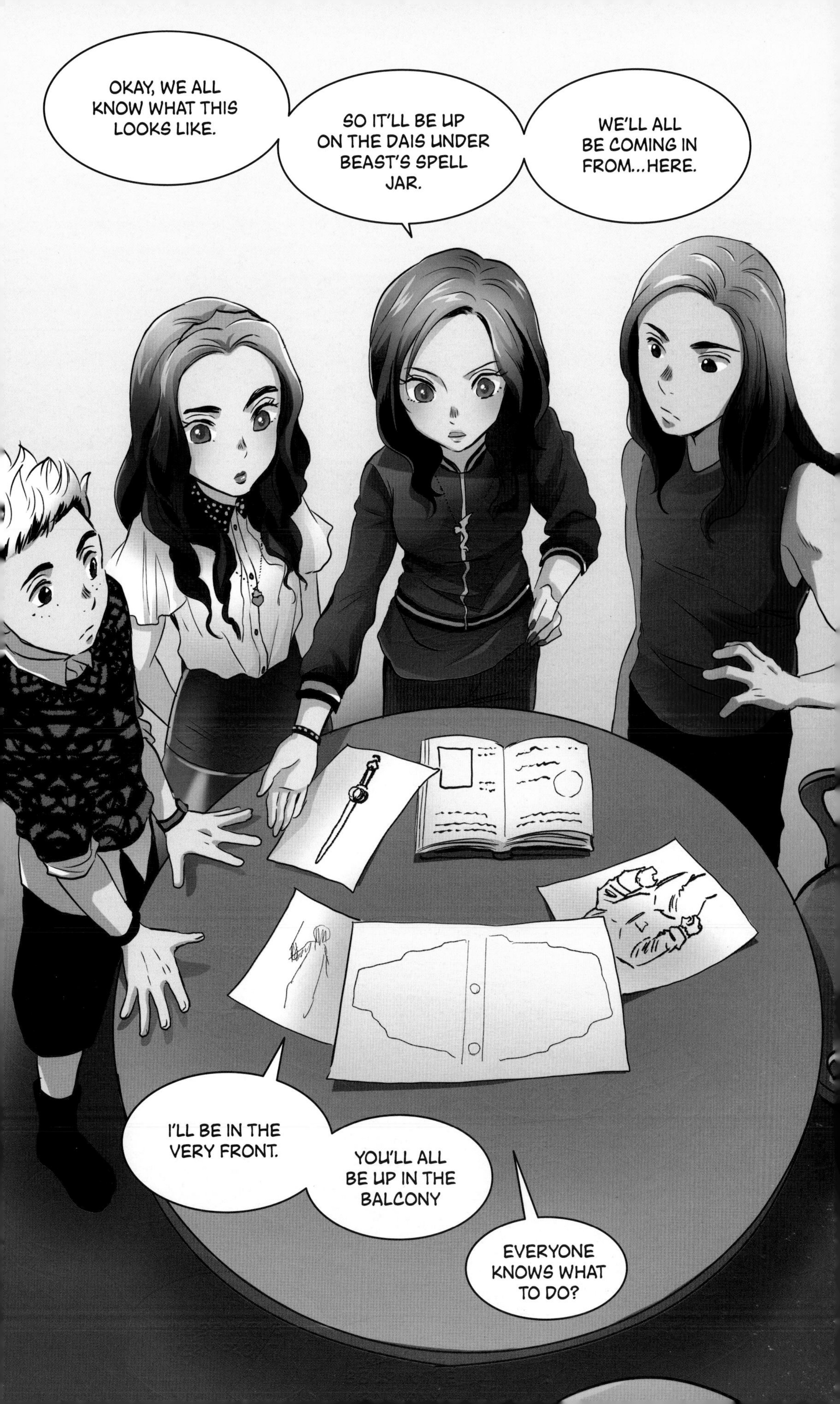
OKAY, WE ALL KNOW WHAT THIS LOOKS LIKE.
SO IT'LL BE UP ON THE DAIS UNDER BEAST'S SPELL JAR.
WE'LL ALL BE COMING IN FROM...HERE.
I'LL BE IN THE VERY FRONT.
YOU'LL ALL BE UP IN THE BALCONY
EVERYONE KNOWS WHAT TO DO?

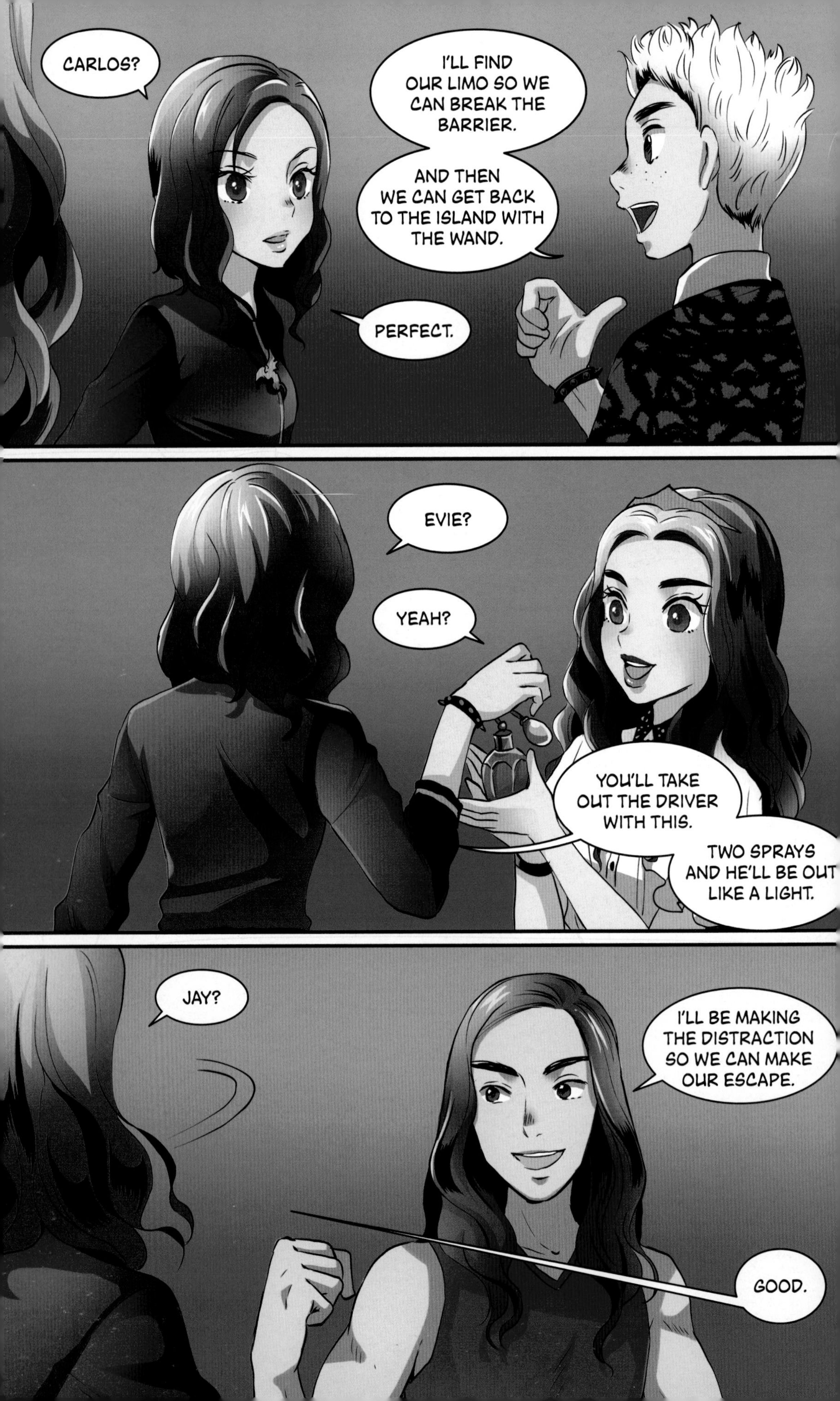
CARLOS?
I'LL FIND OUR LIMO SO WE CAN BREAK THE BARRIER.
AND THEN WE CAN GET BACK TO THE ISLAND WITH THE WAND.
PERFECT.
EVIE?
YEAH?
YOU'LL TAKE OUT THE DRIVER WITH THIS.
TWO SPRAYS AND HE'LL BE OUT LIKE A LIGHT.
JAY?
I'LL BE MAKING THE DISTRACTION SO WE CAN MAKE OUR ESCAPE.
GOOD.

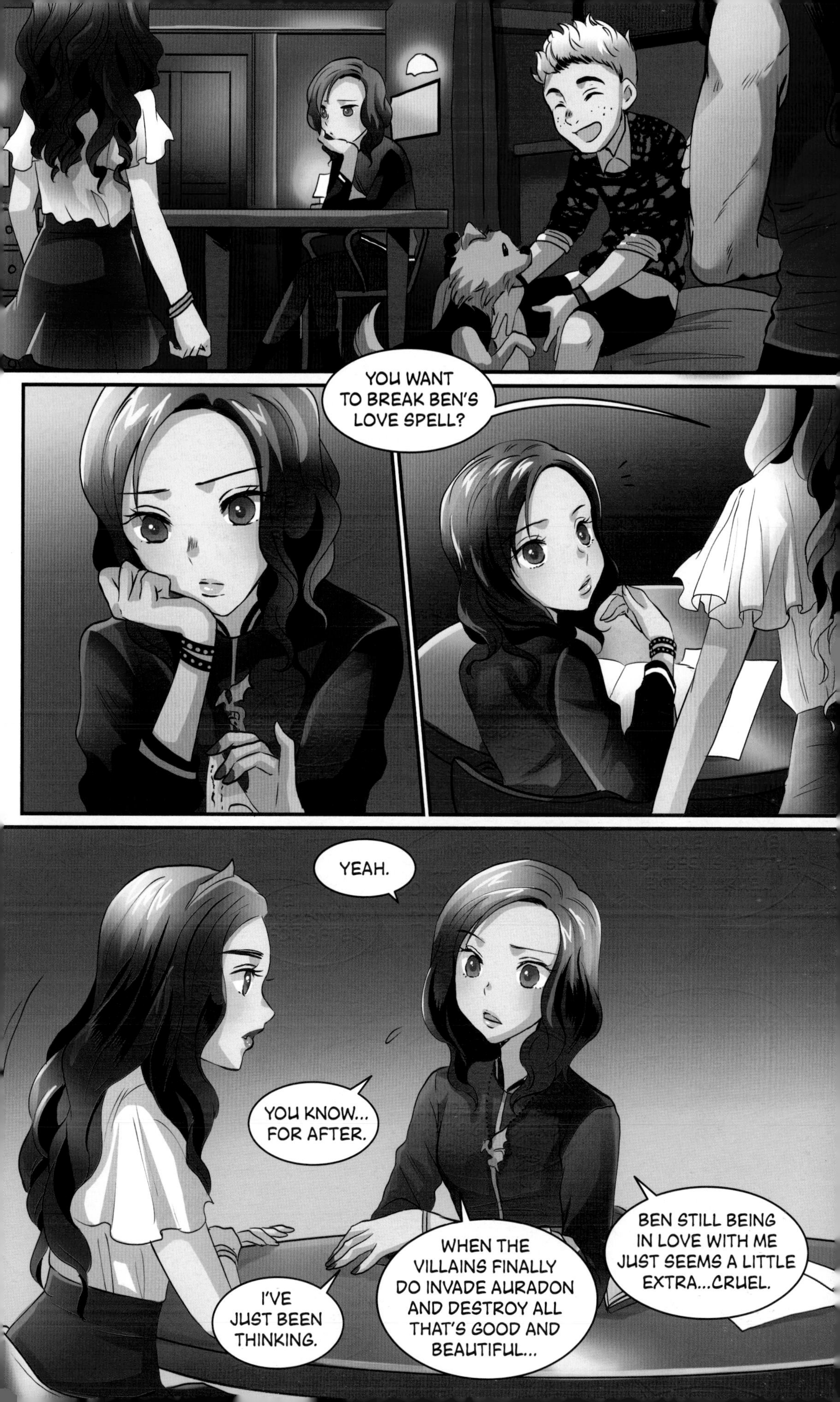
YOU WANT TO BREAK BEN'S LOVE SPELL?
YEAH.
YOU KNOW... FOR AFTER.
I'VE JUST BEEN THINKING.
WHEN THE VILLAINS FINALLY DO INVADE AURADON AND DESTROY ALL THAT'S GOOD AND BEAUTIFUL...
BEN STILL BEING IN LOVE WITH ME JUST SEEMS A LITTLE EXTRA...CRUEL.

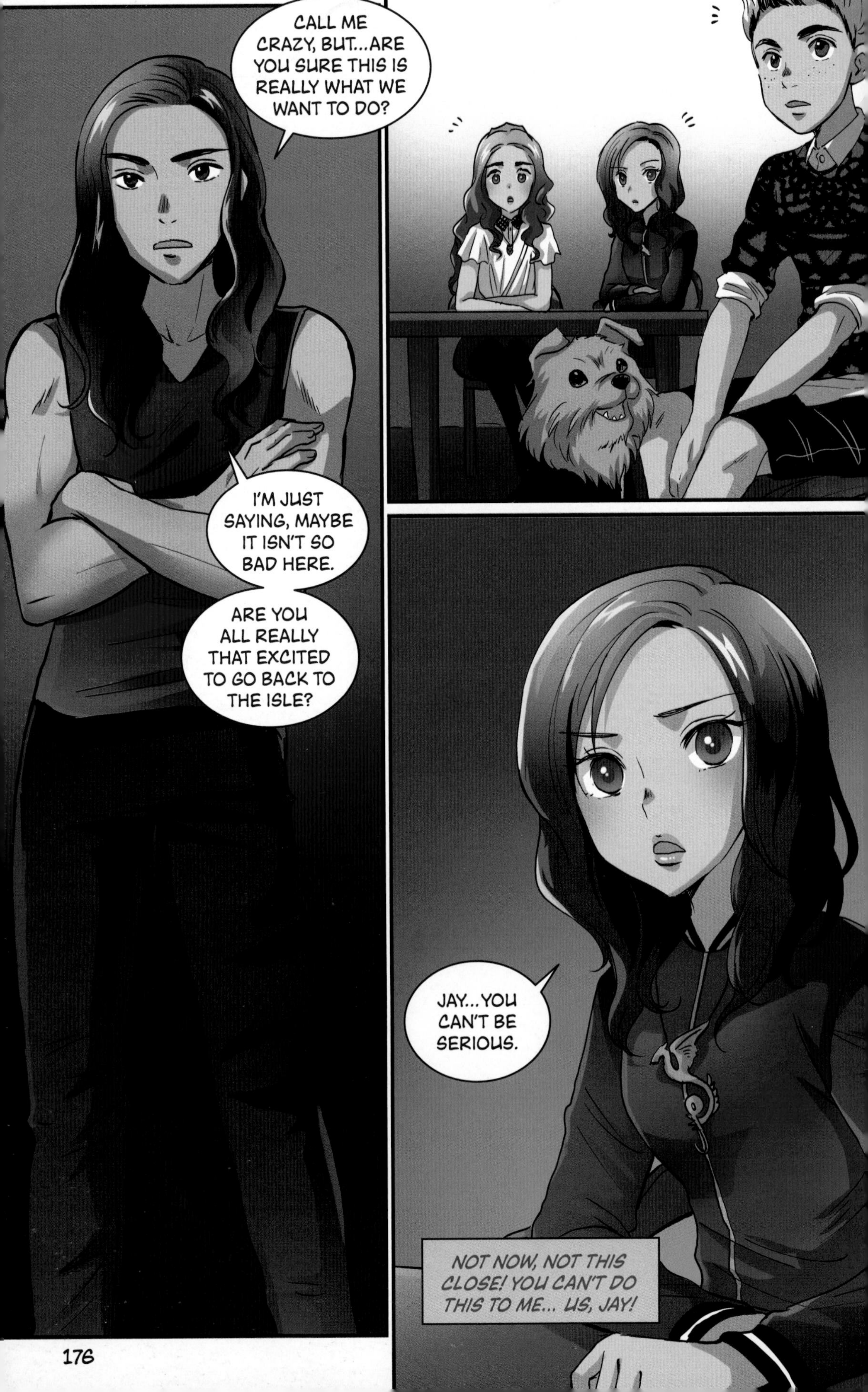
CALL ME CRAZY, BUT...ARE YOU SURE THIS IS REALLY WHAT WE WANT TO DO?
I'M JUST SAYING, MAYBE IT ISN'T SO BAD HERE.
ARE YOU ALL REALLY THAT EXCITED TO GO BACK TO THE ISLE?
JAY...YOU CAN'T BE SERIOUS.
NOT NOW, NOT THIS CLOSE! YOU CAN'T DO THIS TO ME... US, JAY!

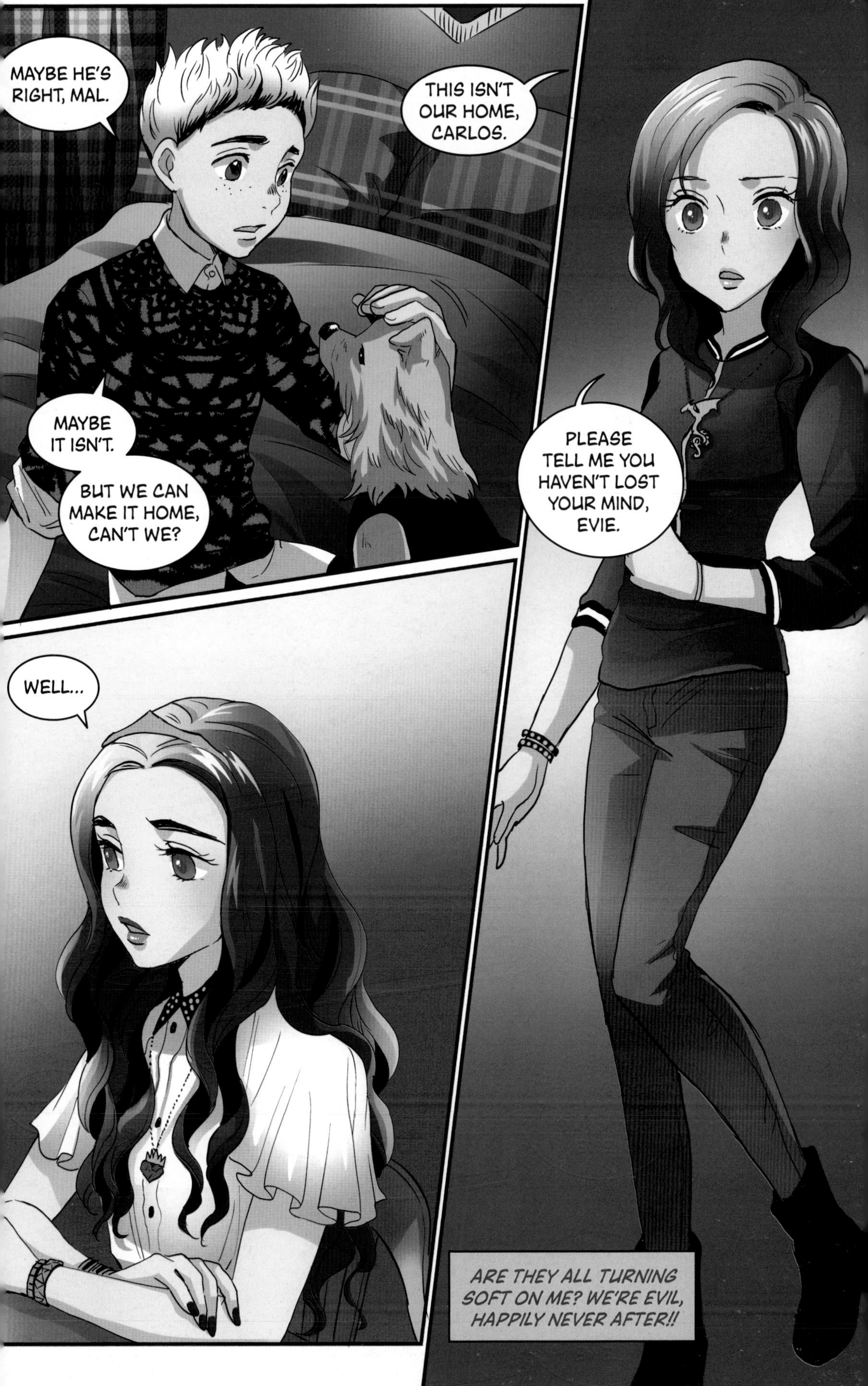
MAYBE HE'S RIGHT, MAL.
THIS ISN'T OUR HOME, CARLOS.
MAYBE IT ISN'T.
BUT WE CAN MAKE IT HOME, CAN'T WE?
PLEASE TELL ME YOU HAVEN'T LOST YOUR MIND, EVIE.
WELL...
ARE THEY ALL TURNING SOFT ON ME? WE'RE EVIL, HAPPILY NEVER AFTER!!

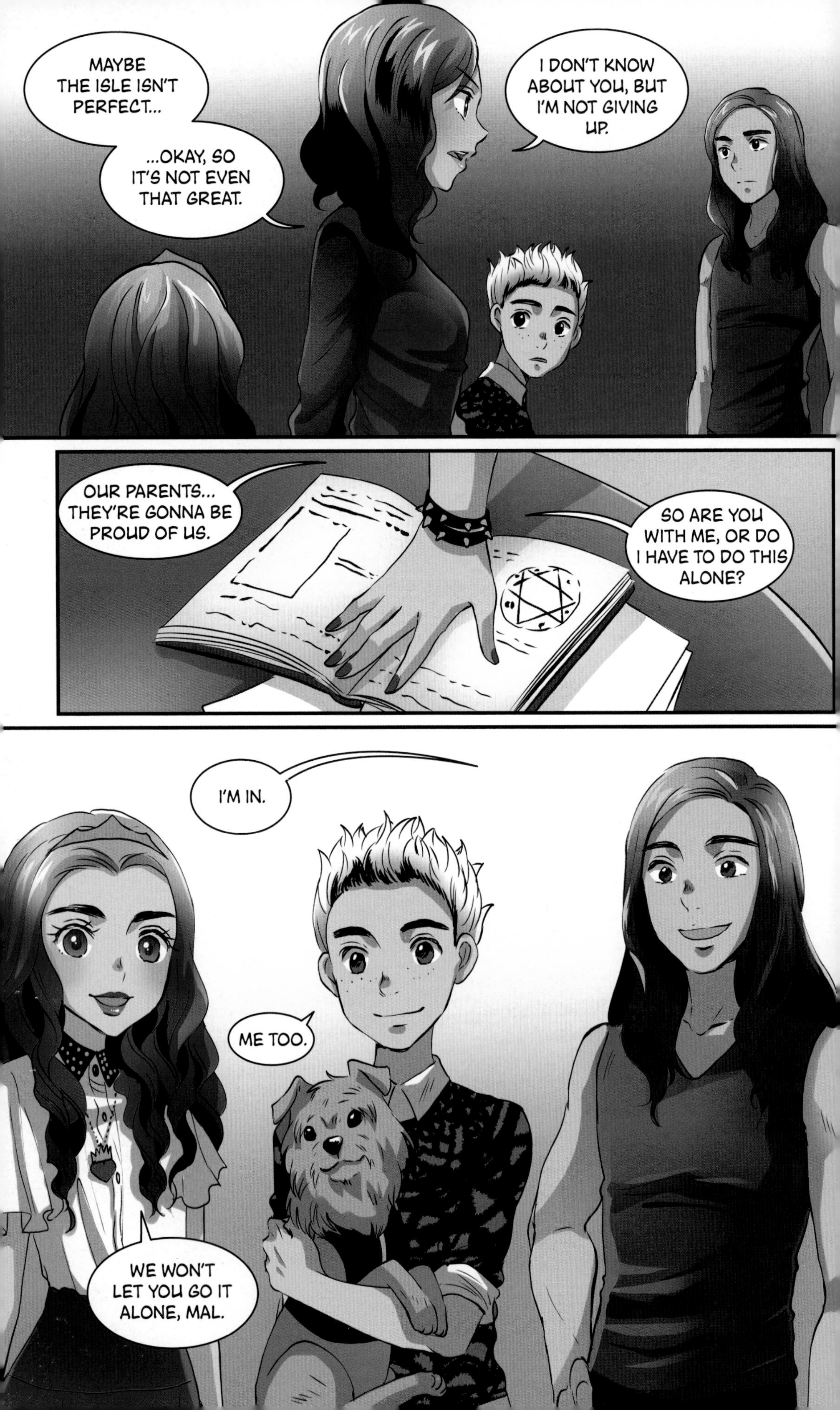
MAYBE THE ISLE ISN'T PERFECT...
...OKAY, SO IT'S NOT EVEN THAT GREAT.
I DON'T KNOW ABOUT YOU, BUT I'M NOT GIVING UP.
OUR PARENTS... THEY'RE GONNA BE PROUD OF US.
SO ARE YOU WITH ME, OR DO I HAVE TO DO THIS ALONE?
I'M IN.
ME TOO.
WE WON'T LET YOU GO IT ALONE, MAL.

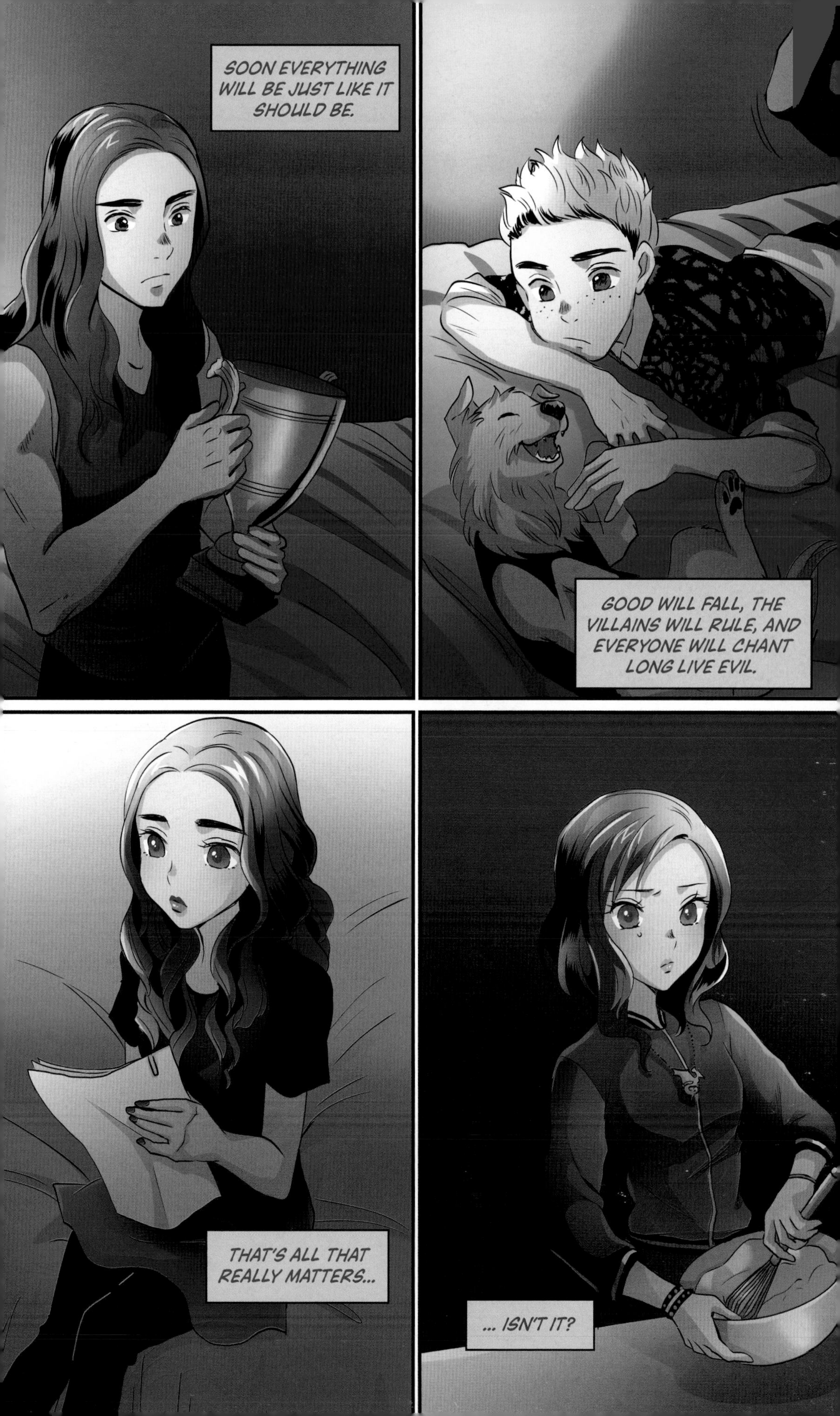
SOON EVERYTHING WILL BE JUST LIKE IT SHOULD BE.
GOOD WILL FALL, THE VILLAINS WILL RULE, AND EVERYONE WILL CHANT LONG LIVE EVIL.
THAT'S ALL THAT REALLY MATTERS...
... ISN'T IT?

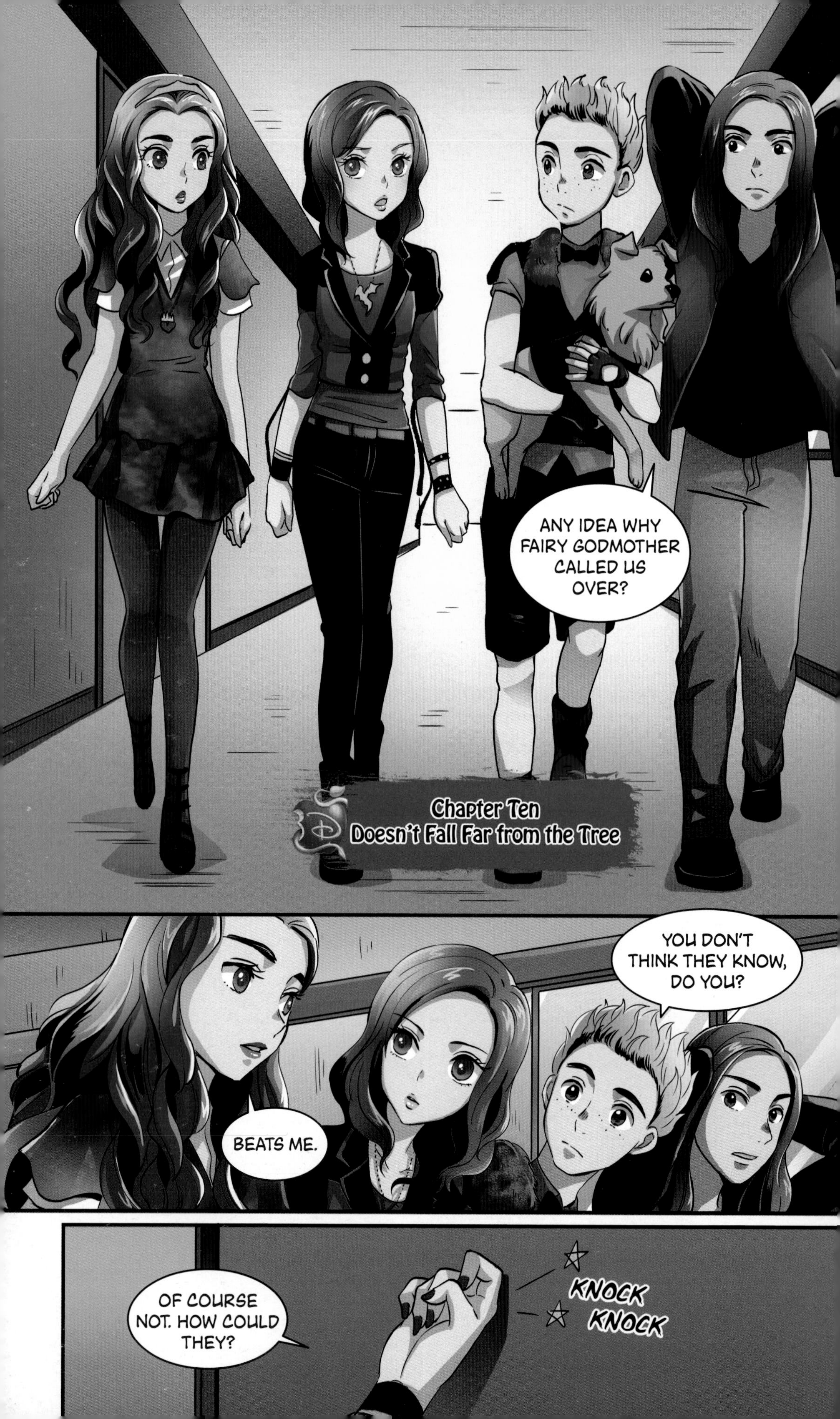
ANY IDEA WHY FAIRY GODMOTHER CALLED US OVER?
Chapter Ten
Doesn't Fall Far from the Tree
YOU DON'T THINK THEY KNOW, DO YOU?
BEATS ME.
OF COURSE NOT. HOW COULD THEY?
KNOCK KNOCK

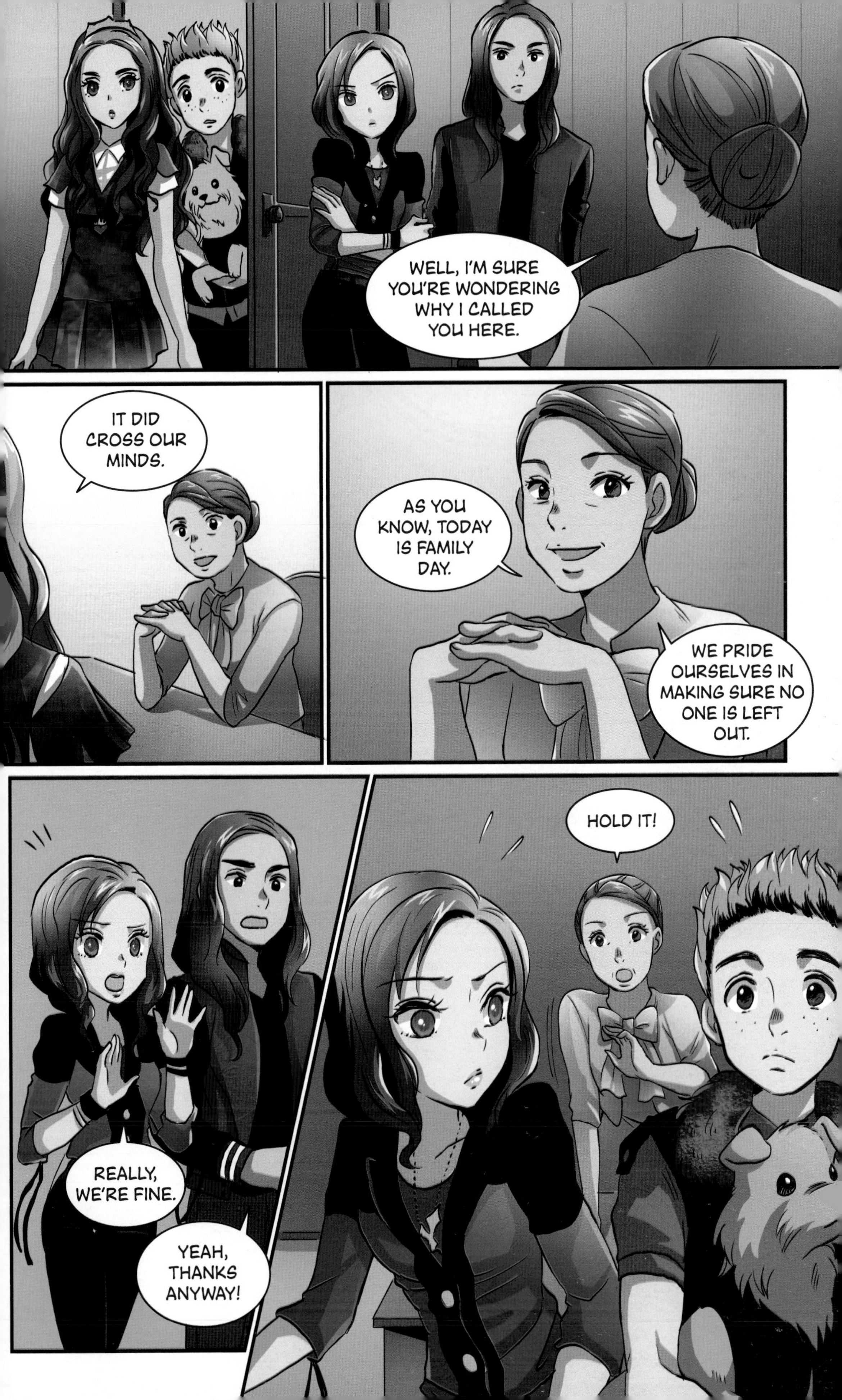
WELL, I'M SURE YOU'RE WONDERING WHY I CALLED YOU HERE.
IT DID CROSS OUR MINDS.
AS YOU KNOW, TODAY IS FAMILY DAY.
WE PRIDE OURSELVES IN MAKING SURE NO ONE IS LEFT OUT.
REALLY, WE'RE FINE.
YEAH, THANKS ANYWAY!
HOLD IT!

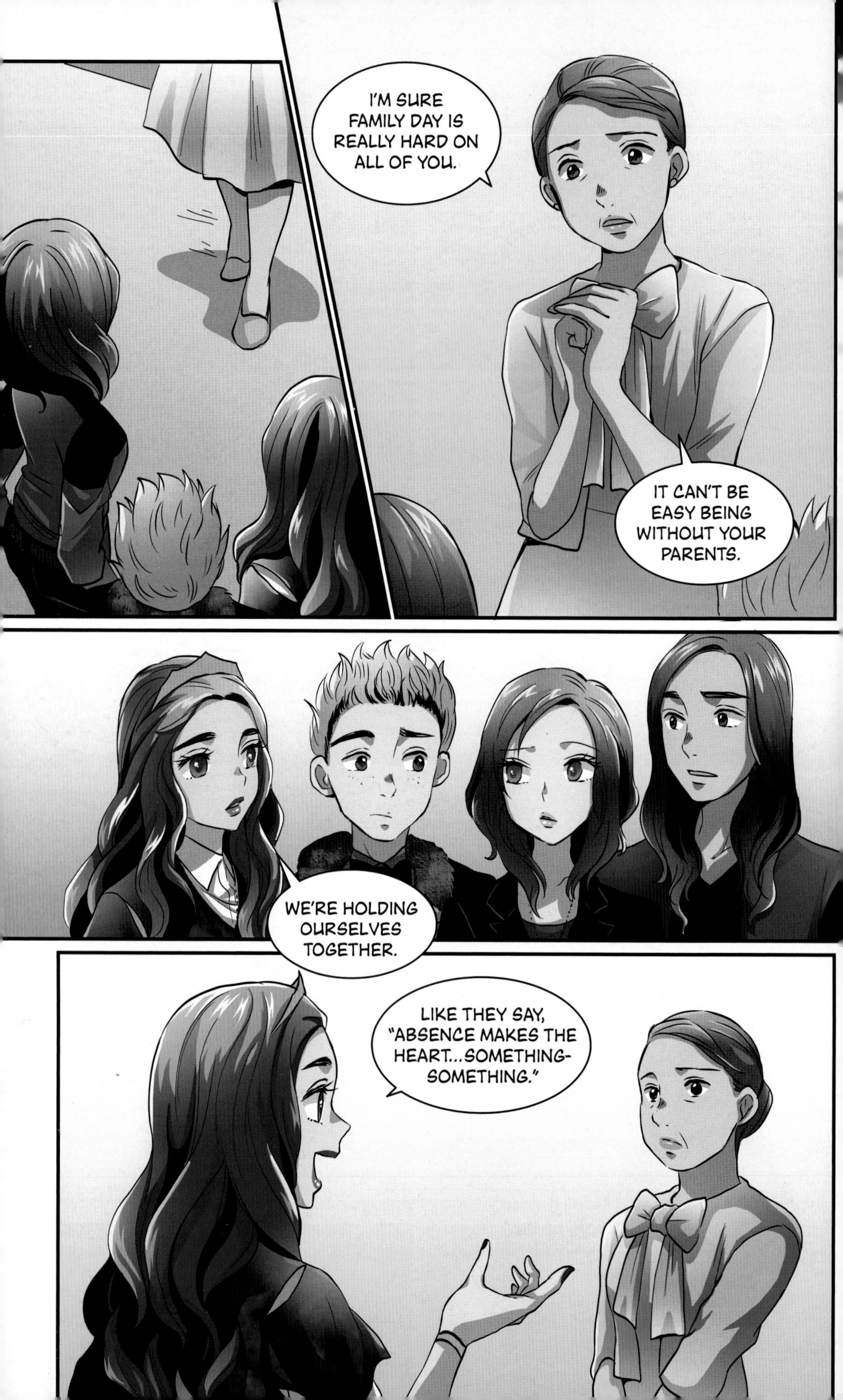
I'M SURE FAMILY DAY IS REALLY HARD ON ALL OF YOU.
IT CAN'T BE EASY BEING WITHOUT YOUR PARENTS.
WE'RE HOLDING OURSELVES TOGETHER.
LIKE THEY SAY, "ABSENCE MAKES THE HEART...SOMETHING-SOMETHING."

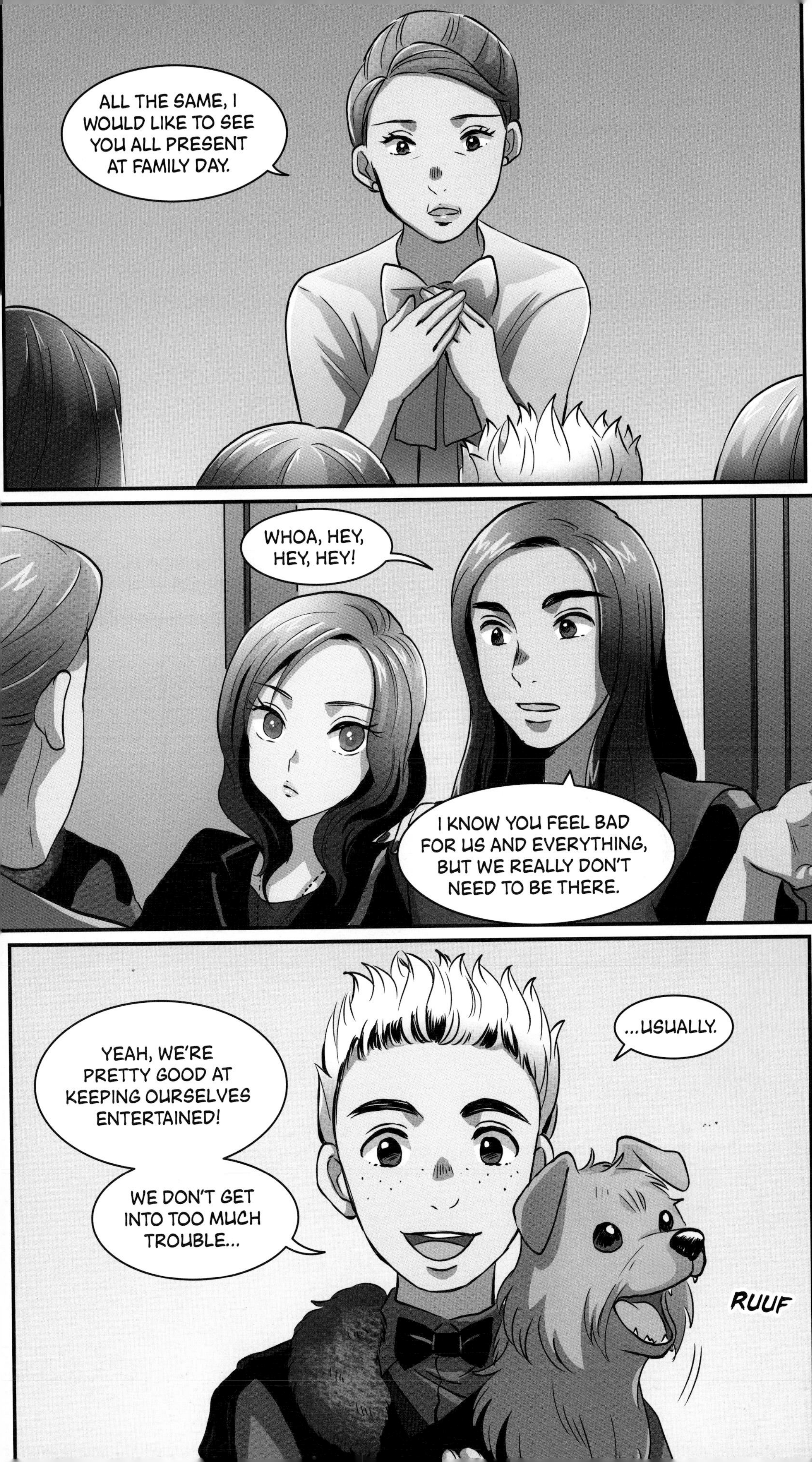
ALL THE SAME, I WOULD LIKE TO SEE YOU ALL PRESENT AT FAMILY DAY.
WHOA, HEY, HEY, HEY!
I KNOW YOU FEEL BAD FOR US AND EVERYTHING, BUT WE REALLY DON'T NEED TO BE THERE.
YEAH, WE'RE PRETTY GOOD AT KEEPING OURSELVES ENTERTAINED!
WE DON'T GET INTO TOO MUCH TROUBLE...
...USUALLY.
RUUF

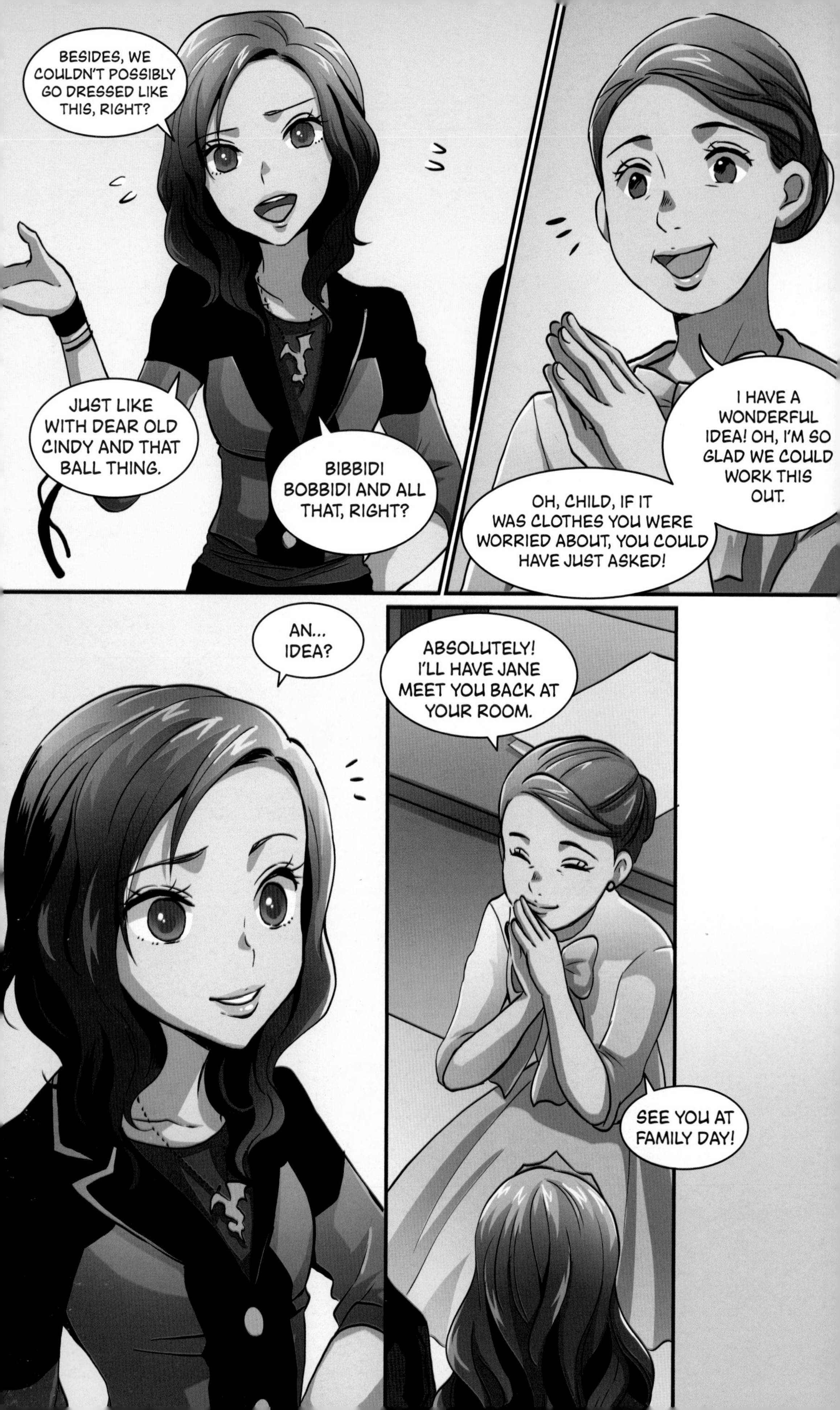
BESIDES, WE COULDN'T POSSIBLY GO DRESSED LIKE THIS, RIGHT?
JUST LIKE WITH DEAR OLD CINDY AND THAT BALL THING.
BIBBIDI BOBBIDI AND ALL THAT, RIGHT?
I HAVE A WONDERFUL IDEA! OH, I'M SO GLAD WE COULD WORK THIS OUT.
OH, CHILD, IF IT WAS CLOTHES YOU WERE WORRIED ABOUT, YOU COULD HAVE JUST ASKED!
AN... IDEA?
ABSOLUTELY! I'LL HAVE JANE MEET YOU BACK AT YOUR ROOM.
SEE YOU AT FAMILY DAY!

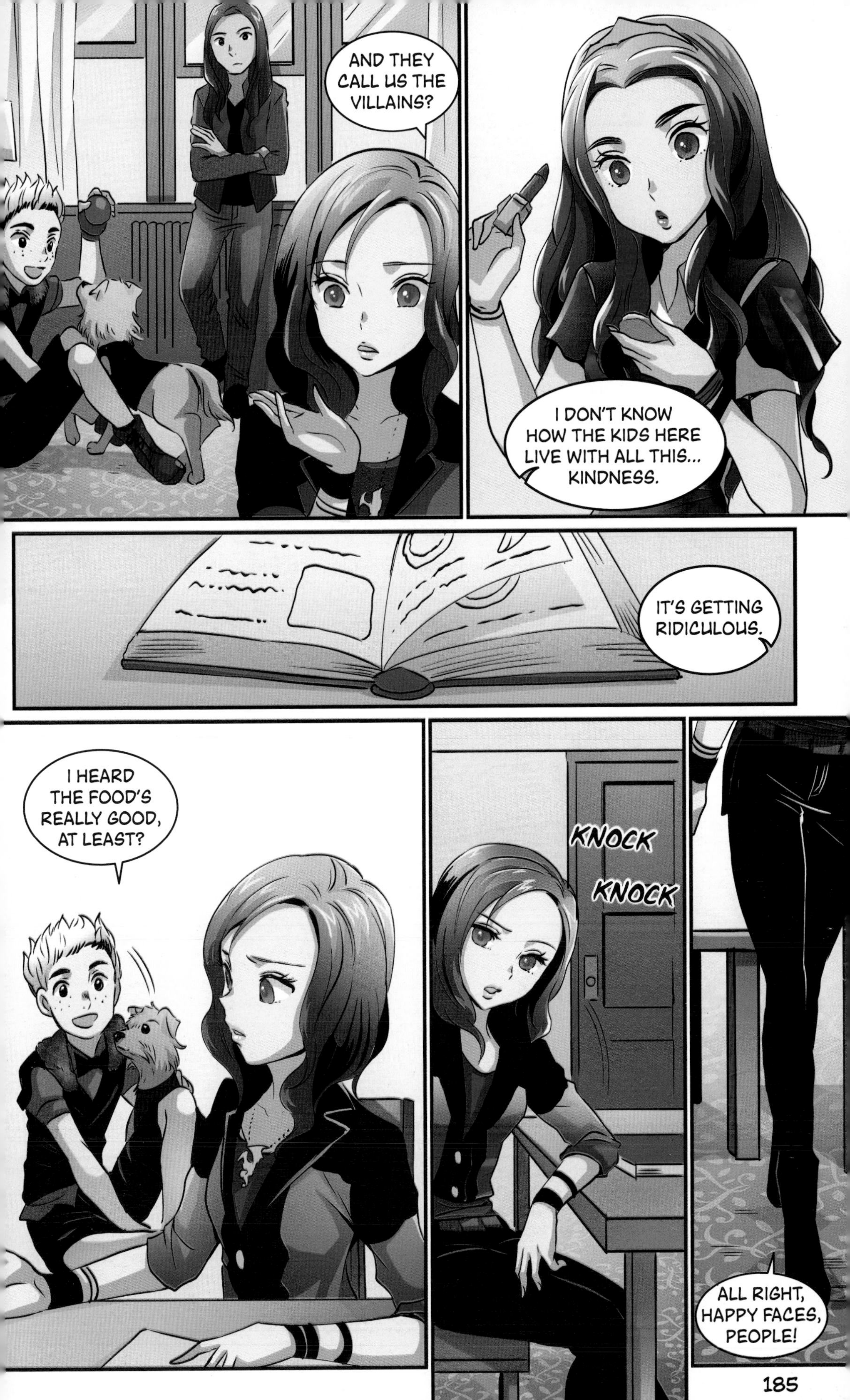
AND THEY CALL US THE VILLAINS?
I DON'T KNOW HOW THE KIDS HERE LIVE WITH ALL THIS... KINDNESS.
IT'S GETTING RIDICULOUS.
I HEARD THE FOOD'S REALLY GOOD, AT LEAST?
KNOCK
KNOCK
ALL RIGHT, HAPPY FACES, PEOPLE!

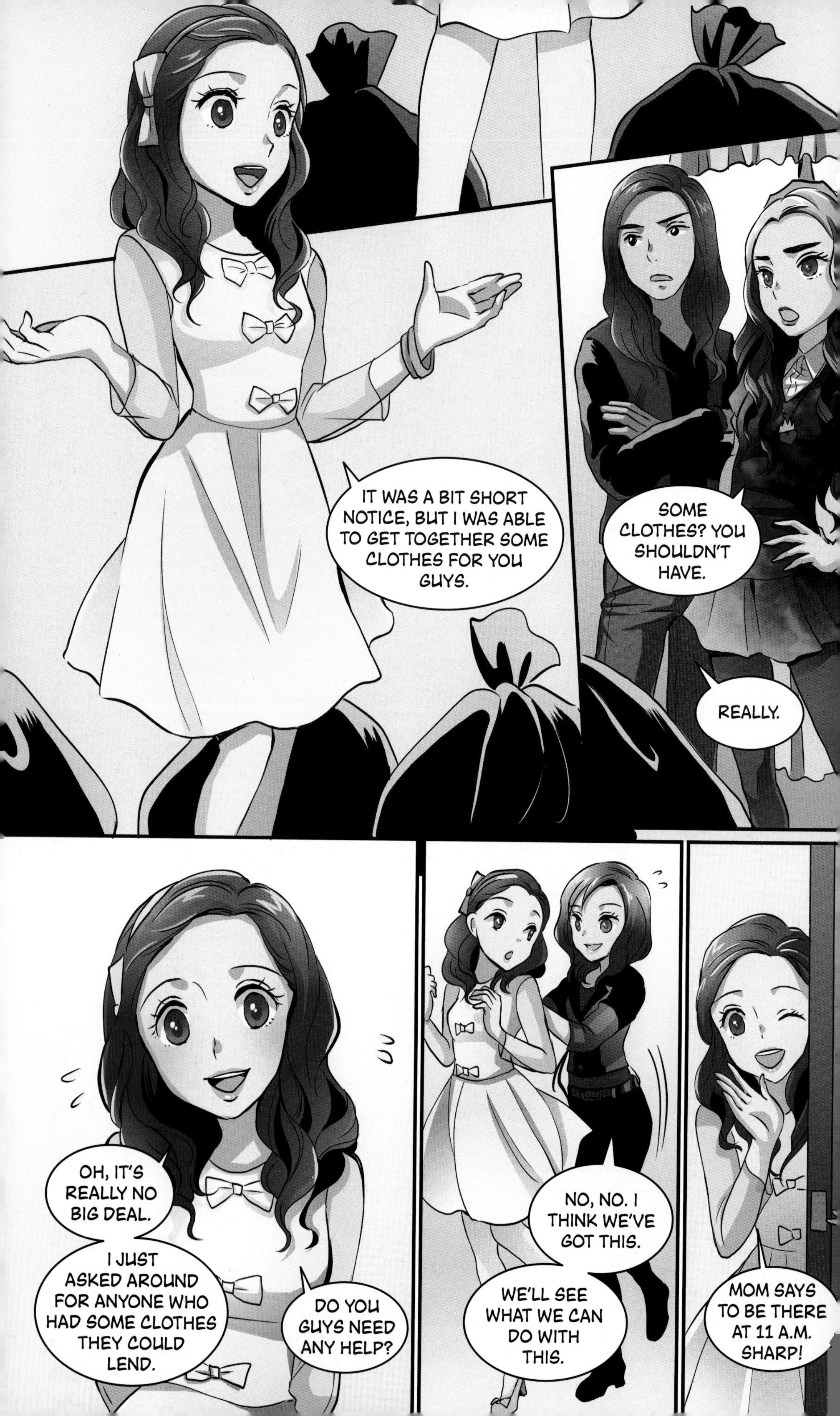
IT WAS A BIT SHORT NOTICE, BUT I WAS ABLE TO GET TOGETHER SOME CLOTHES FOR YOU GUYS.
SOME CLOTHES? YOU SHOULDN'T HAVE.
REALLY.
OH, IT'S REALLY NO BIG DEAL.
I JUST ASKED AROUND FOR ANYONE WHO HAD SOME CLOTHES THEY COULD LEND.
DO YOU GUYS NEED ANY HELP?
NO, NO. I THINK WE'VE GOT THIS.
WE'LL SEE WHAT WE CAN DO WITH THIS.
MOM SAYS TO BE THERE AT 11 A.M. SHARP!

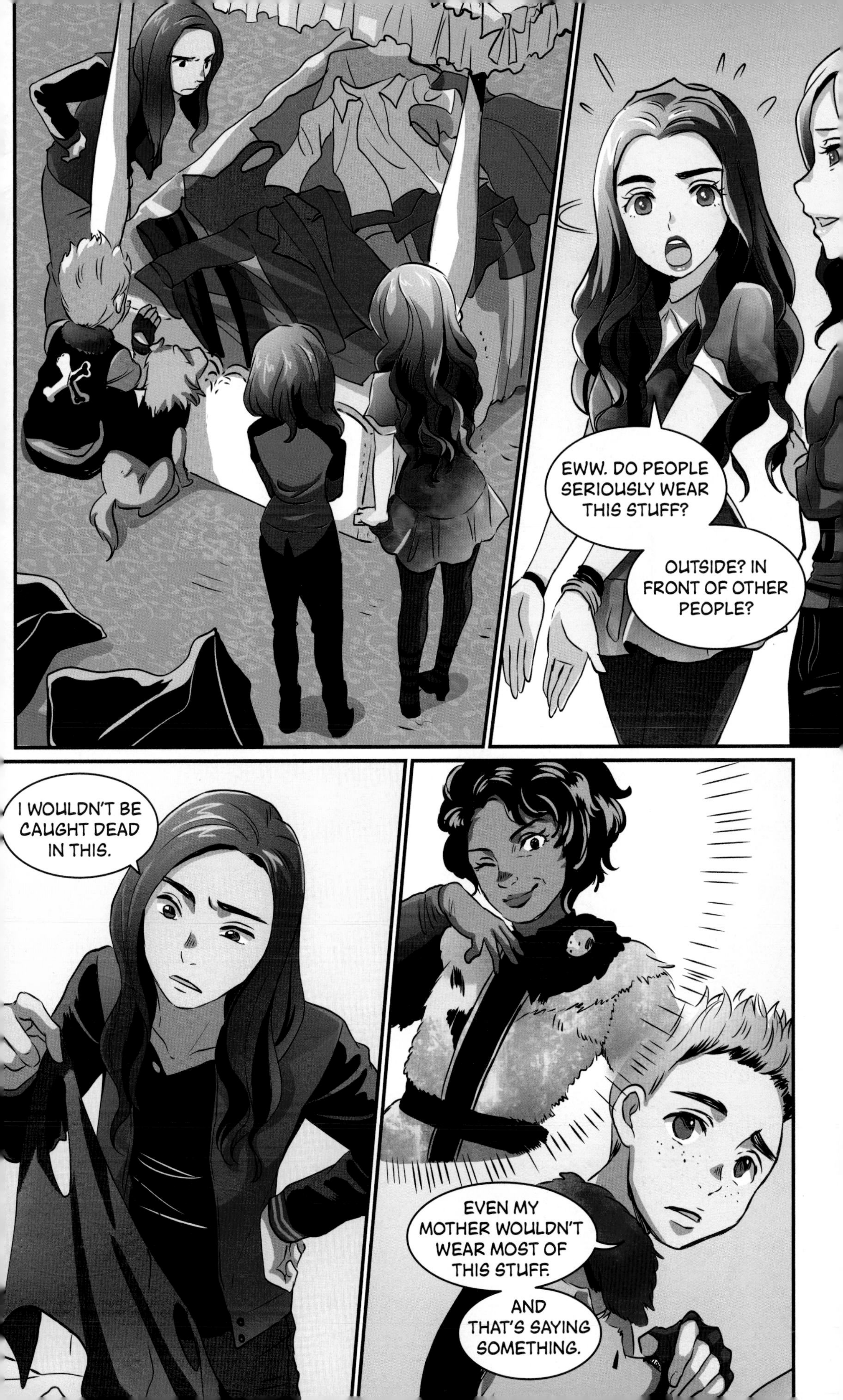
EWW. DO PEOPLE SERIOUSLY WEAR THIS STUFF?
OUTSIDE? IN FRONT OF OTHER PEOPLE?
I WOULDN'T BE CAUGHT DEAD IN THIS.
EVEN MY MOTHER WOULDN'T WEAR MOST OF THIS STUFF.
AND THAT'S SAYING SOMETHING.

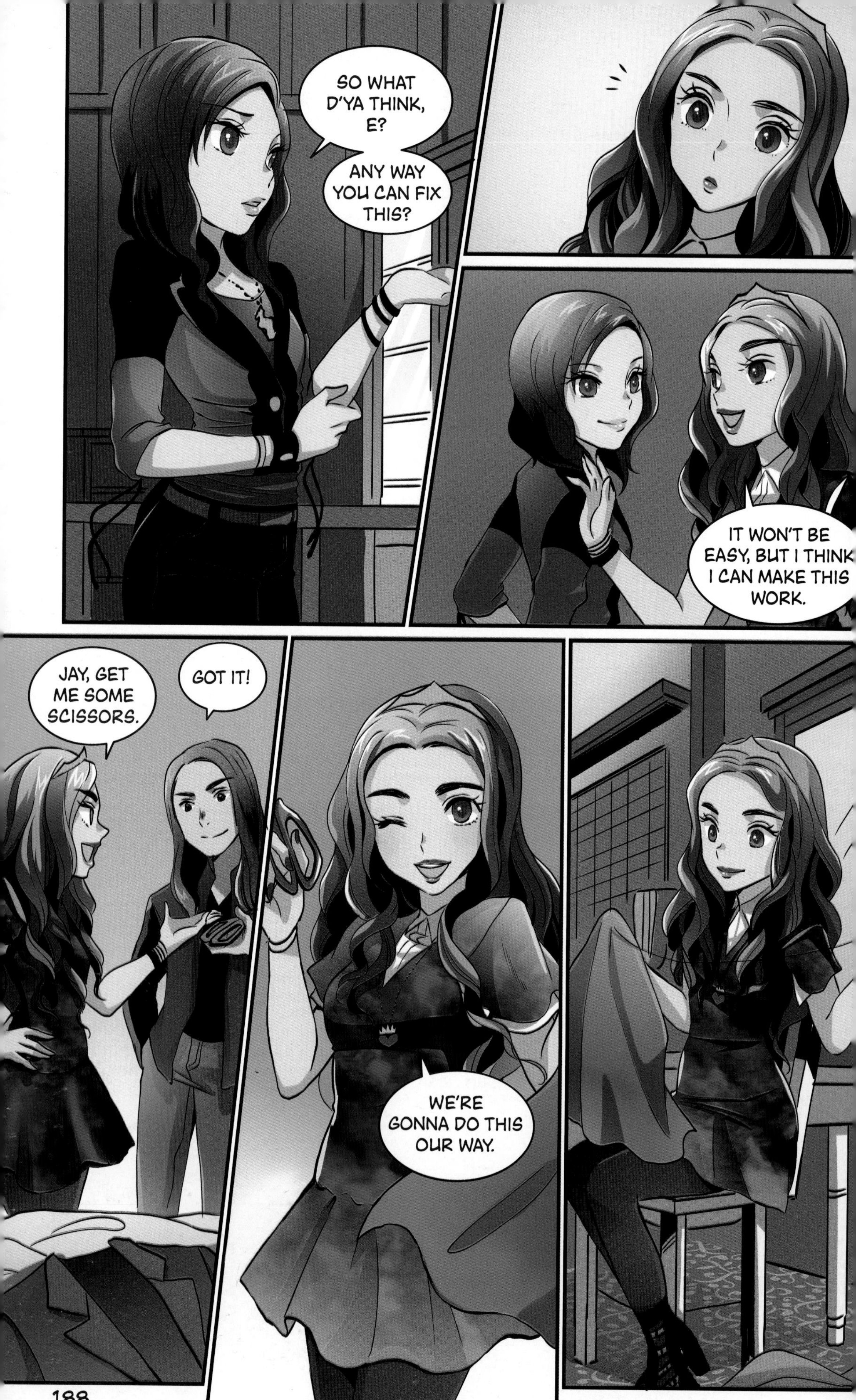
SO WHAT D'YA THINK, E?
ANY WAY YOU CAN FIX THIS?
IT WON'T BE EASY, BUT I THINK I CAN MAKE THIS WORK.
JAY, GET ME SOME SCISSORS.
GOT IT!
WE'RE GONNA DO THIS OUR WAY.

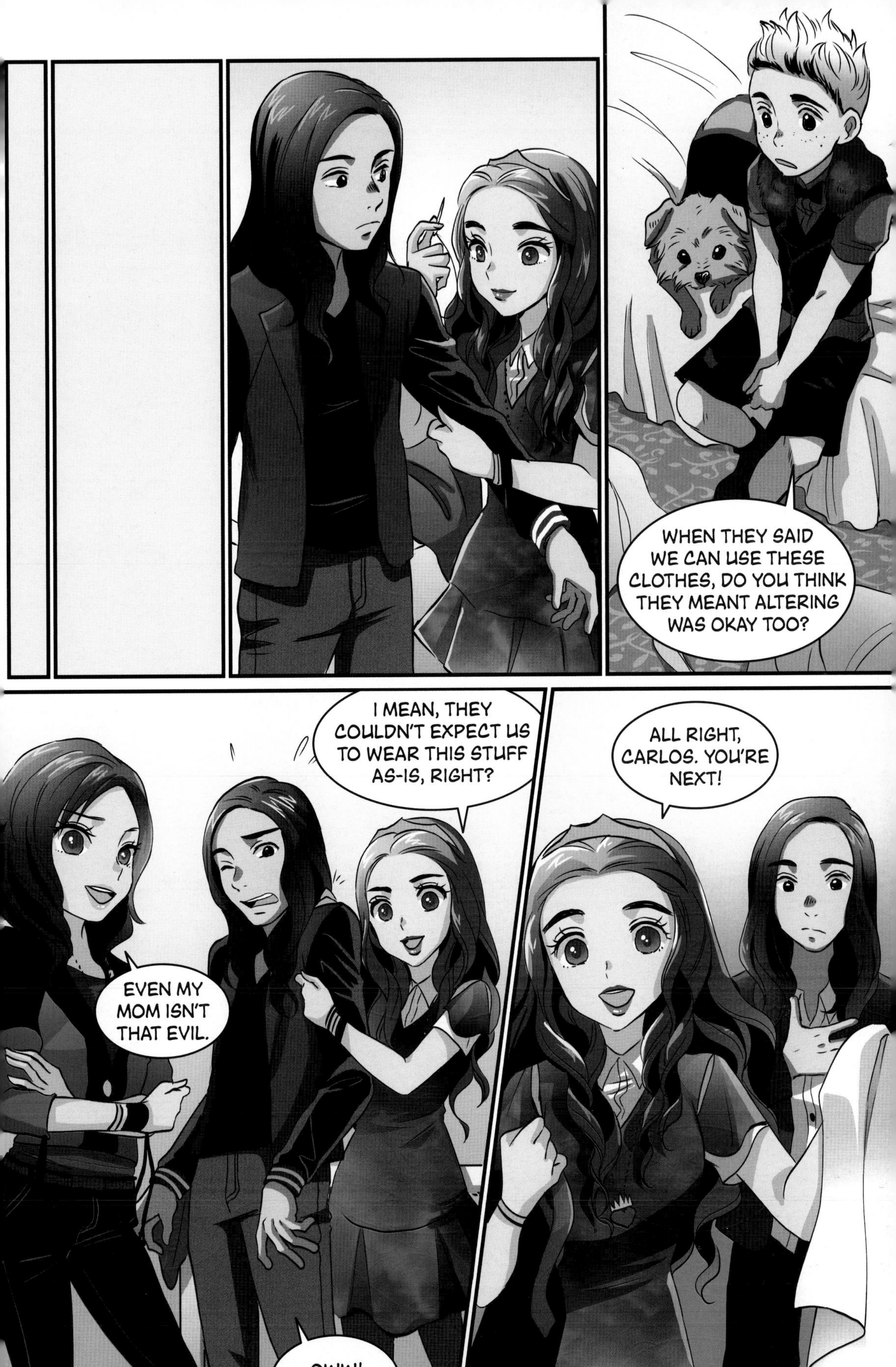
WHEN THEY SAID WE CAN USE THESE CLOTHES, DO YOU THINK THEY MEANT ALTERING WAS OKAY TOO?
I MEAN, THEY COULDN'T EXPECT US TO WEAR THIS STUFF AS-IS, RIGHT?
EVEN MY MOM ISN'T THAT EVIL.
OWW! CAREFUL!
ALL RIGHT, CARLOS. YOU'RE NEXT!

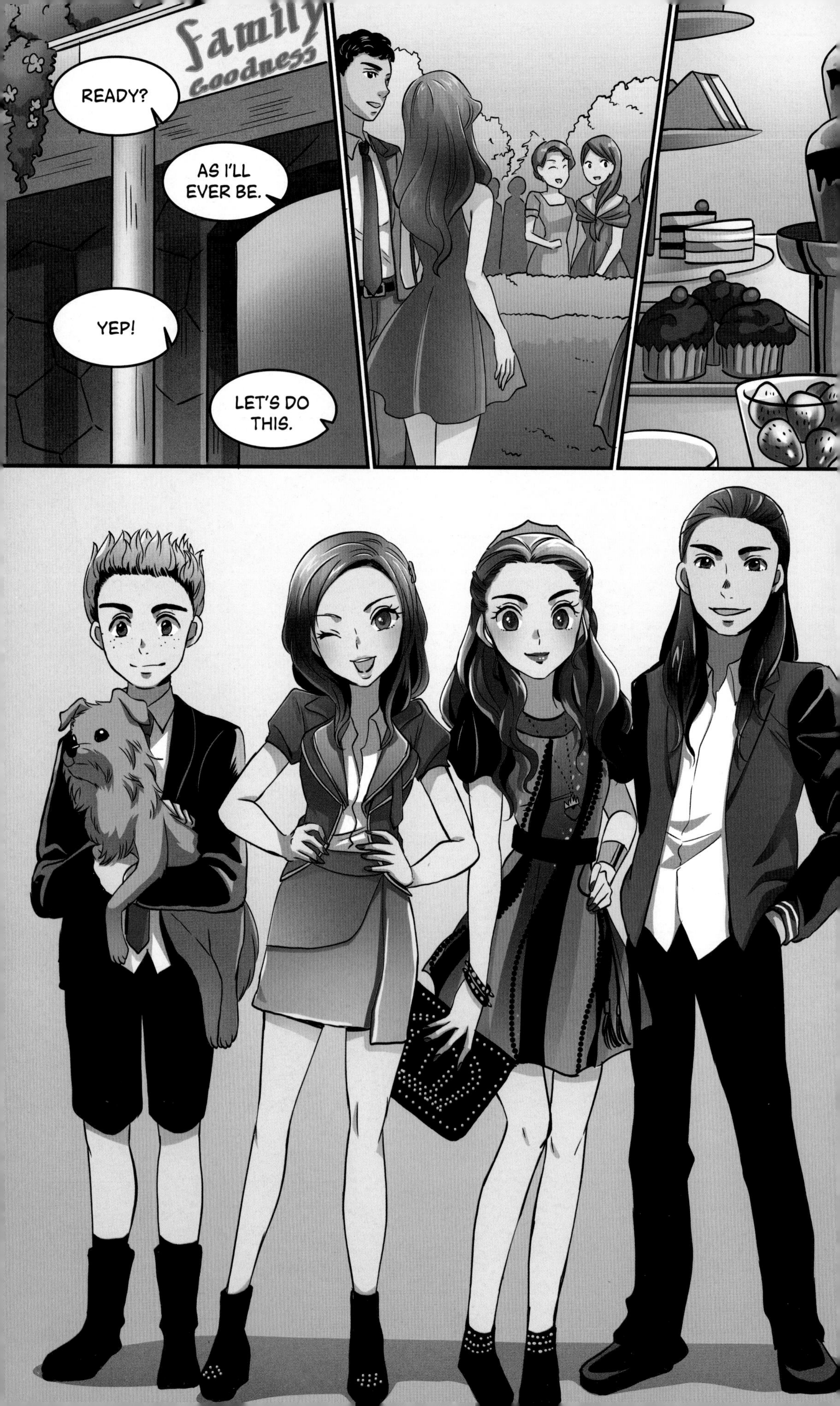
Family
Goodness
READY?
AS I'LL EVER BE.
YEP!
LET'S DO THIS.

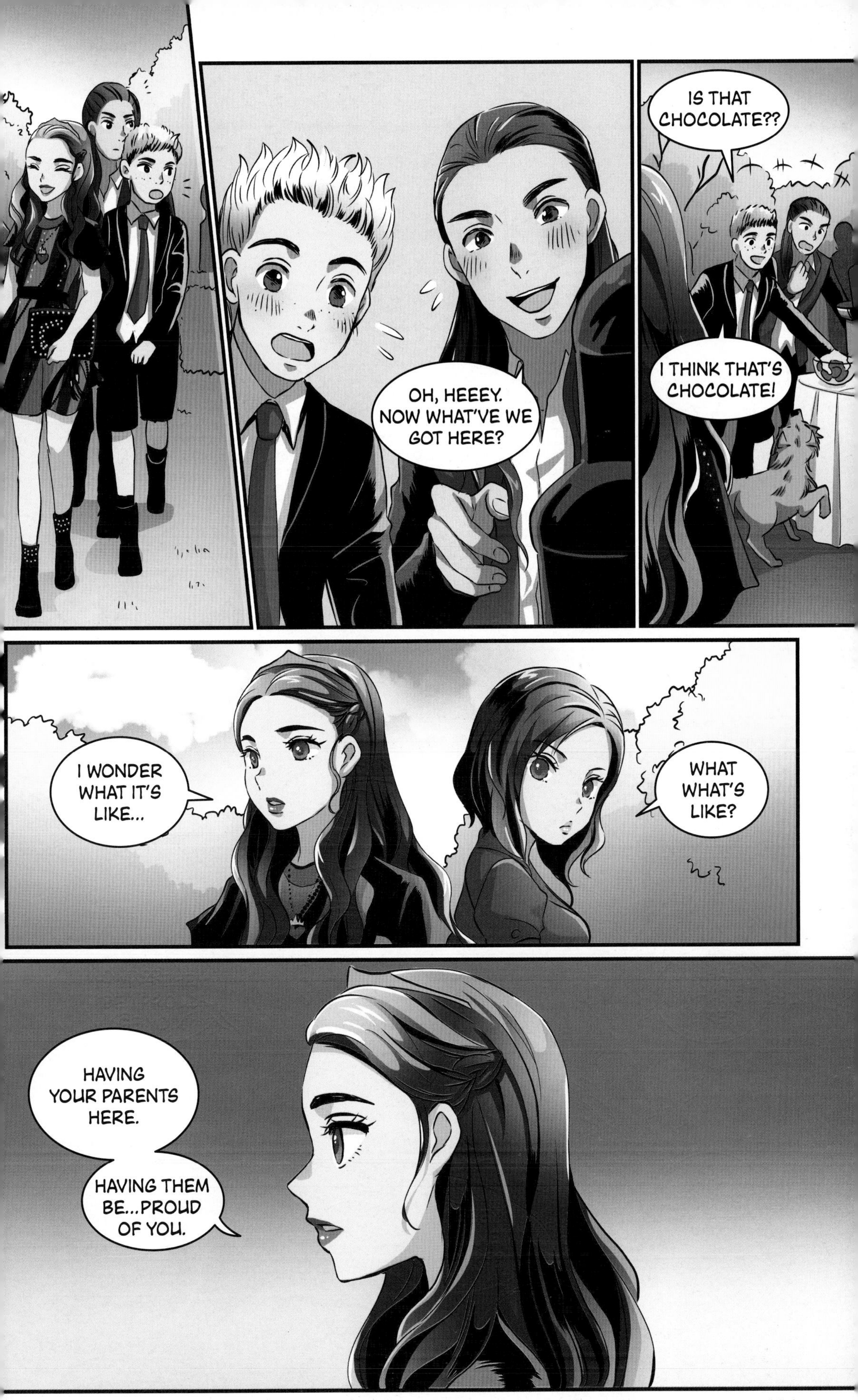
OH, HEEEY. NOW WHAT'VE WE GOT HERE?
IS THAT CHOCOLATE??
I THINK THAT'S CHOCOLATE!
I WONDER WHAT IT'S LIKE...
WHAT WHAT'S LIKE?
HAVING YOUR PARENTS HERE.
HAVING THEM BE...PROUD OF YOU.

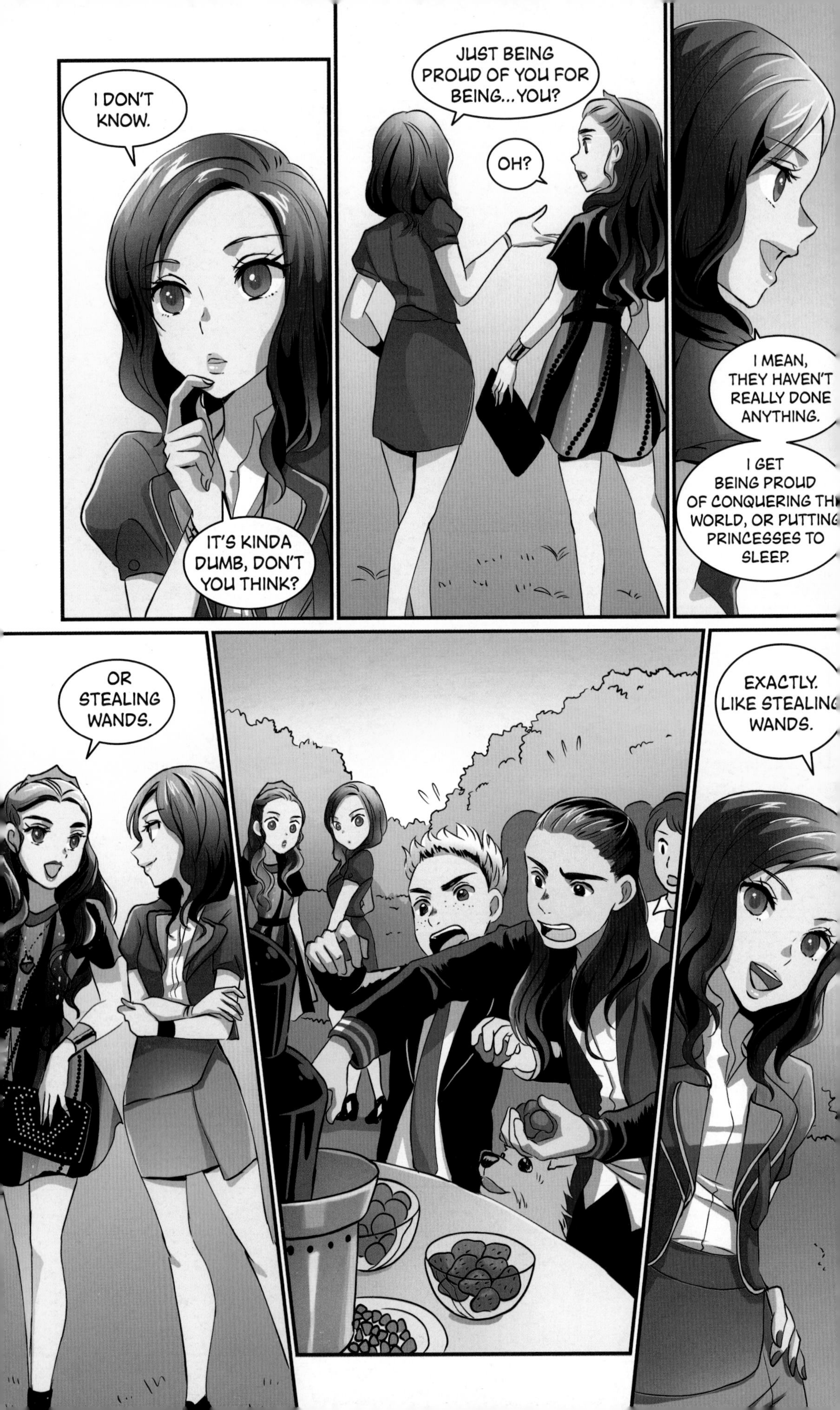
I DON'T KNOW.
IT'S KINDA DUMB, DON'T YOU THINK?
JUST BEING PROUD OF YOU FOR BEING... YOU?
OH?
I MEAN, THEY HAVEN'T REALLY DONE ANYTHING.
I GET BEING PROUD OF CONQUERING TH WORLD, OR PUTTING PRINCESSES TO SLEEP.
OR STEALING WANDS.
EXACTLY. LIKE STEALING WANDS.

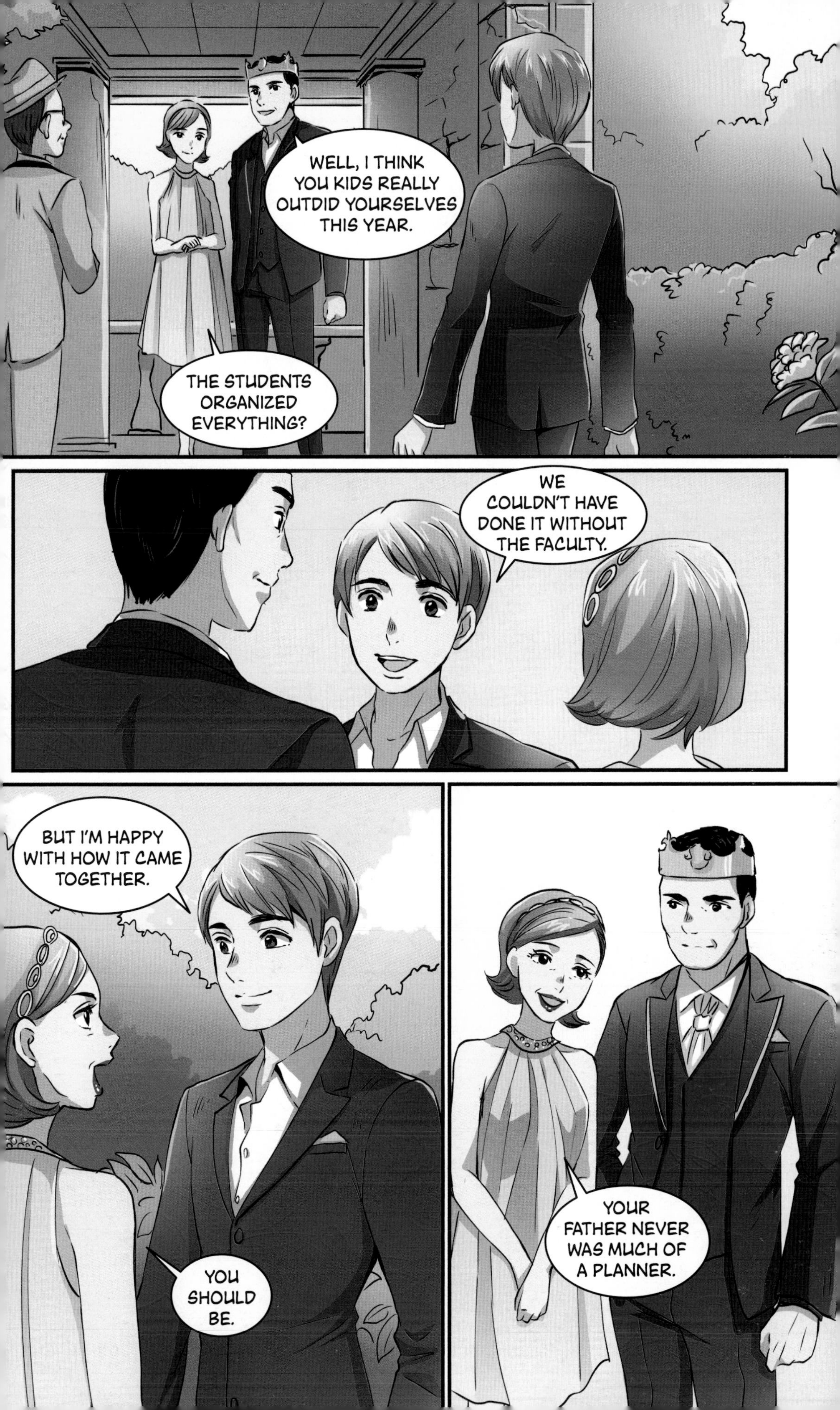
WELL, I THINK YOU KIDS REALLY OUTDID YOURSELVES THIS YEAR.
THE STUDENTS ORGANIZED EVERYTHING?
WE COULDN'T HAVE DONE IT WITHOUT THE FACULTY.
BUT I'M HAPPY WITH HOW IT CAME TOGETHER.
YOU SHOULD BE.
YOUR FATHER NEVER WAS MUCH OF A PLANNER.

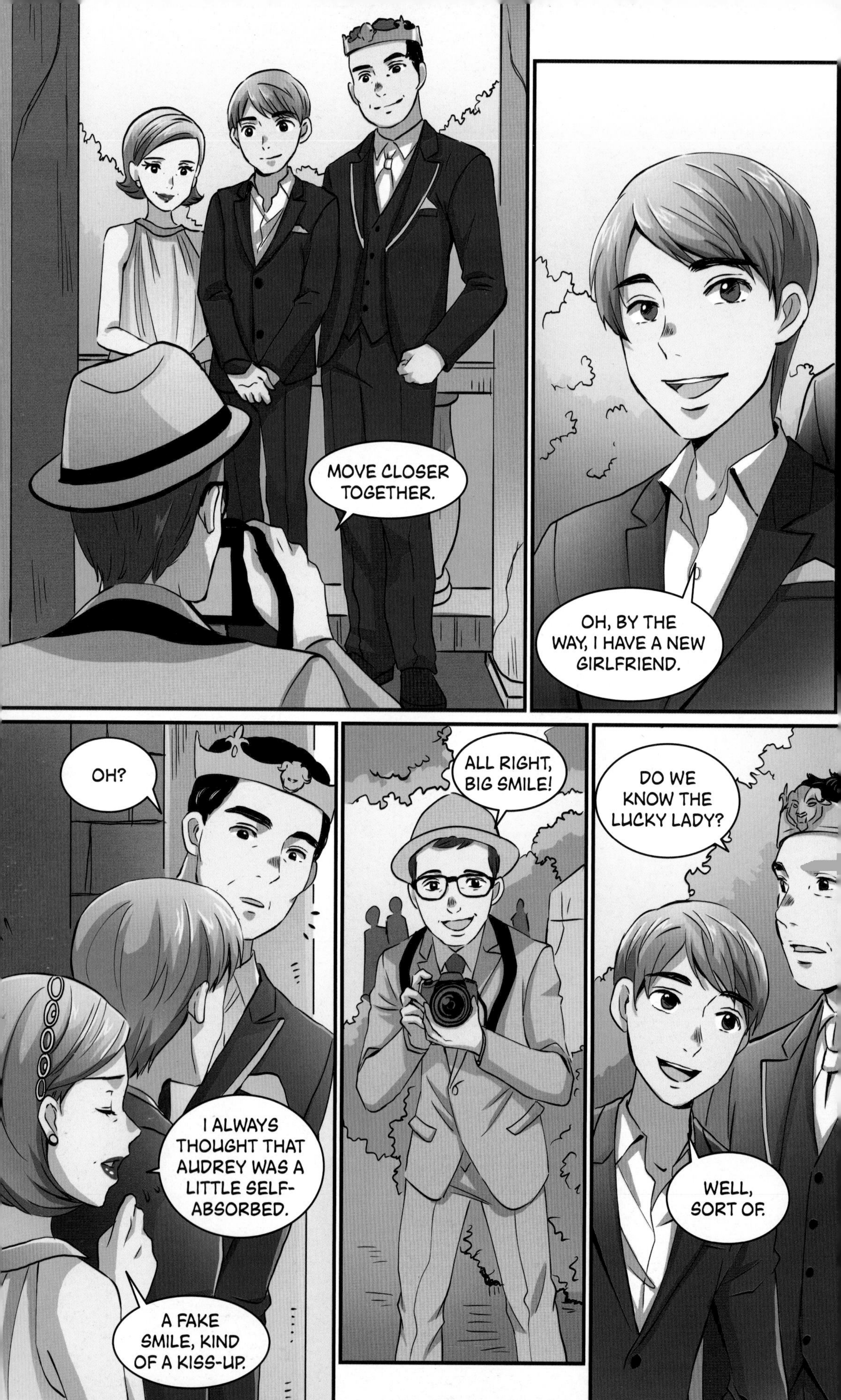
MOVE CLOSER TOGETHER.
OH, BY THE WAY, I HAVE A NEW GIRLFRIEND.
OH?
I ALWAYS THOUGHT THAT AUDREY WAS A LITTLE SELF-ABSORBED.
A FAKE SMILE, KIND OF A KISS-UP.
ALL RIGHT, BIG SMILE!
DO WE KNOW THE LUCKY LADY?
WELL, SORT OF.

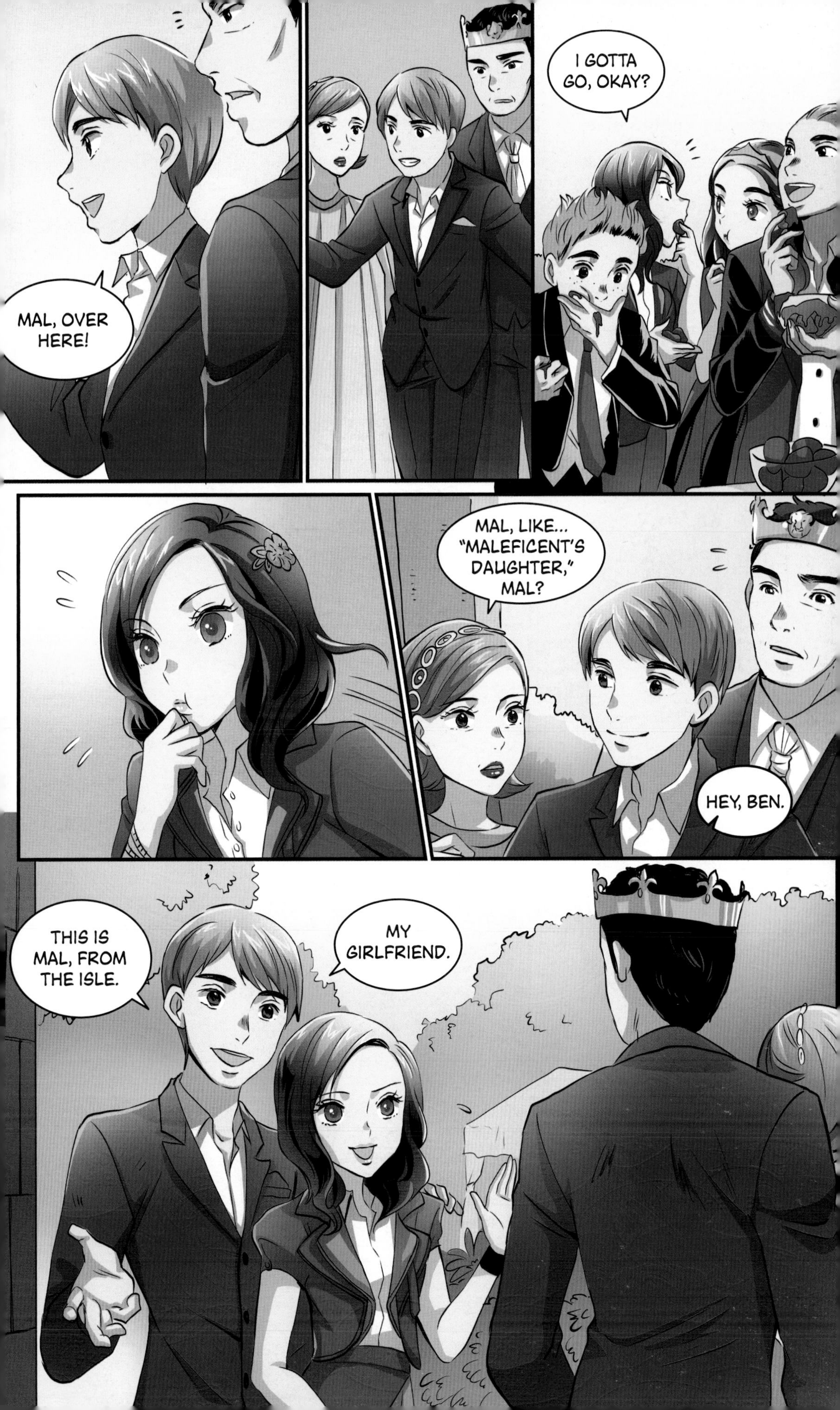
MAL, OVER HERE!
I GOTTA GO, OKAY?
MAL, LIKE... "MALEFICENT'S DAUGHTER," MAL?
HEY, BEN.
THIS IS MAL, FROM THE ISLE.
MY GIRLFRIEND.

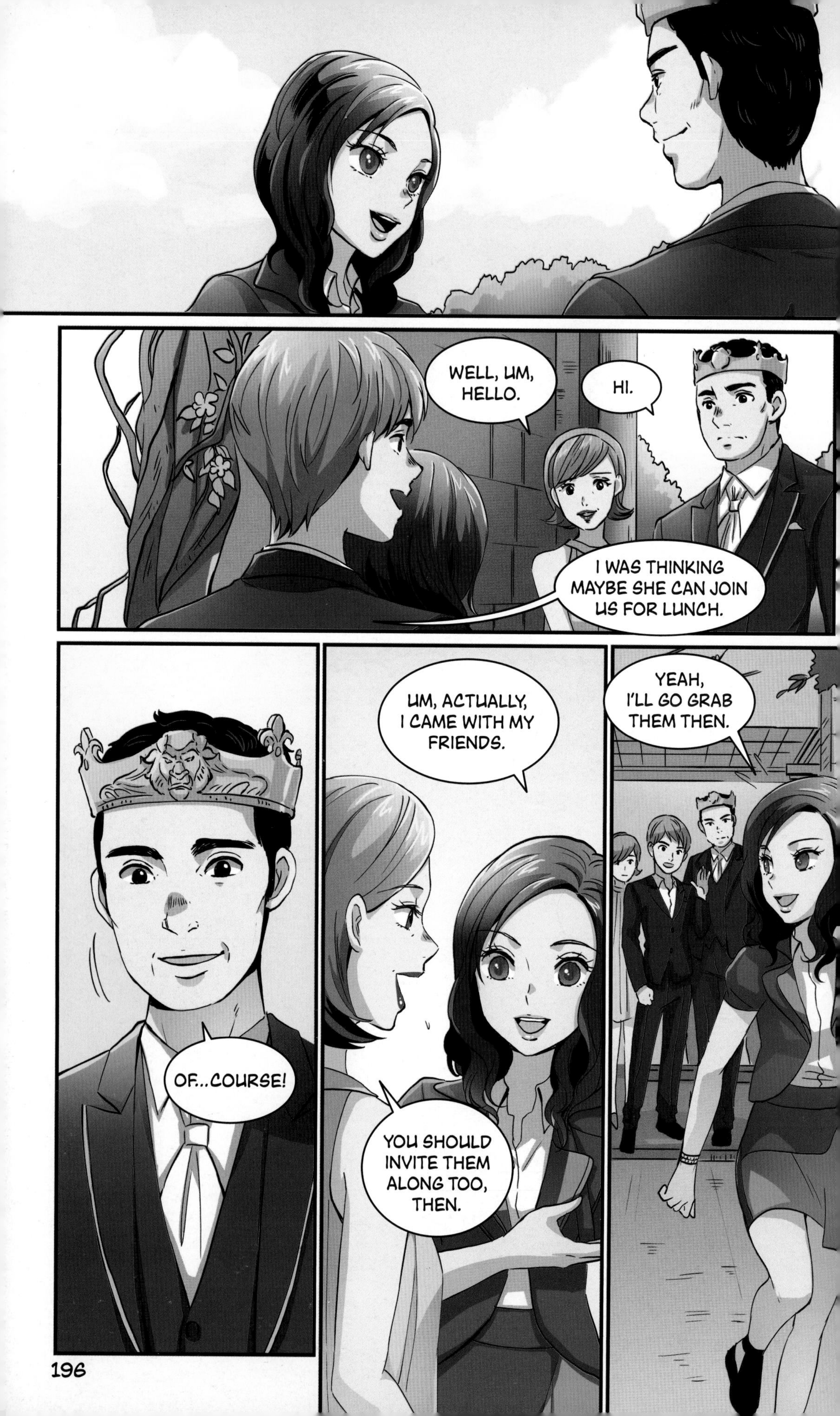
WELL, UM, HELLO.
HI.
I WAS THINKING MAYBE SHE CAN JOIN US FOR LUNCH.
OF...COURSE!
UM, ACTUALLY, I CAME WITH MY FRIENDS.
YOU SHOULD INVITE THEM ALONG TOO, THEN.
YEAH, I'LL GO GRAB THEM THEN.

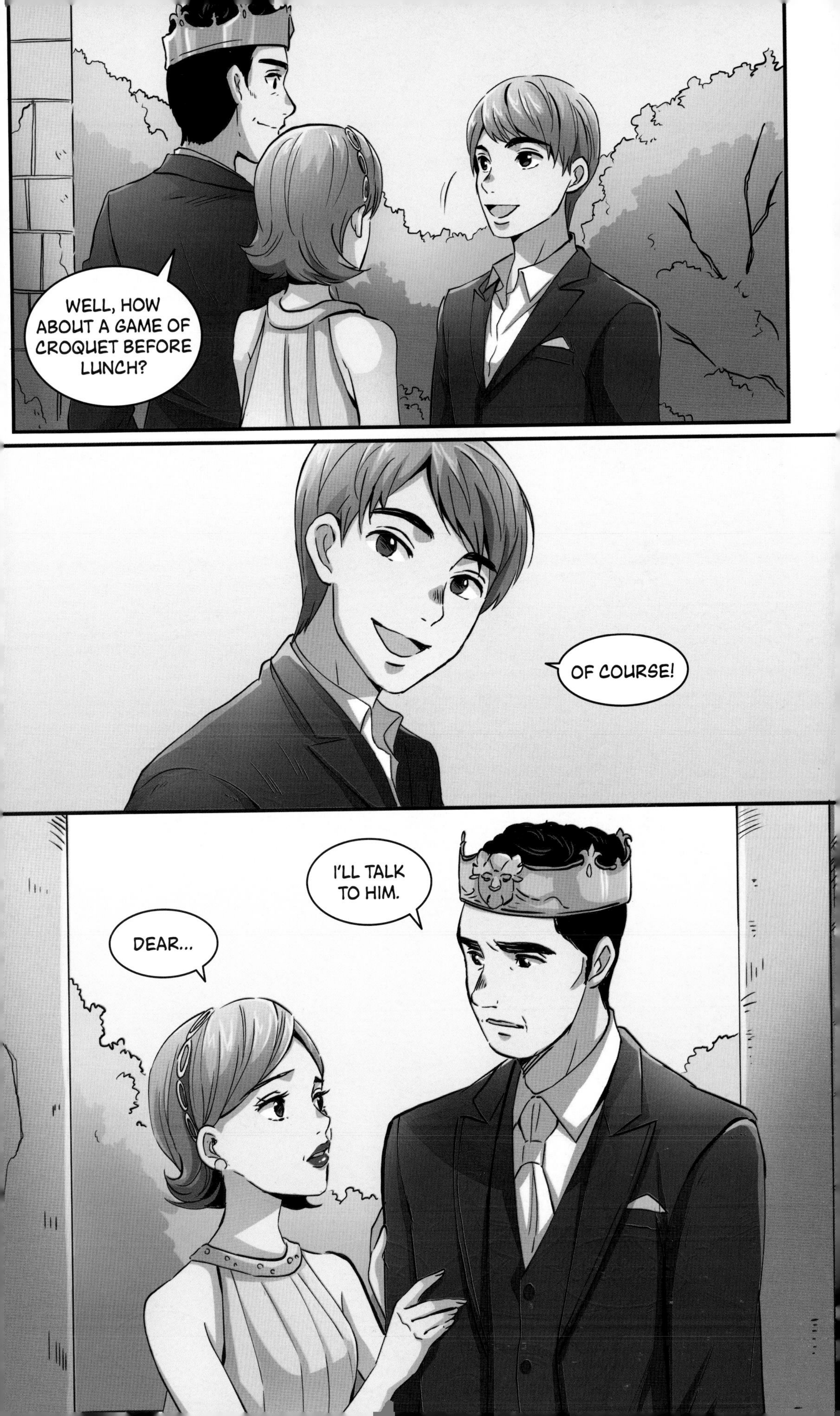
WELL, HOW ABOUT A GAME OF CROQUET BEFORE LUNCH?
OF COURSE!
DEAR...
I'LL TALK TO HIM.

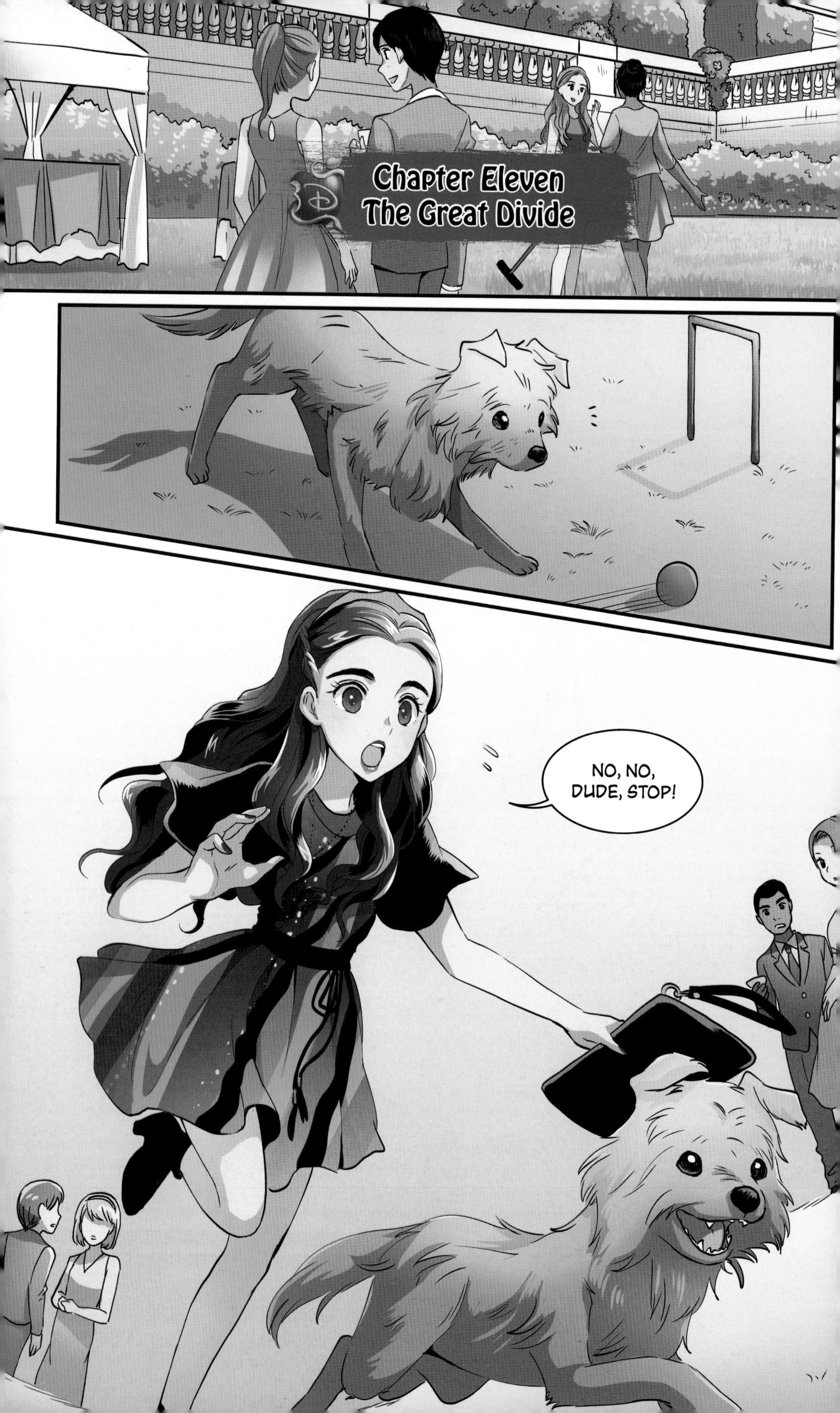
Chapter Eleven
The Great Divide
NO, NO, DUDE, STOP!

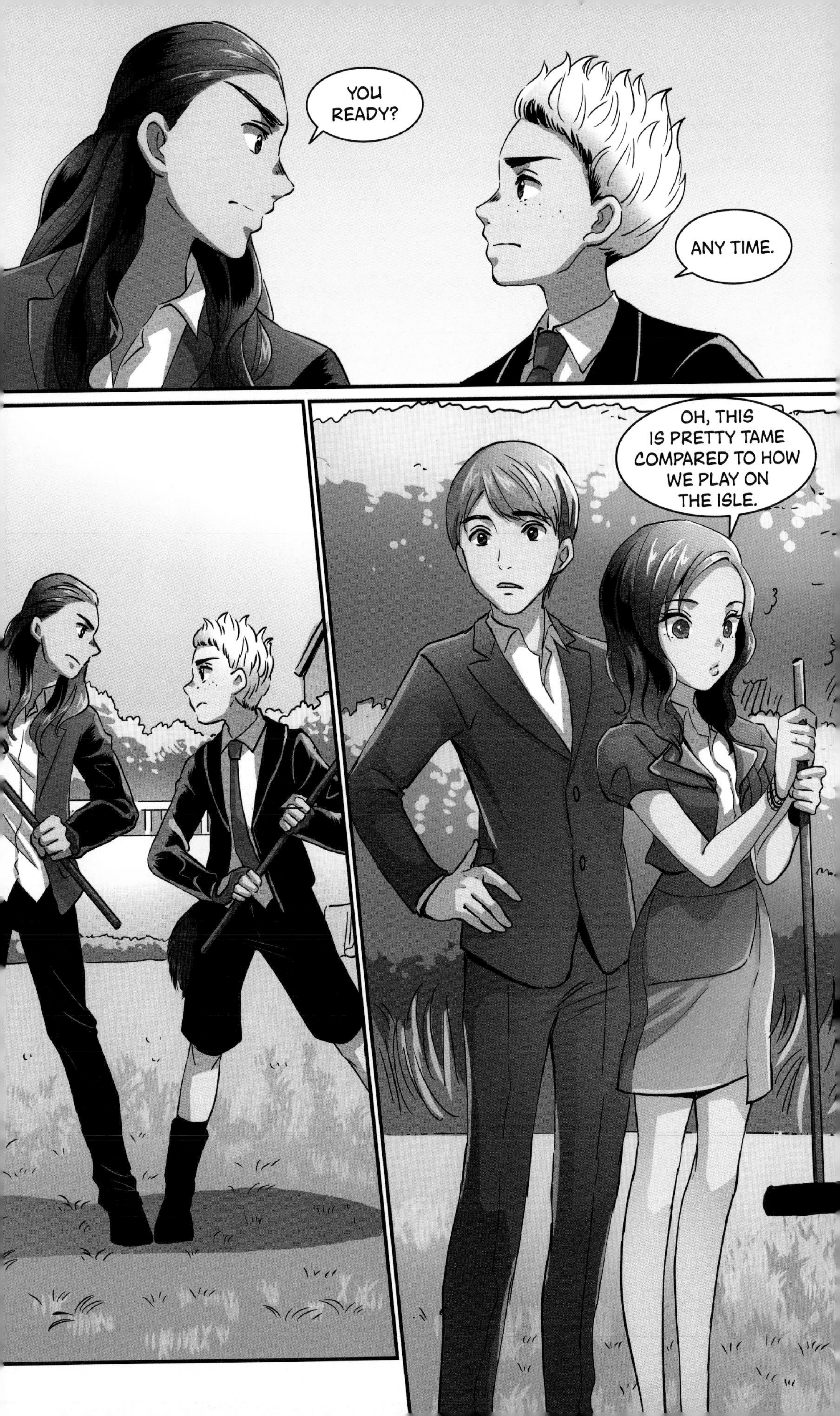
YOU READY?
ANY TIME.
OH, THIS IS PRETTY TAME COMPARED TO HOW WE PLAY ON THE ISLE.

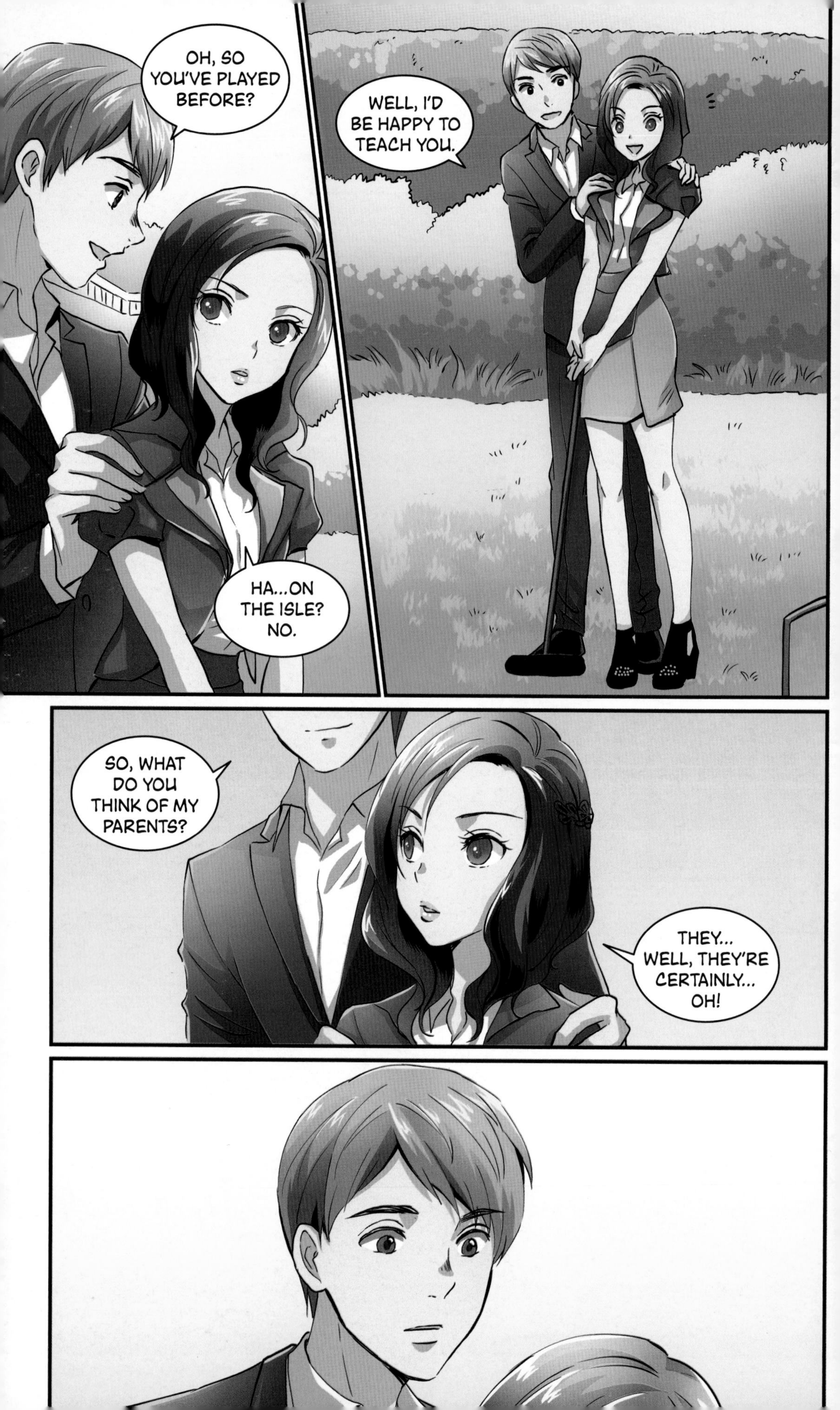
OH, SO YOU'VE PLAYED BEFORE?
HA...ON THE ISLE? NO.
WELL, I'D BE HAPPY TO TEACH YOU.
SO, WHAT DO YOU THINK OF MY PARENTS?
THEY... WELL, THEY'RE CERTAINLY... OH!

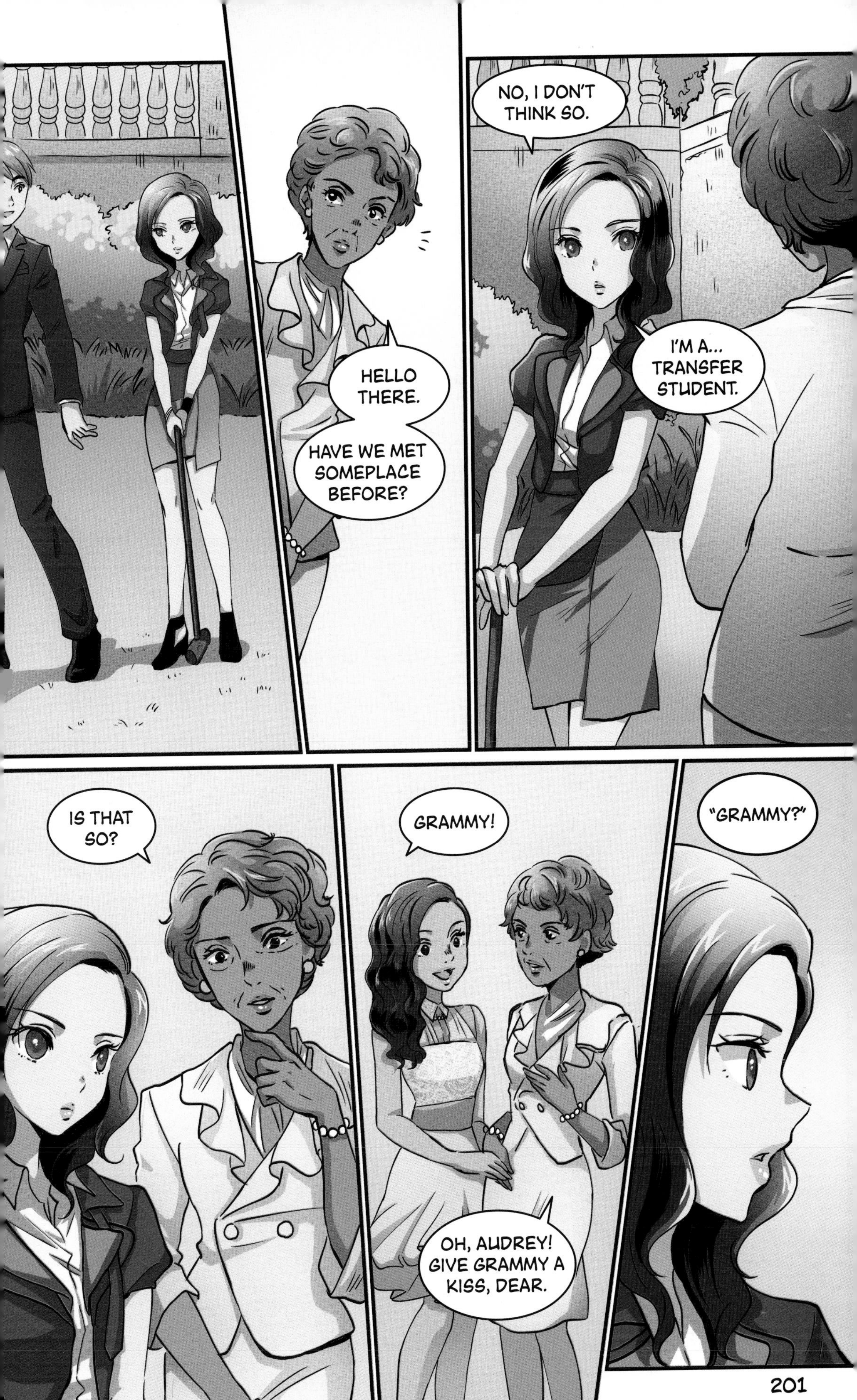
HELLO THERE.
HAVE WE MET SOMEPLACE BEFORE?
NO, I DON'T THINK SO.
I'M A... TRANSFER STUDENT.
IS THAT SO?
GRAMMY!
OH, AUDREY! GIVE GRAMMY A KISS, DEAR.
"GRAMMY?"

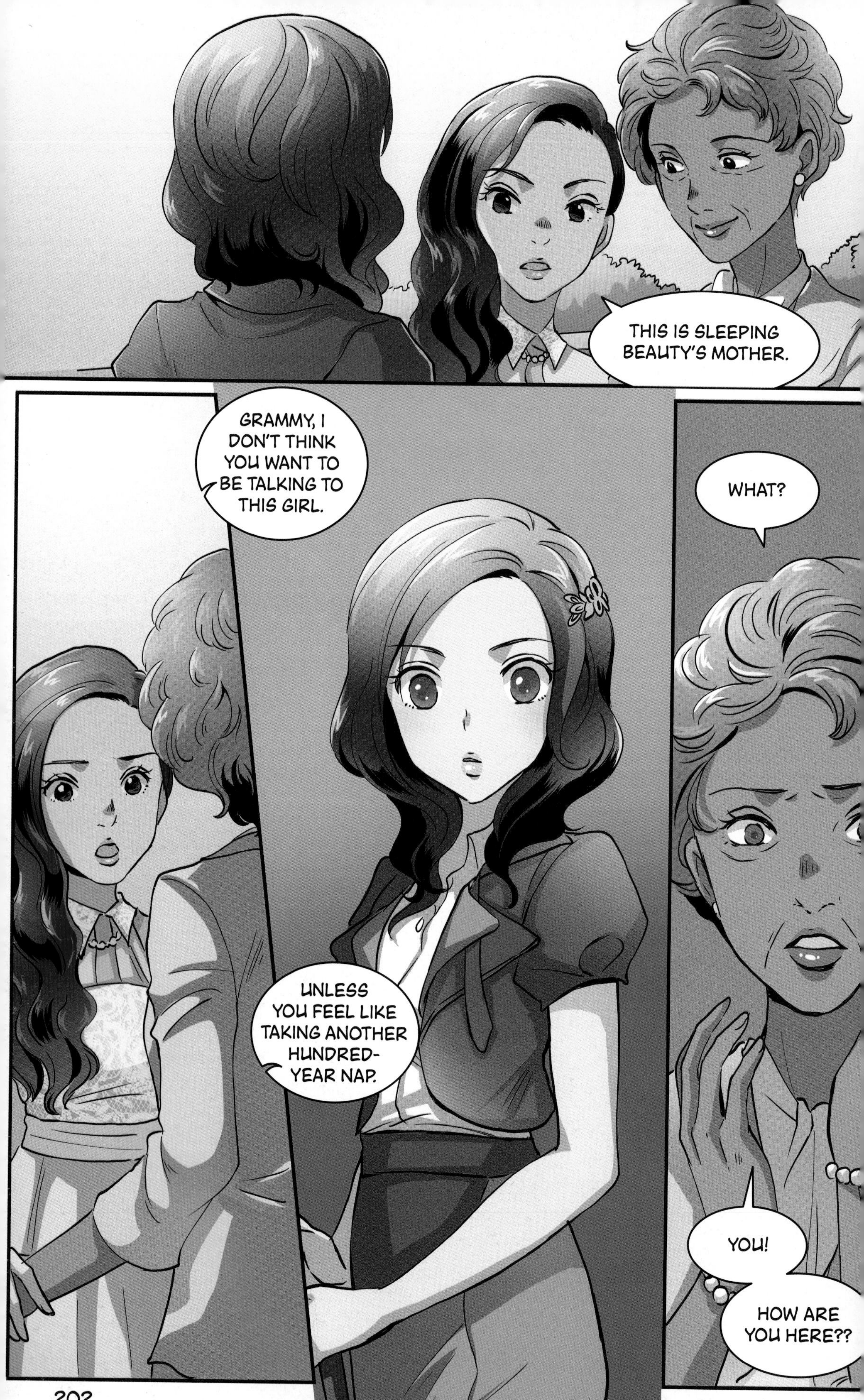
THIS IS SLEEPING BEAUTY'S MOTHER.
GRAMMY, I DON'T THINK YOU WANT TO BE TALKING TO THIS GIRL.
WHAT?
UNLESS YOU FEEL LIKE TAKING ANOTHER HUNDRED-YEAR NAP.
YOU!
HOW ARE YOU HERE??

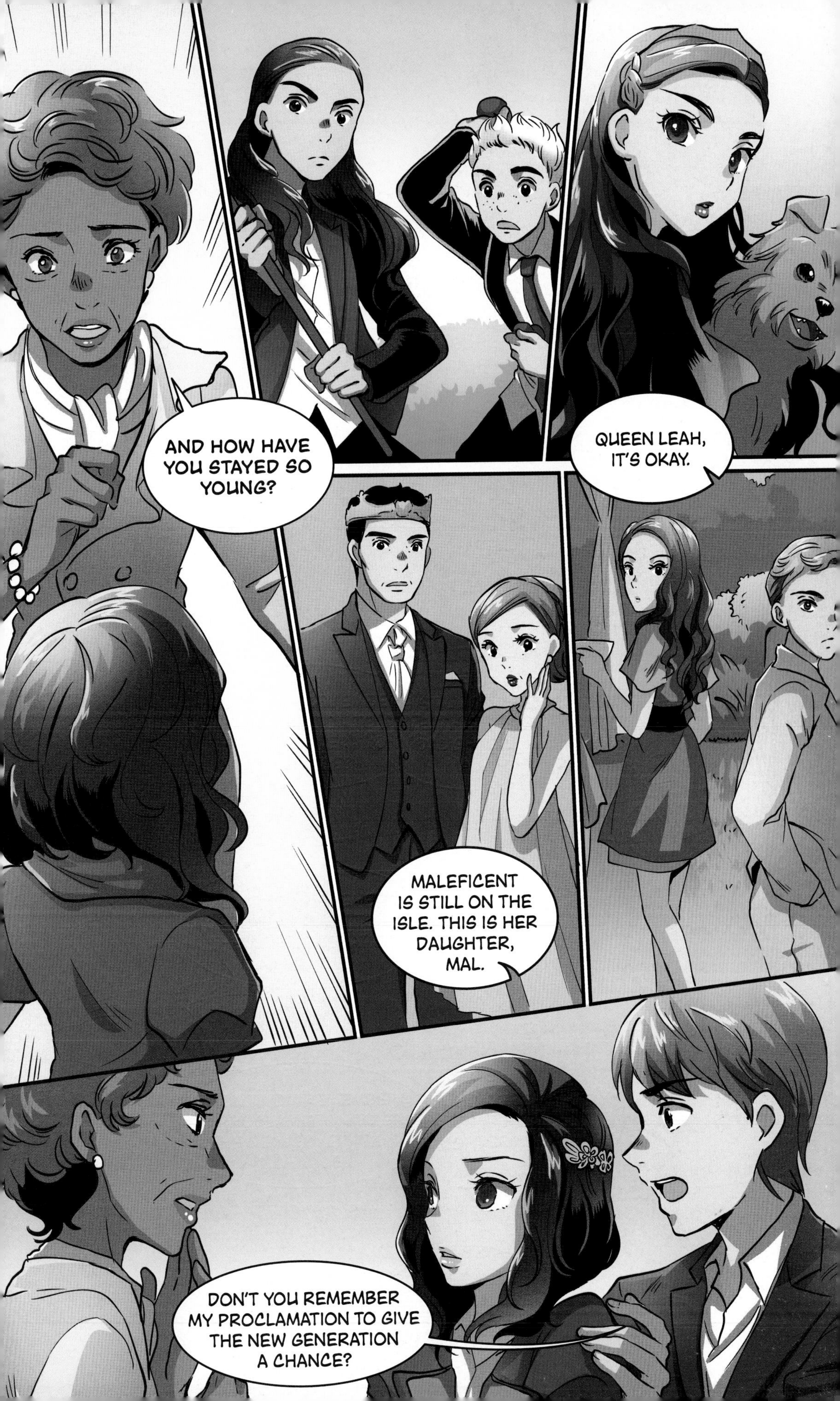
AND HOW HAVE YOU STAYED SO YOUNG?
QUEEN LEAH, IT'S OKAY.
MALEFICENT IS STILL ON THE ISLE. THIS IS HER DAUGHTER, MAL.
DON'T YOU REMEMBER MY PROCLAMATION TO GIVE THE NEW GENERATION A CHANCE?

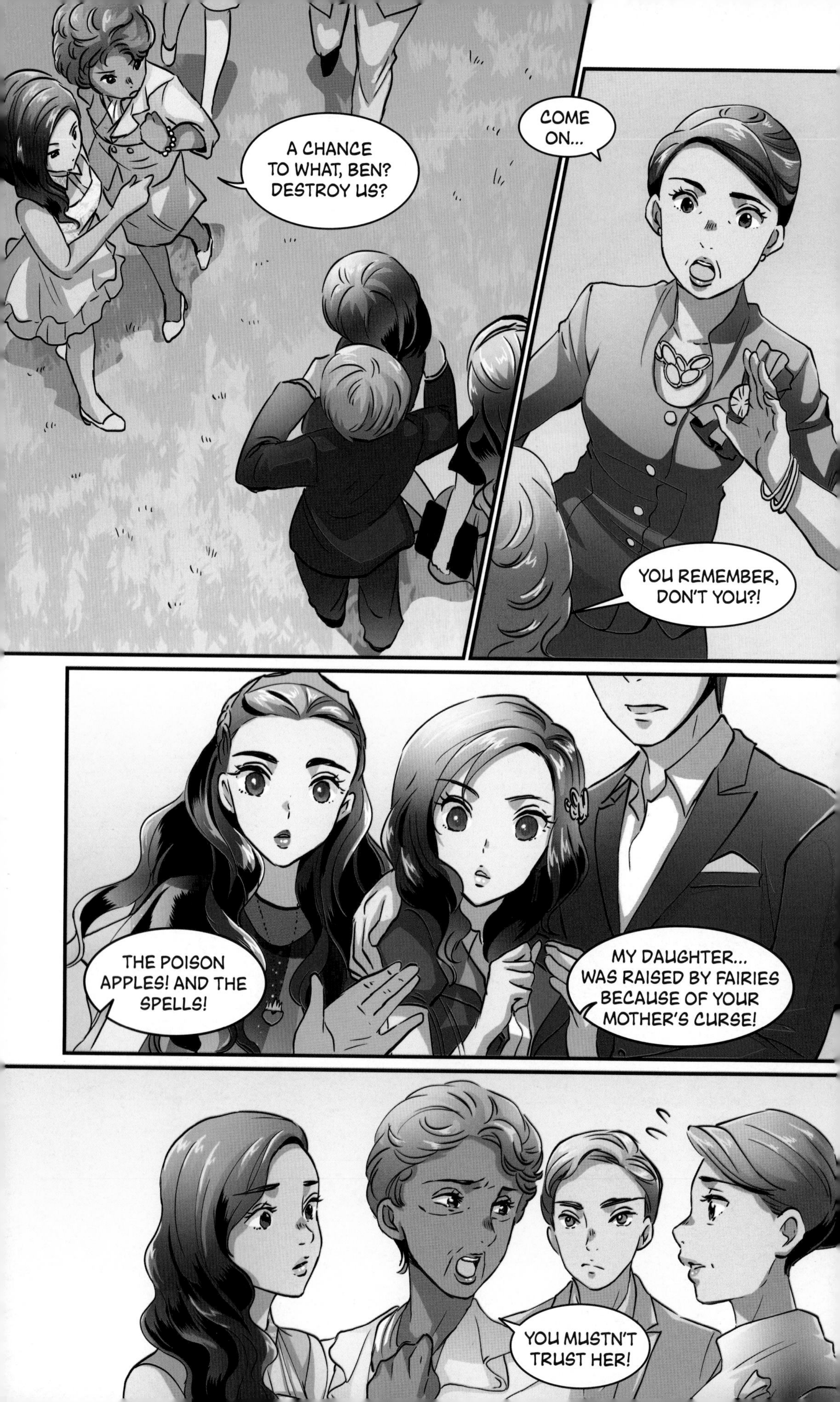
A CHANCE TO WHAT, BEN? DESTROY US?
COME ON...
YOU REMEMBER, DON'T YOU?!
THE POISON APPLES! AND THE SPELLS!
MY DAUGHTER... WAS RAISED BY FAIRIES BECAUSE OF YOUR MOTHER'S CURSE!
YOU MUSTN'T TRUST HER!

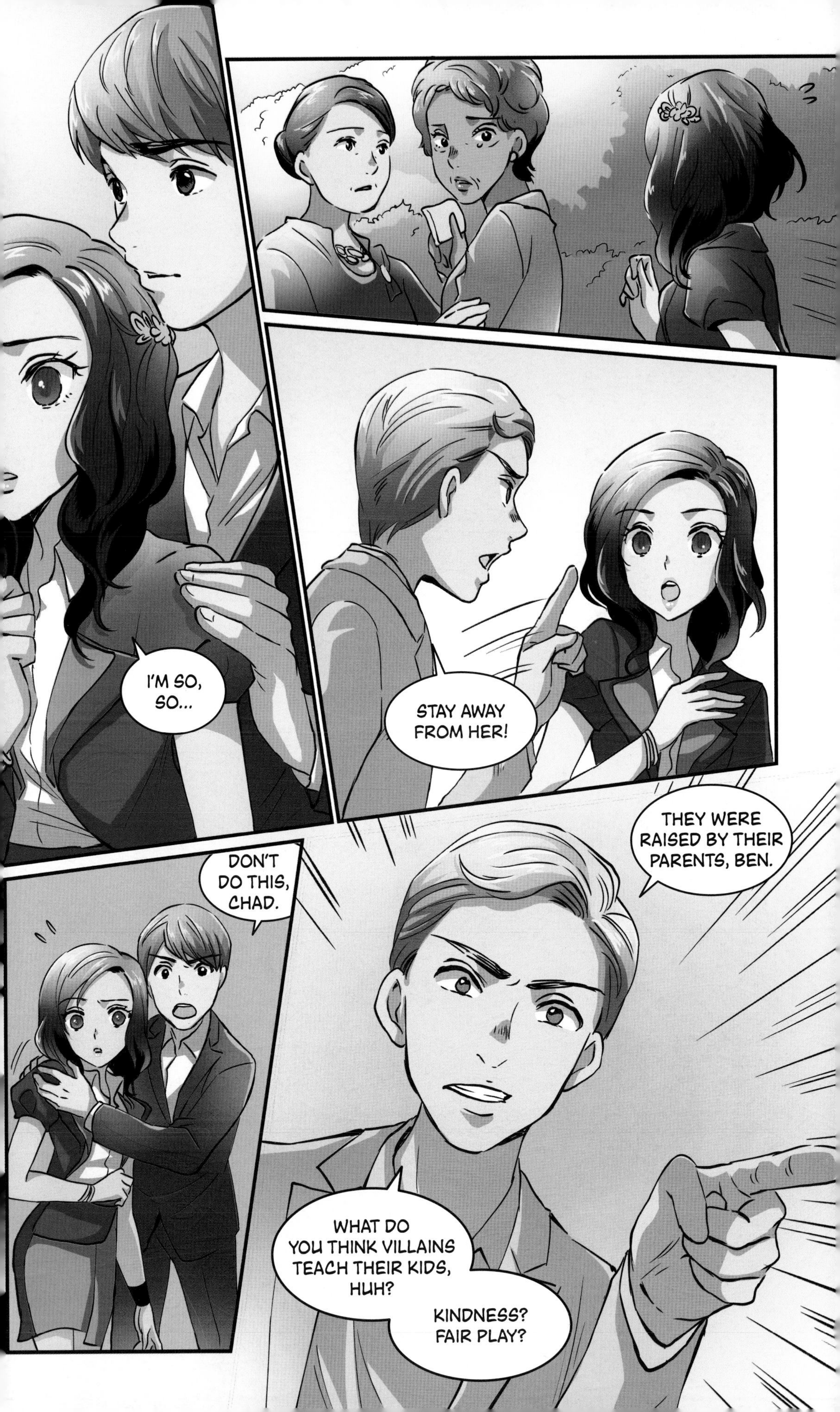
I'M SO, SO...
STAY AWAY FROM HER!
THEY WERE RAISED BY THEIR PARENTS, BEN.
DON'T DO THIS, CHAD.
WHAT DO YOU THINK VILLAINS TEACH THEIR KIDS, HUH?
KINDNESS? FAIR PLAY?

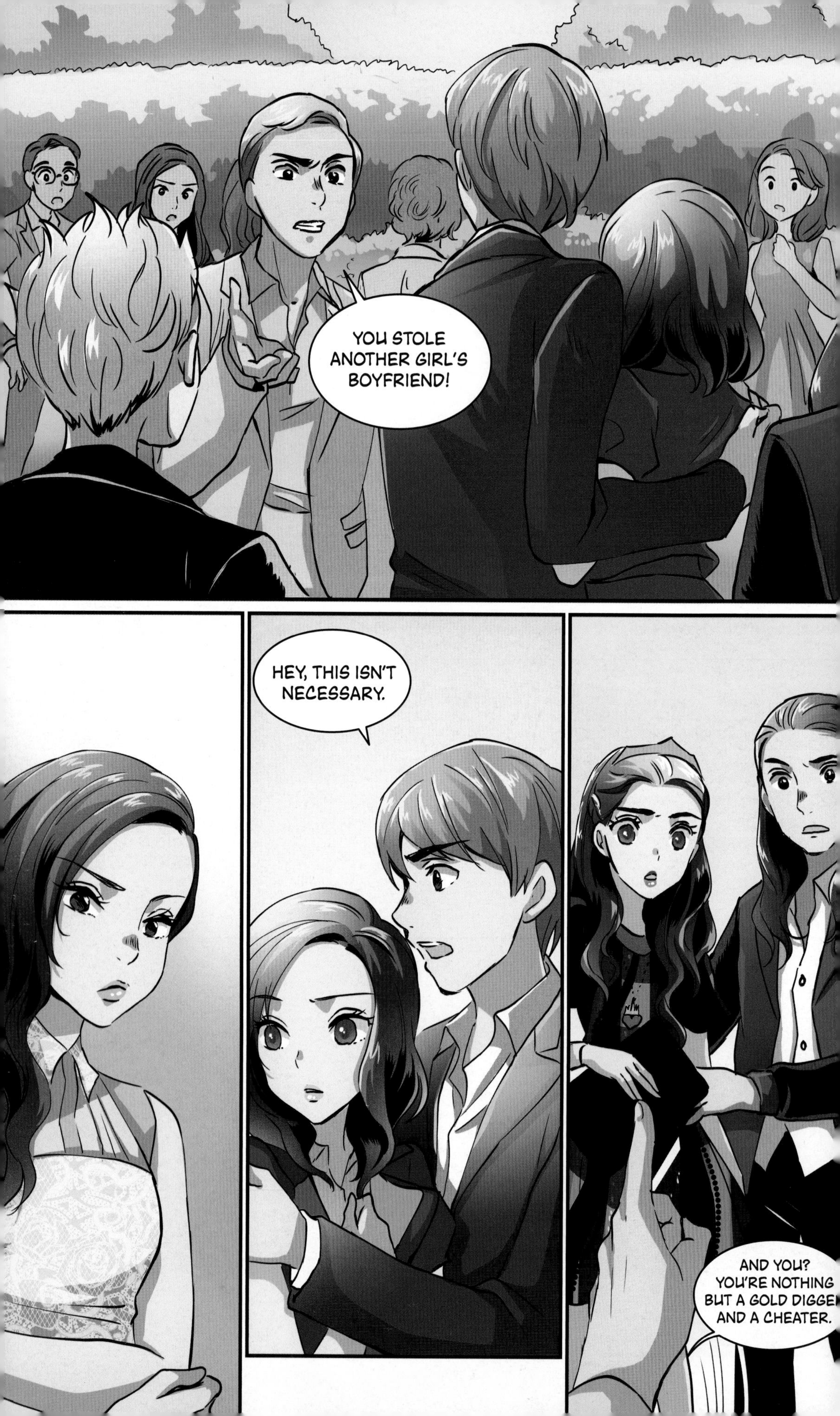
YOU STOLE ANOTHER GIRL'S BOYFRIEND!
HEY, THIS ISN'T NECESSARY.
AND YOU? YOU'RE NOTHING BUT A GOLD DIGGE AND A CHEATER.

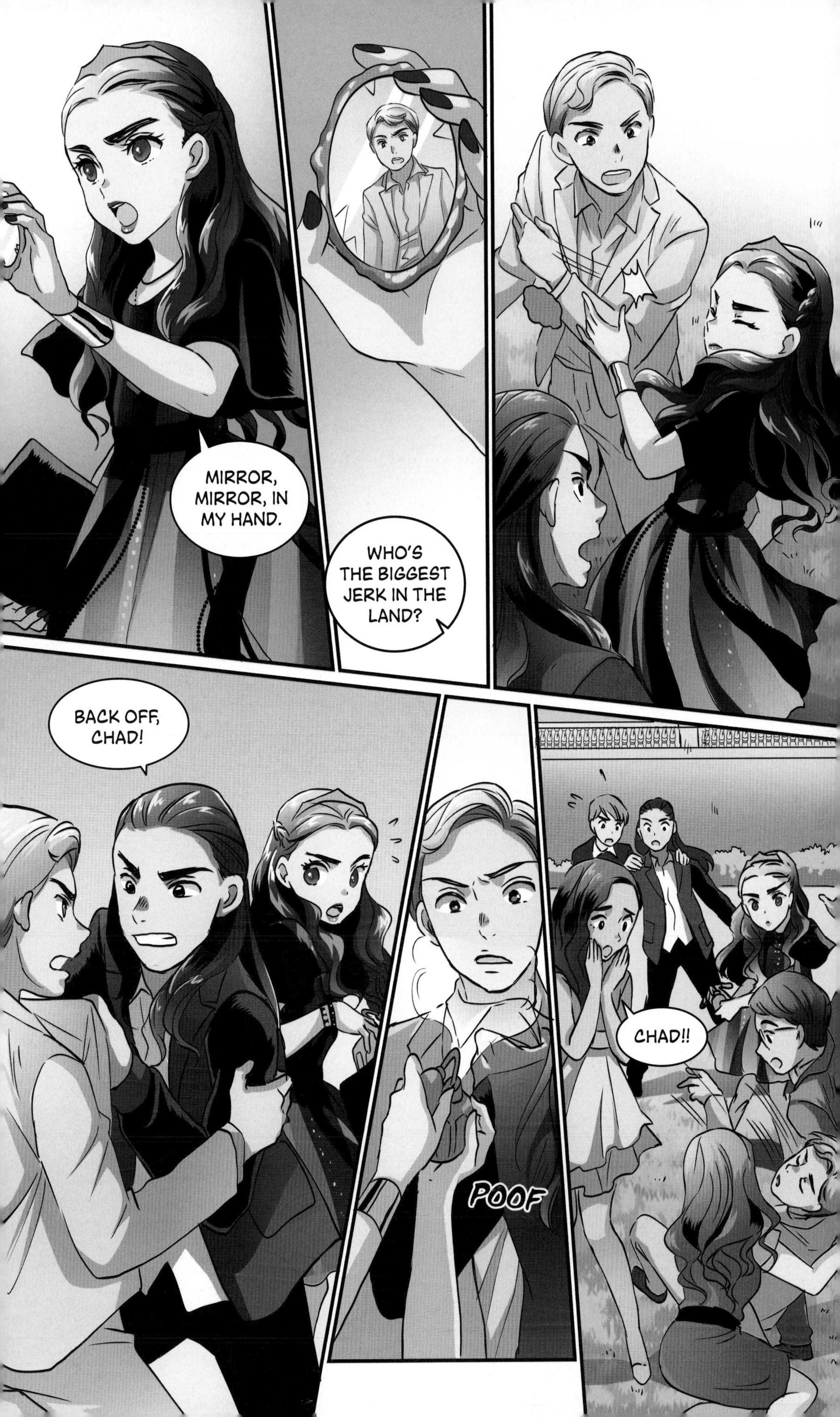
MIRROR, MIRROR, IN MY HAND.
WHO'S THE BIGGEST JERK IN THE LAND?
BACK OFF, CHAD!
POOF
CHAD!!

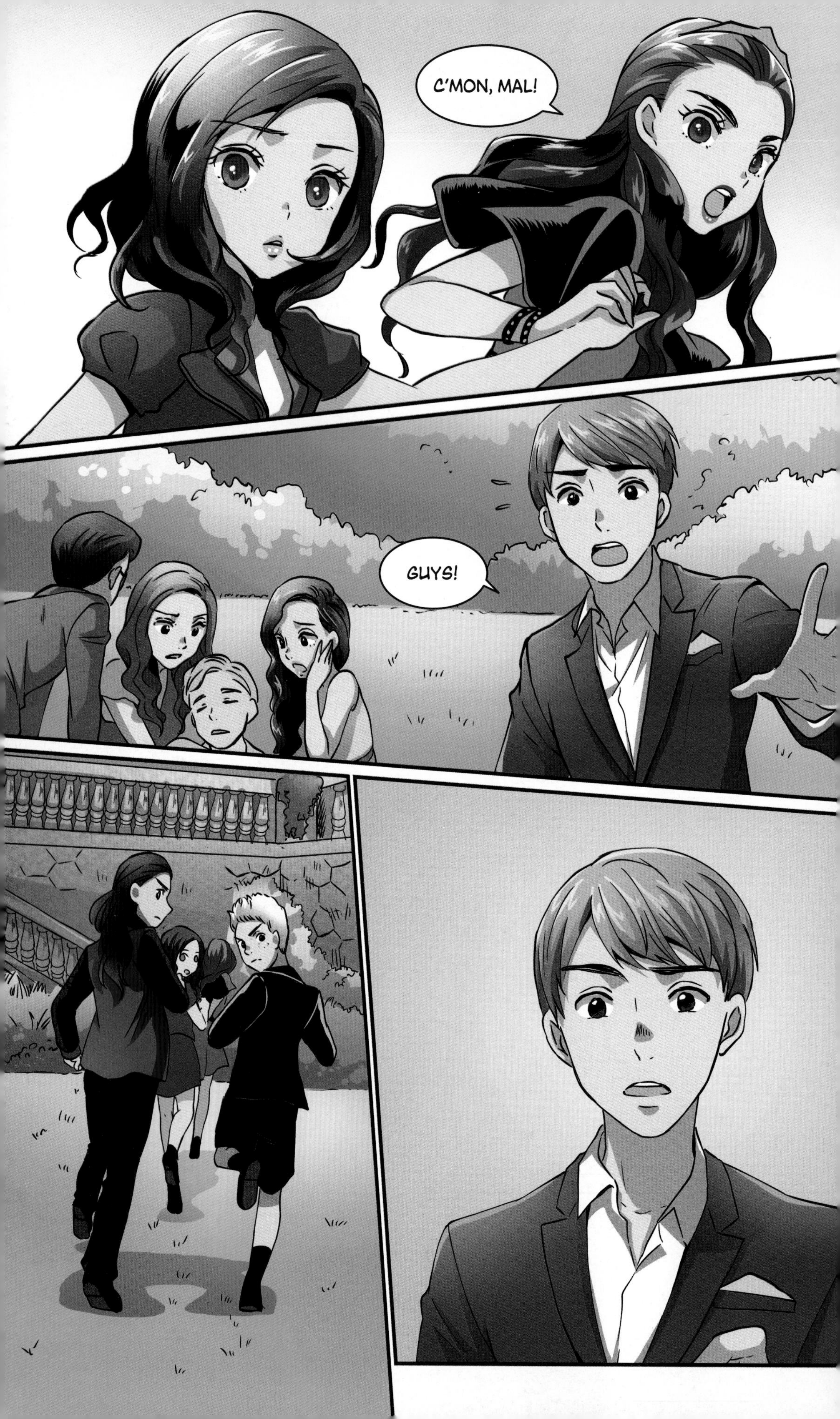
C'MON, MAL!
GUYS!

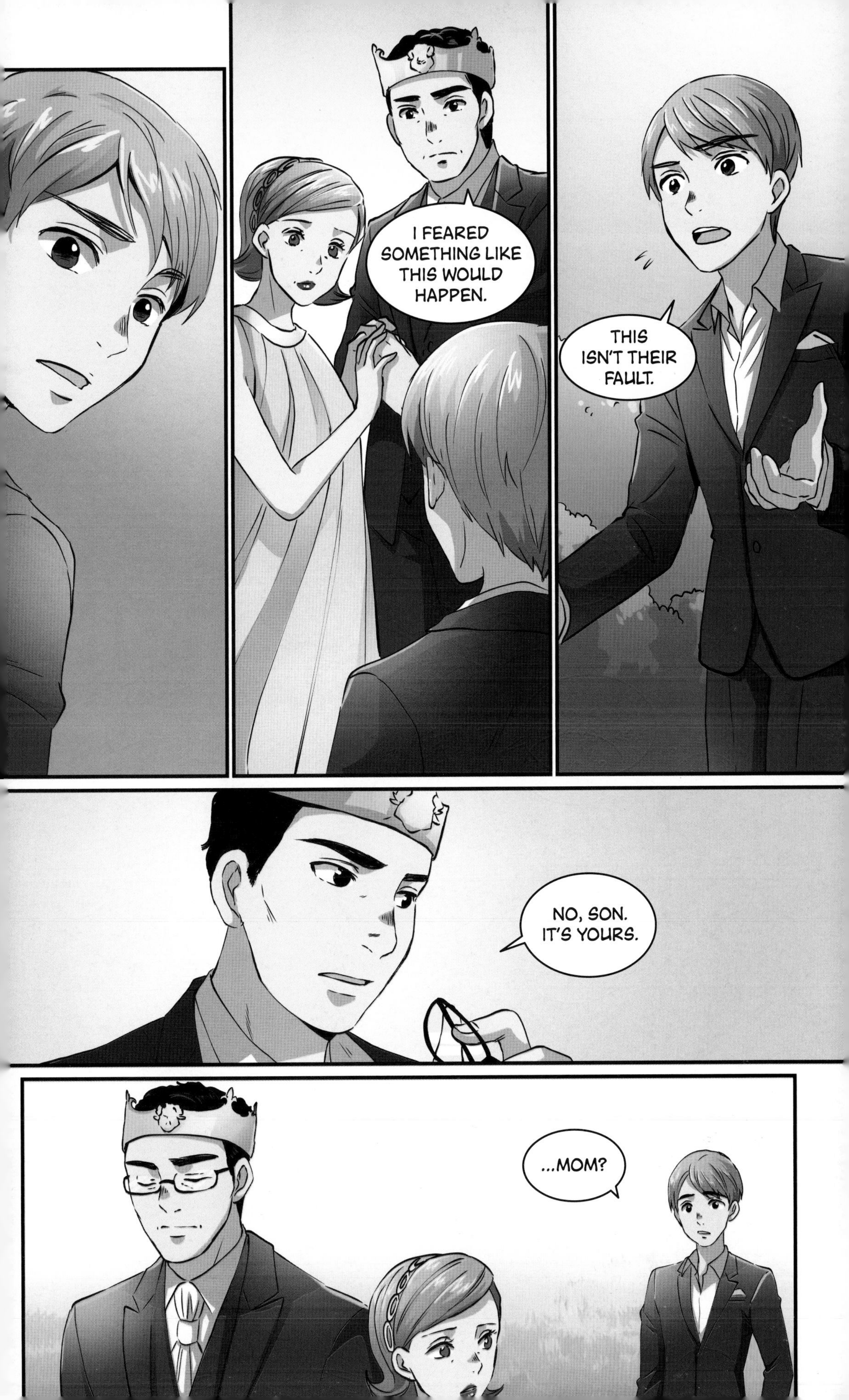
I FEARED SOMETHING LIKE THIS WOULD HAPPEN.
THIS ISN'T THEIR FAULT.
NO, SON. IT'S YOURS.
...MOM?

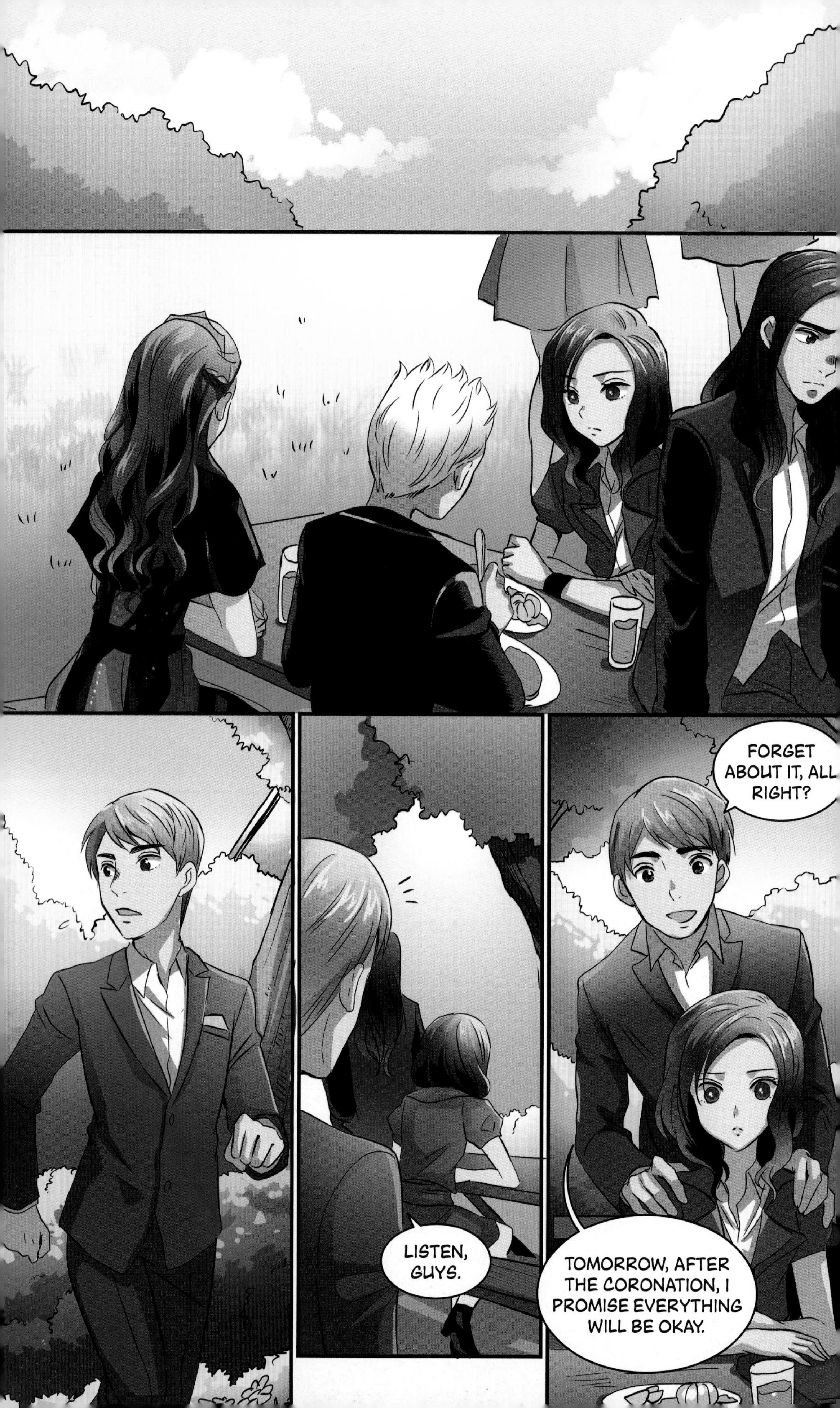
FORGET ABOUT IT, ALL RIGHT?
LISTEN, GUYS.
TOMORROW, AFTER THE CORONATION, I PROMISE EVERYTHING WILL BE OKAY.

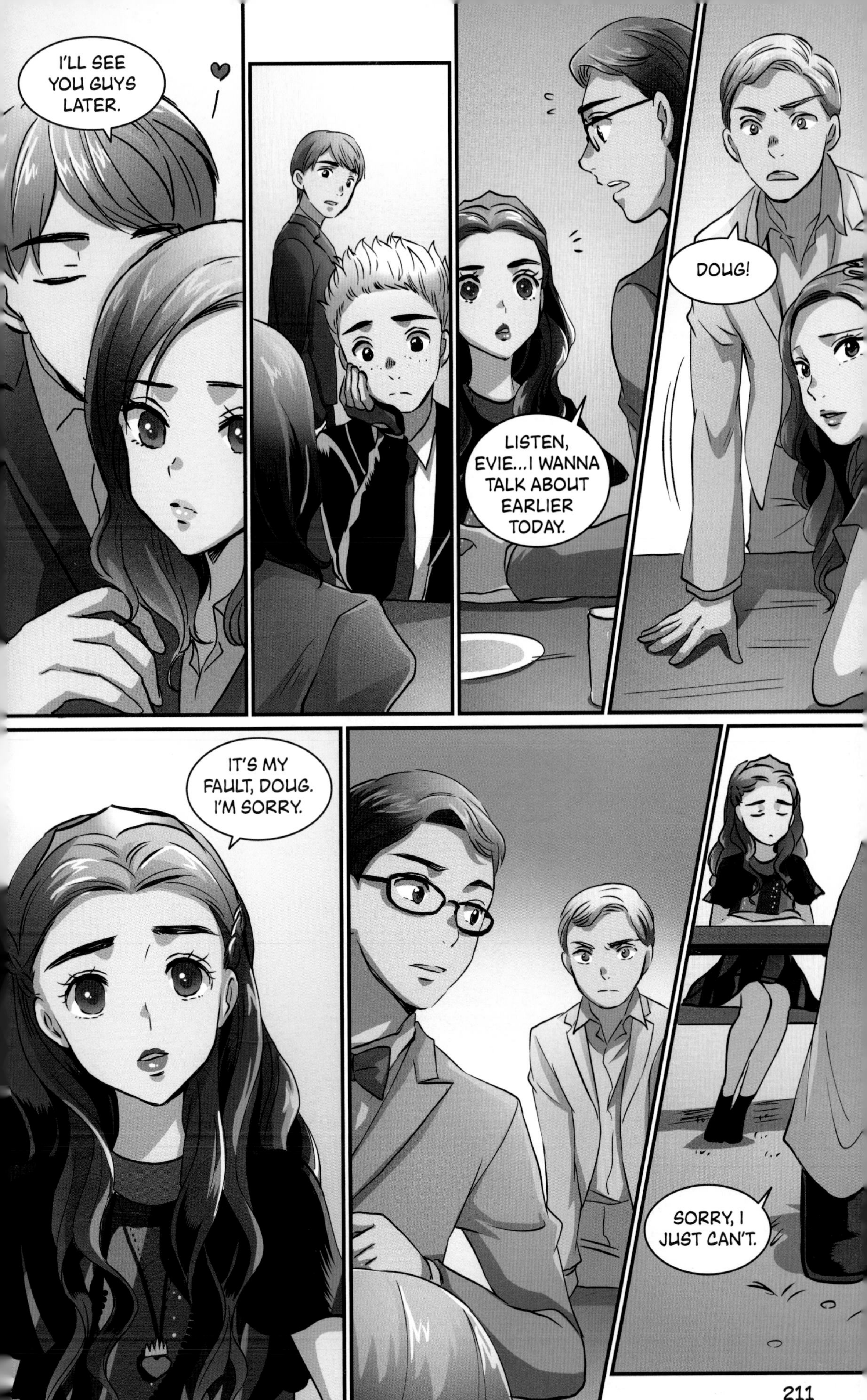
I'LL SEE YOU GUYS LATER.
LISTEN, EVIE...I WANNA TALK ABOUT EARLIER TODAY.
DOUG!
IT'S MY FAULT, DOUG. I'M SORRY.
SORRY, I JUST CAN'T.

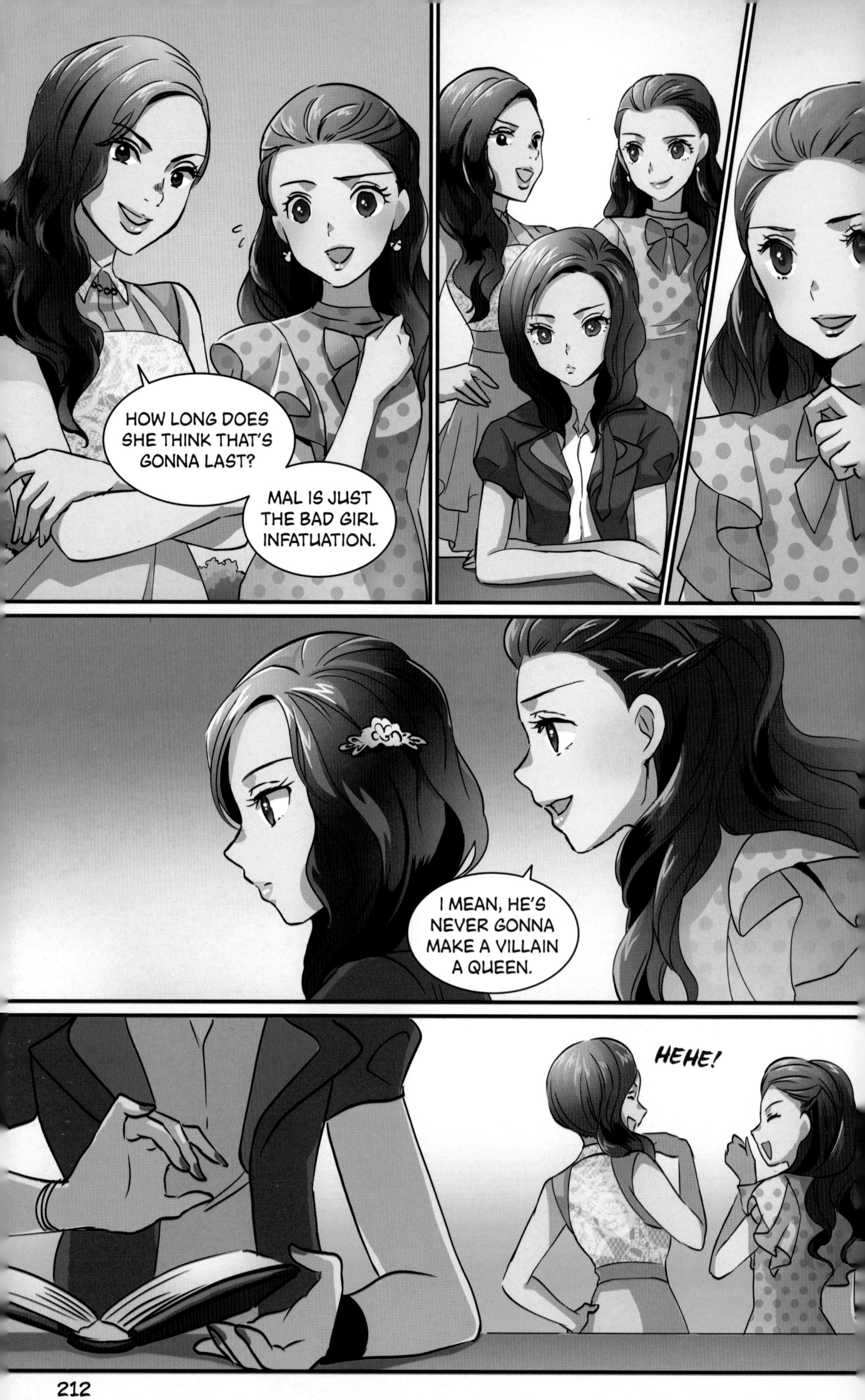
HOW LONG DOES SHE THINK THAT'S GONNA LAST?
MAL IS JUST THE BAD GIRL INFATUATION.
I MEAN, HE'S NEVER GONNA MAKE A VILLAIN A QUEEN.
HEHE!

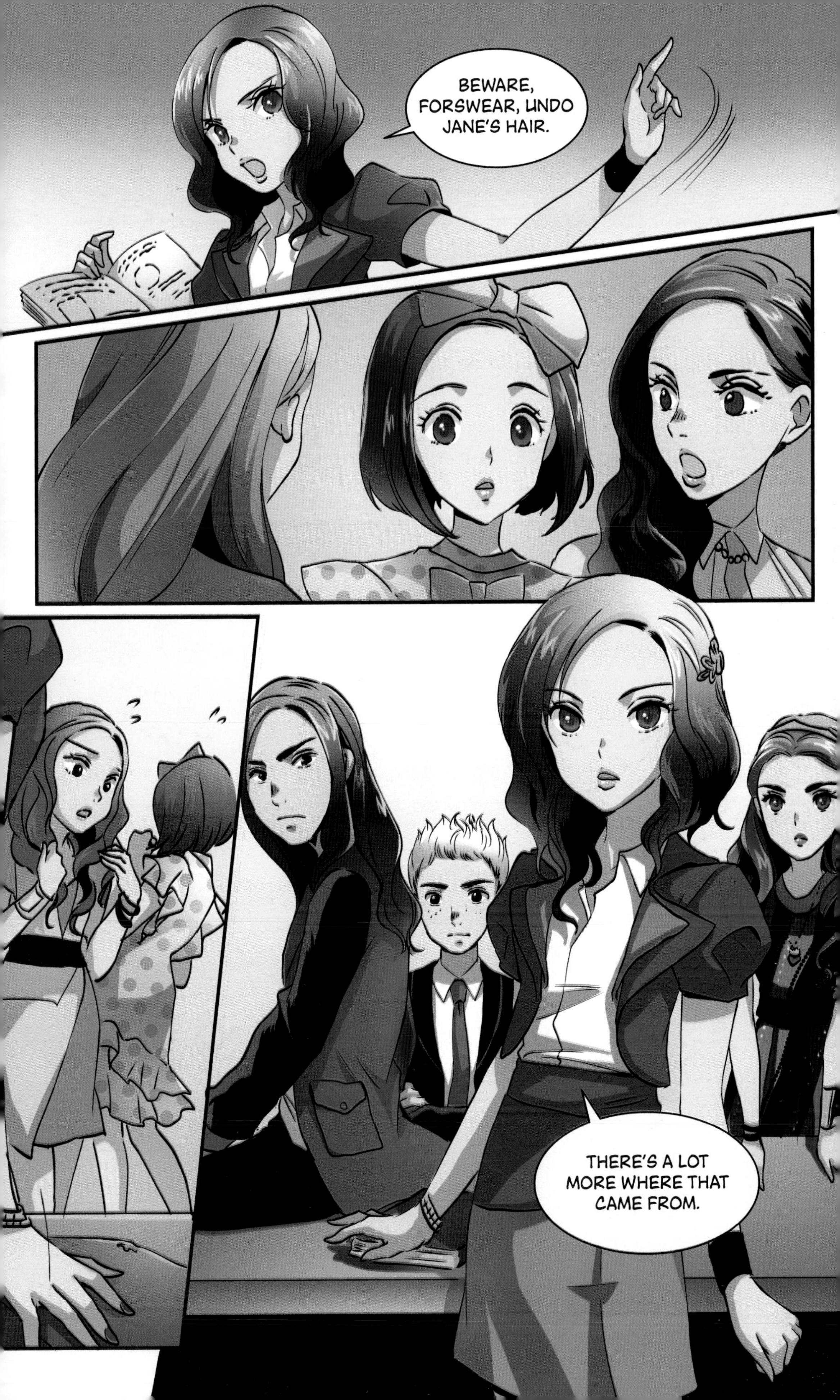
BEWARE, FORSWEAR, UNDO JANE'S HAIR.
THERE'S A LOT MORE WHERE THAT CAME FROM.

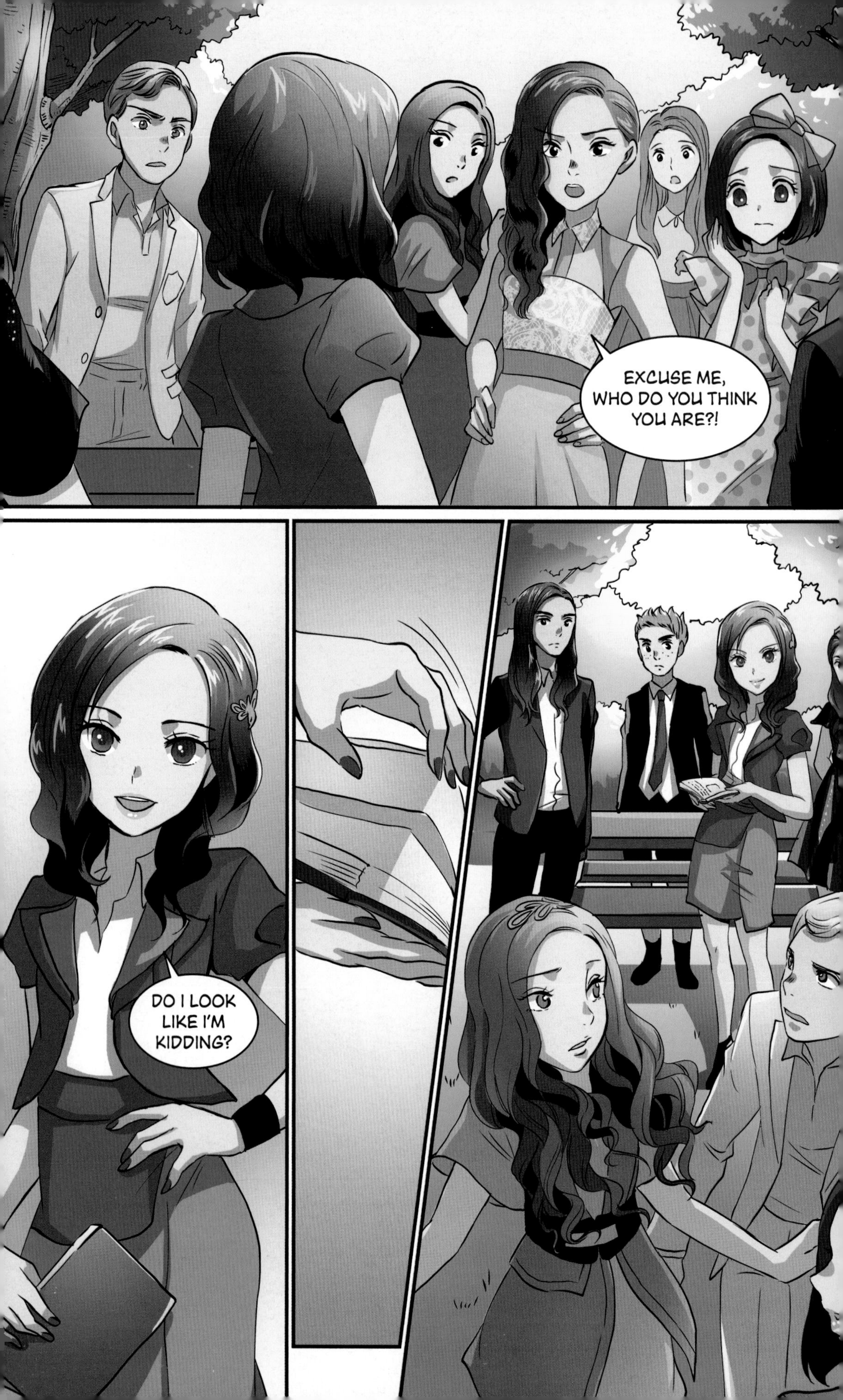
EXCUSE ME, WHO DO YOU THINK YOU ARE?!
DO I LOOK LIKE I'M KIDDING?

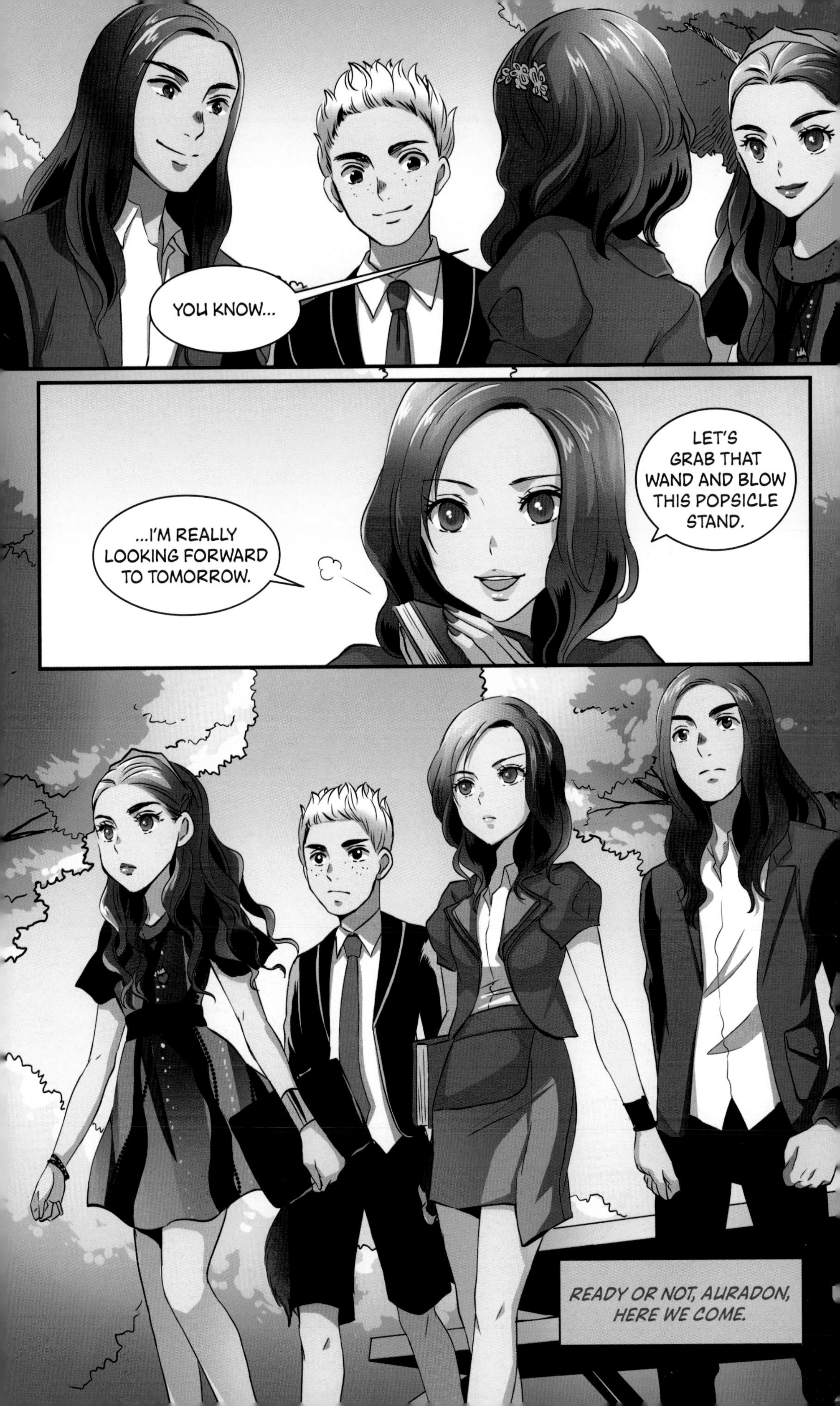
YOU KNOW...
...I'M REALLY LOOKING FORWARD TO TOMORROW.
LET'S GRAB THAT WAND AND BLOW THIS POPSICLE STAND.
READY OR NOT, AURADON, HERE WE COME.

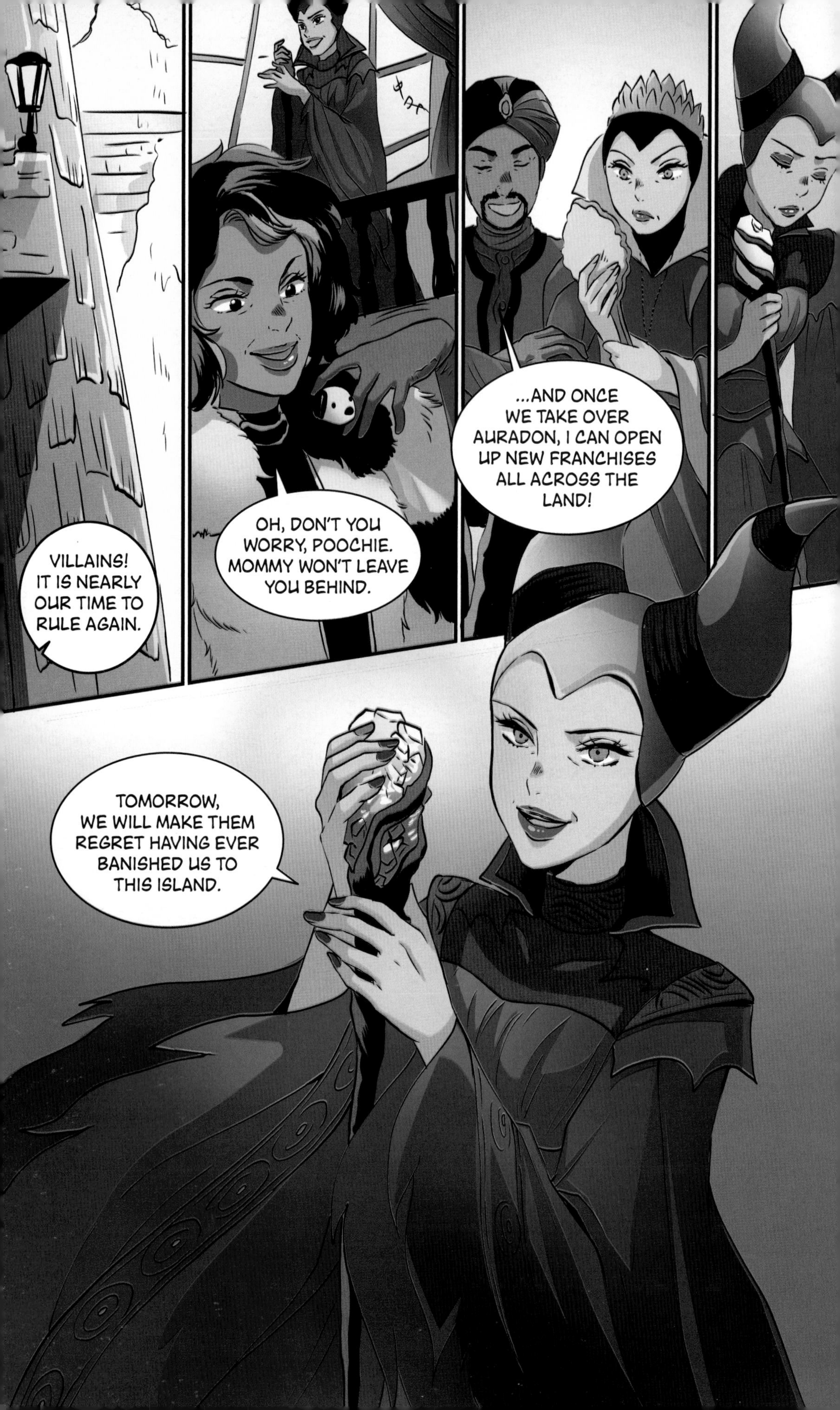
VILLAINS! IT IS NEARLY OUR TIME TO RULE AGAIN.
OH, DON'T YOU WORRY, POOCHIE. MOMMY WON'T LEAVE YOU BEHIND.
...AND ONCE WE TAKE OVER AURADON, I CAN OPEN UP NEW FRANCHISES ALL ACROSS THE LAND!
TOMORROW, WE WILL MAKE THEM REGRET HAVING EVER BANISHED US TO THIS ISLAND.

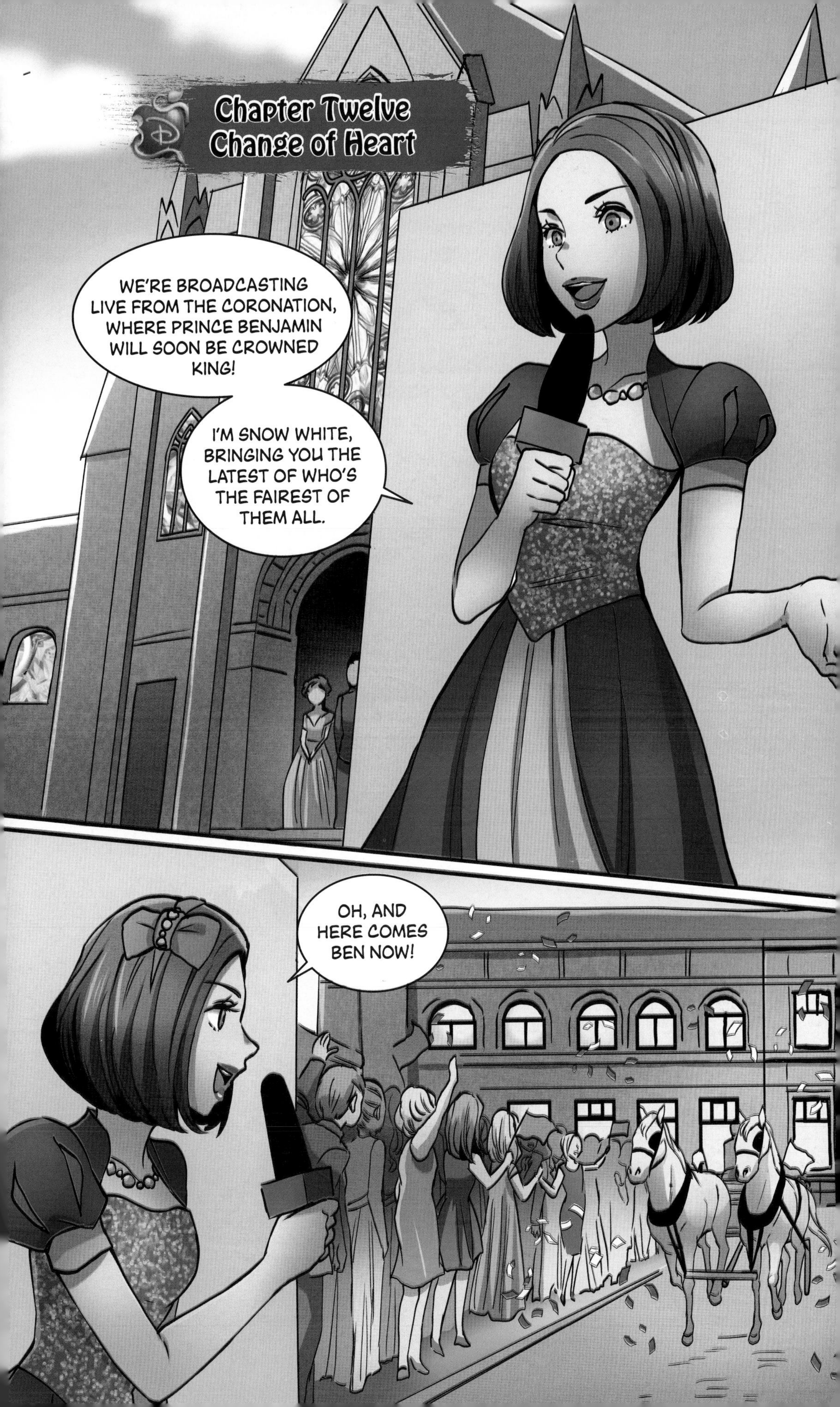
Chapter Twelve
Change of Heart
WE'RE BROADCASTING LIVE FROM THE CORONATION, WHERE PRINCE BENJAMIN WILL SOON BE CROWNED KING!
I'M SNOW WHITE, BRINGING YOU THE LATEST OF WHO'S THE FAIREST OF THEM ALL.
OH, AND HERE COMES BEN NOW!

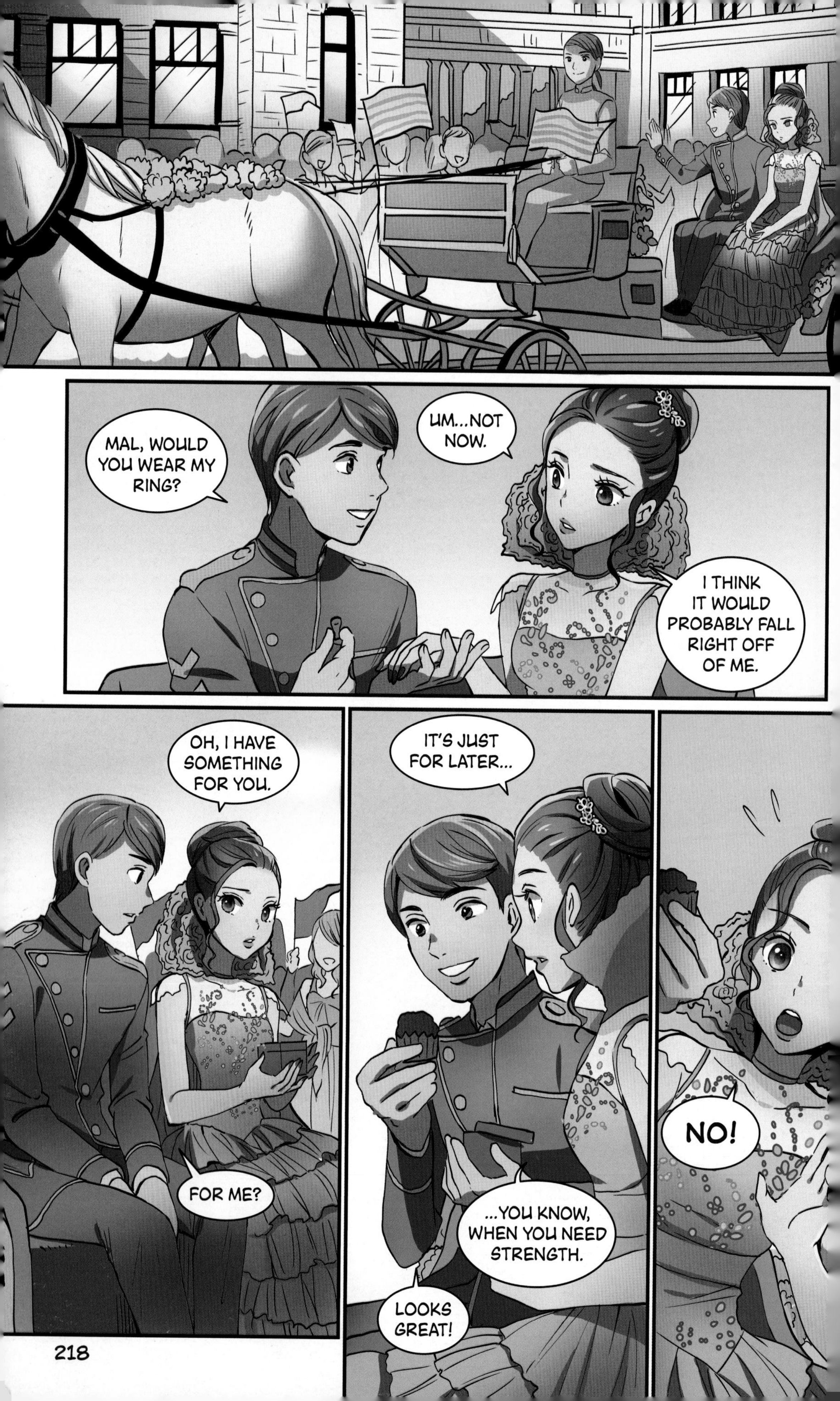
MAL, WOULD YOU WEAR MY RING?
UM...NOT NOW.
I THINK IT WOULD PROBABLY FALL RIGHT OFF OF ME.
OH, I HAVE SOMETHING FOR YOU.
FOR ME?
IT'S JUST FOR LATER...
...YOU KNOW, WHEN YOU NEED STRENGTH.
LOOKS GREAT!
NO!

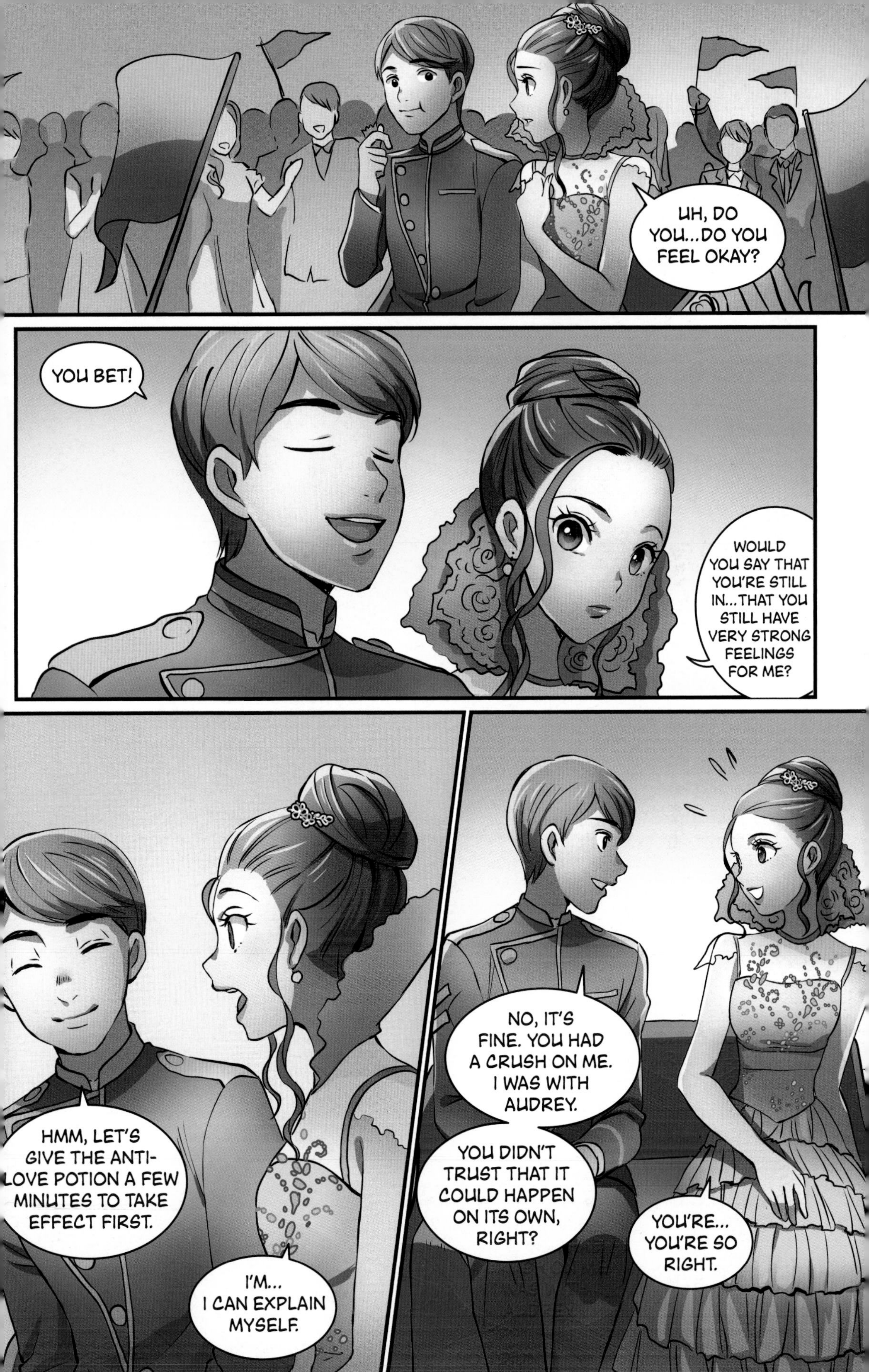
UH, DO YOU...DO YOU FEEL OKAY?
YOU BET!
WOULD YOU SAY THAT YOU'RE STILL IN...THAT YOU STILL HAVE VERY STRONG FEELINGS FOR ME?
HMM, LET'S GIVE THE ANTI-LOVE POTION A FEW MINUTES TO TAKE EFFECT FIRST.
I'M... I CAN EXPLAIN MYSELF.
NO, IT'S FINE. YOU HAD A CRUSH ON ME. I WAS WITH AUDREY.
YOU DIDN'T TRUST THAT IT COULD HAPPEN ON ITS OWN, RIGHT?
YOU'RE... YOU'RE SO RIGHT.

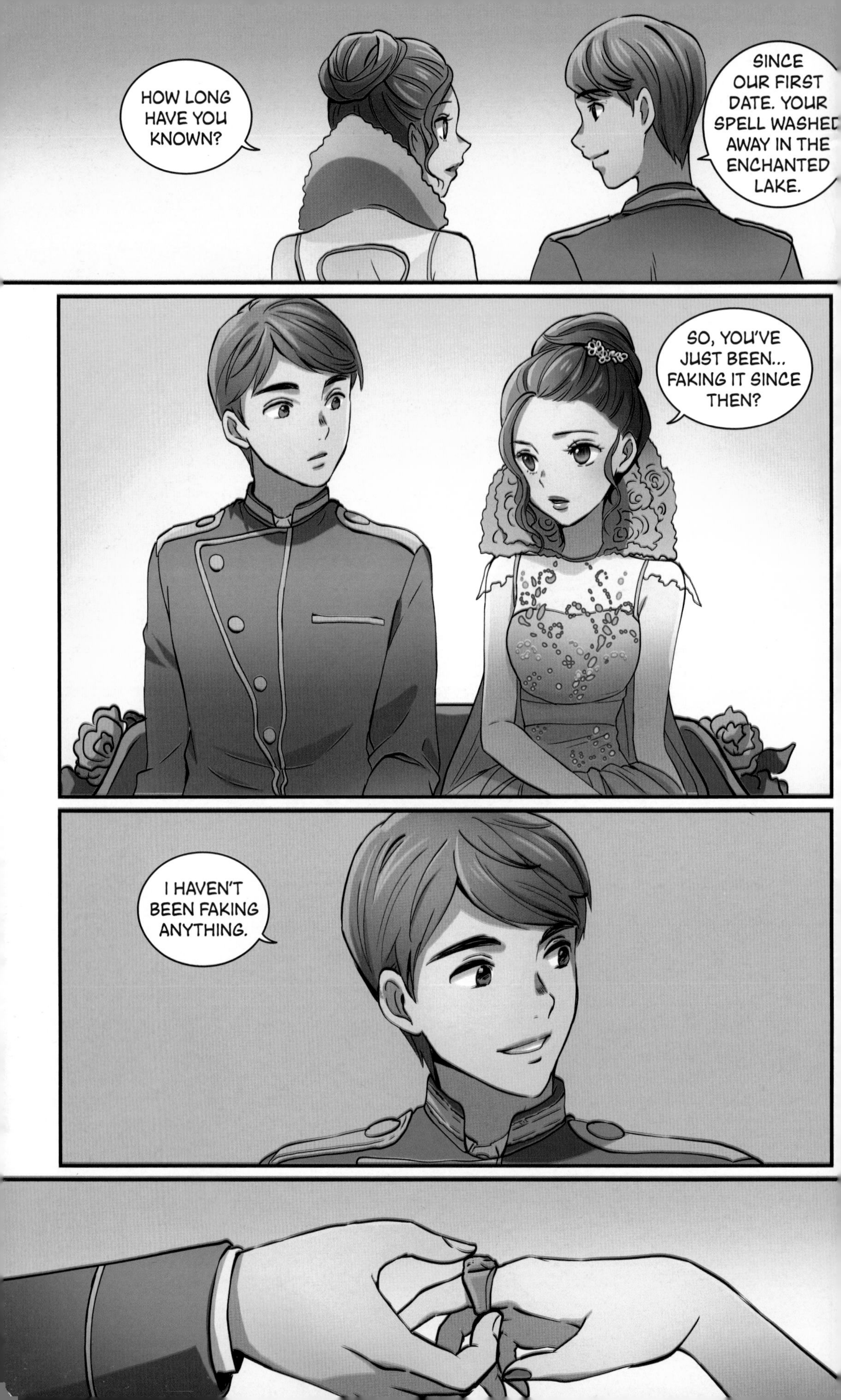
HOW LONG HAVE YOU KNOWN?
SINCE OUR FIRST DATE. YOUR SPELL WASHED AWAY IN THE ENCHANTED LAKE.
SO, YOU'VE JUST BEEN... FAKING IT SINCE THEN?
I HAVEN'T BEEN FAKING ANYTHING.

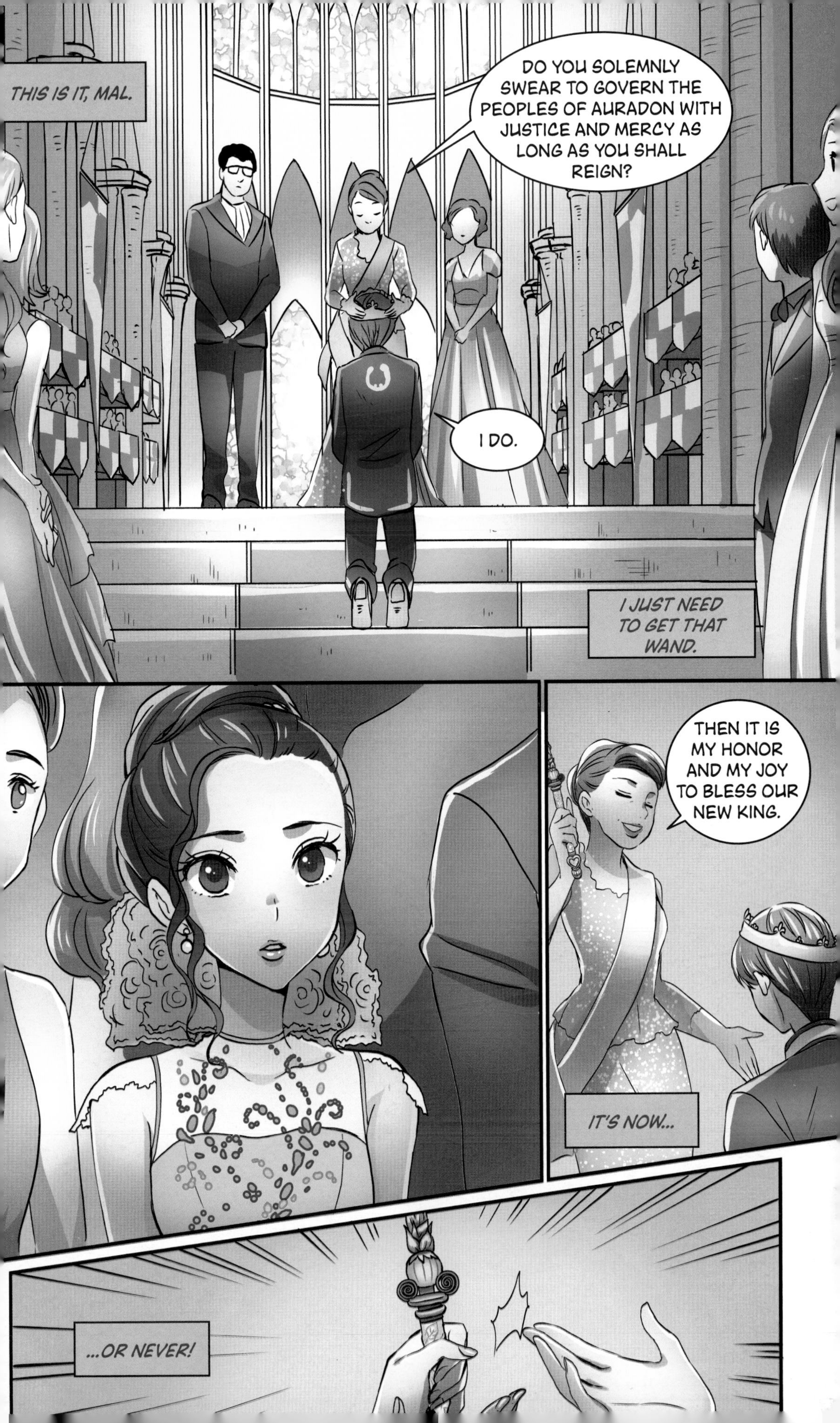
THIS IS IT, MAL.
DO YOU SOLEMNLY SWEAR TO GOVERN THE PEOPLES OF AURADON WITH JUSTICE AND MERCY AS LONG AS YOU SHALL REIGN?
I DO.
I JUST NEED TO GET THAT WAND.
THEN IT IS MY HONOR AND MY JOY TO BLESS OUR NEW KING.
IT'S NOW...
...OR NEVER!

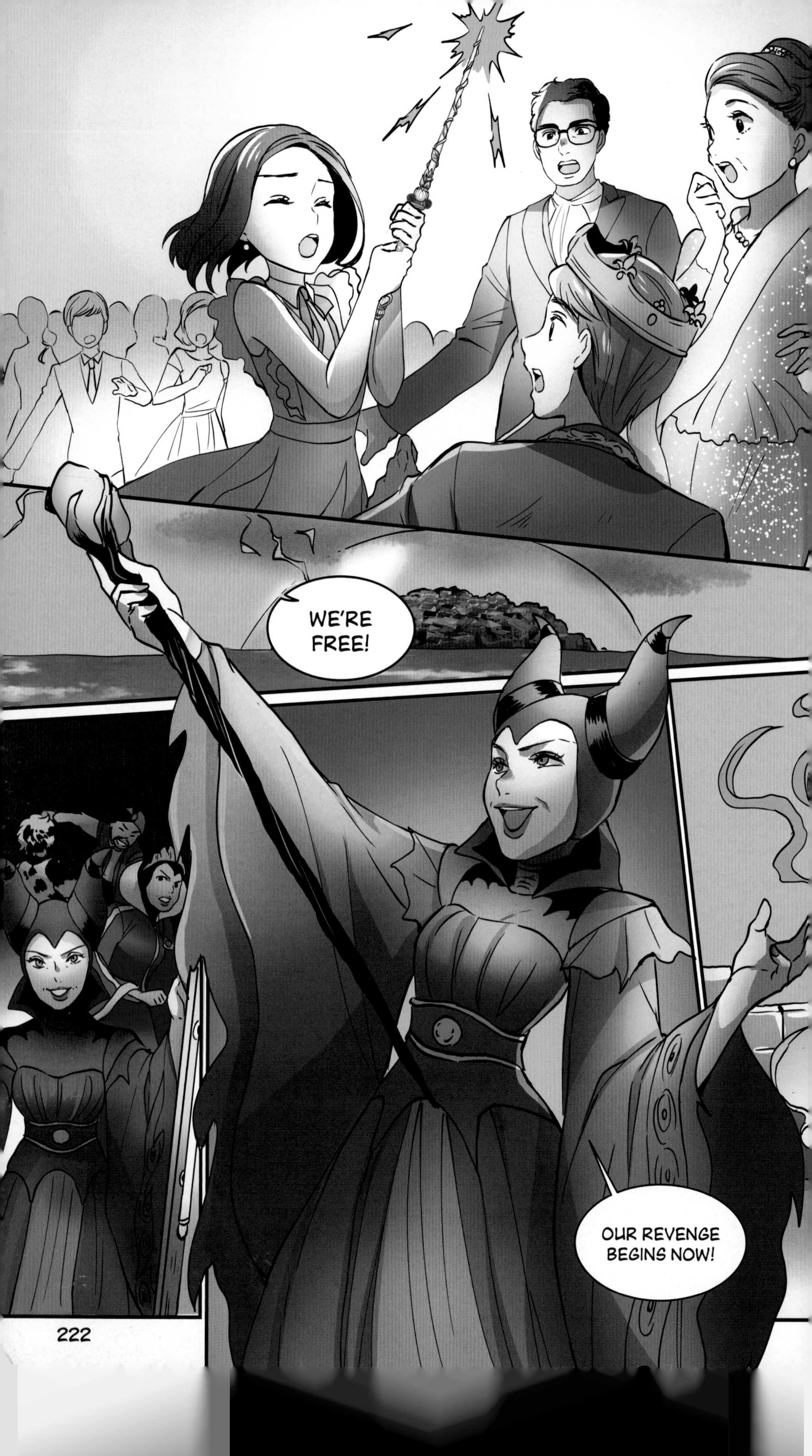
WE'RE FREE!
OUR REVENGE BEGINS NOW!

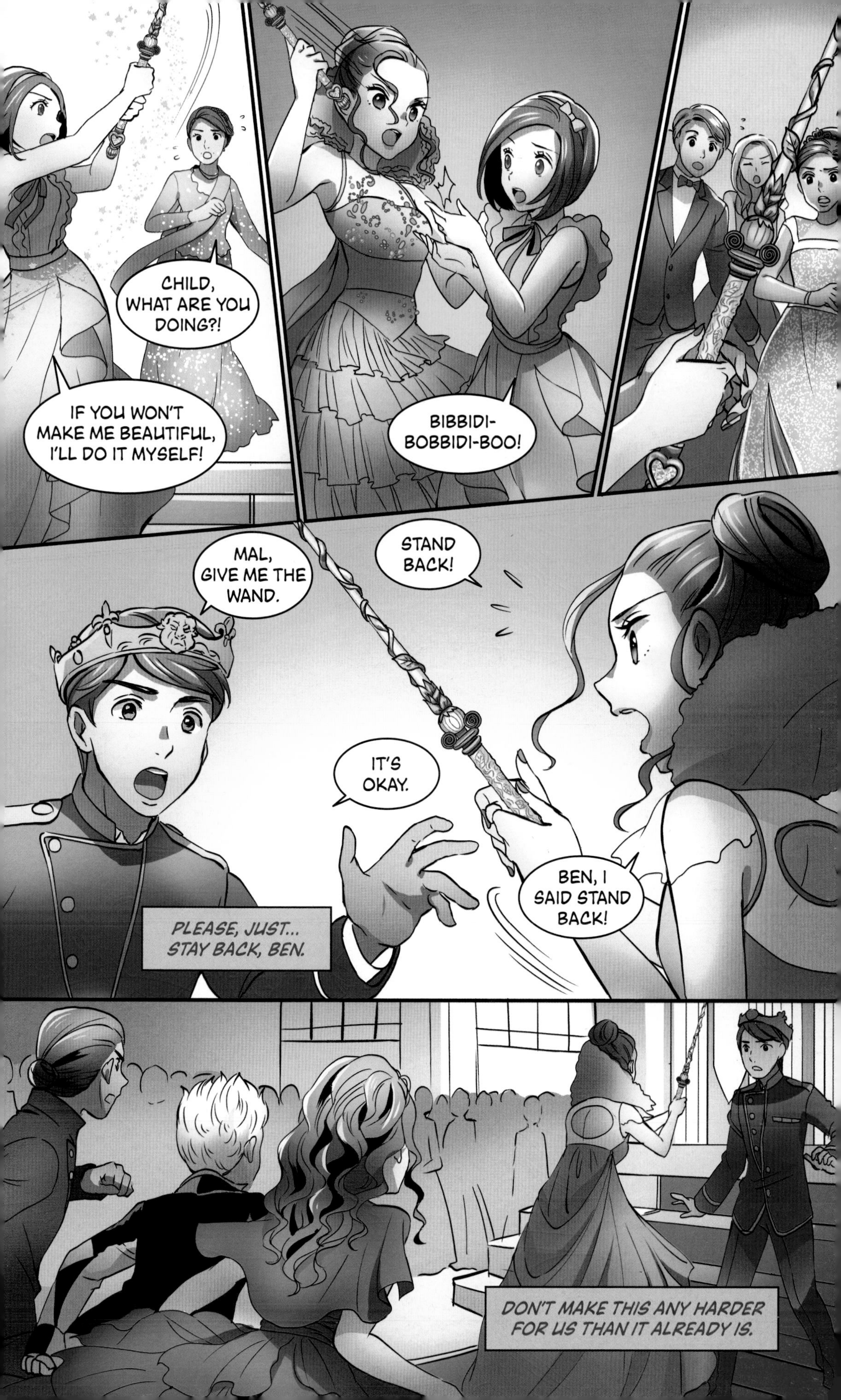
CHILD, WHAT ARE YOU DOING?!
IF YOU WON'T MAKE ME BEAUTIFUL, I'LL DO IT MYSELF!
BIBBIDI-BOBBIDI-BOO!
MAL, GIVE ME THE WAND.
STAND BACK!
IT'S OKAY.
BEN, I SAID STAND BACK!
PLEASE, JUST... STAY BACK, BEN.
DON'T MAKE THIS ANY HARDER FOR US THAN IT ALREADY IS.

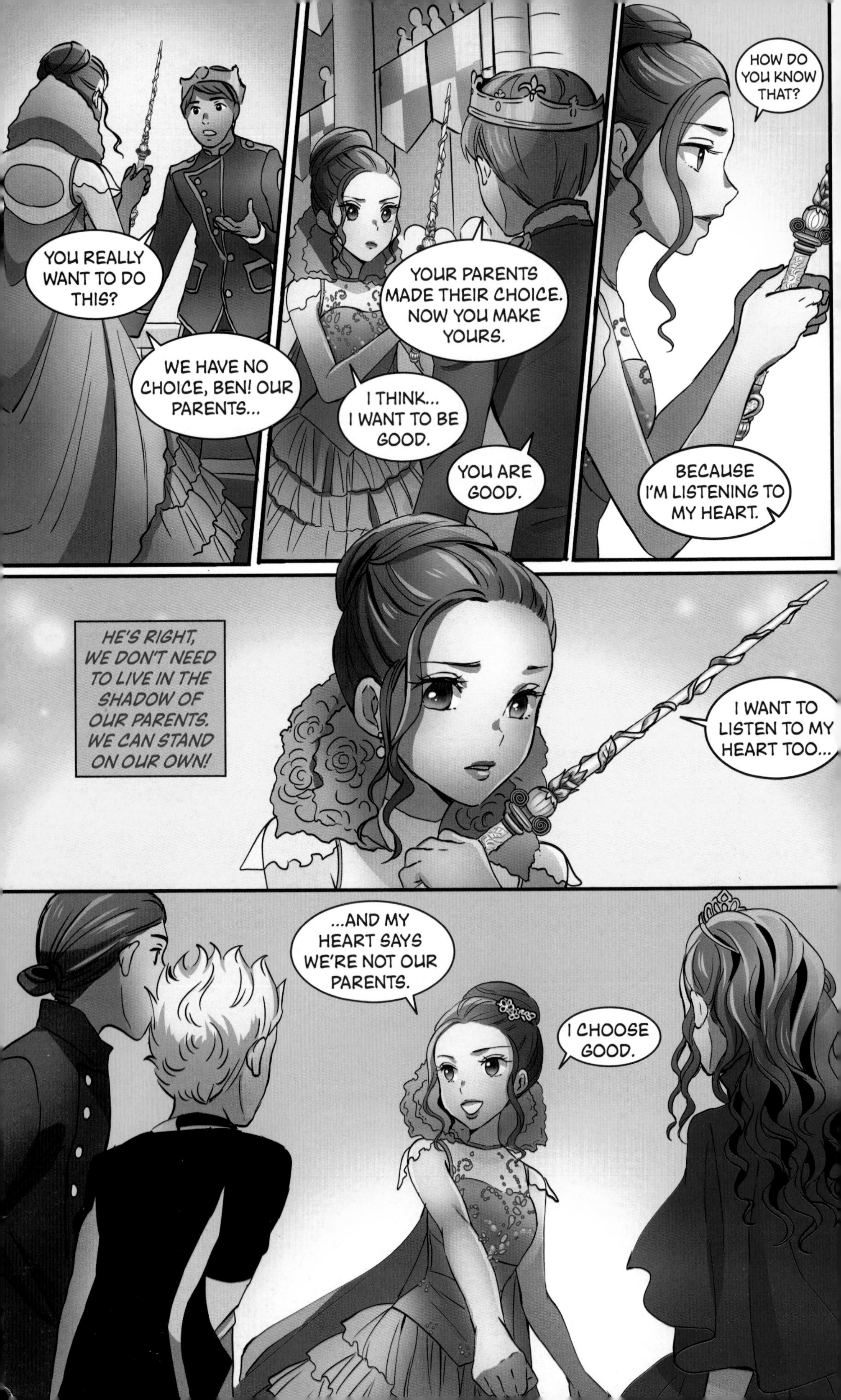
YOU REALLY WANT TO DO THIS?
WE HAVE NO CHOICE, BEN! OUR PARENTS...
YOUR PARENTS MADE THEIR CHOICE. NOW YOU MAKE YOURS.
I THINK... I WANT TO BE GOOD.
YOU ARE GOOD.
HOW DO YOU KNOW THAT?
BECAUSE I'M LISTENING TO MY HEART.
HE'S RIGHT, WE DON'T NEED TO LIVE IN THE SHADOW OF OUR PARENTS. WE CAN STAND ON OUR OWN!
I WANT TO LISTEN TO MY HEART TOO...
...AND MY HEART SAYS WE'RE NOT OUR PARENTS.
I CHOOSE GOOD.

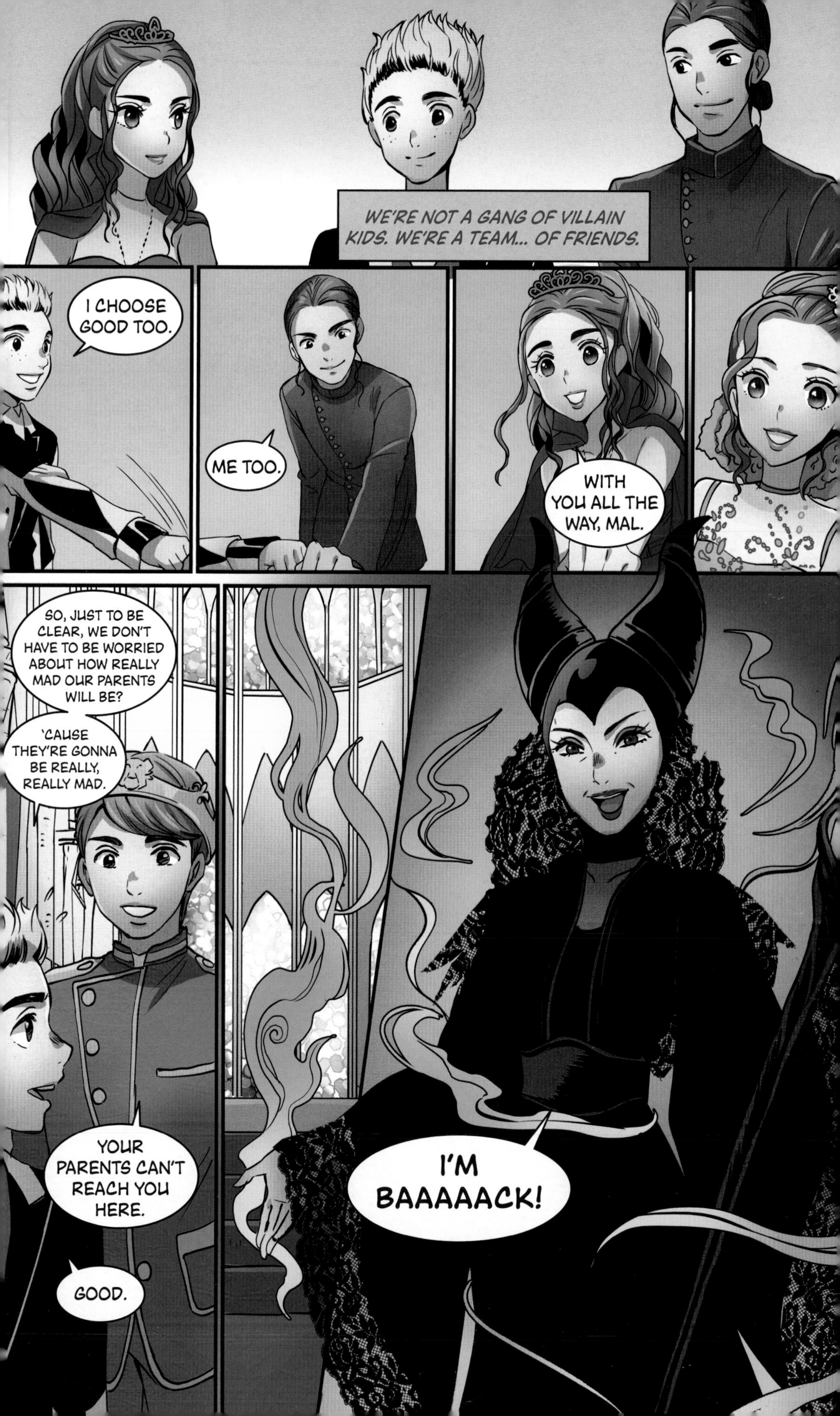
WE'RE NOT A GANG OF VILLAIN KIDS. WE'RE A TEAM... OF FRIENDS.
I CHOOSE GOOD TOO.
ME TOO.
WITH YOU ALL THE WAY, MAL.
SO, JUST TO BE CLEAR, WE DON'T HAVE TO BE WORRIED ABOUT HOW REALLY MAD OUR PARENTS WILL BE?
'CAUSE THEY'RE GONNA BE REALLY, REALLY MAD.
YOUR PARENTS CAN'T REACH YOU HERE.
GOOD.
I'M BAAAAACK!

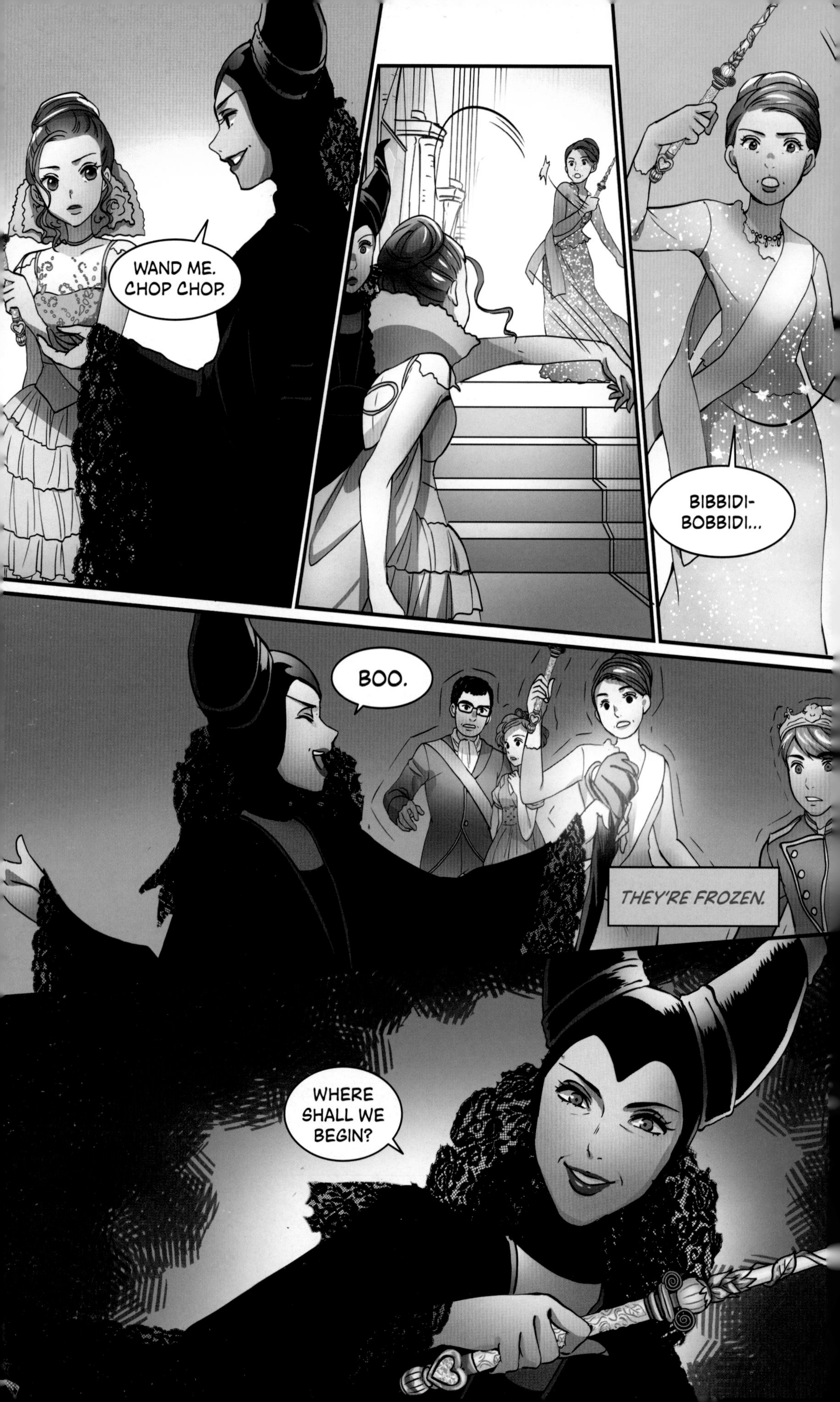
WAND ME. CHOP CHOP.
BIBBIDI-BOBBIDI...
BOO.
THEY'RE FROZEN.
WHERE SHALL WE BEGIN?

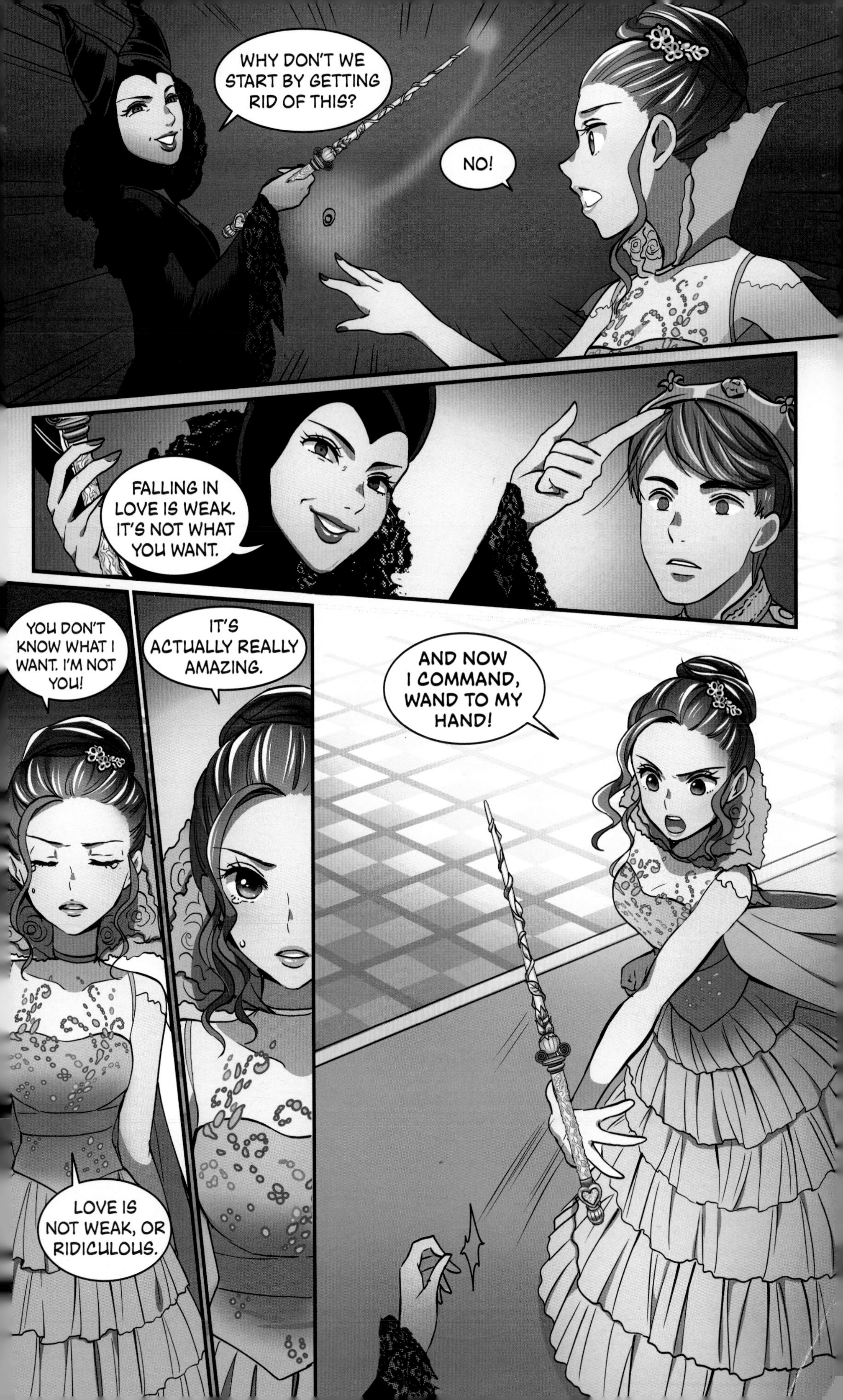
WHY DON'T WE START BY GETTING RID OF THIS?
NO!
FALLING IN LOVE IS WEAK. IT'S NOT WHAT YOU WANT.
YOU DON'T KNOW WHAT I WANT. I'M NOT YOU!
LOVE IS NOT WEAK, OR RIDICULOUS.
IT'S ACTUALLY REALLY AMAZING.
AND NOW I COMMAND, WAND TO MY HAND!

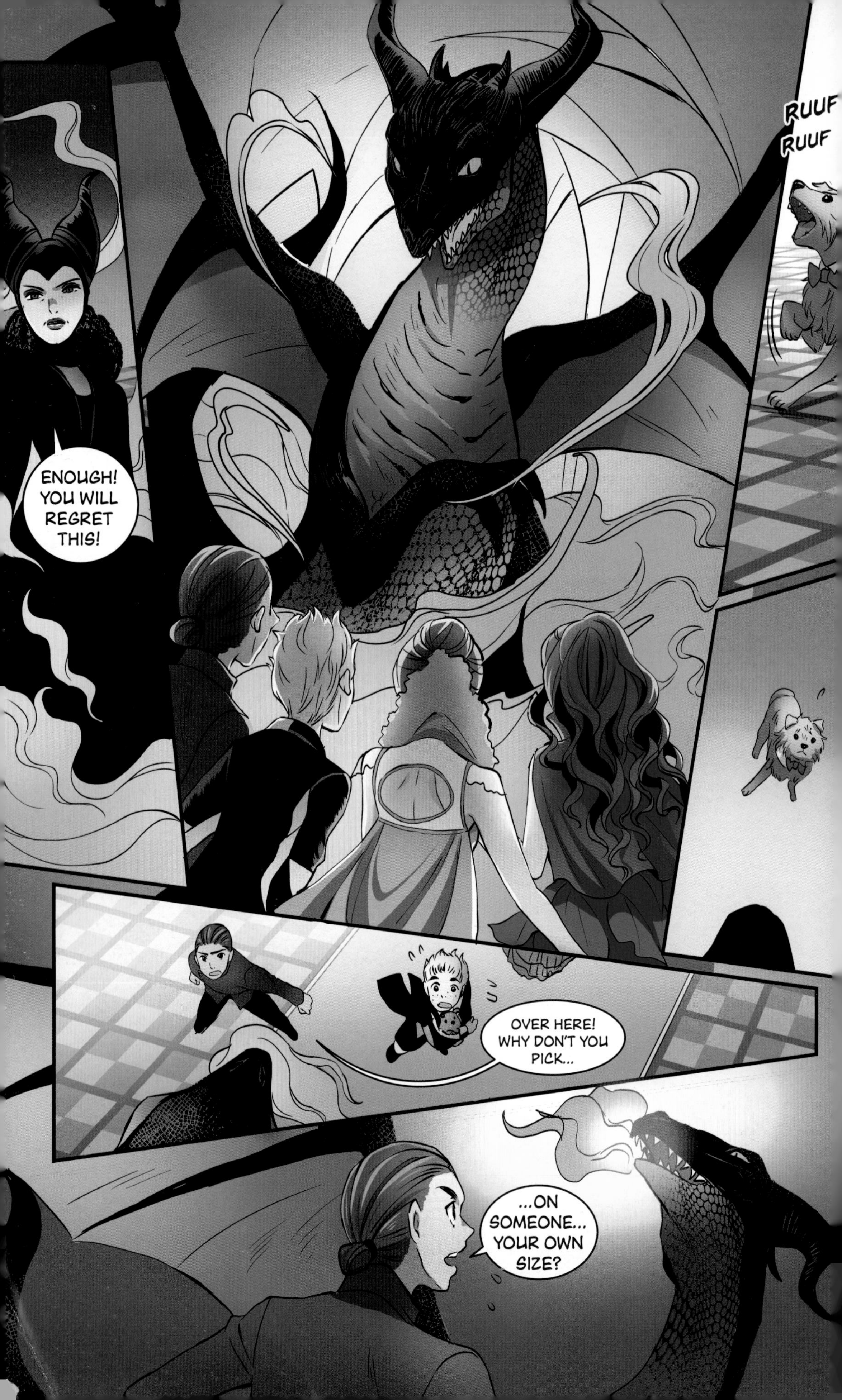
RUUF
RUUF
ENOUGH! YOU WILL REGRET THIS!
OVER HERE! WHY DON'T YOU PICK...
...ON SOMEONE... YOUR OWN SIZE?

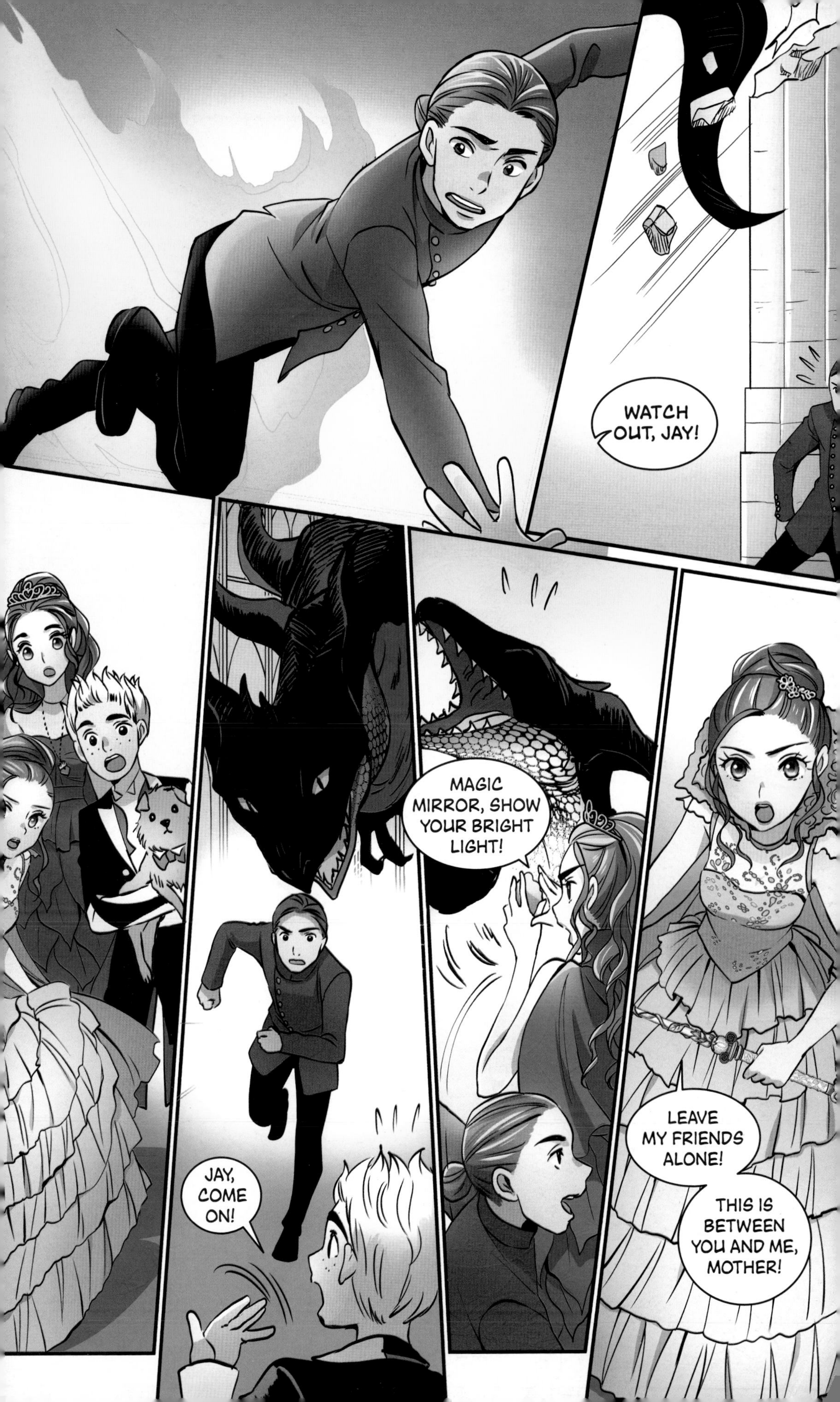
WATCH OUT, JAY!
MAGIC MIRROR, SHOW YOUR BRIGHT LIGHT!
JAY, COME ON!
LEAVE MY FRIENDS ALONE!
THIS IS BETWEEN YOU AND ME, MOTHER!

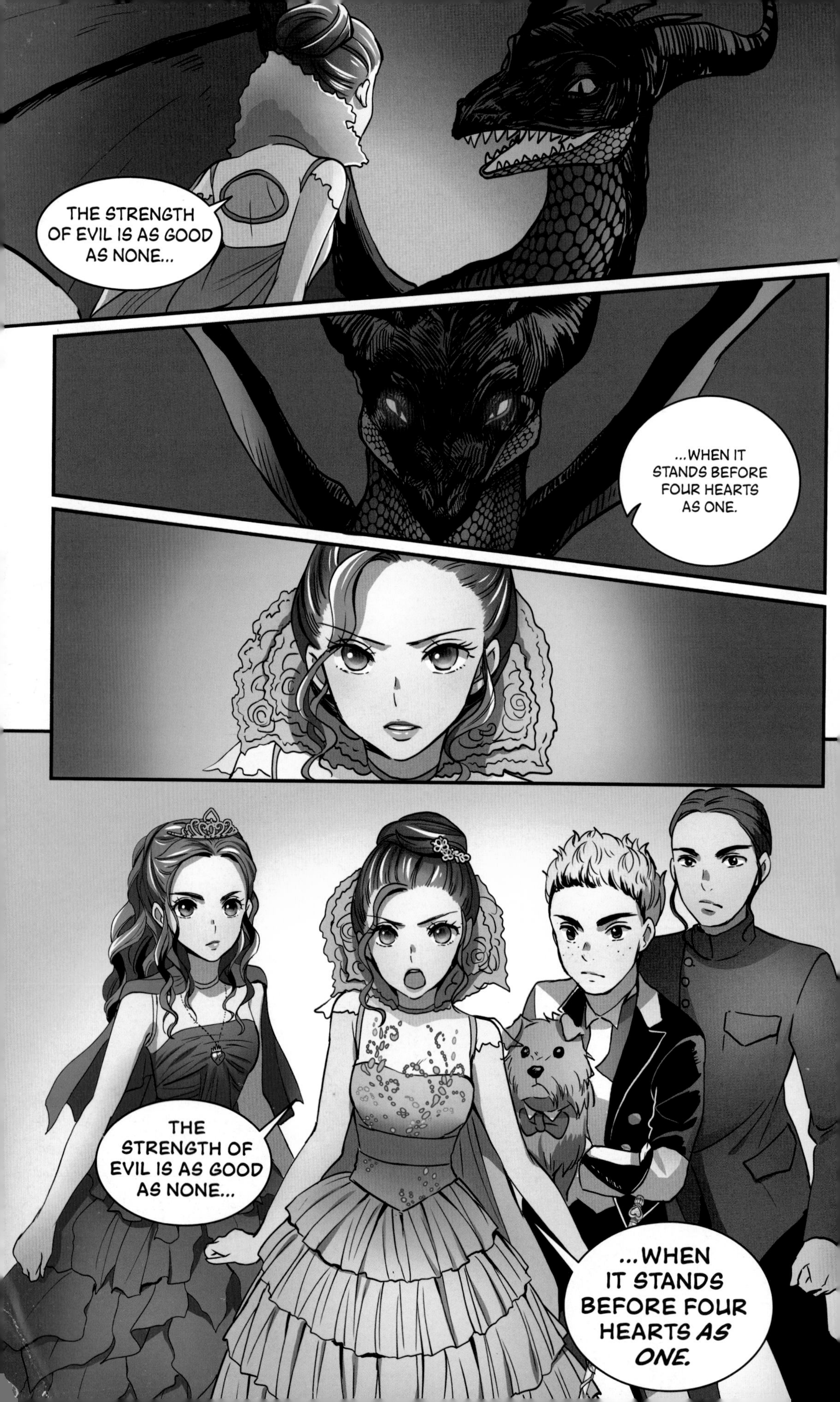
THE STRENGTH OF EVIL IS AS GOOD AS NONE...
...WHEN IT STANDS BEFORE FOUR HEARTS AS ONE.
THE STRENGTH OF EVIL IS AS GOOD AS NONE...
...WHEN IT STANDS BEFORE FOUR HEARTS *AS ONE.*

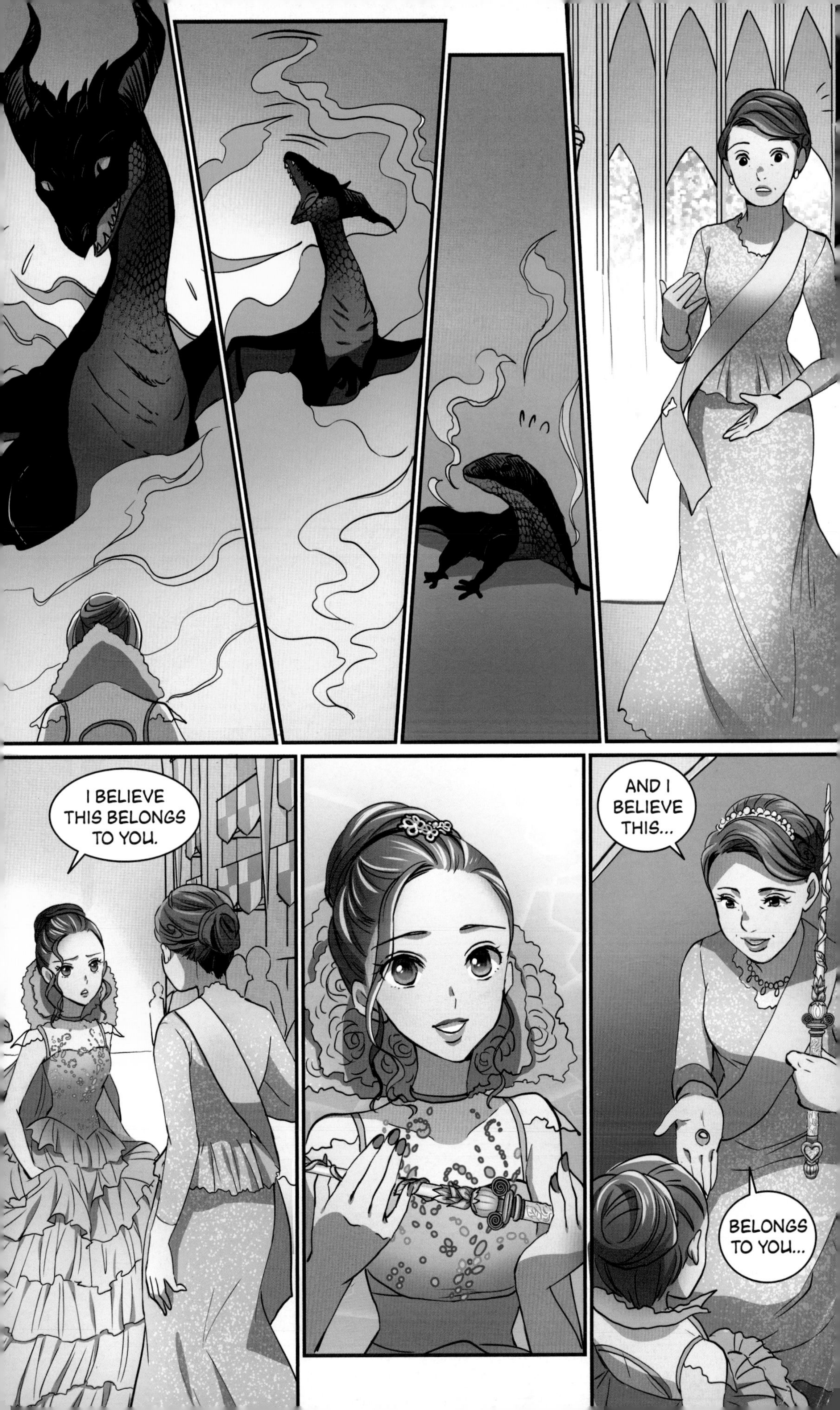
I BELIEVE THIS BELONGS TO YOU.
AND I BELIEVE THIS...
BELONGS TO YOU...

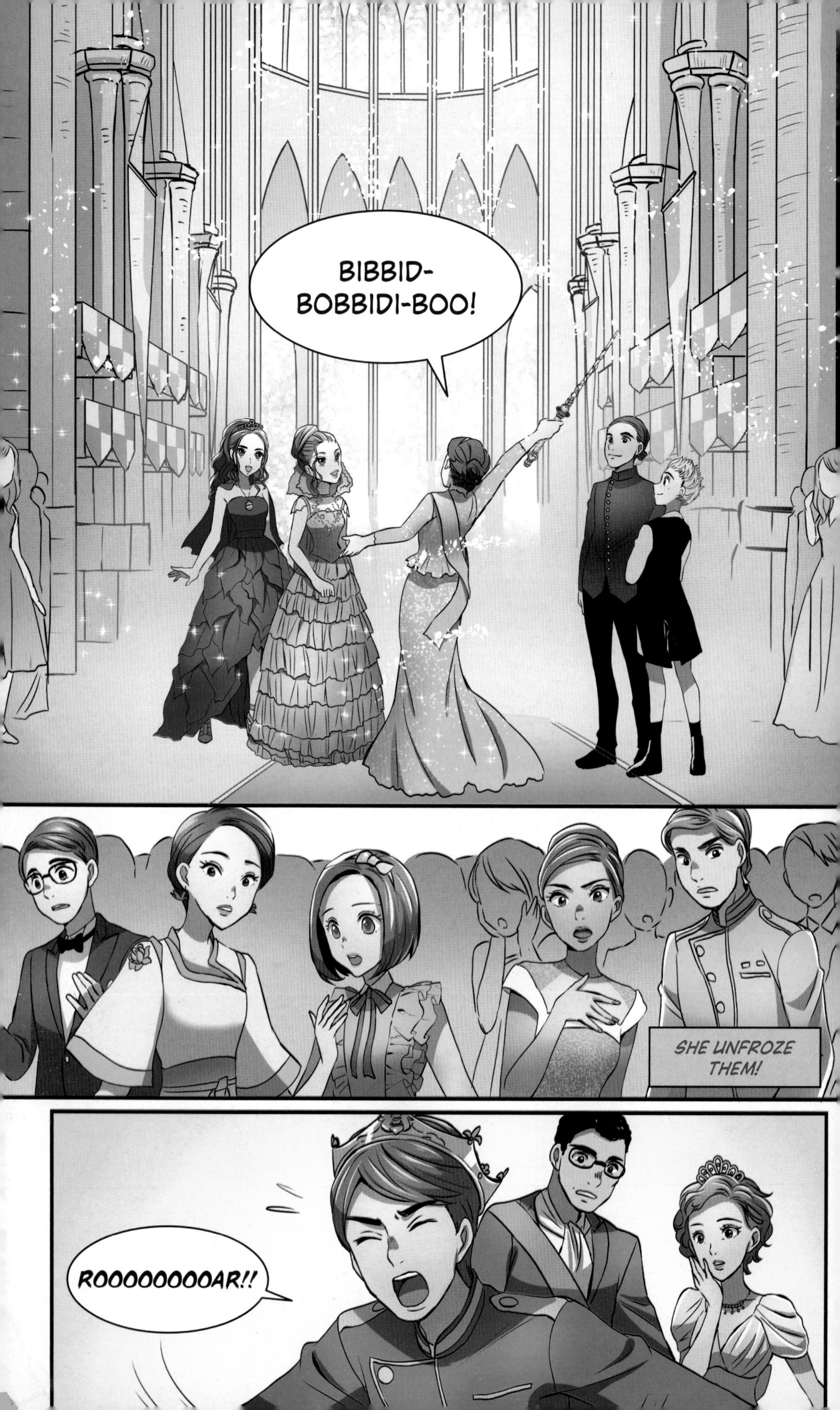
BIBBID-BOBBIDI-BOO!
SHE UNFROZE THEM!
ROOOOOOOOAR!!

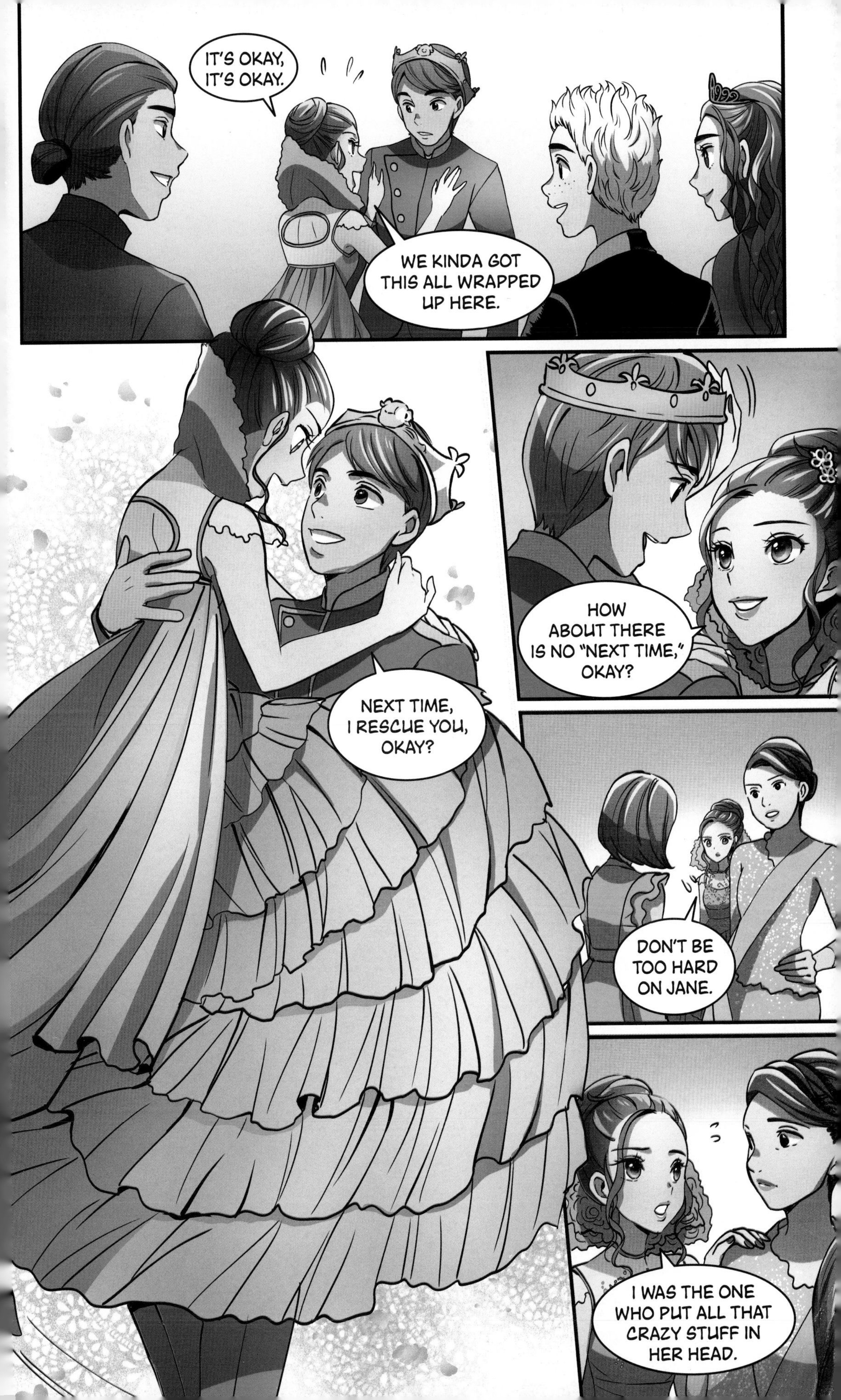
IT'S OKAY, IT'S OKAY.
WE KINDA GOT THIS ALL WRAPPED UP HERE.
NEXT TIME, I RESCUE YOU, OKAY?
HOW ABOUT THERE IS NO "NEXT TIME," OKAY?
DON'T BE TOO HARD ON JANE.
I WAS THE ONE WHO PUT ALL THAT CRAZY STUFF IN HER HEAD.

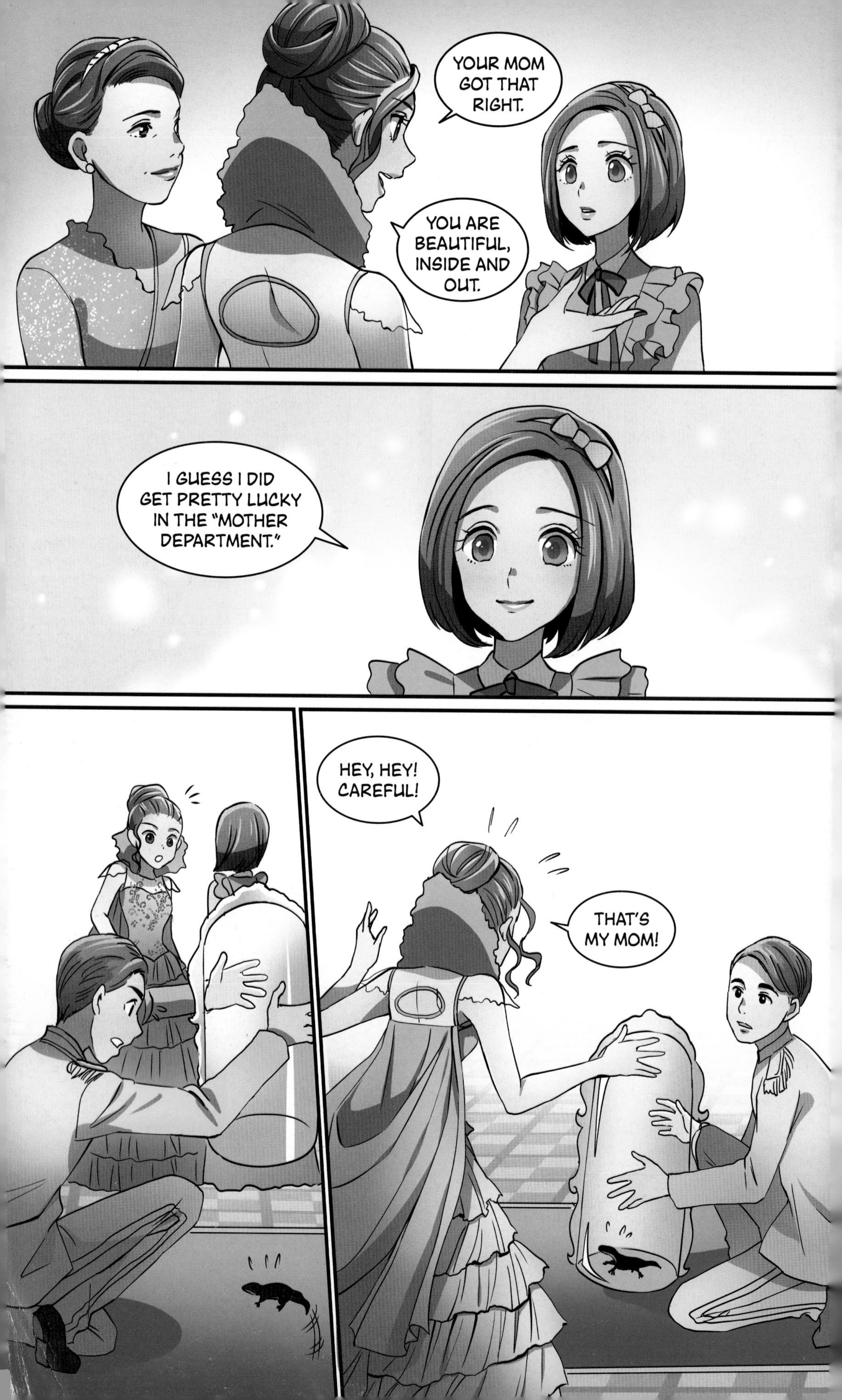
YOUR MOM GOT THAT RIGHT.
YOU ARE BEAUTIFUL, INSIDE AND OUT.
I GUESS I DID GET PRETTY LUCKY IN THE "MOTHER DEPARTMENT."
HEY, HEY! CAREFUL!
THAT'S MY MOM!

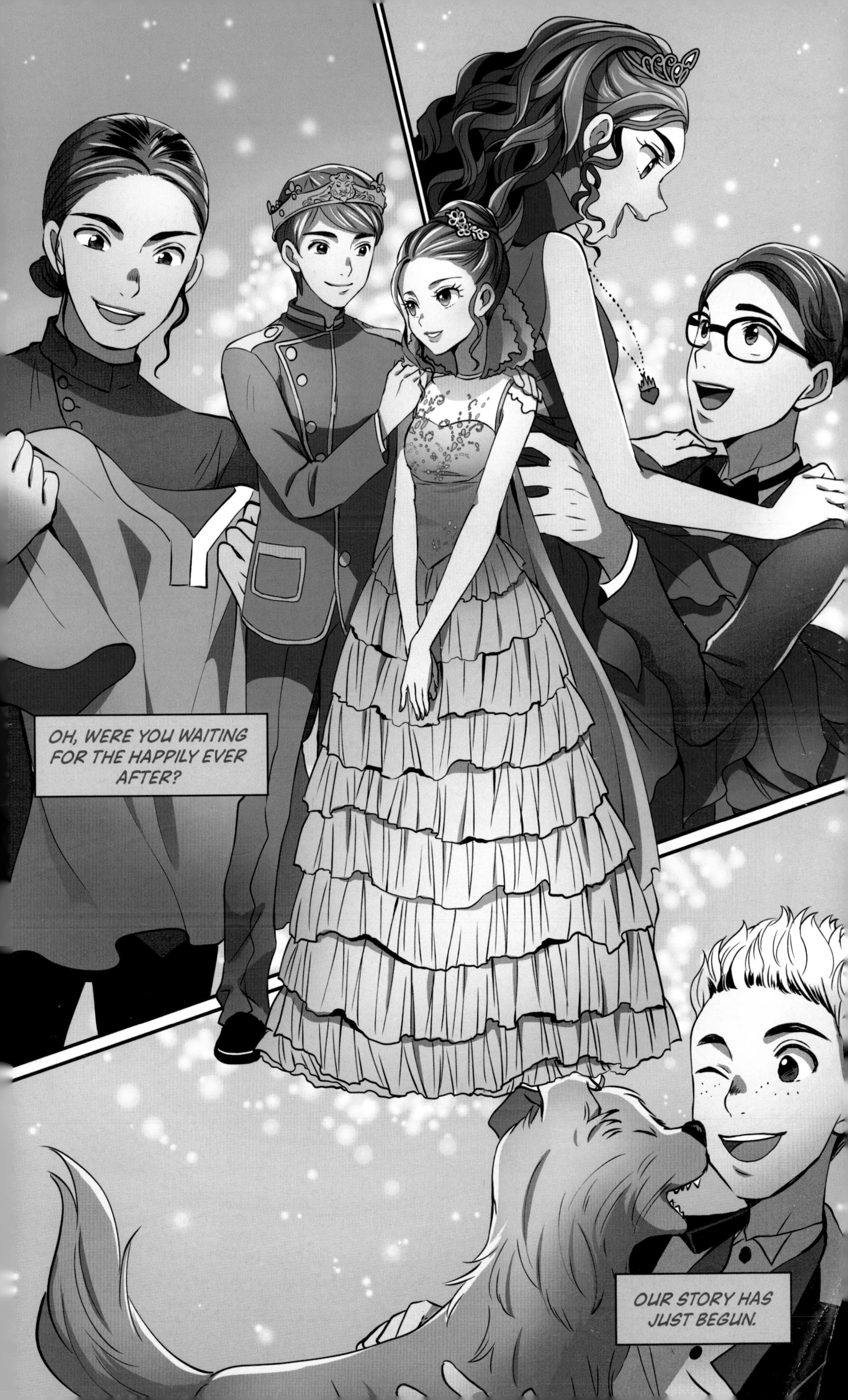
OH, WERE YOU WAITING FOR THE HAPPILY EVER AFTER?
OUR STORY HAS JUST BEGUN.

All New Trilogy!

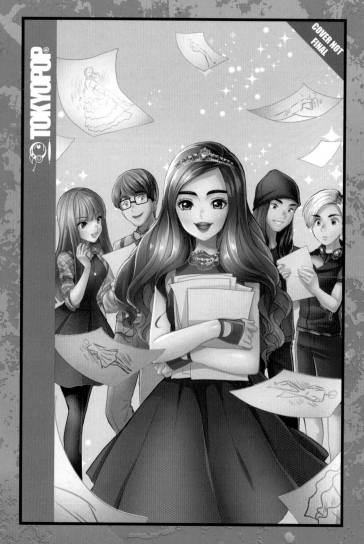

Book 1 coming in July 2018!

The Interscholastic Auradon Fashion Show is the biggest fashion event of the year and students across Auradon are buzzing with anticipation! No one is more excited than Evie, the VKs' resident fashionista and designer extraordinaire! Will Evie be able to reach the top spot? And just how far are the other competitors prepared to go to win first place?

Evie's Wicked Trilogy!

Book 2 coming in September 2018!

Book 3 coming in December 2018!

Find out more about this trilogy at www.TOKYOPOP.com/DisneyManga

Add These Disney Manga to Your Collection Today!

SHOJO
- [ ] DISNEY BEAUTY AND THE BEAST
- [ ] DISNEY KILALA PRINCESS SERIES

FANTASY
- [ ] DISNEY DESCENDANTS SERIES
- [ ] DISNEY TANGLED
- [ ] DISNEY PRINCESS AND THE FROG
- [ ] DISNEY FAIRIES SERIES
- [ ] DISNEY MARIE: MIRIYA AND MARIE

KAWAII
- [ ] DISNEY MAGICAL DANCE
- [ ] DISNEY STITCH! SERIES

PIXAR
- [ ] DISNEY • PIXAR TOY STORY
- [ ] DISNEY • PIXAR MONSTERS, INC.
- [ ] DISNEY • PIXAR WALL-E
- [ ] DISNEY • PIXAR FINDING NEMO

ADVENTURE
- [ ] DISNEY TIM BURTON'S THE NIGHTMARE BEFORE CHRISTMAS
- [ ] DISNEY ALICE IN WONDERLAND
- [ ] DISNEY PIRATES OF THE CARIBBEAN SERIES

TOKYO POP

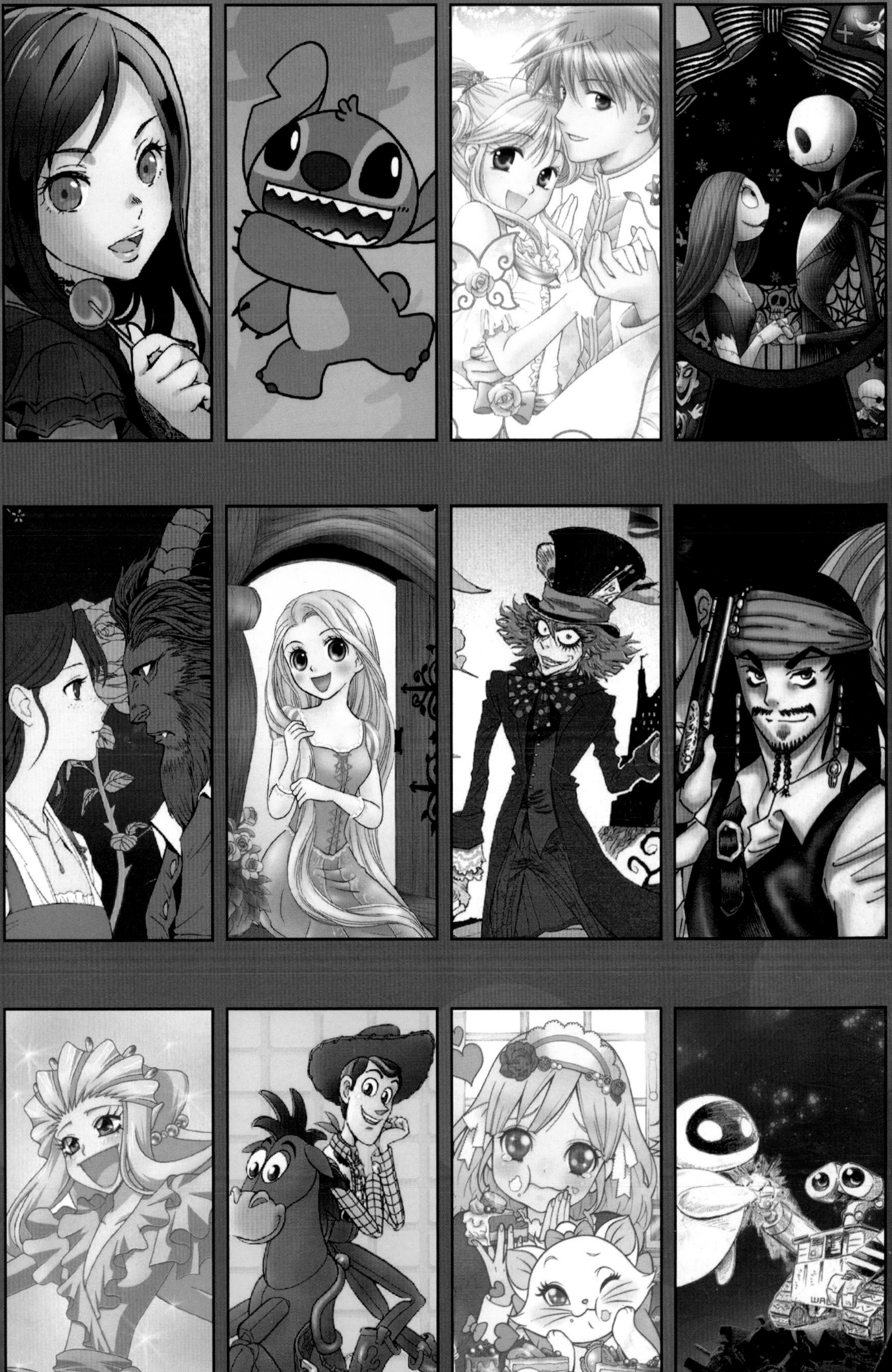

Disney Descendants - The Rotten to the Core Trilogy: The Complete Collection

Art by : Natsuki Minami

Adapted by : Jason Muell

Colorist : juryiaxreiria

Based on the hit Disney Channel original movie *Disney Descendants.*

Directed by : Kenny Ortega

Executive Produced by : Kenny Ortega and Wendy Japhet

Produced by : Tracey Jeffrey

Written by : Josann McGibbon & Sara Parriott

Editorial Associate - Janae Young

Marketing Associate - Kae Winters

Technology and Digital Media Assistant - Phillip Hong

Retouching and Lettering - Vibrraant Publishing Studio

Graphic Designer - Phillip Hong

Copy Editor - Daniella Orihuela-Gruber

Editor - Janae Young

Editor-in-Chief & Publisher - Stu Levy

Digital Media Coordinator - Rico Brenner-Quiñonez

A  Manga

TOKYOPOP and 🐷 are trademarks or registered trademarks of TOKYOPOP Inc.

TOKYOPOP Inc.
5200 W. Century Blvd. Suite 705
Los Angeles, 90045

E-mail: info@TOKYOPOP.com
Come visit us online at www.TOKYOPOP.com

f www.facebook.com/TOKYOPOP
🐦 www.twitter.com/TOKYOPOP
▶ www.youtube.com/TOKYOPOPTV
📌 www.pinterest.com/TOKYOPOP
📷 www.instagram.com/TOKYOPOP
t. TOKYOPOP.tumblr.com

ISBN: 978-1-4278-5721-7
First TOKYOPOP Printing: April 2018
10 9 8 7 6 5 4 3 2 1
Printed in the CANADA